Walt Disney

The Complete Life and Times of $CROOGE M^cDUCK

VOLUME
1

FANTAGRAPHICS

SEATTLE

Publisher: GARY GROTH
Senior Editor: J. MICHAEL CATRON
Designer: JUSTIN ALLAN-SPENCER
Production: PAUL BARESH and PRESTON WHITE
Associate Publisher: ERIC REYNOLDS

Fantagraphics Books, Inc.
7563 Lake City Way NE
Seattle, WA 98115
(800) 657-1100
Fantagraphics.com • Twitter: @fantagraphics • facebook.com/fantagraphics

Special thanks to David Gerstein.

Fourth Printing: July 2022
ISBN 978-1-68396-174-1
Library of Congress Control Number: 2018907540
Printed in China

The Life and Times of Scrooge McDuck by Don Rosa was originally serialized in 12 chapters in Denmark's
Anders And & Co between August 10, 1992, and June 2, 1994. It was revised and corrected by the author and
published in its final form in *The Don Rosa Library* Volume 4 and Volume 5 (Fantagraphics Books, 2015
and 2016). That finalized version is presented here in a single edition for the first time.

Also available:
The Complete Life and Times of Scrooge McDuck Volume 2 (Don Rosa)
Walt Disney's Uncle Scrooge: "Island in the Sky" (Carl Barks)
Mickey Mouse: The Man From Altacraz (Romano Scarpa)
Darkwing Duck: Just Us Justice Ducks (David Cody Weiss, et al.)
Uncle Scrooge: Pie in the Sky (William Van Horn, et al.)
Mickey Mouse: Zombie Coffee (Régis Loisel)
Mickey Mouse: The Greatest Adventures (Floyd Gottfredson, Walt Disney)
Mickey All-Stars (40 international artists, including Giorgio Cavazzano)
The Don Rosa Library Volumes 1-10 (Don Rosa)

Walt Disney

The Complete Life and Times of $crooge McDuck

by

Don Rosa

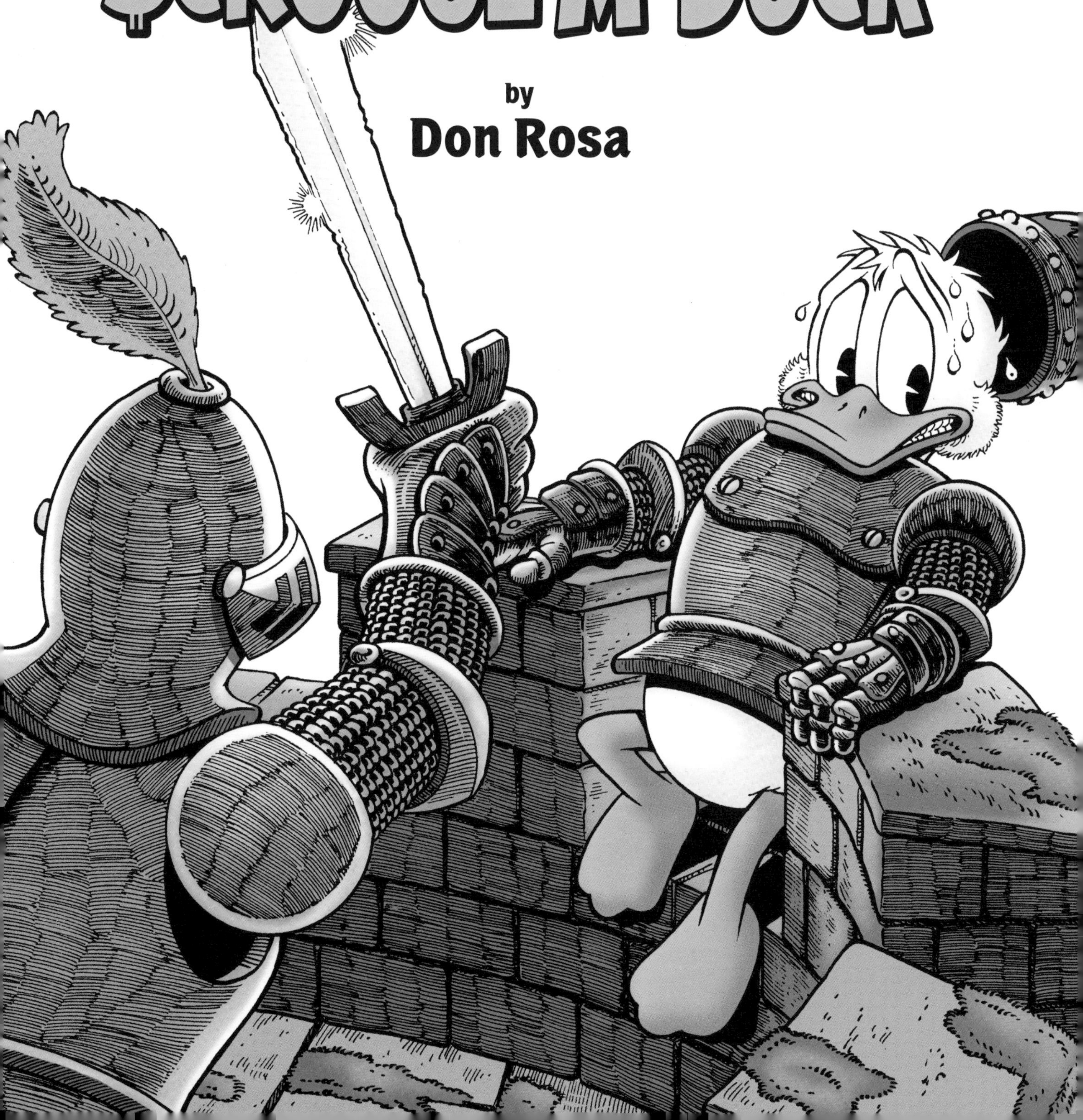

The Ages of Scrooge McDuck

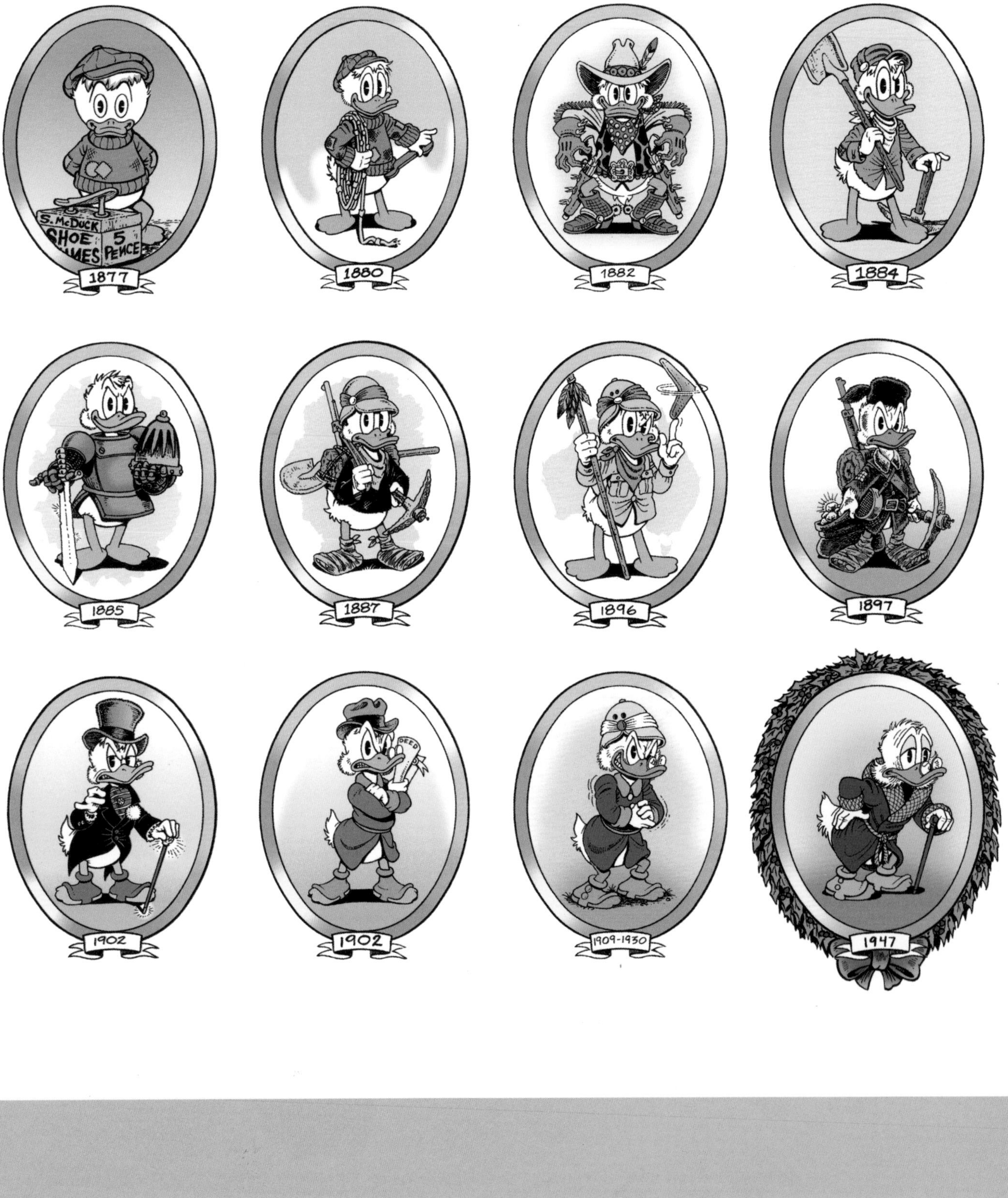
S. McDUCK
SHOE
5
PENCE
1877
1880
1882
1884
1885
1887
1896
1897
1902
DEED
1902
1909-1930
1947

Contents

All stories written and drawn by Don Rosa

Lettering by Todd Klein, Kneon Transitt, Preston White, David Gerstein, Scott Rockwell, and Sindre Wexelsen Goksøyr

Coloring by Susan Daigle-Leach, Kneon Transitt, Scott Rockwell, Egmont, and Digikore Studios

This title includes negative depictions and mistreatment of people or cultures. These stereotypes were wrong then and are wrong now. Rather than remove this content, we want to acknowledge its harmful impact, learn from it, and spark conversation to create a more inclusive future together. Disney is committed to creating stories with inspirational and aspirational themes that reflect the rich diversity of the human experience around the globe. To learn more about how stories have impacted society, please visit www.disney.com/StoriesMatter.

Just for the Fun of It

BY DON ROSA

DID YOU KNOW that Carl Barks's stories of Donald Duck and $crooge McDuck are the most popular and widely printed comics on the planet Earth?

As beloved as Donald Duck is, there is not really much to tell about the early life of such an "everyman" character. But Donald's wealthy Uncle Scrooge? Well, *that's* another story! Perhaps, even, an endless number of stories about how this elderly character became so rich during a long lifetime of high adventure.

The Life and Times of Scrooge McDuck began as a series of 12 stories that I wrote and drew between, roughly, mid-1991 and the end of 1993. The stories appeared first in comics published by the Egmont media company, the vast European publisher which has the license for Carl Barks's original Uncle Scrooge comics stories for most of the world.

BarksDuck fans around the globe seemed eager to read my version (and it's only *my* version) of the life and times of Mr. McDuck when these stories were first published in the early 1990s in the various weekly Duck comics in Europe. Soon thereafter, numerous countries published special collections of these tales of young Scrooge.

On my own bookshelves, I have collected editions of my *The Life and Times of Scrooge McDuck* in nearly 20 different languages. I don't mean the small comic books that feature the individual stories — I mean standalone hardback collections of the 12 original chapters and the later "untold tales," as my editor insists on calling them, or "B-chapters," as I call them.

This book is the first of a two-volume set, presenting the full original 12-part series — complete with all my restorations, revisions, and corrections — as first seen in *The Don Rosa Library*. Volume 2 will contain the additional chapters — the "untold tales" (sigh) — that I later created to please the many Scrooge McDuck fans around the world who wanted more stories of their favorite comics character's early life.

Despite the fact that the modern American readership of Barks's comics is the world's smallest, we are still the reprint leader, with this being the sixth special collection of these stories in the USA. Germany and Italy are tied for second place, with five editions each. The list continues: three collections in France and Poland, two in Finland, Norway, Denmark, Sweden, Greece, Brazil, Spain, Portugal, the Netherlands, and even Java! Finally, I have single collections from the Czech Republic, Hungary, and China. And for all I know, there may be others. Licensed publishers don't need to notify me (or pay me) when these stories are printed.

The point is that I think it's the worldwide popularity of Barks's Scrooge McDuck that has made this series possibly the most internationally reprinted comics stories in history.

But, you may ask, what prompted me to do this series? I am a lifelong McDuck fan, which is why I seized the unexpected opportunity to abandon my family's near-century-old construction company in 1987 to create McDuck adventures. Still, I never intended to undertake a project such as this. But in 1991, I discovered that the Disney company in the United States, which had briefly taken over publishing their own comics for the first time, had decided they wanted to find writers and artists to do a life of Scrooge "miniseries," something fashionable in American comics at the time.

Immediately, I notified my publisher, Egmont, knowing that they had the best writers and artists of these comics in the world. I suggested that to serve Scrooge best, the people who loved and understood the character should be the ones to create such an important series. Knowing what a Scrooge fan I was, they suggested that I should take it on (as I'd hoped!).

The main reason I accepted the assignment was just for the fun of it — the fanboy challenge of taking into account every "fact" concerning Scrooge

McDuck's early life that was ever revealed in one of Carl Barks's classic stories, no matter how minute or obscurely buried the morsel of history might have been. If Scrooge made a comment about his youth in the third balloon of the fifth panel of the seventh page of the second story in some comic book in 1957 — as long as it was a story written by Barks — that fact is mentioned somewhere in this series.

But this series was *not* intended to change the BarksDuck Universe or to otherwise break tradition. On the contrary, it is intended to reaffirm all the elements of all the great Barks Scrooge stories so many citizens of this planet grew up on. And yet, as carefully and authentically as I sought to construct it — basing everything solely on Barks's original works — it was never intended to be anything but my personal telling of the life of Scrooge McDuck.

In order to make the series as accurate as possible, I first made a list of all of those obscure "Barksian facts" about Scrooge that all we Duckfans have faithfully committed to memory over the years. Next, I assembled those facts into a timeline, which I then broke down into 12 logical segments, each dealing with one period of Scrooge's life as already described by Mr. Barks. And since Scrooge is no more my property than that of any other Duckfan, I sent copies of that chart to noted Duckfans around the world (including one Carl Barks) for their comments and help. The end result is the series of stories collected in this book.

Fantagraphics's ten-volume *The Don Rosa Library*, completed in 2018, contains detailed background texts that cover each of these adventures. To keep this (and the following) volume to a manageable size and price, those texts are not repeated herein — but if you're interested, those editions are still available.

Another caveat is that I have learned that some Duckfans hoped that these two volumes would interweave the original 12 chapters of *The Life and Times of Scrooge McDuck* with my additional untold tales and present them in chronological order as to the year each adventure takes place.

But this I cannot allow!

The original 12 chapters form a single, complete narrative. Each chapter accomplishes a certain goal in explaining the importance of that adventure in Scrooge's life. Furthermore, each chapter matches a specific method of presentation in form and content. The additional untold tales that I created in the subsequent years of my so-called cartooning career follow a totally different framing sequence and have no other purpose than to entertain (which is no less a worthy goal, simply different).

So, despite my explanation why it would be a mistake, if you still want to read these two series of adventure stories in chronological order, just buy Volume 2 and read them in *any order* you wish! Ultimately, you are the boss!

But, in whatever order you read these stories, I hope you enjoy this, my ultimate life tribute to the greatest storyteller of the 20th century, Carl Barks. ✻

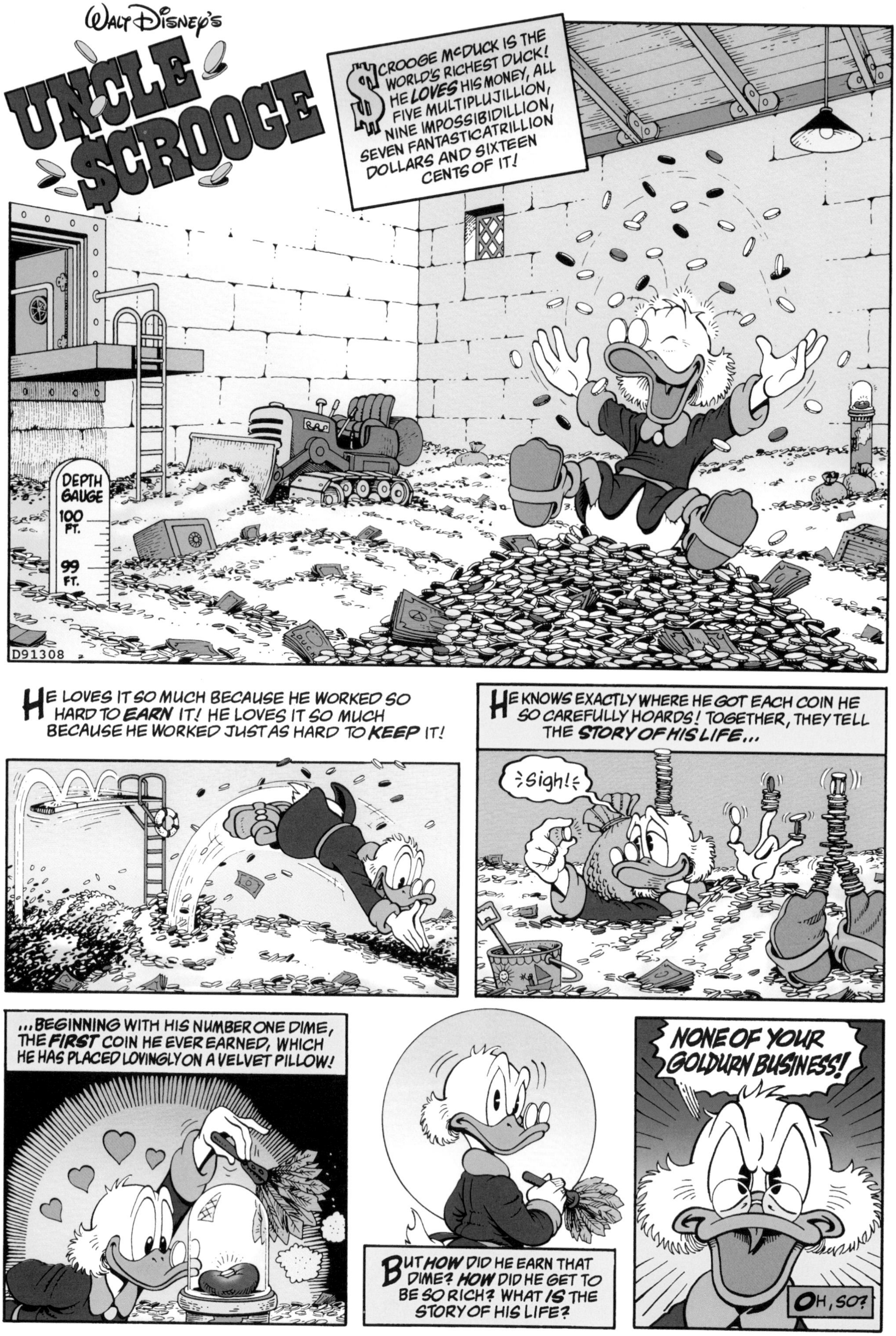
WALT DISNEY'S
UNCLE $CROOGE
$CROOGE McDUCK IS THE WORLD'S RICHEST DUCK! HE LOVES HIS MONEY, ALL FIVE MULTIPLUJILLION, NINE IMPOSSIBIDILLION, SEVEN FANTASTICATRILLION DOLLARS AND SIXTEEN CENTS OF IT!
DEPTH GAUGE
100 FT.
99 FT.
D91308
HE LOVES IT SO MUCH BECAUSE HE WORKED SO HARD TO EARN IT! HE LOVES IT SO MUCH BECAUSE HE WORKED JUST AS HARD TO KEEP IT!
HE KNOWS EXACTLY WHERE HE GOT EACH COIN HE SO CAREFULLY HOARDS! TOGETHER, THEY TELL THE STORY OF HIS LIFE...
Sigh!
...BEGINNING WITH HIS NUMBER ONE DIME, THE FIRST COIN HE EVER EARNED, WHICH HE HAS PLACED LOVINGLY ON A VELVET PILLOW!
BUT HOW DID HE EARN THAT DIME? HOW DID HE GET TO BE SO RICH? WHAT IS THE STORY OF HIS LIFE?
NONE OF YOUR GOLDURN BUSINESS!
OH, SO?

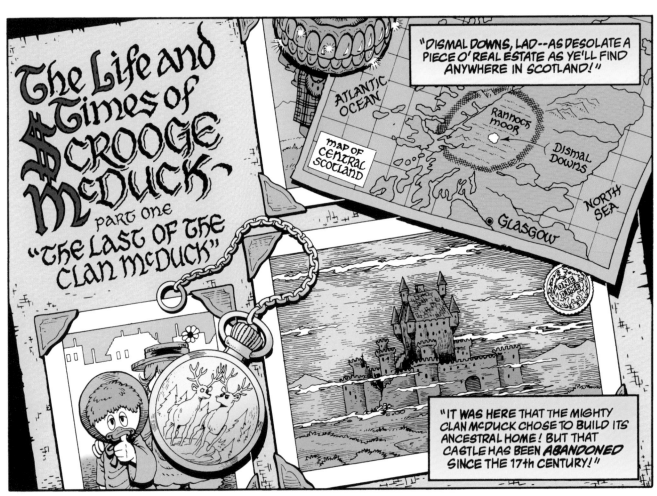

The Life and Times of Scrooge McDuck

PART ONE
"THE LAST OF THE CLAN McDUCK"

"DISMAL DOWNS, LAD--AS DESOLATE A PIECE O' REAL ESTATE AS YE'LL FIND ANYWHERE IN SCOTLAND!"

MAP OF CENTRAL SCOTLAND

ATLANTIC OCEAN

Rannoch Moor

DISMAL DOWNS

NORTH SEA

GLASGOW

"IT WAS HERE THAT THE MIGHTY CLAN McDUCK CHOSE TO BUILD ITS ANCESTRAL HOME! BUT THAT CASTLE HAS BEEN *ABANDONED* SINCE THE 17th CENTURY!"

"NOW, GOLDEN EAGLES NEST IN ITS LOFTY TURRETS, LOOKIN' OUT OE'R A LOST REALM O' OCHRE GRASS AND BRACKEN!"

"AND PTARMIGAN AND GROUSE HIDE HERE IN THE HEATHER O' THE CLAN CEMETERY!"

THERE IT IS, LAD, *CASTLE McDUCK!* IT'S TIME YE LEARNED SOMETHING O' YOUR ANCESTORS! AFTER ALL, 'TIS THE EVE O' YOUR *TENTH* BIRTHDAY!

ARE YE LISTENIN', SCROOGEY?

AYE, POPPA!

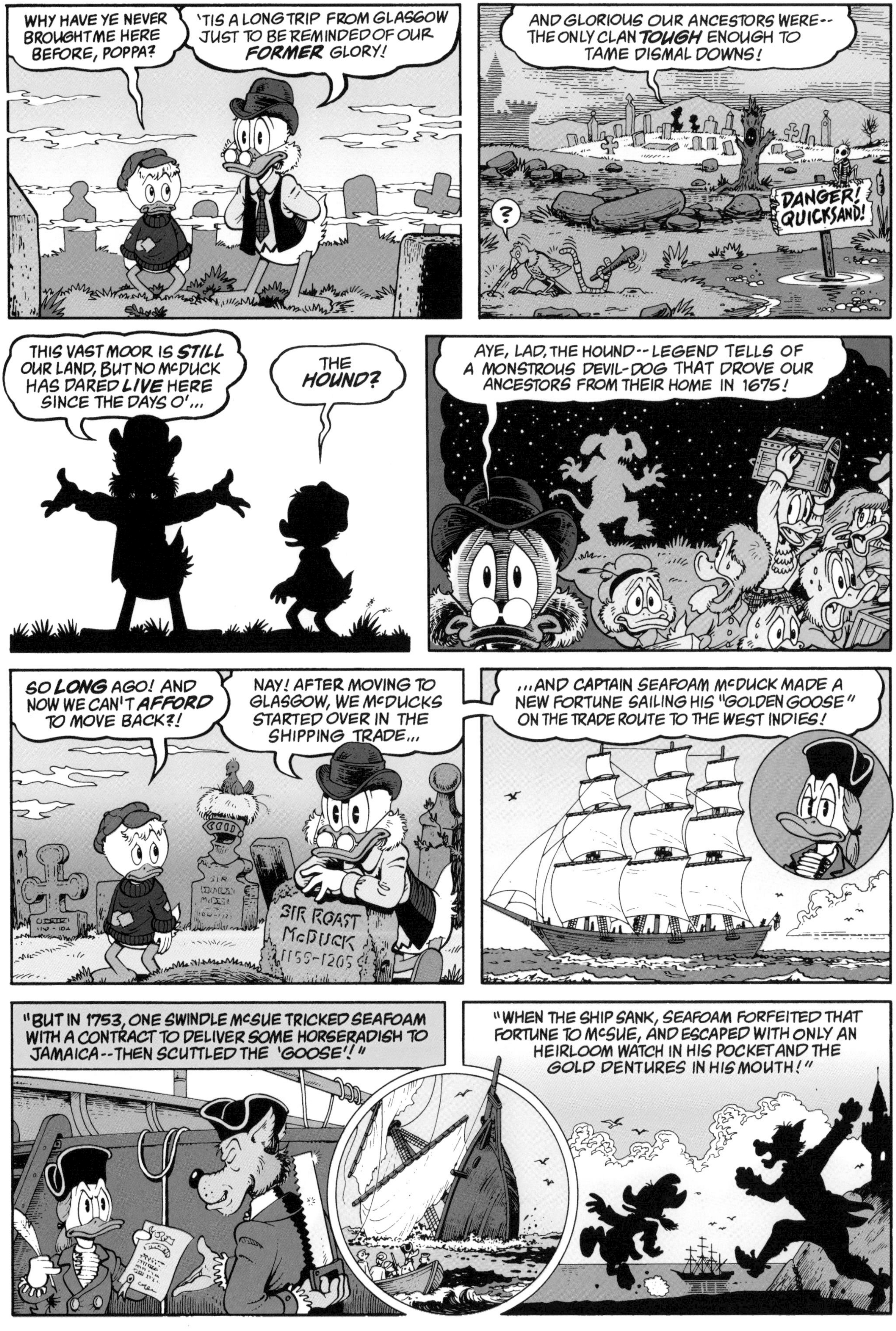
WHY HAVE YE NEVER BROUGHT ME HERE BEFORE, POPPA?
'TIS A LONG TRIP FROM GLASGOW JUST TO BE REMINDED OF OUR FORMER GLORY!
AND GLORIOUS OUR ANCESTORS WERE-- THE ONLY CLAN TOUGH ENOUGH TO TAME DISMAL DOWNS!
?
DANGER! QUICKSAND!
THIS VAST MOOR IS STILL OUR LAND, BUT NO McDUCK HAS DARED LIVE HERE SINCE THE DAYS O'...
THE HOUND?
AYE, LAD, THE HOUND-- LEGEND TELLS OF A MONSTROUS DEVIL-DOG THAT DROVE OUR ANCESTORS FROM THEIR HOME IN 1675!
SO LONG AGO! AND NOW WE CAN'T AFFORD TO MOVE BACK?!
NAY! AFTER MOVING TO GLASGOW, WE McDUCKS STARTED OVER IN THE SHIPPING TRADE...
...AND CAPTAIN SEAFOAM McDUCK MADE A NEW FORTUNE SAILING HIS "GOLDEN GOOSE" ON THE TRADE ROUTE TO THE WEST INDIES!
SIR ROAST McDUCK 1159-1205
"BUT IN 1753, ONE SWINDLE McSUE TRICKED SEAFOAM WITH A CONTRACT TO DELIVER SOME HORSERADISH TO JAMAICA--THEN SCUTTLED THE 'GOOSE'!"
"WHEN THE SHIP SANK, SEAFOAM FORFEITED THAT FORTUNE TO McSUE, AND ESCAPED WITH ONLY AN HEIRLOOM WATCH IN HIS POCKET AND THE GOLD DENTURES IN HIS MOUTH!"

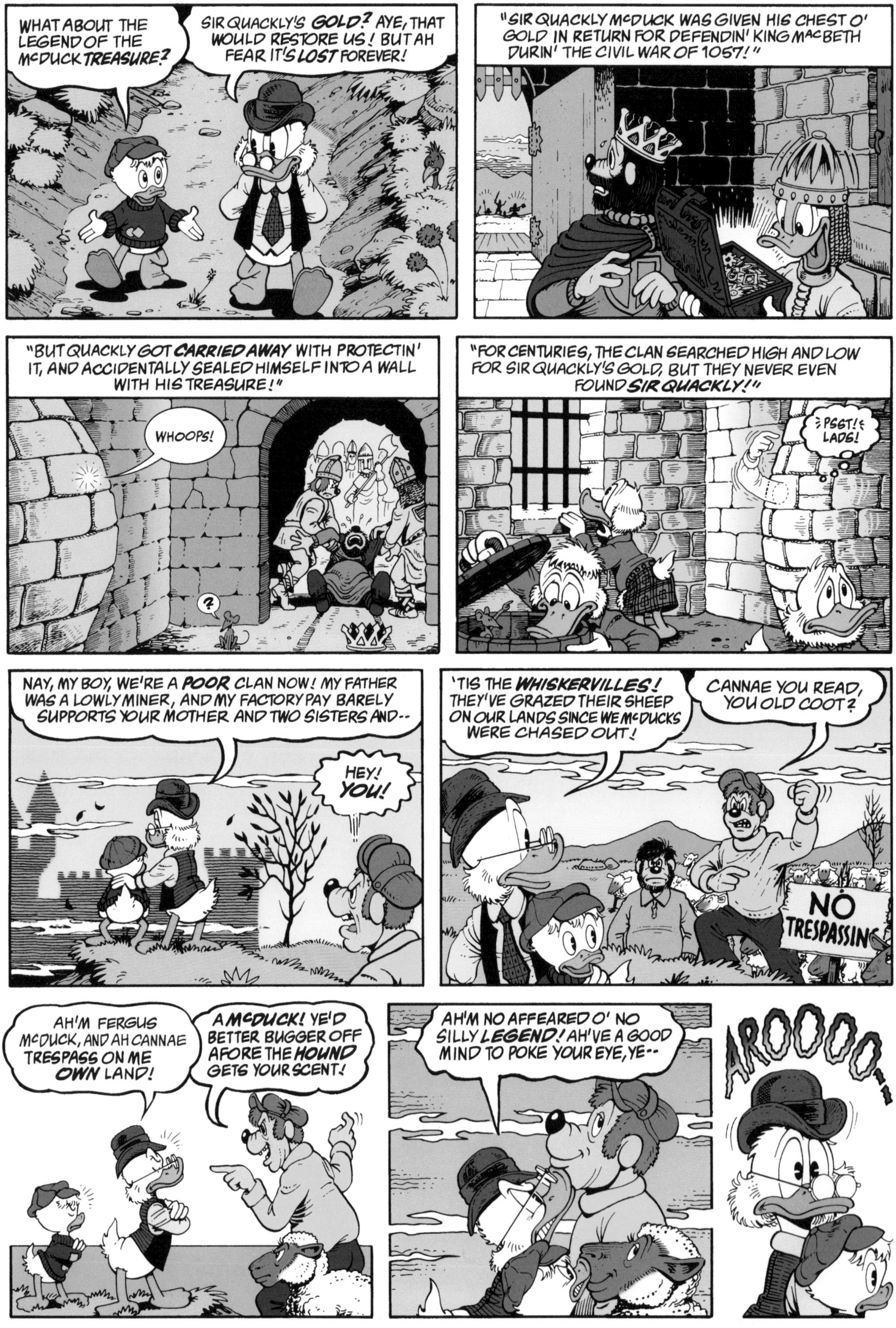
WHAT ABOUT THE LEGEND OF THE McDUCK TREASURE?
SIR QUACKLY'S GOLD? AYE, THAT WOULD RESTORE US! BUT AH FEAR IT'S LOST FOREVER!
"SIR QUACKLY McDUCK WAS GIVEN HIS CHEST O' GOLD IN RETURN FOR DEFENDIN' KING MacBETH DURIN' THE CIVIL WAR OF 1057!"
"BUT QUACKLY GOT CARRIED AWAY WITH PROTECTIN' IT, AND ACCIDENTALLY SEALED HIMSELF INTO A WALL WITH HIS TREASURE!"
WHOOPS!
?
"FOR CENTURIES, THE CLAN SEARCHED HIGH AND LOW FOR SIR QUACKLY'S GOLD, BUT THEY NEVER EVEN FOUND SIR QUACKLY!"
PSST! LADS!
NAY, MY BOY, WE'RE A POOR CLAN NOW! MY FATHER WAS A LOWLY MINER, AND MY FACTORY PAY BARELY SUPPORTS YOUR MOTHER AND TWO SISTERS AND--
HEY! YOU!
'TIS THE WHISKERVILLES! THEY'VE GRAZED THEIR SHEEP ON OUR LANDS SINCE WE McDUCKS WERE CHASED OUT!
CANNAE YOU READ, YOU OLD COOT?
NO TRESPASSIN
AH'M FERGUS McDUCK, AND AH CANNAE TRESPASS ON ME OWN LAND!
A McDUCK! YE'D BETTER BUGGER OFF AFORE THE HOUND GETS YOUR SCENT!
AH'M NO AFFEARED O' NO SILLY LEGEND! AH'VE A GOOD MIND TO POKE YOUR EYE, YE--
AROOOOO...

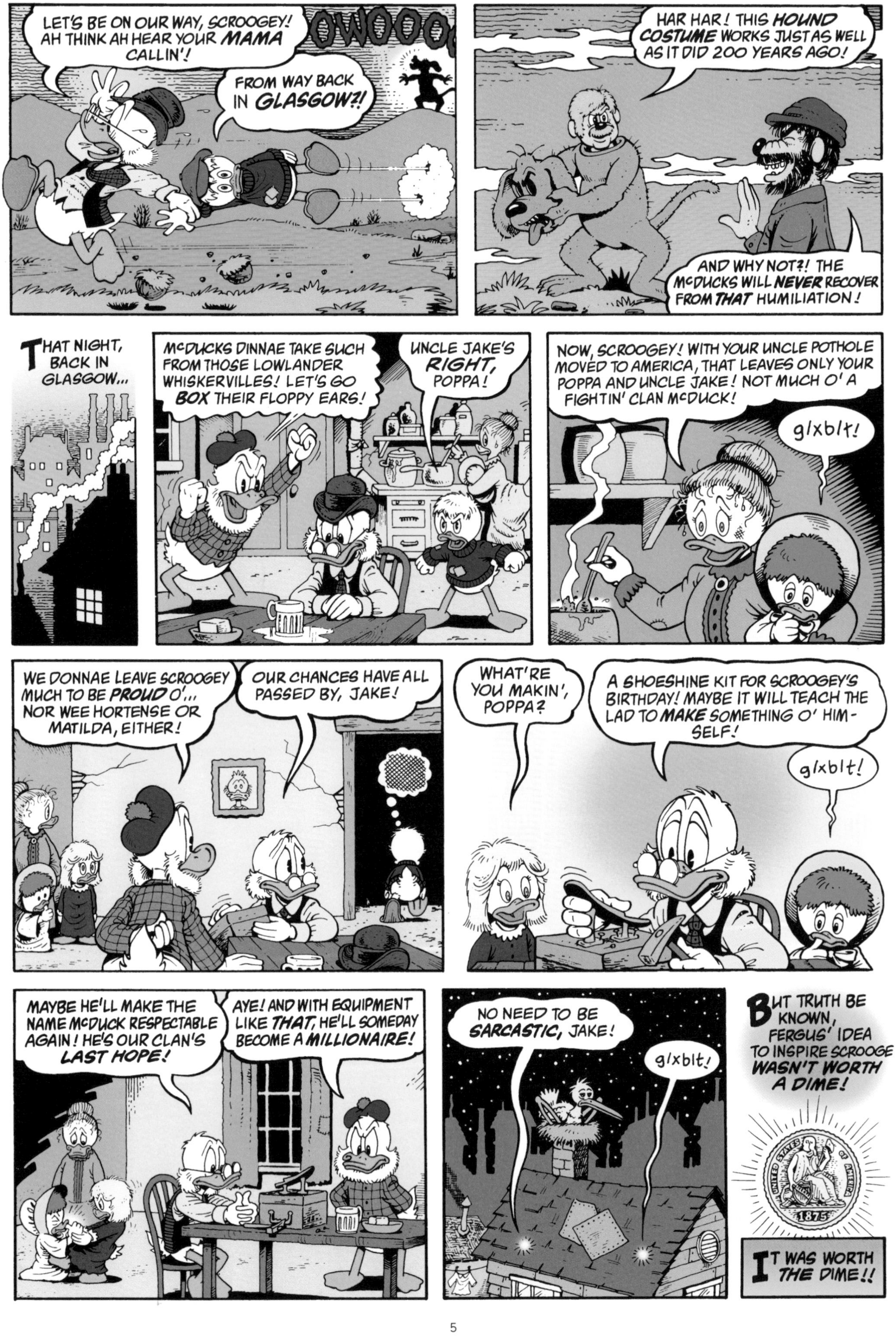
LET'S BE ON OUR WAY, SCROOGEY! AH THINK AH HEAR YOUR MAMA CALLIN'!
OWOOOO
FROM WAY BACK IN GLASGOW?!
HAR HAR! THIS HOUND COSTUME WORKS JUST AS WELL AS IT DID 200 YEARS AGO!
AND WHY NOT?! THE McDUCKS WILL NEVER RECOVER FROM THAT HUMILIATION!
THAT NIGHT, BACK IN GLASGOW...
McDUCKS DINNAE TAKE SUCH FROM THOSE LOWLANDER WHISKERVILLES! LET'S GO BOX THEIR FLOPPY EARS!
UNCLE JAKE'S RIGHT, POPPA!
NOW, SCROOGEY! WITH YOUR UNCLE POTHOLE MOVED TO AMERICA, THAT LEAVES ONLY YOUR POPPA AND UNCLE JAKE! NOT MUCH O' A FIGHTIN' CLAN McDUCK!
g/xbl/t!
WE DONNAE LEAVE SCROOGEY MUCH TO BE PROUD O'... NOR WEE HORTENSE OR MATILDA, EITHER!
OUR CHANCES HAVE ALL PASSED BY, JAKE!
WHAT'RE YOU MAKIN', POPPA?
A SHOESHINE KIT FOR SCROOGEY'S BIRTHDAY! MAYBE IT WILL TEACH THE LAD TO MAKE SOMETHING O' HIM-SELF!
g/xbl/t!
MAYBE HE'LL MAKE THE NAME McDUCK RESPECTABLE AGAIN! HE'S OUR CLAN'S LAST HOPE!
AYE! AND WITH EQUIPMENT LIKE THAT, HE'LL SOMEDAY BECOME A MILLIONAIRE!
NO NEED TO BE SARCASTIC, JAKE!
g/xblt!
BUT TRUTH BE KNOWN, FERGUS' IDEA TO INSPIRE SCROOGE WASN'T WORTH A DIME!
UNITED STATES OF AMERICA
1875
IT WAS WORTH THE DIME!!

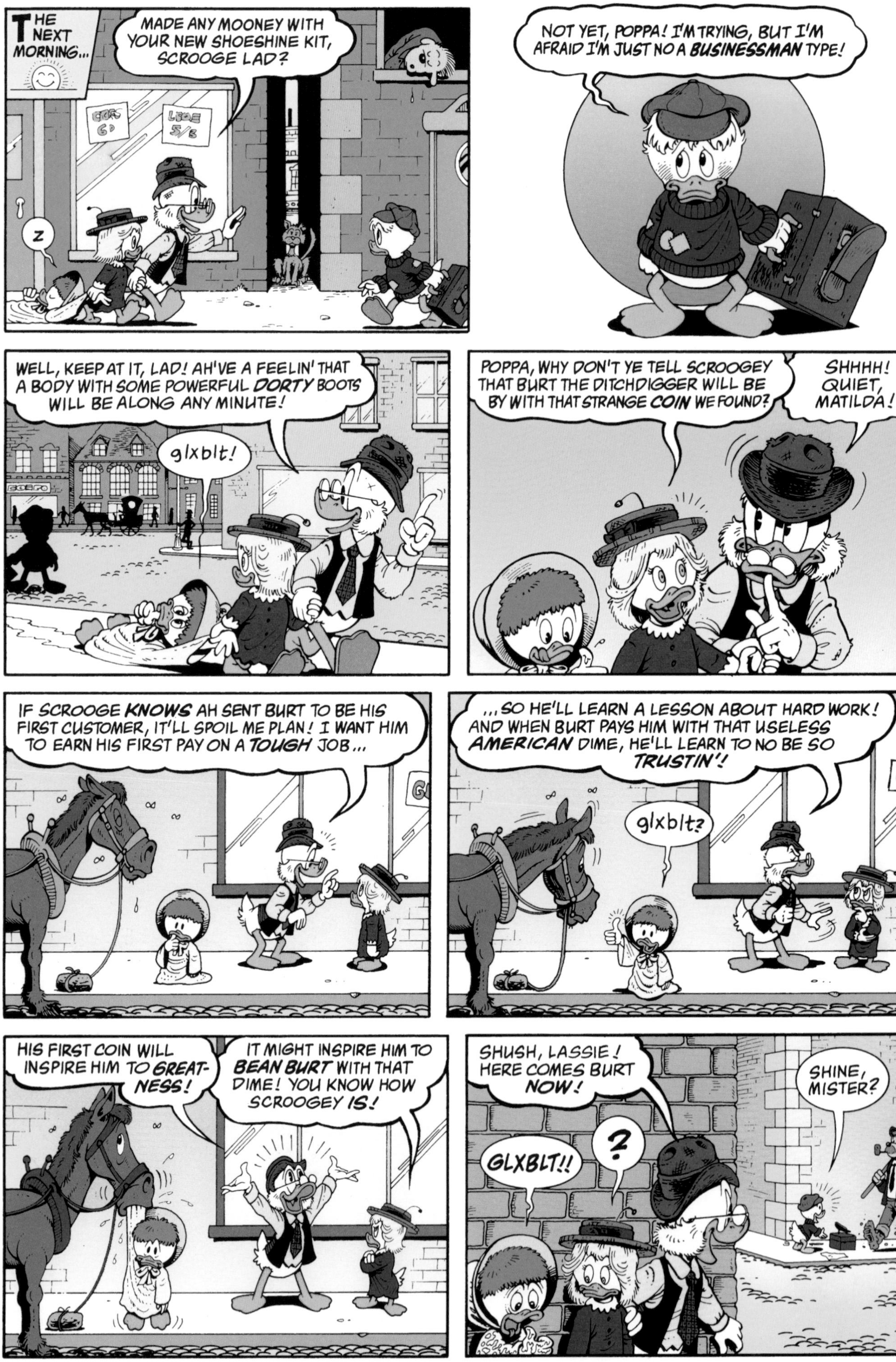
THE NEXT MORNING...
MADE ANY MOONEY WITH YOUR NEW SHOESHINE KIT, SCROOGE LAD?
Z
NOT YET, POPPA! I'M TRYING, BUT I'M AFRAID I'M JUST NO A BUSINESSMAN TYPE!
WELL, KEEP AT IT, LAD! AH'VE A FEELIN' THAT A BODY WITH SOME POWERFUL DORTY BOOTS WILL BE ALONG ANY MINUTE!
glxblt!
POPPA, WHY DON'T YE TELL SCROOGEY THAT BURT THE DITCHDIGGER WILL BE BY WITH THAT STRANGE COIN WE FOUND?
SHHHH! QUIET, MATILDA!
IF SCROOGE KNOWS AH SENT BURT TO BE HIS FIRST CUSTOMER, IT'LL SPOIL ME PLAN! I WANT HIM TO EARN HIS FIRST PAY ON A TOUGH JOB...
...SO HE'LL LEARN A LESSON ABOUT HARD WORK! AND WHEN BURT PAYS HIM WITH THAT USELESS AMERICAN DIME, HE'LL LEARN TO NO BE SO TRUSTIN'!
glxblt?
HIS FIRST COIN WILL INSPIRE HIM TO GREATNESS!
IT MIGHT INSPIRE HIM TO BEAN BURT WITH THAT DIME! YOU KNOW HOW SCROOGEY IS!
SHUSH, LASSIE! HERE COMES BURT NOW!
GLXBLT!!
?
SHINE, MISTER?

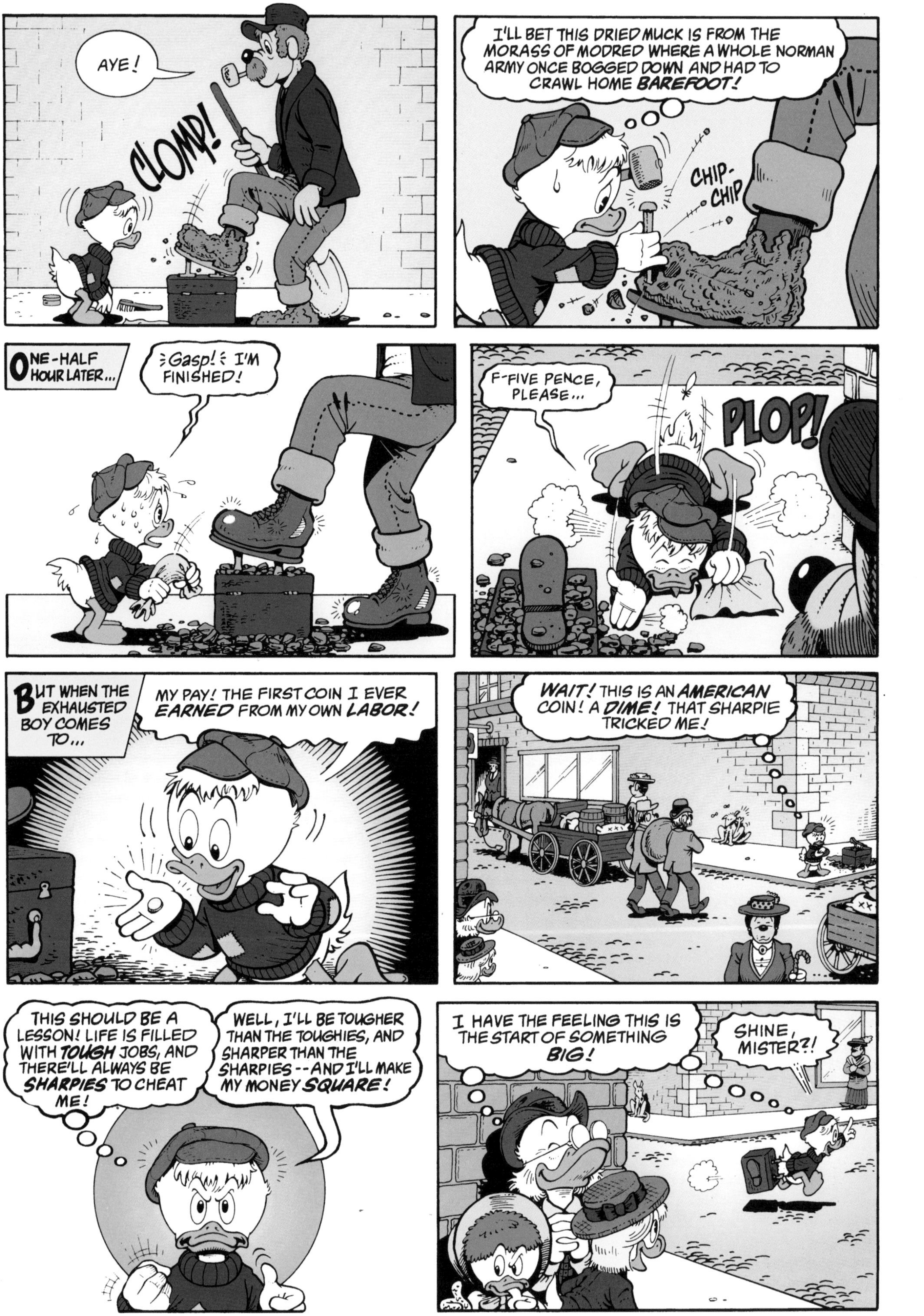
AYE!
CLOMP!
I'LL BET THIS DRIED MUCK IS FROM THE MORASS OF MODRED WHERE A WHOLE NORMAN ARMY ONCE BOGGED DOWN AND HAD TO CRAWL HOME BAREFOOT!
CHIP-CHIP
ONE-HALF HOUR LATER...
Gasp! I'M FINISHED!
F-FIVE PENCE, PLEASE...
PLOP!
BUT WHEN THE EXHAUSTED BOY COMES TO...
MY PAY! THE FIRST COIN I EVER EARNED FROM MY OWN LABOR!
WAIT! THIS IS AN AMERICAN COIN! A DIME! THAT SHARPIE TRICKED ME!
THIS SHOULD BE A LESSON! LIFE IS FILLED WITH TOUGH JOBS, AND THERE'LL ALWAYS BE SHARPIES TO CHEAT ME!
WELL, I'LL BE TOUGHER THAN THE TOUGHIES, AND SHARPER THAN THE SHARPIES--AND I'LL MAKE MY MONEY SQUARE!
I HAVE THE FEELING THIS IS THE START OF SOMETHING BIG!
SHINE, MISTER?!

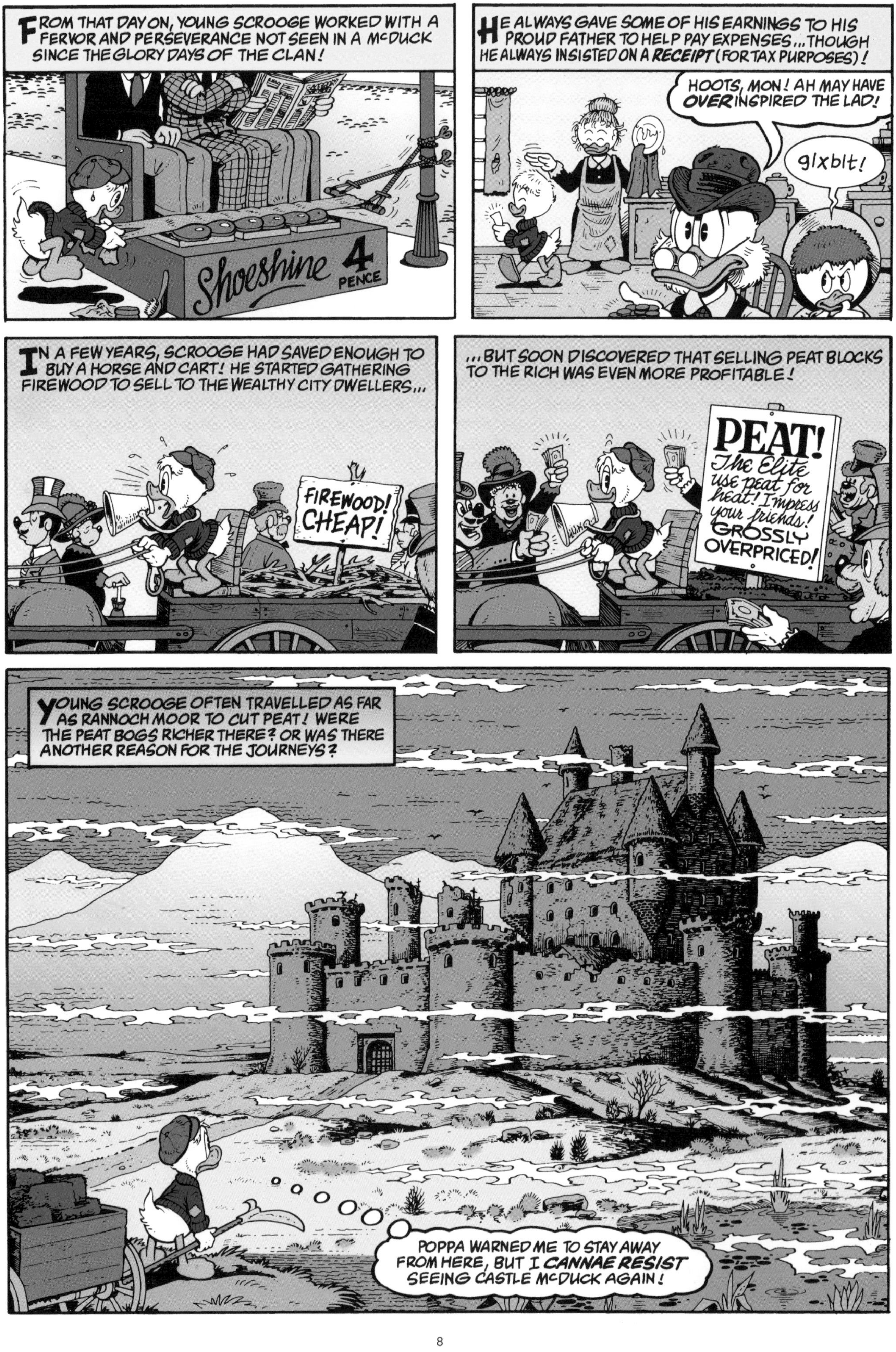
FROM THAT DAY ON, YOUNG SCROOGE WORKED WITH A FERVOR AND PERSEVERANCE NOT SEEN IN A McDUCK SINCE THE GLORY DAYS OF THE CLAN!
Shoeshine 4 PENCE
HE ALWAYS GAVE SOME OF HIS EARNINGS TO HIS PROUD FATHER TO HELP PAY EXPENSES... THOUGH HE ALWAYS INSISTED ON A RECEIPT (FOR TAX PURPOSES)!
HOOTS, MON! AH MAY HAVE OVERINSPIRED THE LAD!
glxblt!
IN A FEW YEARS, SCROOGE HAD SAVED ENOUGH TO BUY A HORSE AND CART! HE STARTED GATHERING FIREWOOD TO SELL TO THE WEALTHY CITY DWELLERS...
FIREWOOD! CHEAP!
...BUT SOON DISCOVERED THAT SELLING PEAT BLOCKS TO THE RICH WAS EVEN MORE PROFITABLE!
PEAT! The Elite use peat for heat! Impress your friends! GROSSLY OVERPRICED!
YOUNG SCROOGE OFTEN TRAVELLED AS FAR AS RANNOCH MOOR TO CUT PEAT! WERE THE PEAT BOGS RICHER THERE? OR WAS THERE ANOTHER REASON FOR THE JOURNEYS?
POPPA WARNED ME TO STAY AWAY FROM HERE, BUT I CANNAE RESIST SEEING CASTLE McDUCK AGAIN!

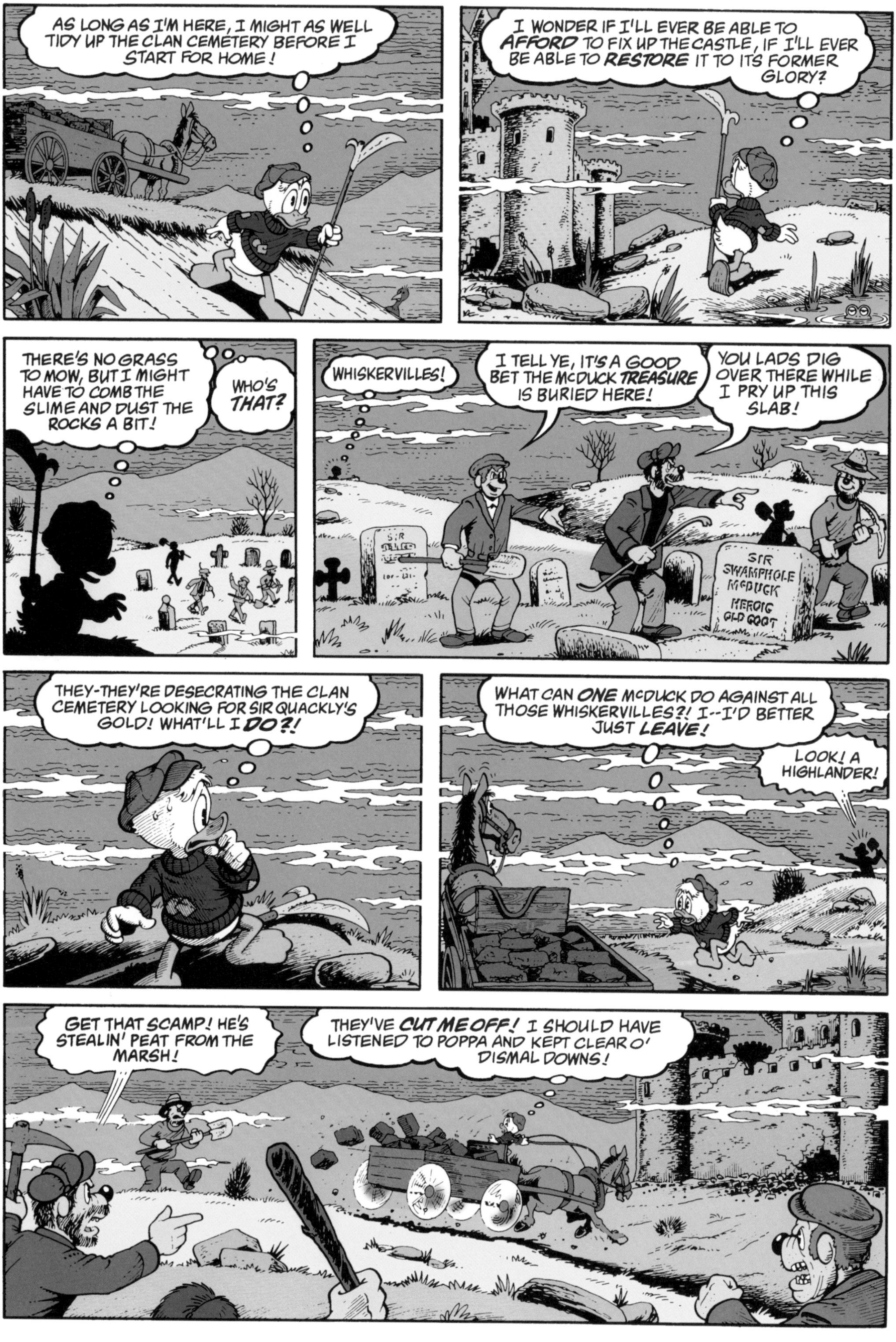
AS LONG AS I'M HERE, I MIGHT AS WELL TIDY UP THE CLAN CEMETERY BEFORE I START FOR HOME!
I WONDER IF I'LL EVER BE ABLE TO AFFORD TO FIX UP THE CASTLE, IF I'LL EVER BE ABLE TO RESTORE IT TO ITS FORMER GLORY?
THERE'S NO GRASS TO MOW, BUT I MIGHT HAVE TO COMB THE SLIME AND DUST THE ROCKS A BIT!
WHO'S THAT?
WHISKERVILLES!
I TELL YE, IT'S A GOOD BET THE McDUCK TREASURE IS BURIED HERE!
YOU LADS DIG OVER THERE WHILE I PRY UP THIS SLAB!
SIR SWAMPHOLE McDUCK HEROIC OLD COOT
THEY-THEY'RE DESECRATING THE CLAN CEMETERY LOOKING FOR SIR QUACKLY'S GOLD! WHAT'LL I DO?!
WHAT CAN ONE McDUCK DO AGAINST ALL THOSE WHISKERVILLES?! I--I'D BETTER JUST LEAVE!
LOOK! A HIGHLANDER!
GET THAT SCAMP! HE'S STEALIN' PEAT FROM THE MARSH!
THEY'VE CUT ME OFF! I SHOULD HAVE LISTENED TO POPPA AND KEPT CLEAR O' DISMAL DOWNS!

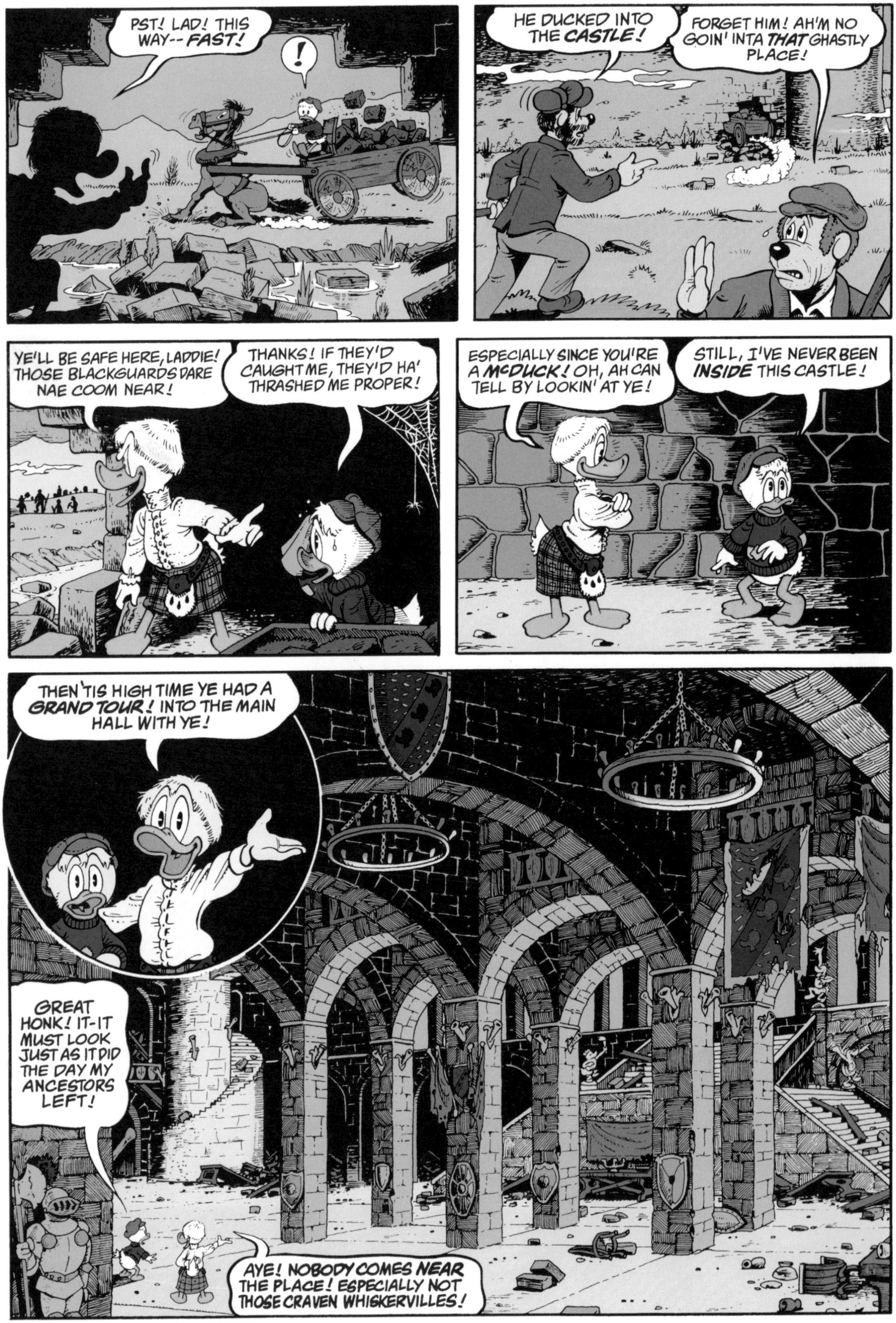
PST! LAD! THIS WAY-- FAST!
!
HE DUCKED INTO THE CASTLE!
FORGET HIM! AH'M NO GOIN' INTA THAT GHASTLY PLACE!
YE'LL BE SAFE HERE, LADDIE! THOSE BLACKGUARDS DARE NAE COOM NEAR!
THANKS! IF THEY'D CAUGHT ME, THEY'D HA' THRASHED ME PROPER!
ESPECIALLY SINCE YOU'RE A McDUCK! OH, AH CAN TELL BY LOOKIN' AT YE!
STILL, I'VE NEVER BEEN INSIDE THIS CASTLE!
THEN 'TIS HIGH TIME YE HAD A GRAND TOUR! INTO THE MAIN HALL WITH YE!
GREAT HONK! IT-IT MUST LOOK JUST AS IT DID THE DAY MY ANCESTORS LEFT!
AYE! NOBODY COMES NEAR THE PLACE! ESPECIALLY NOT THOSE CRAVEN WHISKERVILLES!

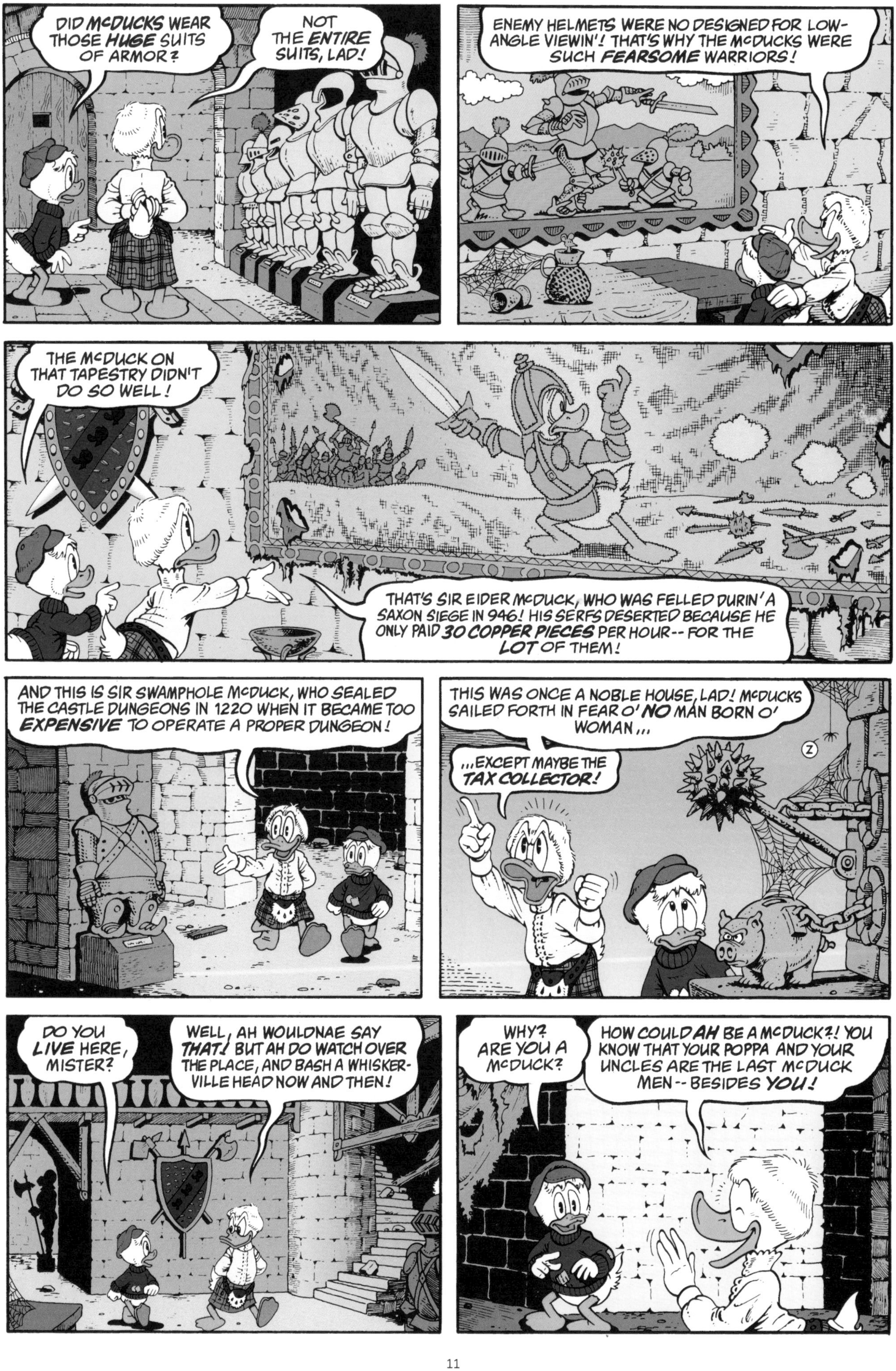
DID McDUCKS WEAR THOSE HUGE SUITS OF ARMOR?
NOT THE ENTIRE SUITS, LAD!
ENEMY HELMETS WERE NO DESIGNED FOR LOW-ANGLE VIEWIN'! THAT'S WHY THE McDUCKS WERE SUCH FEARSOME WARRIORS!
THE McDUCK ON THAT TAPESTRY DIDN'T DO SO WELL!
THAT'S SIR EIDER McDUCK, WHO WAS FELLED DURIN' A SAXON SIEGE IN 946! HIS SERFS DESERTED BECAUSE HE ONLY PAID 30 COPPER PIECES PER HOUR -- FOR THE LOT OF THEM!
AND THIS IS SIR SWAMPHOLE McDUCK, WHO SEALED THE CASTLE DUNGEONS IN 1220 WHEN IT BECAME TOO EXPENSIVE TO OPERATE A PROPER DUNGEON!
THIS WAS ONCE A NOBLE HOUSE, LAD! McDUCKS SAILED FORTH IN FEAR O' NO MAN BORN O' WOMAN...
...EXCEPT MAYBE THE TAX COLLECTOR!
Z
DO YOU LIVE HERE, MISTER?
WELL, AH WOULDNAE SAY THAT! BUT AH DO WATCH OVER THE PLACE, AND BASH A WHISKER-VILLE HEAD NOW AND THEN!
WHY? ARE YOU A McDUCK?
HOW COULD AH BE A McDUCK?! YOU KNOW THAT YOUR POPPA AND YOUR UNCLES ARE THE LAST McDUCK MEN -- BESIDES YOU!

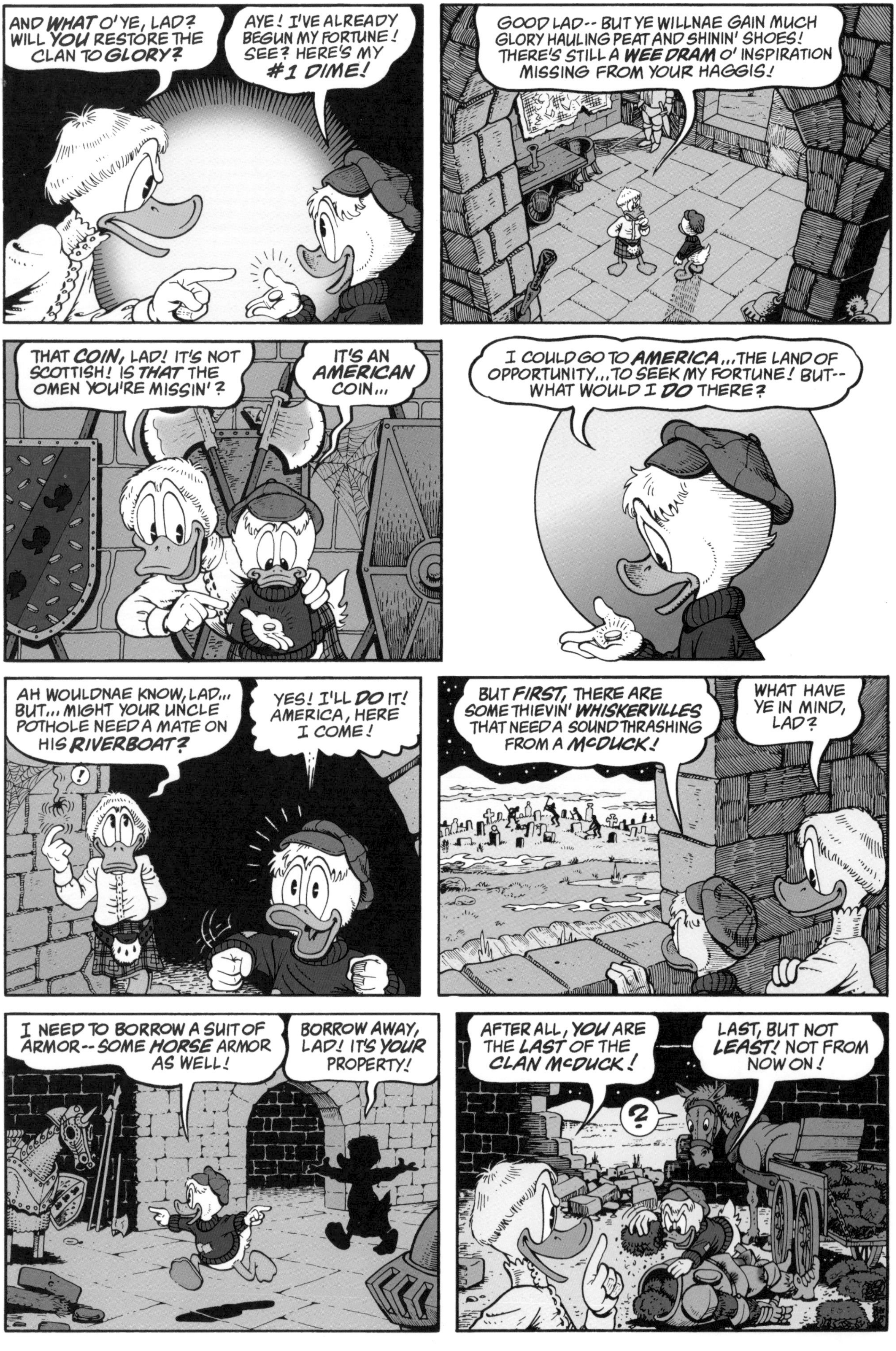
AND WHAT O' YE, LAD? WILL YOU RESTORE THE CLAN TO GLORY?
AYE! I'VE ALREADY BEGUN MY FORTUNE! SEE? HERE'S MY #1 DIME!
GOOD LAD-- BUT YE WILLNAE GAIN MUCH GLORY HAULING PEAT AND SHININ' SHOES! THERE'S STILL A WEE DRAM O' INSPIRATION MISSING FROM YOUR HAGGIS!
THAT COIN, LAD! IT'S NOT SCOTTISH! IS THAT THE OMEN YOU'RE MISSIN'?
IT'S AN AMERICAN COIN...
I COULD GO TO AMERICA... THE LAND OF OPPORTUNITY... TO SEEK MY FORTUNE! BUT-- WHAT WOULD I DO THERE?
AH WOULDNAE KNOW, LAD... BUT... MIGHT YOUR UNCLE POTHOLE NEED A MATE ON HIS RIVERBOAT?
!
YES! I'LL DO IT! AMERICA, HERE I COME!
BUT FIRST, THERE ARE SOME THIEVIN' WHISKERVILLES THAT NEED A SOUND THRASHING FROM A McDUCK!
WHAT HAVE YE IN MIND, LAD?
I NEED TO BORROW A SUIT OF ARMOR-- SOME HORSE ARMOR AS WELL!
BORROW AWAY, LAD! IT'S YOUR PROPERTY!
AFTER ALL, YOU ARE THE LAST OF THE CLAN McDUCK!
?
LAST, BUT NOT LEAST! NOT FROM NOW ON!

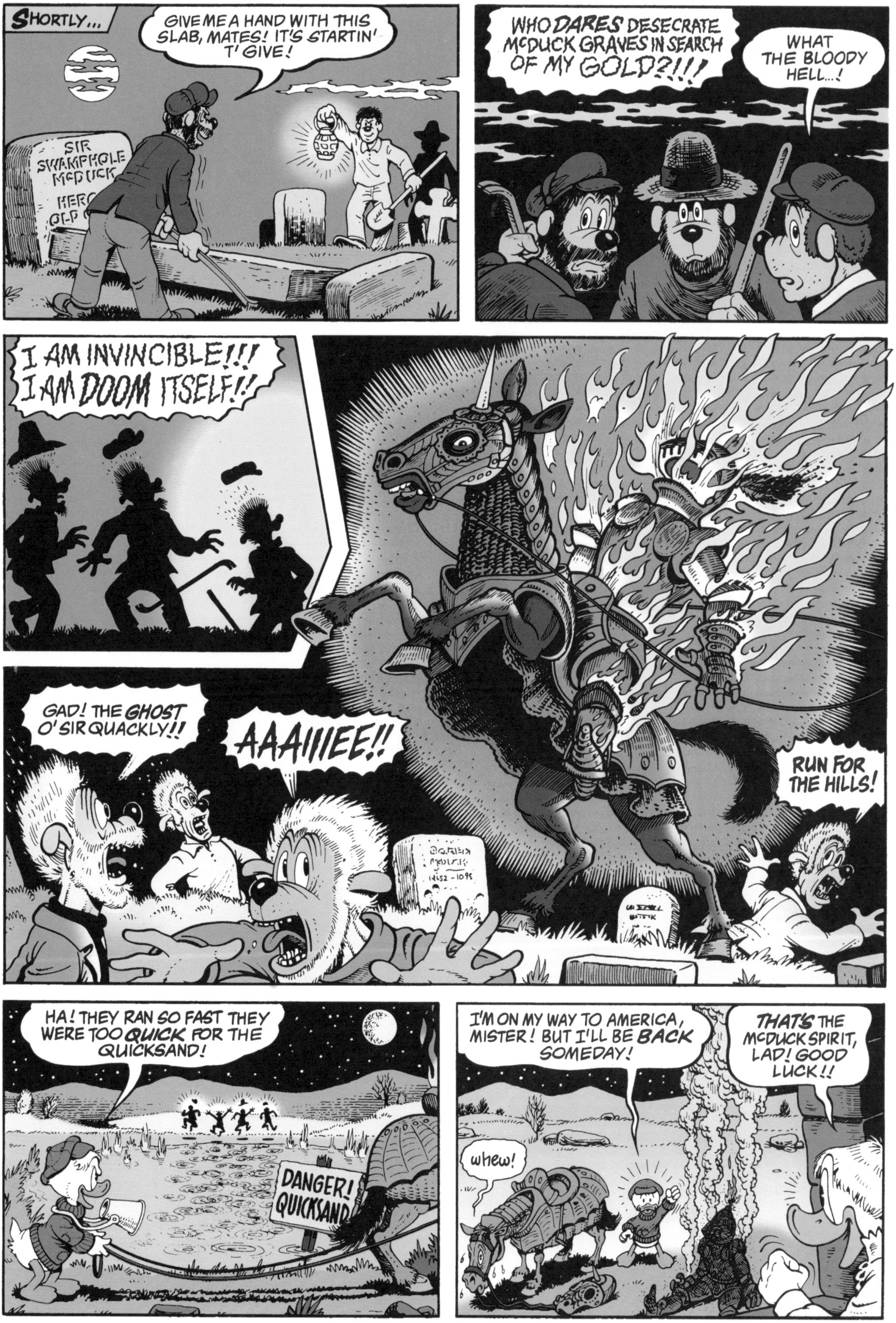
SHORTLY...
GIVE ME A HAND WITH THIS SLAB, MATES! IT'S STARTIN' T' GIVE!
SIR SWAMPHOLE McDUCK
WHO DARES DESECRATE McDUCK GRAVES IN SEARCH OF MY GOLD?!!!
WHAT THE BLOODY HELL...!
I AM INVINCIBLE!!! I AM DOOM ITSELF!!
GAD! THE GHOST O' SIR QUACKLY!!
AAAIIIEE!!
RUN FOR THE HILLS!
HA! THEY RAN SO FAST THEY WERE TOO QUICK FOR THE QUICKSAND!
DANGER! QUICKSAND
I'M ON MY WAY TO AMERICA, MISTER! BUT I'LL BE BACK SOMEDAY!
THAT'S THE McDUCK SPIRIT, LAD! GOOD LUCK!!
whew!

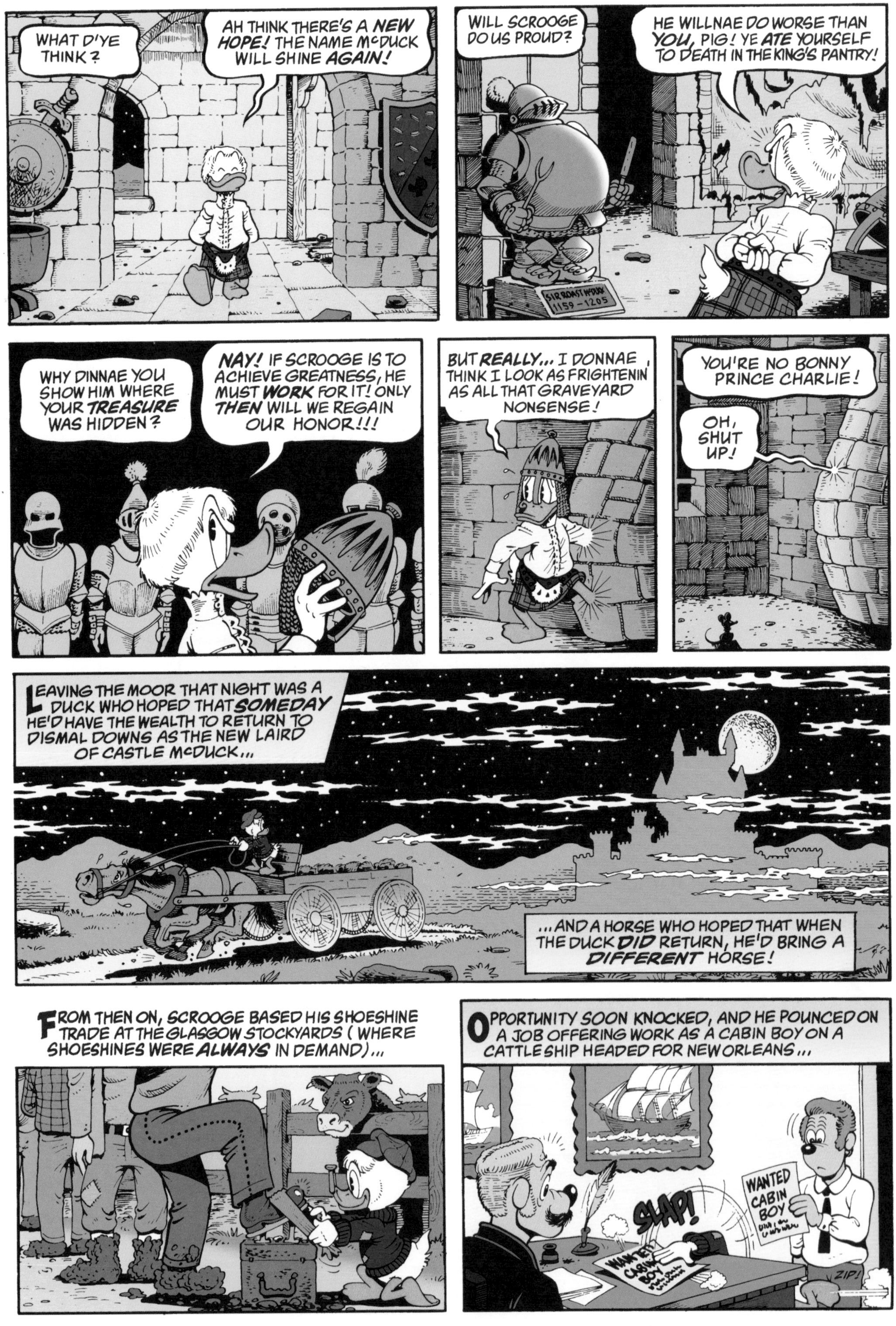
WHAT D'YE THINK?
AH THINK THERE'S A NEW HOPE! THE NAME McDUCK WILL SHINE AGAIN!
WILL SCROOGE DO US PROUD?
HE WILLNAE DO WORSE THAN YOU, PIG! YE ATE YOURSELF TO DEATH IN THE KING'S PANTRY!
SIR ROAST McDUCK 1159 – 1205
WHY DINNAE YOU SHOW HIM WHERE YOUR TREASURE WAS HIDDEN?
NAY! IF SCROOGE IS TO ACHIEVE GREATNESS, HE MUST WORK FOR IT! ONLY THEN WILL WE REGAIN OUR HONOR!!!
BUT REALLY... I DONNAE THINK I LOOK AS FRIGHTENIN' AS ALL THAT GRAVEYARD NONSENSE!
YOU'RE NO BONNY PRINCE CHARLIE!
OH, SHUT UP!
LEAVING THE MOOR THAT NIGHT WAS A DUCK WHO HOPED THAT SOMEDAY HE'D HAVE THE WEALTH TO RETURN TO DISMAL DOWNS AS THE NEW LAIRD OF CASTLE McDUCK...
...AND A HORSE WHO HOPED THAT WHEN THE DUCK DID RETURN, HE'D BRING A DIFFERENT HORSE!
FROM THEN ON, SCROOGE BASED HIS SHOESHINE TRADE AT THE GLASGOW STOCKYARDS (WHERE SHOESHINES WERE ALWAYS IN DEMAND)...
OPPORTUNITY SOON KNOCKED, AND HE POUNCED ON A JOB OFFERING WORK AS A CABIN BOY ON A CATTLESHIP HEADED FOR NEW ORLEANS...
WANTED CABIN BOY
SLAP!
WANTED CABIN BOY
ZIP!

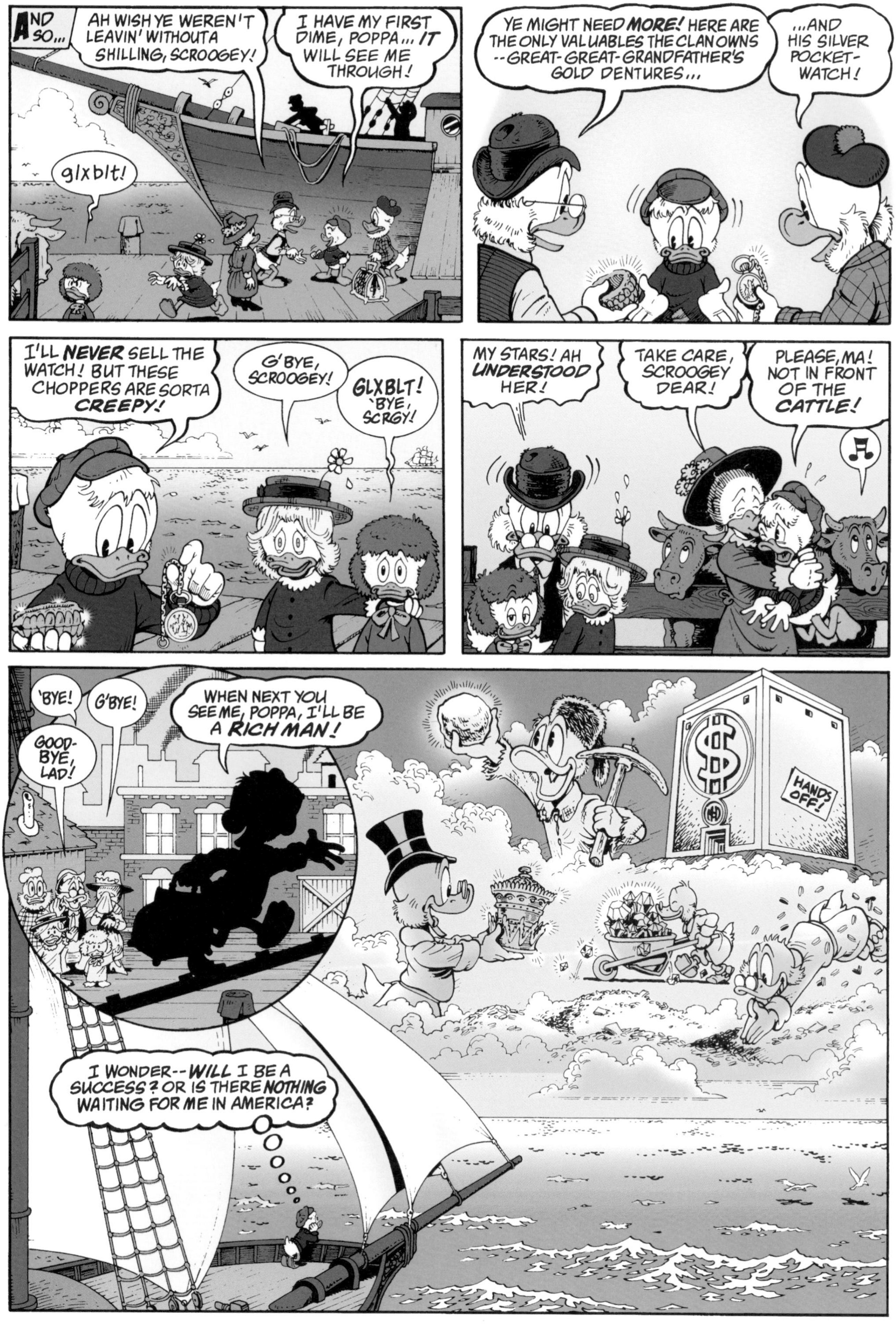
AND SO...
AH WISH YE WEREN'T LEAVIN' WITHOUTA SHILLING, SCROOGEY!
I HAVE MY FIRST DIME, POPPA... IT WILL SEE ME THROUGH!
glxblt!
YE MIGHT NEED MORE! HERE ARE THE ONLY VALUABLES THE CLAN OWNS --GREAT-GREAT-GRANDFATHER'S GOLD DENTURES...
...AND HIS SILVER POCKET-WATCH!
I'LL NEVER SELL THE WATCH! BUT THESE CHOPPERS ARE SORTA CREEPY!
G'BYE, SCROOGEY!
GLXBLT! `BYE, SCRGY!
MY STARS! AH UNDERSTOOD HER!
TAKE CARE, SCROOGEY DEAR!
PLEASE, MA! NOT IN FRONT OF THE CATTLE!
'BYE!
G'BYE!
GOOD-BYE, LAD!
WHEN NEXT YOU SEE ME, POPPA, I'LL BE A RICH MAN!
HANDS OFF!
I WONDER--WILL I BE A SUCCESS? OR IS THERE NOTHING WAITING FOR ME IN AMERICA?

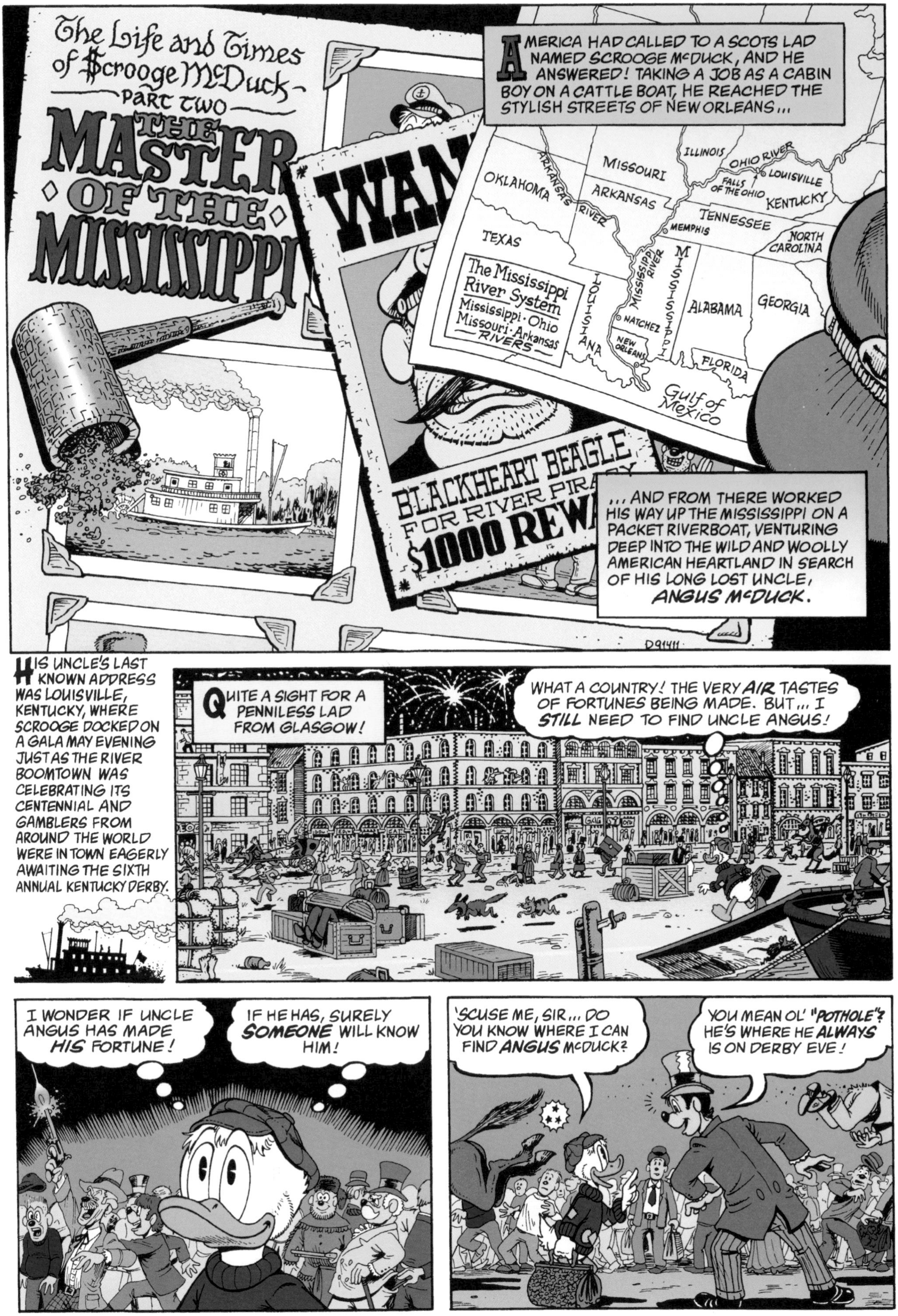
The Life and Times of $crooge McDuck
Part Two
THE MASTER OF THE MISSISSIPPI
AMERICA HAD CALLED TO A SCOTS LAD NAMED SCROOGE McDUCK, AND HE ANSWERED! TAKING A JOB AS A CABIN BOY ON A CATTLE BOAT, HE REACHED THE STYLISH STREETS OF NEW ORLEANS...
WAN
BLACKHEART BEAGLE
FOR RIVER PIRA
$1000 REWA
MISSOURI
ILLINOIS
OHIO RIVER
LOUISVILLE
FALLS OF THE OHIO
KENTUCKY
OKLAHOMA
ARKANSAS RIVER
ARKANSAS
TENNESSEE
MEMPHIS
NORTH CAROLINA
TEXAS
MISSISSIPPI RIVER
MISSISSIPPI
LOUISIANA
NATCHEZ
NEW ORLEANS
ALABAMA
GEORGIA
FLORIDA
Gulf of Mexico
The Mississippi River System
Mississippi · Ohio
Missouri · Arkansas
RIVERS
...AND FROM THERE WORKED HIS WAY UP THE MISSISSIPPI ON A PACKET RIVERBOAT, VENTURING DEEP INTO THE WILD AND WOOLLY AMERICAN HEARTLAND IN SEARCH OF HIS LONG LOST UNCLE, ANGUS McDUCK.
HIS UNCLE'S LAST KNOWN ADDRESS WAS LOUISVILLE, KENTUCKY, WHERE SCROOGE DOCKED ON A GALA MAY EVENING JUST AS THE RIVER BOOMTOWN WAS CELEBRATING ITS CENTENNIAL AND GAMBLERS FROM AROUND THE WORLD WERE IN TOWN EAGERLY AWAITING THE SIXTH ANNUAL KENTUCKY DERBY.
QUITE A SIGHT FOR A PENNILESS LAD FROM GLASGOW!
WHAT A COUNTRY! THE VERY AIR TASTES OF FORTUNES BEING MADE. BUT... I STILL NEED TO FIND UNCLE ANGUS!
I WONDER IF UNCLE ANGUS HAS MADE HIS FORTUNE!
IF HE HAS, SURELY SOMEONE WILL KNOW HIM!
'SCUSE ME, SIR... DO YOU KNOW WHERE I CAN FIND ANGUS McDUCK?
YOU MEAN OL' "POTHOLE"? HE'S WHERE HE ALWAYS IS ON DERBY EVE!

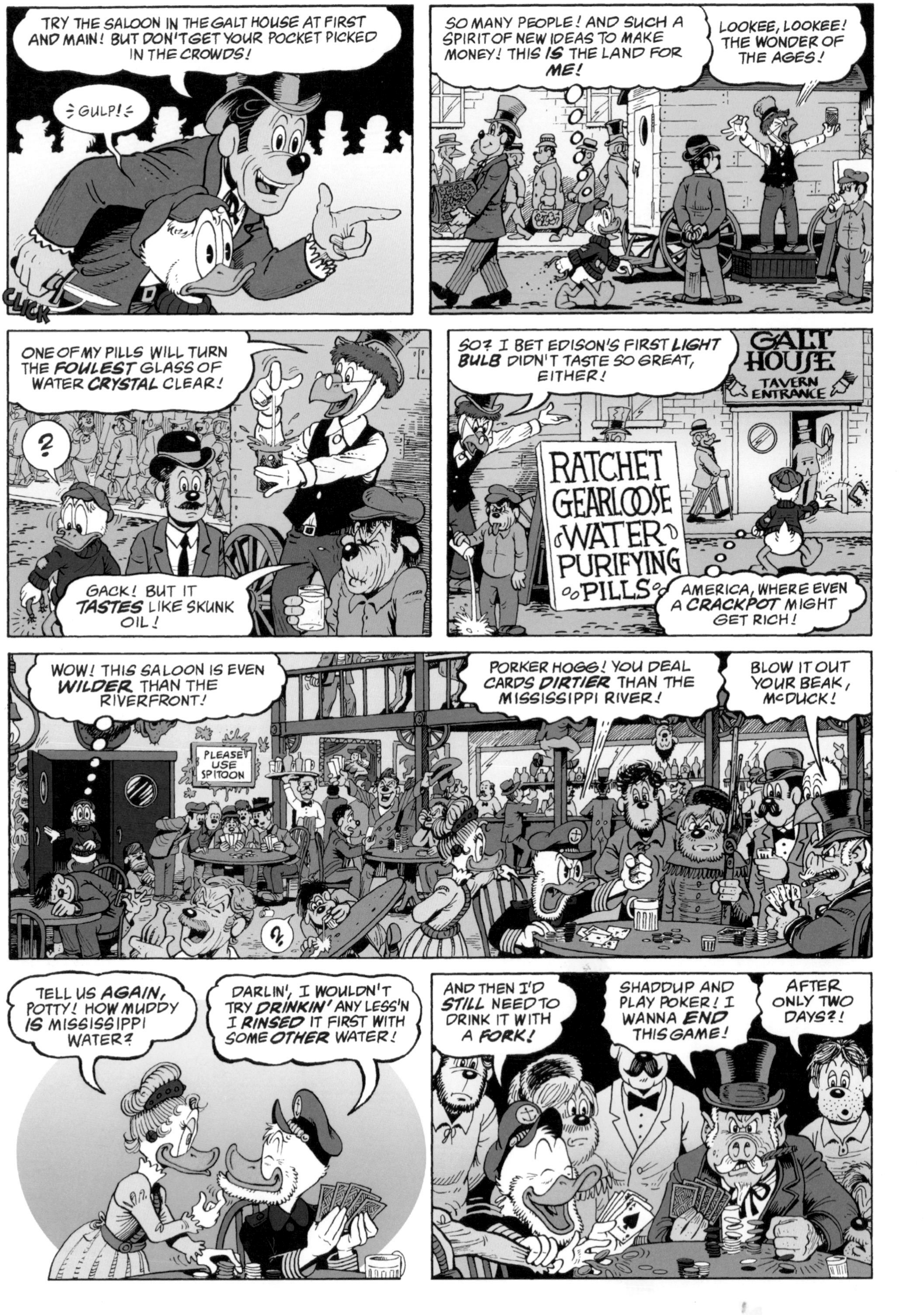
TRY THE SALOON IN THE GALT HOUSE AT FIRST AND MAIN! BUT DON'T GET YOUR POCKET PICKED IN THE CROWDS!
GULP!
CLICK
SO MANY PEOPLE! AND SUCH A SPIRIT OF NEW IDEAS TO MAKE MONEY! THIS IS THE LAND FOR ME!
LOOKEE, LOOKEE! THE WONDER OF THE AGES!
ONE OF MY PILLS WILL TURN THE FOULEST GLASS OF WATER CRYSTAL CLEAR!
?
GACK! BUT IT TASTES LIKE SKUNK OIL!
SO? I BET EDISON'S FIRST LIGHT BULB DIDN'T TASTE SO GREAT, EITHER!
GALT HOUSE
TAVERN ENTRANCE
RATCHET GEARLOOSE WATER PURIFYING PILLS
AMERICA, WHERE EVEN A CRACKPOT MIGHT GET RICH!
WOW! THIS SALOON IS EVEN WILDER THAN THE RIVERFRONT!
PLEASE USE SPITOON
PORKER HOGG! YOU DEAL CARDS DIRTIER THAN THE MISSISSIPPI RIVER!
BLOW IT OUT YOUR BEAK, McDUCK!
?
TELL US AGAIN, POTTY! HOW MUDDY IS MISSISSIPPI WATER?
DARLIN', I WOULDN'T TRY DRINKIN' ANY LESS'N I RINSED IT FIRST WITH SOME OTHER WATER!
AND THEN I'D STILL NEED TO DRINK IT WITH A FORK!
SHADDUP AND PLAY POKER! I WANNA END THIS GAME!
AFTER ONLY TWO DAYS?!

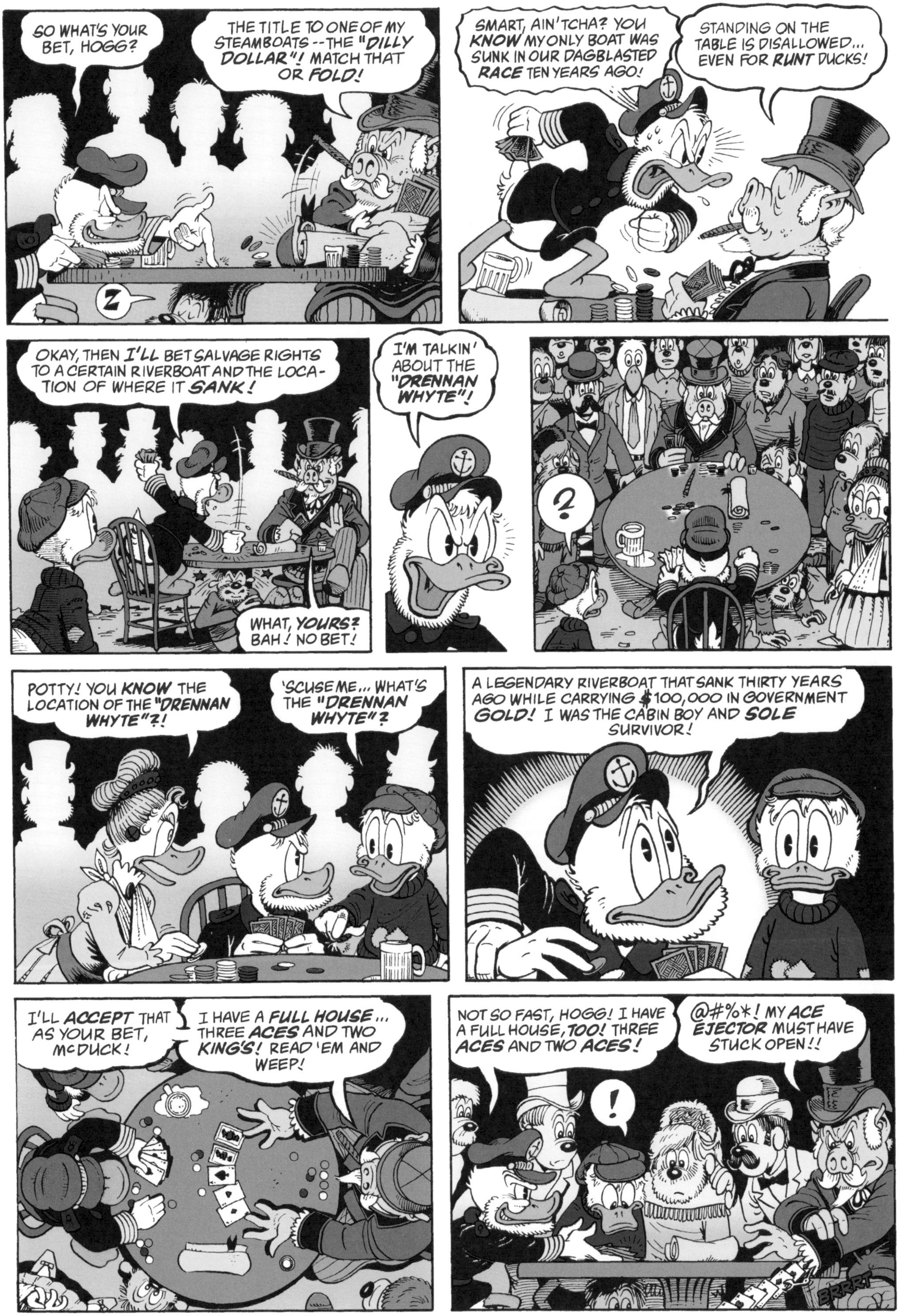
SO WHAT'S YOUR BET, HOGG?
THE TITLE TO ONE OF MY STEAMBOATS -- THE "DILLY DOLLAR"! MATCH THAT OR FOLD!
Z
SMART, AIN'TCHA? YOU KNOW MY ONLY BOAT WAS SUNK IN OUR DAGBLASTED RACE TEN YEARS AGO!
STANDING ON THE TABLE IS DISALLOWED... EVEN FOR RUNT DUCKS!
OKAY, THEN I'LL BET SALVAGE RIGHTS TO A CERTAIN RIVERBOAT AND THE LOCATION OF WHERE IT SANK!
WHAT, YOURS? BAH! NO BET!
I'M TALKIN' ABOUT THE "DRENNAN WHYTE"!
?
POTTY! YOU KNOW THE LOCATION OF THE "DRENNAN WHYTE"?!
'SCUSE ME... WHAT'S THE "DRENNAN WHYTE"?
A LEGENDARY RIVERBOAT THAT SANK THIRTY YEARS AGO WHILE CARRYING $100,000 IN GOVERNMENT GOLD! I WAS THE CABIN BOY AND SOLE SURVIVOR!
I'LL ACCEPT THAT AS YOUR BET, McDUCK!
I HAVE A FULL HOUSE... THREE ACES AND TWO KING'S! READ 'EM AND WEEP!
NOT SO FAST, HOGG! I HAVE A FULL HOUSE, TOO! THREE ACES AND TWO ACES!
!
@#%*! MY ACE EJECTOR MUST HAVE STUCK OPEN!!
BRRRT

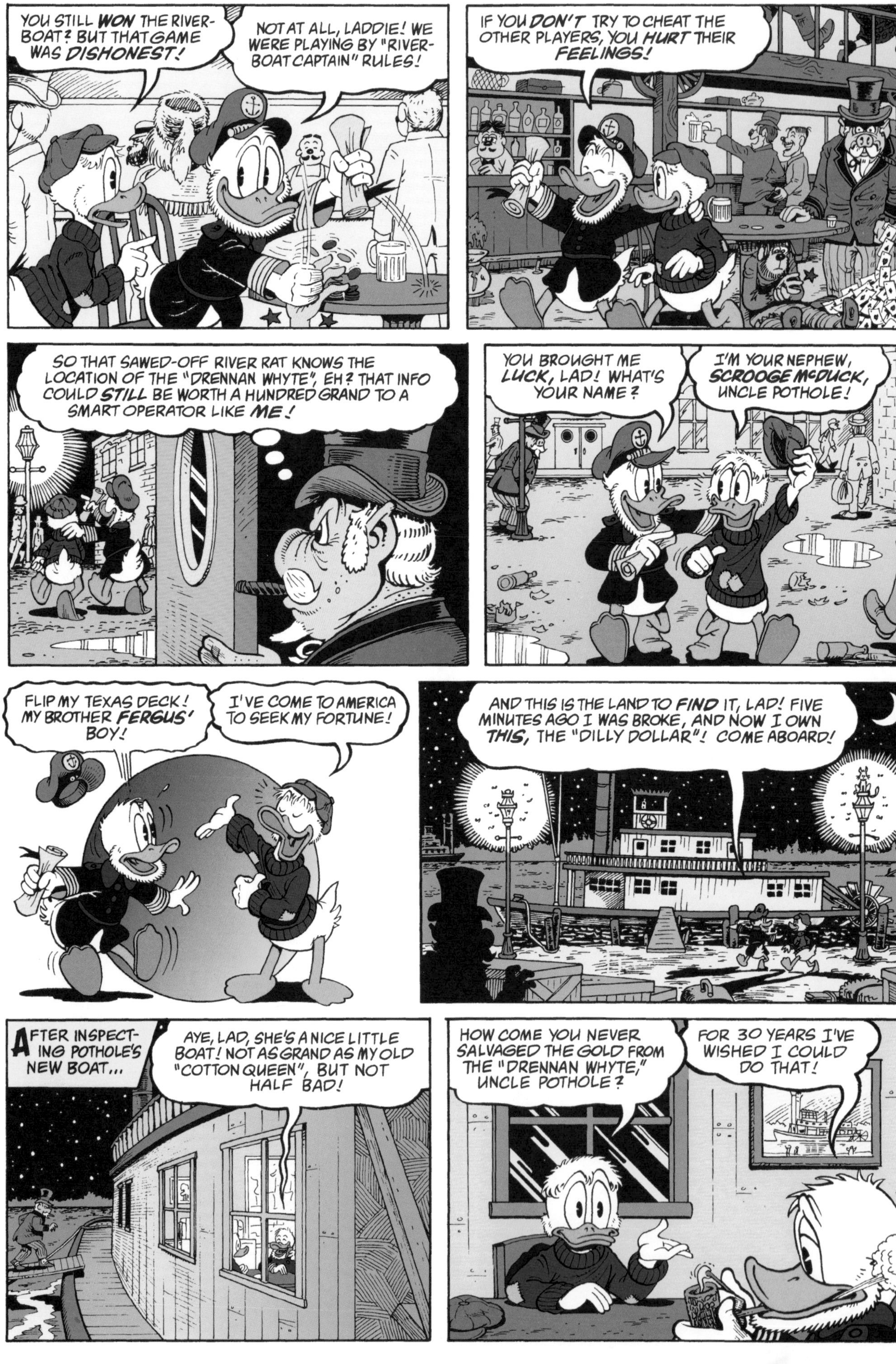
YOU STILL WON THE RIVER-BOAT? BUT THAT GAME WAS DISHONEST!
NOT AT ALL, LADDIE! WE WERE PLAYING BY "RIVER-BOAT CAPTAIN" RULES!
IF YOU DON'T TRY TO CHEAT THE OTHER PLAYERS, YOU HURT THEIR FEELINGS!
SO THAT SAWED-OFF RIVER RAT KNOWS THE LOCATION OF THE "DRENNAN WHYTE", EH? THAT INFO COULD STILL BE WORTH A HUNDRED GRAND TO A SMART OPERATOR LIKE ME!
YOU BROUGHT ME LUCK, LAD! WHAT'S YOUR NAME?
I'M YOUR NEPHEW, SCROOGE McDUCK, UNCLE POTHOLE!
FLIP MY TEXAS DECK! MY BROTHER FERGUS' BOY!
I'VE COME TO AMERICA TO SEEK MY FORTUNE!
AND THIS IS THE LAND TO FIND IT, LAD! FIVE MINUTES AGO I WAS BROKE, AND NOW I OWN THIS, THE "DILLY DOLLAR"! COME ABOARD!
AFTER INSPECTING POTHOLE'S NEW BOAT...
AYE, LAD, SHE'S A NICE LITTLE BOAT! NOT AS GRAND AS MY OLD "COTTON QUEEN", BUT NOT HALF BAD!
HOW COME YOU NEVER SALVAGED THE GOLD FROM THE "DRENNAN WHYTE," UNCLE POTHOLE?
FOR 30 YEARS I'VE WISHED I COULD DO THAT!

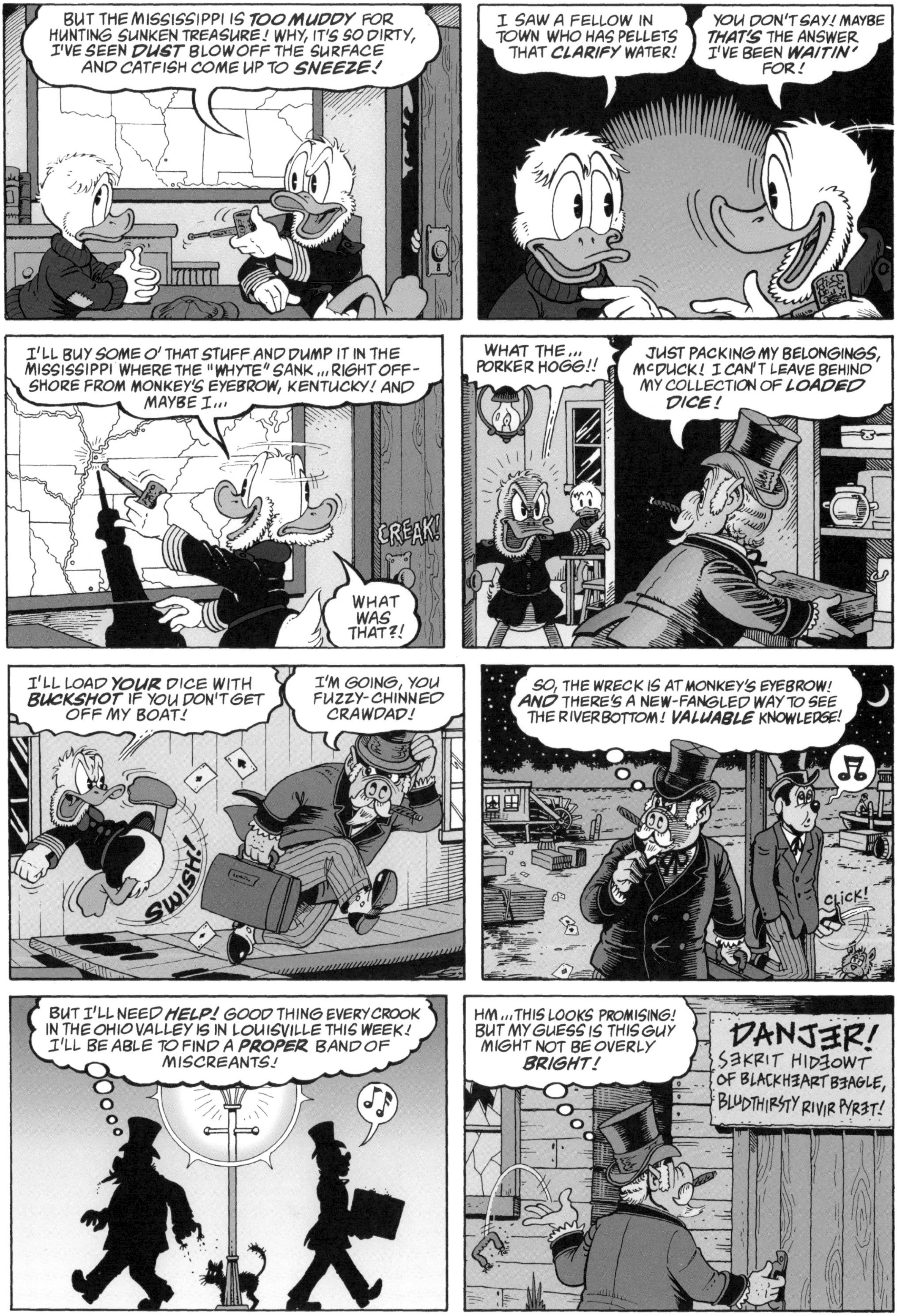
BUT THE MISSISSIPPI IS TOO MUDDY FOR HUNTING SUNKEN TREASURE! WHY, IT'S SO DIRTY, I'VE SEEN DUST BLOW OFF THE SURFACE AND CATFISH COME UP TO SNEEZE!
I SAW A FELLOW IN TOWN WHO HAS PELLETS THAT CLARIFY WATER!
YOU DON'T SAY! MAYBE THAT'S THE ANSWER I'VE BEEN WAITIN' FOR!
I'LL BUY SOME O' THAT STUFF AND DUMP IT IN THE MISSISSIPPI WHERE THE "WHYTE" SANK ... RIGHT OFF-SHORE FROM MONKEY'S EYEBROW, KENTUCKY! AND MAYBE I...
CREAK!
WHAT WAS THAT?!
WHAT THE... PORKER HOGG!!
JUST PACKING MY BELONGINGS, McDUCK! I CAN'T LEAVE BEHIND MY COLLECTION OF LOADED DICE!
I'LL LOAD YOUR DICE WITH BUCKSHOT IF YOU DON'T GET OFF MY BOAT!
I'M GOING, YOU FUZZY-CHINNED CRAWDAD!
SWISH!
SO, THE WRECK IS AT MONKEY'S EYEBROW! AND THERE'S A NEW-FANGLED WAY TO SEE THE RIVERBOTTOM! VALUABLE KNOWLEDGE!
CLICK!
BUT I'LL NEED HELP! GOOD THING EVERY CROOK IN THE OHIO VALLEY IS IN LOUISVILLE THIS WEEK! I'LL BE ABLE TO FIND A PROPER BAND OF MISCREANTS!
HM... THIS LOOKS PROMISING! BUT MY GUESS IS THIS GUY MIGHT NOT BE OVERLY BRIGHT!
DANJER! SEKRIT HIDEOWT OF BLACKHEART BEAGLE, BLUDTHIRSTY RIVIR PYRET!

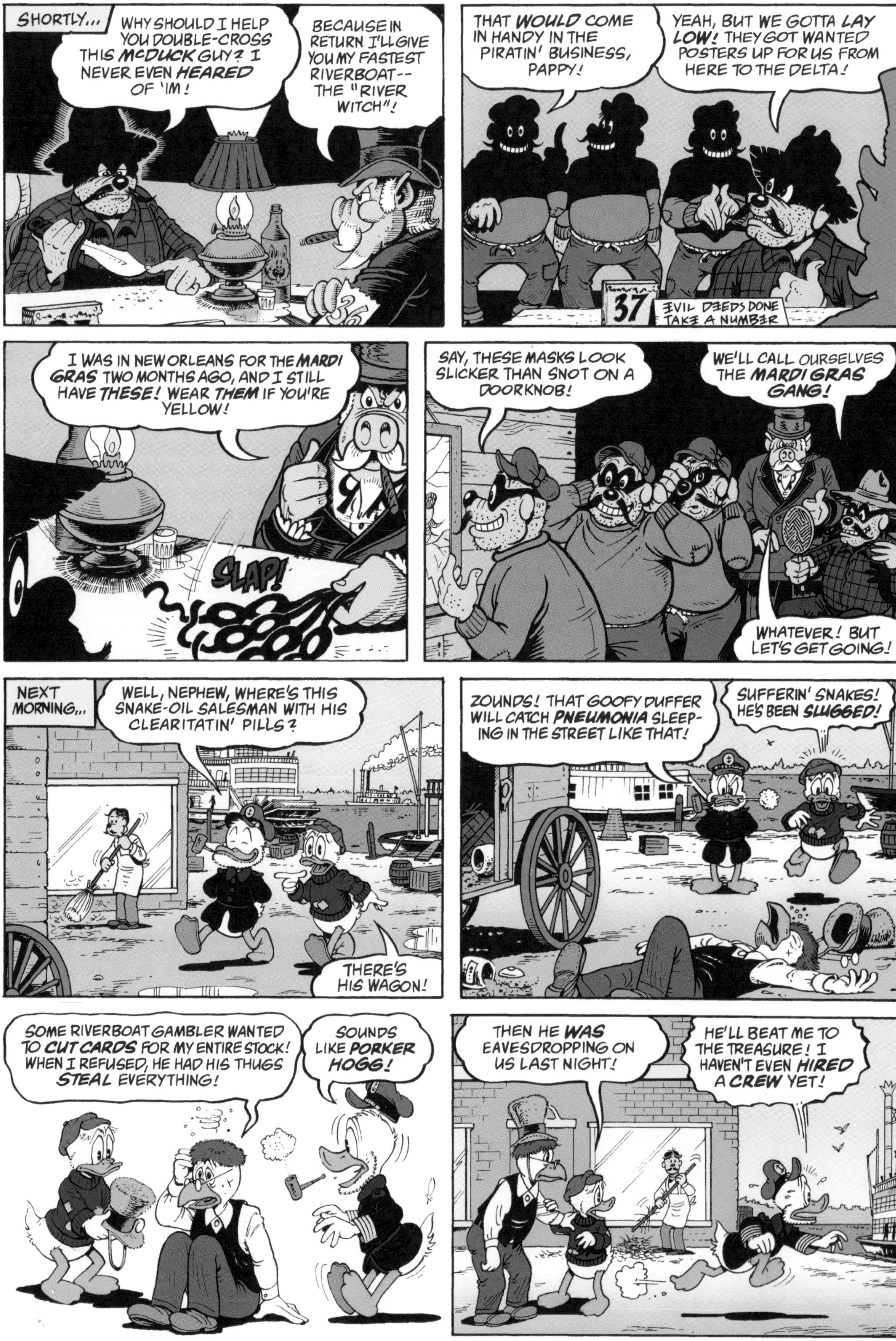
SHORTLY...
WHY SHOULD I HELP YOU DOUBLE-CROSS THIS McDUCK GUY? I NEVER EVEN HEARED OF 'IM!
BECAUSE IN RETURN I'LL GIVE YOU MY FASTEST RIVERBOAT-- THE "RIVER WITCH"!
THAT WOULD COME IN HANDY IN THE PIRATIN' BUSINESS, PAPPY!
YEAH, BUT WE GOTTA LAY LOW! THEY GOT WANTED POSTERS UP FOR US FROM HERE TO THE DELTA!
37
EVIL DEEDS DONE
TAKE A NUMBER
I WAS IN NEW ORLEANS FOR THE MARDI GRAS TWO MONTHS AGO, AND I STILL HAVE THESE! WEAR THEM IF YOU'RE YELLOW!
SLAP!
SAY, THESE MASKS LOOK SLICKER THAN SNOT ON A DOORKNOB!
WE'LL CALL OURSELVES THE MARDI GRAS GANG!
WHATEVER! BUT LET'S GET GOING!
NEXT MORNING...
WELL, NEPHEW, WHERE'S THIS SNAKE-OIL SALESMAN WITH HIS CLEARITATIN' PILLS?
THERE'S HIS WAGON!
ZOUNDS! THAT GOOFY DUFFER WILL CATCH PNEUMONIA SLEEPING IN THE STREET LIKE THAT!
SUFFERIN' SNAKES! HE'S BEEN SLUGGED!
SOME RIVERBOAT GAMBLER WANTED TO CUT CARDS FOR MY ENTIRE STOCK! WHEN I REFUSED, HE HAD HIS THUGS STEAL EVERYTHING!
SOUNDS LIKE PORKER HOGG!
THEN HE WAS EAVESDROPPING ON US LAST NIGHT!
HE'LL BEAT ME TO THE TREASURE! I HAVEN'T EVEN HIRED A CREW YET!

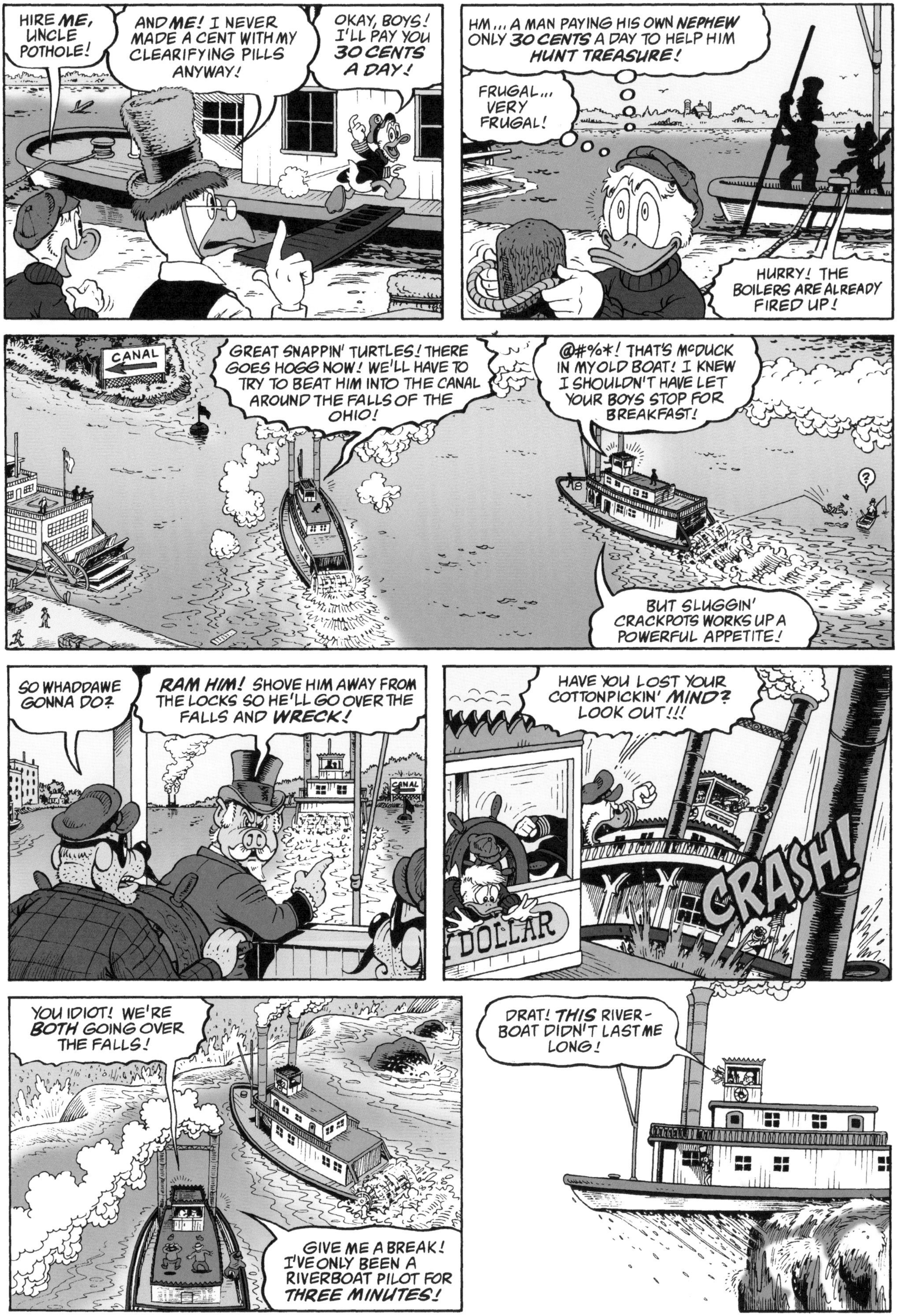
HIRE ME, UNCLE POTHOLE!
AND ME! I NEVER MADE A CENT WITH MY CLEARIFYING PILLS ANYWAY!
OKAY, BOYS! I'LL PAY YOU 30 CENTS A DAY!
HM... A MAN PAYING HIS OWN NEPHEW ONLY 30 CENTS A DAY TO HELP HIM HUNT TREASURE!
FRUGAL... VERY FRUGAL!
HURRY! THE BOILERS ARE ALREADY FIRED UP!
CANAL
GREAT SNAPPIN' TURTLES! THERE GOES HOGG NOW! WE'LL HAVE TO TRY TO BEAT HIM INTO THE CANAL AROUND THE FALLS OF THE OHIO!
@#%*! THAT'S McDUCK IN MY OLD BOAT! I KNEW I SHOULDN'T HAVE LET YOUR BOYS STOP FOR BREAKFAST!
BUT SLUGGIN' CRACKPOTS WORKS UP A POWERFUL APPETITE!
SO WHADDAWE GONNA DO?
RAM HIM! SHOVE HIM AWAY FROM THE LOCKS SO HE'LL GO OVER THE FALLS AND WRECK!
CANAL
HAVE YOU LOST YOUR COTTONPICKIN' MIND? LOOK OUT!!!
DOLLAR
CRASH!
YOU IDIOT! WE'RE BOTH GOING OVER THE FALLS!
GIVE ME A BREAK! I'VE ONLY BEEN A RIVERBOAT PILOT FOR THREE MINUTES!
DRAT! THIS RIVER-BOAT DIDN'T LAST ME LONG!

SPLASH!

FLOP!

WHEEEEEEE!

ZIP!

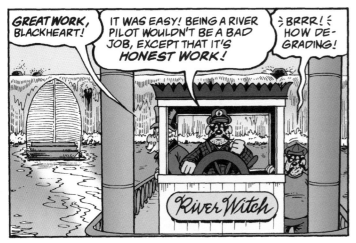

GREAT WORK, BLACKHEART!

IT WAS EASY! BEING A RIVER PILOT WOULDN'T BE A BAD JOB, EXCEPT THAT IT'S *HONEST WORK!*

BRRR! HOW DE-GRADING!

River Witch

AND I GOTTA ADMIT IT RILES ME ALTOGETHER SPECIAL WHEN IT'S ON THE *CEILING!*

YOU WERE RIGHT, UNCLE POTHOLE! THIS WATER IS *MUDDY!*

SOON...

OUR JOB IS REMOVING RIVER SNAGS, *NOT* FLIPPING RIVERBOATS!

CHUG-CHUG-CHUG!

CREEAK!

SORRY... SLIGHT NAVIGATION ERROR! WON'T HAPPEN AGAIN!

GOVERNMENT SNAG BOAT

SPLASH!

OOF!

24

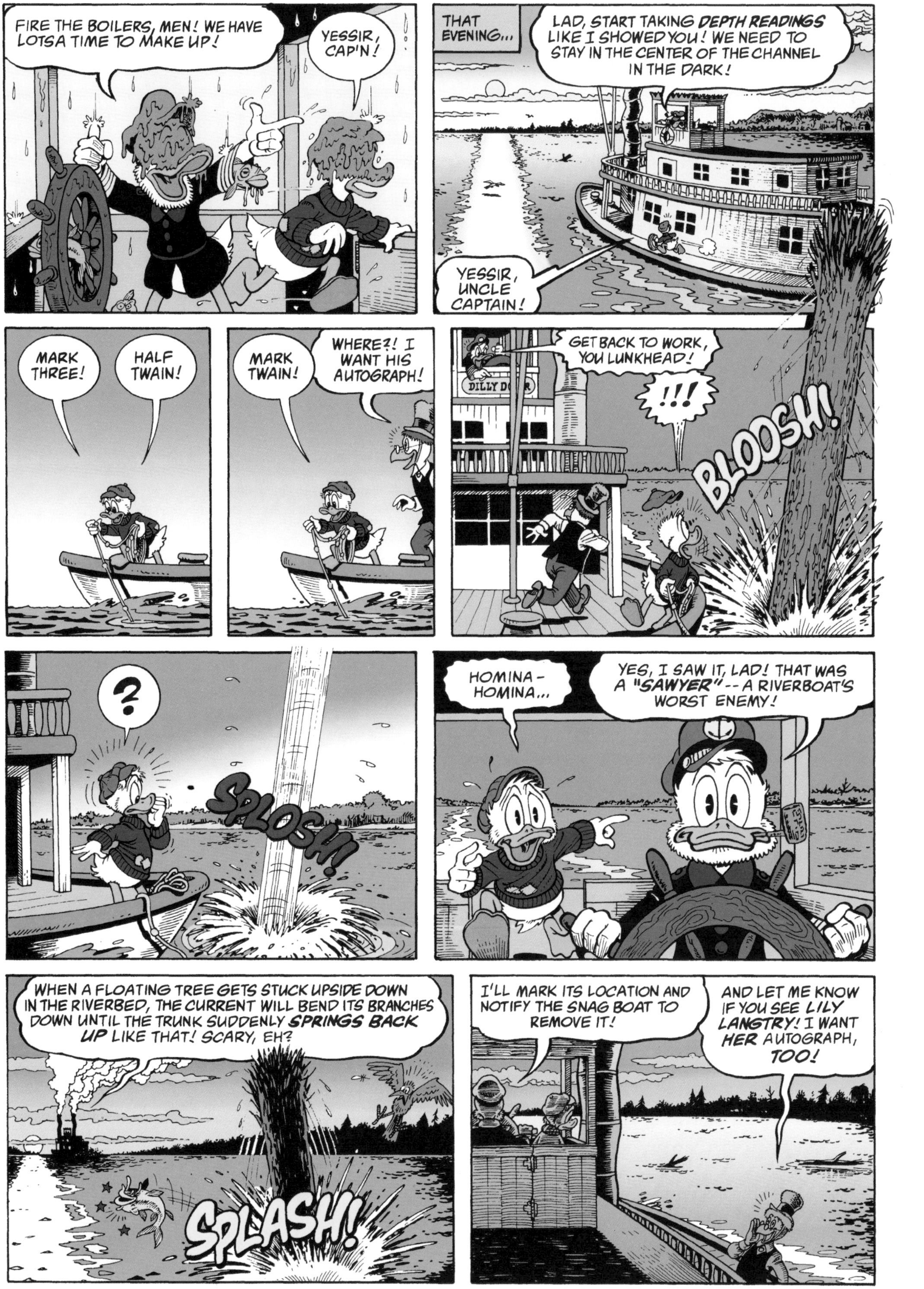
FIRE THE BOILERS, MEN! WE HAVE LOTSA TIME TO MAKE UP!
YESSIR, CAP'N!
THAT EVENING...
LAD, START TAKING DEPTH READINGS LIKE I SHOWED YOU! WE NEED TO STAY IN THE CENTER OF THE CHANNEL IN THE DARK!
YESSIR, UNCLE CAPTAIN!
MARK THREE!
HALF TWAIN!
MARK TWAIN!
WHERE?! I WANT HIS AUTOGRAPH!
GET BACK TO WORK, YOU LUNKHEAD!
!!!
DILLY DO
BLOOSH!
?
SPLOSH!
HOMINA-HOMINA...
YES, I SAW IT, LAD! THAT WAS A "SAWYER" -- A RIVERBOAT'S WORST ENEMY!
WHEN A FLOATING TREE GETS STUCK UPSIDE DOWN IN THE RIVERBED, THE CURRENT WILL BEND ITS BRANCHES DOWN UNTIL THE TRUNK SUDDENLY SPRINGS BACK UP LIKE THAT! SCARY, EH?
SPLASH!
I'LL MARK ITS LOCATION AND NOTIFY THE SNAG BOAT TO REMOVE IT!
AND LET ME KNOW IF YOU SEE LILY LANGTRY! I WANT HER AUTOGRAPH, TOO!

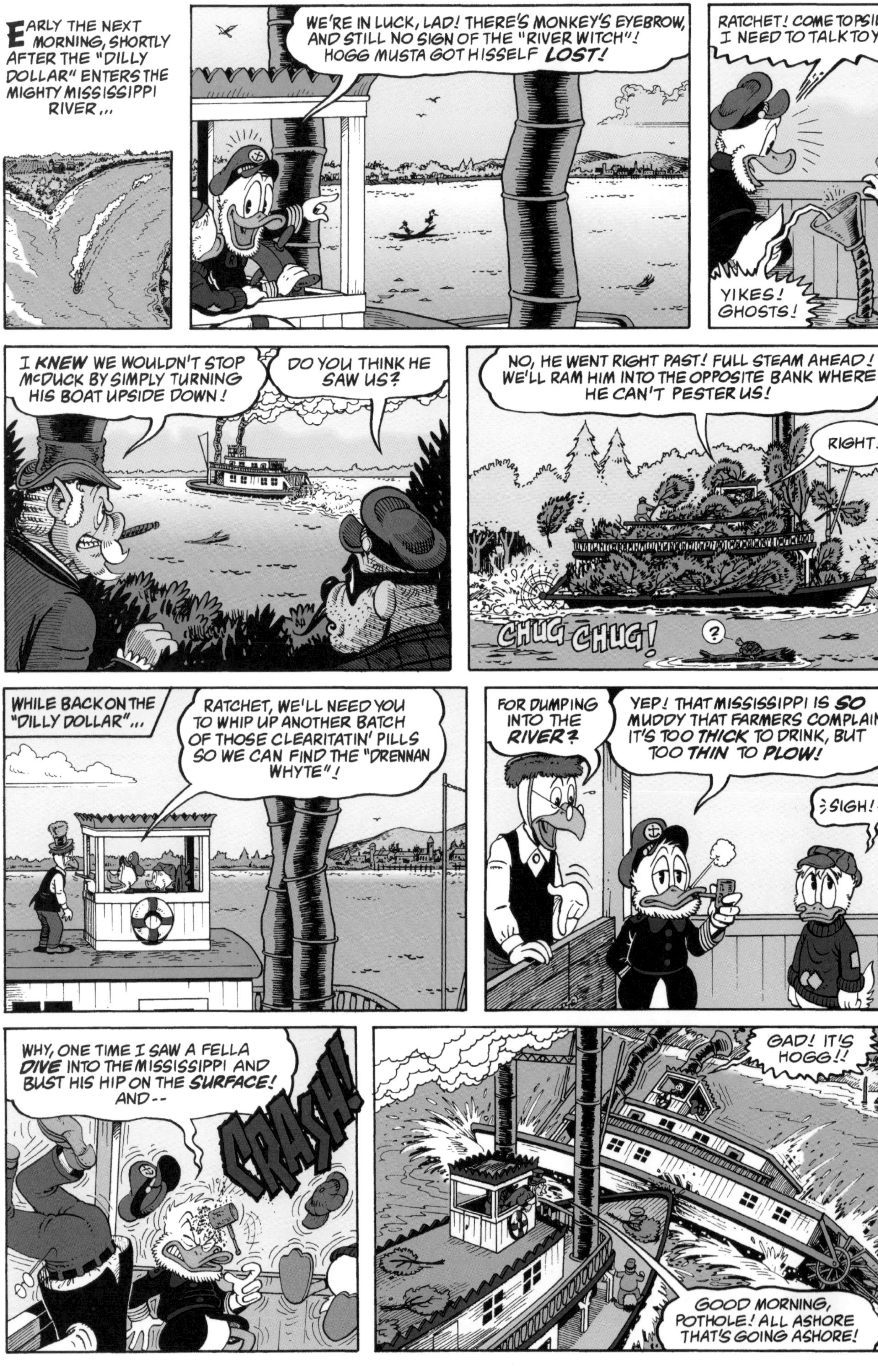
EARLY THE NEXT MORNING, SHORTLY AFTER THE "DILLY DOLLAR" ENTERS THE MIGHTY MISSISSIPPI RIVER,..
WE'RE IN LUCK, LAD! THERE'S MONKEY'S EYEBROW, AND STILL NO SIGN OF THE "RIVER WITCH"! HOGG MUSTA GOT HISSELF LOST!
RATCHET! COME TOPSIDE! I NEED TO TALK TO YOU!
YIKES! GHOSTS!
I KNEW WE WOULDN'T STOP McDUCK BY SIMPLY TURNING HIS BOAT UPSIDE DOWN!
DO YOU THINK HE SAW US?
NO, HE WENT RIGHT PAST! FULL STEAM AHEAD! WE'LL RAM HIM INTO THE OPPOSITE BANK WHERE HE CAN'T PESTER US!
RIGHT!
CHUG CHUG!
?
WHILE BACK ON THE "DILLY DOLLAR",..
RATCHET, WE'LL NEED YOU TO WHIP UP ANOTHER BATCH OF THOSE CLEARITATIN' PILLS SO WE CAN FIND THE "DRENNAN WHYTE"!
FOR DUMPING INTO THE RIVER?
YEP! THAT MISSISSIPPI IS SO MUDDY THAT FARMERS COMPLAIN IT'S TOO THICK TO DRINK, BUT TOO THIN TO PLOW!
SIGH!
WHY, ONE TIME I SAW A FELLA DIVE INTO THE MISSISSIPPI AND BUST HIS HIP ON THE SURFACE! AND--
CRASH!
GAD! IT'S HOGG!!
GOOD MORNING, POTHOLE! ALL ASHORE THAT'S GOING ASHORE!

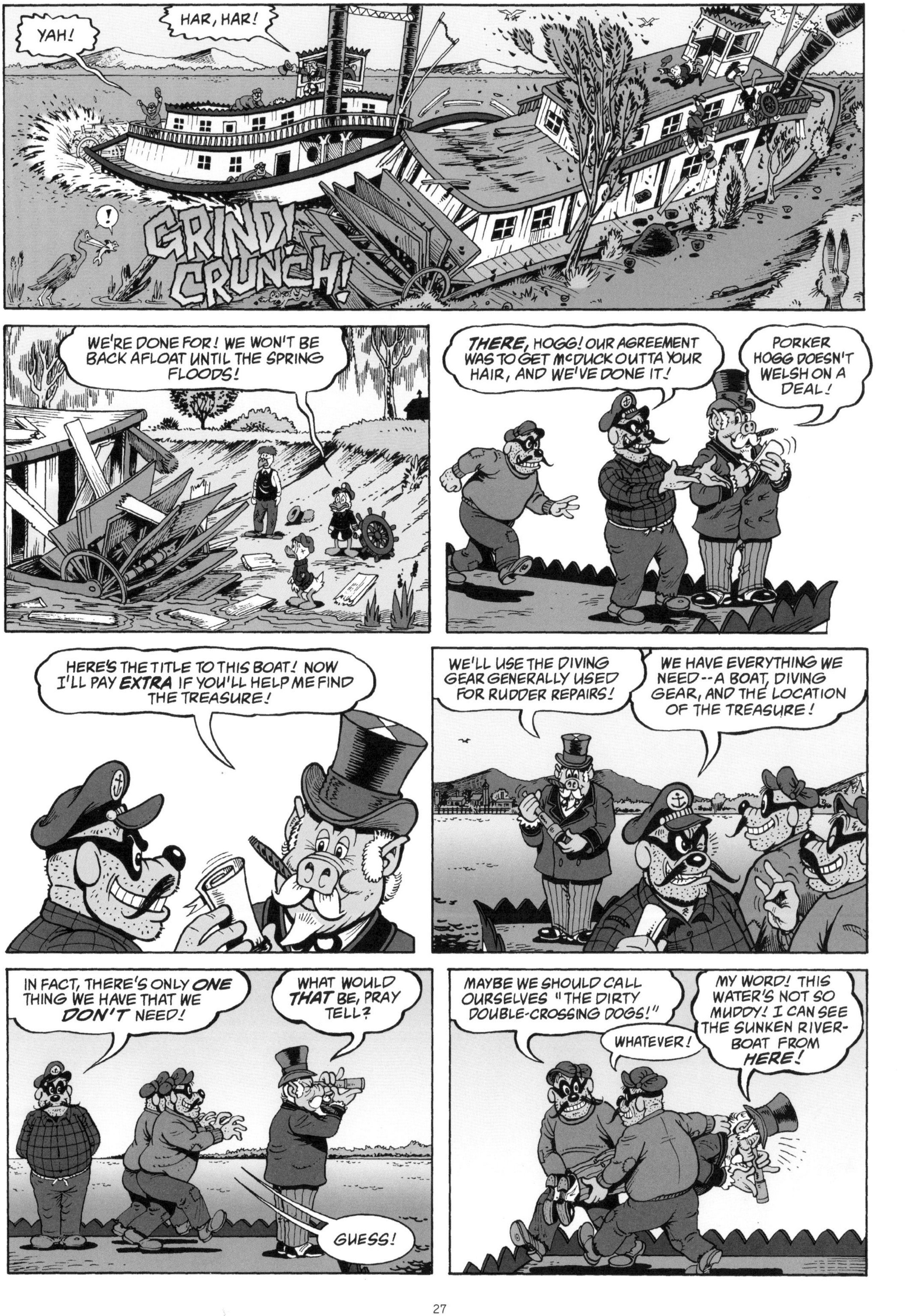
YAH!
HAR, HAR!
GRIND! CRUNCH!
!
WE'RE DONE FOR! WE WON'T BE BACK AFLOAT UNTIL THE SPRING FLOODS!
THERE, HOGG! OUR AGREEMENT WAS TO GET McDUCK OUTTA YOUR HAIR, AND WE'VE DONE IT!
PORKER HOGG DOESN'T WELSH ON A DEAL!
HERE'S THE TITLE TO THIS BOAT! NOW I'LL PAY EXTRA IF YOU'LL HELP ME FIND THE TREASURE!
WE'LL USE THE DIVING GEAR GENERALLY USED FOR RUDDER REPAIRS!
WE HAVE EVERYTHING WE NEED--A BOAT, DIVING GEAR, AND THE LOCATION OF THE TREASURE!
IN FACT, THERE'S ONLY ONE THING WE HAVE THAT WE DON'T NEED!
WHAT WOULD THAT BE, PRAY TELL?
GUESS!
MAYBE WE SHOULD CALL OURSELVES "THE DIRTY DOUBLE-CROSSING DOGS!"
WHATEVER!
MY WORD! THIS WATER'S NOT SO MUDDY! I CAN SEE THE SUNKEN RIVER-BOAT FROM HERE!

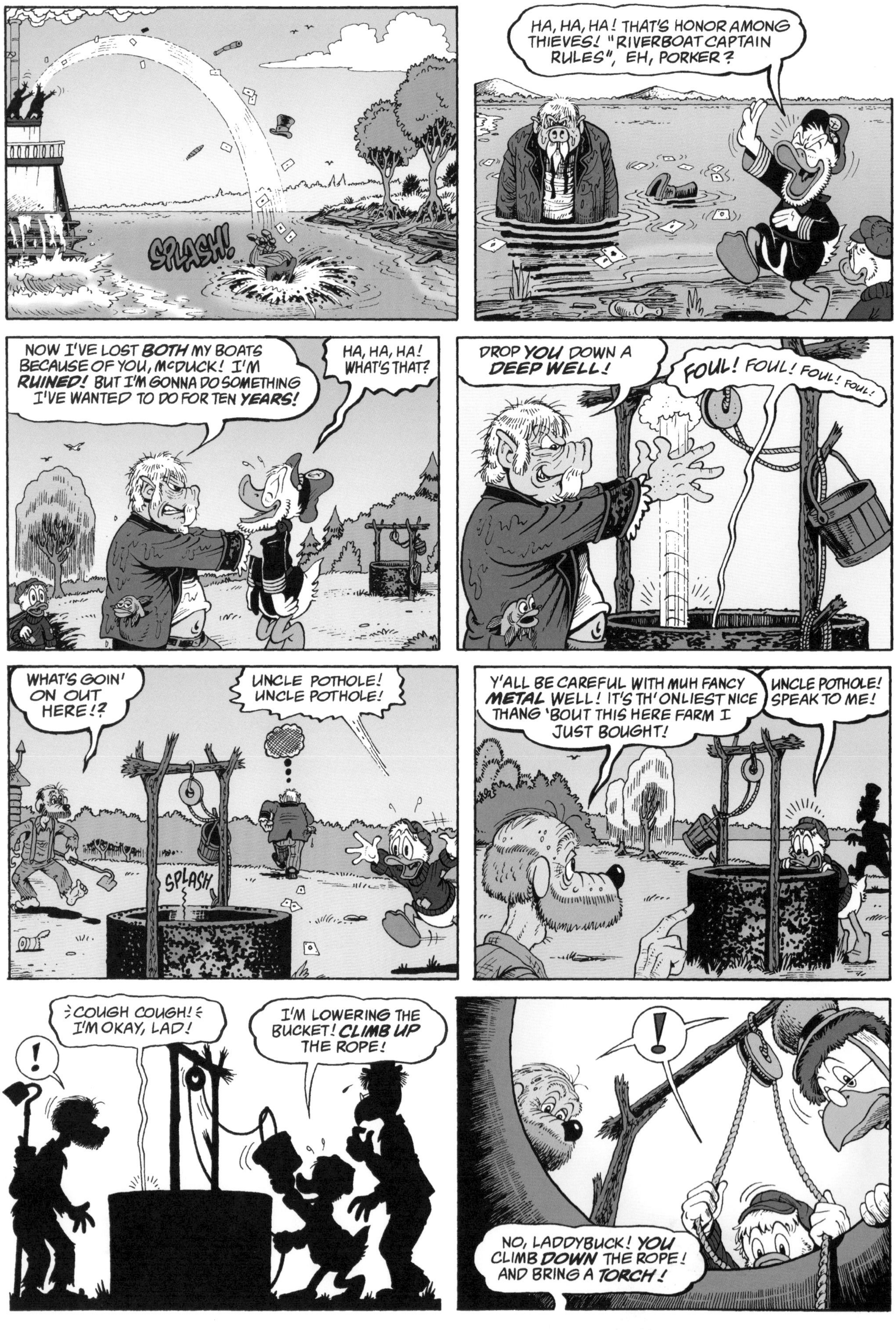
SPLASH!
HA, HA, HA! THAT'S HONOR AMONG THIEVES! "RIVERBOAT CAPTAIN RULES", EH, PORKER?
NOW I'VE LOST BOTH MY BOATS BECAUSE OF YOU, McDUCK! I'M RUINED! BUT I'M GONNA DO SOMETHING I'VE WANTED TO DO FOR TEN YEARS!
HA, HA, HA! WHAT'S THAT?
DROP YOU DOWN A DEEP WELL!
FOUL! FOUL! FOUL! FOUL!
WHAT'S GOIN' ON OUT HERE!?
UNCLE POTHOLE! UNCLE POTHOLE!
SPLASH
Y'ALL BE CAREFUL WITH MUH FANCY METAL WELL! IT'S TH' ONLIEST NICE THANG 'BOUT THIS HERE FARM I JUST BOUGHT!
UNCLE POTHOLE! SPEAK TO ME!
!
COUGH COUGH! I'M OKAY, LAD!
I'M LOWERING THE BUCKET! CLIMB UP THE ROPE!
!
NO, LADDYBUCK! YOU CLIMB DOWN THE ROPE! AND BRING A TORCH!

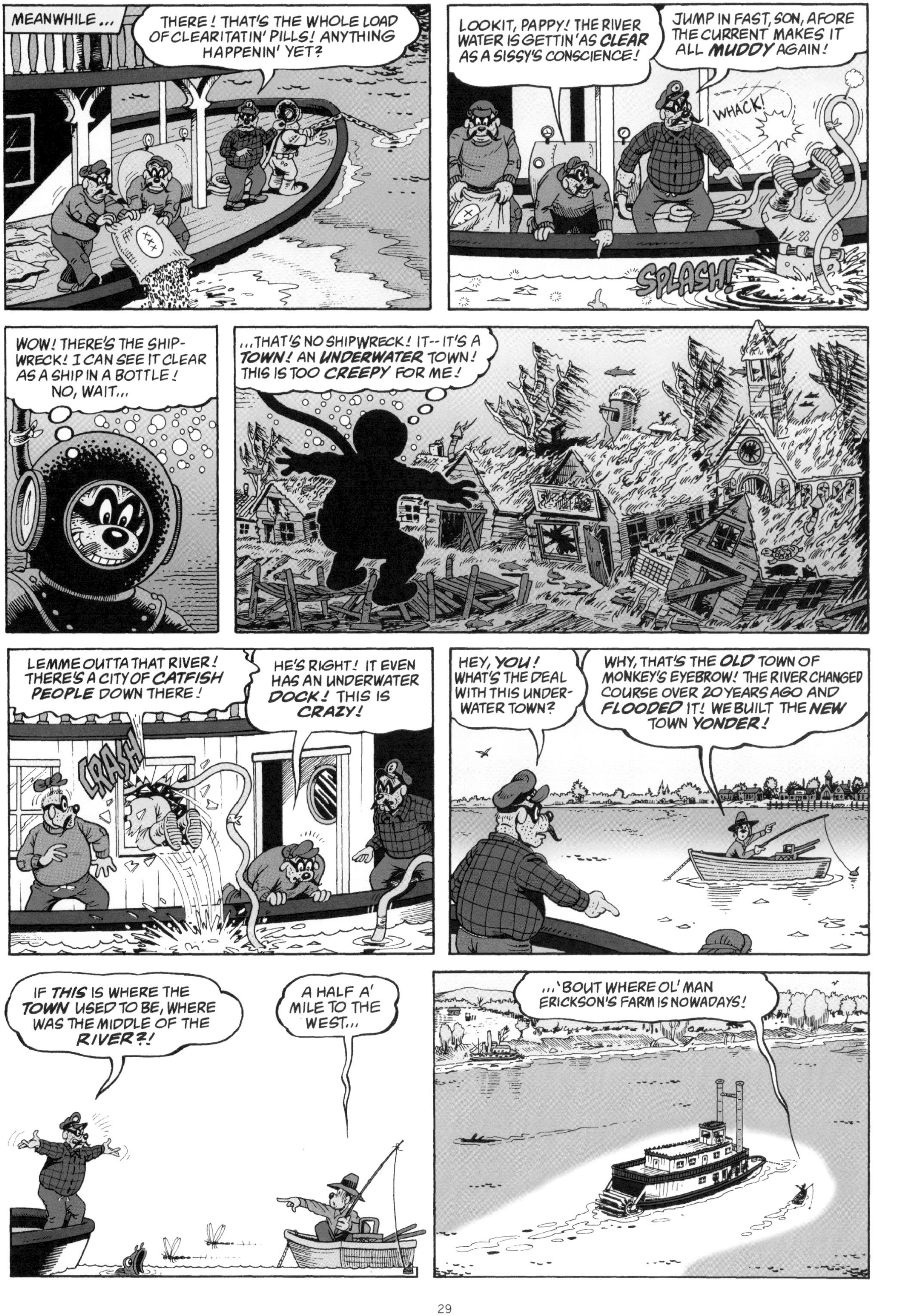
MEANWHILE...
THERE! THAT'S THE WHOLE LOAD OF CLEARITATIN' PILLS! ANYTHING HAPPENIN' YET?
LOOKIT, PAPPY! THE RIVER WATER IS GETTIN' AS CLEAR AS A SISSY'S CONSCIENCE!
JUMP IN FAST, SON, AFORE THE CURRENT MAKES IT ALL MUDDY AGAIN!
WHACK!
SPLASH!
WOW! THERE'S THE SHIPWRECK! I CAN SEE IT CLEAR AS A SHIP IN A BOTTLE! NO, WAIT...
...THAT'S NO SHIPWRECK! IT-- IT'S A TOWN! AN UNDERWATER TOWN! THIS IS TOO CREEPY FOR ME!
LEMME OUTTA THAT RIVER! THERE'S A CITY OF CATFISH PEOPLE DOWN THERE!
HE'S RIGHT! IT EVEN HAS AN UNDERWATER DOCK! THIS IS CRAZY!
CRASH
HEY, YOU! WHAT'S THE DEAL WITH THIS UNDERWATER TOWN?
WHY, THAT'S THE OLD TOWN OF MONKEY'S EYEBROW! THE RIVER CHANGED COURSE OVER 20 YEARS AGO AND FLOODED IT! WE BUILT THE NEW TOWN YONDER!
IF THIS IS WHERE THE TOWN USED TO BE, WHERE WAS THE MIDDLE OF THE RIVER?!
A HALF A' MILE TO THE WEST...
...'BOUT WHERE OL' MAN ERICKSON'S FARM IS NOWADAYS!

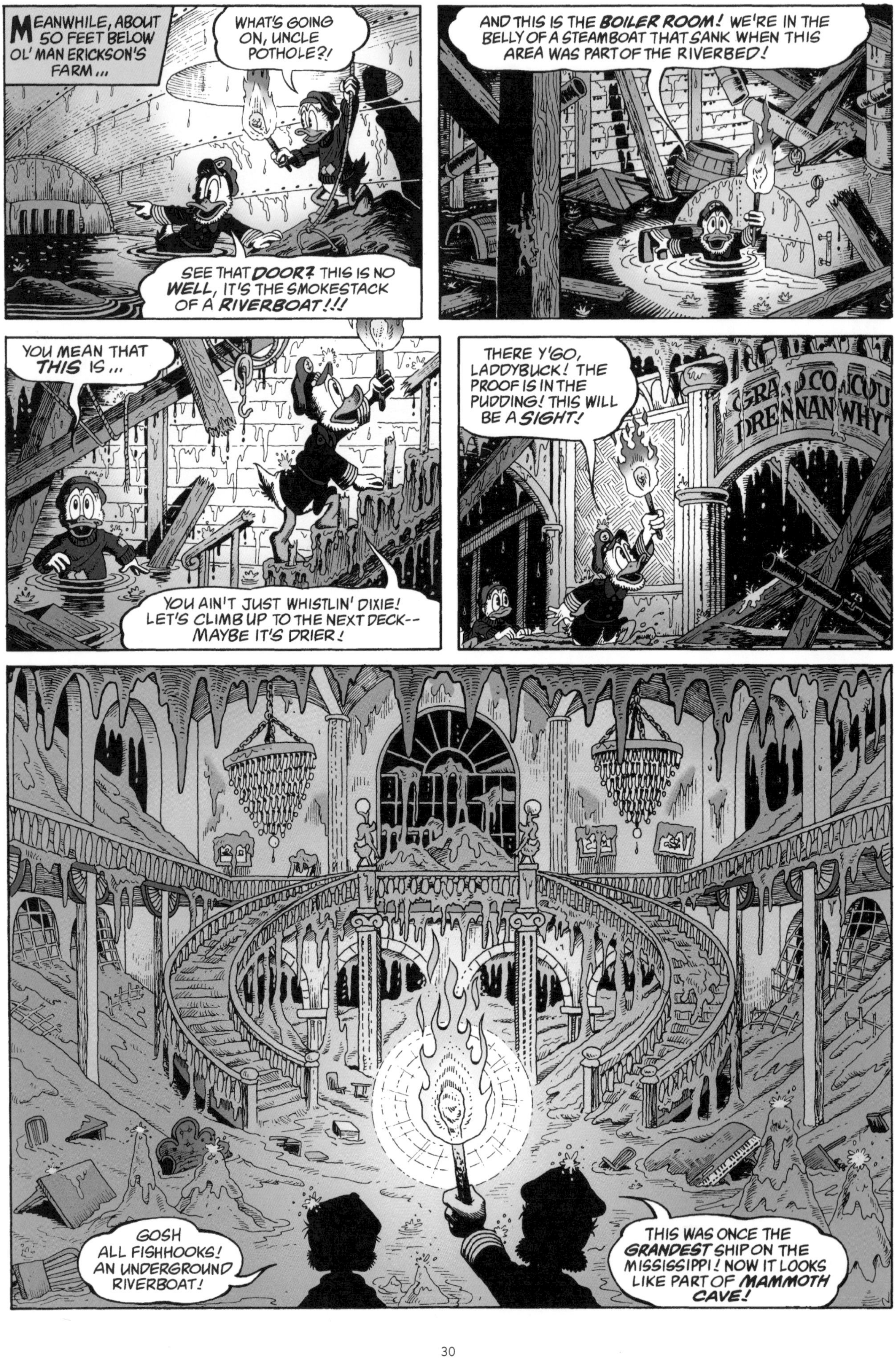
MEANWHILE, ABOUT 50 FEET BELOW OL' MAN ERICKSON'S FARM...
WHAT'S GOING ON, UNCLE POTHOLE?!
SEE THAT DOOR? THIS IS NO WELL, IT'S THE SMOKESTACK OF A RIVERBOAT!!!
AND THIS IS THE BOILER ROOM! WE'RE IN THE BELLY OF A STEAMBOAT THAT SANK WHEN THIS AREA WAS PART OF THE RIVERBED!
YOU MEAN THAT THIS IS...
YOU AIN'T JUST WHISTLIN' DIXIE! LET'S CLIMB UP TO THE NEXT DECK--MAYBE IT'S DRIER!
THERE Y'GO, LADDYBUCK! THE PROOF IS IN THE PUDDING! THIS WILL BE A SIGHT!
GOSH ALL FISHHOOKS! AN UNDERGROUND RIVERBOAT!
THIS WAS ONCE THE GRANDEST SHIP ON THE MISSISSIPPI! NOW IT LOOKS LIKE PART OF MAMMOTH CAVE!

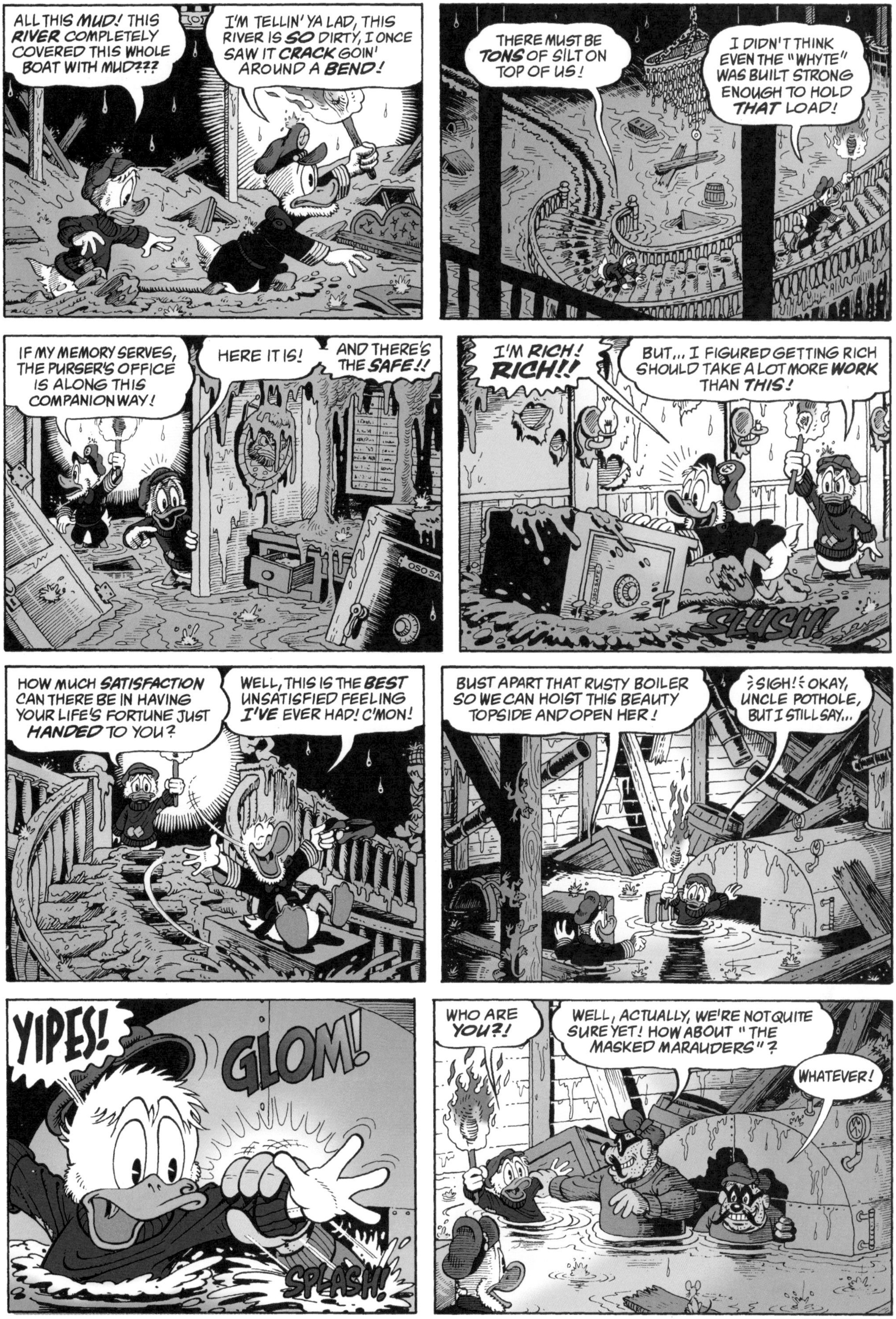

ALL THIS MUD! THIS RIVER COMPLETELY COVERED THIS WHOLE BOAT WITH MUD???
I'M TELLIN' YA LAD, THIS RIVER IS SO DIRTY, I ONCE SAW IT CRACK GOIN' AROUND A BEND!
THERE MUST BE TONS OF SILT ON TOP OF US!
I DIDN'T THINK EVEN THE "WHYTE" WAS BUILT STRONG ENOUGH TO HOLD THAT LOAD!
IF MY MEMORY SERVES, THE PURSER'S OFFICE IS ALONG THIS COMPANIONWAY!
HERE IT IS!
AND THERE'S THE SAFE!!
I'M RICH! RICH!!
BUT... I FIGURED GETTING RICH SHOULD TAKE A LOT MORE WORK THAN THIS!
SLUSH!
HOW MUCH SATISFACTION CAN THERE BE IN HAVING YOUR LIFE'S FORTUNE JUST HANDED TO YOU?
WELL, THIS IS THE BEST UNSATISFIED FEELING I'VE EVER HAD! C'MON!
BUST APART THAT RUSTY BOILER SO WE CAN HOIST THIS BEAUTY TOPSIDE AND OPEN HER!
SIGH! OKAY, UNCLE POTHOLE, BUT I STILL SAY...
YIPES!
GLOM!
SPLASH!
WHO ARE YOU?!
WELL, ACTUALLY, WE'RE NOT QUITE SURE YET! HOW ABOUT "THE MASKED MARAUDERS"?
WHATEVER!

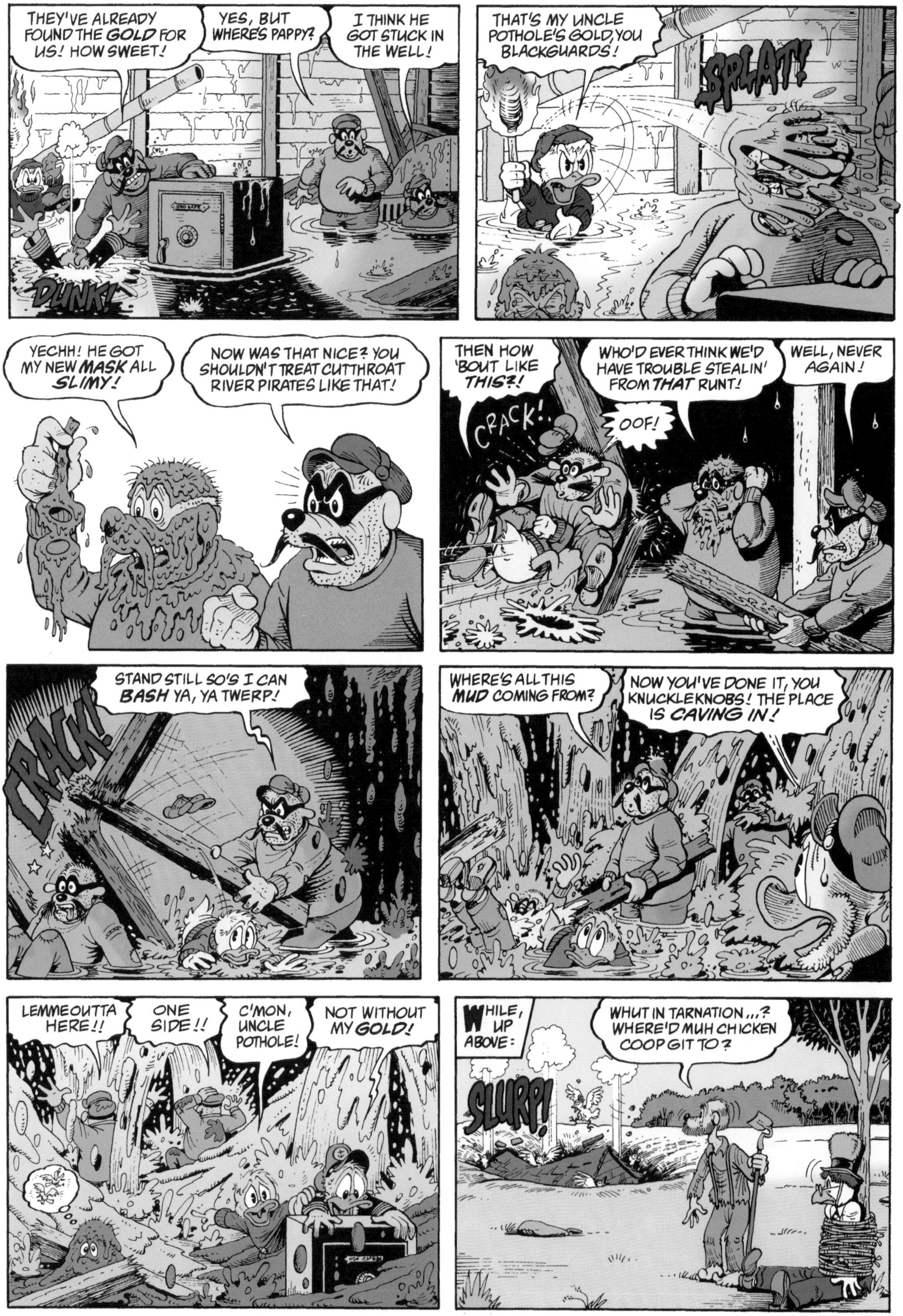
THEY'VE ALREADY FOUND THE GOLD FOR US! HOW SWEET!
YES, BUT WHERE'S PAPPY?
I THINK HE GOT STUCK IN THE WELL!
DUNK!
THAT'S MY UNCLE POTHOLE'S GOLD, YOU BLACKGUARDS!
SPLAT!
YECHH! HE GOT MY NEW MASK ALL SLIMY!
NOW WAS THAT NICE? YOU SHOULDN'T TREAT CUTTHROAT RIVER PIRATES LIKE THAT!
THEN HOW 'BOUT LIKE THIS?!
CRACK!
WHO'D EVER THINK WE'D HAVE TROUBLE STEALIN' FROM THAT RUNT!
OOF!
WELL, NEVER AGAIN!
STAND STILL SO'S I CAN BASH YA, YA TWERP!
CRACK!
WHERE'S ALL THIS MUD COMING FROM?
NOW YOU'VE DONE IT, YOU KNUCKLEKNOBS! THE PLACE IS CAVING IN!
LEMMEOUTTA HERE!!
ONE SIDE!!
C'MON, UNCLE POTHOLE!
NOT WITHOUT MY GOLD!
WHILE, UP ABOVE:
WHUT IN TARNATION...? WHERE'D MUH CHICKEN COOP GIT TO?
SLURP!

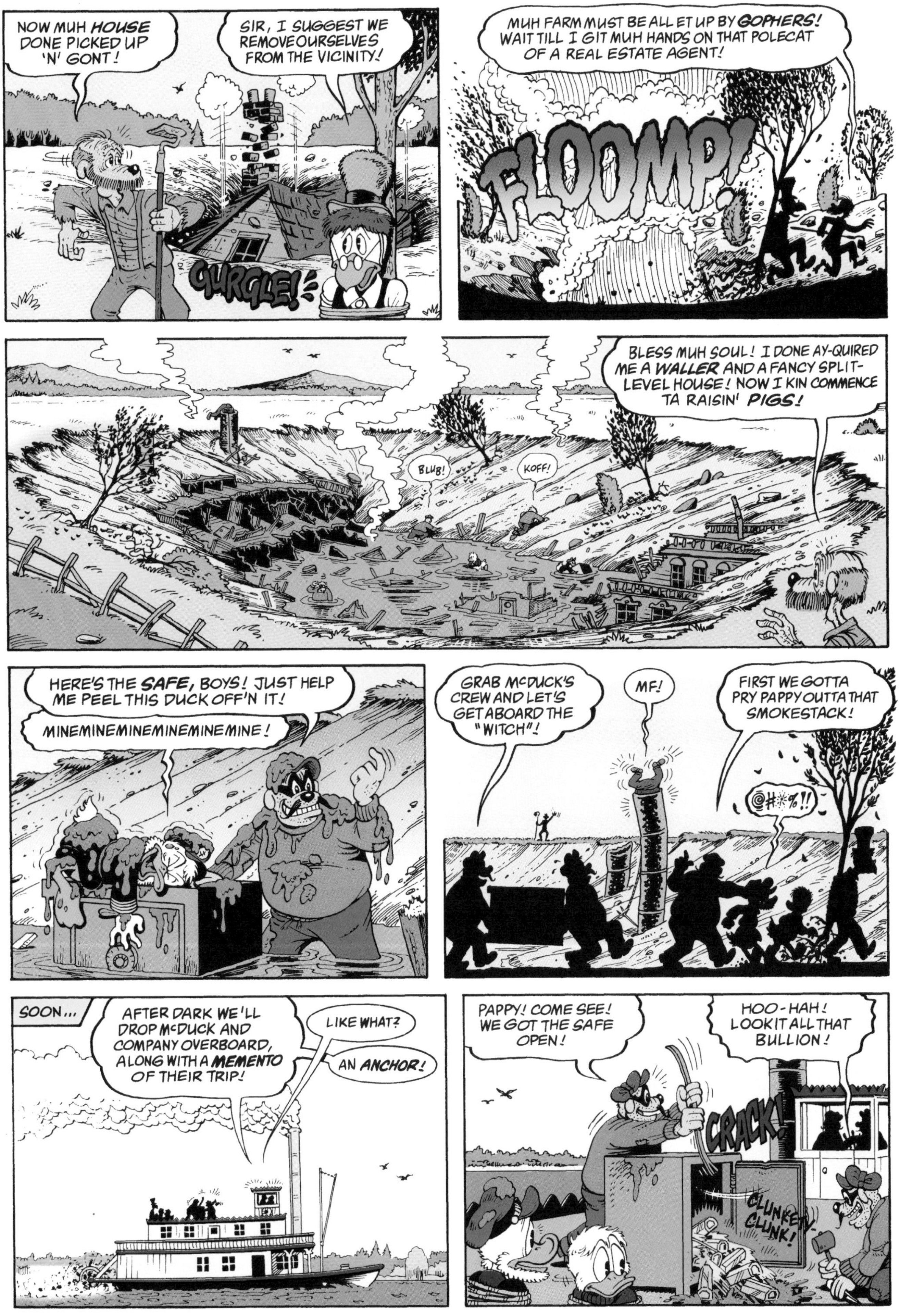
NOW MUH HOUSE DONE PICKED UP 'N' GONT!
SIR, I SUGGEST WE REMOVE OURSELVES FROM THE VICINITY!
GURGLE!
MUH FARM MUST BE ALL ET UP BY GOPHERS! WAIT TILL I GIT MUH HANDS ON THAT POLECAT OF A REAL ESTATE AGENT!
FLOOMP!
BLESS MUH SOUL! I DONE AY-QUIRED ME A WALLER AND A FANCY SPLIT-LEVEL HOUSE! NOW I KIN COMMENCE TA RAISIN' PIGS!
BLUB!
KOFF!
HERE'S THE SAFE, BOYS! JUST HELP ME PEEL THIS DUCK OFF'N IT!
MINEMINEMINEMINEMINEMINE!
GRAB McDUCK'S CREW AND LET'S GET ABOARD THE "WITCH"!
MF!
FIRST WE GOTTA PRY PAPPY OUTTA THAT SMOKESTACK!
@#*%!!
SOON...
AFTER DARK WE'LL DROP McDUCK AND COMPANY OVERBOARD, ALONG WITH A MEMENTO OF THEIR TRIP!
LIKE WHAT?
AN ANCHOR!
PAPPY! COME SEE! WE GOT THE SAFE OPEN!
HOO-HAH! LOOKIT ALL THAT BULLION!
CRACK!
CLUNKETY CLUNK!

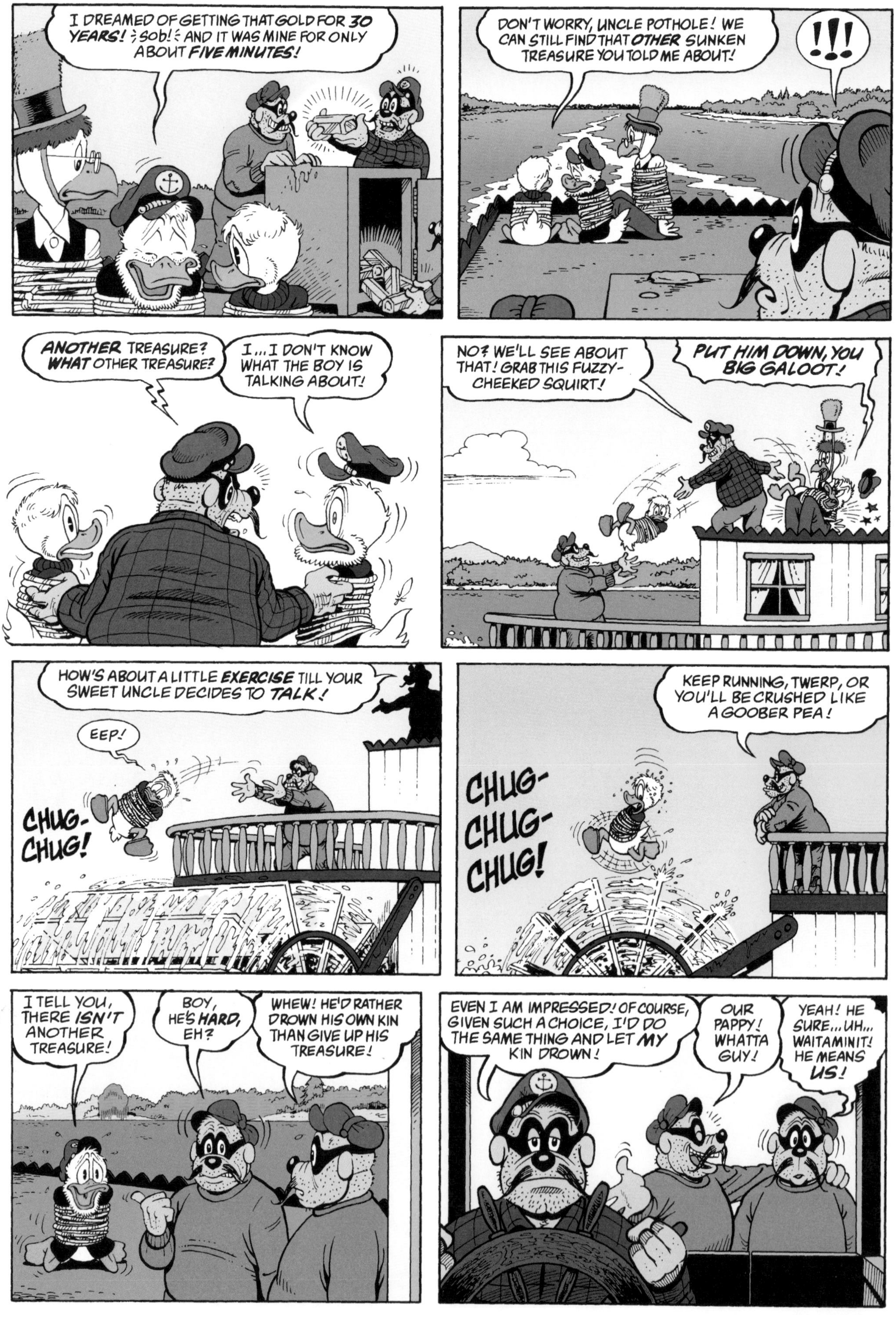
I DREAMED OF GETTING THAT GOLD FOR 30 YEARS! ⸗SOB!⸗ AND IT WAS MINE FOR ONLY ABOUT FIVE MINUTES!
DON'T WORRY, UNCLE POTHOLE! WE CAN STILL FIND THAT OTHER SUNKEN TREASURE YOU TOLD ME ABOUT!
!!!
ANOTHER TREASURE? WHAT OTHER TREASURE?
I... I DON'T KNOW WHAT THE BOY IS TALKING ABOUT!
NO? WE'LL SEE ABOUT THAT! GRAB THIS FUZZY-CHEEKED SQUIRT!
PUT HIM DOWN, YOU BIG GALOOT!
HOW'S ABOUT A LITTLE EXERCISE TILL YOUR SWEET UNCLE DECIDES TO TALK!
EEP!
CHUG-CHUG!
KEEP RUNNING, TWERP, OR YOU'LL BE CRUSHED LIKE A GOOBER PEA!
CHUG-CHUG-CHUG!
I TELL YOU, THERE ISN'T ANOTHER TREASURE!
BOY, HE'S HARD, EH?
WHEW! HE'D RATHER DROWN HIS OWN KIN THAN GIVE UP HIS TREASURE!
EVEN I AM IMPRESSED! OF COURSE, GIVEN SUCH A CHOICE, I'D DO THE SAME THING AND LET MY KIN DROWN!
OUR PAPPY! WHATTA GUY!
YEAH! HE SURE... UH... WAITAMINIT! HE MEANS US!

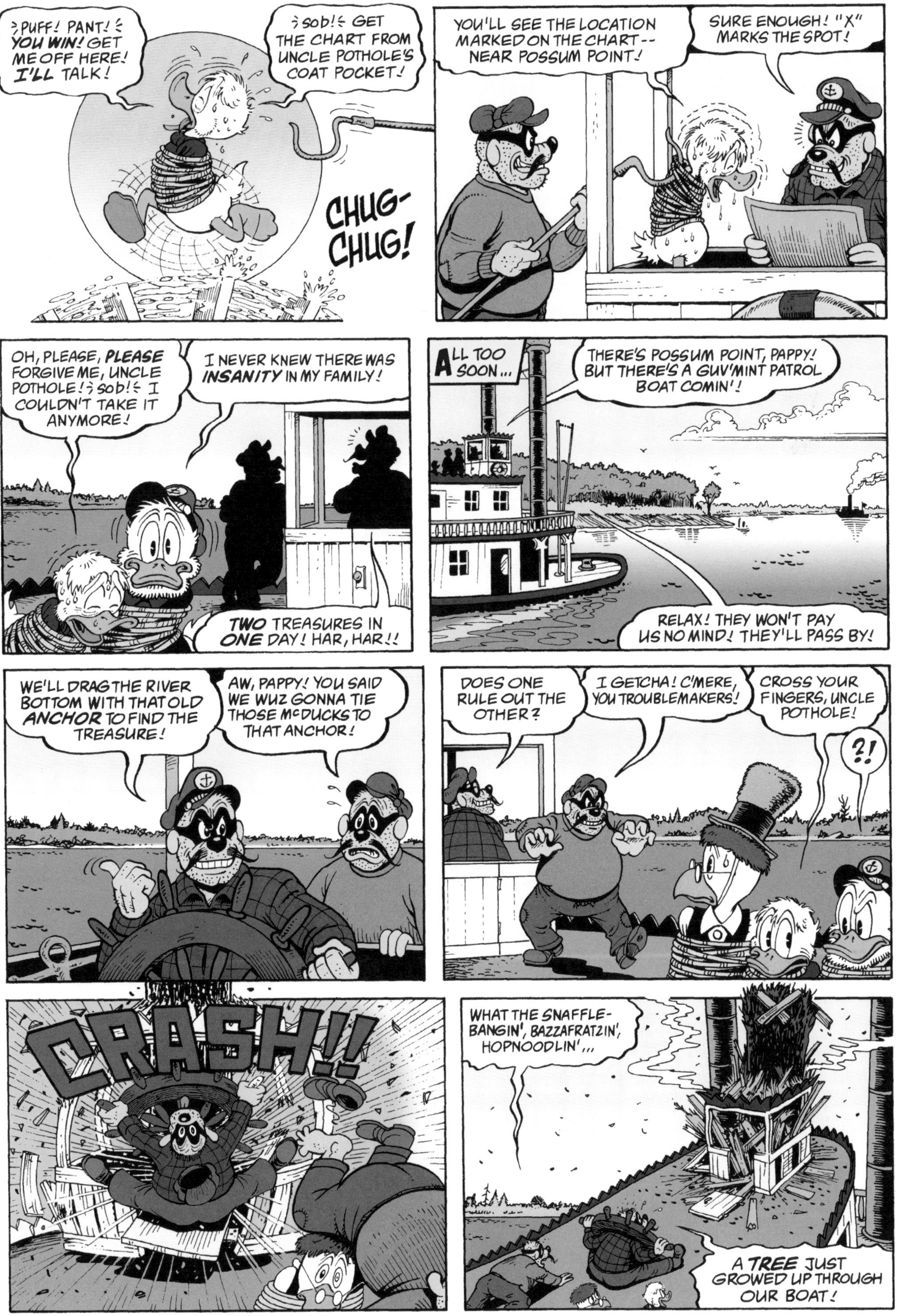

PUFF! PANT! YOU WIN! GET ME OFF HERE! I'LL TALK!
SOB! GET THE CHART FROM UNCLE POTHOLE'S COAT POCKET!
CHUG-CHUG!
YOU'LL SEE THE LOCATION MARKED ON THE CHART-- NEAR POSSUM POINT!
SURE ENOUGH! "X" MARKS THE SPOT!
OH, PLEASE, PLEASE FORGIVE ME, UNCLE POTHOLE! SOB! I COULDN'T TAKE IT ANYMORE!
I NEVER KNEW THERE WAS INSANITY IN MY FAMILY!
TWO TREASURES IN ONE DAY! HAR, HAR!!
ALL TOO SOON...
THERE'S POSSUM POINT, PAPPY! BUT THERE'S A GUV'MINT PATROL BOAT COMIN'!
RELAX! THEY WON'T PAY US NO MIND! THEY'LL PASS BY!
WE'LL DRAG THE RIVER BOTTOM WITH THAT OLD ANCHOR TO FIND THE TREASURE!
AW, PAPPY! YOU SAID WE WUZ GONNA TIE THOSE McDUCKS TO THAT ANCHOR!
DOES ONE RULE OUT THE OTHER?
I GETCHA! C'MERE, YOU TROUBLEMAKERS!
CROSS YOUR FINGERS, UNCLE POTHOLE!
?!
CRASH!!
WHAT THE SNAFFLE-BANGIN', BAZZAFRATZIN', HOPNOODLIN',...
A TREE JUST GROWED UP THROUGH OUR BOAT!

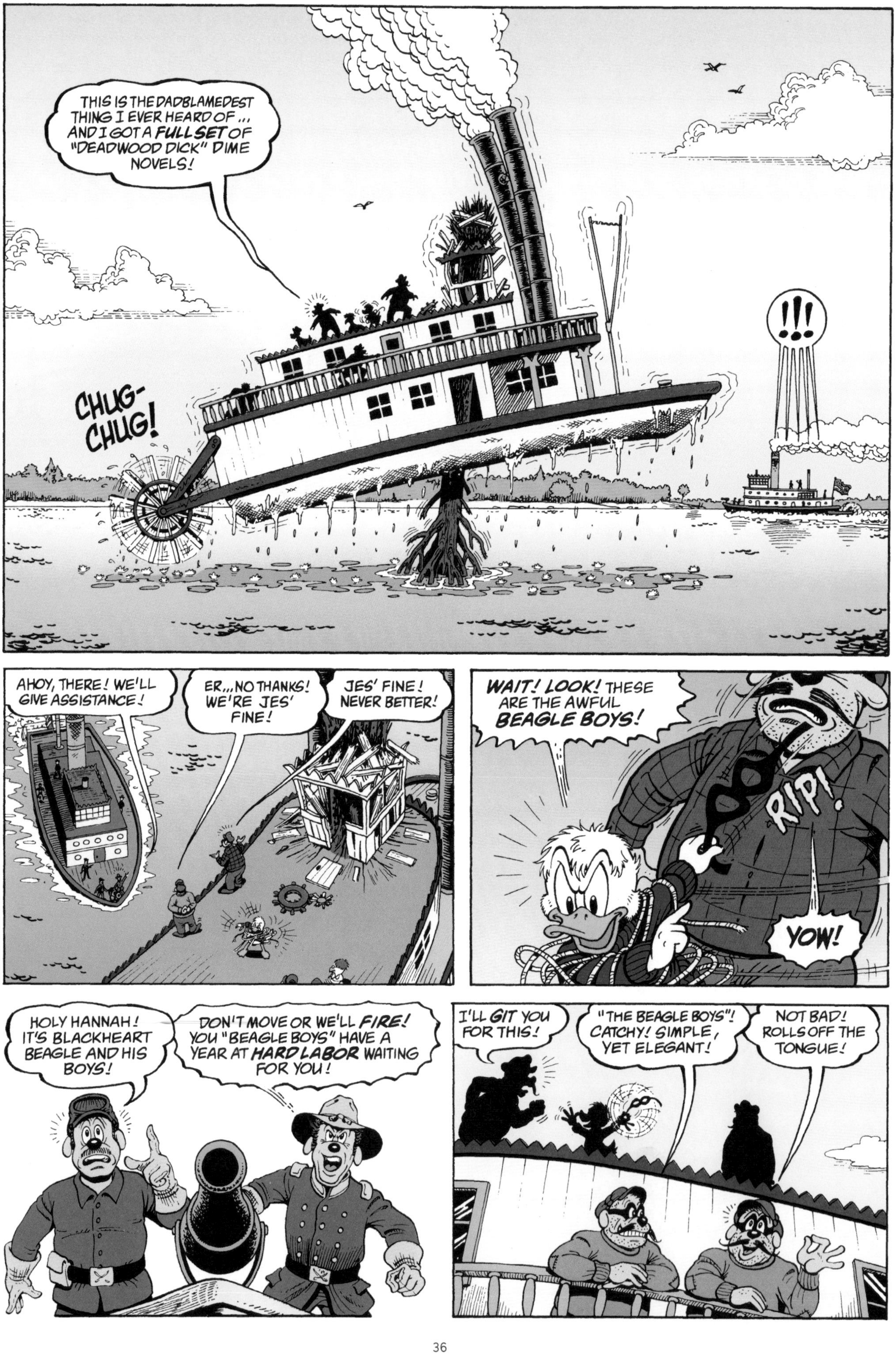

THIS IS THE DADBLAMEDEST THING I EVER HEARD OF ... AND I GOT A FULL SET OF "DEADWOOD DICK" DIME NOVELS!
CHUG-CHUG!
!!!
AHOY, THERE! WE'LL GIVE ASSISTANCE!
ER... NO THANKS! WE'RE JES' FINE!
JES' FINE! NEVER BETTER!
WAIT! LOOK! THESE ARE THE AWFUL BEAGLE BOYS!
RIP!
YOW!
HOLY HANNAH! IT'S BLACKHEART BEAGLE AND HIS BOYS!
DON'T MOVE OR WE'LL FIRE! YOU "BEAGLE BOYS" HAVE A YEAR AT HARD LABOR WAITING FOR YOU!
I'LL GIT YOU FOR THIS!
"THE BEAGLE BOYS"! CATCHY! SIMPLE, YET ELEGANT!
NOT BAD! ROLLS OFF THE TONGUE!

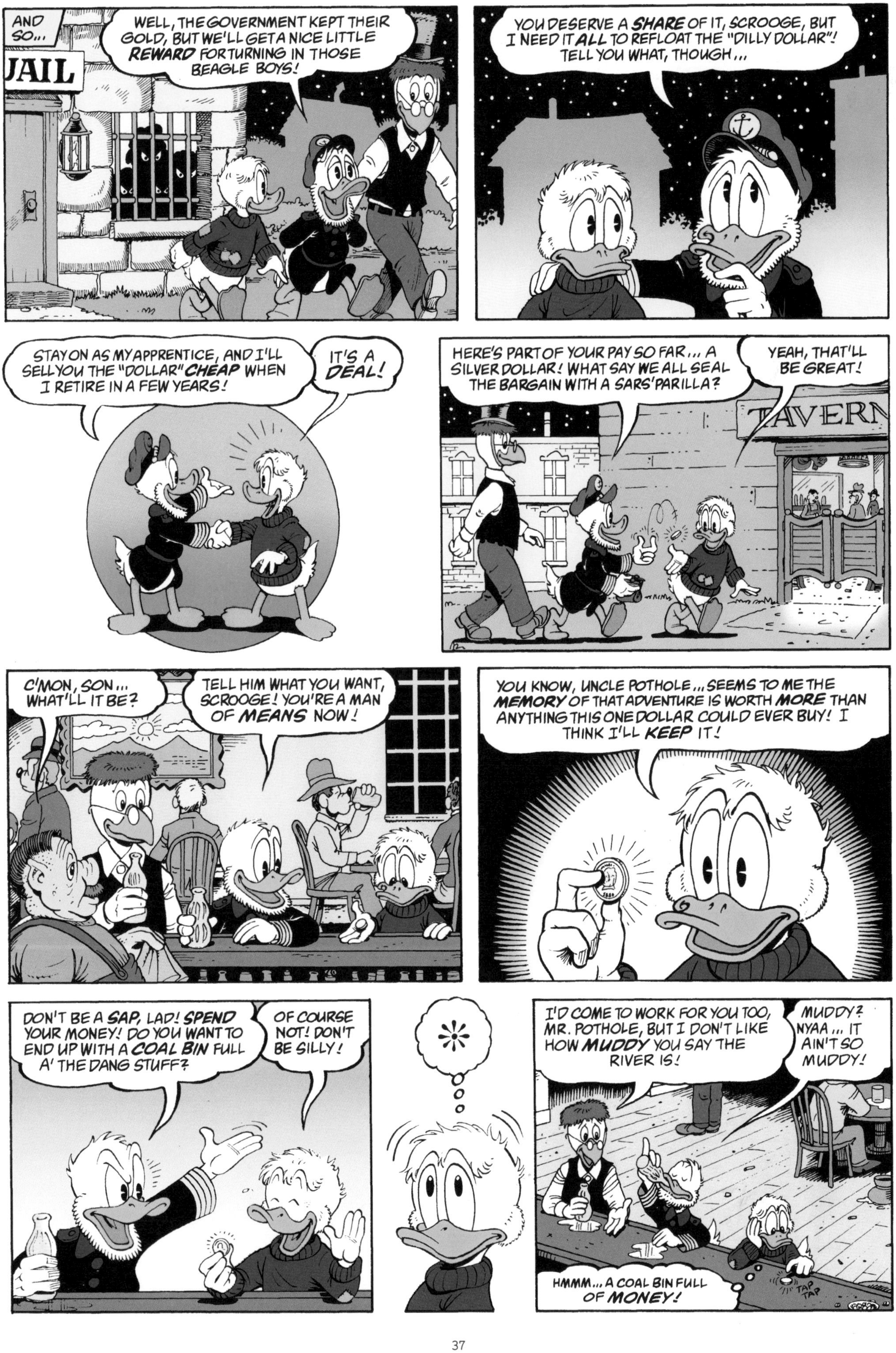
AND SO...
WELL, THE GOVERNMENT KEPT THEIR GOLD, BUT WE'LL GET A NICE LITTLE REWARD FOR TURNING IN THOSE BEAGLE BOYS!
JAIL
YOU DESERVE A SHARE OF IT, SCROOGE, BUT I NEED IT ALL TO REFLOAT THE "DILLY DOLLAR"! TELL YOU WHAT, THOUGH...
STAY ON AS MY APPRENTICE, AND I'LL SELL YOU THE "DOLLAR" CHEAP WHEN I RETIRE IN A FEW YEARS!
IT'S A DEAL!
HERE'S PART OF YOUR PAY SO FAR... A SILVER DOLLAR! WHAT SAY WE ALL SEAL THE BARGAIN WITH A SARS'PARILLA?
YEAH, THAT'LL BE GREAT!
TAVERN
C'MON, SON... WHAT'LL IT BE?
TELL HIM WHAT YOU WANT, SCROOGE! YOU'RE A MAN OF MEANS NOW!
YOU KNOW, UNCLE POTHOLE... SEEMS TO ME THE MEMORY OF THAT ADVENTURE IS WORTH MORE THAN ANYTHING THIS ONE DOLLAR COULD EVER BUY! I THINK I'LL KEEP IT!
DON'T BE A SAP, LAD! SPEND YOUR MONEY! DO YOU WANT TO END UP WITH A COAL BIN FULL A' THE DANG STUFF?
OF COURSE NOT! DON'T BE SILLY!
I'D COME TO WORK FOR YOU TOO, MR. POTHOLE, BUT I DON'T LIKE HOW MUDDY YOU SAY THE RIVER IS!
MUDDY? NYAA... IT AIN'T SO MUDDY!
HMMM... A COAL BIN FULL OF MONEY!
TAP TAP

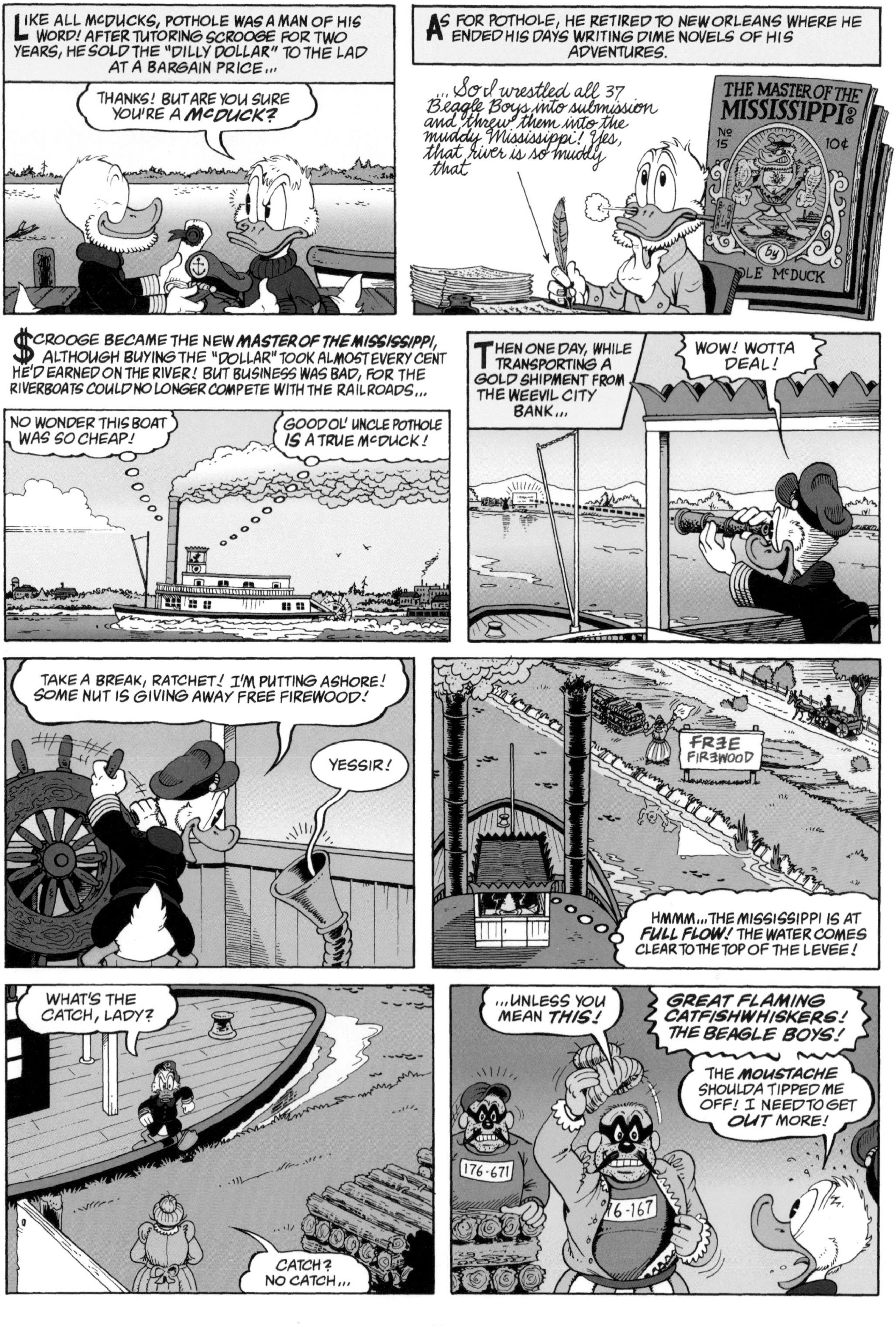
LIKE ALL McDUCKS, POTHOLE WAS A MAN OF HIS WORD! AFTER TUTORING SCROOGE FOR TWO YEARS, HE SOLD THE "DILLY DOLLAR" TO THE LAD AT A BARGAIN PRICE...
THANKS! BUT ARE YOU SURE YOU'RE A McDUCK?
AS FOR POTHOLE, HE RETIRED TO NEW ORLEANS WHERE HE ENDED HIS DAYS WRITING DIME NOVELS OF HIS ADVENTURES.
...So I wrestled all 37 Beagle Boys into submission and threw them into the muddy Mississippi! Yes, that river is so muddy that
THE MASTER OF THE MISSISSIPPI
№ 15
10¢
by
LE McDUCK
SCROOGE BECAME THE NEW MASTER OF THE MISSISSIPPI, ALTHOUGH BUYING THE "DOLLAR" TOOK ALMOST EVERY CENT HE'D EARNED ON THE RIVER! BUT BUSINESS WAS BAD, FOR THE RIVERBOATS COULD NO LONGER COMPETE WITH THE RAILROADS...
NO WONDER THIS BOAT WAS SO CHEAP!
GOOD OL' UNCLE POTHOLE IS A TRUE McDUCK!
THEN ONE DAY, WHILE TRANSPORTING A GOLD SHIPMENT FROM THE WEEVIL CITY BANK...
WOW! WOTTA DEAL!
TAKE A BREAK, RATCHET! I'M PUTTING ASHORE! SOME NUT IS GIVING AWAY FREE FIREWOOD!
YESSIR!
FR∃E FIR∃WOOD
HMMM... THE MISSISSIPPI IS AT FULL FLOW! THE WATER COMES CLEAR TO THE TOP OF THE LEVEE!
WHAT'S THE CATCH, LADY?
CATCH? NO CATCH...
...UNLESS YOU MEAN THIS!
GREAT FLAMING CATFISHWHISKERS! THE BEAGLE BOYS!
THE MOUSTACHE SHOULDA TIPPED ME OFF! I NEED TO GET OUT MORE!
176-671
176-167

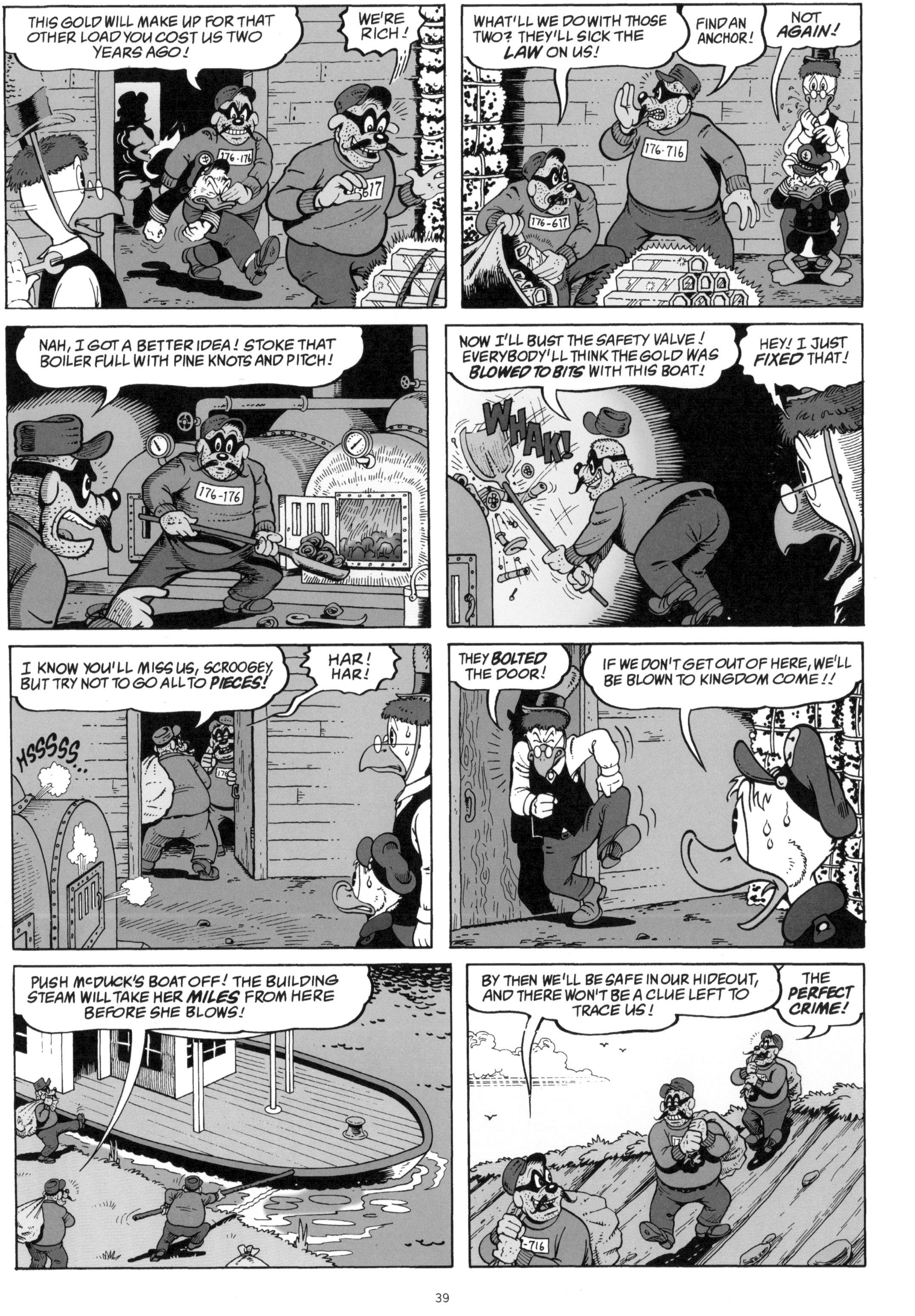
THIS GOLD WILL MAKE UP FOR THAT OTHER LOAD YOU COST US TWO YEARS AGO!
WE'RE RICH!
WHAT'LL WE DO WITH THOSE TWO? THEY'LL SICK THE LAW ON US!
FIND AN ANCHOR!
NOT AGAIN!
NAH, I GOT A BETTER IDEA! STOKE THAT BOILER FULL WITH PINE KNOTS AND PITCH!
NOW I'LL BUST THE SAFETY VALVE! EVERYBODY'LL THINK THE GOLD WAS BLOWED TO BITS WITH THIS BOAT!
WHAK!
HEY! I JUST FIXED THAT!
I KNOW YOU'LL MISS US, SCROOGEY, BUT TRY NOT TO GO ALL TO PIECES!
HAR! HAR!
HSSSSS...
THEY BOLTED THE DOOR!
IF WE DON'T GET OUT OF HERE, WE'LL BE BLOWN TO KINGDOM COME!!
PUSH McDUCK'S BOAT OFF! THE BUILDING STEAM WILL TAKE HER MILES FROM HERE BEFORE SHE BLOWS!
BY THEN WE'LL BE SAFE IN OUR HIDEOUT, AND THERE WON'T BE A CLUE LEFT TO TRACE US!
THE PERFECT CRIME!

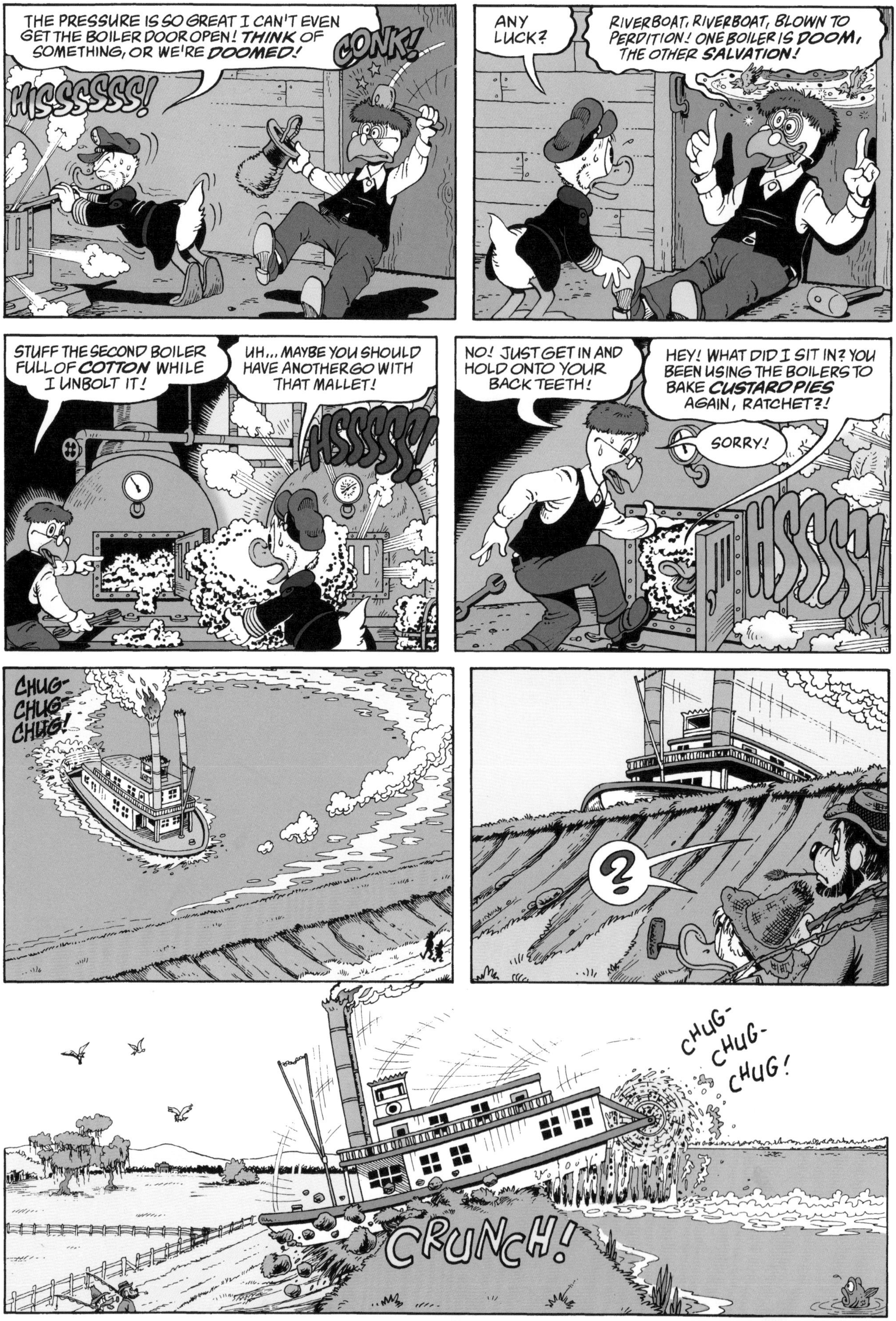

THE PRESSURE IS SO GREAT I CAN'T EVEN GET THE BOILER DOOR OPEN! THINK OF SOMETHING, OR WE'RE DOOMED!
HISSSSSS!
CONK!
ANY LUCK?
RIVERBOAT, RIVERBOAT, BLOWN TO PERDITION! ONE BOILER IS DOOM, THE OTHER SALVATION!
STUFF THE SECOND BOILER FULL OF COTTON WHILE I UNBOLT IT!
UH... MAYBE YOU SHOULD HAVE ANOTHER GO WITH THAT MALLET!
HSSSSS!
NO! JUST GET IN AND HOLD ONTO YOUR BACK TEETH!
HEY! WHAT DID I SIT IN? YOU BEEN USING THE BOILERS TO BAKE CUSTARD PIES AGAIN, RATCHET?!
SORRY!
HSSSS!
CHUG-CHUG-CHUG!
?
CHUG-CHUG-CHUG!
CRUNCH!

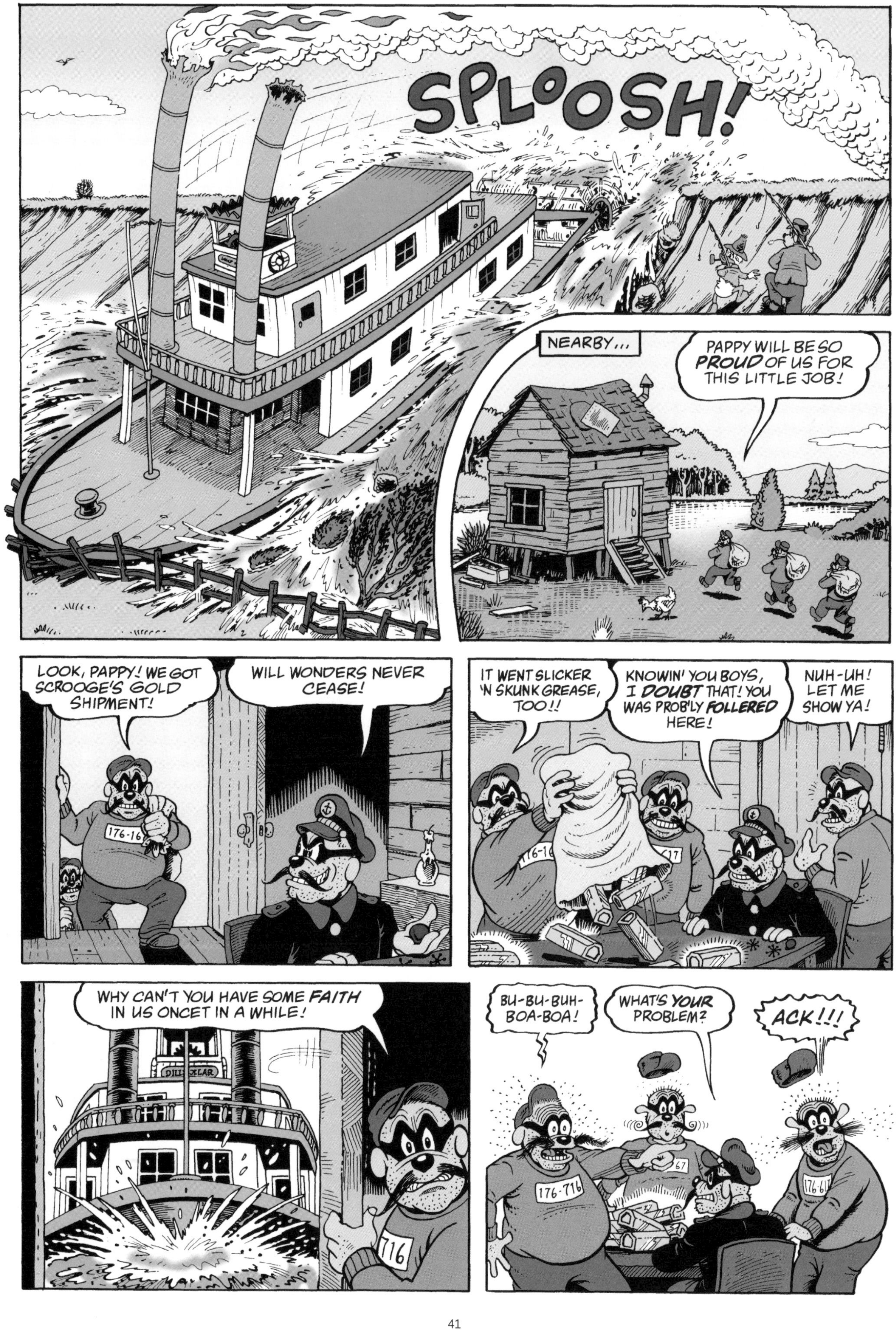
SPLOOSH!
NEARBY...
PAPPY WILL BE SO PROUD OF US FOR THIS LITTLE JOB!
LOOK, PAPPY! WE GOT SCROOGE'S GOLD SHIPMENT!
WILL WONDERS NEVER CEASE!
IT WENT SLICKER 'N SKUNK GREASE, TOO!!
KNOWIN' YOU BOYS, I DOUBT THAT! YOU WAS PROB'LY FOLLERED HERE!
NUH-UH! LET ME SHOW YA!
WHY CAN'T YOU HAVE SOME FAITH IN US ONCET IN A WHILE!
BU-BU-BUH-BOA-BOA!
WHAT'S YOUR PROBLEM?
ACK!!!

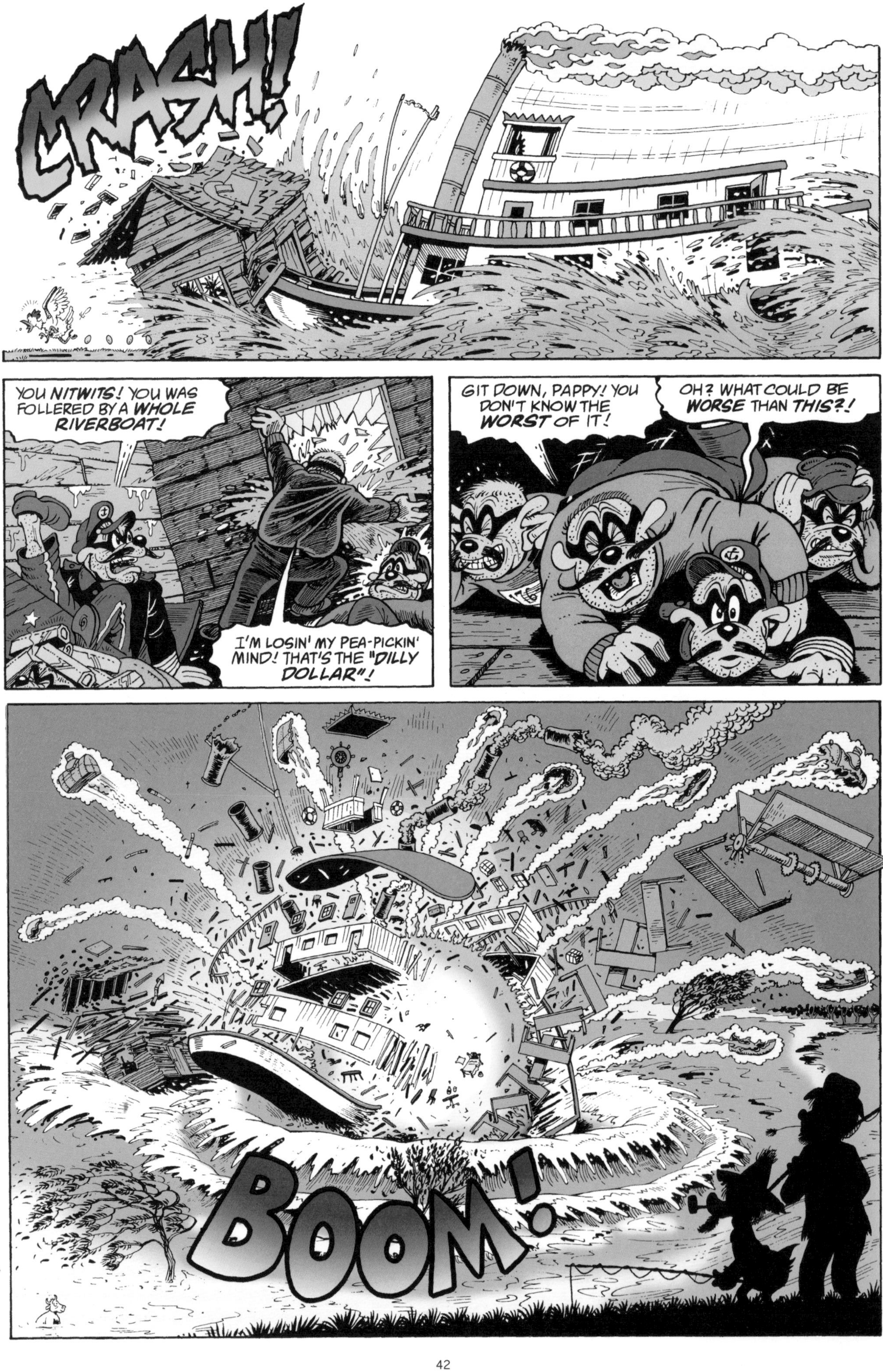
CRASH!
YOU NITWITS! YOU WAS FOLLERED BY A WHOLE RIVERBOAT!
I'M LOSIN' MY PEA-PICKIN' MIND! THAT'S THE "DILLY DOLLAR"!
GIT DOWN, PAPPY! YOU DON'T KNOW THE WORST OF IT!
OH? WHAT COULD BE WORSE THAN THIS?!
BOOM!

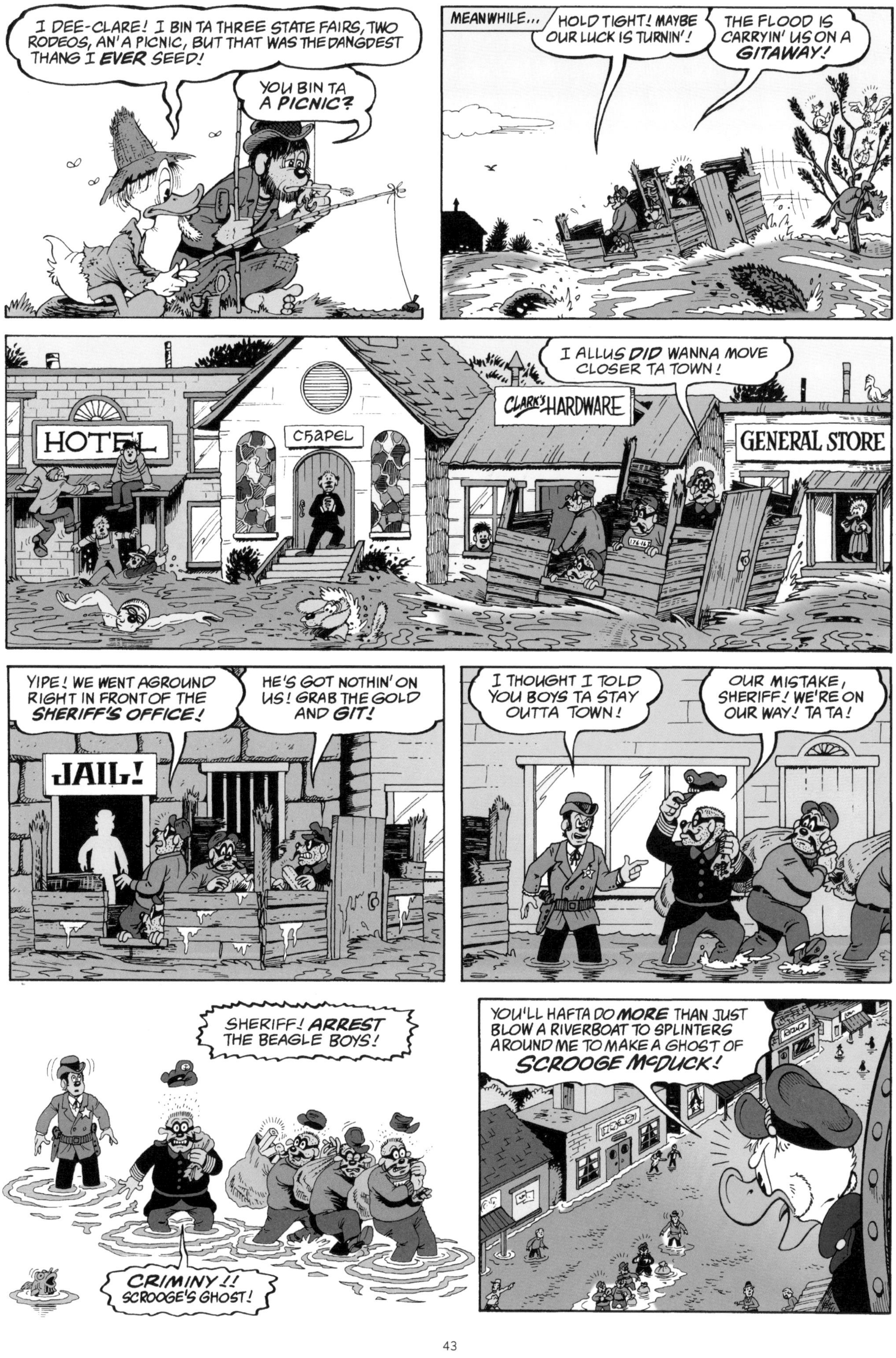

I DEE-CLARE! I BIN TA THREE STATE FAIRS, TWO RODEOS, AN' A PICNIC, BUT THAT WAS THE DANGDEST THANG I EVER SEED!
YOU BIN TA A PICNIC?
MEANWHILE...
HOLD TIGHT! MAYBE OUR LUCK IS TURNIN'!
THE FLOOD IS CARRYIN' US ON A GITAWAY!
HOTEL
CHAPEL
CLARK'S HARDWARE
GENERAL STORE
I ALLUS DID WANNA MOVE CLOSER TA TOWN!
YIPE! WE WENT AGROUND RIGHT IN FRONT OF THE SHERIFF'S OFFICE!
HE'S GOT NOTHIN' ON US! GRAB THE GOLD AND GIT!
JAIL!
I THOUGHT I TOLD YOU BOYS TA STAY OUTTA TOWN!
OUR MISTAKE, SHERIFF! WE'RE ON OUR WAY! TA TA!
SHERIFF! ARREST THE BEAGLE BOYS!
CRIMINY!! SCROOGE'S GHOST!
YOU'LL HAFTA DO MORE THAN JUST BLOW A RIVERBOAT TO SPLINTERS AROUND ME TO MAKE A GHOST OF SCROOGE McDUCK!

LOCK 'EM UP! THOSE PIRATES ARE GUILTY OF STEALING GOLD, DEMOLISHING A RIVERBOAT WITHOUT A PERMIT, AND DRESSING UP IN *WOMEN'S CLOTHING!*

CURSES! BACK TO PRISON!

AT LEAST WE'RE BETTER OFF THAN McDUCK!

YEAH! HAH.... HE'S SO BROKE, WE BEAGLE BOYS WILL NEVER HAVE TO BOTHER ROBBING *HIM* AGAIN!

HAVE I LOST MY JOB ON THE "DILLY DOLLAR", MR. McDUCK?

YES, UNLESS YOU WANT TO GET INTO THE *MATCH STICK* BUSINESS!

NO, I THINK I'LL OPEN UP A CUSTARD PIE SHOP! WHAT ABOUT YOU?

WELL, THE DAYS OF THE RIVERBOAT ARE OVER! IT'S TIME TO SEEK MY FORTUNE ELSEWHERE!

I'VE ONLY GOT A FEW DOLLARS TO MY NAME, BUT AT LEAST I STILL HAVE THE HEIRLOOMS I LEFT SCOTLAND WITH! I'LL JUST START OVER FROM SCRATCH AGAIN!

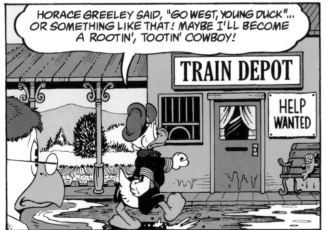

HORACE GREELEY SAID, "GO WEST, YOUNG DUCK"... OR SOMETHING LIKE THAT! MAYBE I'LL BECOME A ROOTIN', TOOTIN' COWBOY!

TRAIN DEPOT

HELP WANTED

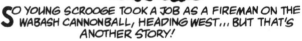

*S*O YOUNG SCROOGE TOOK A JOB AS A FIREMAN ON THE WABASH CANNONBALL, HEADING WEST.... BUT THAT'S ANOTHER STORY!

"...SO MUDDY THAT I SOLD MY RIVERBOAT AND LAID RAILROAD TRACK ON THE RIVER SURFACE!"

OH, BROTHER!

THE MASTER OF THE *MISSISSIPPI!*

POTHOLE McDUCK

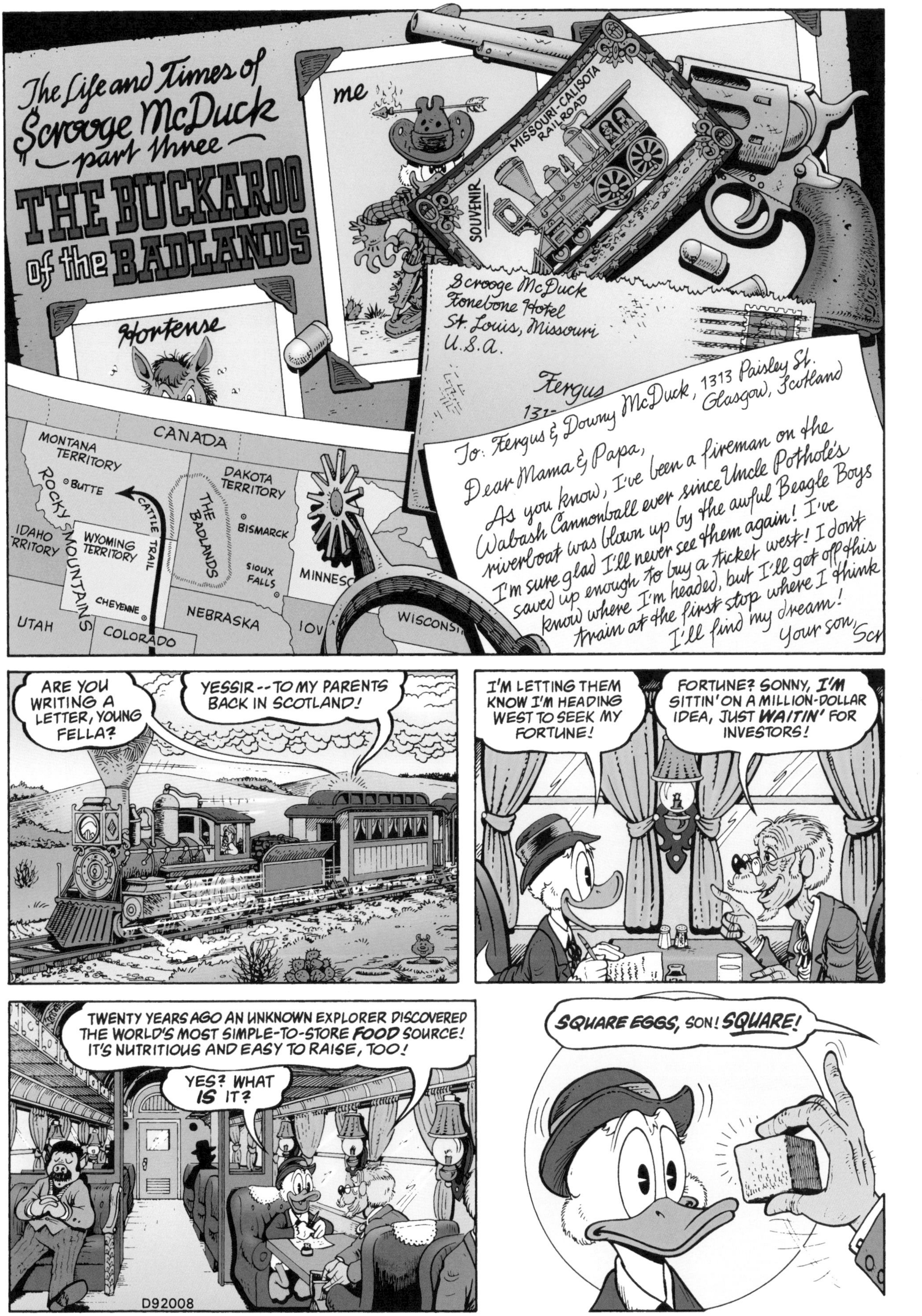
The Life and Times of Scrooge McDuck part three
THE BUCKAROO of the BADLANDS
me
Hortense
MISSOURI-CALISOTA RAILROAD
SOUVENIR
Scrooge McDuck
Fonebone Hotel
St. Louis, Missouri
U.S.A.
Fergus
CANADA
MONTANA TERRITORY
BUTTE
ROCKY MOUNTAINS
CATTLE TRAIL
DAKOTA TERRITORY
THE BADLANDS
BISMARCK
IDAHO TERRITORY
WYOMING TERRITORY
SIOUX FALLS
MINNESO
CHEYENNE
NEBRASKA
UTAH
COLORADO
IOW
WISCONSI
To: Fergus & Downy McDuck, 1313 Paisley St. Glasgow, Scotland
Dear Mama & Papa,
As you know, I've been a fireman on the Wabash Cannonball ever since Uncle Pothole's riverboat was blown up by the awful Beagle Boys. I'm sure glad I'll never see them again! I've saved up enough to buy a ticket west! I don't know where I'm headed, but I'll get off this train at the first stop where I think I'll find my dream!
Your son, Scr
ARE YOU WRITING A LETTER, YOUNG FELLA?
YESSIR -- TO MY PARENTS BACK IN SCOTLAND!
I'M LETTING THEM KNOW I'M HEADING WEST TO SEEK MY FORTUNE!
FORTUNE? SONNY, I'M SITTIN' ON A MILLION-DOLLAR IDEA, JUST WAITIN' FOR INVESTORS!
TWENTY YEARS AGO AN UNKNOWN EXPLORER DISCOVERED THE WORLD'S MOST SIMPLE-TO-STORE FOOD SOURCE! IT'S NUTRITIOUS AND EASY TO RAISE, TOO!
YES? WHAT IS IT?
D92008
SQUARE EGGS, SON! SQUARE!

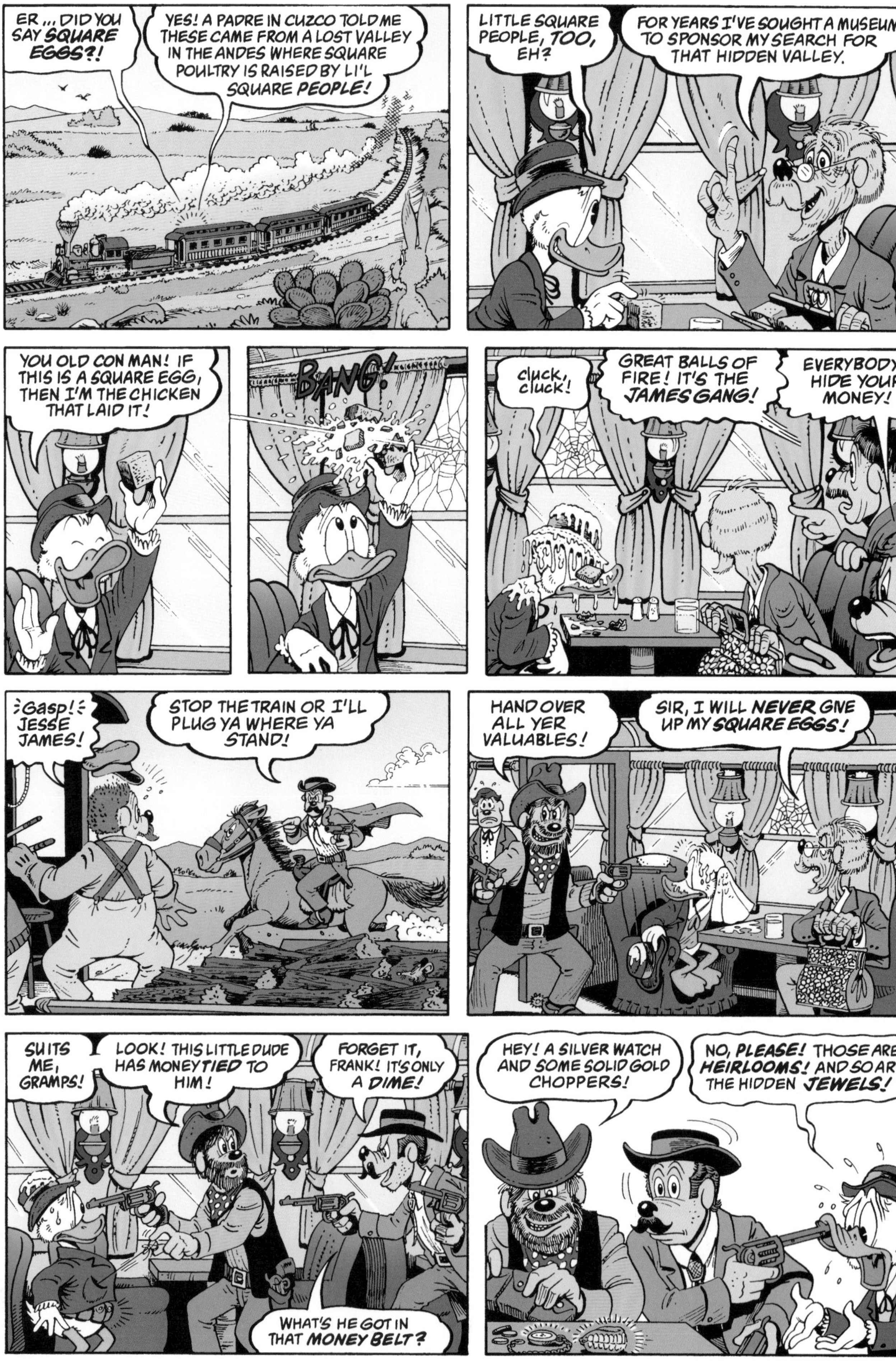
ER... DID YOU SAY SQUARE EGGS?!
YES! A PADRE IN CUZCO TOLD ME THESE CAME FROM A LOST VALLEY IN THE ANDES WHERE SQUARE POULTRY IS RAISED BY LI'L SQUARE PEOPLE!
LITTLE SQUARE PEOPLE, TOO, EH?
FOR YEARS I'VE SOUGHT A MUSEUM TO SPONSOR MY SEARCH FOR THAT HIDDEN VALLEY.
YOU OLD CON MAN! IF THIS IS A SQUARE EGG, THEN I'M THE CHICKEN THAT LAID IT!
BANG!
cluck, cluck!
GREAT BALLS OF FIRE! IT'S THE JAMES GANG!
EVERYBODY HIDE YOUR MONEY!
Gasp! JESSE JAMES!
STOP THE TRAIN OR I'LL PLUG YA WHERE YA STAND!
HAND OVER ALL YER VALUABLES!
SIR, I WILL NEVER GIVE UP MY SQUARE EGGS!
SUITS ME, GRAMPS!
LOOK! THIS LITTLE DUDE HAS MONEY TIED TO HIM!
FORGET IT, FRANK! IT'S ONLY A DIME!
WHAT'S HE GOT IN THAT MONEY BELT?
HEY! A SILVER WATCH AND SOME SOLID GOLD CHOPPERS!
NO, PLEASE! THOSE ARE HEIRLOOMS! AND SO ARE THE HIDDEN JEWELS!

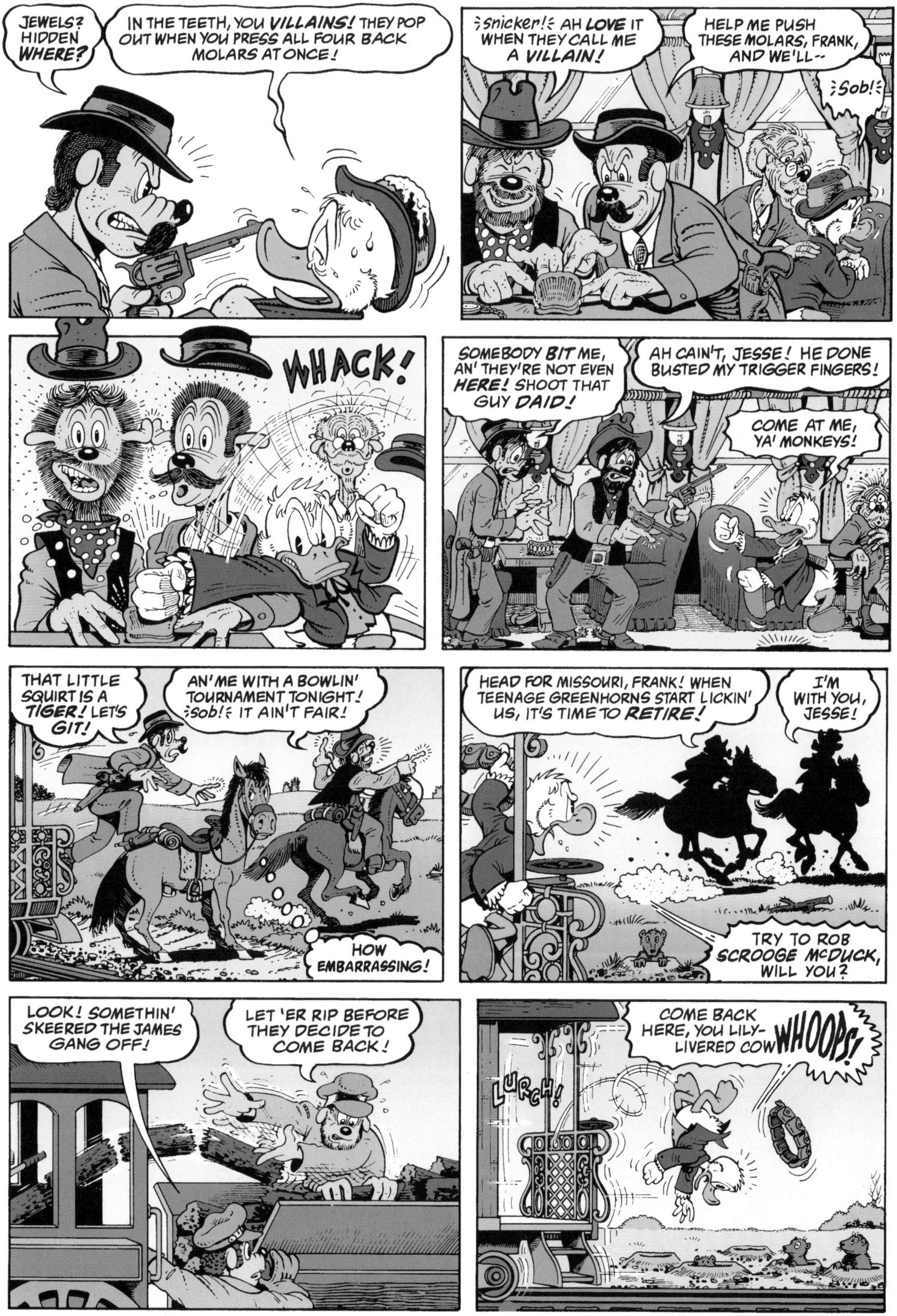
JEWELS? HIDDEN WHERE?
IN THE TEETH, YOU VILLAINS! THEY POP OUT WHEN YOU PRESS ALL FOUR BACK MOLARS AT ONCE!
¡Snicker!¡ AH LOVE IT WHEN THEY CALL ME A VILLAIN!
HELP ME PUSH THESE MOLARS, FRANK, AND WE'LL--
¡Sob!¡
WHACK!
SOMEBODY BIT ME, AN' THEY'RE NOT EVEN HERE! SHOOT THAT GUY DAID!
AH CAIN'T, JESSE! HE DONE BUSTED MY TRIGGER FINGERS!
COME AT ME, YA' MONKEYS!
THAT LITTLE SQUIRT IS A TIGER! LET'S GIT!
AN' ME WITH A BOWLIN' TOURNAMENT TONIGHT! ¡Sob!¡ IT AIN'T FAIR!
HOW EMBARRASSING!
HEAD FOR MISSOURI, FRANK! WHEN TEENAGE GREENHORNS START LICKIN' US, IT'S TIME TO RETIRE!
I'M WITH YOU, JESSE!
TRY TO ROB SCROOGE McDUCK, WILL YOU?
LOOK! SOMETHIN' SKEERED THE JAMES GANG OFF!
LET 'ER RIP BEFORE THEY DECIDE TO COME BACK!
LURCH!
COME BACK HERE, YOU LILY-LIVERED COW
WHOOPS!

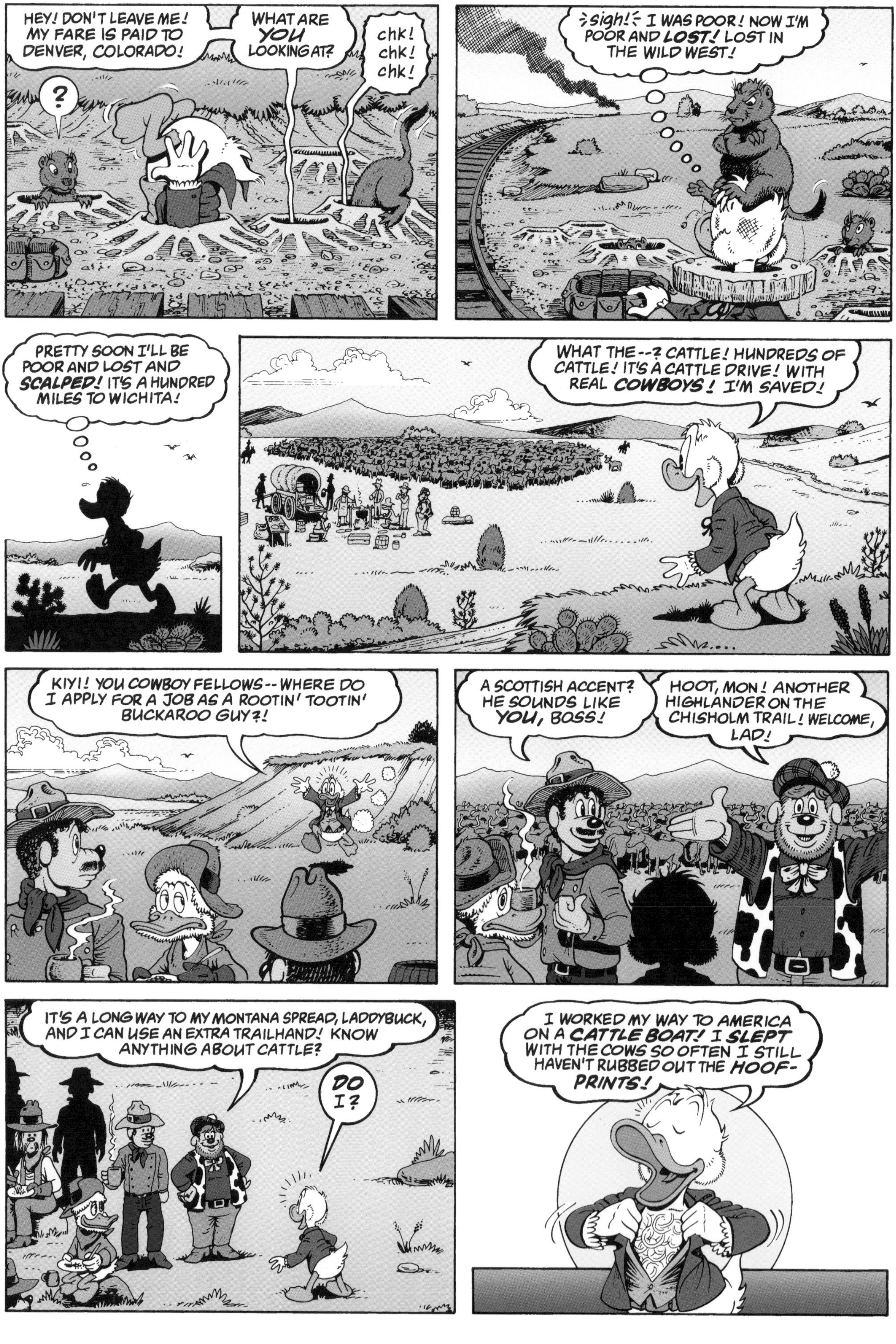

HEY! DON'T LEAVE ME! MY FARE IS PAID TO DENVER, COLORADO!
WHAT ARE YOU LOOKING AT?
chk! chk! chk!
?
sigh! I WAS POOR! NOW I'M POOR AND LOST! LOST IN THE WILD WEST!
PRETTY SOON I'LL BE POOR AND LOST AND SCALPED! IT'S A HUNDRED MILES TO WICHITA!
WHAT THE--? CATTLE! HUNDREDS OF CATTLE! IT'S A CATTLE DRIVE! WITH REAL COWBOYS! I'M SAVED!
KIYI! YOU COWBOY FELLOWS--WHERE DO I APPLY FOR A JOB AS A ROOTIN' TOOTIN' BUCKAROO GUY?!
A SCOTTISH ACCENT? HE SOUNDS LIKE YOU, BOSS!
HOOT, MON! ANOTHER HIGHLANDER ON THE CHISHOLM TRAIL! WELCOME, LAD!
IT'S A LONG WAY TO MY MONTANA SPREAD, LADDYBUCK, AND I CAN USE AN EXTRA TRAILHAND! KNOW ANYTHING ABOUT CATTLE?
DO I?
I WORKED MY WAY TO AMERICA ON A CATTLE BOAT! I SLEPT WITH THE COWS SO OFTEN I STILL HAVEN'T RUBBED OUT THE HOOF-PRINTS!

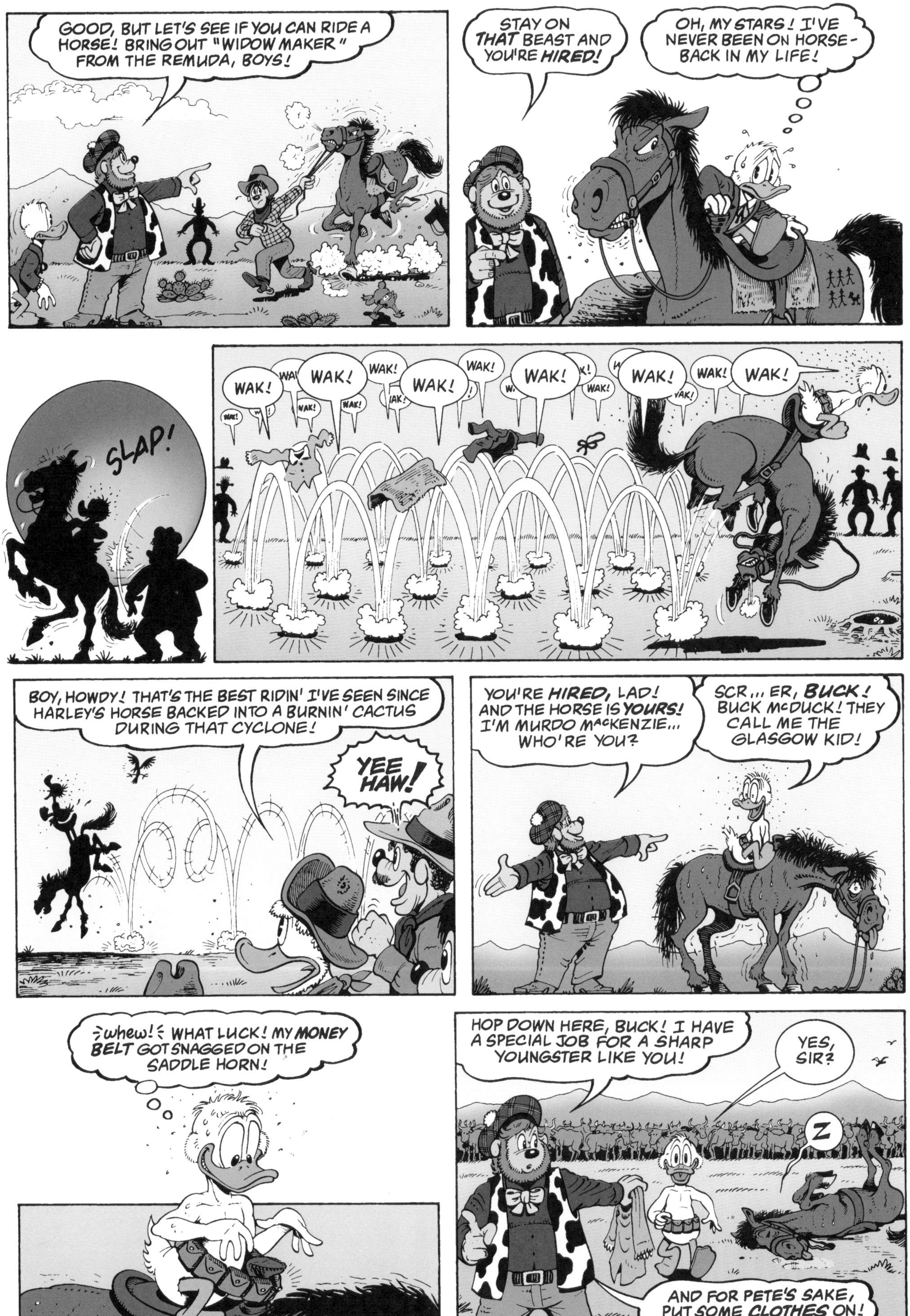
GOOD, BUT LET'S SEE IF YOU CAN RIDE A HORSE! BRING OUT "WIDOW MAKER" FROM THE REMUDA, BOYS!
STAY ON THAT BEAST AND YOU'RE HIRED!
OH, MY STARS! I'VE NEVER BEEN ON HORSE-BACK IN MY LIFE!
SLAP!
WAK!
WAK!
WAK!
WAK!
WAK!
WAK!
WAK!
WAK!
WAK!
WAK!
BOY, HOWDY! THAT'S THE BEST RIDIN' I'VE SEEN SINCE HARLEY'S HORSE BACKED INTO A BURNIN' CACTUS DURING THAT CYCLONE!
YEE HAW!
YOU'RE HIRED, LAD! AND THE HORSE IS YOURS! I'M MURDO MACKENZIE... WHO'RE YOU?
SCR... ER, BUCK! BUCK McDUCK! THEY CALL ME THE GLASGOW KID!
whew! WHAT LUCK! MY MONEY BELT GOT SNAGGED ON THE SADDLE HORN!
HOP DOWN HERE, BUCK! I HAVE A SPECIAL JOB FOR A SHARP YOUNGSTER LIKE YOU!
YES, SIR?
Z
AND FOR PETE'S SAKE, PUT SOME CLOTHES ON!

I PAID A FORTUNE TO IMPORT THIS PRIZE ANGUS BULL FROM *SCOTLAND!* I WANT *YOU* TO TAKE CHARGE OF HIM!

?!

BUT, BOSS! *WE'RE* RAMRODDIN' VINDICATOR!

NOT ANYMORE! YOU McVIPER BOYS CAN WORK WITH THE REGULAR HERD NOW!

@#%@*! NOW IT WON'T BE SO EASY TO RUSTLE THAT CHAMPEEN ANGUS!

SHH! DON'T WORRY! THE RIGHT TIME WILL COME!

Dear Mama & Papa,
Your son is a cowboy! Enclosed is a photo of me with all my cowboy clothes and six-shooters and other buckaroo stuff!

me

rgus & Downy McDuc!
Paisley St
w,

Of course, we cowpokes don't always wear all this equipment when we ride the range and punch cows!

THERE GOES BUCK, SHOWIN' OFF AGAIN! WOTTA GUY!

The wild west is all you've heard! On our cattle drive to Mr. Mackenzie's ranch in the Montana Territory, the Rocky Mountains are always to the west! They make the Scottish mountains look like molehills!

And you should see the molehills here!

And the weather is just as amazing! One day it was raining so hard that I think I saw some trout swim by at about shoulder level!

?

52

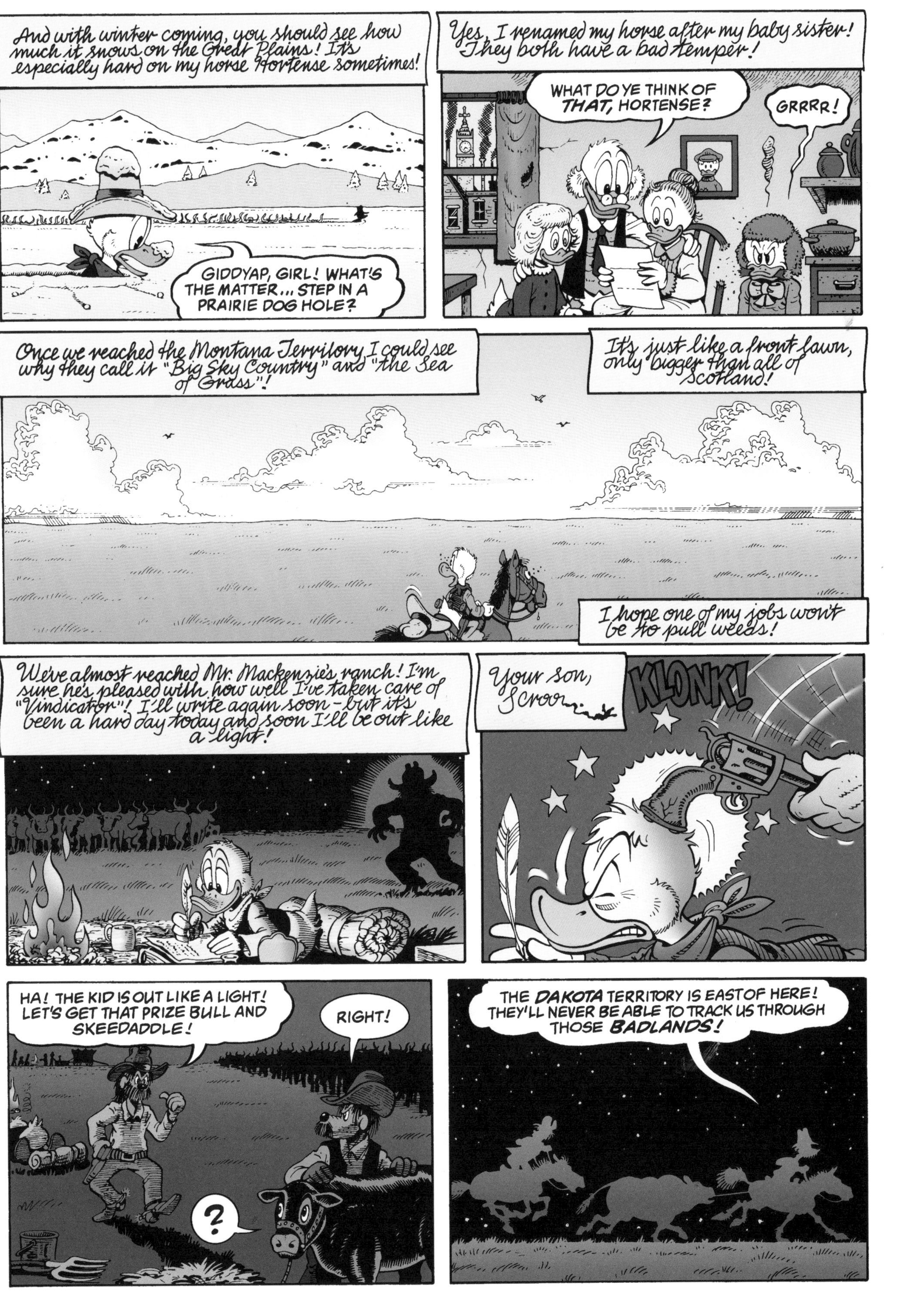

And with winter coming, you should see how much it snows on the Great Plains! It's especially hard on my horse Hortense sometimes!
GIDDYAP, GIRL! WHAT'S THE MATTER... STEP IN A PRAIRIE DOG HOLE?
Yes, I renamed my horse after my baby sister! They both have a bad temper!
WHAT DO YE THINK OF THAT, HORTENSE?
GRRRR!
Once we reached the Montana Territory I could see why they call it "Big Sky Country" and "the Sea of Grass"!
It's just like a front lawn, only bigger than all of Scotland!
I hope one of my jobs won't be to pull weeds!
We've almost reached Mr. Mackenzie's ranch! I'm sure he's pleased with how well I've taken care of "Vindicator"! I'll write again soon - but it's been a hard day today and soon I'll be out like a light!
Your son, Scroo
KLONK!
HA! THE KID IS OUT LIKE A LIGHT! LET'S GET THAT PRIZE BULL AND SKEEDADDLE!
RIGHT!
?
THE DAKOTA TERRITORY IS EAST OF HERE! THEY'LL NEVER BE ABLE TO TRACK US THROUGH THOSE BADLANDS!

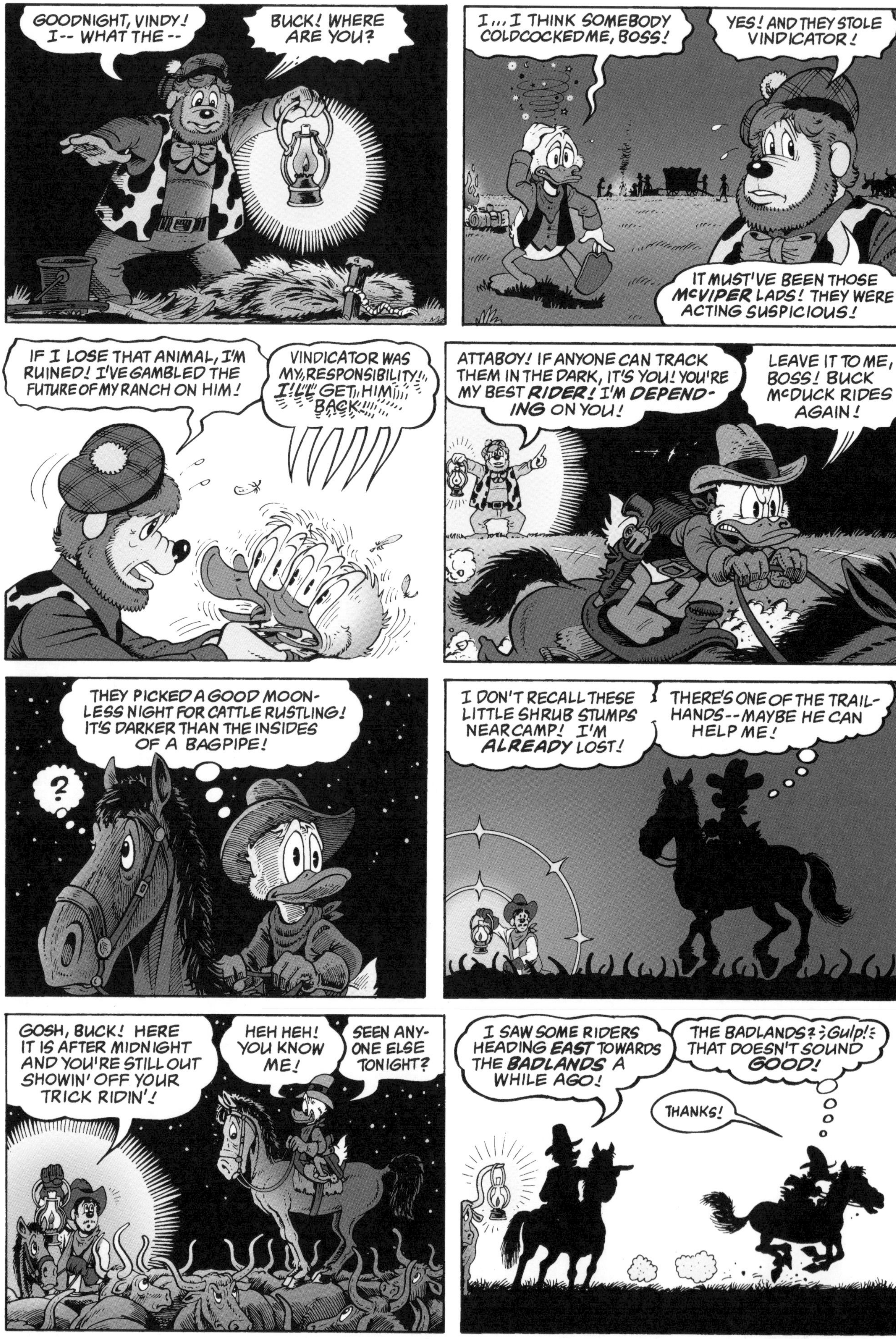
GOODNIGHT, VINDY! I-- WHAT THE --
BUCK! WHERE ARE YOU?
I... I THINK SOMEBODY COLDCOCKED ME, BOSS!
YES! AND THEY STOLE VINDICATOR!
IT MUST'VE BEEN THOSE McVIPER LADS! THEY WERE ACTING SUSPICIOUS!
IF I LOSE THAT ANIMAL, I'M RUINED! I'VE GAMBLED THE FUTURE OF MY RANCH ON HIM!
VINDICATOR WAS MY RESPONSIBILITY! I'LL GET HIM BACK!
ATTABOY! IF ANYONE CAN TRACK THEM IN THE DARK, IT'S YOU! YOU'RE MY BEST RIDER! I'M DEPENDING ON YOU!
LEAVE IT TO ME, BOSS! BUCK McDUCK RIDES AGAIN!
THEY PICKED A GOOD MOONLESS NIGHT FOR CATTLE RUSTLING! IT'S DARKER THAN THE INSIDES OF A BAGPIPE!
?
I DON'T RECALL THESE LITTLE SHRUB STUMPS NEAR CAMP! I'M ALREADY LOST!
THERE'S ONE OF THE TRAIL-HANDS--MAYBE HE CAN HELP ME!
GOSH, BUCK! HERE IT IS AFTER MIDNIGHT AND YOU'RE STILL OUT SHOWIN' OFF YOUR TRICK RIDIN'!
HEH HEH! YOU KNOW ME!
SEEN ANYONE ELSE TONIGHT?
I SAW SOME RIDERS HEADING EAST TOWARDS THE BADLANDS A WHILE AGO!
THANKS!
THE BADLANDS? Gulp! THAT DOESN'T SOUND GOOD!

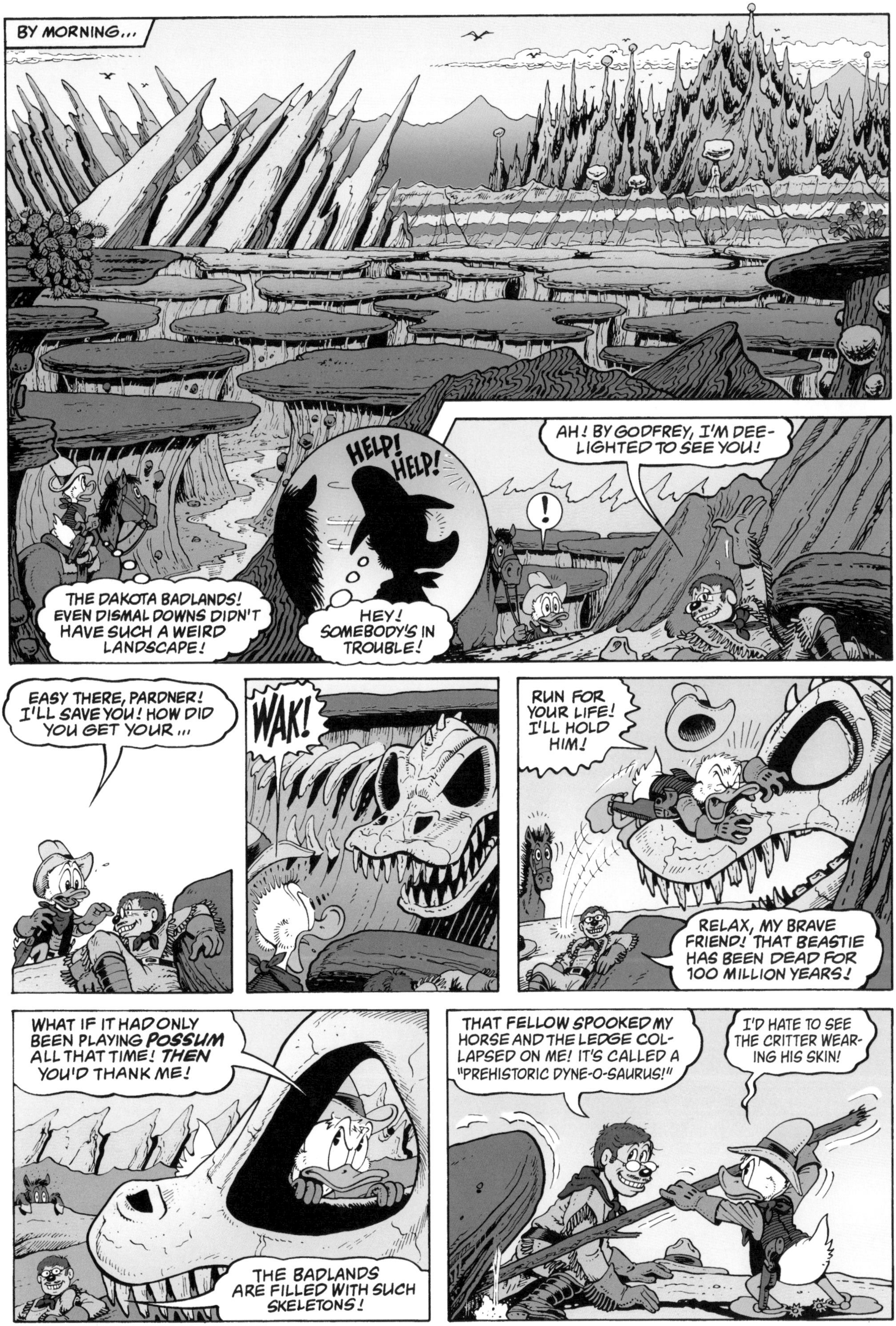
BY MORNING...
HELP! HELP!
THE DAKOTA BADLANDS! EVEN DISMAL DOWNS DIDN'T HAVE SUCH A WEIRD LANDSCAPE!
HEY! SOMEBODY'S IN TROUBLE!
!
AH! BY GODFREY, I'M DEE-LIGHTED TO SEE YOU!
EASY THERE, PARDNER! I'LL SAVE YOU! HOW DID YOU GET YOUR...
WAK!
RUN FOR YOUR LIFE! I'LL HOLD HIM!
RELAX, MY BRAVE FRIEND! THAT BEASTIE HAS BEEN DEAD FOR 100 MILLION YEARS!
WHAT IF IT HAD ONLY BEEN PLAYING POSSUM ALL THAT TIME! THEN YOU'D THANK ME!
THE BADLANDS ARE FILLED WITH SUCH SKELETONS!
THAT FELLOW SPOOKED MY HORSE AND THE LEDGE COL-LAPSED ON ME! IT'S CALLED A "PREHISTORIC DYNE-O-SAURUS!"
I'D HATE TO SEE THE CRITTER WEAR-ING HIS SKIN!

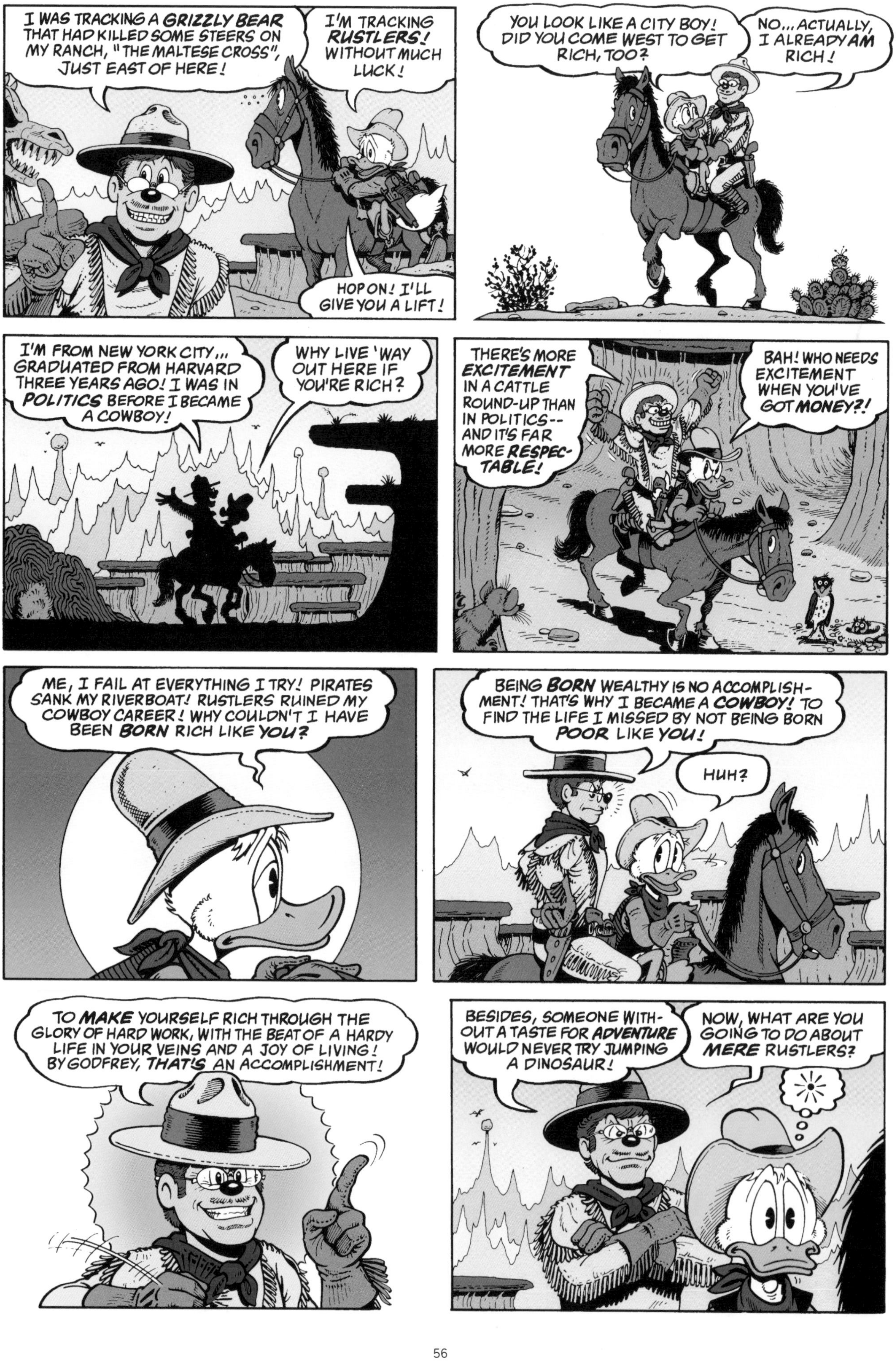
I WAS TRACKING A GRIZZLY BEAR THAT HAD KILLED SOME STEERS ON MY RANCH, "THE MALTESE CROSS", JUST EAST OF HERE!
I'M TRACKING RUSTLERS! WITHOUT MUCH LUCK!
HOP ON! I'LL GIVE YOU A LIFT!
YOU LOOK LIKE A CITY BOY! DID YOU COME WEST TO GET RICH, TOO?
NO... ACTUALLY, I ALREADY AM RICH!
I'M FROM NEW YORK CITY... GRADUATED FROM HARVARD THREE YEARS AGO! I WAS IN POLITICS BEFORE I BECAME A COWBOY!
WHY LIVE 'WAY OUT HERE IF YOU'RE RICH?
THERE'S MORE EXCITEMENT IN A CATTLE ROUND-UP THAN IN POLITICS-- AND IT'S FAR MORE RESPECTABLE!
BAH! WHO NEEDS EXCITEMENT WHEN YOU'VE GOT MONEY?!
ME, I FAIL AT EVERYTHING I TRY! PIRATES SANK MY RIVERBOAT! RUSTLERS RUINED MY COWBOY CAREER! WHY COULDN'T I HAVE BEEN BORN RICH LIKE YOU?
BEING BORN WEALTHY IS NO ACCOMPLISHMENT! THAT'S WHY I BECAME A COWBOY! TO FIND THE LIFE I MISSED BY NOT BEING BORN POOR LIKE YOU!
HUH?
TO MAKE YOURSELF RICH THROUGH THE GLORY OF HARD WORK, WITH THE BEAT OF A HARDY LIFE IN YOUR VEINS AND A JOY OF LIVING! BY GODFREY, THAT'S AN ACCOMPLISHMENT!
BESIDES, SOMEONE WITHOUT A TASTE FOR ADVENTURE WOULD NEVER TRY JUMPING A DINOSAUR!
NOW, WHAT ARE YOU GOING TO DO ABOUT MERE RUSTLERS?

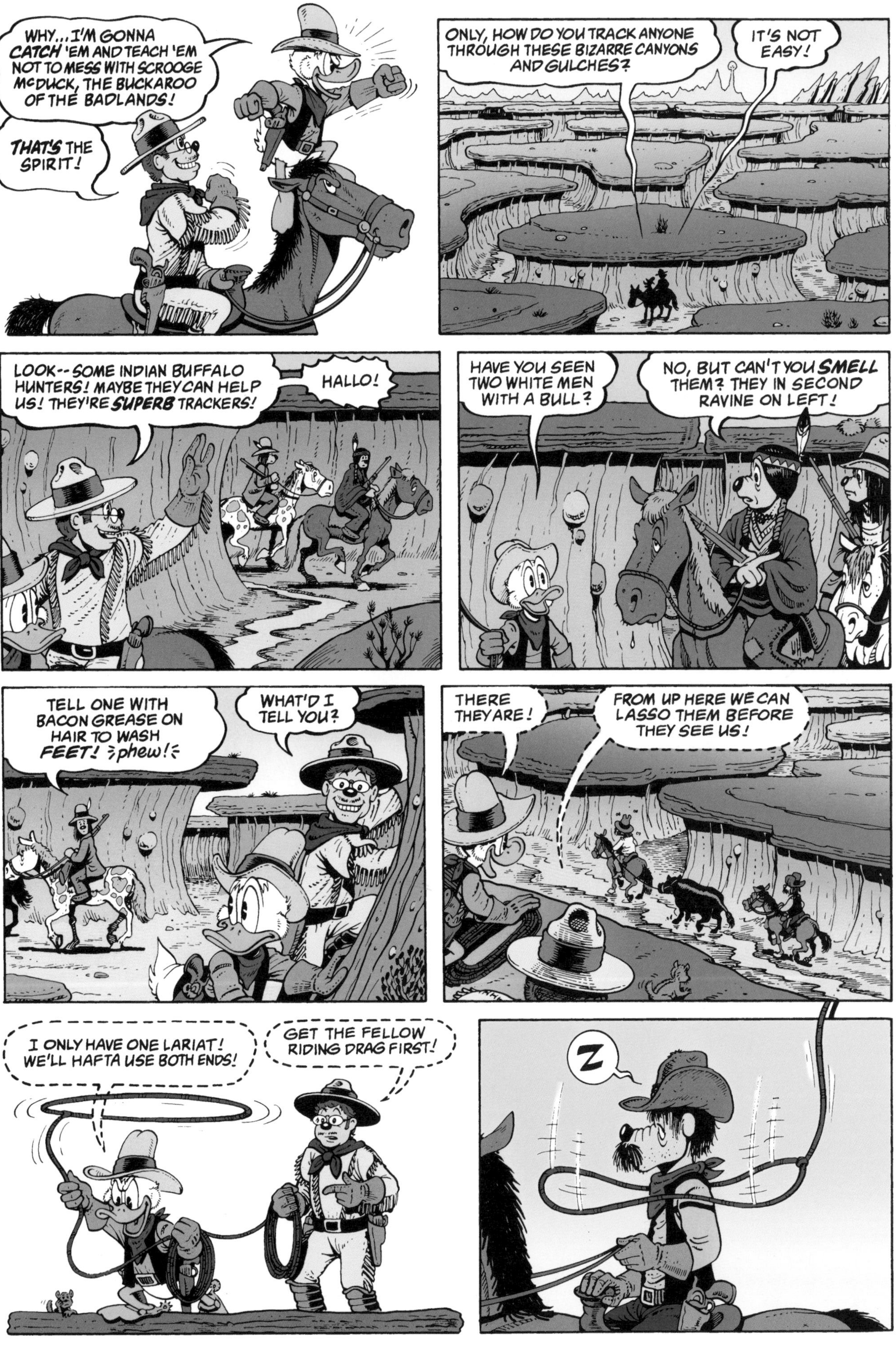
WHY... I'M GONNA CATCH 'EM AND TEACH 'EM NOT TO MESS WITH SCROOGE McDUCK, THE BUCKAROO OF THE BADLANDS!
THAT'S THE SPIRIT!
ONLY, HOW DO YOU TRACK ANYONE THROUGH THESE BIZARRE CANYONS AND GULCHES?
IT'S NOT EASY!
LOOK-- SOME INDIAN BUFFALO HUNTERS! MAYBE THEY CAN HELP US! THEY'RE SUPERB TRACKERS!
HALLO!
HAVE YOU SEEN TWO WHITE MEN WITH A BULL?
NO, BUT CAN'T YOU SMELL THEM? THEY IN SECOND RAVINE ON LEFT!
TELL ONE WITH BACON GREASE ON HAIR TO WASH FEET! phew!
WHAT'D I TELL YOU?
THERE THEY ARE!
FROM UP HERE WE CAN LASSO THEM BEFORE THEY SEE US!
I ONLY HAVE ONE LARIAT! WE'LL HAFTA USE BOTH ENDS!
GET THE FELLOW RIDING DRAG FIRST!
Z

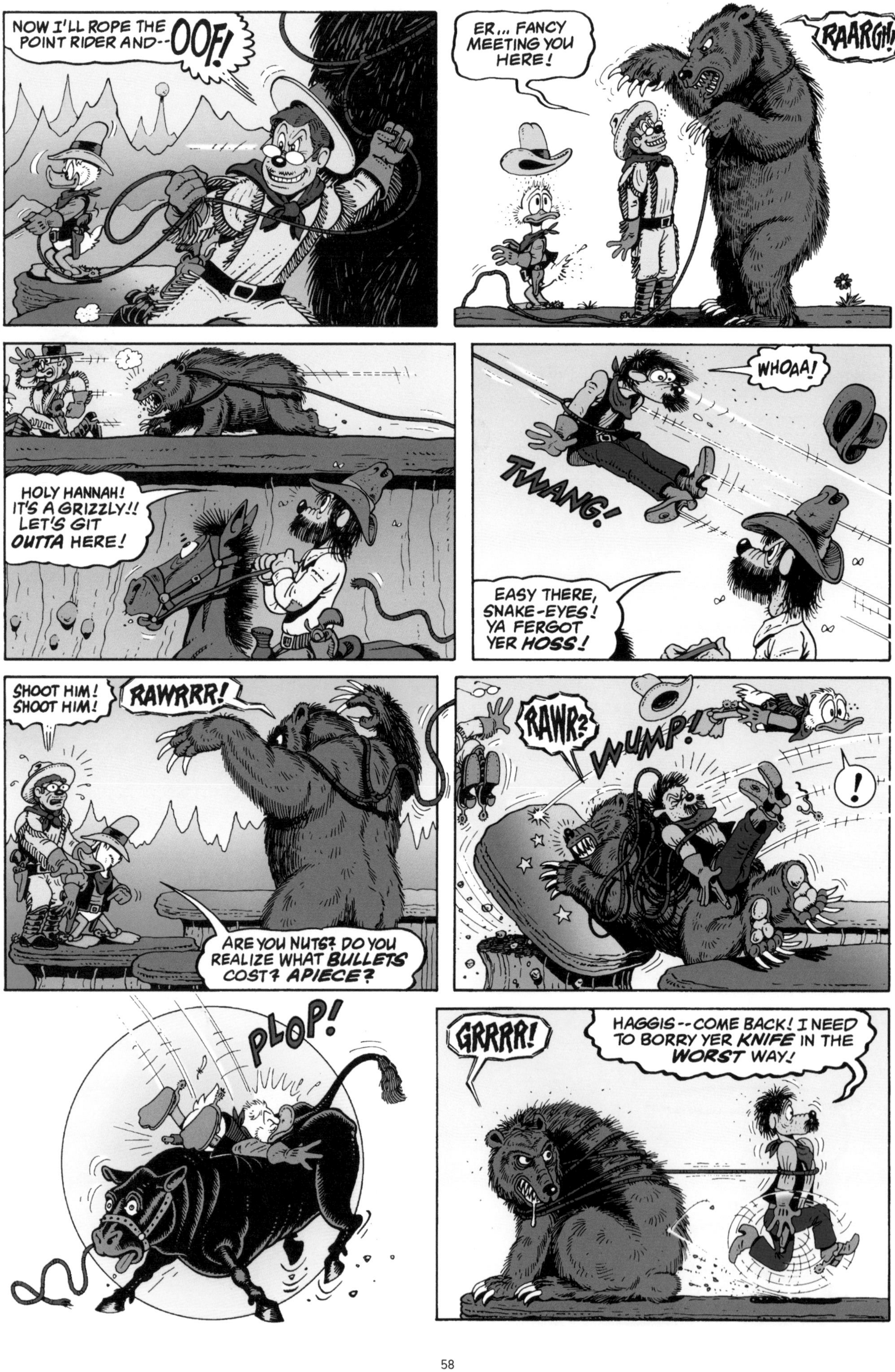
NOW I'LL ROPE THE POINT RIDER AND--OOF!
ER... FANCY MEETING YOU HERE!
RAARGH!
HOLY HANNAH! IT'S A GRIZZLY!! LET'S GIT OUTTA HERE!
WHOAA!
TWANG!
EASY THERE, SNAKE-EYES! YA FERGOT YER HOSS!
SHOOT HIM! SHOOT HIM!
RAWRRR!
ARE YOU NUTS? DO YOU REALIZE WHAT BULLETS COST? APIECE?
RAWR?
WUMP!
!
PLOP!
GRRRR!
HAGGIS--COME BACK! I NEED TO BORRY YER KNIFE IN THE WORST WAY!

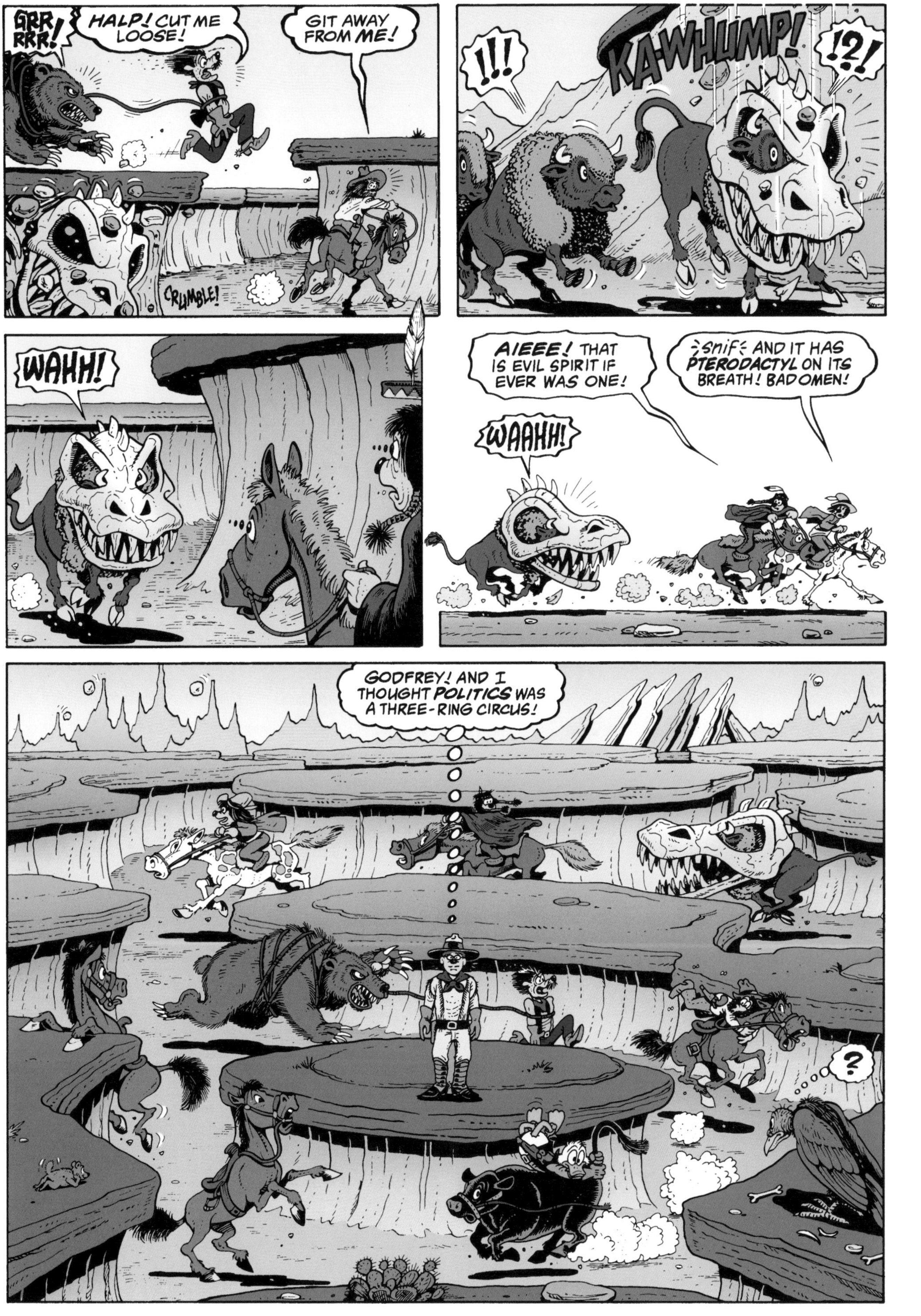
GRR RRR!
HALP! CUT ME LOOSE!
GIT AWAY FROM ME!
CRUMBLE!
!!!
KA-WHUMP!
!?!
WAHH!
AIEEE! THAT IS EVIL SPIRIT IF EVER WAS ONE!
snif AND IT HAS PTERODACTYL ON ITS BREATH! BAD OMEN!
WAAHH!
GODFREY! AND I THOUGHT POLITICS WAS A THREE-RING CIRCUS!
?

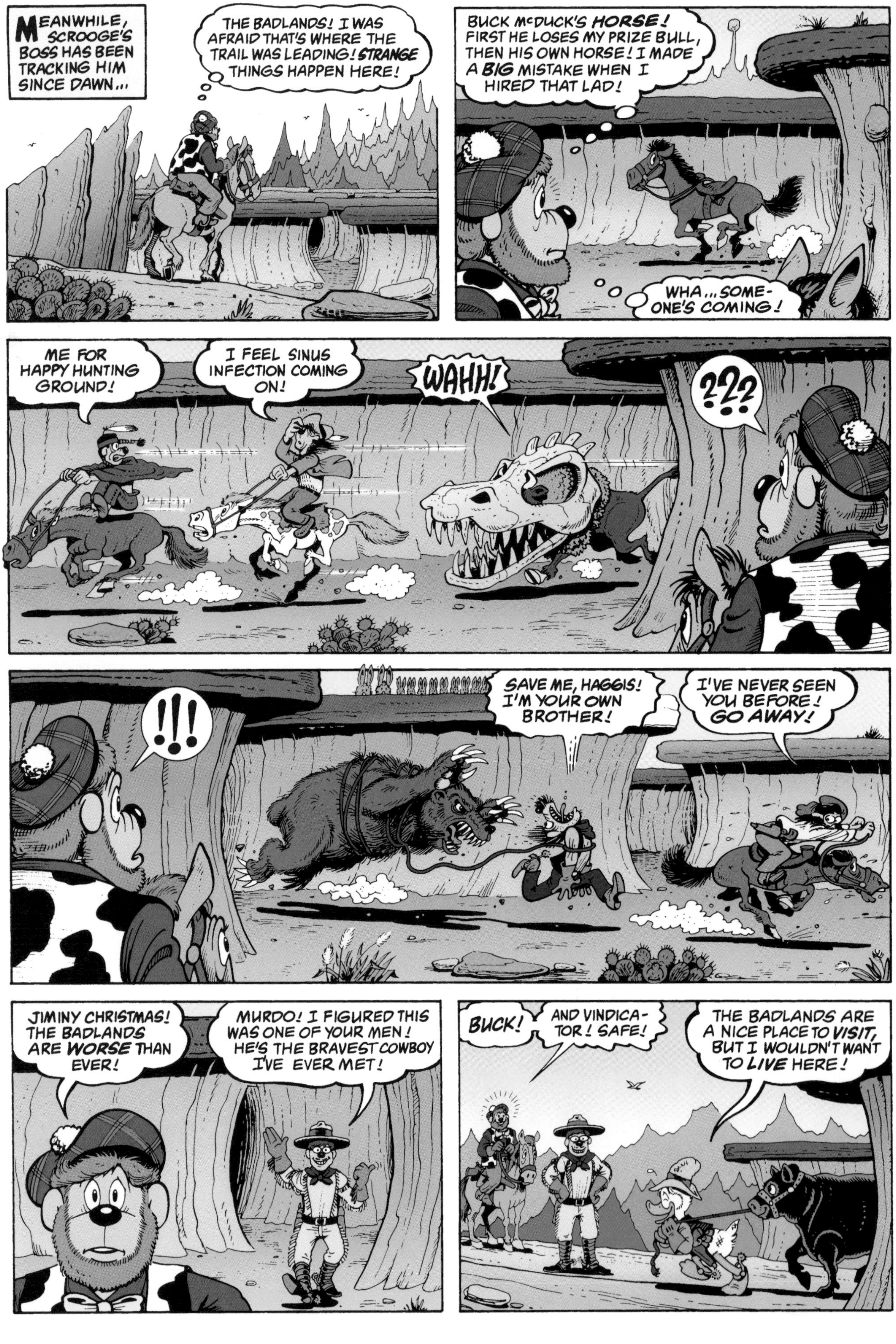
MEANWHILE, SCROOGE'S BOSS HAS BEEN TRACKING HIM SINCE DAWN...
THE BADLANDS! I WAS AFRAID THAT'S WHERE THE TRAIL WAS LEADING! STRANGE THINGS HAPPEN HERE!
BUCK McDUCK'S HORSE! FIRST HE LOSES MY PRIZE BULL, THEN HIS OWN HORSE! I MADE A BIG MISTAKE WHEN I HIRED THAT LAD!
WHA... SOME-ONE'S COMING!
ME FOR HAPPY HUNTING GROUND!
I FEEL SINUS INFECTION COMING ON!
WAHH!
???
!!!
SAVE ME, HAGGIS! I'M YOUR OWN BROTHER!
I'VE NEVER SEEN YOU BEFORE! GO AWAY!
JIMINY CHRISTMAS! THE BADLANDS ARE WORSE THAN EVER!
MURDO! I FIGURED THIS WAS ONE OF YOUR MEN! HE'S THE BRAVEST COWBOY I'VE EVER MET!
BUCK!
AND VINDICA-TOR! SAFE!
THE BADLANDS ARE A NICE PLACE TO VISIT, BUT I WOULDN'T WANT TO LIVE HERE!

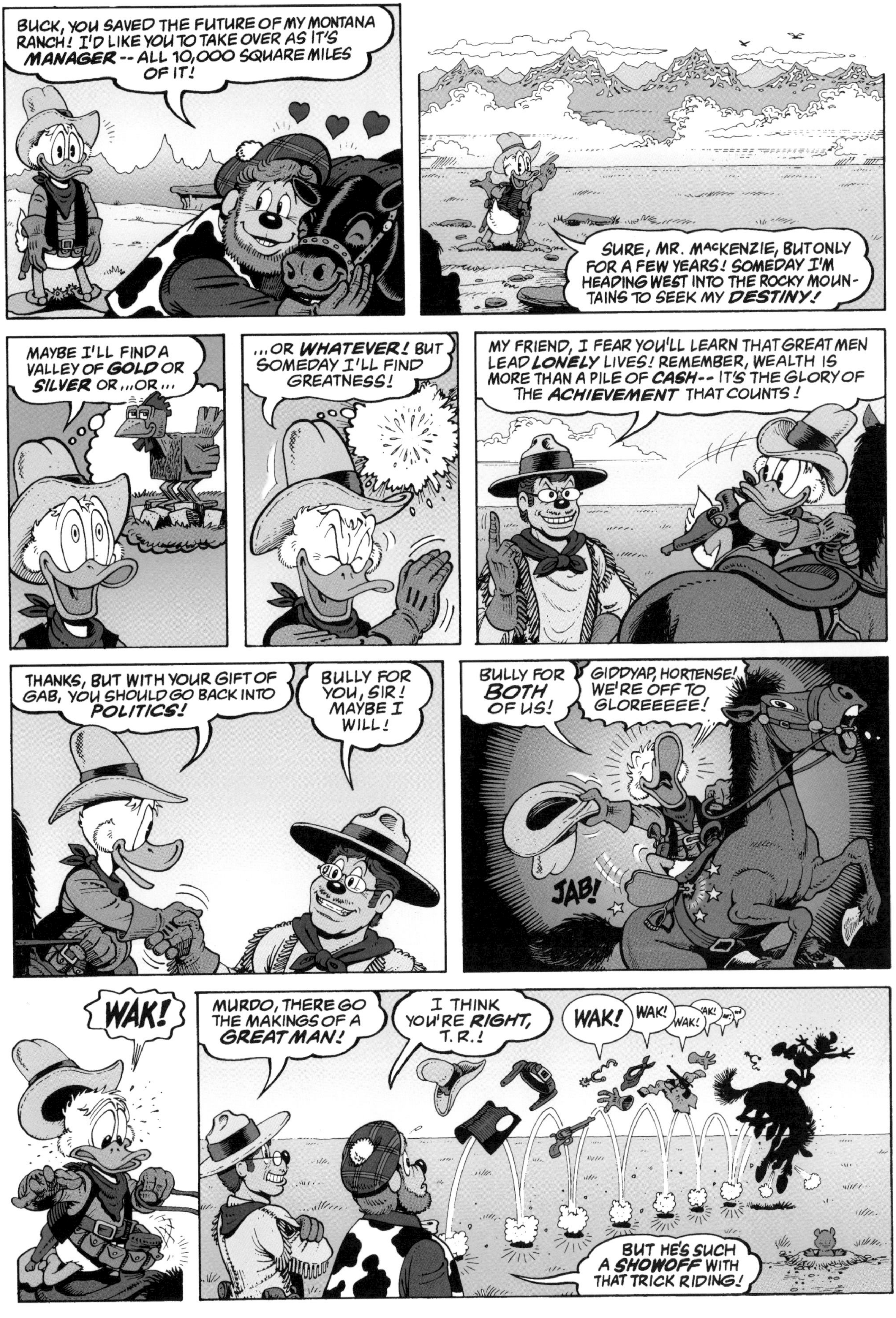
BUCK, YOU SAVED THE FUTURE OF MY MONTANA RANCH! I'D LIKE YOU TO TAKE OVER AS IT'S MANAGER -- ALL 10,000 SQUARE MILES OF IT!
SURE, MR. MACKENZIE, BUT ONLY FOR A FEW YEARS! SOMEDAY I'M HEADING WEST INTO THE ROCKY MOUNTAINS TO SEEK MY DESTINY!
MAYBE I'LL FIND A VALLEY OF GOLD OR SILVER OR ... OR ...
... OR WHATEVER! BUT SOMEDAY I'LL FIND GREATNESS!
MY FRIEND, I FEAR YOU'LL LEARN THAT GREAT MEN LEAD LONELY LIVES! REMEMBER, WEALTH IS MORE THAN A PILE OF CASH -- IT'S THE GLORY OF THE ACHIEVEMENT THAT COUNTS!
THANKS, BUT WITH YOUR GIFT OF GAB, YOU SHOULD GO BACK INTO POLITICS!
BULLY FOR YOU, SIR! MAYBE I WILL!
BULLY FOR BOTH OF US!
GIDDYAP, HORTENSE! WE'RE OFF TO GLOREEEEE!
JAB!
WAK!
MURDO, THERE GO THE MAKINGS OF A GREAT MAN!
I THINK YOU'RE RIGHT, T. R.!
WAK!
WAK!
WAK!
WAK!
BUT HE'S SUCH A SHOWOFF WITH THAT TRICK RIDING!

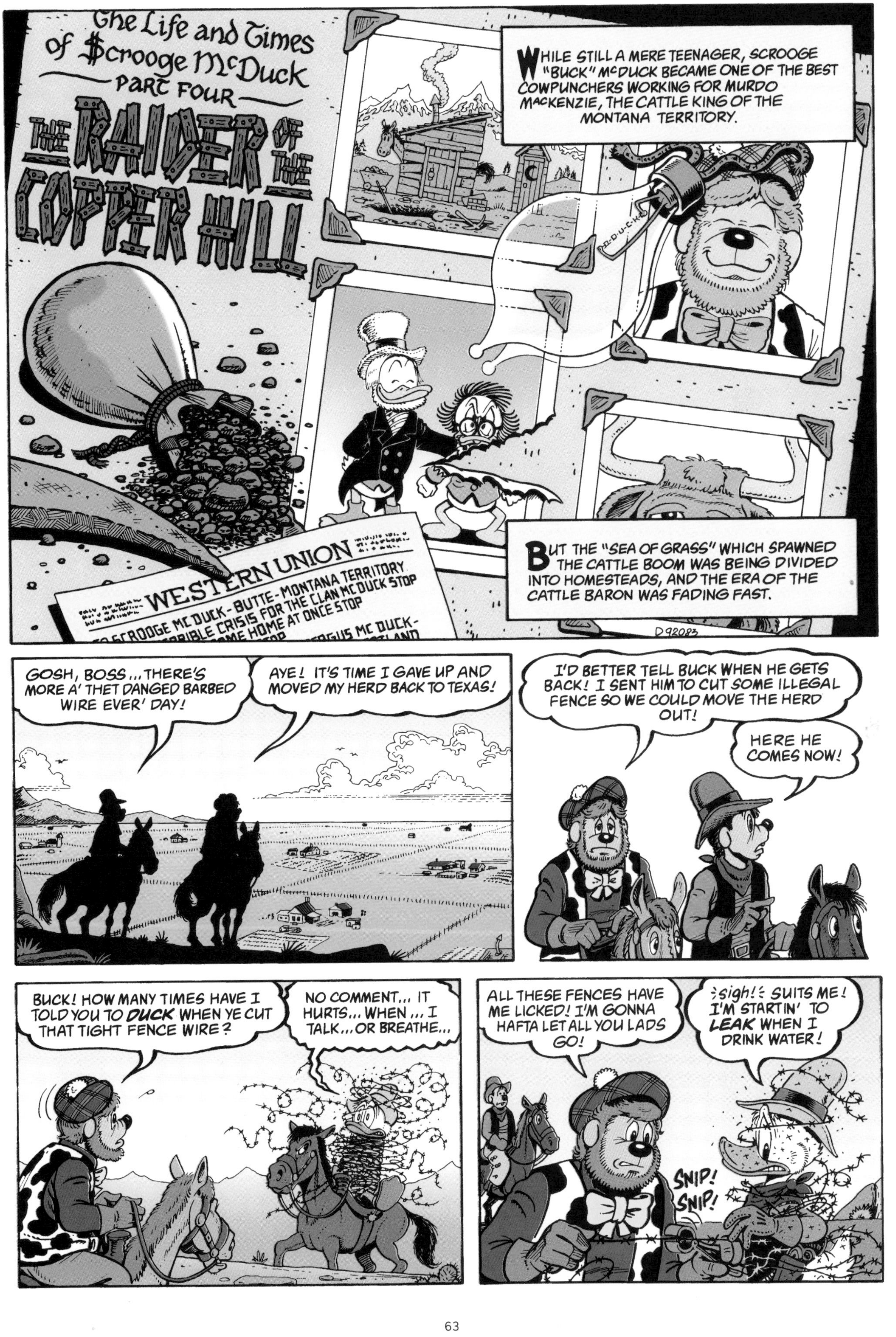
The Life and Times of $crooge McDuck
PART FOUR
THE RAIDER OF THE COPPER HILL
WHILE STILL A MERE TEENAGER, SCROOGE "BUCK" McDUCK BECAME ONE OF THE BEST COWPUNCHERS WORKING FOR MURDO MACKENZIE, THE CATTLE KING OF THE MONTANA TERRITORY.
WESTERN UNION
SCROOGE MC DUCK- BUTTE-MONTANA TERRITORY
TERRIBLE CRISIS FOR THE CLAN MC DUCK STOP
BUT THE "SEA OF GRASS" WHICH SPAWNED THE CATTLE BOOM WAS BEING DIVIDED INTO HOMESTEADS, AND THE ERA OF THE CATTLE BARON WAS FADING FAST.
D 92083
GOSH, BOSS... THERE'S MORE A' THET DANGED BARBED WIRE EVER' DAY!
AYE! IT'S TIME I GAVE UP AND MOVED MY HERD BACK TO TEXAS!
I'D BETTER TELL BUCK WHEN HE GETS BACK! I SENT HIM TO CUT SOME ILLEGAL FENCE SO WE COULD MOVE THE HERD OUT!
HERE HE COMES NOW!
BUCK! HOW MANY TIMES HAVE I TOLD YOU TO DUCK WHEN YE CUT THAT TIGHT FENCE WIRE?
NO COMMENT... IT HURTS... WHEN... I TALK... OR BREATHE...
ALL THESE FENCES HAVE ME LICKED! I'M GONNA HAFTA LET ALL YOU LADS GO!
sigh! SUITS ME! I'M STARTIN' TO LEAK WHEN I DRINK WATER!
SNIP! SNIP!

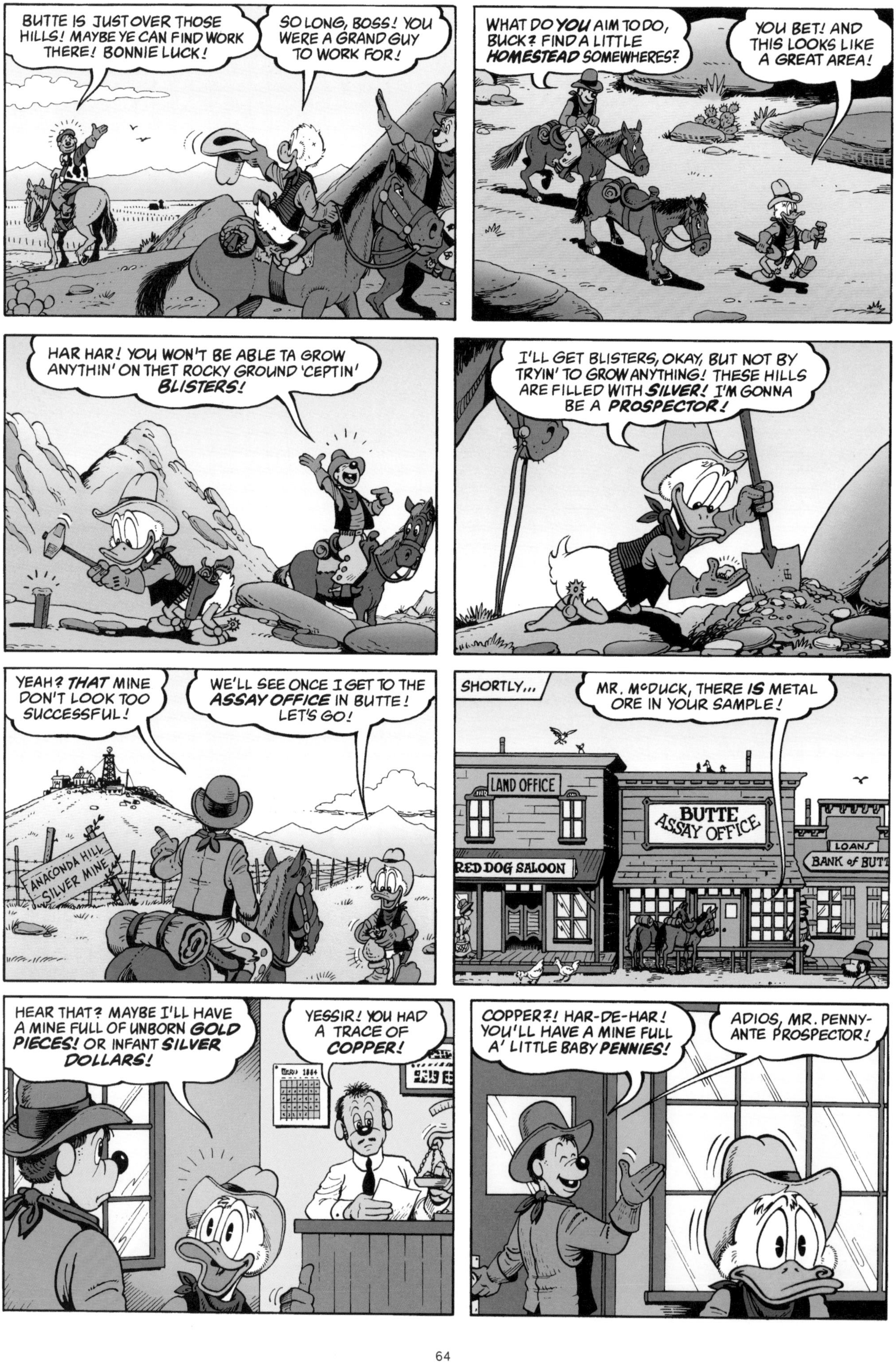
BUTTE IS JUST OVER THOSE HILLS! MAYBE YE CAN FIND WORK THERE! BONNIE LUCK!
SO LONG, BOSS! YOU WERE A GRAND GUY TO WORK FOR!
WHAT DO YOU AIM TO DO, BUCK? FIND A LITTLE HOMESTEAD SOMEWHERES?
YOU BET! AND THIS LOOKS LIKE A GREAT AREA!
HAR HAR! YOU WON'T BE ABLE TA GROW ANYTHIN' ON THET ROCKY GROUND 'CEPTIN' BLISTERS!
I'LL GET BLISTERS, OKAY, BUT NOT BY TRYIN' TO GROW ANYTHING! THESE HILLS ARE FILLED WITH SILVER! I'M GONNA BE A PROSPECTOR!
YEAH? THAT MINE DON'T LOOK TOO SUCCESSFUL!
WE'LL SEE ONCE I GET TO THE ASSAY OFFICE IN BUTTE! LET'S GO!
ANACONDA HILL SILVER MINE
SHORTLY...
MR. McDUCK, THERE IS METAL ORE IN YOUR SAMPLE!
LAND OFFICE
BUTTE ASSAY OFFICE
RED DOG SALOON
LOANS
BANK of BUTT
HEAR THAT? MAYBE I'LL HAVE A MINE FULL OF UNBORN GOLD PIECES! OR INFANT SILVER DOLLARS!
YESSIR! YOU HAD A TRACE OF COPPER!
COPPER?! HAR-DE-HAR! YOU'LL HAVE A MINE FULL A' LITTLE BABY PENNIES!
ADIOS, MR. PENNY-ANTE PROSPECTOR!

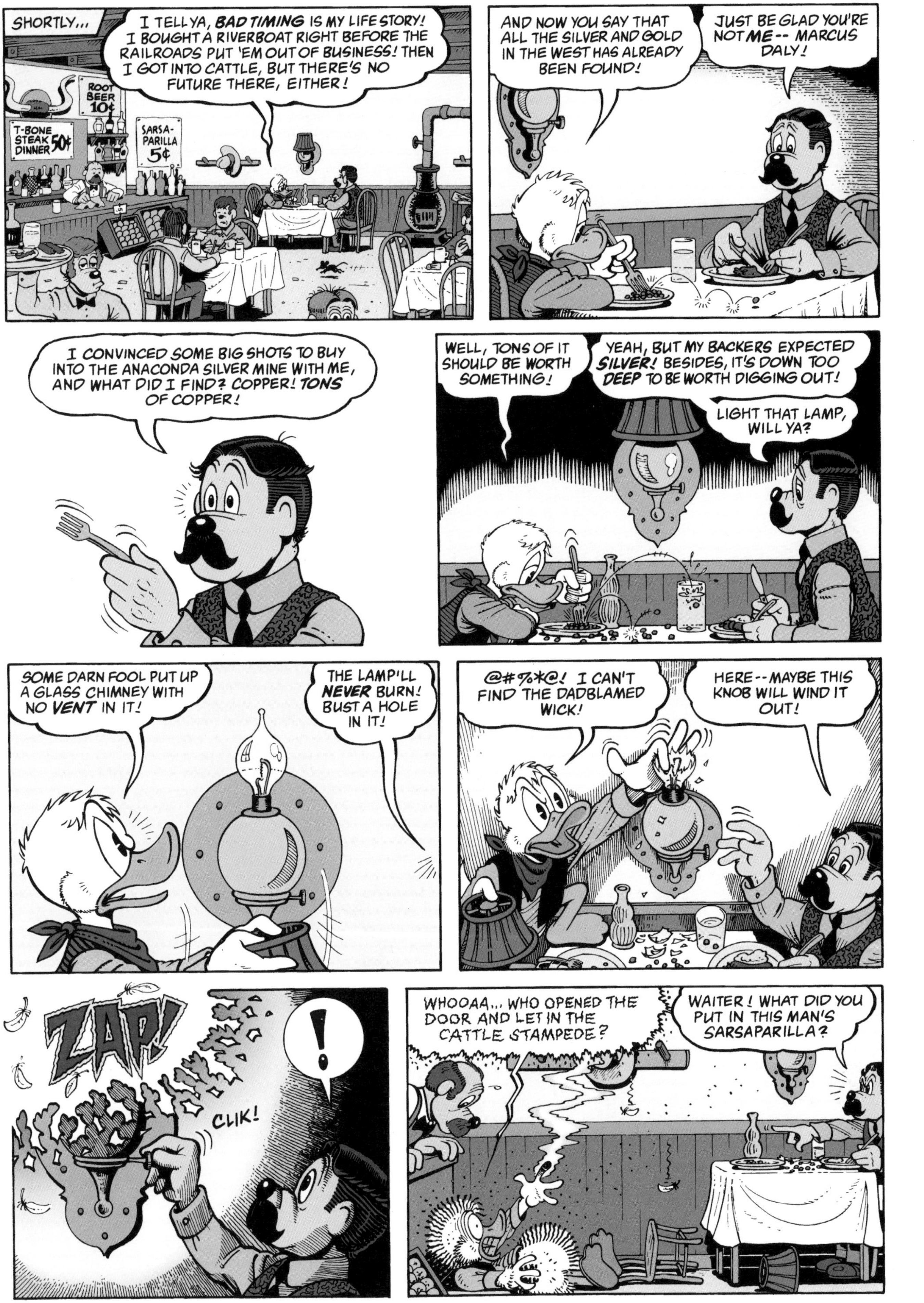
SHORTLY...
I TELL YA, BAD TIMING IS MY LIFE STORY! I BOUGHT A RIVERBOAT RIGHT BEFORE THE RAILROADS PUT 'EM OUT OF BUSINESS! THEN I GOT INTO CATTLE, BUT THERE'S NO FUTURE THERE, EITHER!
ROOT BEER 10¢
T-BONE STEAK DINNER 50¢
SARSA-PARILLA 5¢
AND NOW YOU SAY THAT ALL THE SILVER AND GOLD IN THE WEST HAS ALREADY BEEN FOUND!
JUST BE GLAD YOU'RE NOT ME -- MARCUS DALY!
I CONVINCED SOME BIG SHOTS TO BUY INTO THE ANACONDA SILVER MINE WITH ME, AND WHAT DID I FIND? COPPER! TONS OF COPPER!
WELL, TONS OF IT SHOULD BE WORTH SOMETHING!
YEAH, BUT MY BACKERS EXPECTED SILVER! BESIDES, IT'S DOWN TOO DEEP TO BE WORTH DIGGING OUT!
LIGHT THAT LAMP, WILL YA?
SOME DARN FOOL PUT UP A GLASS CHIMNEY WITH NO VENT IN IT!
THE LAMP'LL NEVER BURN! BUST A HOLE IN IT!
@#%*@! I CAN'T FIND THE DADBLAMED WICK!
HERE -- MAYBE THIS KNOB WILL WIND IT OUT!
ZAP!
!
CLIK!
WHOOAA... WHO OPENED THE DOOR AND LET IN THE CATTLE STAMPEDE?
WAITER! WHAT DID YOU PUT IN THIS MAN'S SARSAPARILLA?

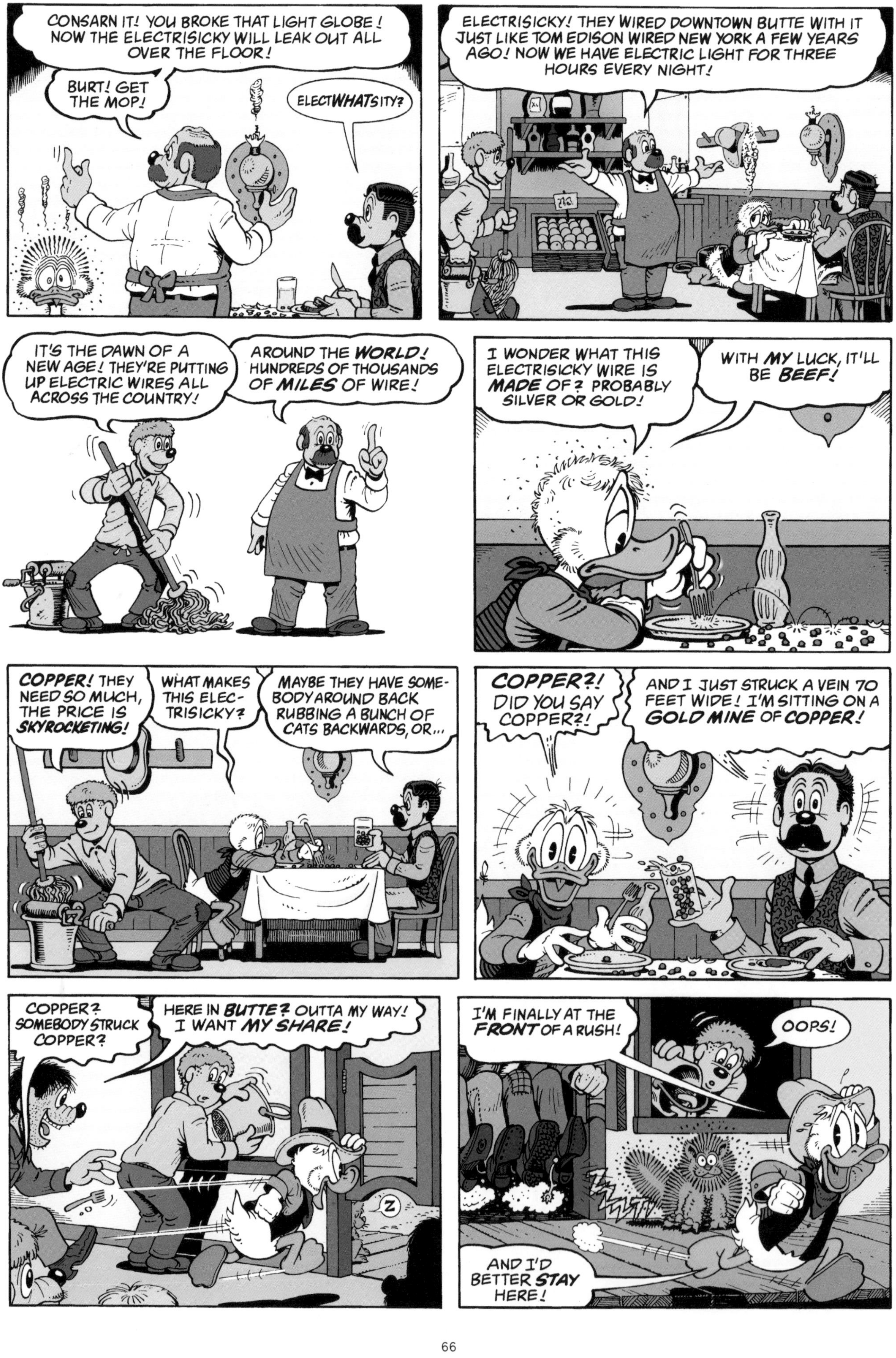
CONSARN IT! YOU BROKE THAT LIGHT GLOBE! NOW THE ELECTRISICKY WILL LEAK OUT ALL OVER THE FLOOR!
BURT! GET THE MOP!
ELECTWHATSITY?
ELECTRISICKY! THEY WIRED DOWNTOWN BUTTE WITH IT JUST LIKE TOM EDISON WIRED NEW YORK A FEW YEARS AGO! NOW WE HAVE ELECTRIC LIGHT FOR THREE HOURS EVERY NIGHT!
IT'S THE DAWN OF A NEW AGE! THEY'RE PUTTING UP ELECTRIC WIRES ALL ACROSS THE COUNTRY!
AROUND THE WORLD! HUNDREDS OF THOUSANDS OF MILES OF WIRE!
I WONDER WHAT THIS ELECTRISICKY WIRE IS MADE OF? PROBABLY SILVER OR GOLD!
WITH MY LUCK, IT'LL BE BEEF!
COPPER! THEY NEED SO MUCH, THE PRICE IS SKYROCKETING!
WHAT MAKES THIS ELECTRISICKY?
MAYBE THEY HAVE SOMEBODY AROUND BACK RUBBING A BUNCH OF CATS BACKWARDS, OR...
COPPER?! DID YOU SAY COPPER?!
AND I JUST STRUCK A VEIN 70 FEET WIDE! I'M SITTING ON A GOLD MINE OF COPPER!
COPPER? SOMEBODY STRUCK COPPER?
HERE IN BUTTE? OUTTA MY WAY! I WANT MY SHARE!
Z
I'M FINALLY AT THE FRONT OF A RUSH!
OOPS!
AND I'D BETTER STAY HERE!

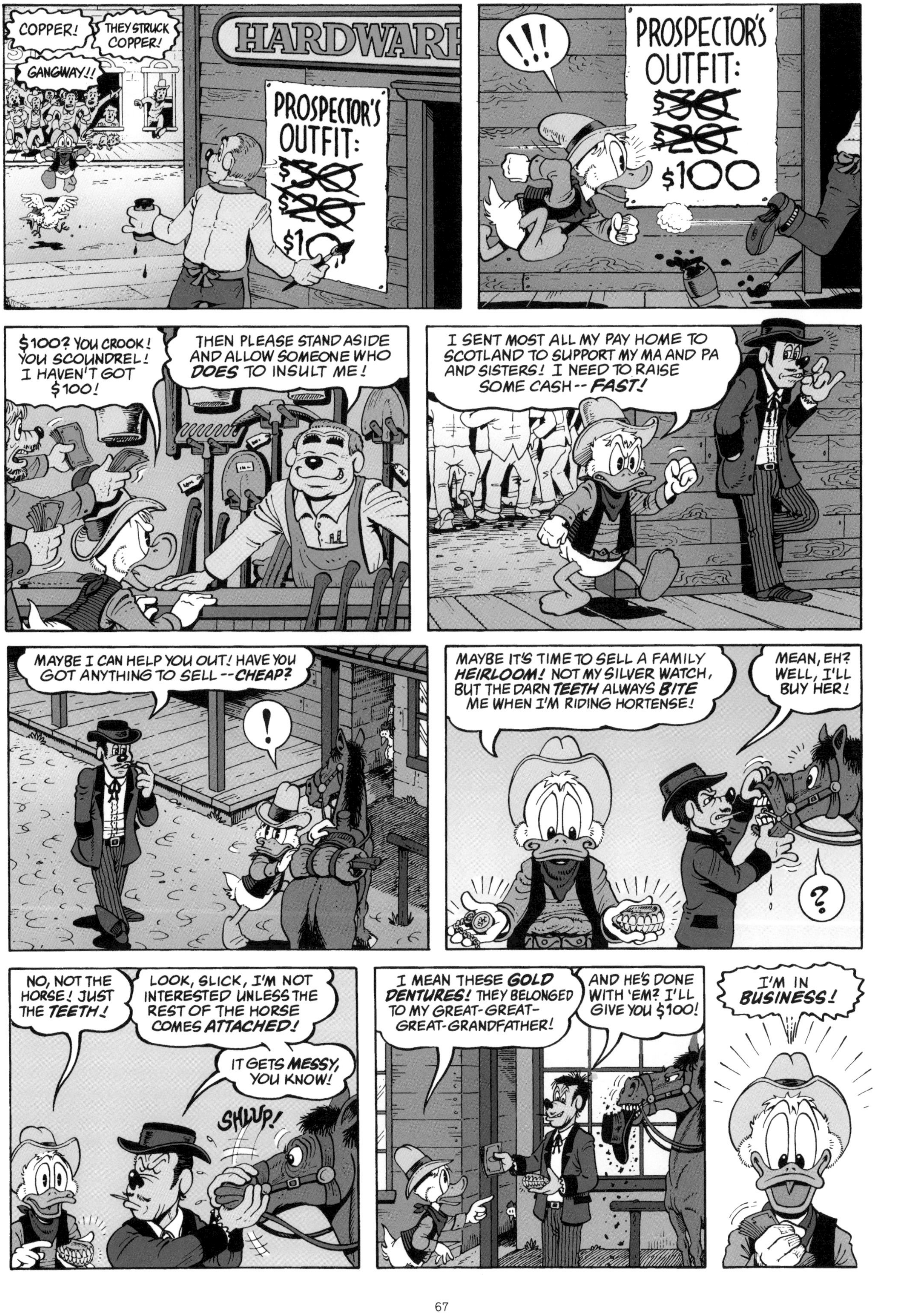
COPPER!
THEY STRUCK COPPER!
GANGWAY!!
HARDWARE
PROSPECTOR'S OUTFIT: $30 $20 $10
!!!
PROSPECTOR'S OUTFIT: $30 $20 $100
$100? YOU CROOK! YOU SCOUNDREL! I HAVEN'T GOT $100!
THEN PLEASE STAND ASIDE AND ALLOW SOMEONE WHO DOES TO INSULT ME!
I SENT MOST ALL MY PAY HOME TO SCOTLAND TO SUPPORT MY MA AND PA AND SISTERS! I NEED TO RAISE SOME CASH -- FAST!
MAYBE I CAN HELP YOU OUT! HAVE YOU GOT ANYTHING TO SELL -- CHEAP?
!
MAYBE IT'S TIME TO SELL A FAMILY HEIRLOOM! NOT MY SILVER WATCH, BUT THE DARN TEETH ALWAYS BITE ME WHEN I'M RIDING HORTENSE!
MEAN, EH? WELL, I'LL BUY HER!
?
NO, NOT THE HORSE! JUST THE TEETH!
LOOK, SLICK, I'M NOT INTERESTED UNLESS THE REST OF THE HORSE COMES ATTACHED!
IT GETS MESSY, YOU KNOW!
SHLUP!
I MEAN THESE GOLD DENTURES! THEY BELONGED TO MY GREAT-GREAT-GREAT-GRANDFATHER!
AND HE'S DONE WITH 'EM? I'LL GIVE YOU $100!
I'M IN BUSINESS!

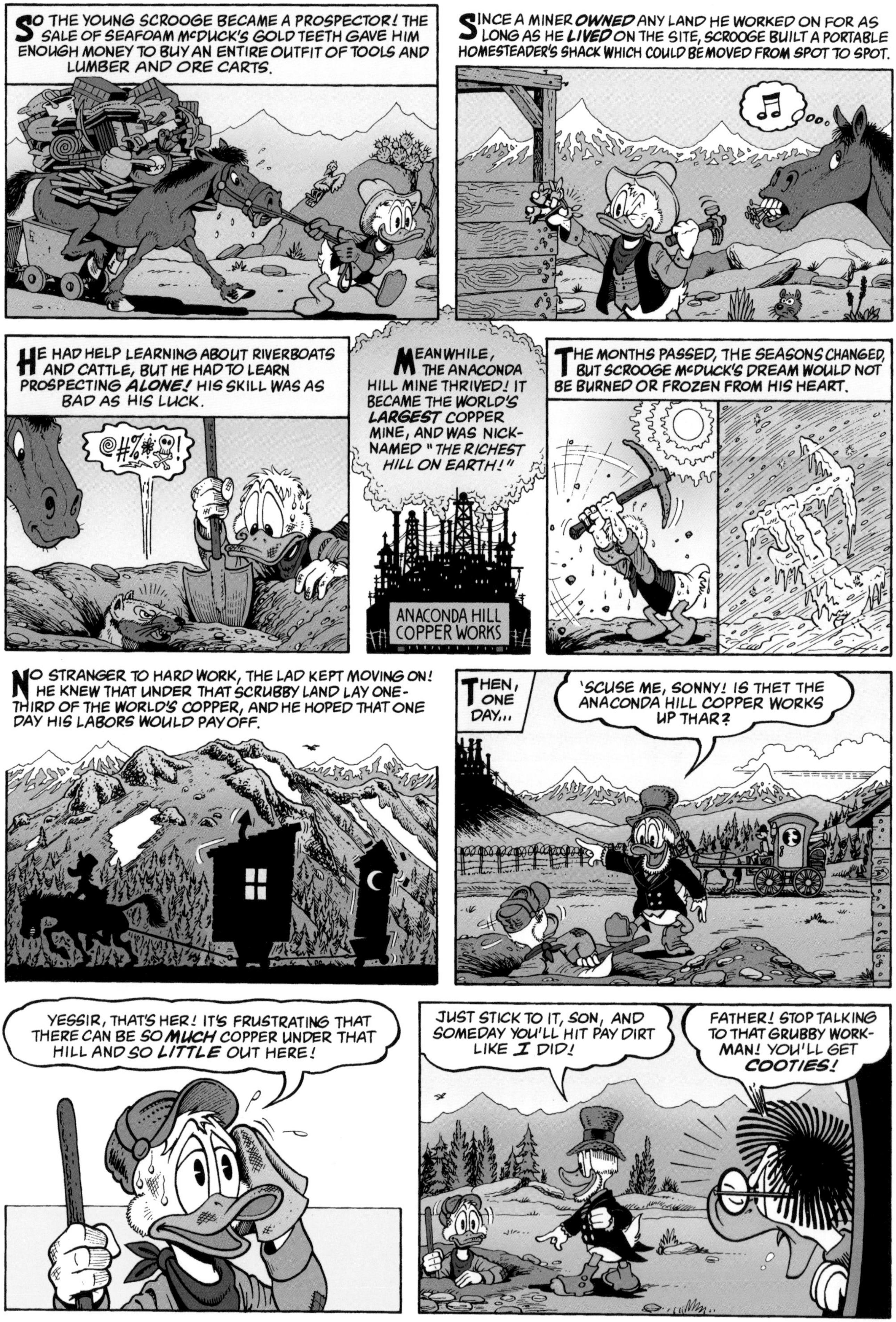
SO THE YOUNG SCROOGE BECAME A PROSPECTOR! THE SALE OF SEAFOAM McDUCK'S GOLD TEETH GAVE HIM ENOUGH MONEY TO BUY AN ENTIRE OUTFIT OF TOOLS AND LUMBER AND ORE CARTS.
SINCE A MINER OWNED ANY LAND HE WORKED ON FOR AS LONG AS HE LIVED ON THE SITE, SCROOGE BUILT A PORTABLE HOMESTEADER'S SHACK WHICH COULD BE MOVED FROM SPOT TO SPOT.
HE HAD HELP LEARNING ABOUT RIVERBOATS AND CATTLE, BUT HE HAD TO LEARN PROSPECTING ALONE! HIS SKILL WAS AS BAD AS HIS LUCK.
MEANWHILE, THE ANACONDA HILL MINE THRIVED! IT BECAME THE WORLD'S LARGEST COPPER MINE, AND WAS NICK-NAMED "THE RICHEST HILL ON EARTH!"
ANACONDA HILL COPPER WORKS
THE MONTHS PASSED, THE SEASONS CHANGED, BUT SCROOGE McDUCK'S DREAM WOULD NOT BE BURNED OR FROZEN FROM HIS HEART.
NO STRANGER TO HARD WORK, THE LAD KEPT MOVING ON! HE KNEW THAT UNDER THAT SCRUBBY LAND LAY ONE-THIRD OF THE WORLD'S COPPER, AND HE HOPED THAT ONE DAY HIS LABORS WOULD PAY OFF.
THEN, ONE DAY...
'SCUSE ME, SONNY! IS THET THE ANACONDA HILL COPPER WORKS UP THAR?
YESSIR, THAT'S HER! IT'S FRUSTRATING THAT THERE CAN BE SO MUCH COPPER UNDER THAT HILL AND SO LITTLE OUT HERE!
JUST STICK TO IT, SON, AND SOMEDAY YOU'LL HIT PAY DIRT LIKE I DID!
FATHER! STOP TALKING TO THAT GRUBBY WORK-MAN! YOU'LL GET COOTIES!

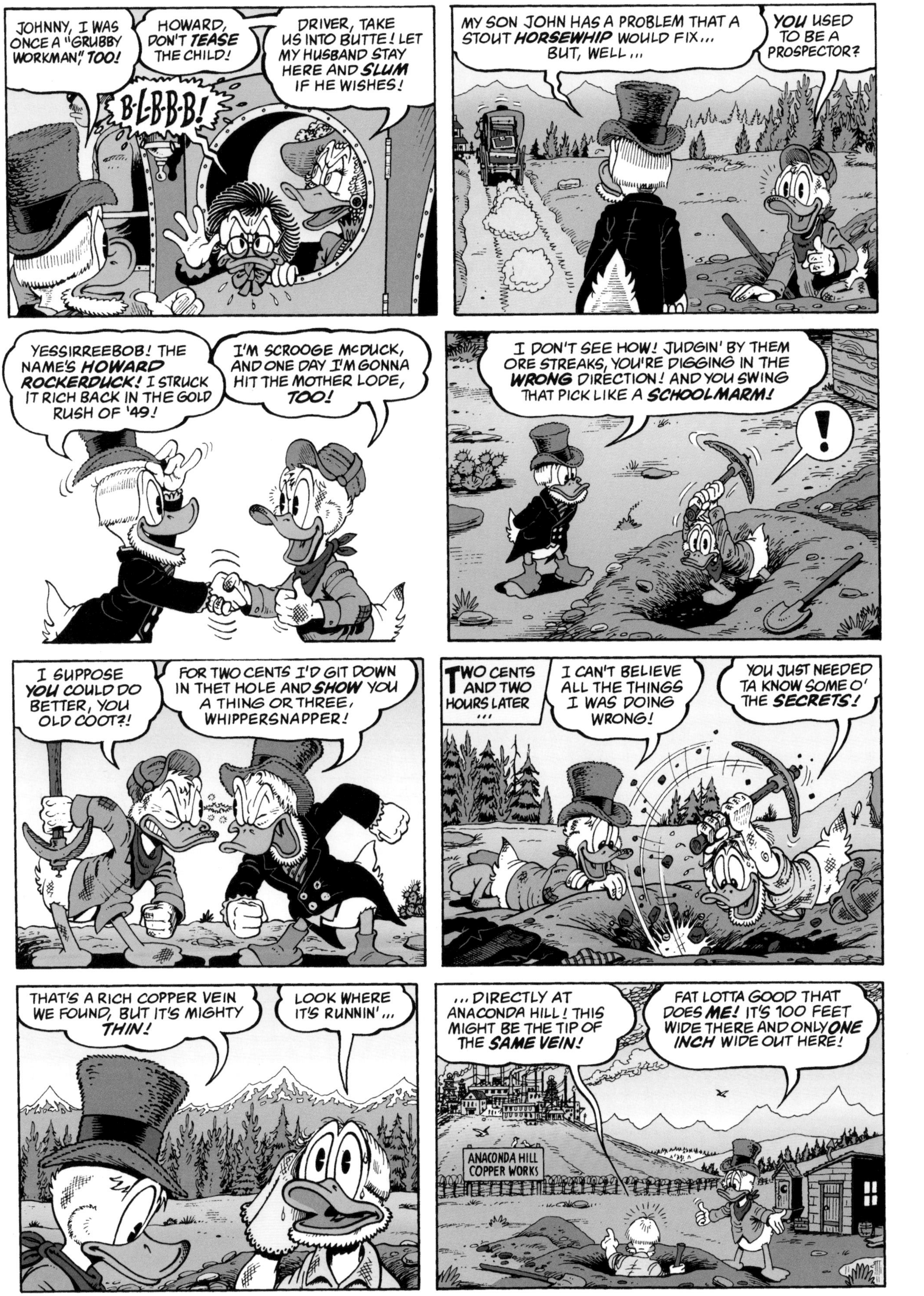
JOHNNY, I WAS ONCE A "GRUBBY WORKMAN," TOO!
HOWARD, DON'T TEASE THE CHILD!
DRIVER, TAKE US INTO BUTTE! LET MY HUSBAND STAY HERE AND SLUM IF HE WISHES!
B-L-B-B-B!
MY SON JOHN HAS A PROBLEM THAT A STOUT HORSEWHIP WOULD FIX... BUT, WELL...
YOU USED TO BE A PROSPECTOR?
YESSIRREEBOB! THE NAME'S HOWARD ROCKERDUCK! I STRUCK IT RICH BACK IN THE GOLD RUSH OF '49!
I'M SCROOGE McDUCK, AND ONE DAY I'M GONNA HIT THE MOTHER LODE, TOO!
I DON'T SEE HOW! JUDGIN' BY THEM ORE STREAKS, YOU'RE DIGGING IN THE WRONG DIRECTION! AND YOU SWING THAT PICK LIKE A SCHOOLMARM!
!
I SUPPOSE YOU COULD DO BETTER, YOU OLD COOT?!
FOR TWO CENTS I'D GIT DOWN IN THET HOLE AND SHOW YOU A THING OR THREE, WHIPPERSNAPPER!
TWO CENTS AND TWO HOURS LATER ...
I CAN'T BELIEVE ALL THE THINGS I WAS DOING WRONG!
YOU JUST NEEDED TA KNOW SOME O' THE SECRETS!
THAT'S A RICH COPPER VEIN WE FOUND, BUT IT'S MIGHTY THIN!
LOOK WHERE IT'S RUNNIN'...
...DIRECTLY AT ANACONDA HILL! THIS MIGHT BE THE TIP OF THE SAME VEIN!
FAT LOTTA GOOD THAT DOES ME! IT'S 100 FEET WIDE THERE AND ONLY ONE INCH WIDE OUT HERE!
ANACONDA HILL COPPER WORKS

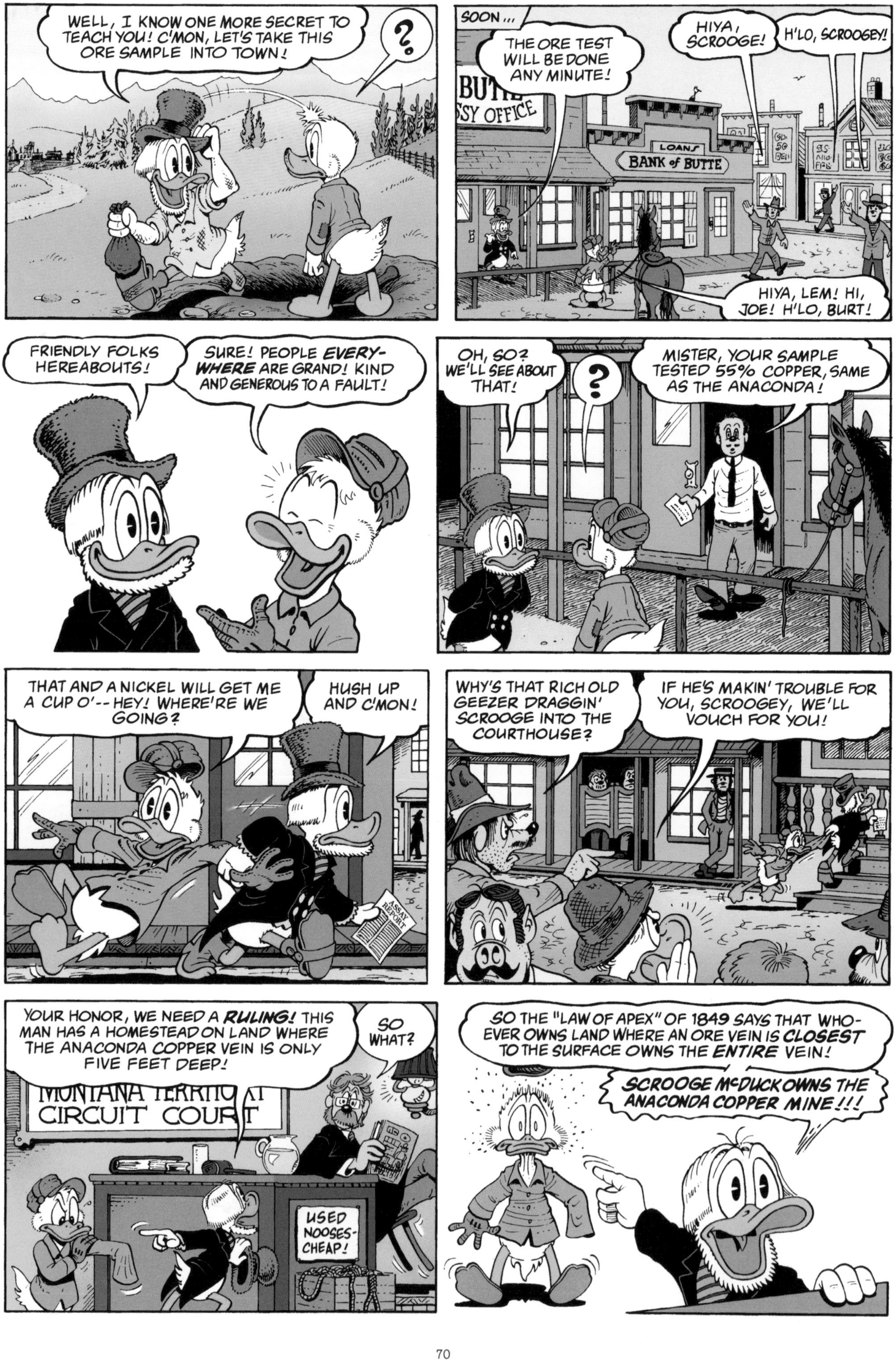
WELL, I KNOW ONE MORE SECRET TO TEACH YOU! C'MON, LET'S TAKE THIS ORE SAMPLE INTO TOWN!
?
SOON...
BUTTE ASSAY OFFICE
LOANS
BANK of BUTTE
THE ORE TEST WILL BE DONE ANY MINUTE!
HIYA, SCROOGE!
H'LO, SCROOGEY!
HIYA, LEM! HI, JOE! H'LO, BURT!
FRIENDLY FOLKS HEREABOUTS!
SURE! PEOPLE EVERYWHERE ARE GRAND! KIND AND GENEROUS TO A FAULT!
OH, SO? WE'LL SEE ABOUT THAT!
?
MISTER, YOUR SAMPLE TESTED 55% COPPER, SAME AS THE ANACONDA!
THAT AND A NICKEL WILL GET ME A CUP O'-- HEY! WHERE'RE WE GOING?
HUSH UP AND C'MON!
ASSAY REPORT
WHY'S THAT RICH OLD GEEZER DRAGGIN' SCROOGE INTO THE COURTHOUSE?
IF HE'S MAKIN' TROUBLE FOR YOU, SCROOGEY, WE'LL VOUCH FOR YOU!
YOUR HONOR, WE NEED A RULING! THIS MAN HAS A HOMESTEAD ON LAND WHERE THE ANACONDA COPPER VEIN IS ONLY FIVE FEET DEEP!
SO WHAT?
CIRCUIT COURT
USED NOOSES-CHEAP!
SO THE "LAW OF APEX" OF 1849 SAYS THAT WHOEVER OWNS LAND WHERE AN ORE VEIN IS CLOSEST TO THE SURFACE OWNS THE ENTIRE VEIN!
SCROOGE McDUCK OWNS THE ANACONDA COPPER MINE!!!

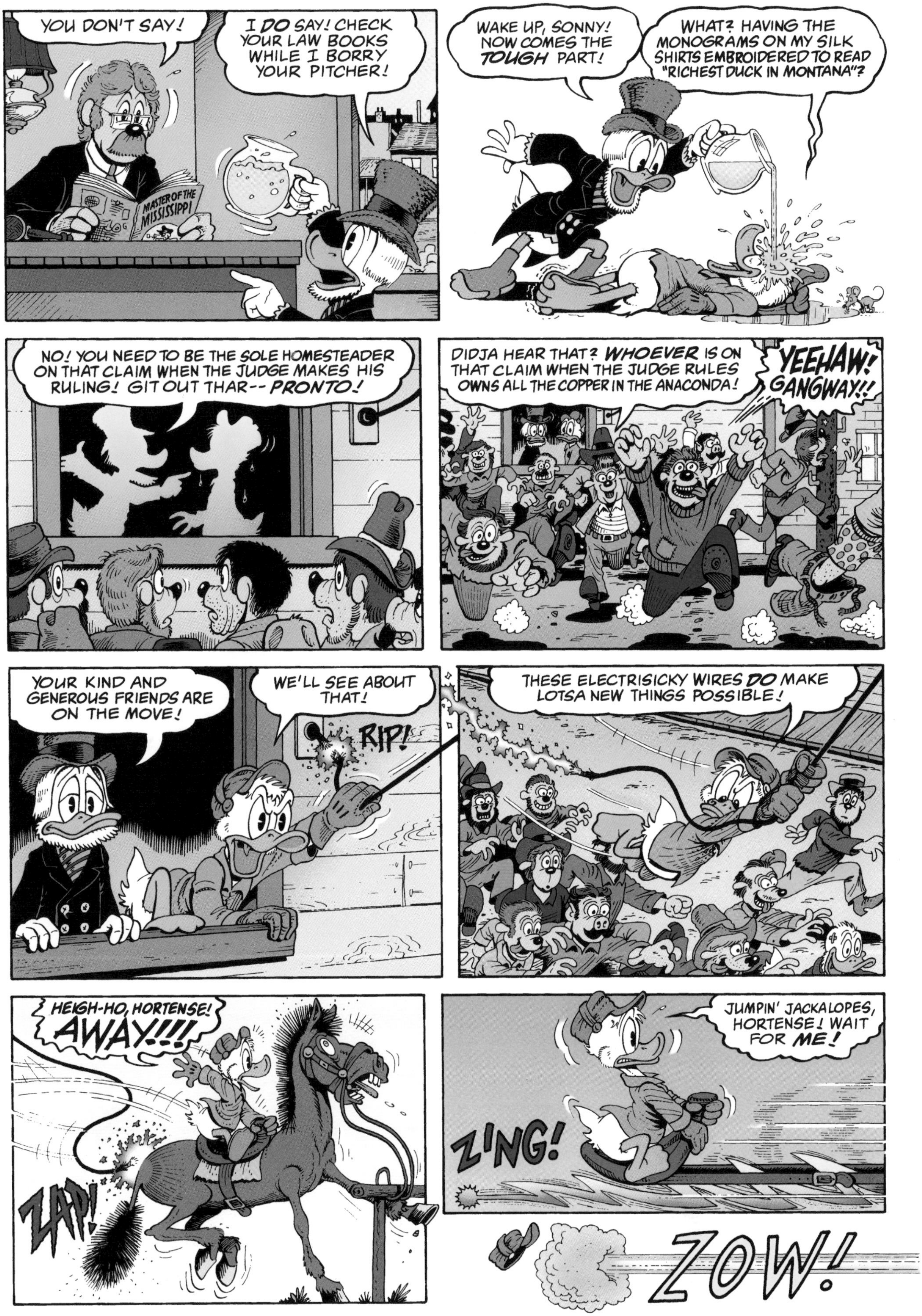
YOU DON'T SAY!
I DO SAY! CHECK YOUR LAW BOOKS WHILE I BORRY YOUR PITCHER!
MASTER OF THE MISSISSIPPI
WAKE UP, SONNY! NOW COMES THE TOUGH PART!
WHAT? HAVING THE MONOGRAMS ON MY SILK SHIRTS EMBROIDERED TO READ "RICHEST DUCK IN MONTANA"?
NO! YOU NEED TO BE THE SOLE HOMESTEADER ON THAT CLAIM WHEN THE JUDGE MAKES HIS RULING! GIT OUT THAR-- PRONTO!
DIDJA HEAR THAT? WHOEVER IS ON THAT CLAIM WHEN THE JUDGE RULES OWNS ALL THE COPPER IN THE ANACONDA!
YEEHAW! GANGWAY!!
YOUR KIND AND GENEROUS FRIENDS ARE ON THE MOVE!
WE'LL SEE ABOUT THAT!
RIP!
THESE ELECTRISICKY WIRES DO MAKE LOTSA NEW THINGS POSSIBLE!
HEIGH-HO, HORTENSE! AWAY!!!
ZAP!
JUMPIN' JACKALOPES, HORTENSE! WAIT FOR ME!
Z'NG!
ZOW!

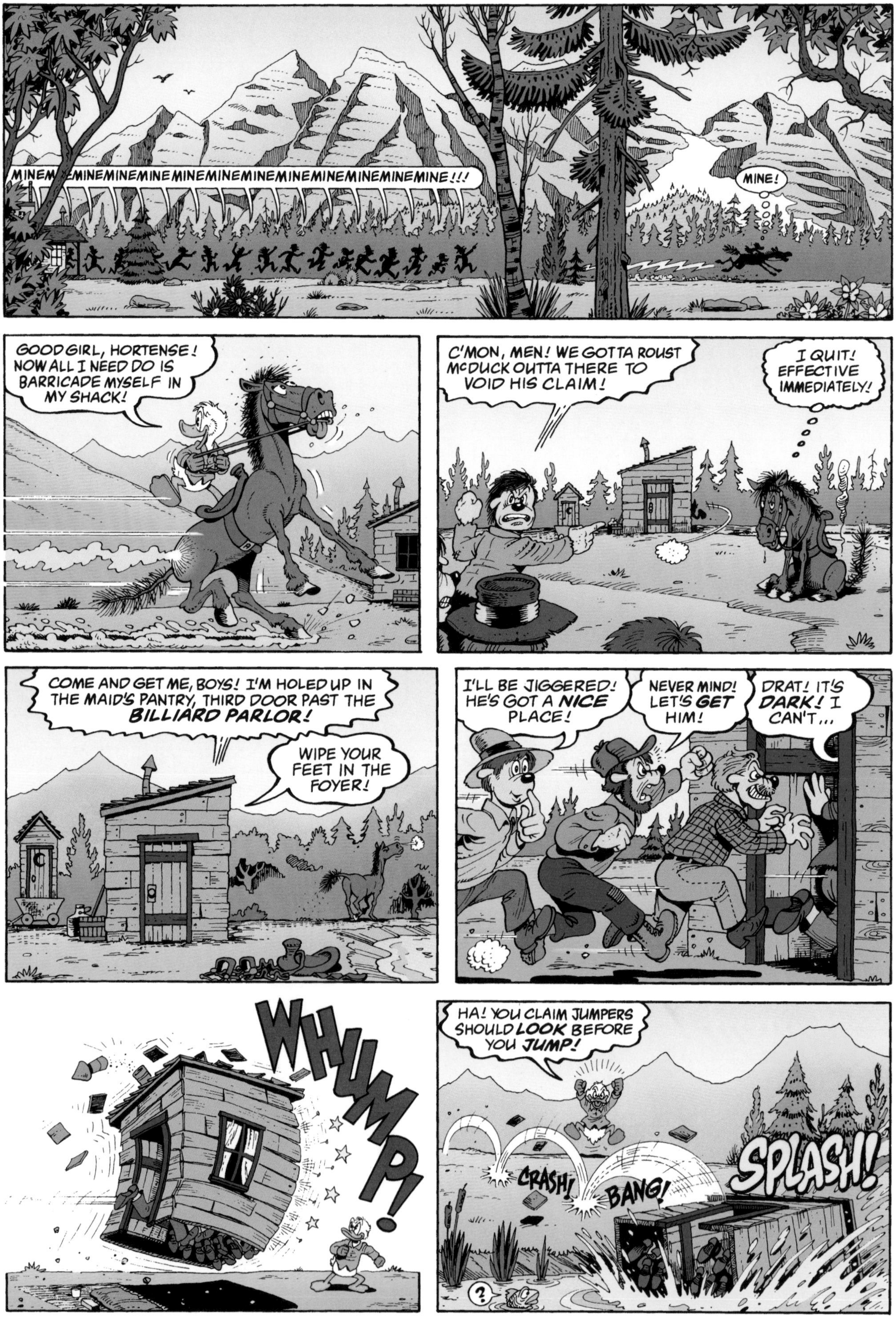
MINEMINEMINEMINEMINEMINEMINEMINEMINEMINEMINEMINEMINE!!!
MINE!
GOOD GIRL, HORTENSE! NOW ALL I NEED DO IS BARRICADE MYSELF IN MY SHACK!
C'MON, MEN! WE GOTTA ROUST McDUCK OUTTA THERE TO VOID HIS CLAIM!
I QUIT! EFFECTIVE IMMEDIATELY!
COME AND GET ME, BOYS! I'M HOLED UP IN THE MAID'S PANTRY, THIRD DOOR PAST THE BILLIARD PARLOR!
WIPE YOUR FEET IN THE FOYER!
I'LL BE JIGGERED! HE'S GOT A NICE PLACE!
NEVER MIND! LET'S GET HIM!
DRAT! IT'S DARK! I CAN'T...
WHUMP!
HA! YOU CLAIM JUMPERS SHOULD LOOK BEFORE YOU JUMP!
CRASH!
BANG!
SPLASH!
?

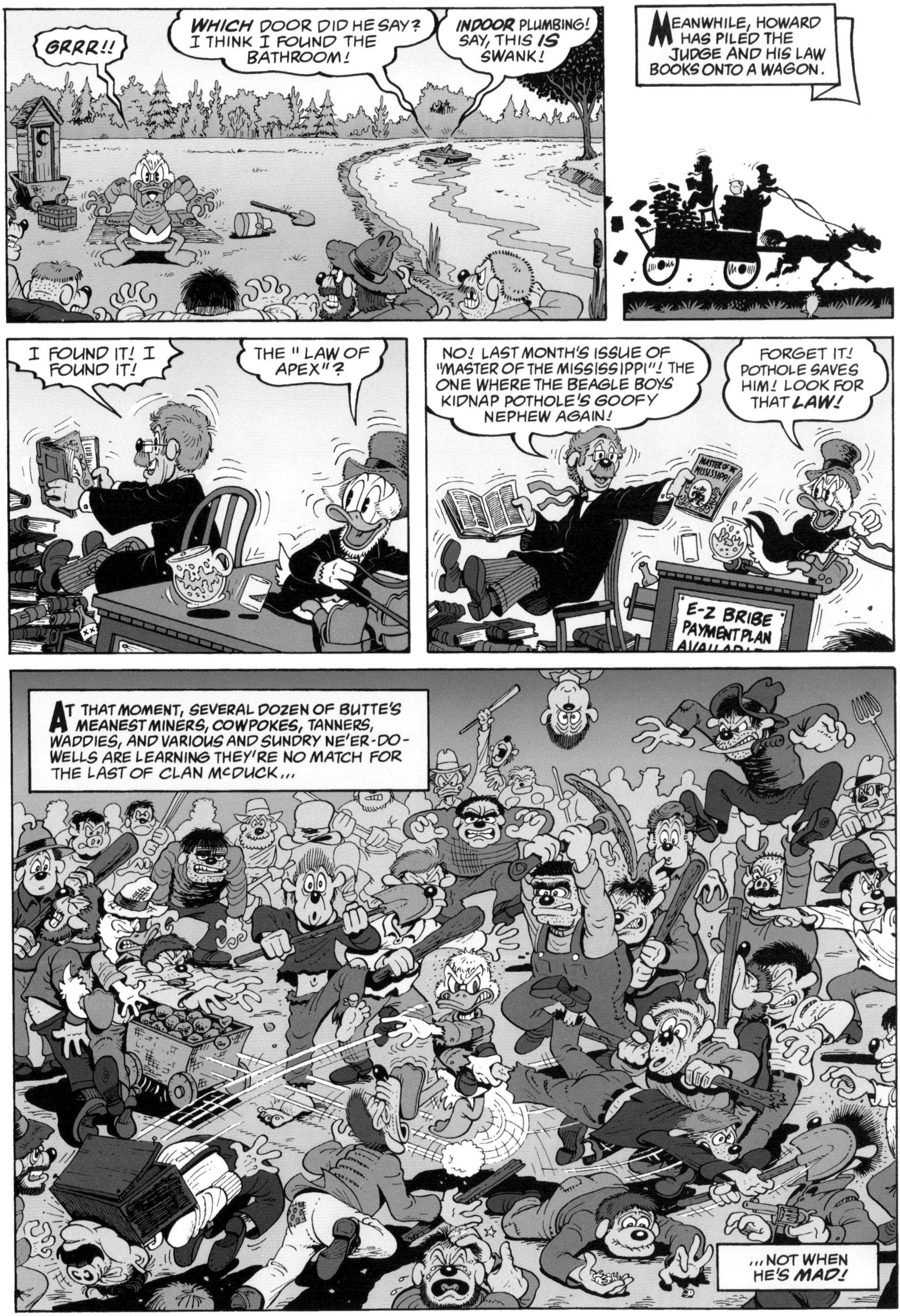
GRRR!!
WHICH DOOR DID HE SAY? I THINK I FOUND THE BATHROOM!
INDOOR PLUMBING! SAY, THIS IS SWANK!
MEANWHILE, HOWARD HAS PILED THE JUDGE AND HIS LAW BOOKS ONTO A WAGON.
I FOUND IT! I FOUND IT!
THE "LAW OF APEX"?
NO! LAST MONTH'S ISSUE OF "MASTER OF THE MISSISSIPPI"! THE ONE WHERE THE BEAGLE BOYS KIDNAP POTHOLE'S GOOFY NEPHEW AGAIN!
FORGET IT! POTHOLE SAVES HIM! LOOK FOR THAT LAW!
E-Z BRIBE PAYMENT PLAN
AT THAT MOMENT, SEVERAL DOZEN OF BUTTE'S MEANEST MINERS, COWPOKES, TANNERS, WADDIES, AND VARIOUS AND SUNDRY NE'ER-DO-WELLS ARE LEARNING THEY'RE NO MATCH FOR THE LAST OF CLAN McDUCK...
...NOT WHEN HE'S MAD!

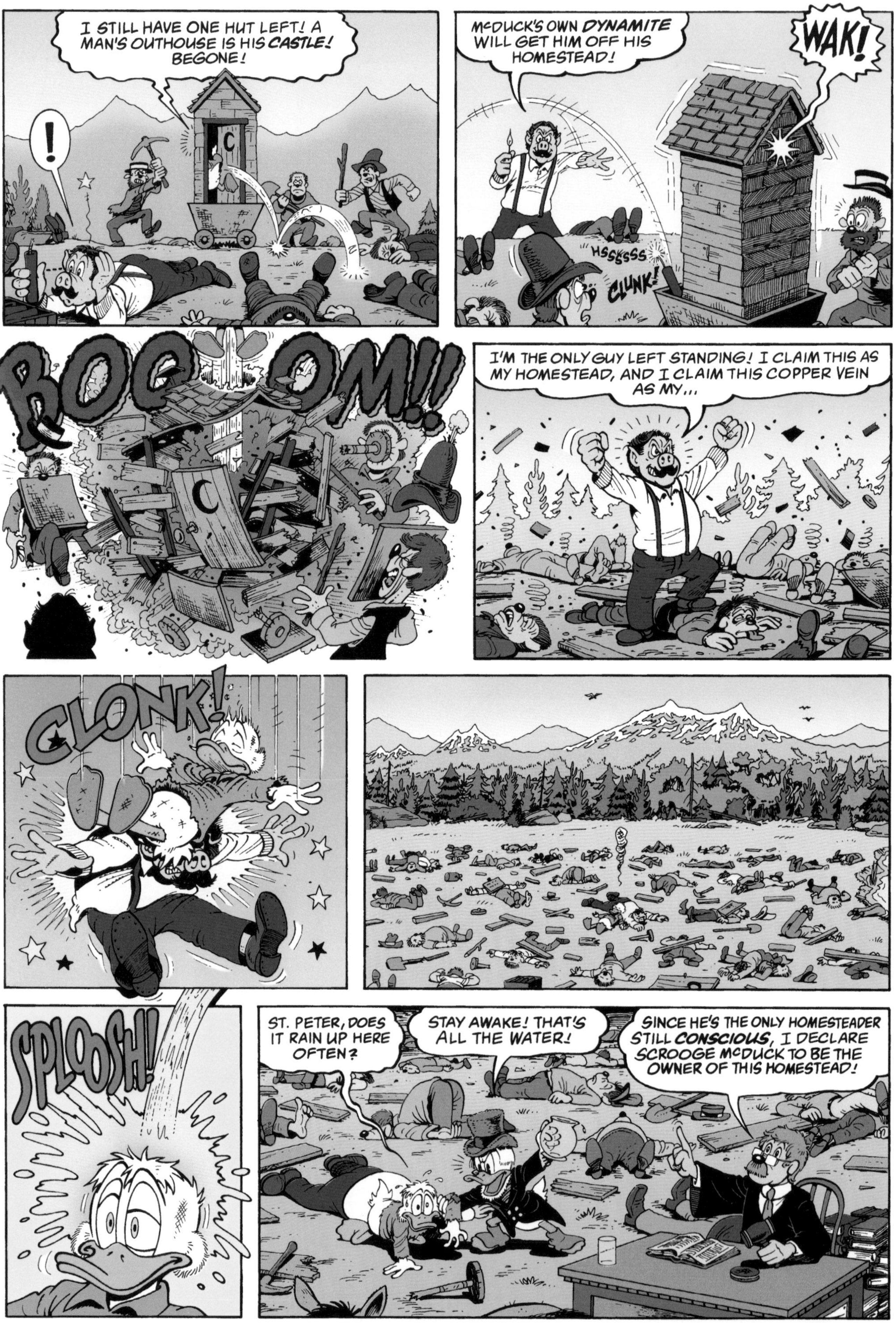

I STILL HAVE ONE HUT LEFT! A MAN'S OUTHOUSE IS HIS CASTLE! BEGONE!
!
McDUCK'S OWN DYNAMITE WILL GET HIM OFF HIS HOMESTEAD!
WAK!
HSSSSSS
CLUNK!
BOOOOM!!
I'M THE ONLY GUY LEFT STANDING! I CLAIM THIS AS MY HOMESTEAD, AND I CLAIM THIS COPPER VEIN AS MY...
CLONK!
SPLOOSH!
ST. PETER, DOES IT RAIN UP HERE OFTEN?
STAY AWAKE! THAT'S ALL THE WATER!
SINCE HE'S THE ONLY HOMESTEADER STILL CONSCIOUS, I DECLARE SCROOGE McDUCK TO BE THE OWNER OF THIS HOMESTEAD!

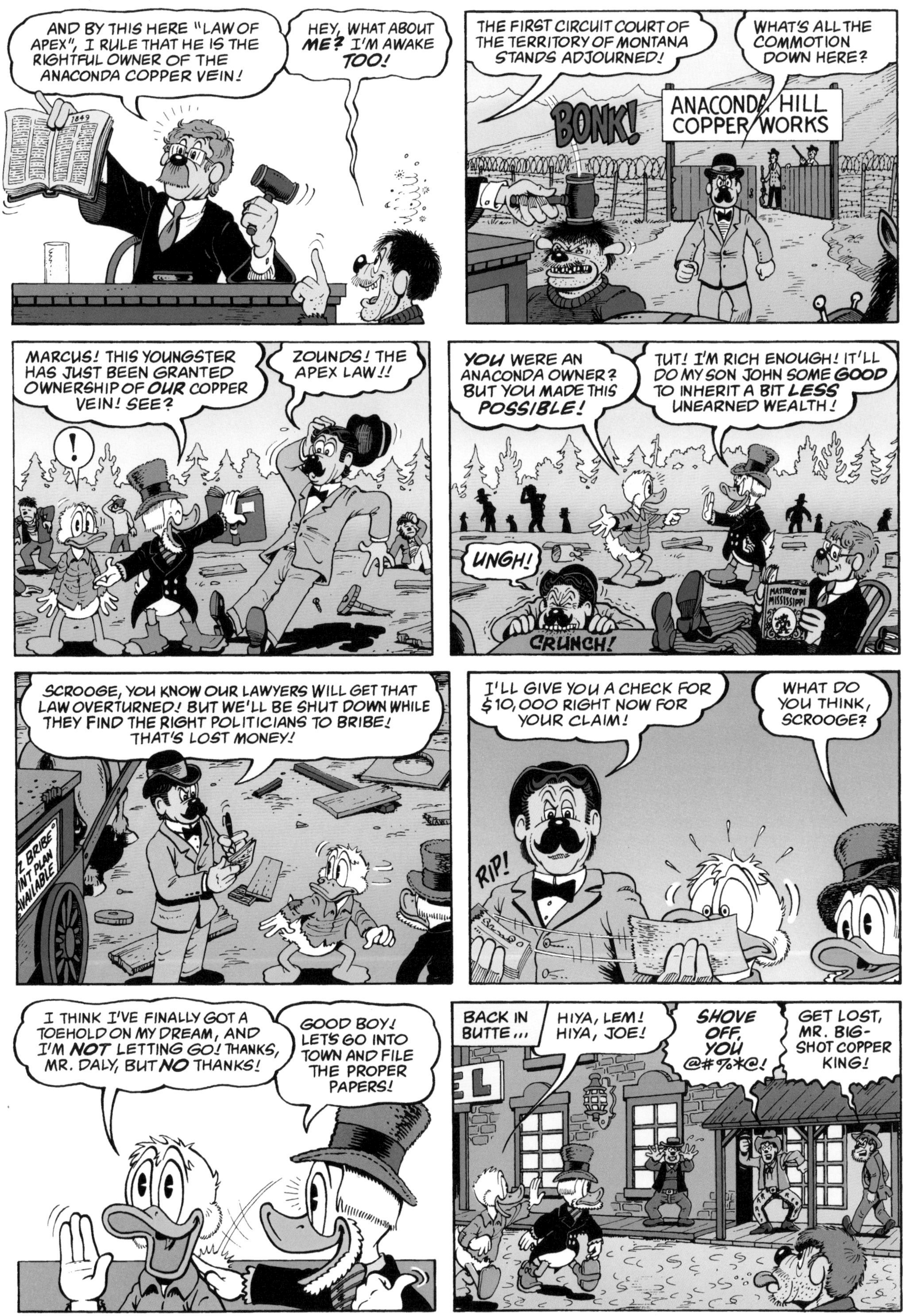
AND BY THIS HERE "LAW OF APEX", I RULE THAT HE IS THE RIGHTFUL OWNER OF THE ANACONDA COPPER VEIN!
1849
HEY, WHAT ABOUT ME? I'M AWAKE TOO!
THE FIRST CIRCUIT COURT OF THE TERRITORY OF MONTANA STANDS ADJOURNED!
WHAT'S ALL THE COMMOTION DOWN HERE?
BONK!
ANACONDA HILL COPPER WORKS
MARCUS! THIS YOUNGSTER HAS JUST BEEN GRANTED OWNERSHIP OF OUR COPPER VEIN! SEE?
!
ZOUNDS! THE APEX LAW!!
YOU WERE AN ANACONDA OWNER? BUT YOU MADE THIS POSSIBLE!
TUT! I'M RICH ENOUGH! IT'LL DO MY SON JOHN SOME GOOD TO INHERIT A BIT LESS UNEARNED WEALTH!
UNGH!
MASTER OF THE MISSISSIPPI
CRUNCH!
SCROOGE, YOU KNOW OUR LAWYERS WILL GET THAT LAW OVERTURNED! BUT WE'LL BE SHUT DOWN WHILE THEY FIND THE RIGHT POLITICIANS TO BRIBE! THAT'S LOST MONEY!
I'LL GIVE YOU A CHECK FOR $10,000 RIGHT NOW FOR YOUR CLAIM!
WHAT DO YOU THINK, SCROOGE?
RIP!
I THINK I'VE FINALLY GOT A TOEHOLD ON MY DREAM, AND I'M NOT LETTING GO! THANKS, MR. DALY, BUT NO THANKS!
GOOD BOY! LET'S GO INTO TOWN AND FILE THE PROPER PAPERS!
BACK IN BUTTE...
HIYA, LEM! HIYA, JOE!
SHOVE OFF, YOU @#%*@!
GET LOST, MR. BIG-SHOT COPPER KING!

THEY WERE MY *FRIENDS!* WHAT DID I *DO?*

YOU GOT *RICH,* SON! BEST GET USED TO IT LIKE ⸮sigh⸮ I DID!

YOU'LL HAVE THEIR *RESPECT,* BUT NO LONGER THEIR *LOVE!*

AH, WHO NEEDS 'EM? I'LL HAVE *MONEY!*

I HOPE I WASN'T *WRONG* ABOUT YOU, SON!

TELEGRAM! TELEGRAM FOR THAT RICH, MISERABLE SCROOGE M°DUCK!

!

I HOPE YOU AREN'T EXPECTING A *TIP!*

TELEGRAM FOR THAT RICH, MISERABLE, *STINGY* SCROOGE M°DUCK!

GLOM!

WHY, I OUGHTA HAUL OFF AND--

ULP!

WESTERN UNION

TO SCROOGE MCDUCK-BUTTE-MONTANA TERRITORY

SON - TERRIBLE CRISIS FOR THE CLAN MCDUCK STOP NEED CASH STOP COME HOME AT ONCE STOP DON'T STOP STOP -FERGUS MCDUCK-GLASGOW-SCOTLAND

IT'S NOT FAIR! NO SOONER DO I FIND SUCCESS THAN I'M FORCED TO *QUIT!*

BUT IT LOOKS LIKE YOUR FAMILY NEEDS YOU!

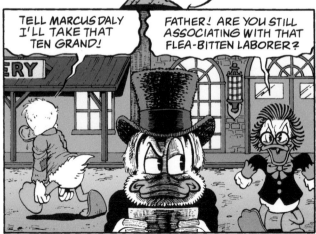

TELL MARCUS DALY I'LL TAKE THAT TEN GRAND!

FATHER! ARE YOU STILL ASSOCIATING WITH THAT FLEA-BITTEN LABORER?

YOUR FATHER SENT YOU OVER HERE TO BUY HIM A HORSEWHIP?

YES! AND YOU'D BETTER SNAP TO IT, LACKEY! HE'S A *RICH MAN!*

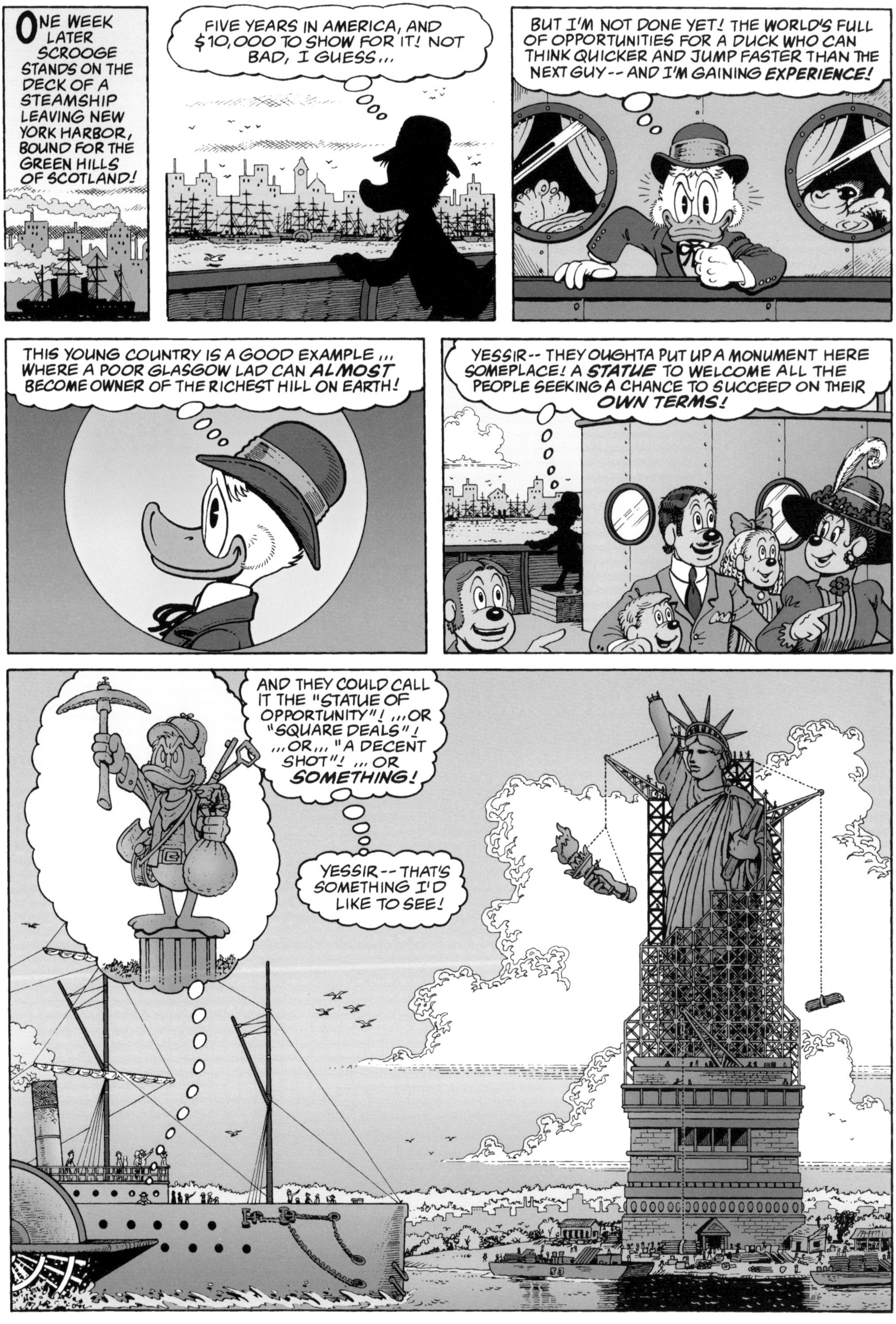
ONE WEEK LATER SCROOGE STANDS ON THE DECK OF A STEAMSHIP LEAVING NEW YORK HARBOR, BOUND FOR THE GREEN HILLS OF SCOTLAND!
FIVE YEARS IN AMERICA, AND $10,000 TO SHOW FOR IT! NOT BAD, I GUESS...
BUT I'M NOT DONE YET! THE WORLD'S FULL OF OPPORTUNITIES FOR A DUCK WHO CAN THINK QUICKER AND JUMP FASTER THAN THE NEXT GUY -- AND I'M GAINING EXPERIENCE!
THIS YOUNG COUNTRY IS A GOOD EXAMPLE... WHERE A POOR GLASGOW LAD CAN ALMOST BECOME OWNER OF THE RICHEST HILL ON EARTH!
YESSIR -- THEY OUGHTA PUT UP A MONUMENT HERE SOMEPLACE! A STATUE TO WELCOME ALL THE PEOPLE SEEKING A CHANCE TO SUCCEED ON THEIR OWN TERMS!
AND THEY COULD CALL IT THE "STATUE OF OPPORTUNITY"! ...OR "SQUARE DEALS"! ...OR... "A DECENT SHOT"! ...OR SOMETHING!
YESSIR -- THAT'S SOMETHING I'D LIKE TO SEE!

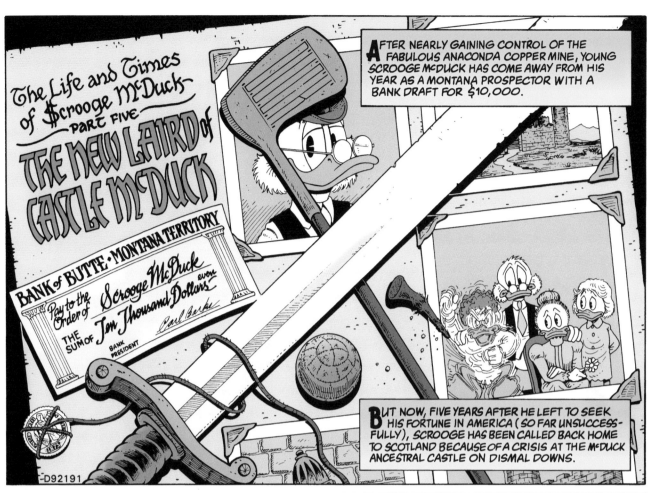

The Life and Times of $crooge McDuck
PART FIVE

THE NEW LAIRD OF CASTLE McDUCK

BANK OF BUTTE · MONTANA TERRITORY

Pay to the Order of Scrooge McDuck
THE SUM OF Ten Thousand Dollars even

BANK PRESIDENT

Carl Barks

D92191

AFTER NEARLY GAINING CONTROL OF THE FABULOUS ANACONDA COPPER MINE, YOUNG SCROOGE McDUCK HAS COME AWAY FROM HIS YEAR AS A MONTANA PROSPECTOR WITH A BANK DRAFT FOR $10,000.

BUT NOW, FIVE YEARS AFTER HE LEFT TO SEEK HIS FORTUNE IN AMERICA (SO FAR UNSUCCESS-FULLY), SCROOGE HAS BEEN CALLED BACK HOME TO SCOTLAND BECAUSE OF A CRISIS AT THE McDUCK ANCESTRAL CASTLE ON DISMAL DOWNS.

BAHROOM!

HURRY, SCROOGEY! YE KNOW WHAT TH' LEGENDS SAY ABOOT TH' *DEMON HOUND* O' DISMAL DOWNS!!

DON'T WORRY, MA! WE'LL SOON BE INSIDE THE CASTLE COURT-YARD!

I HOPE POPPA AND UNCLE JAKE ARE STILL THERE HOLDING OFF THE WHISKERVILLES!

AYE! AN' YORE WEE SISTER HORTENSE AS WELL!

WHAT'S THIS-- A POSTER?

NOTICE: PUBLIC SALE

I'LL HAFTA USE THOSE NEW *SPECS* I BOUGHT IN GLASGOW TO READ IT!

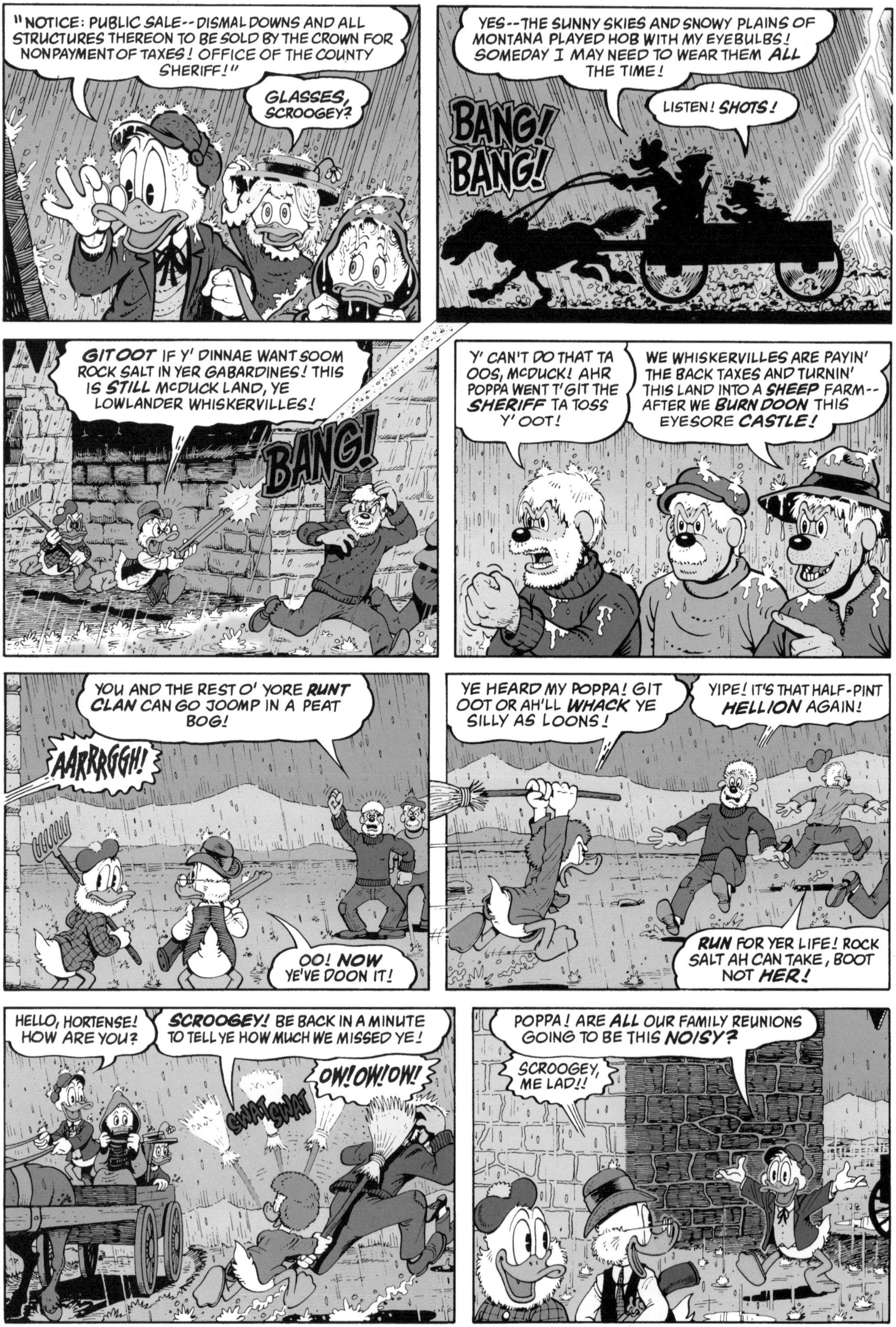
"NOTICE: PUBLIC SALE--DISMAL DOWNS AND ALL STRUCTURES THEREON TO BE SOLD BY THE CROWN FOR NONPAYMENT OF TAXES! OFFICE OF THE COUNTY SHERIFF!"
GLASSES, SCROOGEY?
YES--THE SUNNY SKIES AND SNOWY PLAINS OF MONTANA PLAYED HOB WITH MY EYEBULBS! SOMEDAY I MAY NEED TO WEAR THEM ALL THE TIME!
BANG! BANG!
LISTEN! SHOTS!
GIT OOT IF Y' DINNAE WANT SOOM ROCK SALT IN YER GABARDINES! THIS IS STILL McDUCK LAND, YE LOWLANDER WHISKERVILLES!
BANG!
Y' CAN'T DO THAT TA OOS, McDUCK! AHR POPPA WENT T' GIT THE SHERIFF TA TOSS Y' OOT!
WE WHISKERVILLES ARE PAYIN' THE BACK TAXES AND TURNIN' THIS LAND INTO A SHEEP FARM--AFTER WE BURN DOON THIS EYESORE CASTLE!
YOU AND THE REST O' YORE RUNT CLAN CAN GO JOOMP IN A PEAT BOG!
AARRRGGH!
OO! NOW YE'VE DOON IT!
YE HEARD MY POPPA! GIT OOT OR AH'LL WHACK YE SILLY AS LOONS!
YIPE! IT'S THAT HALF-PINT HELLION AGAIN!
RUN FOR YER LIFE! ROCK SALT AH CAN TAKE, BOOT NOT HER!
HELLO, HORTENSE! HOW ARE YOU?
SCROOGEY! BE BACK IN A MINUTE TO TELL YE HOW MUCH WE MISSED YE!
SWAT! SWAT!
OW! OW! OW!
POPPA! ARE ALL OUR FAMILY REUNIONS GOING TO BE THIS NOISY?
SCROOGEY, ME LAD!!

AH'M SOO GLAD YE'RE HOME, SCROOGEY! WE McDUCKS MOOST STICK TOGETHER IN THIS CRISIS!

THAT'S A CINCH NOW, POPPA! I HAD A *CREAM CHEESE* SANDWICH IN MY POCKET!

JAKE, YOU TAKE TH' WOMEN BACK TO TOWN! THERE'LL BE *TROUBLE* HERE, NO DOOT!

AYE, FERGUS... *IF* I CAN CATCH HORTENSE!

FROM WHOSE SIDE O' THE CLAN DOES HORTENSE GIT HER *TEMPER?*

AH DINNAE KNOW, BOOT AH HOPE SHE DOESNAE PASS IT ON TO *HER* BAIRN!

CAUTION! PEAT BOG

IT'S LIKE THIS, LAD-- WE McDUCKS WERE CHASED OOT O' DISMAL DOWNS BY THE HOUND, BOOT OUR ANCESTORS ALL POOLED THEIR INCOMES TO KEEP UP THE ESTATE *TAXES!*

I KNOW, POPPA!

THERE'S ONLY JAKE AND ME LEFT NOW, LAD! WE FINALLY FELL SO FAR BEHIND IN THE PAYMENTS THAT WE'RE ABOOT TO LOSE THE LAND! AND TO THE *WHISKERVILLES*, NO LESS! IT'S UNTHINKABLE!

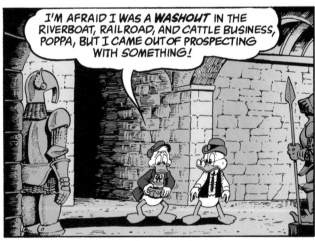

I'M AFRAID I WAS A *WASHOUT* IN THE RIVERBOAT, RAILROAD, AND CATTLE BUSINESS, POPPA, BUT I CAME OUT OF PROSPECTING WITH SOMETHING!

FROM WHAT MA SAID, THIS BANK DRAFT WILL *JUST* PAY OFF OUR TAXES! I'LL BE FLAT BROKE AGAIN!

EXCEPT FOR MY *FIRST DIME!* ≿Sigh≾ MAYBE SOMEDAY IT WILL INSPIRE ME TO *ACCOMPLISH* SOMETHING!

YE'VE SAVED OUR ANCESTRAL *CASTLE*, LAD! THAT'S *SOOMTHIN' GRAND!*

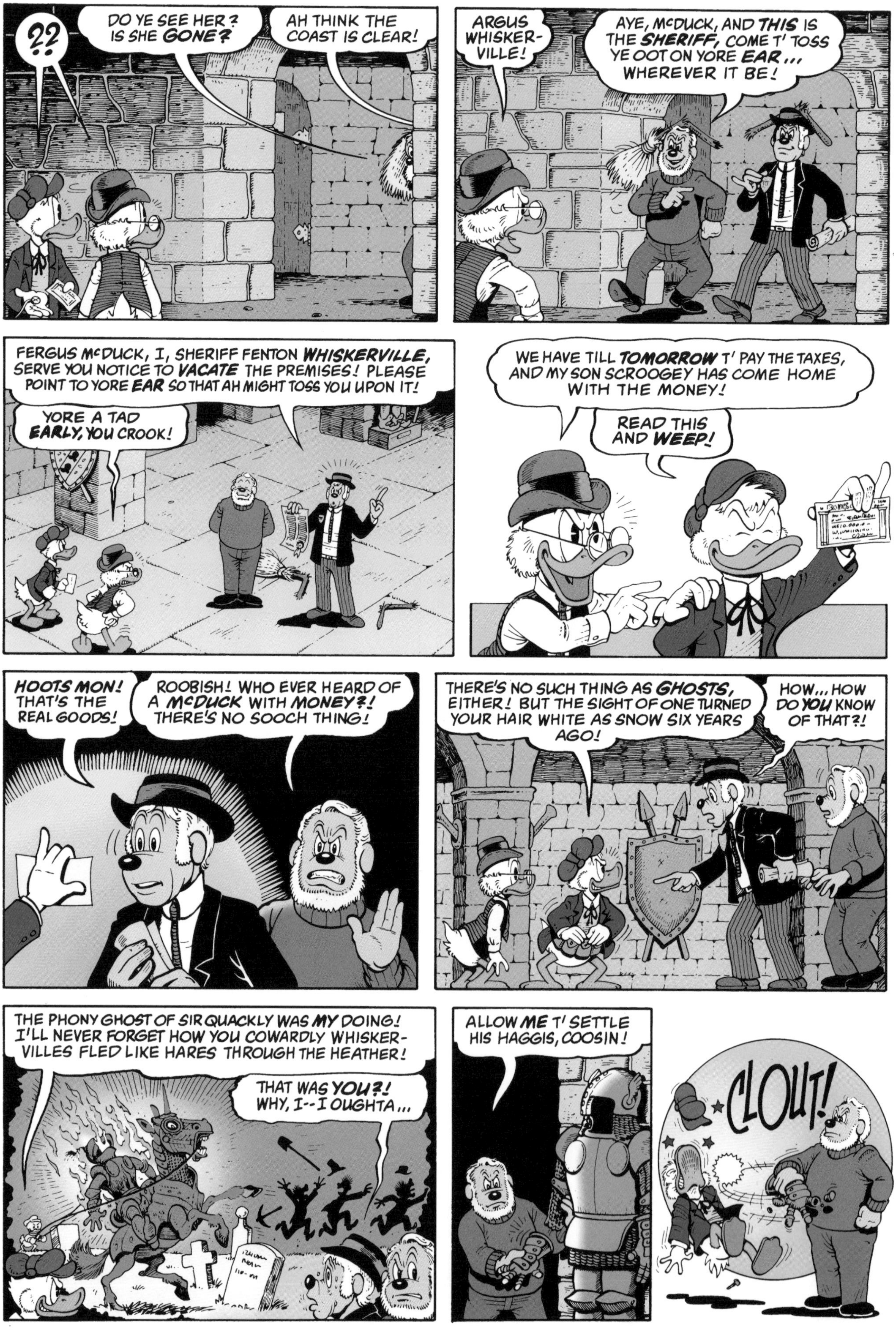
??
DO YE SEE HER? IS SHE GONE?
AH THINK THE COAST IS CLEAR!
ARGUS WHISKER-VILLE!
AYE, McDUCK, AND THIS IS THE SHERIFF, COME T' TOSS YE OOT ON YORE EAR... WHEREVER IT BE!
FERGUS McDUCK, I, SHERIFF FENTON WHISKERVILLE, SERVE YOU NOTICE TO VACATE THE PREMISES! PLEASE POINT TO YORE EAR SO THAT AH MIGHT TOSS YOU UPON IT!
YORE A TAD EARLY, YOU CROOK!
WE HAVE TILL TOMORROW T' PAY THE TAXES, AND MY SON SCROOGEY HAS COME HOME WITH THE MONEY!
READ THIS AND WEEP!
HOOTS MON! THAT'S THE REAL GOODS!
ROOBISH! WHO EVER HEARD OF A McDUCK WITH MONEY?! THERE'S NO SOOCH THING!
THERE'S NO SUCH THING AS GHOSTS, EITHER! BUT THE SIGHT OF ONE TURNED YOUR HAIR WHITE AS SNOW SIX YEARS AGO!
HOW... HOW DO YOU KNOW OF THAT?!
THE PHONY GHOST OF SIR QUACKLY WAS MY DOING! I'LL NEVER FORGET HOW YOU COWARDLY WHISKER-VILLES FLED LIKE HARES THROUGH THE HEATHER!
THAT WAS YOU?! WHY, I--I OUGHTA...
ALLOW ME T' SETTLE HIS HAGGIS, COOSIN!
CLOUT!

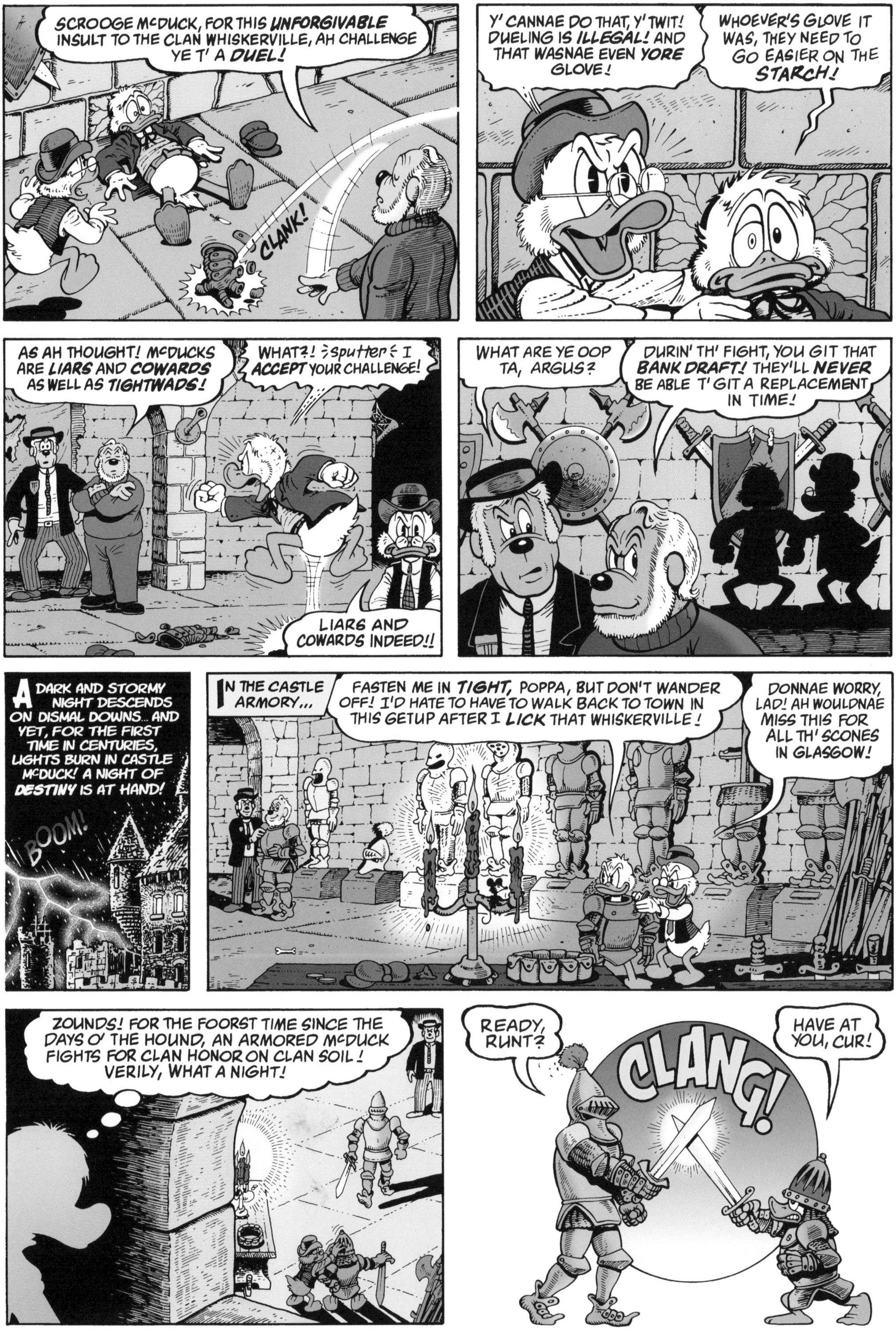
SCROOGE McDUCK, FOR THIS UNFORGIVABLE INSULT TO THE CLAN WHISKERVILLE, AH CHALLENGE YE T' A DUEL!
CLANK!
Y' CANNAE DO THAT, Y' TWIT! DUELING IS ILLEGAL! AND THAT WASNAE EVEN YORE GLOVE!
WHOEVER'S GLOVE IT WAS, THEY NEED TO GO EASIER ON THE STARCH!
AS AH THOUGHT! McDUCKS ARE LIARS AND COWARDS AS WELL AS TIGHTWADS!
WHAT?! sputter I ACCEPT YOUR CHALLENGE!
LIARS AND COWARDS INDEED!!
WHAT ARE YE OOP TA, ARGUS?
DURIN' TH' FIGHT, YOU GIT THAT BANK DRAFT! THEY'LL NEVER BE ABLE T' GIT A REPLACEMENT IN TIME!
A DARK AND STORMY NIGHT DESCENDS ON DISMAL DOWNS... AND YET, FOR THE FIRST TIME IN CENTURIES, LIGHTS BURN IN CASTLE McDUCK! A NIGHT OF DESTINY IS AT HAND!
BOOM!
IN THE CASTLE ARMORY...
FASTEN ME IN TIGHT, POPPA, BUT DON'T WANDER OFF! I'D HATE TO HAVE TO WALK BACK TO TOWN IN THIS GETUP AFTER I LICK THAT WHISKERVILLE!
DONNAE WORRY, LAD! AH WOULDNAE MISS THIS FOR ALL TH' SCONES IN GLASGOW!
ZOUNDS! FOR THE FOORST TIME SINCE THE DAYS O' THE HOUND, AN ARMORED McDUCK FIGHTS FOR CLAN HONOR ON CLAN SOIL! VERILY, WHAT A NIGHT!
READY, RUNT?
CLANG!
HAVE AT YOU, CUR!

GAD! YE-YE'RE GOOD WITH THAT BLADE, Y' FUZZY-CHEEKED VOLE!
WHACK!
MY REFLEXES ARE HONED FROM FIGHTING KEELBOAT PIRATES ON THE MISSISSIPPI AND RUSTLERS ON THE CHISHOLM TRAIL!
CLANG!
BUFFALO BILL HIMSELF TAUGHT ME HOW TO KNIFE-FIGHT INJUN STYLE...
EEK!
SNIP!
...AND AFTER THE LAST MATCH I HAD WITH SITTING BULL AT THE WILD WEST SHOW, HE STOPPED SITTING FOR A MONTH!
SWAK!
YOWTCH!
GREAT FLAMING TUMBLE-WEEDS! LOOK OUT!
HACK!
YOU'RE SUPPOSED TO HIT ME, NOT THE FURNITURE! DON'T YOU REALIZE THE RESALE VALUE OF THAT CHAIR IS GOING TO BE NIL?
HE DINNAE COOM PAST HERE, SON!
sniff sniff snf
WHAT AYR Y' DOIN', LAD?
THE BLACKFEET INDIANS TAUGHT ME TO HUNT PRAIRIE WEASELS BY SCENT!
CREEEAK...
SO EITHER A RAT CRAWLED INTO THAT LAST SUIT OF ARMOR AND DIED...
...OR IT'S CHOCK FULL OF WHISKERVILLE!
BONK!
STAND STILL! I CAN'T FIGHT A ONE-MAN DUEL!

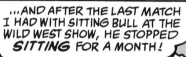

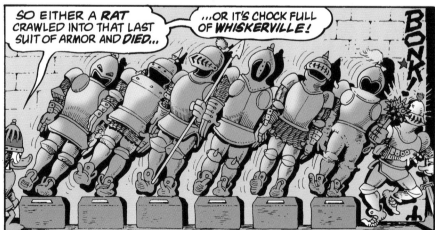

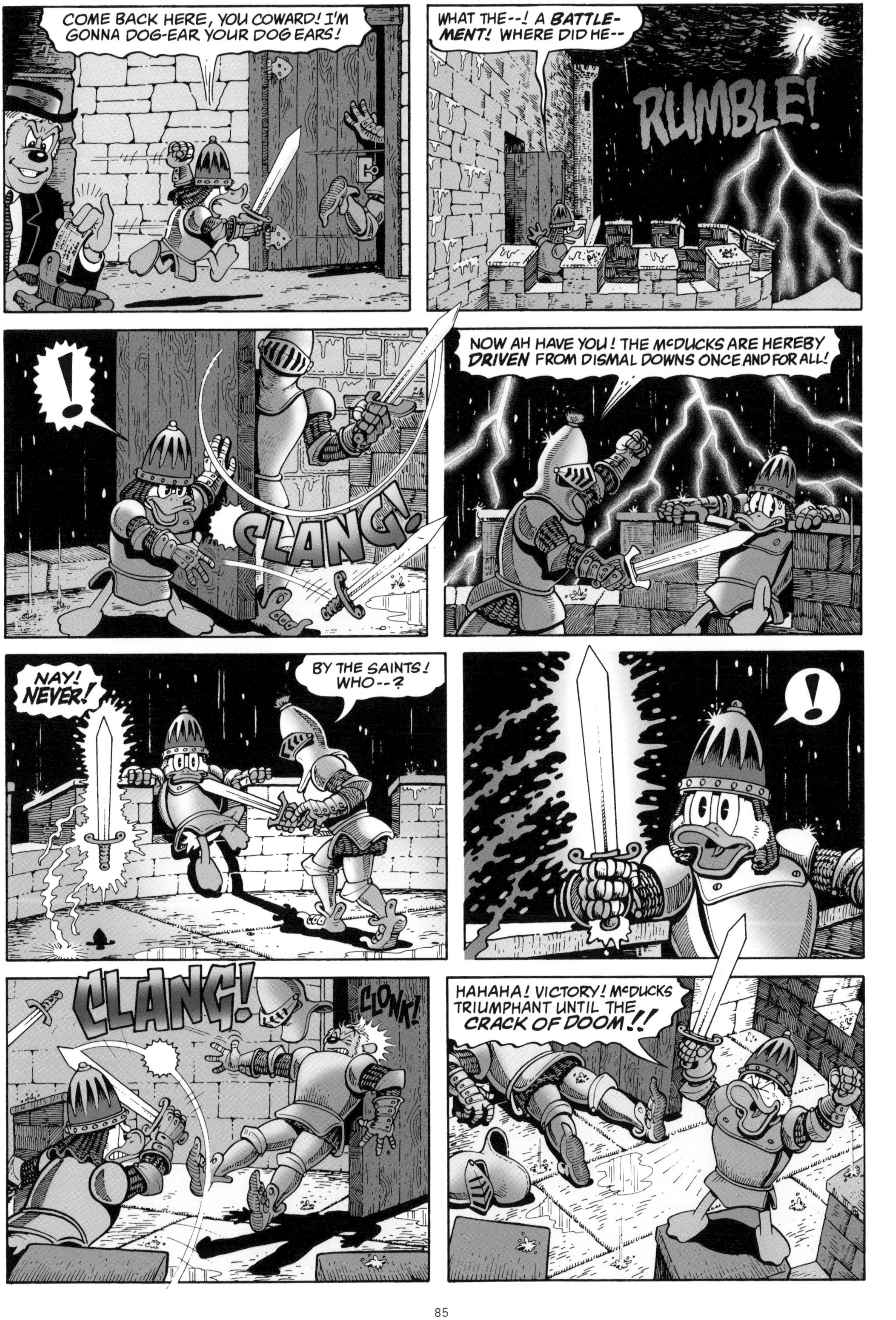

COME BACK HERE, YOU COWARD! I'M GONNA DOG-EAR YOUR DOG EARS!
WHAT THE--! A BATTLE-MENT! WHERE DID HE--
RUMBLE!
!
CLANG!
NOW AH HAVE YOU! THE McDUCKS ARE HEREBY DRIVEN FROM DISMAL DOWNS ONCE AND FOR ALL!
NAY! NEVER!
BY THE SAINTS! WHO--?
!
CLANG!
CLONK!
HAHAHA! VICTORY! McDUCKS TRIUMPHANT UNTIL THE CRACK OF DOOM!!

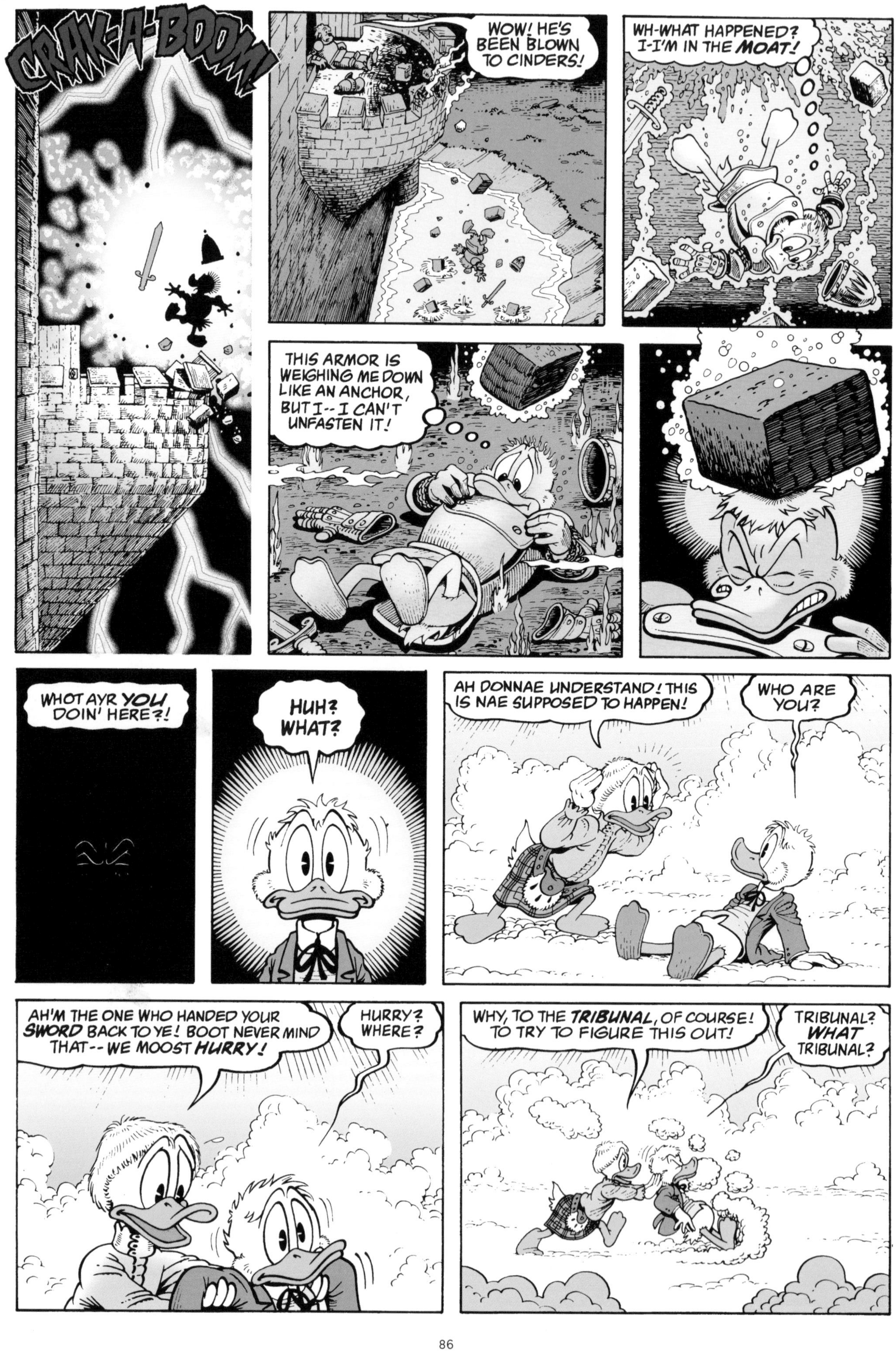
CRAK-A-BOOM!
WOW! HE'S BEEN BLOWN TO CINDERS!
WH-WHAT HAPPENED? I-I'M IN THE MOAT!
THIS ARMOR IS WEIGHING ME DOWN LIKE AN ANCHOR, BUT I-- I CAN'T UNFASTEN IT!
WHOT AYR YOU DOIN' HERE?!
HUH? WHAT?
AH DONNAE UNDERSTAND! THIS IS NAE SUPPOSED TO HAPPEN!
WHO ARE YOU?
AH'M THE ONE WHO HANDED YOUR SWORD BACK TO YE! BOOT NEVER MIND THAT-- WE MOOST HURRY!
HURRY? WHERE?
WHY, TO THE TRIBUNAL, OF COURSE! TO TRY TO FIGURE THIS OUT!
TRIBUNAL? WHAT TRIBUNAL?

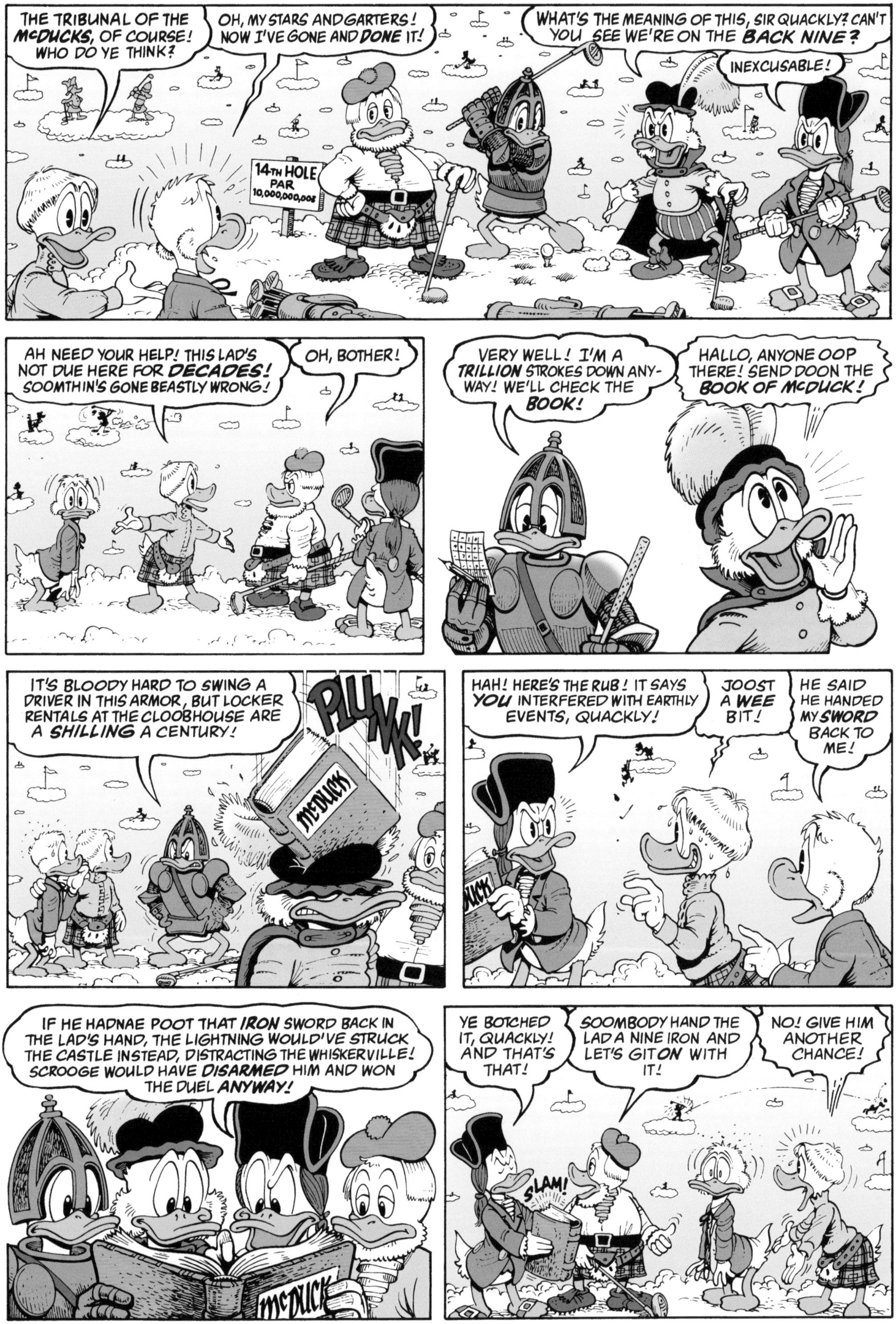
THE TRIBUNAL OF THE McDUCKS, OF COURSE! WHO DO YE THINK?
OH, MY STARS AND GARTERS! NOW I'VE GONE AND DONE IT!
WHAT'S THE MEANING OF THIS, SIR QUACKLY? CAN'T YOU SEE WE'RE ON THE BACK NINE?
INEXCUSABLE!
14TH HOLE PAR 10,000,000,008
AH NEED YOUR HELP! THIS LAD'S NOT DUE HERE FOR DECADES! SOOMTHIN'S GONE BEASTLY WRONG!
OH, BOTHER!
VERY WELL! I'M A TRILLION STROKES DOWN ANY-WAY! WE'LL CHECK THE BOOK!
HALLO, ANYONE OOP THERE! SEND DOON THE BOOK OF McDUCK!
IT'S BLOODY HARD TO SWING A DRIVER IN THIS ARMOR, BUT LOCKER RENTALS AT THE CLOOBHOUSE ARE A SHILLING A CENTURY!
PLUNK!
McDUCK
HAH! HERE'S THE RUB! IT SAYS YOU INTERFERED WITH EARTHLY EVENTS, QUACKLY!
JOOST A WEE BIT!
HE SAID HE HANDED MY SWORD BACK TO ME!
IF HE HADNAE POOT THAT IRON SWORD BACK IN THE LAD'S HAND, THE LIGHTNING WOULD'VE STRUCK THE CASTLE INSTEAD, DISTRACTING THE WHISKERVILLE! SCROOGE WOULD HAVE DISARMED HIM AND WON THE DUEL ANYWAY!
McDUCK
YE BOTCHED IT, QUACKLY! AND THAT'S THAT!
SOOMBODY HAND THE LAD A NINE IRON AND LET'S GIT ON WITH IT!
NO! GIVE HIM ANOTHER CHANCE!
SLAM!

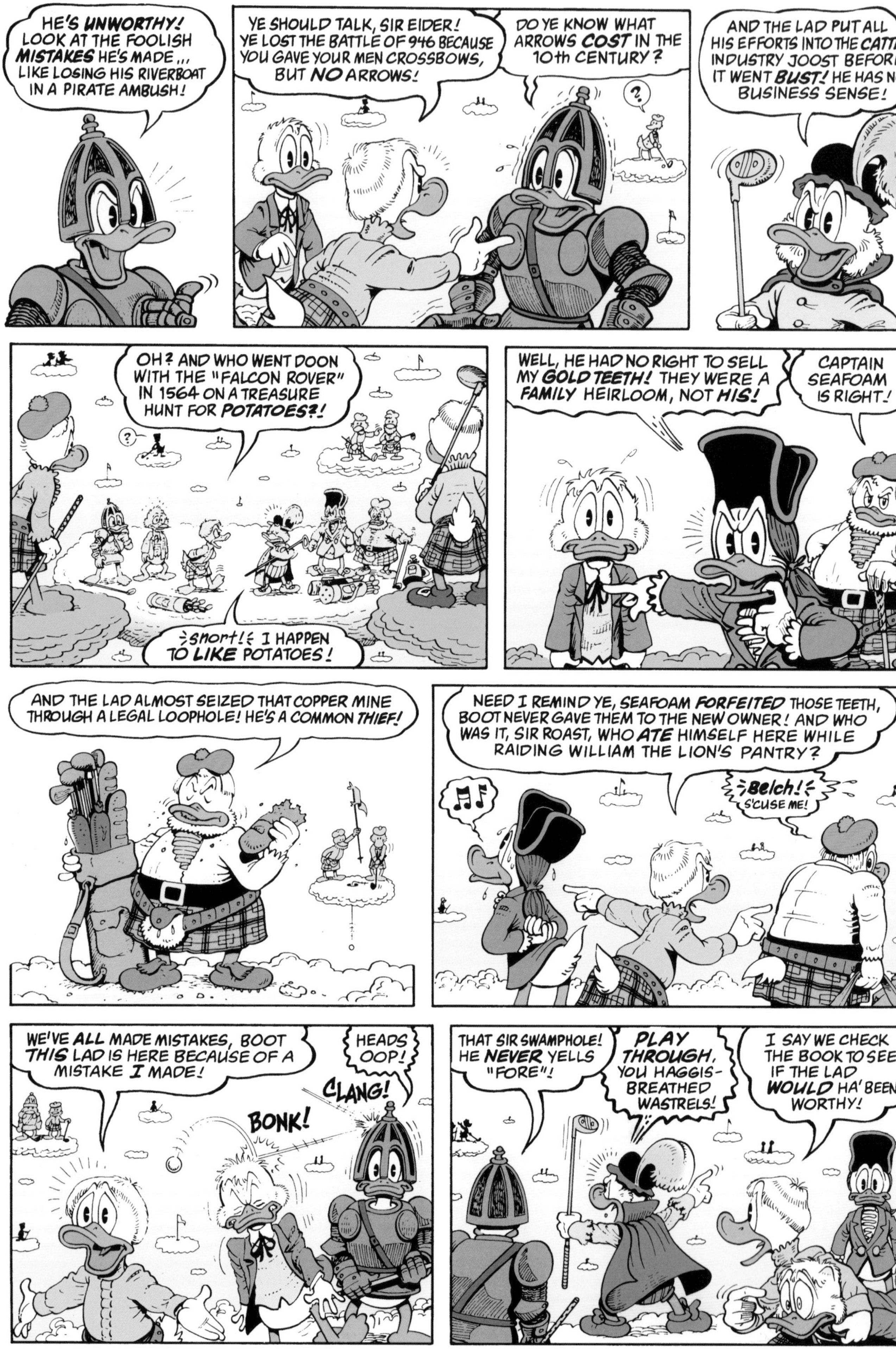
HE'S UNWORTHY! LOOK AT THE FOOLISH MISTAKES HE'S MADE... LIKE LOSING HIS RIVERBOAT IN A PIRATE AMBUSH!
YE SHOULD TALK, SIR EIDER! YE LOST THE BATTLE OF 946 BECAUSE YOU GAVE YOUR MEN CROSSBOWS, BUT NO ARROWS!
DO YE KNOW WHAT ARROWS COST IN THE 10th CENTURY?
?
AND THE LAD PUT ALL HIS EFFORTS INTO THE CATTLE INDUSTRY JOOST BEFORE IT WENT BUST! HE HAS NO BUSINESS SENSE!
OH? AND WHO WENT DOON WITH THE "FALCON ROVER" IN 1564 ON A TREASURE HUNT FOR POTATOES?!
?
SNORT! I HAPPEN TO LIKE POTATOES!
WELL, HE HAD NO RIGHT TO SELL MY GOLD TEETH! THEY WERE A FAMILY HEIRLOOM, NOT HIS!
CAPTAIN SEAFOAM IS RIGHT!
AND THE LAD ALMOST SEIZED THAT COPPER MINE THROUGH A LEGAL LOOPHOLE! HE'S A COMMON THIEF!
NEED I REMIND YE, SEAFOAM FORFEITED THOSE TEETH, BOOT NEVER GAVE THEM TO THE NEW OWNER! AND WHO WAS IT, SIR ROAST, WHO ATE HIMSELF HERE WHILE RAIDING WILLIAM THE LION'S PANTRY?
BELCH! S'CUSE ME!
WE'VE ALL MADE MISTAKES, BOOT THIS LAD IS HERE BECAUSE OF A MISTAKE I MADE!
HEADS OOP!
CLANG!
BONK!
THAT SIR SWAMPHOLE! HE NEVER YELLS "FORE"!
PLAY THROUGH, YOU HAGGIS-BREATHED WASTRELS!
I SAY WE CHECK THE BOOK TO SEE IF THE LAD WOULD HA' BEEN WORTHY!

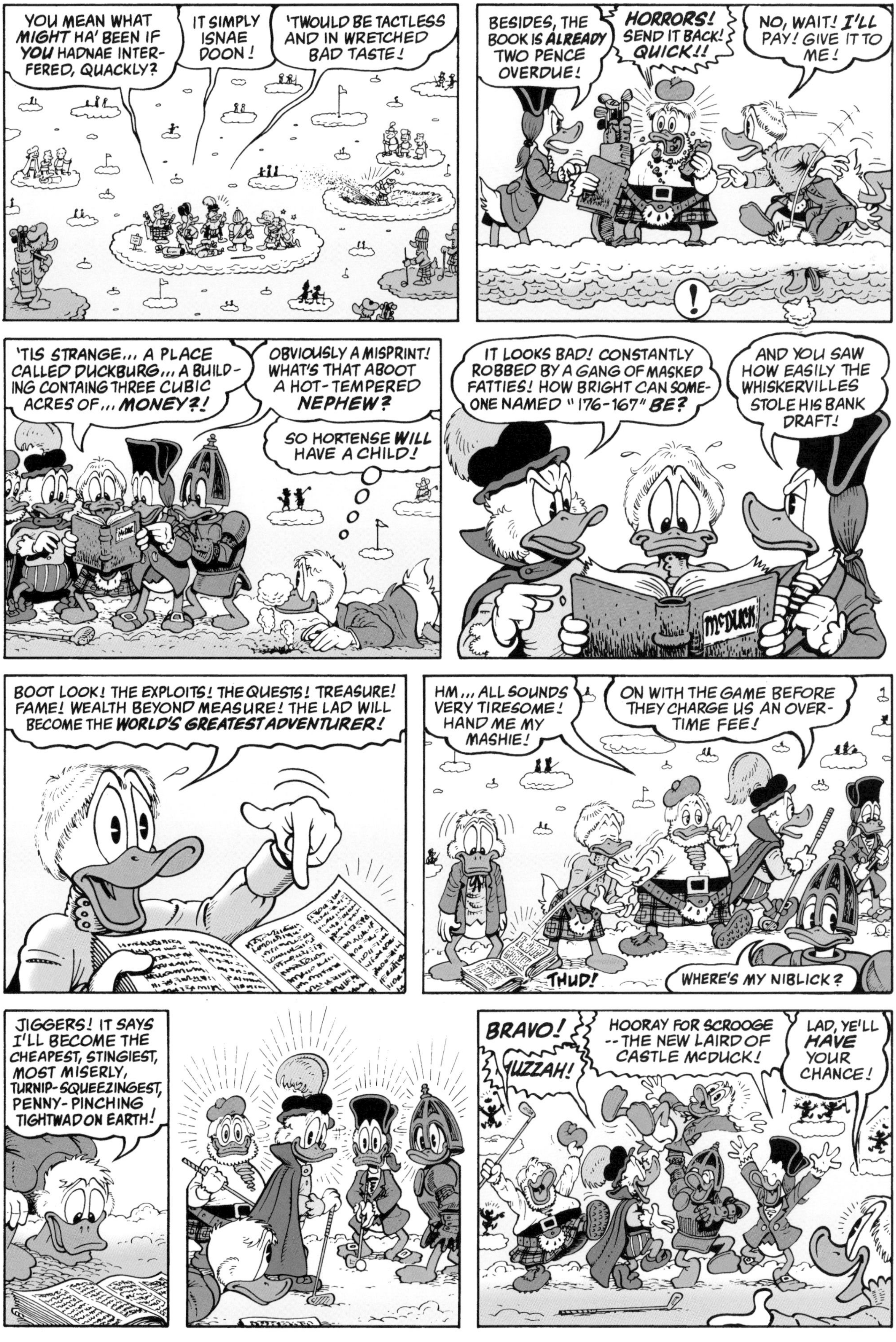

YOU MEAN WHAT MIGHT HA' BEEN IF YOU HADNAE INTERFERED, QUACKLY?
IT SIMPLY ISNAE DOON!
'TWOULD BE TACTLESS AND IN WRETCHED BAD TASTE!
BESIDES, THE BOOK IS ALREADY TWO PENCE OVERDUE!
HORRORS! SEND IT BACK! QUICK!!
NO, WAIT! I'LL PAY! GIVE IT TO ME!
!
'TIS STRANGE... A PLACE CALLED DUCKBURG... A BUILDING CONTAING THREE CUBIC ACRES OF... MONEY?!
OBVIOUSLY A MISPRINT! WHAT'S THAT ABOOT A HOT-TEMPERED NEPHEW?
SO HORTENSE WILL HAVE A CHILD!
IT LOOKS BAD! CONSTANTLY ROBBED BY A GANG OF MASKED FATTIES! HOW BRIGHT CAN SOMEONE NAMED "176-167" BE?
AND YOU SAW HOW EASILY THE WHISKERVILLES STOLE HIS BANK DRAFT!
McDUCK
BOOT LOOK! THE EXPLOITS! THE QUESTS! TREASURE! FAME! WEALTH BEYOND MEASURE! THE LAD WILL BECOME THE WORLD'S GREATEST ADVENTURER!
HM... ALL SOUNDS VERY TIRESOME! HAND ME MY MASHIE!
ON WITH THE GAME BEFORE THEY CHARGE US AN OVERTIME FEE!
THUD!
WHERE'S MY NIBLICK?
JIGGERS! IT SAYS I'LL BECOME THE CHEAPEST, STINGIEST, MOST MISERLY, TURNIP-SQUEEZINGEST, PENNY-PINCHING TIGHTWAD ON EARTH!
BRAVO!
HUZZAH!
HOORAY FOR SCROOGE --THE NEW LAIRD OF CASTLE McDUCK!
LAD, YE'LL HAVE YOUR CHANCE!

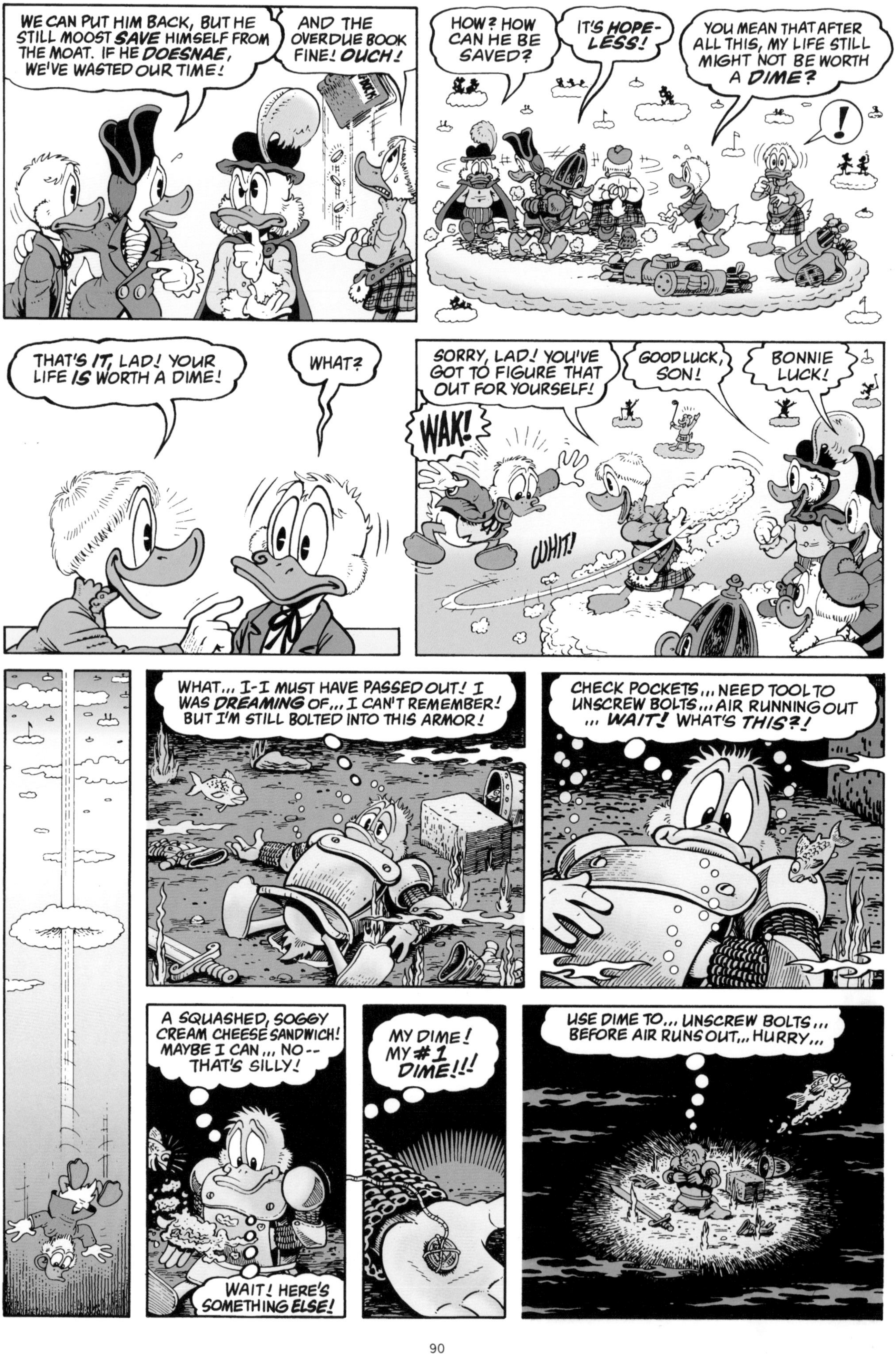
WE CAN PUT HIM BACK, BUT HE STILL MOOST SAVE HIMSELF FROM THE MOAT. IF HE DOESNAE, WE'VE WASTED OUR TIME!
AND THE OVERDUE BOOK FINE! OUCH!
HOW? HOW CAN HE BE SAVED?
IT'S HOPE-LESS!
YOU MEAN THAT AFTER ALL THIS, MY LIFE STILL MIGHT NOT BE WORTH A DIME?
!
THAT'S IT, LAD! YOUR LIFE IS WORTH A DIME!
WHAT?
SORRY, LAD! YOU'VE GOT TO FIGURE THAT OUT FOR YOURSELF!
GOOD LUCK, SON!
BONNIE LUCK!
WAK!
WHIT!
WHAT... I-I MUST HAVE PASSED OUT! I WAS DREAMING OF... I CAN'T REMEMBER! BUT I'M STILL BOLTED INTO THIS ARMOR!
CHECK POCKETS... NEED TOOL TO UNSCREW BOLTS... AIR RUNNING OUT ... WAIT! WHAT'S THIS?!
A SQUASHED, SOGGY CREAM CHEESE SANDWICH! MAYBE I CAN... NO-- THAT'S SILLY!
WAIT! HERE'S SOMETHING ELSE!
MY DIME! MY #1 DIME!!!
USE DIME TO... UNSCREW BOLTS... BEFORE AIR RUNS OUT... HURRY...

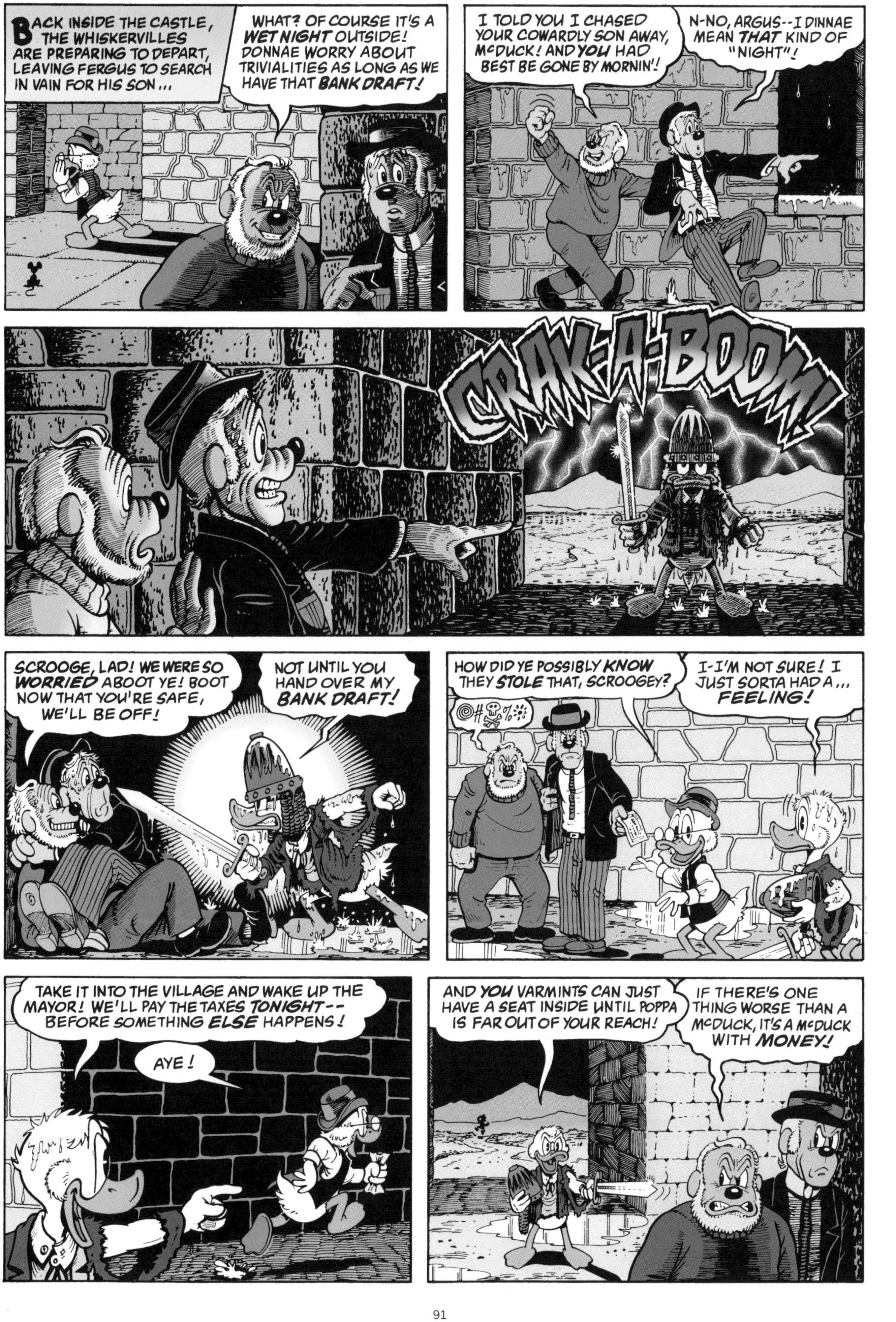
BACK INSIDE THE CASTLE, THE WHISKERVILLES ARE PREPARING TO DEPART, LEAVING FERGUS TO SEARCH IN VAIN FOR HIS SON...
WHAT? OF COURSE IT'S A WET NIGHT OUTSIDE! DONNAE WORRY ABOUT TRIVIALITIES AS LONG AS WE HAVE THAT BANK DRAFT!
I TOLD YOU I CHASED YOUR COWARDLY SON AWAY, McDUCK! AND YOU HAD BEST BE GONE BY MORNIN'!
N-NO, ARGUS--I DINNAE MEAN THAT KIND OF "NIGHT"!
CRAK-A-BOOM!
SCROOGE, LAD! WE WERE SO WORRIED ABOOT YE! BOOT NOW THAT YOU'RE SAFE, WE'LL BE OFF!
NOT UNTIL YOU HAND OVER MY BANK DRAFT!
HOW DID YE POSSIBLY KNOW THEY STOLE THAT, SCROOGEY?
I-I'M NOT SURE! I JUST SORTA HAD A... FEELING!
TAKE IT INTO THE VILLAGE AND WAKE UP THE MAYOR! WE'LL PAY THE TAXES TONIGHT-- BEFORE SOMETHING ELSE HAPPENS!
AYE!
AND YOU VARMINTS CAN JUST HAVE A SEAT INSIDE UNTIL POPPA IS FAR OUT OF YOUR REACH!
IF THERE'S ONE THING WORSE THAN A McDUCK, IT'S A McDUCK WITH MONEY!

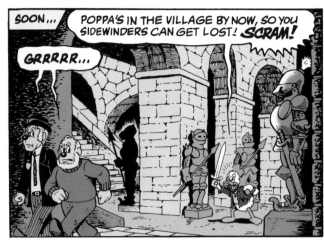

SOON... POPPA'S IN THE VILLAGE BY NOW, SO YOU SIDEWINDERS CAN GET LOST! *SCRAM!*

GRRRRR...

LISTEN, FENTON -- IF WE CANNAE STEAL THE BANK DRAFT, WHAT'S THE NEXT BEST THING?

STEAL THE *BANK?* AH DONNAE KNOW, ARGUS -- THAT'S A *BIG BANK!*

NO, IDIOT! WE'LL GIT RID OF WHO THE DRAFT IS *PAYABLE* TO -- *SCROOGE!* FOR *CERTAIN* THIS TIME!

BOOT WILL IT PUT THEM OUT OF OUR HAIR FOR GOOD? WHO'LL POP UP NEXT?

NOBODY! SCROOGE IS THE *LAST* OF THE CLAN McDUCK!

AYE -- BOOT HE'S THE LAST OF A *LONG* LINE...

...AND WE'RE ALL *PROUD* OF HIM!

AAAAIIIII!!!

HUH?

??! WHAT'S ALL THIS STRINGY *WHITE* STUFF?

WHAT THE SAM HILL'S GOING *ON* HERE? ⸮Gulp!⸜ IF I DIDN'T KNOW BETTER, I'D THINK THIS PLACE WAS...

...HAUNTED! ⸮shiver!⸜

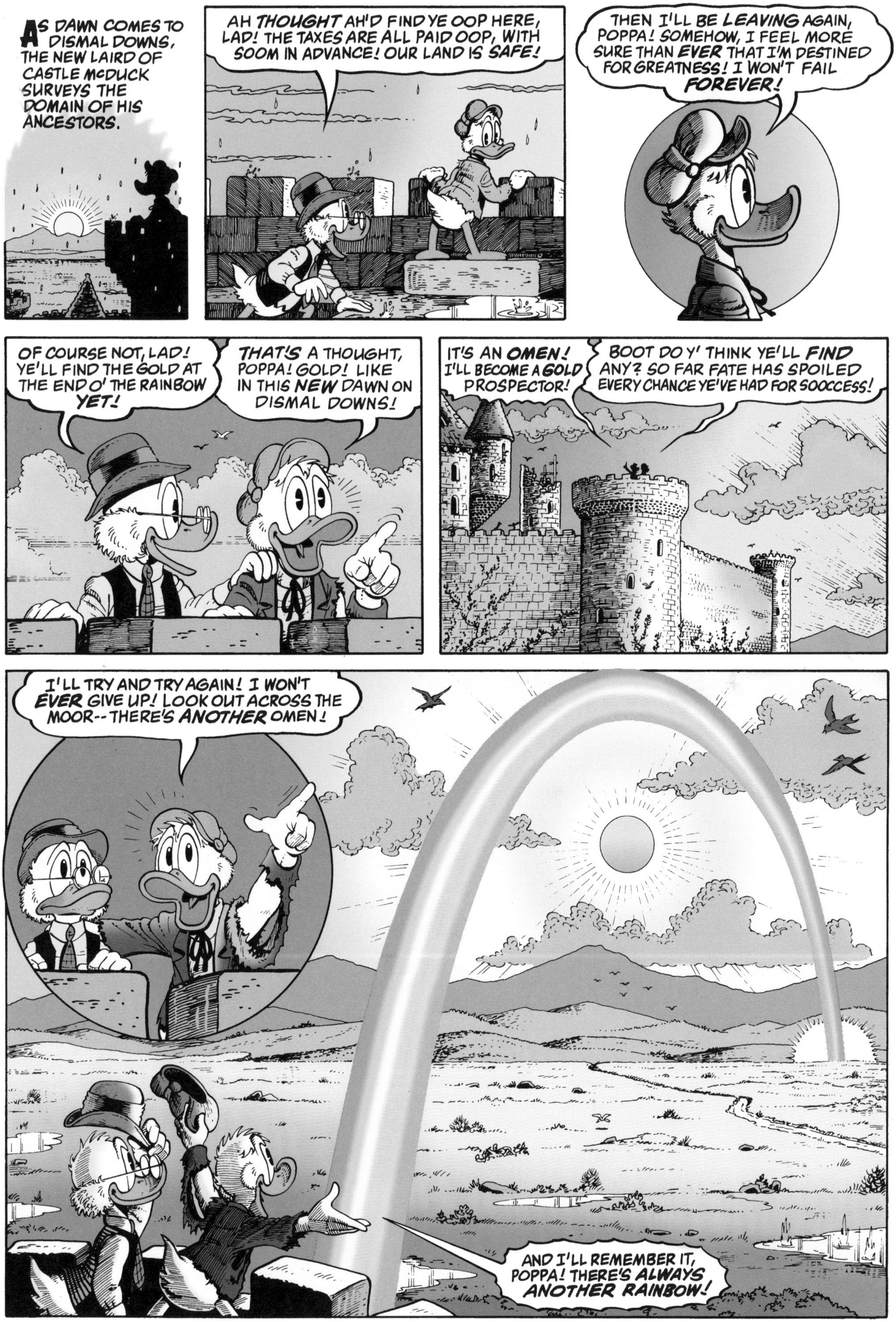
AS DAWN COMES TO DISMAL DOWNS, THE NEW LAIRD OF CASTLE McDUCK SURVEYS THE DOMAIN OF HIS ANCESTORS.
AH THOUGHT AH'D FIND YE OOP HERE, LAD! THE TAXES ARE ALL PAID OOP, WITH SOOM IN ADVANCE! OUR LAND IS SAFE!
THEN I'LL BE LEAVING AGAIN, POPPA! SOMEHOW, I FEEL MORE SURE THAN EVER THAT I'M DESTINED FOR GREATNESS! I WON'T FAIL FOREVER!
OF COURSE NOT, LAD! YE'LL FIND THE GOLD AT THE END O' THE RAINBOW YET!
THAT'S A THOUGHT, POPPA! GOLD! LIKE IN THIS NEW DAWN ON DISMAL DOWNS!
IT'S AN OMEN! I'LL BECOME A GOLD PROSPECTOR!
BOOT DO Y' THINK YE'LL FIND ANY? SO FAR FATE HAS SPOILED EVERY CHANCE YE'VE HAD FOR SOOCCESS!
I'LL TRY AND TRY AGAIN! I WON'T EVER GIVE UP! LOOK OUT ACROSS THE MOOR-- THERE'S ANOTHER OMEN!
AND I'LL REMEMBER IT, POPPA! THERE'S ALWAYS ANOTHER RAINBOW!

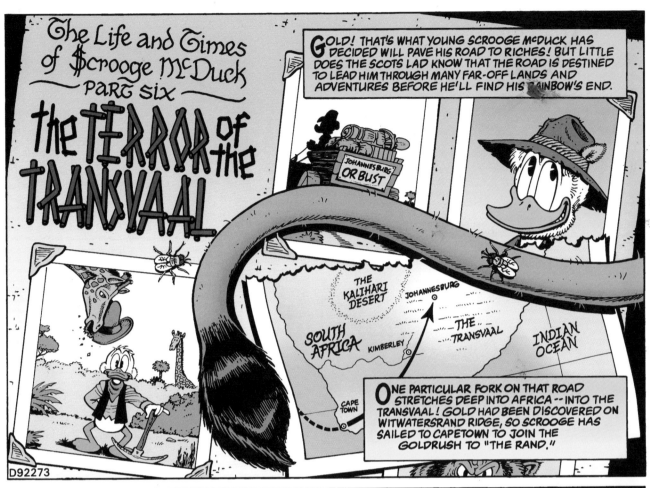

The Life and Times of $crooge McDuck — PART SIX

THE TERROR OF THE TRANSVAAL

GOLD! THAT'S WHAT YOUNG SCROOGE McDUCK HAS DECIDED WILL PAVE HIS ROAD TO RICHES! BUT LITTLE DOES THE SCOTS LAD KNOW THAT THE ROAD IS DESTINED TO LEAD HIM THROUGH MANY FAR-OFF LANDS AND ADVENTURES BEFORE HE'LL FIND HIS RAINBOW'S END.

JOHANNESBURG OR BUST

THE KALIHARI DESERT — JOHANNESBURG — THE TRANSVAAL — SOUTH AFRICA — KIMBERLEY — CAPE TOWN — INDIAN OCEAN

ONE PARTICULAR FORK ON THAT ROAD STRETCHES DEEP INTO AFRICA -- INTO THE TRANSVAAL! GOLD HAD BEEN DISCOVERED ON WITWATERSRAND RIDGE, SO SCROOGE HAS SAILED TO CAPETOWN TO JOIN THE GOLDRUSH TO "THE RAND."

D92273

AFTER LONG DAYS OF JOUNCING ALONG THE RUGGED TRAIL IN A BULLOCK CART...

AH! THERE'S KIMBERLEY! I'M OVER HALFWAY TO THE RAND!

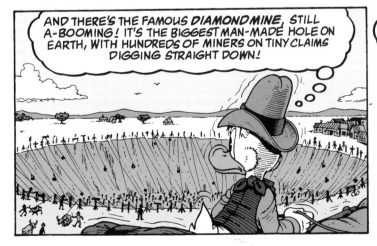

AND THERE'S THE FAMOUS DIAMOND MINE, STILL A-BOOMING! IT'S THE BIGGEST MAN-MADE HOLE ON EARTH, WITH HUNDREDS OF MINERS ON TINY CLAIMS DIGGING STRAIGHT DOWN!

BAH! TOO MUCH HUBBUB! TOO MANY PEOPLE! I'LL FIND A HOLE THAT BIG FILLED WITH GOLD... AND ALL MINE!

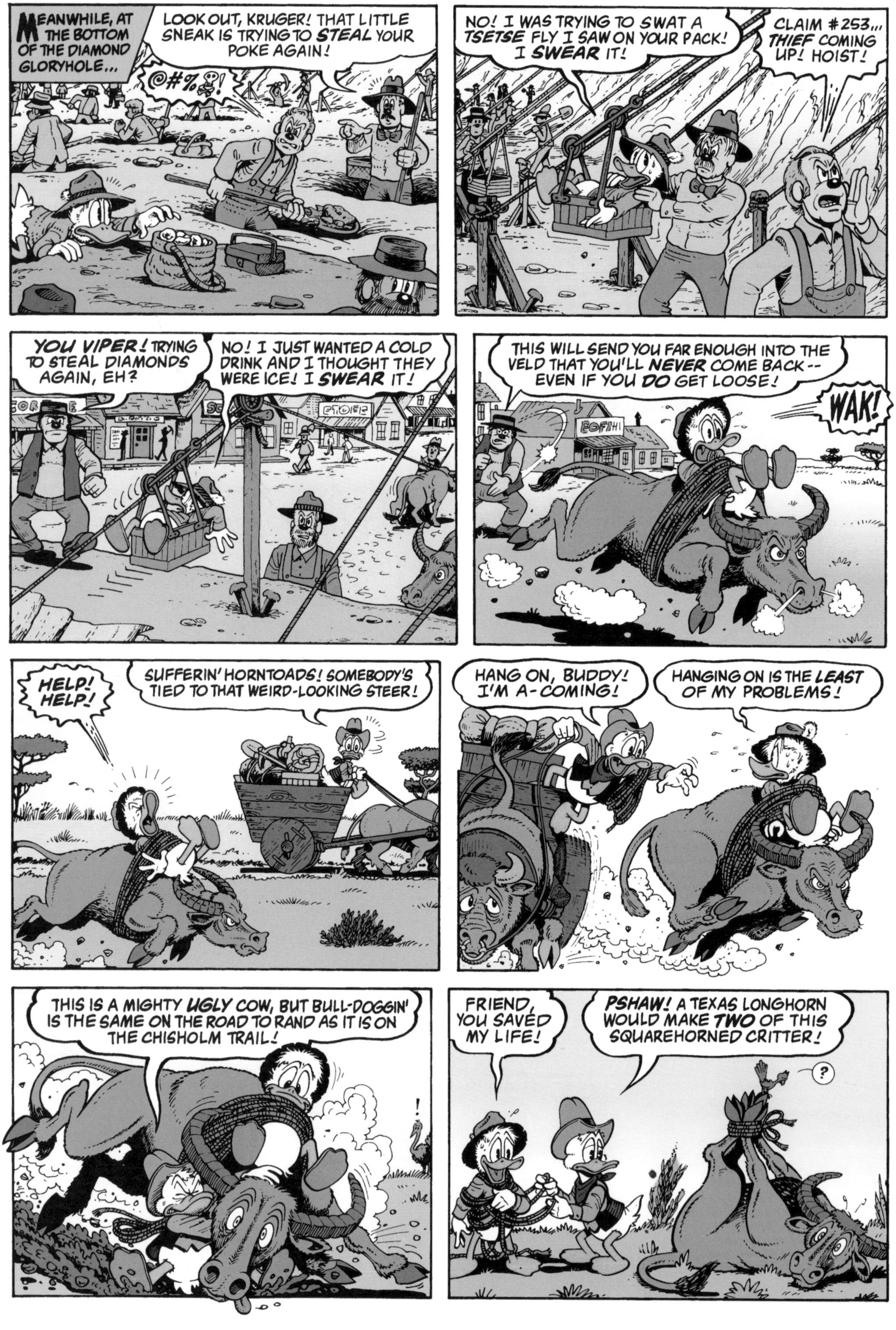
MEANWHILE, AT THE BOTTOM OF THE DIAMOND GLORYHOLE...
LOOK OUT, KRUGER! THAT LITTLE SNEAK IS TRYING TO STEAL YOUR POKE AGAIN!
@#%☠!
NO! I WAS TRYING TO SWAT A TSETSE FLY I SAW ON YOUR PACK! I SWEAR IT!
CLAIM #253... THIEF COMING UP! HOIST!
YOU VIPER! TRYING TO STEAL DIAMONDS AGAIN, EH?
NO! I JUST WANTED A COLD DRINK AND I THOUGHT THEY WERE ICE! I SWEAR IT!
THIS WILL SEND YOU FAR ENOUGH INTO THE VELD THAT YOU'LL NEVER COME BACK -- EVEN IF YOU DO GET LOOSE!
WAK!
HELP! HELP!
SUFFERIN' HORNTOADS! SOMEBODY'S TIED TO THAT WEIRD-LOOKING STEER!
HANG ON, BUDDY! I'M A-COMING!
HANGING ON IS THE LEAST OF MY PROBLEMS!
THIS IS A MIGHTY UGLY COW, BUT BULL-DOGGIN' IS THE SAME ON THE ROAD TO RAND AS IT IS ON THE CHISHOLM TRAIL!
!
FRIEND, YOU SAVED MY LIFE!
PSHAW! A TEXAS LONGHORN WOULD MAKE TWO OF THIS SQUAREHORNED CRITTER!
?

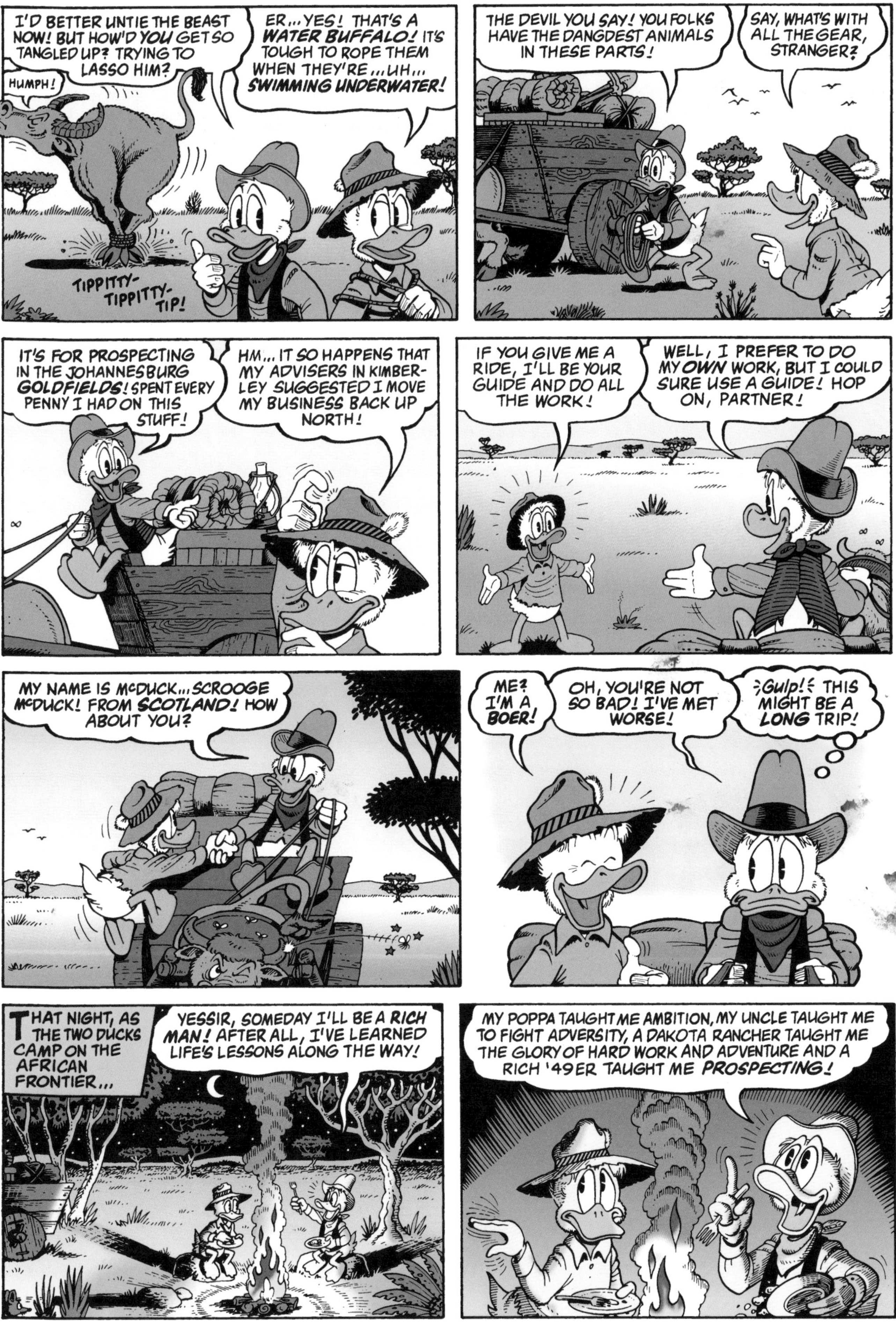
I'D BETTER UNTIE THE BEAST NOW! BUT HOW'D YOU GET SO TANGLED UP? TRYING TO LASSO HIM?
ER... YES! THAT'S A WATER BUFFALO! IT'S TOUGH TO ROPE THEM WHEN THEY'RE ...UH... SWIMMING UNDERWATER!
HUMPH!
TIPPITTY-TIPPITTY-TIP!
THE DEVIL YOU SAY! YOU FOLKS HAVE THE DANGDEST ANIMALS IN THESE PARTS!
SAY, WHAT'S WITH ALL THE GEAR, STRANGER?
IT'S FOR PROSPECTING IN THE JOHANNESBURG GOLDFIELDS! SPENT EVERY PENNY I HAD ON THIS STUFF!
HM... IT SO HAPPENS THAT MY ADVISERS IN KIMBERLEY SUGGESTED I MOVE MY BUSINESS BACK UP NORTH!
IF YOU GIVE ME A RIDE, I'LL BE YOUR GUIDE AND DO ALL THE WORK!
WELL, I PREFER TO DO MY OWN WORK, BUT I COULD SURE USE A GUIDE! HOP ON, PARTNER!
MY NAME IS McDUCK... SCROOGE McDUCK! FROM SCOTLAND! HOW ABOUT YOU?
ME? I'M A BOER!
OH, YOU'RE NOT SO BAD! I'VE MET WORSE!
Gulp! THIS MIGHT BE A LONG TRIP!
THAT NIGHT, AS THE TWO DUCKS CAMP ON THE AFRICAN FRONTIER...
YESSIR, SOMEDAY I'LL BE A RICH MAN! AFTER ALL, I'VE LEARNED LIFE'S LESSONS ALONG THE WAY!
MY POPPA TAUGHT ME AMBITION, MY UNCLE TAUGHT ME TO FIGHT ADVERSITY, A DAKOTA RANCHER TAUGHT ME THE GLORY OF HARD WORK AND ADVENTURE AND A RICH '49ER TAUGHT ME PROSPECTING!

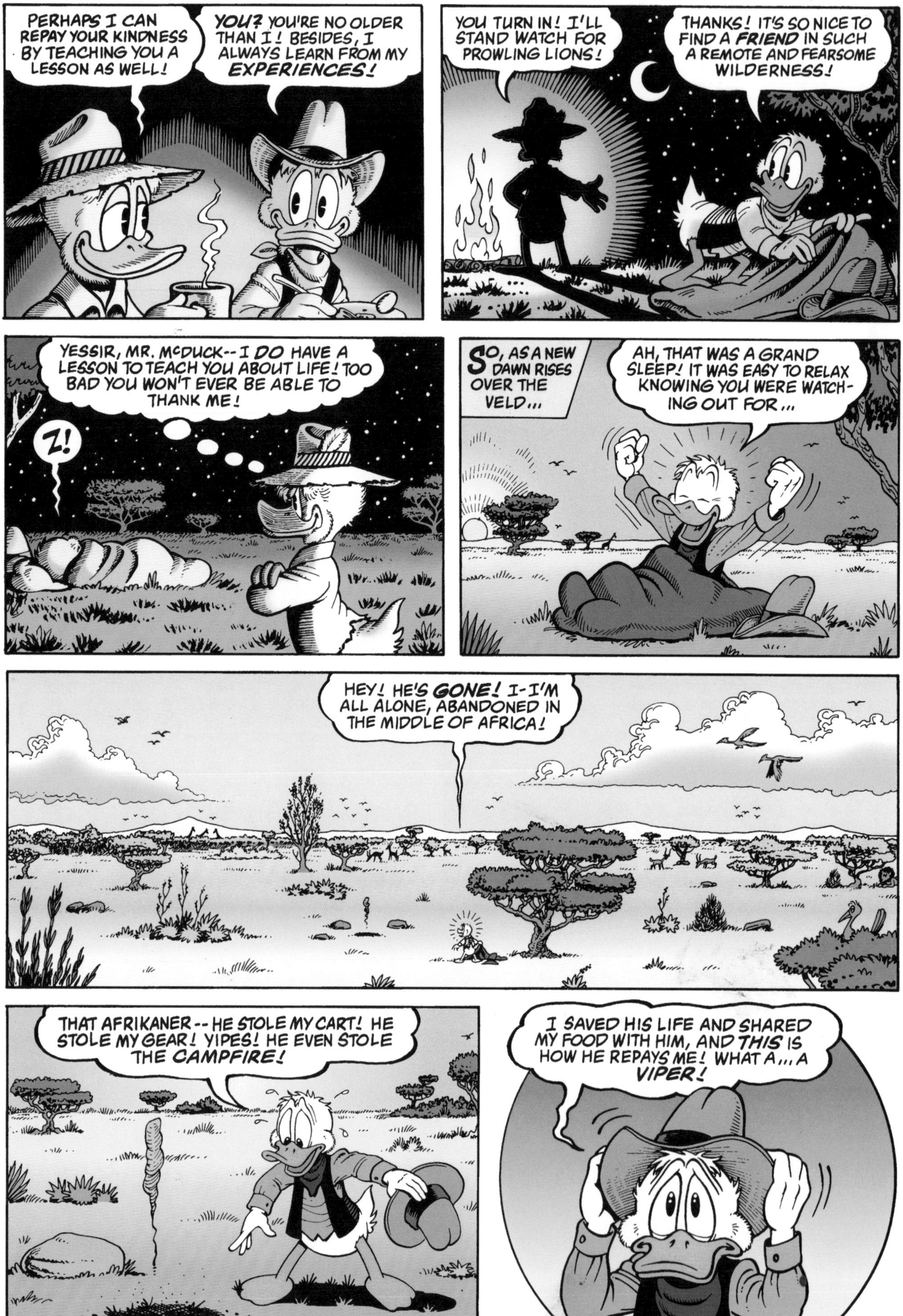
PERHAPS I CAN REPAY YOUR KINDNESS BY TEACHING YOU A LESSON AS WELL!
YOU? YOU'RE NO OLDER THAN I! BESIDES, I ALWAYS LEARN FROM MY EXPERIENCES!
YOU TURN IN! I'LL STAND WATCH FOR PROWLING LIONS!
THANKS! IT'S SO NICE TO FIND A FRIEND IN SUCH A REMOTE AND FEARSOME WILDERNESS!
YESSIR, MR. McDUCK-- I DO HAVE A LESSON TO TEACH YOU ABOUT LIFE! TOO BAD YOU WON'T EVER BE ABLE TO THANK ME!
Z!
SO, AS A NEW DAWN RISES OVER THE VELD...
AH, THAT WAS A GRAND SLEEP! IT WAS EASY TO RELAX KNOWING YOU WERE WATCHING OUT FOR...
HEY! HE'S GONE! I-I'M ALL ALONE, ABANDONED IN THE MIDDLE OF AFRICA!
THAT AFRIKANER-- HE STOLE MY CART! HE STOLE MY GEAR! YIPES! HE EVEN STOLE THE CAMPFIRE!
I SAVED HIS LIFE AND SHARED MY FOOD WITH HIM, AND THIS IS HOW HE REPAYS ME! WHAT A... A VIPER!

I SURVIVED BEING LOST IN THE WILDERNESS BEFORE, BUT THAT WAS IN *KANSAS!* ≳Gulp!≲ I WONDER IF THEY HAVE ANYTHING HERE AS *FEROCIOUS* AS A *COUGAR!*

ROAR!

OH, MY!! I'M NOT IN KANSAS ANY MORE!

AT LEAST THERE'S NOTHING AROUND AS *BIG* AS A MONTANA *GRIZZLY BEAR!*

WAAUUEEGAH!

WAK!

WHEREVER I GO, THERE ARE BLACKGUARDS WHO WANT TO *STEAL* THEIR FORTUNE RATHER THAN *WORK* FOR IT!

EVEN SO, THERE WAS NO MISTAKING THE INTENT OF CROOKS LIKE THE BEAGLE BOYS WITH THEIR *CORNY MASKS!* THEY WERE VILLAINS AND *PROUD* OF IT!

BUT FOR HIS SHEER *TREACHERY*, THAT AFRIKANER KID IS THE *WORST* SCOUNDREL I'VE EVER MET!

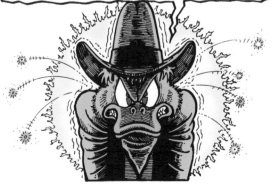

WELL, HE TAUGHT ME A LESSON, ALL RIGHT! AND IF I SOMEHOW MANAGE TO *LIVE* THROUGH THIS, I'LL TEACH *HIM* ONE IN RETURN! NAMELY...

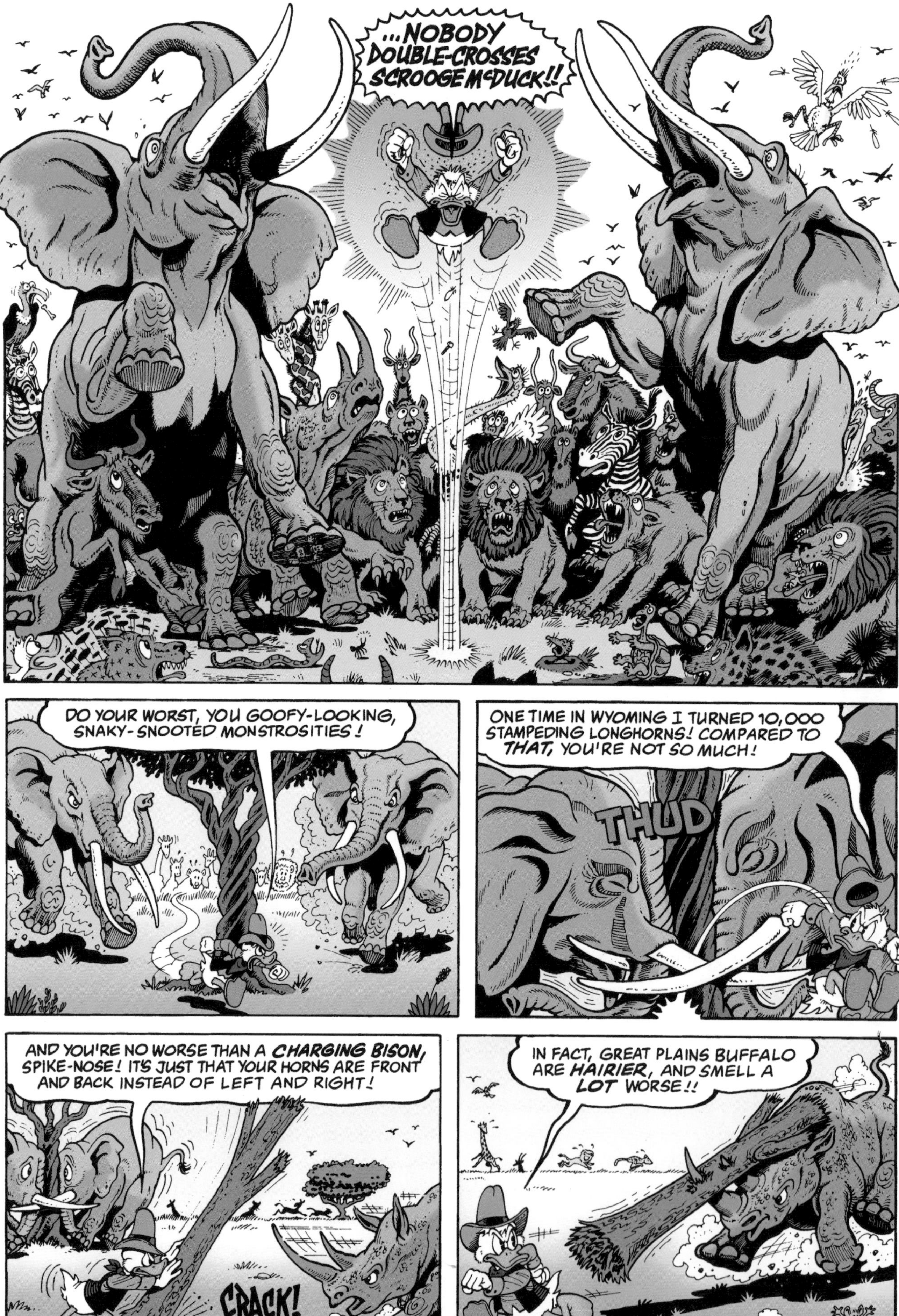
...NOBODY DOUBLE-CROSSES SCROOGE McDUCK!!
DO YOUR WORST, YOU GOOFY-LOOKING, SNAKY-SNOOTED MONSTROSITIES!
ONE TIME IN WYOMING I TURNED 10,000 STAMPEDING LONGHORNS! COMPARED TO THAT, YOU'RE NOT SO MUCH!
THUD
AND YOU'RE NO WORSE THAN A CHARGING BISON, SPIKE-NOSE! IT'S JUST THAT YOUR HORNS ARE FRONT AND BACK INSTEAD OF LEFT AND RIGHT!
CRACK!
IN FACT, GREAT PLAINS BUFFALO ARE HAIRIER, AND SMELL A LOT WORSE!!

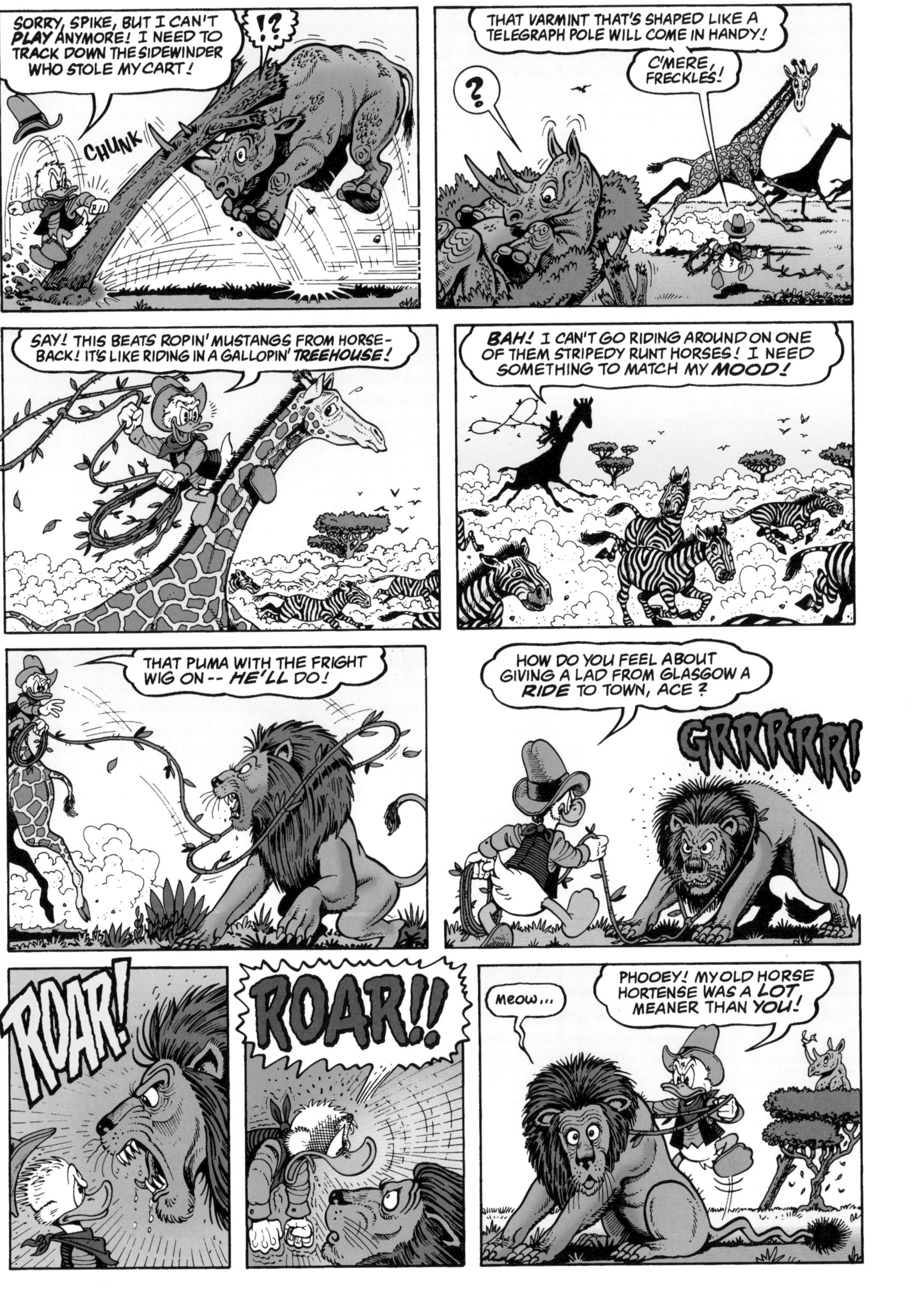

SORRY, SPIKE, BUT I CAN'T PLAY ANYMORE! I NEED TO TRACK DOWN THE SIDEWINDER WHO STOLE MY CART!
!?
CHUNK
THAT VARMINT THAT'S SHAPED LIKE A TELEGRAPH POLE WILL COME IN HANDY!
?
C'MERE, FRECKLES!
SAY! THIS BEATS ROPIN' MUSTANGS FROM HORSE-BACK! IT'S LIKE RIDING IN A GALLOPIN' TREEHOUSE!
BAH! I CAN'T GO RIDING AROUND ON ONE OF THEM STRIPEDY RUNT HORSES! I NEED SOMETHING TO MATCH MY MOOD!
THAT PUMA WITH THE FRIGHT WIG ON -- HE'LL DO!
HOW DO YOU FEEL ABOUT GIVING A LAD FROM GLASGOW A RIDE TO TOWN, ACE?
GRRRRR!
ROAR!
ROAR!!
Meow...
PHOOEY! MY OLD HORSE HORTENSE WAS A LOT MEANER THAN YOU!

GIDDYAP! I'LL SHOW THE HOTTENTOTS HOW TO *ROOT 'N' TOOT!*

FIRST MASTER OF THE MISSISSIPPI! THEN BUCKAROO OF THE BADLANDS! NOW I'M THE *TERROR OF THE TRANSVAAL!*

YEEHAW! BUCK McDUCK *RIDES AGAIN!*

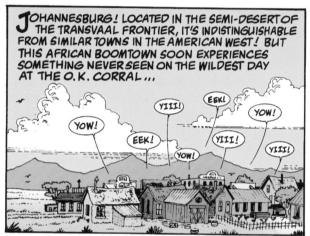

JOHANNESBURG! LOCATED IN THE SEMI-DESERT OF THE TRANSVAAL FRONTIER, IT'S INDISTINGUISHABLE FROM SIMILAR TOWNS IN THE AMERICAN WEST! BUT THIS AFRICAN BOOMTOWN SOON EXPERIENCES SOMETHING NEVER SEEN ON THE WILDEST DAY AT THE O.K. CORRAL...

YOW!
EEK!
YIII!
YOW!
EEK!
YIII!
YOW!
YIII!

HMPH! I RECKON THESE YOKELS HAVE NEVER SEEN A *REAL COWBOY* BEFORE!

=SNORT!=

HAH! THERE'S MY CART! FIRST OFF, I NEED TO GET SOMETHING OUT OF MY BAGS!

STABLES

WHERE'S THE CHICKEN-HEART WHO LEFT THIS CART HERE?

HE ZAID HE VAS GOING TO DER POOB TO FIND A BOYER VOR DOT CART EN GEAR!

THEN I'M GOING THERE TO DISCUSS THE *OWNERSHIP* OF THESE *SIX-SHOOTERS* WITH HIM! WILL YOU WATCH MY MOUNT FOR A FEW MINUTES?

ZERTAINLY! DOT'S MINE CHOB!

DON'T LET HIM GET UP ON THE FURNITURE! HE'S GOT *CLAWS* LIKE NOBODY'S BUSINESS!

YAAAH!!

snarl!!

I'LL TEACH THAT POLECAT HE CAN'T DRY GULCH SCROOGE McDUCK!

"DO NOT FORSAKE ME, OH MAH DARLIN'"...

MEANWHILE, INSIDE THE PUB...

BLIMEY! SO AFTER YOU SAVED THE BLOKE'S LIFE, THE FILTHY BEGGAR TRIED TO STEAL YOUR CART?

YES! BUT I FOUGHT HIM OFF! AND HIS GANG OF THUGS, TOO!

YESSIR! MINE IS AS THE STRENGTH OF TEN BECAUSE MY HEART IS PURE!

YOU'RE FULL OF PURE SOMETHING, ALL RIGHT!

HEY, KID!

FREE LUNCH TODAY— ½ PRICE

THERE'S A COWBOY COMIN'!... SAYS HE'S LOOKIN' FOR YOU!

A "COWBOY"? WHAT'S THAT? SOME KIND OF APPRENTICE MILKMAN?

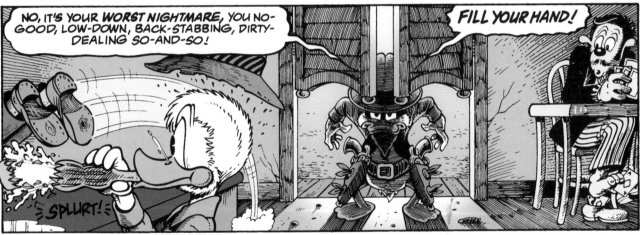

NO, IT'S YOUR WORST NIGHTMARE, YOU NO-GOOD, LOW-DOWN, BACK-STABBING, DIRTY-DEALING SO-AND-SO!

FILL YOUR HAND!

SPLURT!

SCROOGE! I'M SO GLAD YOU'RE ALL RIGHT! I WAS ABDUCTED BY A BAND OF ZULU WARRIORS WITH BIG, NASTY SPEARS! I SWEAR IT!

!!!

CUT THE YAMMER!

I TOLD YOU I LEARN FROM EXPERIENCE! I WON'T TRUST YOU TWICE! FROM NOW ON, I WON'T TRUST ANYBODY ONCE!

WHIT! WHIT! WHIT!

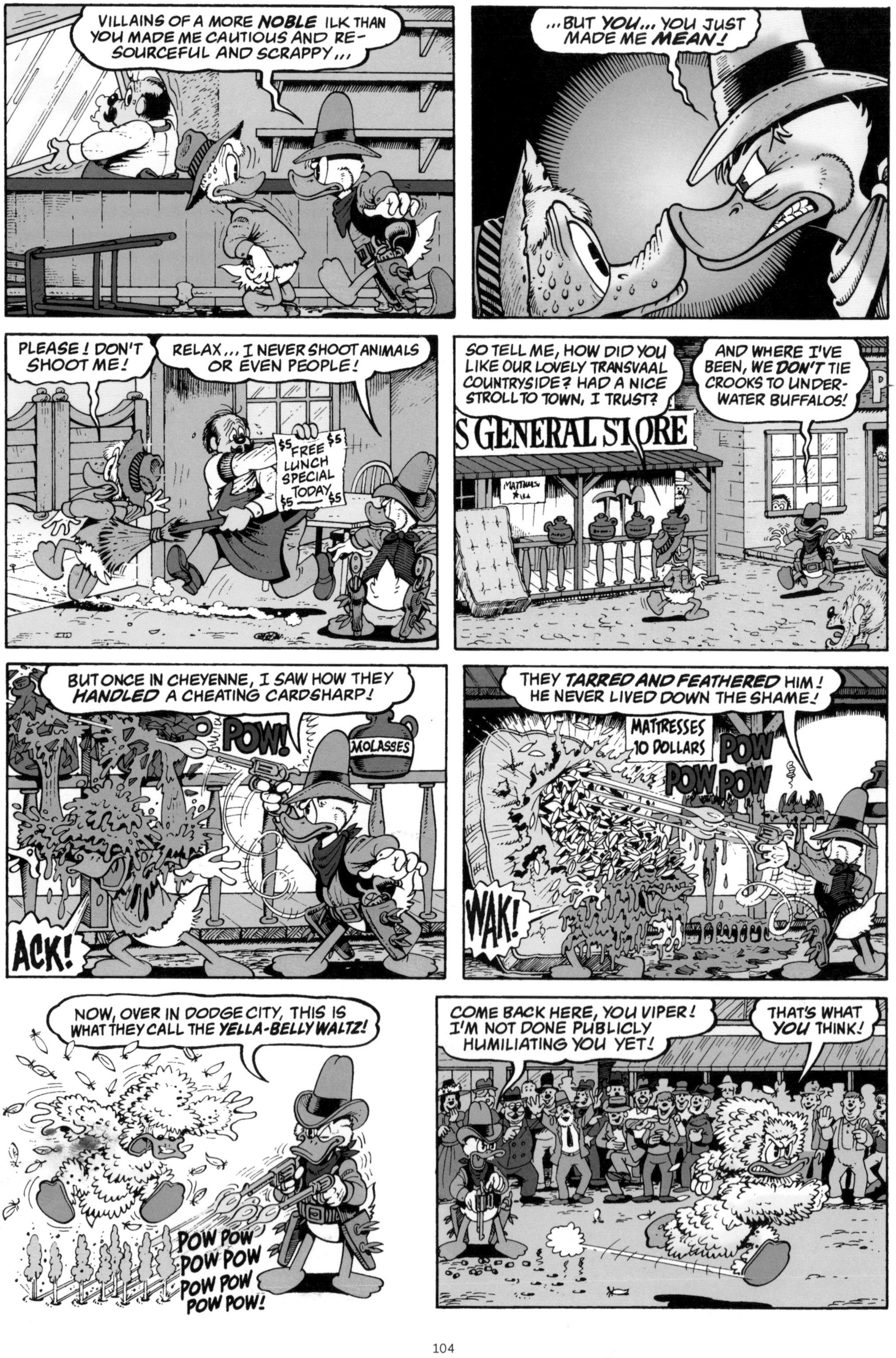
VILLAINS OF A MORE NOBLE ILK THAN YOU MADE ME CAUTIOUS AND RESOURCEFUL AND SCRAPPY...
...BUT YOU... YOU JUST MADE ME MEAN!
PLEASE! DON'T SHOOT ME!
RELAX... I NEVER SHOOT ANIMALS OR EVEN PEOPLE!
$5 FREE LUNCH SPECIAL TODAY $5
SO TELL ME, HOW DID YOU LIKE OUR LOVELY TRANSVAAL COUNTRYSIDE? HAD A NICE STROLL TO TOWN, I TRUST?
AND WHERE I'VE BEEN, WE DON'T TIE CROOKS TO UNDERWATER BUFFALOS!
S GENERAL STORE
BUT ONCE IN CHEYENNE, I SAW HOW THEY HANDLED A CHEATING CARDSHARP!
POW!
MOLASSES
ACK!
THEY TARRED AND FEATHERED HIM! HE NEVER LIVED DOWN THE SHAME!
MATTRESSES 10 DOLLARS
POW
POW POW
WAK!
NOW, OVER IN DODGE CITY, THIS IS WHAT THEY CALL THE YELLA-BELLY WALTZ!
POW POW
POW POW
POW POW
POW POW!
COME BACK HERE, YOU VIPER! I'M NOT DONE PUBLICLY HUMILIATING YOU YET!
THAT'S WHAT YOU THINK!

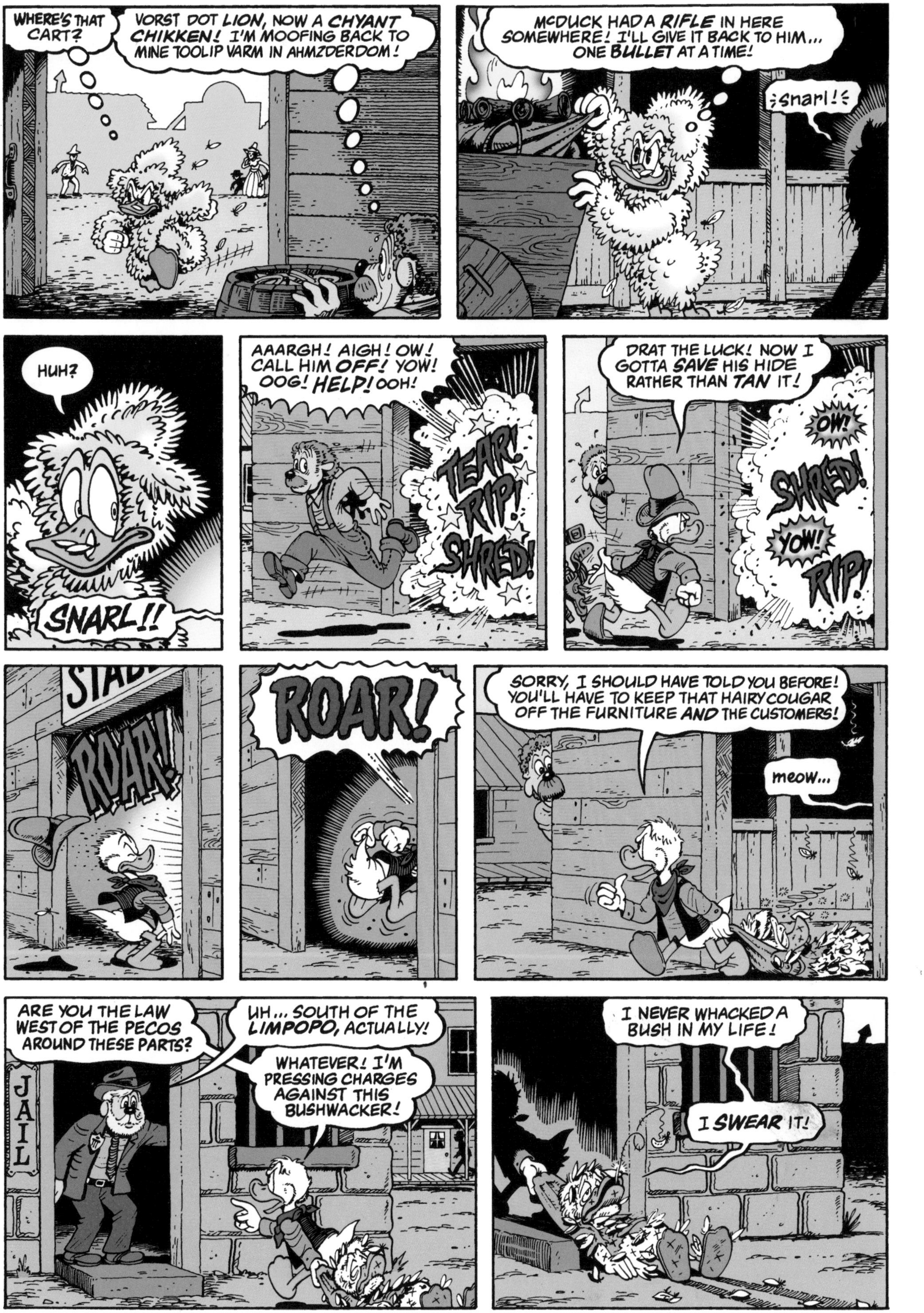
WHERE'S THAT CART?
VORST DOT LION, NOW A CHYANT CHIKKEN! I'M MOOFING BACK TO MINE TOOLIP VARM IN AHMZDERDOM!
McDUCK HAD A RIFLE IN HERE SOMEWHERE! I'LL GIVE IT BACK TO HIM... ONE BULLET AT A TIME!
Snarl!
HUH?
SNARL!!
AAARGH! AIGH! OW! CALL HIM OFF! YOW! OOG! HELP! OOH!
TEAR! RIP! SHRED!
DRAT THE LUCK! NOW I GOTTA SAVE HIS HIDE RATHER THAN TAN IT!
OW! SHRED! YOW! RIP!
ROAR!
ROAR!
SORRY, I SHOULD HAVE TOLD YOU BEFORE! YOU'LL HAVE TO KEEP THAT HAIRY COUGAR OFF THE FURNITURE AND THE CUSTOMERS!
meow...
ARE YOU THE LAW WEST OF THE PECOS AROUND THESE PARTS?
UH... SOUTH OF THE LIMPOPO, ACTUALLY!
WHATEVER! I'M PRESSING CHARGES AGAINST THIS BUSHWACKER!
JAIL
I NEVER WHACKED A BUSH IN MY LIFE!
I SWEAR IT!

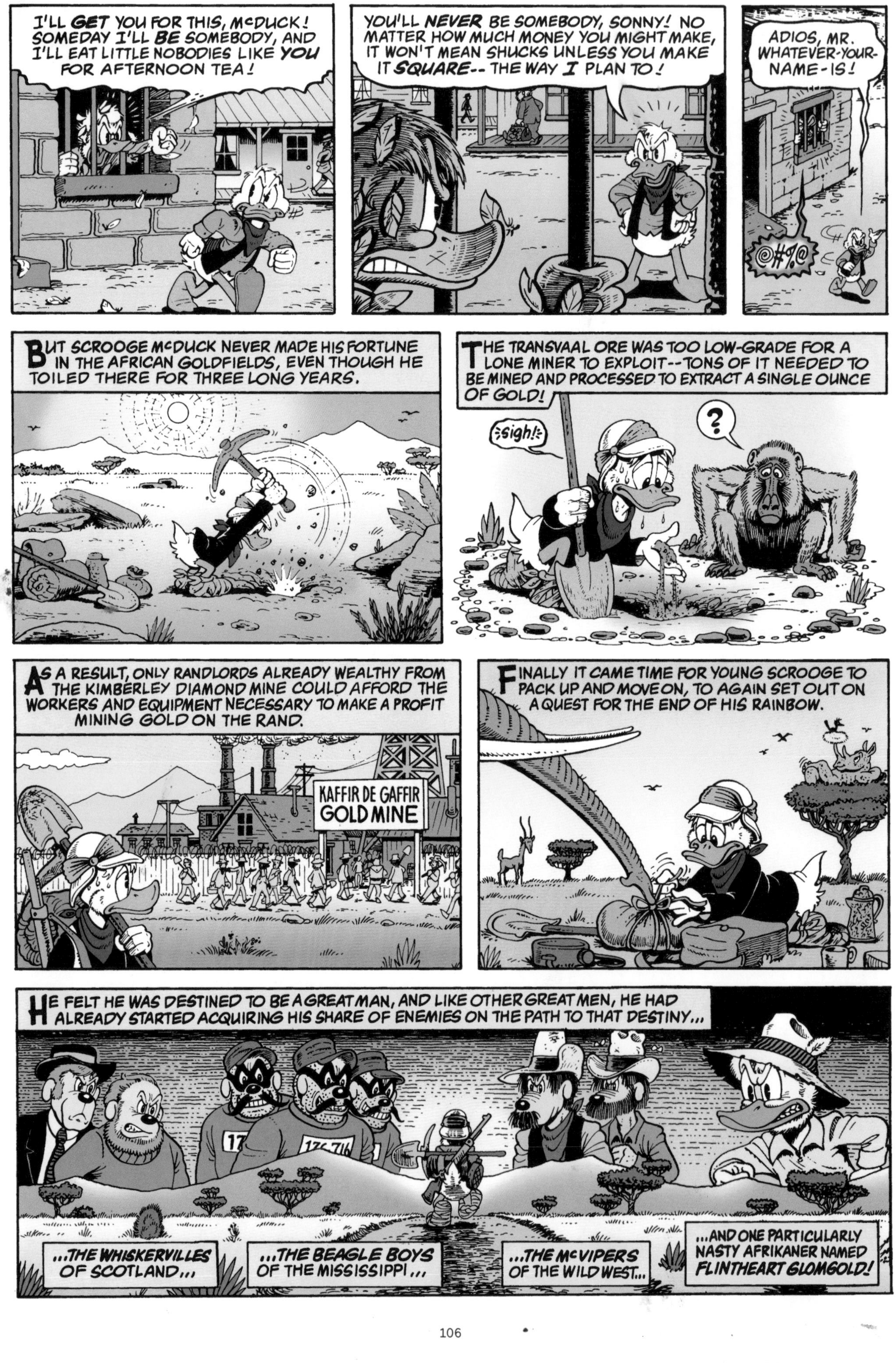

I'LL GET YOU FOR THIS, McDUCK! SOMEDAY I'LL BE SOMEBODY, AND I'LL EAT LITTLE NOBODIES LIKE YOU FOR AFTERNOON TEA!
YOU'LL NEVER BE SOMEBODY, SONNY! NO MATTER HOW MUCH MONEY YOU MIGHT MAKE, IT WON'T MEAN SHUCKS UNLESS YOU MAKE IT SQUARE-- THE WAY I PLAN TO!
ADIOS, MR. WHATEVER-YOUR-NAME-IS!
@#%@
BUT SCROOGE McDUCK NEVER MADE HIS FORTUNE IN THE AFRICAN GOLDFIELDS, EVEN THOUGH HE TOILED THERE FOR THREE LONG YEARS.
THE TRANSVAAL ORE WAS TOO LOW-GRADE FOR A LONE MINER TO EXPLOIT--TONS OF IT NEEDED TO BE MINED AND PROCESSED TO EXTRACT A SINGLE OUNCE OF GOLD!
sigh!
?
AS A RESULT, ONLY RANDLORDS ALREADY WEALTHY FROM THE KIMBERLEY DIAMOND MINE COULD AFFORD THE WORKERS AND EQUIPMENT NECESSARY TO MAKE A PROFIT MINING GOLD ON THE RAND.
KAFFIR DE GAFFIR GOLD MINE
FINALLY IT CAME TIME FOR YOUNG SCROOGE TO PACK UP AND MOVE ON, TO AGAIN SET OUT ON A QUEST FOR THE END OF HIS RAINBOW.
HE FELT HE WAS DESTINED TO BE A GREAT MAN, AND LIKE OTHER GREAT MEN, HE HAD ALREADY STARTED ACQUIRING HIS SHARE OF ENEMIES ON THE PATH TO THAT DESTINY...
176-716
...THE WHISKERVILLES OF SCOTLAND...
...THE BEAGLE BOYS OF THE MISSISSIPPI...
...THE McVIPERS OF THE WILD WEST...
...AND ONE PARTICULARLY NASTY AFRIKANER NAMED FLINTHEART GLOMGOLD!

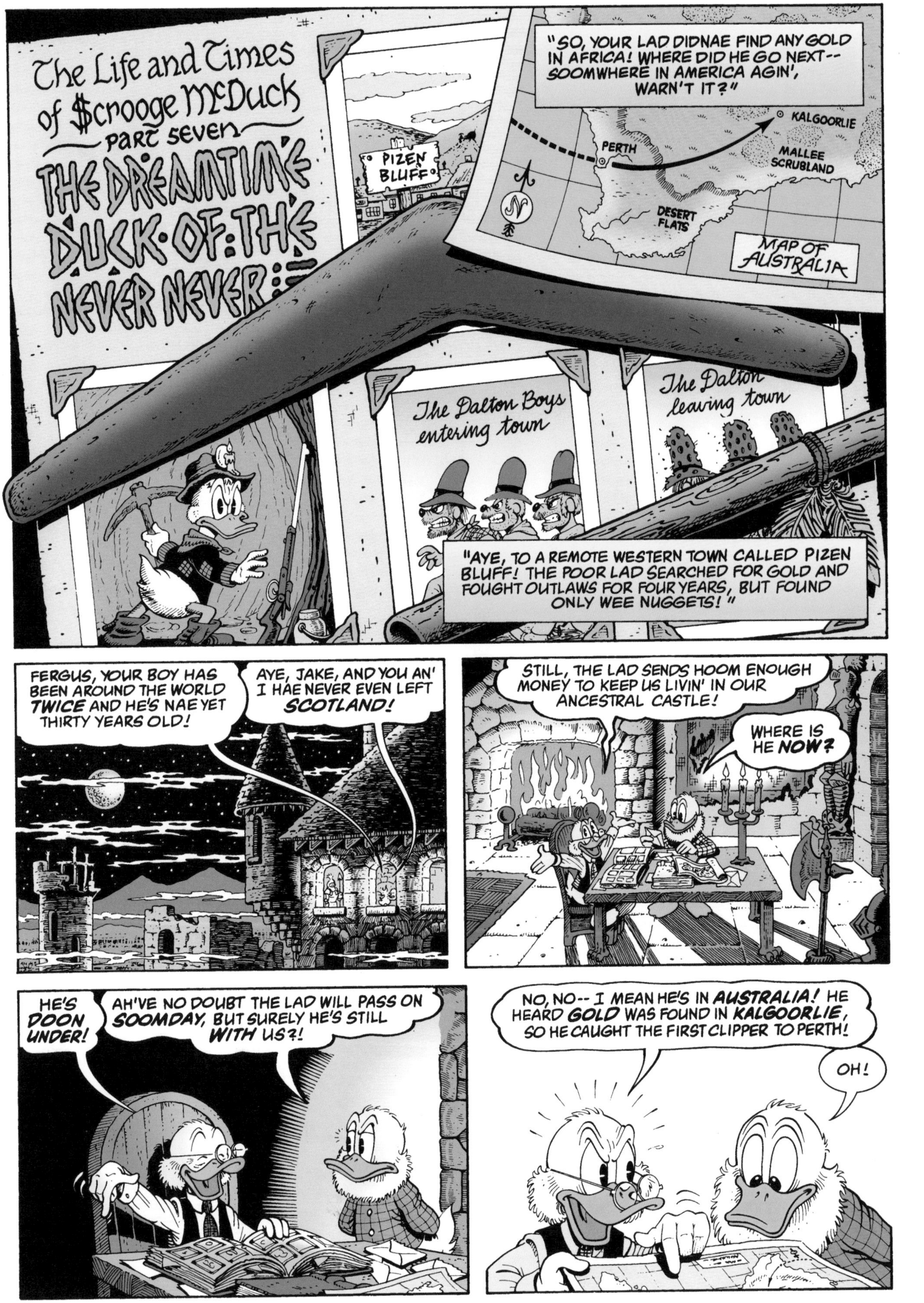

The Life and Times of $crooge McDuck
PART SEVEN
THE DREAMTIME DUCK OF THE NEVER NEVER
"SO, YOUR LAD DIDNAE FIND ANY GOLD IN AFRICA! WHERE DID HE GO NEXT-- SOOMWHERE IN AMERICA AGIN', WARN'T IT?"
KALGOORLIE
PERTH
MALLEE SCRUBLAND
DESERT FLATS
MAP OF AUSTRALIA
PIZEN BLUFF
The Dalton Boys entering town
The Dalton leaving town
"AYE, TO A REMOTE WESTERN TOWN CALLED PIZEN BLUFF! THE POOR LAD SEARCHED FOR GOLD AND FOUGHT OUTLAWS FOR FOUR YEARS, BUT FOUND ONLY WEE NUGGETS!"
FERGUS, YOUR BOY HAS BEEN AROUND THE WORLD TWICE AND HE'S NAE YET THIRTY YEARS OLD!
AYE, JAKE, AND YOU AN' I HAE NEVER EVEN LEFT SCOTLAND!
STILL, THE LAD SENDS HOOM ENOUGH MONEY TO KEEP US LIVIN' IN OUR ANCESTRAL CASTLE!
WHERE IS HE NOW?
HE'S DOON UNDER!
AH'VE NO DOUBT THE LAD WILL PASS ON SOOMDAY, BUT SURELY HE'S STILL WITH US?!
NO, NO-- I MEAN HE'S IN AUSTRALIA! HE HEARD GOLD WAS FOUND IN KALGOORLIE, SO HE CAUGHT THE FIRST CLIPPER TO PERTH!
OH!

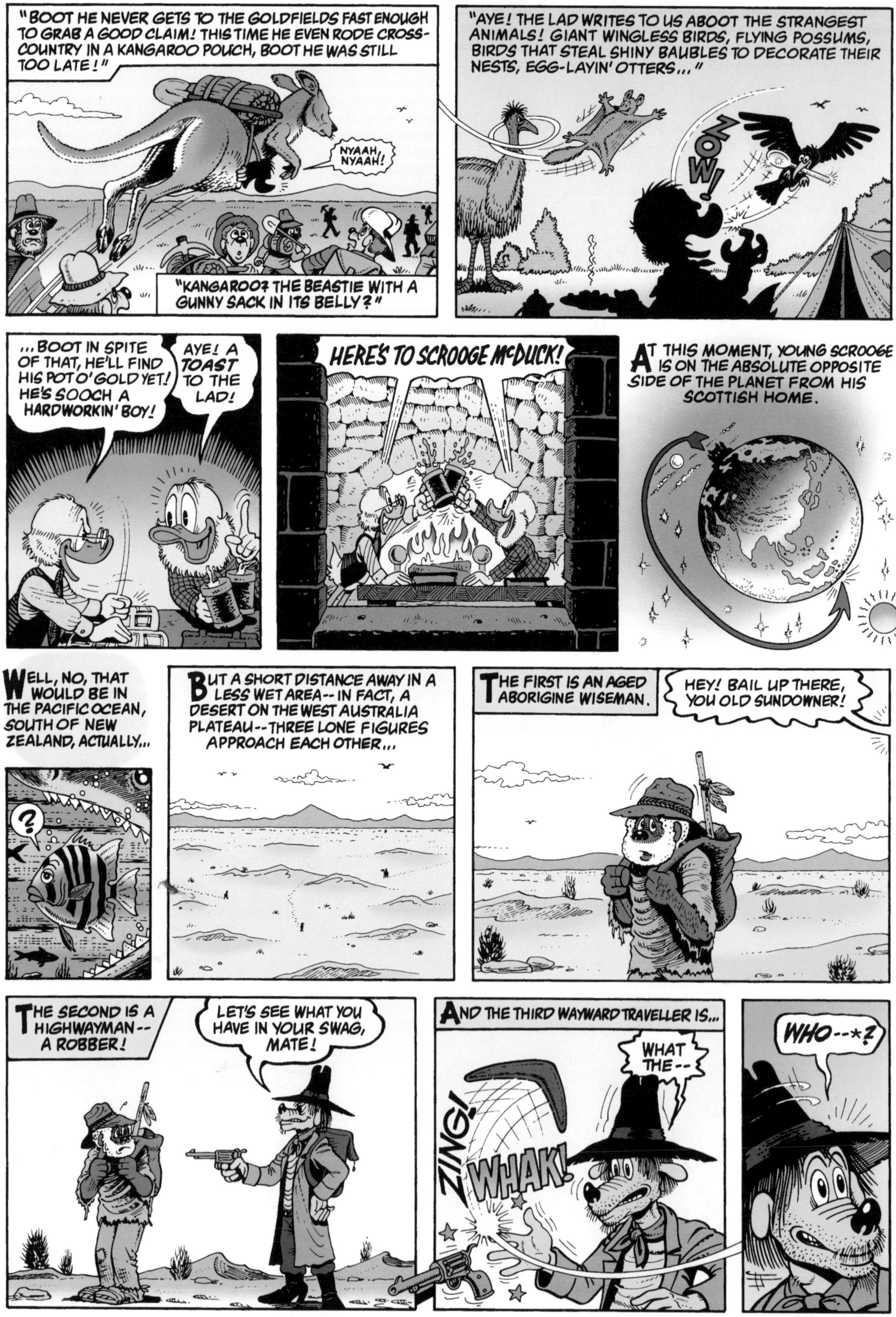
"BOOT HE NEVER GETS TO THE GOLDFIELDS FAST ENOUGH TO GRAB A GOOD CLAIM! THIS TIME HE EVEN RODE CROSS-COUNTRY IN A KANGAROO POUCH, BOOT HE WAS STILL TOO LATE!"
NYAAH, NYAAH!
"KANGAROO? THE BEASTIE WITH A GUNNY SACK IN ITS BELLY?"
"AYE! THE LAD WRITES TO US ABOOT THE STRANGEST ANIMALS! GIANT WINGLESS BIRDS, FLYING POSSUMS, BIRDS THAT STEAL SHINY BAUBLES TO DECORATE THEIR NESTS, EGG-LAYIN' OTTERS..."
ZOW!
...BOOT IN SPITE OF THAT, HE'LL FIND HIS POT O' GOLD YET! HE'S SOOCH A HARDWORKIN' BOY!
AYE! A TOAST TO THE LAD!
HERE'S TO SCROOGE McDUCK!
AT THIS MOMENT, YOUNG SCROOGE IS ON THE ABSOLUTE OPPOSITE SIDE OF THE PLANET FROM HIS SCOTTISH HOME.
WELL, NO, THAT WOULD BE IN THE PACIFIC OCEAN, SOUTH OF NEW ZEALAND, ACTUALLY...
?
BUT A SHORT DISTANCE AWAY IN A LESS WET AREA-- IN FACT, A DESERT ON THE WEST AUSTRALIA PLATEAU--THREE LONE FIGURES APPROACH EACH OTHER...
THE FIRST IS AN AGED ABORIGINE WISEMAN.
HEY! BAIL UP THERE, YOU OLD SUNDOWNER!
THE SECOND IS A HIGHWAYMAN-- A ROBBER!
LET'S SEE WHAT YOU HAVE IN YOUR SWAG, MATE!
AND THE THIRD WAYWARD TRAVELLER IS...
WHAT THE--
ZING!
WHAK!
WHO--*?

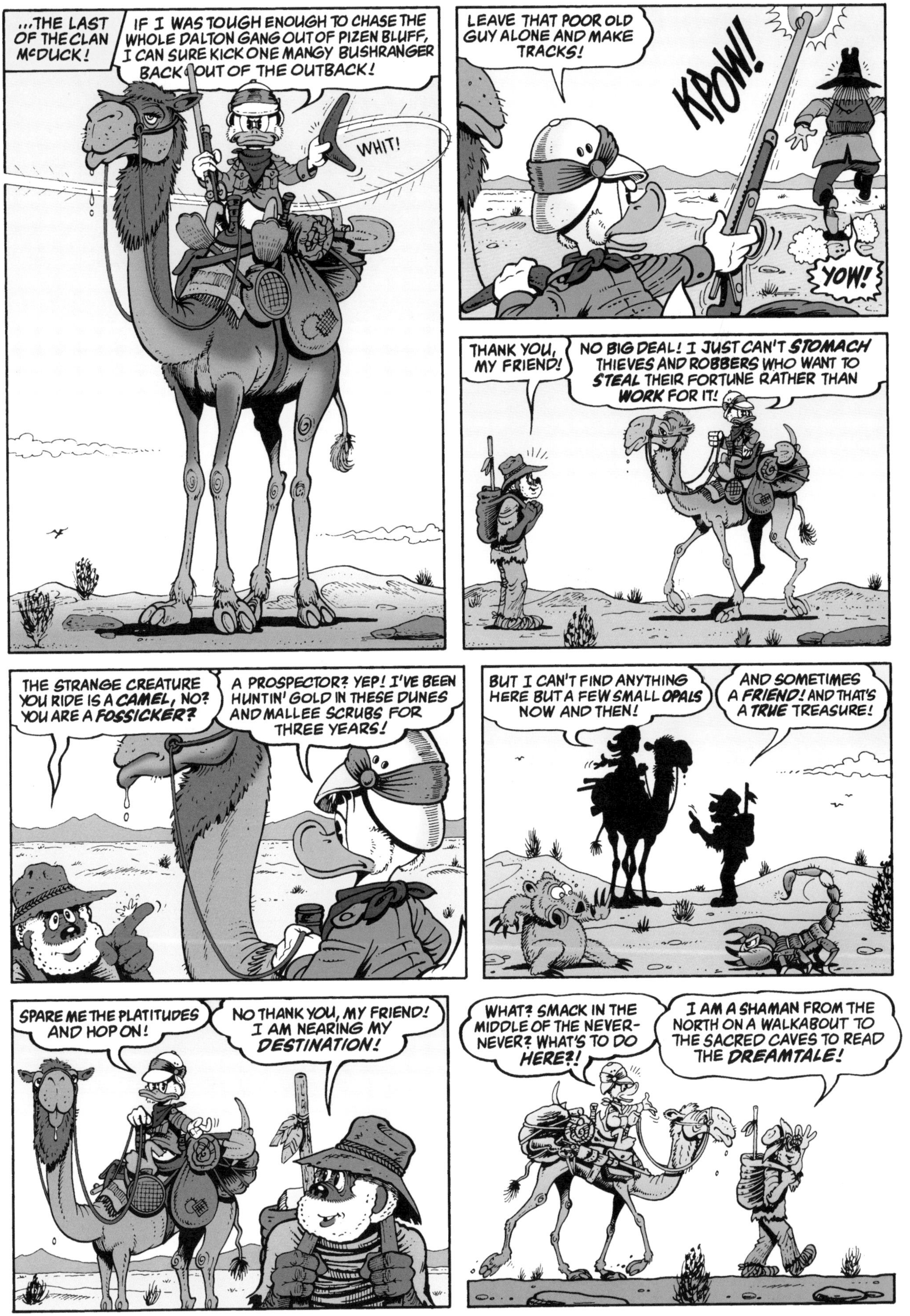
...THE LAST OF THE CLAN McDUCK!
IF I WAS TOUGH ENOUGH TO CHASE THE WHOLE DALTON GANG OUT OF PIZEN BLUFF, I CAN SURE KICK ONE MANGY BUSHRANGER BACK OUT OF THE OUTBACK!
WHIT!
LEAVE THAT POOR OLD GUY ALONE AND MAKE TRACKS!
KPOW!
YOW!
THANK YOU, MY FRIEND!
NO BIG DEAL! I JUST CAN'T STOMACH THIEVES AND ROBBERS WHO WANT TO STEAL THEIR FORTUNE RATHER THAN WORK FOR IT!
THE STRANGE CREATURE YOU RIDE IS A CAMEL, NO? YOU ARE A FOSSICKER?
A PROSPECTOR? YEP! I'VE BEEN HUNTIN' GOLD IN THESE DUNES AND MALLEE SCRUBS FOR THREE YEARS!
BUT I CAN'T FIND ANYTHING HERE BUT A FEW SMALL OPALS NOW AND THEN!
AND SOMETIMES A FRIEND! AND THAT'S A TRUE TREASURE!
SPARE ME THE PLATITUDES AND HOP ON!
NO THANK YOU, MY FRIEND! I AM NEARING MY DESTINATION!
WHAT? SMACK IN THE MIDDLE OF THE NEVER-NEVER? WHAT'S TO DO HERE?!
I AM A SHAMAN FROM THE NORTH ON A WALKABOUT TO THE SACRED CAVES TO READ THE DREAMTALE!

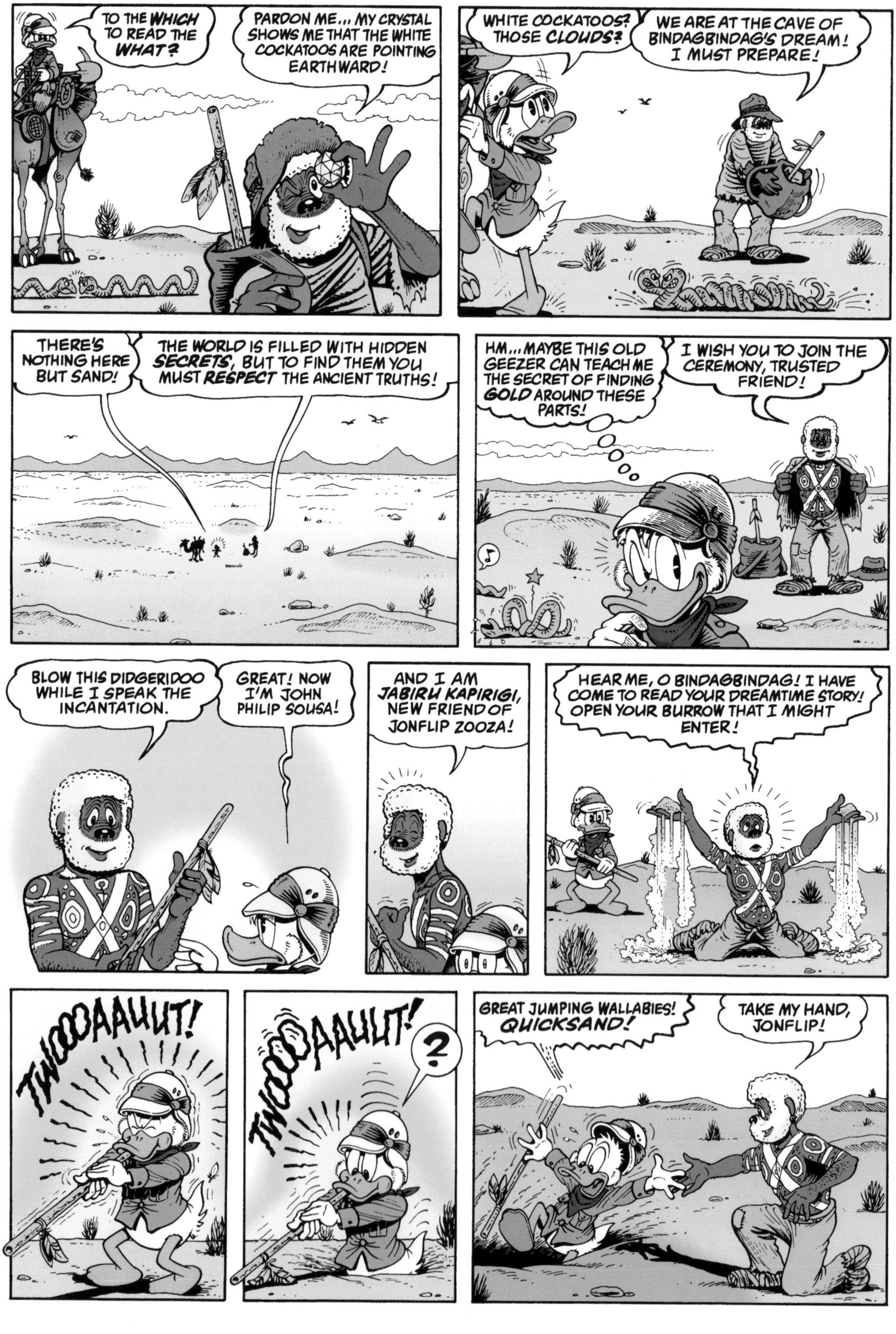
TO THE WHICH TO READ THE WHAT?
PARDON ME... MY CRYSTAL SHOWS ME THAT THE WHITE COCKATOOS ARE POINTING EARTHWARD!
WHITE COCKATOOS? THOSE CLOUDS?
WE ARE AT THE CAVE OF BINDAGBINDAG'S DREAM! I MUST PREPARE!
THERE'S NOTHING HERE BUT SAND!
THE WORLD IS FILLED WITH HIDDEN SECRETS, BUT TO FIND THEM YOU MUST RESPECT THE ANCIENT TRUTHS!
HM... MAYBE THIS OLD GEEZER CAN TEACH ME THE SECRET OF FINDING GOLD AROUND THESE PARTS!
I WISH YOU TO JOIN THE CEREMONY, TRUSTED FRIEND!
BLOW THIS DIDGERIDOO WHILE I SPEAK THE INCANTATION.
GREAT! NOW I'M JOHN PHILIP SOUSA!
AND I AM JABIRU KAPIRIGI, NEW FRIEND OF JONFLIP ZOOZA!
HEAR ME, O BINDAGBINDAG! I HAVE COME TO READ YOUR DREAMTIME STORY! OPEN YOUR BURROW THAT I MIGHT ENTER!
TWOOOAAUUT!
TWOOOAAUUT!
?
GREAT JUMPING WALLABIES! QUICKSAND!
TAKE MY HAND, JONFLIP!

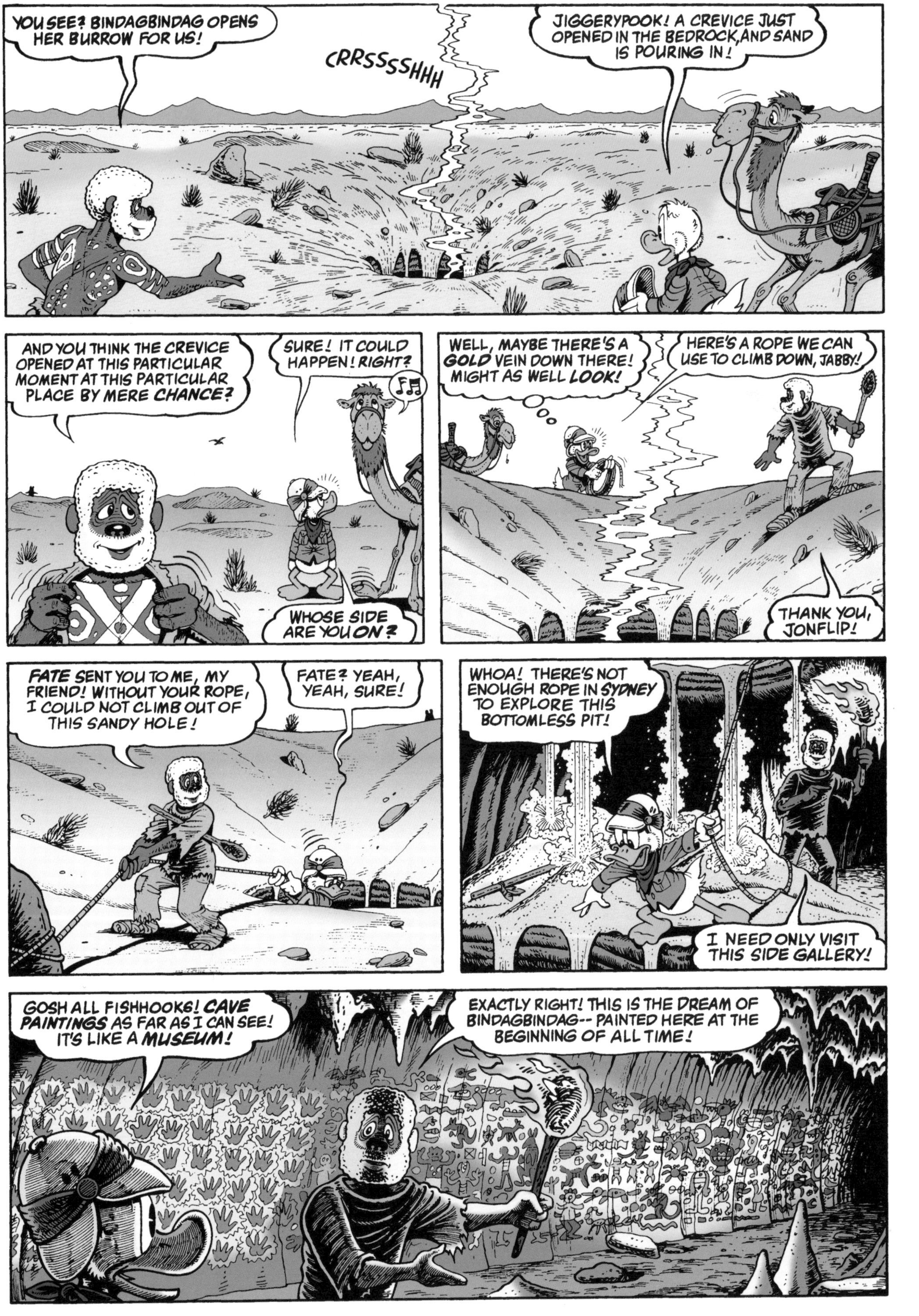
YOU SEE? BINDAGBINDAG OPENS HER BURROW FOR US!
CRRSSSSHHH
JIGGERYPOOK! A CREVICE JUST OPENED IN THE BEDROCK, AND SAND IS POURING IN!
AND YOU THINK THE CREVICE OPENED AT THIS PARTICULAR MOMENT AT THIS PARTICULAR PLACE BY MERE CHANCE?
SURE! IT COULD HAPPEN! RIGHT?
WHOSE SIDE ARE YOU ON?
WELL, MAYBE THERE'S A GOLD VEIN DOWN THERE! MIGHT AS WELL LOOK!
HERE'S A ROPE WE CAN USE TO CLIMB DOWN, JABBY!
THANK YOU, JONFLIP!
FATE SENT YOU TO ME, MY FRIEND! WITHOUT YOUR ROPE, I COULD NOT CLIMB OUT OF THIS SANDY HOLE!
FATE? YEAH, YEAH, SURE!
WHOA! THERE'S NOT ENOUGH ROPE IN SYDNEY TO EXPLORE THIS BOTTOMLESS PIT!
I NEED ONLY VISIT THIS SIDE GALLERY!
GOSH ALL FISHHOOKS! CAVE PAINTINGS AS FAR AS I CAN SEE! IT'S LIKE A MUSEUM!
EXACTLY RIGHT! THIS IS THE DREAM OF BINDAGBINDAG-- PAINTED HERE AT THE BEGINNING OF ALL TIME!

WHAT'S WITH ALL THE **HANDPRINTS?**

IT IS THE **LOG!** I MUST SIGN IT AS HAVE MY ANCESTORS ON EACH TRIP TO THIS CAVE!

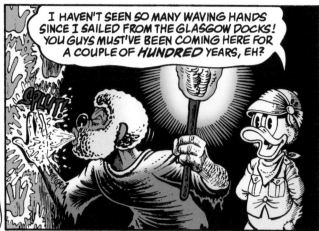

I HAVEN'T SEEN SO MANY WAVING HANDS SINCE I SAILED FROM THE GLASGOW DOCKS! YOU GUYS MUST'VE BEEN COMING HERE FOR A COUPLE OF **HUNDRED** YEARS, EH?

SPLIT!

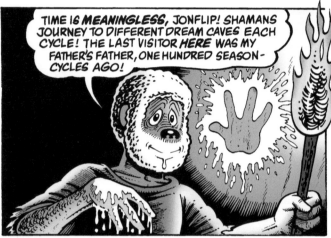

TIME IS **MEANINGLESS**, JONFLIP! SHAMANS JOURNEY TO DIFFERENT DREAM CAVES EACH CYCLE! THE LAST VISITOR **HERE** WAS MY FATHER'S FATHER, ONE HUNDRED SEASON-CYCLES AGO!

⸘GLEEP!⸘ SEVERAL HUNDRED VISITS--THAT'S OVER **20,000** YEARS!

DREAMTIME WAS NOT **LAST WEEK**, JONFLIP!

⸘shudder!⸘ THESE PAINTINGS WERE MADE MORE THAN TWO HUNDRED **CENTURIES** AGO?!

THAT DOES NOT CHANGE THEIR **TRUTH**, MY FRIEND! SHALL I **READ** FOR YOU?

HM... THAT'LL GIVE ME A CHANCE TO CHECK FOR **ORE** VEINS!

READ AWAY, JABBY!

HERE IS THE DREAM I AM TO READ ON THIS VISIT!

IT TELLS OF KAKADU THE DINGO. HE STEALS THE CROCODILE **EGG** FROM ITS NEST!

BUT THE GREAT PLATYPUS **CHASES** KAKADU...

...AND IRRIA, THE BLACK COCKATOO, SENDS BUNYIP, THE WATER MONSTER, AFTER THE EGG THIEF!

BUNYIP **CHASES** THE DINGO...

...AND THE GREAT PLATYPUS **FINDS** THE SACRED EGG, BUT **LOSES** HIS FIRSTBORN IN THE FIGHT!

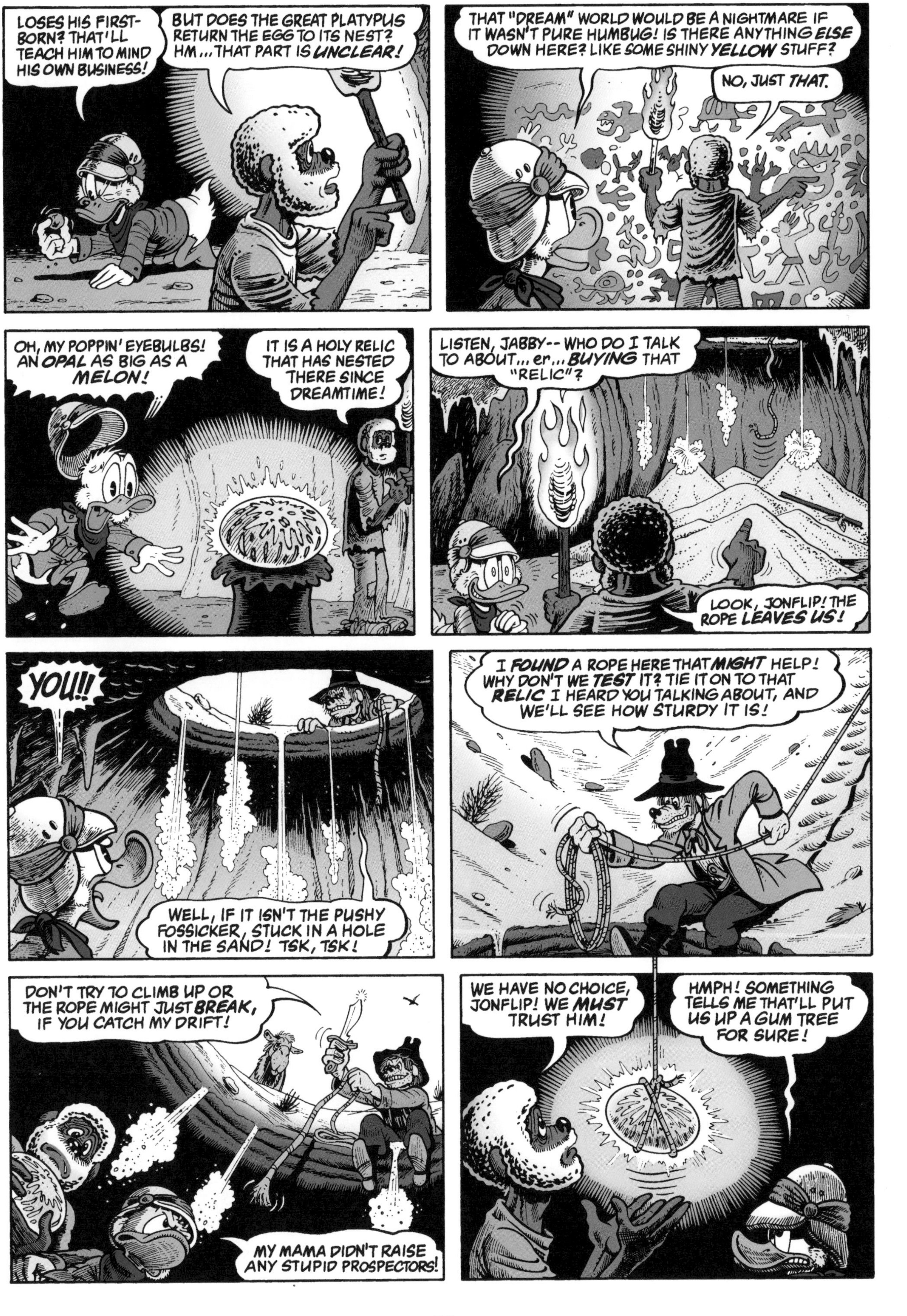
LOSES HIS FIRST-BORN? THAT'LL TEACH HIM TO MIND HIS OWN BUSINESS!
BUT DOES THE GREAT PLATYPUS RETURN THE EGG TO ITS NEST? HM... THAT PART IS UNCLEAR!
THAT "DREAM" WORLD WOULD BE A NIGHTMARE IF IT WASN'T PURE HUMBUG! IS THERE ANYTHING ELSE DOWN HERE? LIKE SOME SHINY YELLOW STUFF?
NO, JUST THAT.
OH, MY POPPIN' EYEBULBS! AN OPAL AS BIG AS A MELON!
IT IS A HOLY RELIC THAT HAS NESTED THERE SINCE DREAMTIME!
LISTEN, JABBY-- WHO DO I TALK TO ABOUT... er... BUYING THAT "RELIC"?
LOOK, JONFLIP! THE ROPE LEAVES US!
YOU!!
WELL, IF IT ISN'T THE PUSHY FOSSICKER, STUCK IN A HOLE IN THE SAND! TSK, TSK!
I FOUND A ROPE HERE THAT MIGHT HELP! WHY DON'T WE TEST IT? TIE IT ON TO THAT RELIC I HEARD YOU TALKING ABOUT, AND WE'LL SEE HOW STURDY IT IS!
DON'T TRY TO CLIMB UP OR THE ROPE MIGHT JUST BREAK, IF YOU CATCH MY DRIFT!
MY MAMA DIDN'T RAISE ANY STUPID PROSPECTORS!
WE HAVE NO CHOICE, JONFLIP! WE MUST TRUST HIM!
HMPH! SOMETHING TELLS ME THAT'LL PUT US UP A GUM TREE FOR SURE!

GOOD ON YA', MATE! HERE'S YOUR ROPE!

YOU SEE, JONFLIP! HE *IS* A MAN OF HONOR!

OOPS! IT SLIPPED!

HIS MOMMA DIDN'T RAISE ANY *STUPID* CHICKEN-HEARTED SKUNKS!

COME BACK HERE, YOU #%*@!!!

NO WORRIES! I'LL GO BRING BACK *MORE* ROPE! DON'T GO AWAY NOW! HA HA HA HA!

THUD!

WAIT, MY FRIEND! WE WILL TOSS YOU THE END OF *THIS* ROPE!

SKIP IT, JABBY! SKIP IT!

DO NOT DESPAIR, JONFLIP! THIS MUST ALL BE PART OF OUR DREAM DESTINY!

NOT *MINE*, IT'S NOT! BESIDES, I'M *THINKING*!

AND I THINK I HAVE AN *IDEA*! WHERE'S YOUR DIDGERIDOO? AHA!

GOOD IDEA, JONFLIP! MUSIC IS RESTFUL WHEN YOU'RE UP A GUM TREE!

WAAOOGH!

?

TIME PASSES ...LOUDLY!

YOU'RE A NICE FELLOW, JONFLIP, BUT I'VE HEARD SWEETER DIDGERI-DOOING!

WAAOOGH!

WAAOOGH!

WAAOOGH?

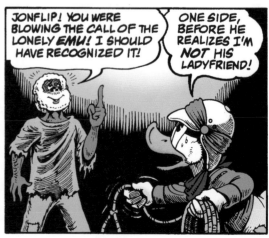

JONFLIP! YOU WERE BLOWING THE CALL OF THE LONELY *EMU*! I SHOULD HAVE RECOGNIZED IT!

ONE SIDE, BEFORE HE REALIZES I'M *NOT* HIS LADYFRIEND!

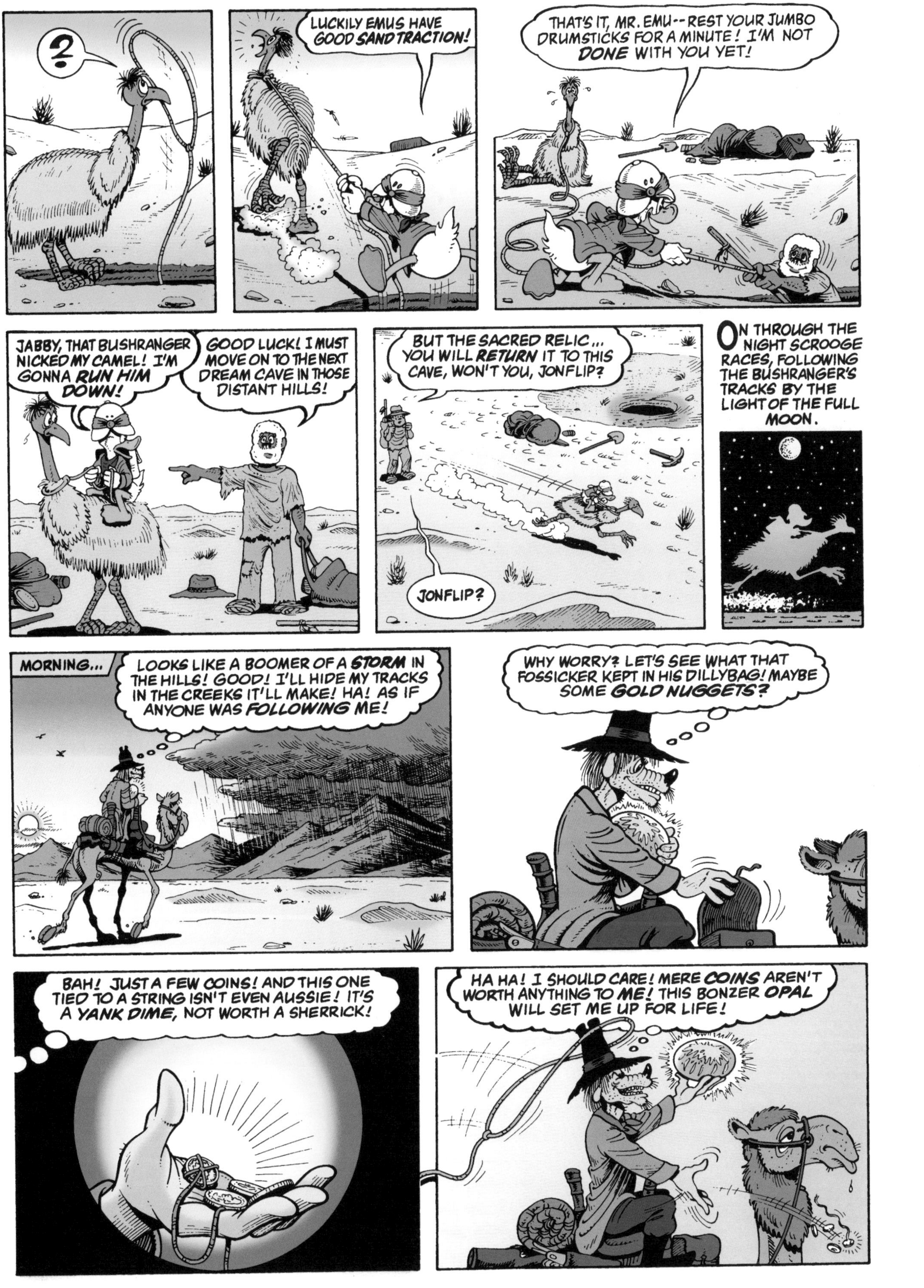
?
LUCKILY EMUS HAVE GOOD SAND TRACTION!
THAT'S IT, MR. EMU--REST YOUR JUMBO DRUMSTICKS FOR A MINUTE! I'M NOT DONE WITH YOU YET!
JABBY, THAT BUSHRANGER NICKED MY CAMEL! I'M GONNA RUN HIM DOWN!
GOOD LUCK! I MUST MOVE ON TO THE NEXT DREAM CAVE IN THOSE DISTANT HILLS!
BUT THE SACRED RELIC... YOU WILL RETURN IT TO THIS CAVE, WON'T YOU, JONFLIP?
JONFLIP?
ON THROUGH THE NIGHT SCROOGE RACES, FOLLOWING THE BUSHRANGER'S TRACKS BY THE LIGHT OF THE FULL MOON.
MORNING...
LOOKS LIKE A BOOMER OF A STORM IN THE HILLS! GOOD! I'LL HIDE MY TRACKS IN THE CREEKS IT'LL MAKE! HA! AS IF ANYONE WAS FOLLOWING ME!
WHY WORRY? LET'S SEE WHAT THAT FOSSICKER KEPT IN HIS DILLYBAG! MAYBE SOME GOLD NUGGETS?
BAH! JUST A FEW COINS! AND THIS ONE TIED TO A STRING ISN'T EVEN AUSSIE! IT'S A YANK DIME, NOT WORTH A SHERRICK!
HA HA! I SHOULD CARE! MERE COINS AREN'T WORTH ANYTHING TO ME! THIS BONZER OPAL WILL SET ME UP FOR LIFE!

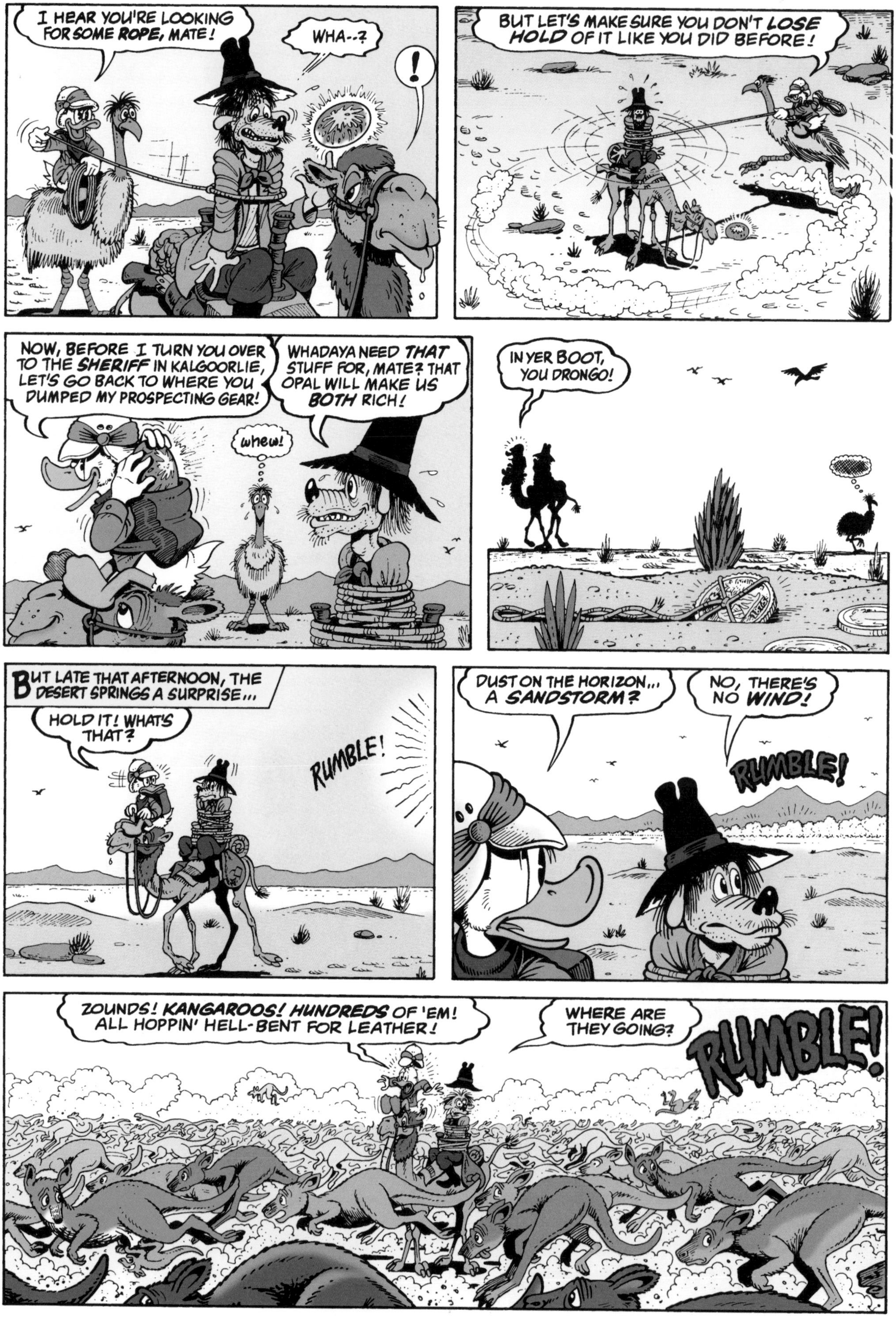

I HEAR YOU'RE LOOKING FOR SOME ROPE, MATE!
WHA--?
!
BUT LET'S MAKE SURE YOU DON'T LOSE HOLD OF IT LIKE YOU DID BEFORE!
NOW, BEFORE I TURN YOU OVER TO THE SHERIFF IN KALGOORLIE, LET'S GO BACK TO WHERE YOU DUMPED MY PROSPECTING GEAR!
WHADAYA NEED THAT STUFF FOR, MATE? THAT OPAL WILL MAKE US BOTH RICH!
whew!
IN YER BOOT, YOU DRONGO!
BUT LATE THAT AFTERNOON, THE DESERT SPRINGS A SURPRISE...
HOLD IT! WHAT'S THAT?
RUMBLE!
DUST ON THE HORIZON... A SANDSTORM?
NO, THERE'S NO WIND!
RUMBLE!
ZOUNDS! KANGAROOS! HUNDREDS OF 'EM! ALL HOPPIN' HELL-BENT FOR LEATHER!
WHERE ARE THEY GOING?
RUMBLE!

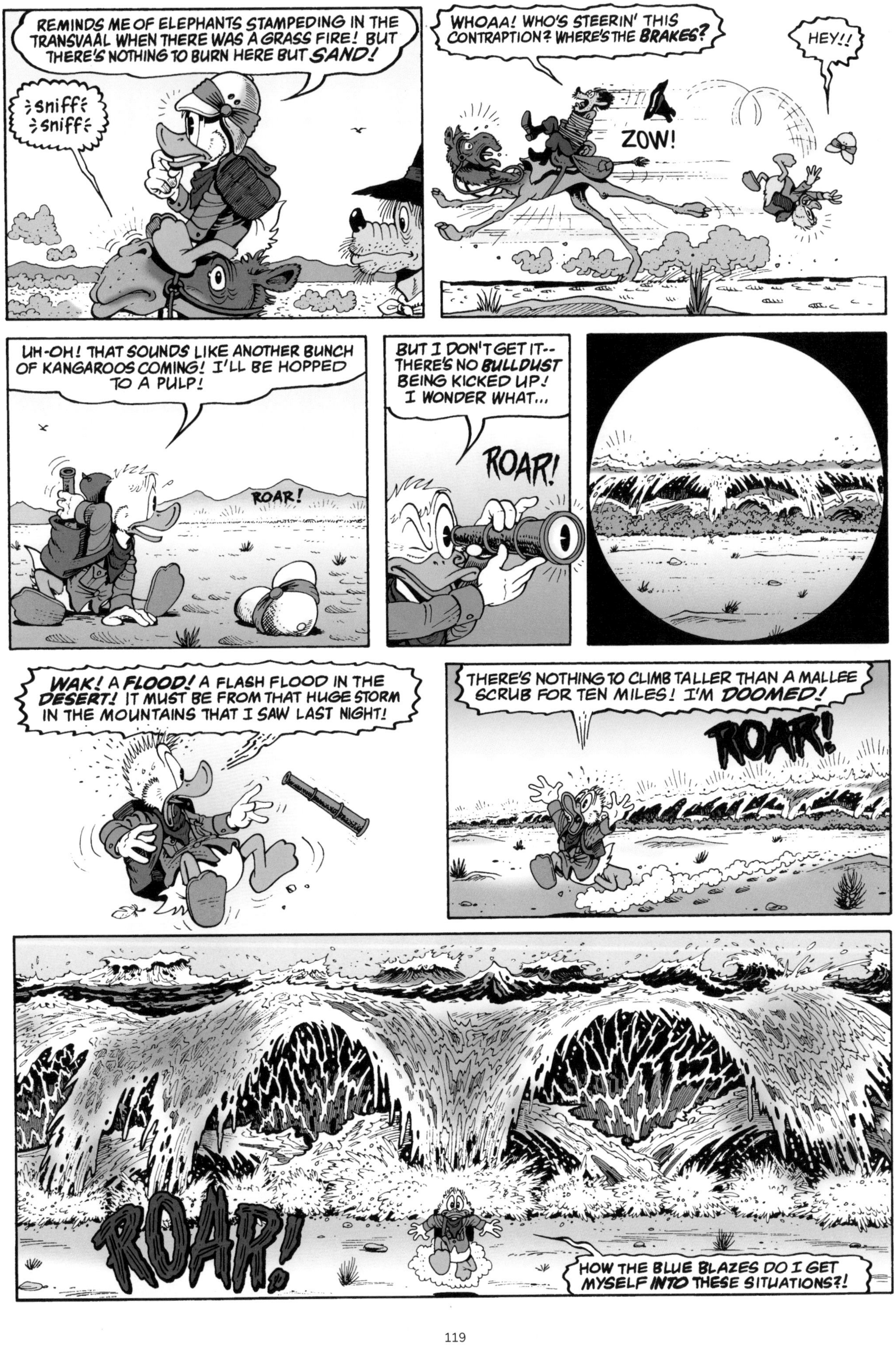
REMINDS ME OF ELEPHANTS STAMPEDING IN THE TRANSVAAL WHEN THERE WAS A GRASS FIRE! BUT THERE'S NOTHING TO BURN HERE BUT SAND!
sniff sniff
WHOAA! WHO'S STEERIN' THIS CONTRAPTION? WHERE'S THE BRAKES?
HEY!!
ZOW!
UH-OH! THAT SOUNDS LIKE ANOTHER BUNCH OF KANGAROOS COMING! I'LL BE HOPPED TO A PULP!
ROAR!
BUT I DON'T GET IT-- THERE'S NO BULLDUST BEING KICKED UP! I WONDER WHAT...
ROAR!
WAK! A FLOOD! A FLASH FLOOD IN THE DESERT! IT MUST BE FROM THAT HUGE STORM IN THE MOUNTAINS THAT I SAW LAST NIGHT!
THERE'S NOTHING TO CLIMB TALLER THAN A MALLEE SCRUB FOR TEN MILES! I'M DOOMED!
ROAR!
ROAR!
HOW THE BLUE BLAZES DO I GET MYSELF INTO THESE SITUATIONS?!

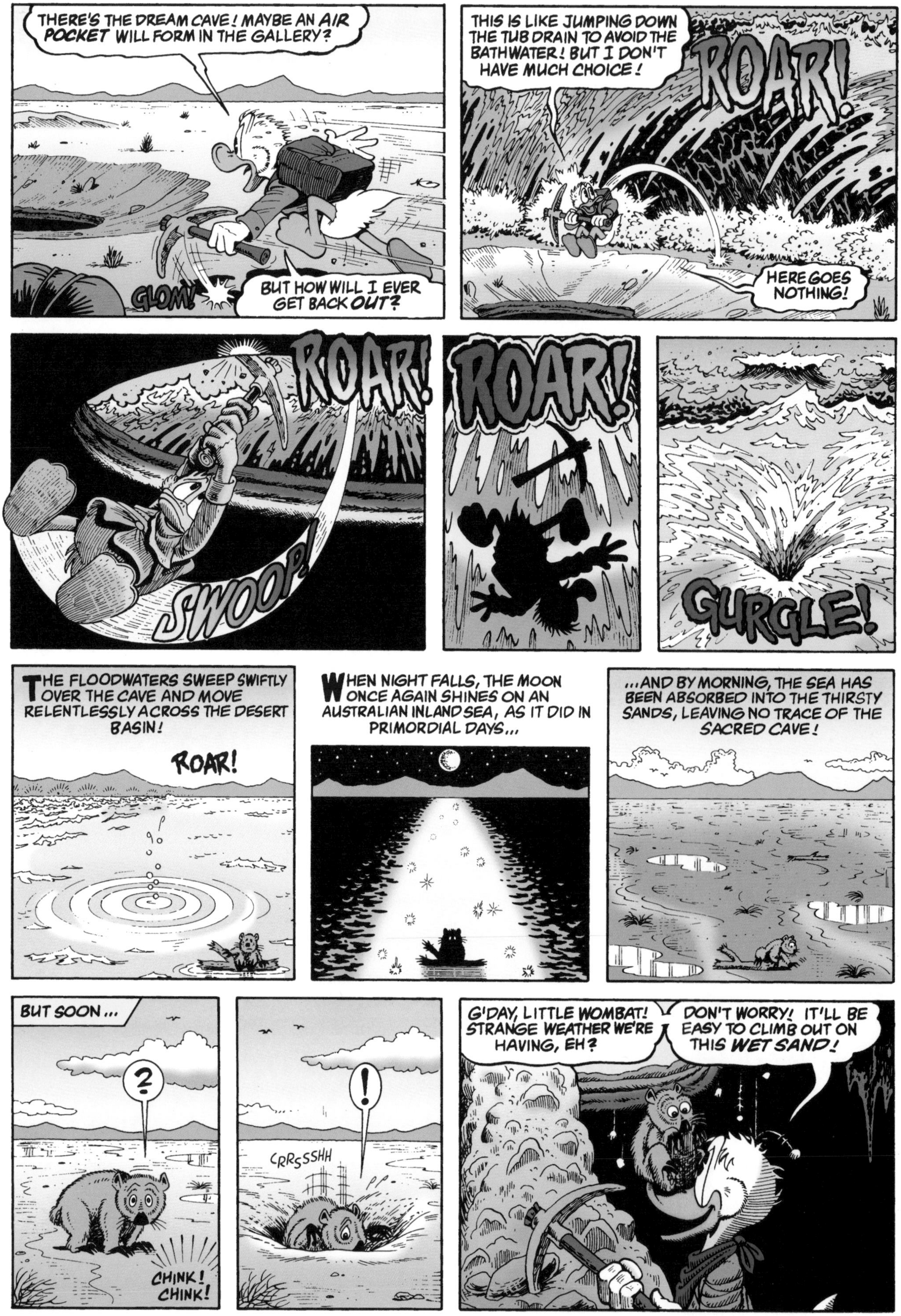

THERE'S THE DREAM CAVE! MAYBE AN AIR POCKET WILL FORM IN THE GALLERY?
GLOM!
BUT HOW WILL I EVER GET BACK OUT?
THIS IS LIKE JUMPING DOWN THE TUB DRAIN TO AVOID THE BATHWATER! BUT I DON'T HAVE MUCH CHOICE!
ROAR!
HERE GOES NOTHING!
ROAR!
SWOOP!
ROAR!
GURGLE!
THE FLOODWATERS SWEEP SWIFTLY OVER THE CAVE AND MOVE RELENTLESSLY ACROSS THE DESERT BASIN!
ROAR!
WHEN NIGHT FALLS, THE MOON ONCE AGAIN SHINES ON AN AUSTRALIAN INLAND SEA, AS IT DID IN PRIMORDIAL DAYS...
...AND BY MORNING, THE SEA HAS BEEN ABSORBED INTO THE THIRSTY SANDS, LEAVING NO TRACE OF THE SACRED CAVE!
BUT SOON...
?
CHINK! CHINK!
!
CRRSSSHH
G'DAY, LITTLE WOMBAT! STRANGE WEATHER WE'RE HAVING, EH?
DON'T WORRY! IT'LL BE EASY TO CLIMB OUT ON THIS WET SAND!

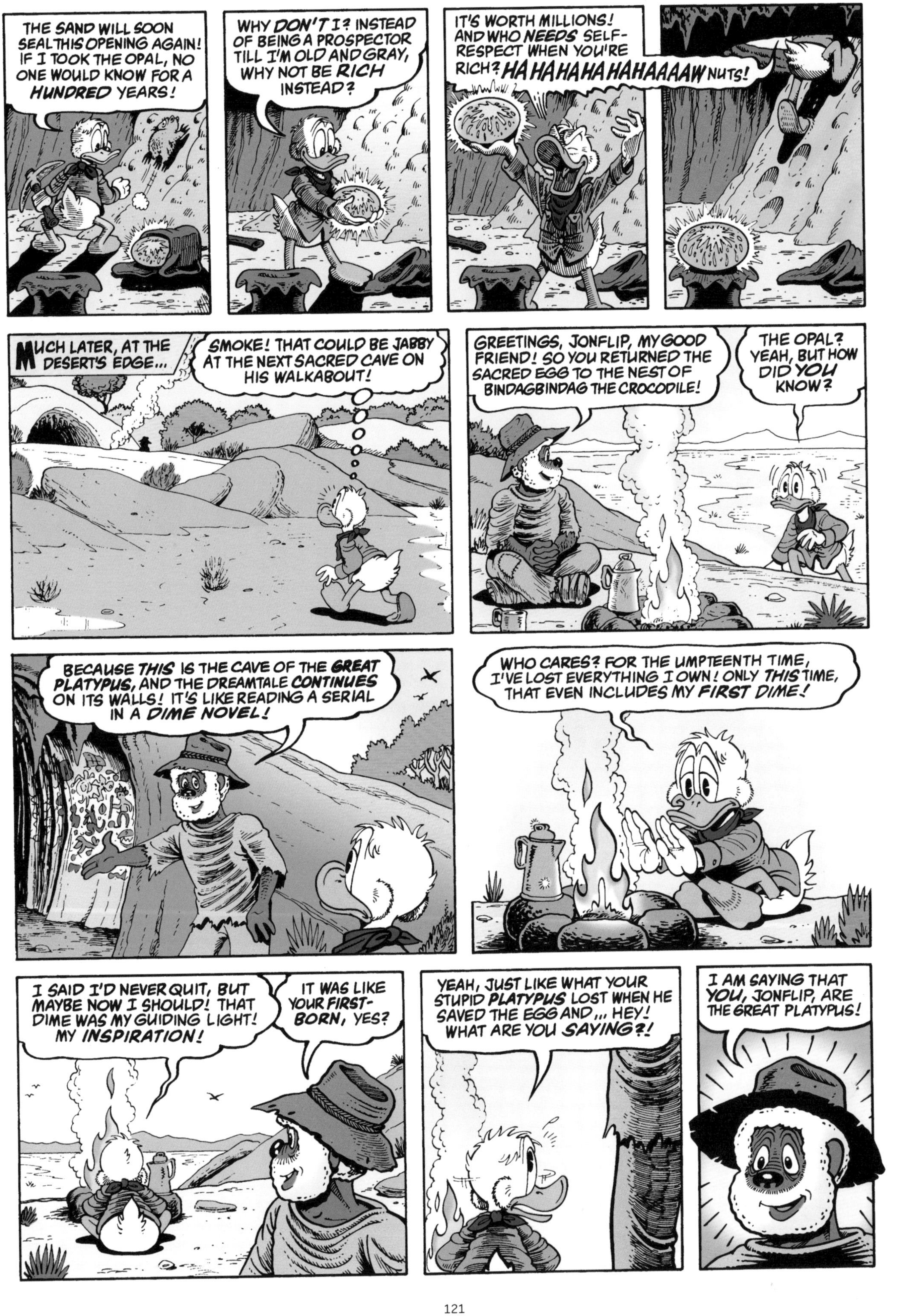
THE SAND WILL SOON SEAL THIS OPENING AGAIN! IF I TOOK THE OPAL, NO ONE WOULD KNOW FOR A HUNDRED YEARS!
WHY DON'T I? INSTEAD OF BEING A PROSPECTOR TILL I'M OLD AND GRAY, WHY NOT BE RICH INSTEAD?
IT'S WORTH MILLIONS! AND WHO NEEDS SELF-RESPECT WHEN YOU'RE RICH? HA HA HA HA HA HAHAAAAW NUTS!
MUCH LATER, AT THE DESERT'S EDGE...
SMOKE! THAT COULD BE JABBY AT THE NEXT SACRED CAVE ON HIS WALKABOUT!
GREETINGS, JONFLIP, MY GOOD FRIEND! SO YOU RETURNED THE SACRED EGG TO THE NEST OF BINDAGBINDAG THE CROCODILE!
THE OPAL? YEAH, BUT HOW DID YOU KNOW?
BECAUSE THIS IS THE CAVE OF THE GREAT PLATYPUS, AND THE DREAMTALE CONTINUES ON ITS WALLS! IT'S LIKE READING A SERIAL IN A DIME NOVEL!
WHO CARES? FOR THE UMPTEENTH TIME, I'VE LOST EVERYTHING I OWN! ONLY THIS TIME, THAT EVEN INCLUDES MY FIRST DIME!
I SAID I'D NEVER QUIT, BUT MAYBE NOW I SHOULD! THAT DIME WAS MY GUIDING LIGHT! MY INSPIRATION!
IT WAS LIKE YOUR FIRST-BORN, YES?
YEAH, JUST LIKE WHAT YOUR STUPID PLATYPUS LOST WHEN HE SAVED THE EGG AND... HEY! WHAT ARE YOU SAYING?!
I AM SAYING THAT YOU, JONFLIP, ARE THE GREAT PLATYPUS!

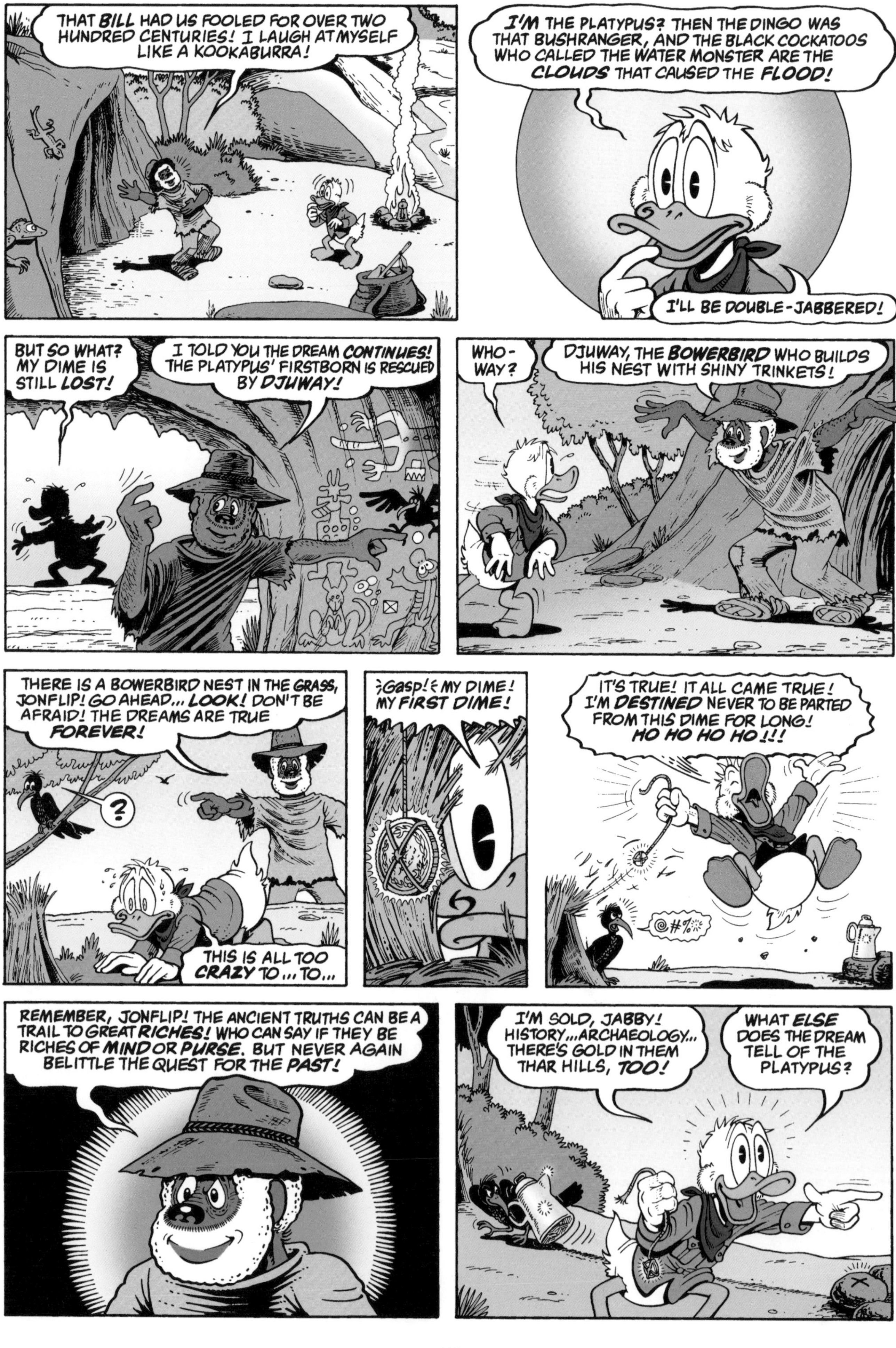
THAT BILL HAD US FOOLED FOR OVER TWO HUNDRED CENTURIES! I LAUGH AT MYSELF LIKE A KOOKABURRA!
I'M THE PLATYPUS? THEN THE DINGO WAS THAT BUSHRANGER, AND THE BLACK COCKATOOS WHO CALLED THE WATER MONSTER ARE THE CLOUDS THAT CAUSED THE FLOOD!
I'LL BE DOUBLE-JABBERED!
BUT SO WHAT? MY DIME IS STILL LOST!
I TOLD YOU THE DREAM CONTINUES! THE PLATYPUS' FIRSTBORN IS RESCUED BY DJUWAY!
WHO-WAY?
DJUWAY, THE BOWERBIRD WHO BUILDS HIS NEST WITH SHINY TRINKETS!
THERE IS A BOWERBIRD NEST IN THE GRASS, JONFLIP! GO AHEAD... LOOK! DON'T BE AFRAID! THE DREAMS ARE TRUE FOREVER!
?
THIS IS ALL TOO CRAZY TO... TO...
Gasp! MY DIME! MY FIRST DIME!
IT'S TRUE! IT ALL CAME TRUE! I'M DESTINED NEVER TO BE PARTED FROM THIS DIME FOR LONG! HO HO HO HO!!!
@#%
REMEMBER, JONFLIP! THE ANCIENT TRUTHS CAN BE A TRAIL TO GREAT RICHES! WHO CAN SAY IF THEY BE RICHES OF MIND OR PURSE. BUT NEVER AGAIN BELITTLE THE QUEST FOR THE PAST!
I'M SOLD, JABBY! HISTORY... ARCHAEOLOGY... THERE'S GOLD IN THEM THAR HILLS, TOO!
WHAT ELSE DOES THE DREAM TELL OF THE PLATYPUS?

IT SAYS THAT, AS A REWARD FOR HIS NOBLE DEED, THE GREAT PLATYPUS WAS ALLOWED TO SEE HIS DREAM THROUGH THE CRYSTAL EYE -- AND THE LIGHT BECKONED HIM!

A CRYSTAL EYE? LIKE *YOUR* CRYSTAL?

WE SHALL SEE! HOLD THE CRYSTAL NEAR THE PAINTING AND I SHALL CAST SUNLIGHT UPON IT WITH YOUR COIN!

WHAT'S THIS? COLORED LIGHTS? LIKE THE *NORTHERN LIGHTS* I ONCE SAW FROM THE MONTANA ROCKIES? THE AURORA BOREALIS?

IS THE DREAM TELLING ME TO HEAD NORTH OF THE *ROCKY MOUNTAINS?*

PERHAPS THAT IS WHAT YOU ARE TELLING *YOURSELF!* WE MUST EACH READ THE TRUTH OF OUR *OWN* DREAM!

TO ME IT LOOKED LIKE PRETTY *DRAPES!* I THOUGHT PERHAPS YOU SHOULD BECOME AN *INTERIOR* DECORATOR!

MAYBE THIS IS THE CHANCE I'VE BEEN SEARCHING FOR -- TO BE *ON THE SPOT* WHEN SOMETHING HAPPENS!

SO LONG, JABBIE! I'M SAILING BACK TO *AMERICA* AND HEADING *NORTH...*

...*NORTH TO THE YUKON!*

GOOD LUCK TO YOU, JONFLIP! I MUST STAY AND READ THE REST OF THE *DREAMTALE!*

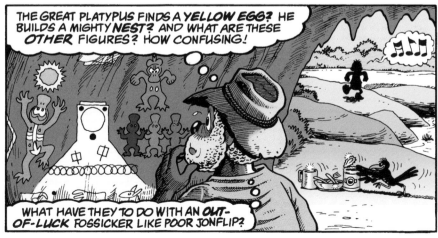

THE GREAT PLATYPUS FINDS A *YELLOW EGG?* HE BUILDS A MIGHTY *NEST?* AND WHAT ARE THESE *OTHER* FIGURES? HOW CONFUSING!

WHAT HAVE THEY TO DO WITH AN *OUT-OF-LUCK* FOSSICKER LIKE POOR JONFLIP?

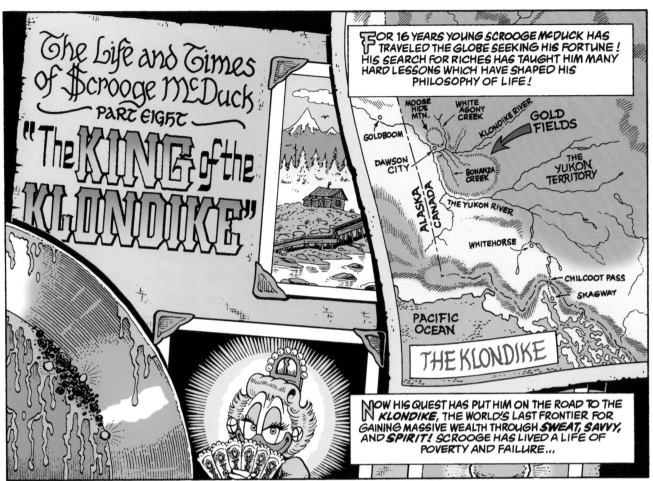

The Life and Times of Scrooge McDuck
PART EIGHT
"The KING of the KLONDIKE"

FOR 16 YEARS YOUNG SCROOGE McDUCK HAS TRAVELED THE GLOBE SEEKING HIS FORTUNE! HIS SEARCH FOR RICHES HAS TAUGHT HIM MANY HARD LESSONS WHICH HAVE SHAPED HIS PHILOSOPHY OF LIFE!

MOOSE HIDE MTN. · WHITE AGONY CREEK · KLONDIKE RIVER · GOLD FIELDS · GOLDBOOM · DAWSON CITY · BONANZA CREEK · THE YUKON TERRITORY · ALASKA · CANADA · THE YUKON RIVER · WHITEHORSE · CHILCOOT PASS · SKAGWAY · PACIFIC OCEAN · THE KLONDIKE

NOW HIS QUEST HAS PUT HIM ON THE ROAD TO THE KLONDIKE, THE WORLD'S LAST FRONTIER FOR GAINING MASSIVE WEALTH THROUGH SWEAT, SAVVY, AND SPIRIT! SCROOGE HAS LIVED A LIFE OF POVERTY AND FAILURE...

...THAT LIFE IS NEARING AN END!

SKAGWAY, ALASKA!

FINALLY -- THE LAND OF THE NORTHERN LIGHTS! I'VE STOKED BOILERS THE WHOLE 7500 MILES FROM PERTH TO GET HERE!

SO THAT'S ALASKA! AND ACROSS THE COASTAL MOUNTAINS, CANADA! TIME TO COLLECT MY BACK PAY AND GET GOING!

THE SOUTHERN CROSS · PERTH

THERE Y'GO, MATE -- $100! BUT I HATES T' LOSE YA! YOU WUZ THE HARDEST WORKER I EVER HAD!

SORRY, CAP'N! I'M NOT A COAL CHUCKER -- I'M A GOLD HUNTER!

AN ARGONAUT, EH? GOOD ON YA! BUT HAVE YOU ARRANGED A RIDE TO SHORE? THE MUD FLAT KEEPS US A GOOD HALF MILE OUT!

NO TIME! I'LL HAFTA IMPROVISE!

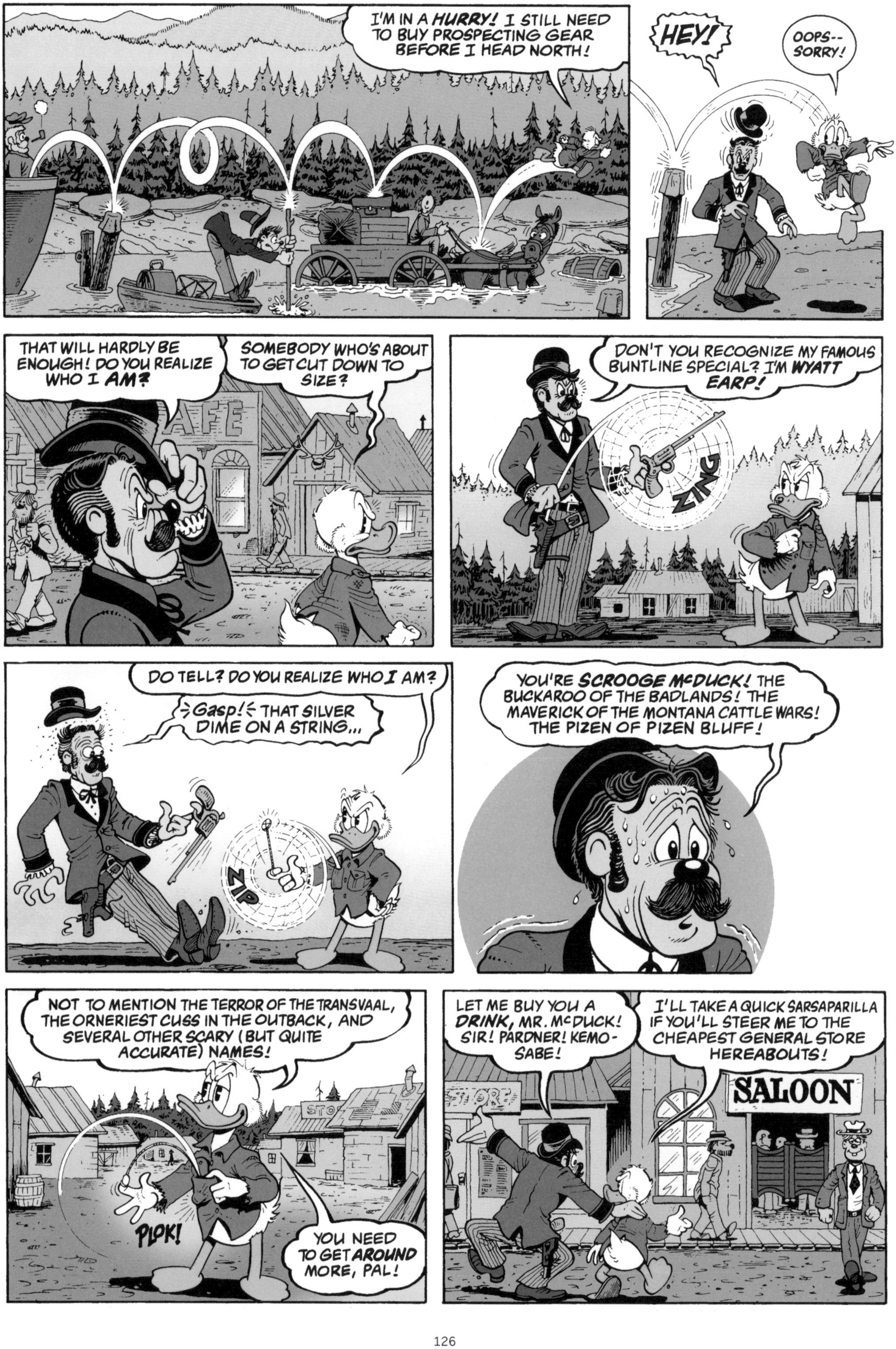
I'M IN A HURRY! I STILL NEED TO BUY PROSPECTING GEAR BEFORE I HEAD NORTH!
HEY!
OOPS-- SORRY!
THAT WILL HARDLY BE ENOUGH! DO YOU REALIZE WHO I AM?
SOMEBODY WHO'S ABOUT TO GET CUT DOWN TO SIZE?
AFE
DON'T YOU RECOGNIZE MY FAMOUS BUNTLINE SPECIAL? I'M WYATT EARP!
ZING
DO TELL? DO YOU REALIZE WHO I AM?
Gasp! THAT SILVER DIME ON A STRING...
ZIP
YOU'RE SCROOGE McDUCK! THE BUCKAROO OF THE BADLANDS! THE MAVERICK OF THE MONTANA CATTLE WARS! THE PIZEN OF PIZEN BLUFF!
NOT TO MENTION THE TERROR OF THE TRANSVAAL, THE ORNERIEST CUSS IN THE OUTBACK, AND SEVERAL OTHER SCARY (BUT QUITE ACCURATE) NAMES!
PLOK!
YOU NEED TO GET AROUND MORE, PAL!
LET ME BUY YOU A DRINK, MR. McDUCK! SIR! PARDNER! KEMO-SABE!
I'LL TAKE A QUICK SARSAPARILLA IF YOU'LL STEER ME TO THE CHEAPEST GENERAL STORE HEREABOUTS!
SALOON

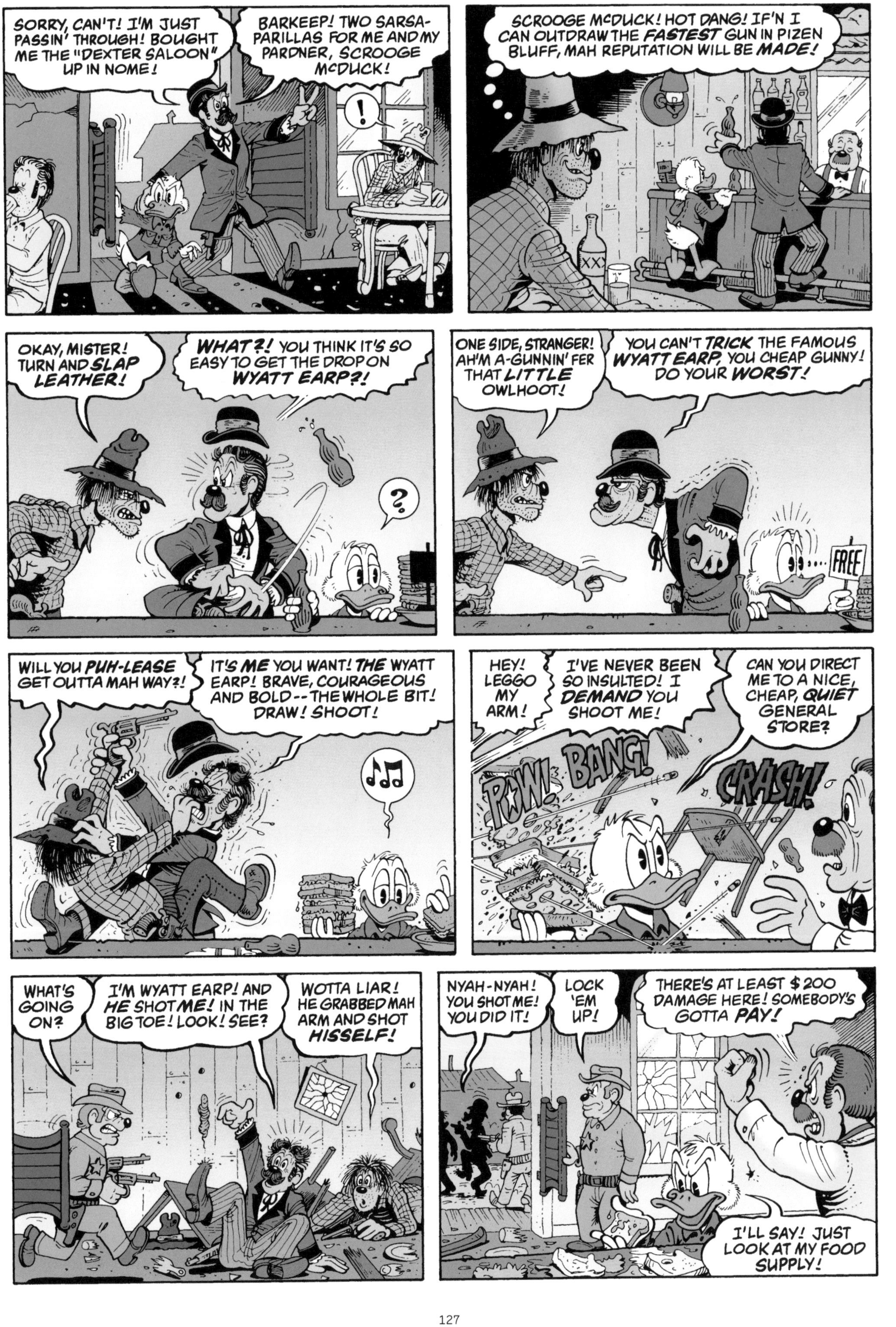
SORRY, CAN'T! I'M JUST PASSIN' THROUGH! BOUGHT ME THE "DEXTER SALOON" UP IN NOME!
BARKEEP! TWO SARSA-PARILLAS FOR ME AND MY PARDNER, SCROOGE McDUCK!
!
SCROOGE McDUCK! HOT DANG! IF'N I CAN OUTDRAW THE FASTEST GUN IN PIZEN BLUFF, MAH REPUTATION WILL BE MADE!
XXX
OKAY, MISTER! TURN AND SLAP LEATHER!
WHAT?! YOU THINK IT'S SO EASY TO GET THE DROP ON WYATT EARP?!
?
ONE SIDE, STRANGER! AH'M A-GUNNIN' FER THAT LITTLE OWLHOOT!
YOU CAN'T TRICK THE FAMOUS WYATT EARP, YOU CHEAP GUNNY! DO YOUR WORST!
FREE
WILL YOU PUH-LEASE GET OUTTA MAH WAY?!
IT'S ME YOU WANT! THE WYATT EARP! BRAVE, COURAGEOUS AND BOLD -- THE WHOLE BIT! DRAW! SHOOT!
HEY! LEGGO MY ARM!
I'VE NEVER BEEN SO INSULTED! I DEMAND YOU SHOOT ME!
CAN YOU DIRECT ME TO A NICE, CHEAP, QUIET GENERAL STORE?
POW! BANG! CRASH!
WHAT'S GOING ON?
I'M WYATT EARP! AND HE SHOT ME! IN THE BIG TOE! LOOK! SEE?
WOTTA LIAR! HE GRABBED MAH ARM AND SHOT HISSELF!
NYAH-NYAH! YOU SHOT ME! YOU DID IT!
LOCK 'EM UP!
THERE'S AT LEAST $200 DAMAGE HERE! SOMEBODY'S GOTTA PAY!
I'LL SAY! JUST LOOK AT MY FOOD SUPPLY!

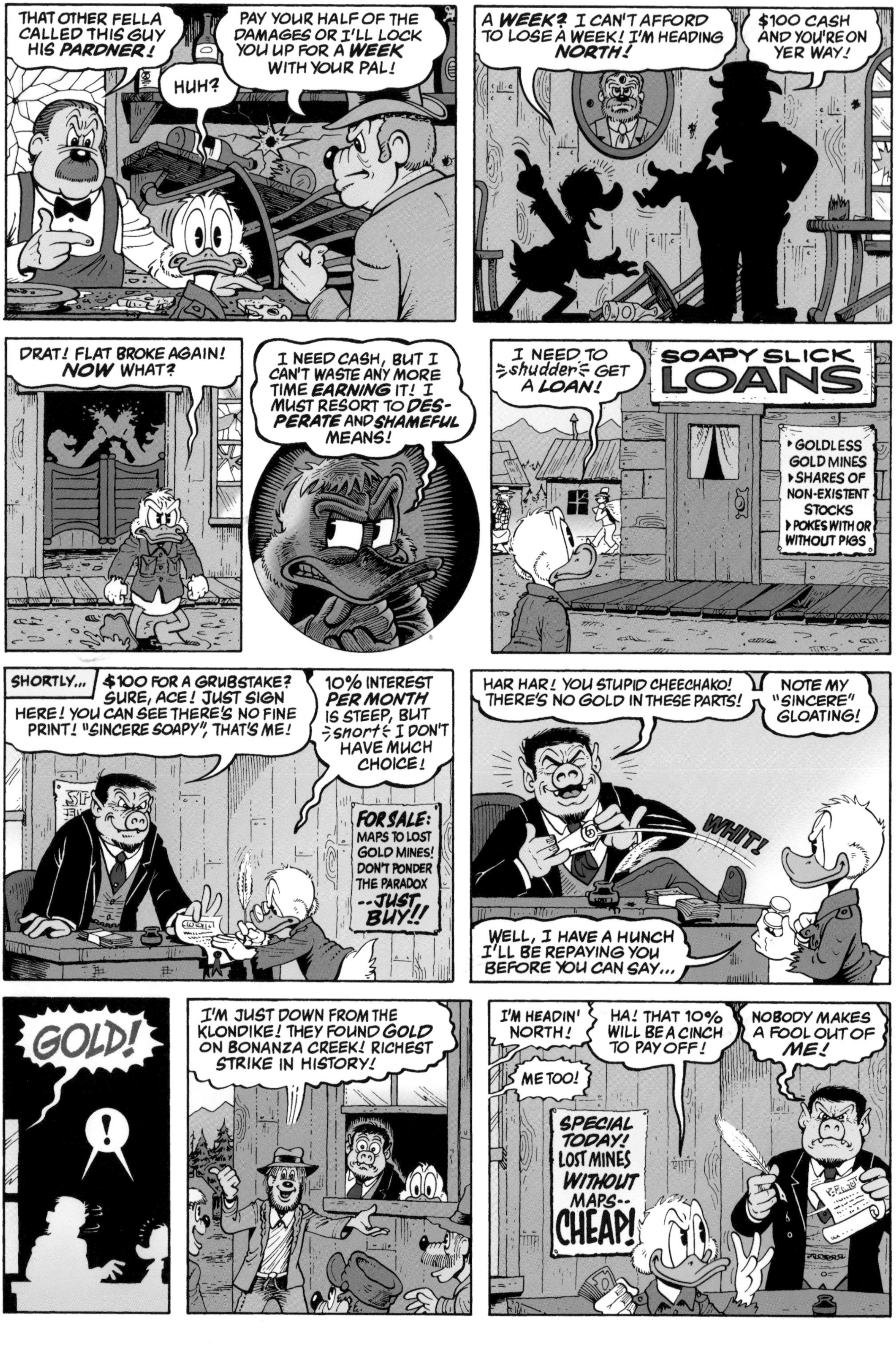
THAT OTHER FELLA CALLED THIS GUY HIS PARDNER!
HUH?
PAY YOUR HALF OF THE DAMAGES OR I'LL LOCK YOU UP FOR A WEEK WITH YOUR PAL!
A WEEK? I CAN'T AFFORD TO LOSE A WEEK! I'M HEADING NORTH!
$100 CASH AND YOU'RE ON YER WAY!
DRAT! FLAT BROKE AGAIN! NOW WHAT?
I NEED CASH, BUT I CAN'T WASTE ANY MORE TIME EARNING IT! I MUST RESORT TO DESPERATE AND SHAMEFUL MEANS!
I NEED TO =shudder= GET A LOAN!
SOAPY SLICK LOANS
▸GOLDLESS GOLD MINES ▸SHARES OF NON-EXISTENT STOCKS ▸POKES WITH OR WITHOUT PIGS
SHORTLY...
$100 FOR A GRUBSTAKE? SURE, ACE! JUST SIGN HERE! YOU CAN SEE THERE'S NO FINE PRINT! "SINCERE SOAPY", THAT'S ME!
10% INTEREST PER MONTH IS STEEP, BUT =snort= I DON'T HAVE MUCH CHOICE!
FOR SALE: MAPS TO LOST GOLD MINES! DON'T PONDER THE PARADOX --JUST BUY!!
HAR HAR! YOU STUPID CHEECHAKO! THERE'S NO GOLD IN THESE PARTS!
NOTE MY "SINCERE" GLOATING!
WHIT!
WELL, I HAVE A HUNCH I'LL BE REPAYING YOU BEFORE YOU CAN SAY...
GOLD!
!
I'M JUST DOWN FROM THE KLONDIKE! THEY FOUND GOLD ON BONANZA CREEK! RICHEST STRIKE IN HISTORY!
I'M HEADIN' NORTH!
ME TOO!
HA! THAT 10% WILL BE A CINCH TO PAY OFF!
NOBODY MAKES A FOOL OUT OF ME!
SPECIAL TODAY! LOST MINES WITHOUT MAPS-- CHEAP!

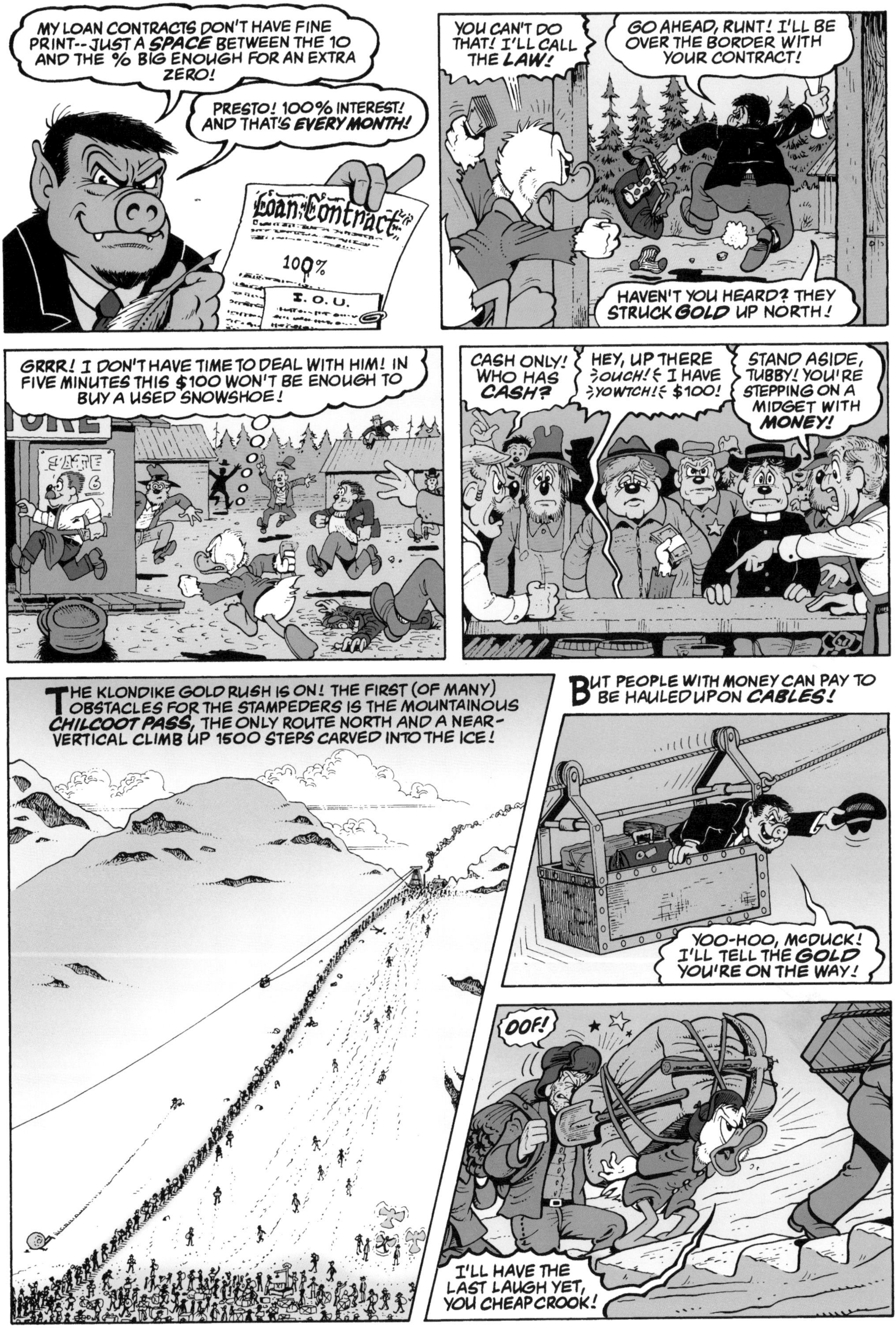

MY LOAN CONTRACTS DON'T HAVE FINE PRINT--JUST A SPACE BETWEEN THE 10 AND THE % BIG ENOUGH FOR AN EXTRA ZERO!
PRESTO! 100% INTEREST! AND THAT'S EVERY MONTH!
Loan Contract
100%
I.O.U.
YOU CAN'T DO THAT! I'LL CALL THE LAW!
GO AHEAD, RUNT! I'LL BE OVER THE BORDER WITH YOUR CONTRACT!
HAVEN'T YOU HEARD? THEY STRUCK GOLD UP NORTH!
GRRR! I DON'T HAVE TIME TO DEAL WITH HIM! IN FIVE MINUTES THIS $100 WON'T BE ENOUGH TO BUY A USED SNOWSHOE!
CASH ONLY! WHO HAS CASH?
HEY, UP THERE OUCH! I HAVE YOWTCH! $100!
STAND ASIDE, TUBBY! YOU'RE STEPPING ON A MIDGET WITH MONEY!
THE KLONDIKE GOLD RUSH IS ON! THE FIRST (OF MANY) OBSTACLES FOR THE STAMPEDERS IS THE MOUNTAINOUS CHILCOOT PASS, THE ONLY ROUTE NORTH AND A NEAR-VERTICAL CLIMB UP 1500 STEPS CARVED INTO THE ICE!
BUT PEOPLE WITH MONEY CAN PAY TO BE HAULED UP ON CABLES!
YOO-HOO, McDUCK! I'LL TELL THE GOLD YOU'RE ON THE WAY!
OOF!
I'LL HAVE THE LAST LAUGH YET, YOU CHEAP CROOK!

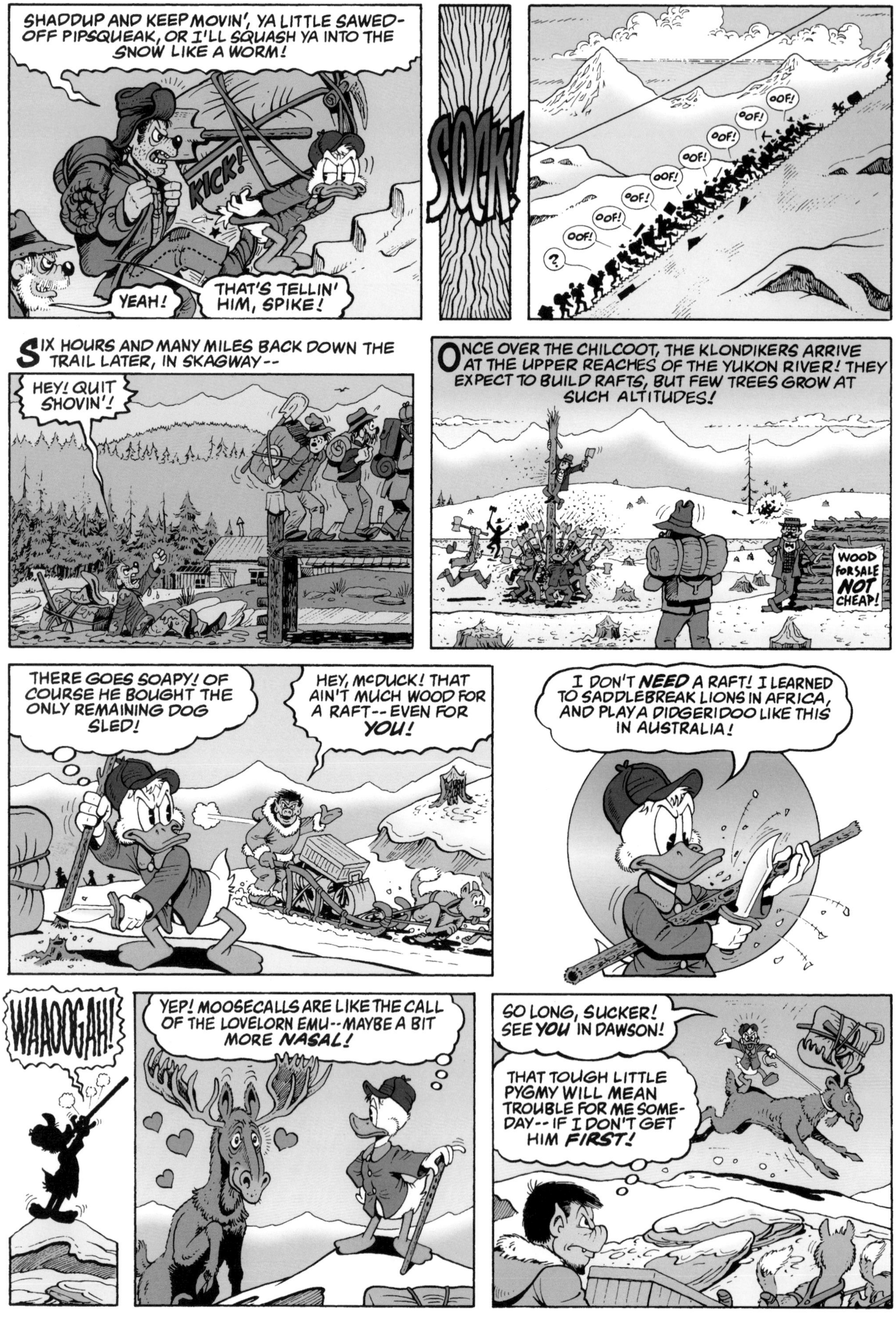
SHADDUP AND KEEP MOVIN', YA LITTLE SAWED-OFF PIPSQUEAK, OR I'LL SQUASH YA INTO THE SNOW LIKE A WORM!
KICK!
YEAH!
THAT'S TELLIN' HIM, SPIKE!
SOCK!
OOF!
OOF!
OOF!
OOF!
OOF!
OOF!
OOF!
OOF!
?
SIX HOURS AND MANY MILES BACK DOWN THE TRAIL LATER, IN SKAGWAY--
HEY! QUIT SHOVIN'!
ONCE OVER THE CHILCOOT, THE KLONDIKERS ARRIVE AT THE UPPER REACHES OF THE YUKON RIVER! THEY EXPECT TO BUILD RAFTS, BUT FEW TREES GROW AT SUCH ALTITUDES!
WOOD FOR SALE NOT CHEAP!
THERE GOES SOAPY! OF COURSE HE BOUGHT THE ONLY REMAINING DOG SLED!
HEY, McDUCK! THAT AIN'T MUCH WOOD FOR A RAFT-- EVEN FOR YOU!
I DON'T NEED A RAFT! I LEARNED TO SADDLEBREAK LIONS IN AFRICA, AND PLAY A DIDGERIDOO LIKE THIS IN AUSTRALIA!
WAAOOGAH!
YEP! MOOSECALLS ARE LIKE THE CALL OF THE LOVELORN EMU--MAYBE A BIT MORE NASAL!
SO LONG, SUCKER! SEE YOU IN DAWSON!
THAT TOUGH LITTLE PYGMY WILL MEAN TROUBLE FOR ME SOMEDAY-- IF I DON'T GET HIM FIRST!

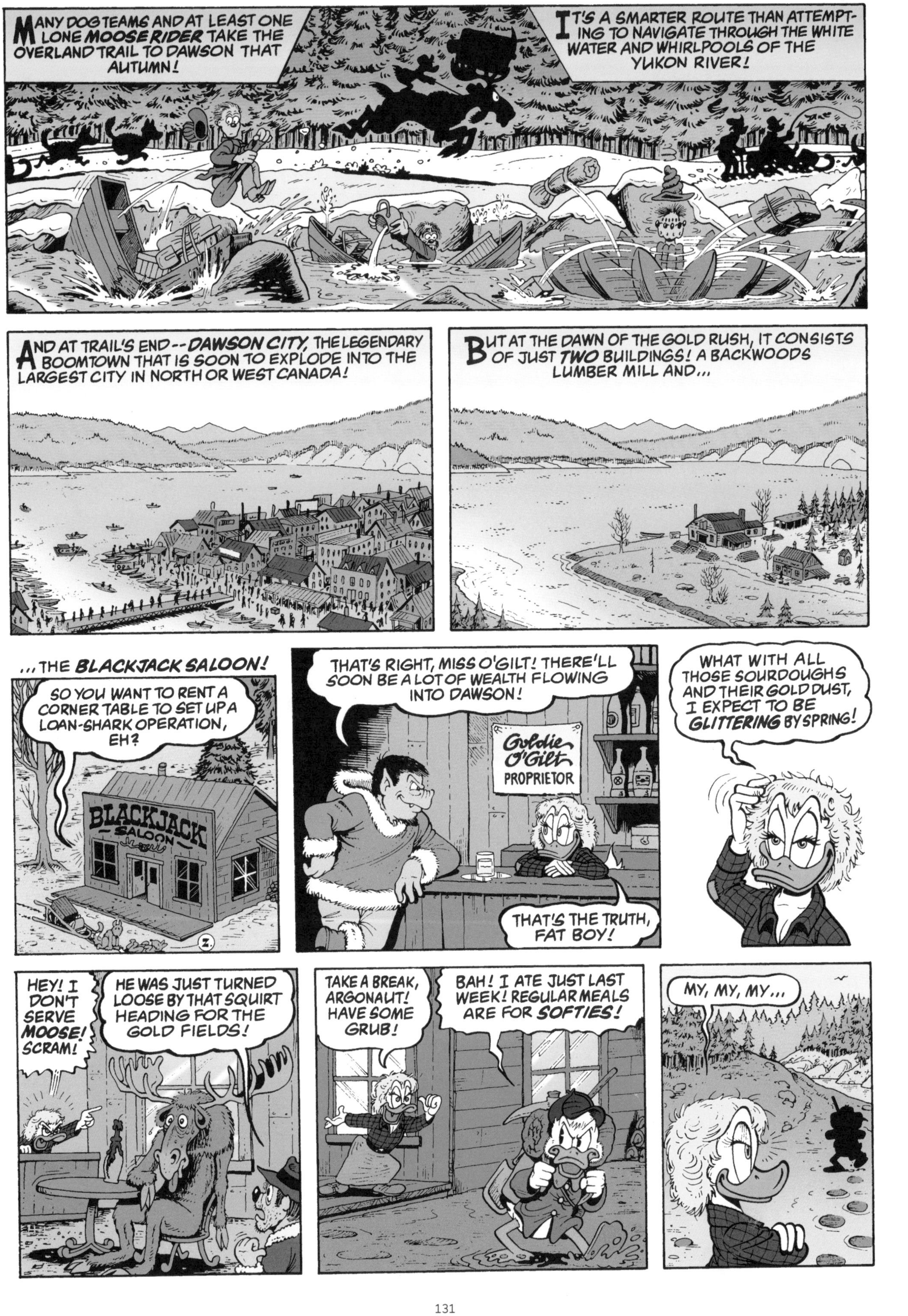
MANY DOG TEAMS AND AT LEAST ONE LONE MOOSE RIDER TAKE THE OVERLAND TRAIL TO DAWSON THAT AUTUMN!
IT'S A SMARTER ROUTE THAN ATTEMPTING TO NAVIGATE THROUGH THE WHITE WATER AND WHIRLPOOLS OF THE YUKON RIVER!
AND AT TRAIL'S END--DAWSON CITY, THE LEGENDARY BOOMTOWN THAT IS SOON TO EXPLODE INTO THE LARGEST CITY IN NORTH OR WEST CANADA!
BUT AT THE DAWN OF THE GOLD RUSH, IT CONSISTS OF JUST TWO BUILDINGS! A BACKWOODS LUMBER MILL AND...
...THE BLACKJACK SALOON!
SO YOU WANT TO RENT A CORNER TABLE TO SET UP A LOAN-SHARK OPERATION, EH?
BLACKJACK SALOON
THAT'S RIGHT, MISS O'GILT! THERE'LL SOON BE A LOT OF WEALTH FLOWING INTO DAWSON!
Goldie O'Gilt PROPRIETOR
THAT'S THE TRUTH, FAT BOY!
WHAT WITH ALL THOSE SOURDOUGHS AND THEIR GOLD DUST, I EXPECT TO BE GLITTERING BY SPRING!
HEY! I DON'T SERVE MOOSE! SCRAM!
HE WAS JUST TURNED LOOSE BY THAT SQUIRT HEADING FOR THE GOLD FIELDS!
TAKE A BREAK, ARGONAUT! HAVE SOME GRUB!
BAH! I ATE JUST LAST WEEK! REGULAR MEALS ARE FOR SOFTIES!
MY, MY, MY...

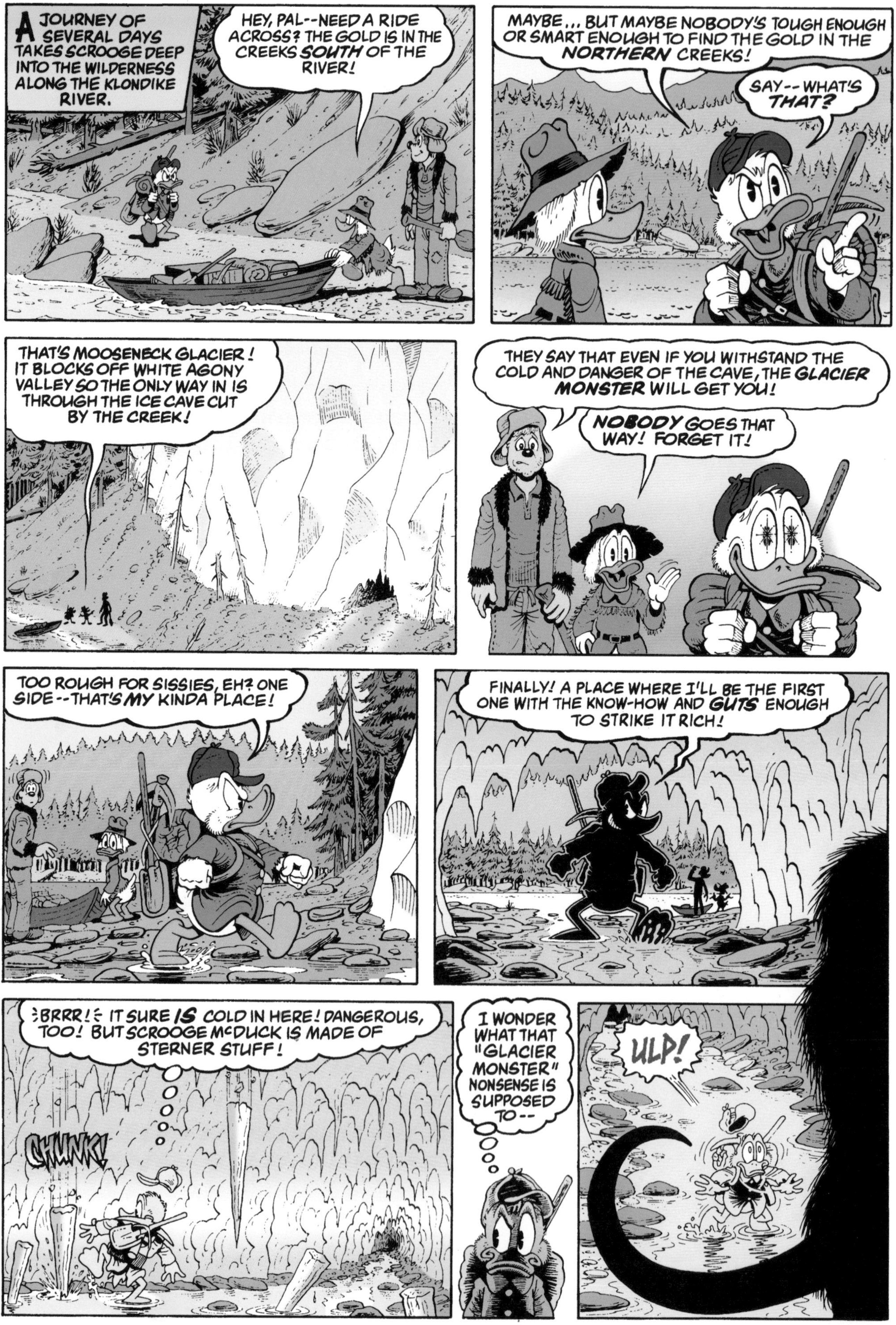

A JOURNEY OF SEVERAL DAYS TAKES SCROOGE DEEP INTO THE WILDERNESS ALONG THE KLONDIKE RIVER.
HEY, PAL--NEED A RIDE ACROSS? THE GOLD IS IN THE CREEKS SOUTH OF THE RIVER!
MAYBE... BUT MAYBE NOBODY'S TOUGH ENOUGH OR SMART ENOUGH TO FIND THE GOLD IN THE NORTHERN CREEKS!
SAY--WHAT'S THAT?
THAT'S MOOSENECK GLACIER! IT BLOCKS OFF WHITE AGONY VALLEY SO THE ONLY WAY IN IS THROUGH THE ICE CAVE CUT BY THE CREEK!
THEY SAY THAT EVEN IF YOU WITHSTAND THE COLD AND DANGER OF THE CAVE, THE GLACIER MONSTER WILL GET YOU!
NOBODY GOES THAT WAY! FORGET IT!
TOO ROUGH FOR SISSIES, EH? ONE SIDE--THAT'S MY KINDA PLACE!
FINALLY! A PLACE WHERE I'LL BE THE FIRST ONE WITH THE KNOW-HOW AND GUTS ENOUGH TO STRIKE IT RICH!
BRRR! IT SURE IS COLD IN HERE! DANGEROUS, TOO! BUT SCROOGE McDUCK IS MADE OF STERNER STUFF!
CHUNK!
I WONDER WHAT THAT "GLACIER MONSTER" NONSENSE IS SUPPOSED TO--
ULP!

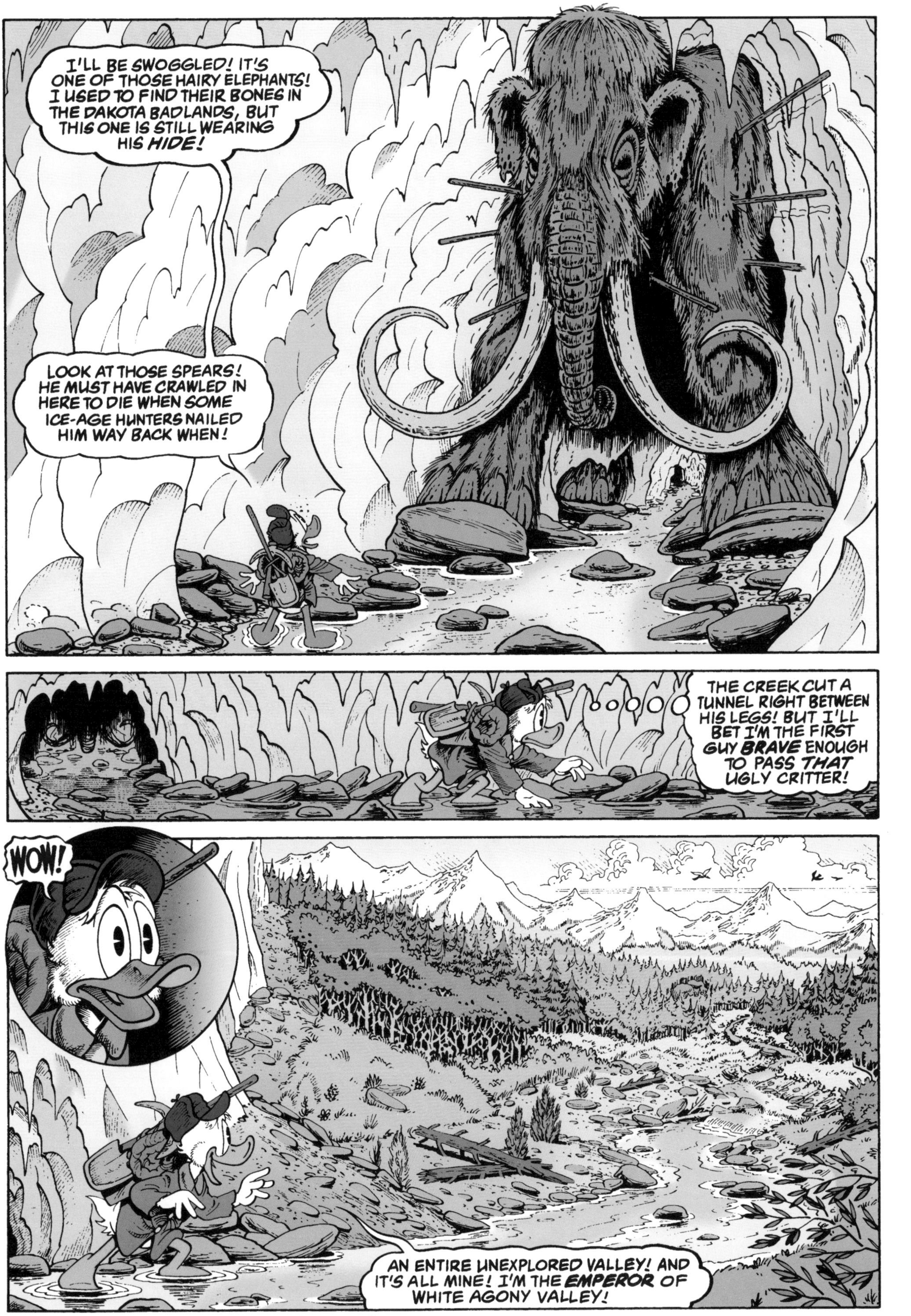
I'LL BE SWOGGLED! IT'S ONE OF THOSE HAIRY ELEPHANTS! I USED TO FIND THEIR BONES IN THE DAKOTA BADLANDS, BUT THIS ONE IS STILL WEARING HIS HIDE!
LOOK AT THOSE SPEARS! HE MUST HAVE CRAWLED IN HERE TO DIE WHEN SOME ICE-AGE HUNTERS NAILED HIM WAY BACK WHEN!
THE CREEK CUT A TUNNEL RIGHT BETWEEN HIS LEGS! BUT I'LL BET I'M THE FIRST GUY BRAVE ENOUGH TO PASS THAT UGLY CRITTER!
WOW!
AN ENTIRE UNEXPLORED VALLEY! AND IT'S ALL MINE! I'M THE EMPEROR OF WHITE AGONY VALLEY!

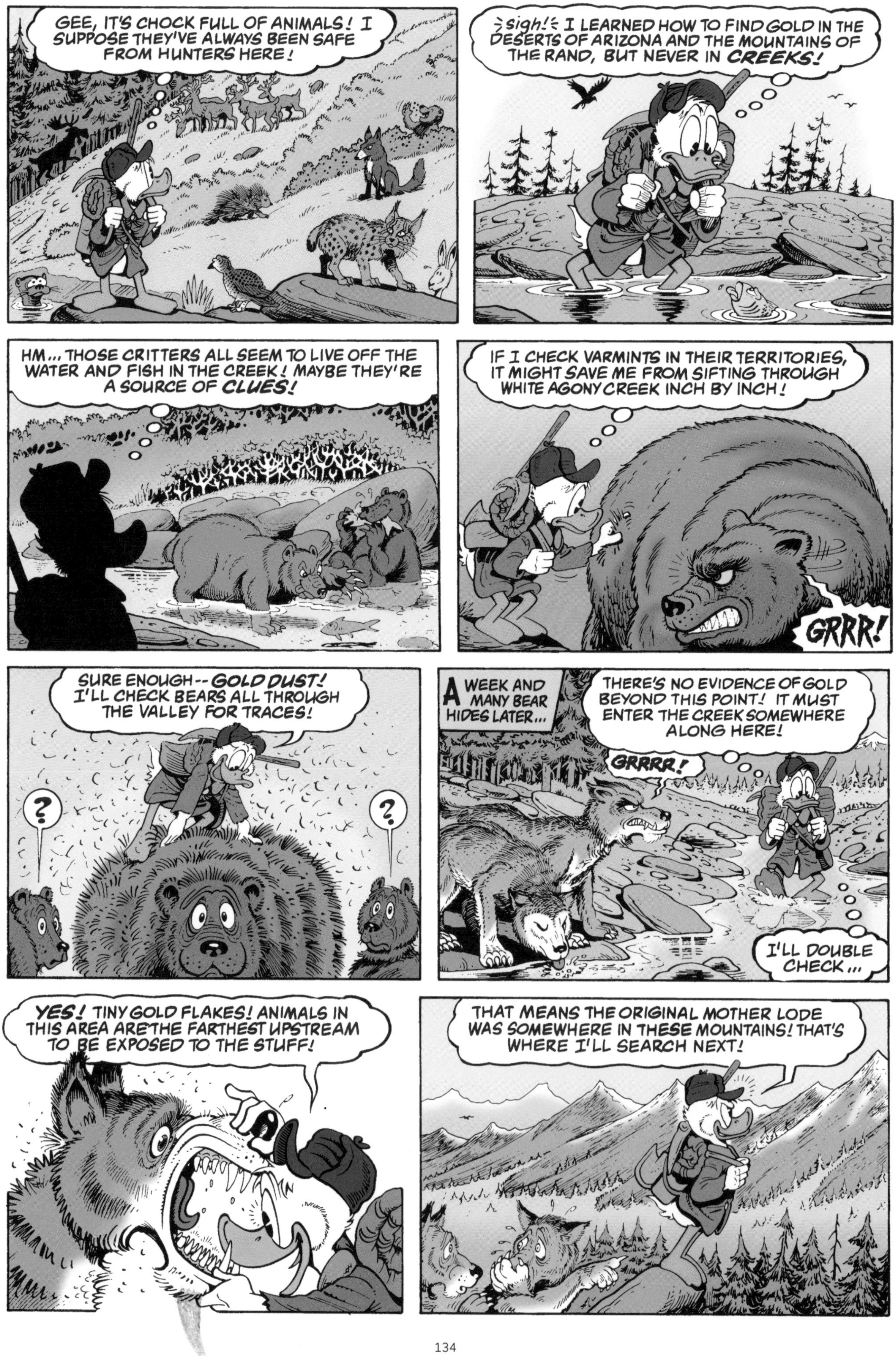
GEE, IT'S CHOCK FULL OF ANIMALS! I SUPPOSE THEY'VE ALWAYS BEEN SAFE FROM HUNTERS HERE!
sigh! I LEARNED HOW TO FIND GOLD IN THE DESERTS OF ARIZONA AND THE MOUNTAINS OF THE RAND, BUT NEVER IN CREEKS!
HM... THOSE CRITTERS ALL SEEM TO LIVE OFF THE WATER AND FISH IN THE CREEK! MAYBE THEY'RE A SOURCE OF CLUES!
IF I CHECK VARMINTS IN THEIR TERRITORIES, IT MIGHT SAVE ME FROM SIFTING THROUGH WHITE AGONY CREEK INCH BY INCH!
GRRR!
SURE ENOUGH -- GOLD DUST! I'LL CHECK BEARS ALL THROUGH THE VALLEY FOR TRACES!
?
?
A WEEK AND MANY BEAR HIDES LATER...
THERE'S NO EVIDENCE OF GOLD BEYOND THIS POINT! IT MUST ENTER THE CREEK SOMEWHERE ALONG HERE!
GRRRR!
I'LL DOUBLE CHECK...
YES! TINY GOLD FLAKES! ANIMALS IN THIS AREA ARE THE FARTHEST UPSTREAM TO BE EXPOSED TO THE STUFF!
THAT MEANS THE ORIGINAL MOTHER LODE WAS SOMEWHERE IN THESE MOUNTAINS! THAT'S WHERE I'LL SEARCH NEXT!

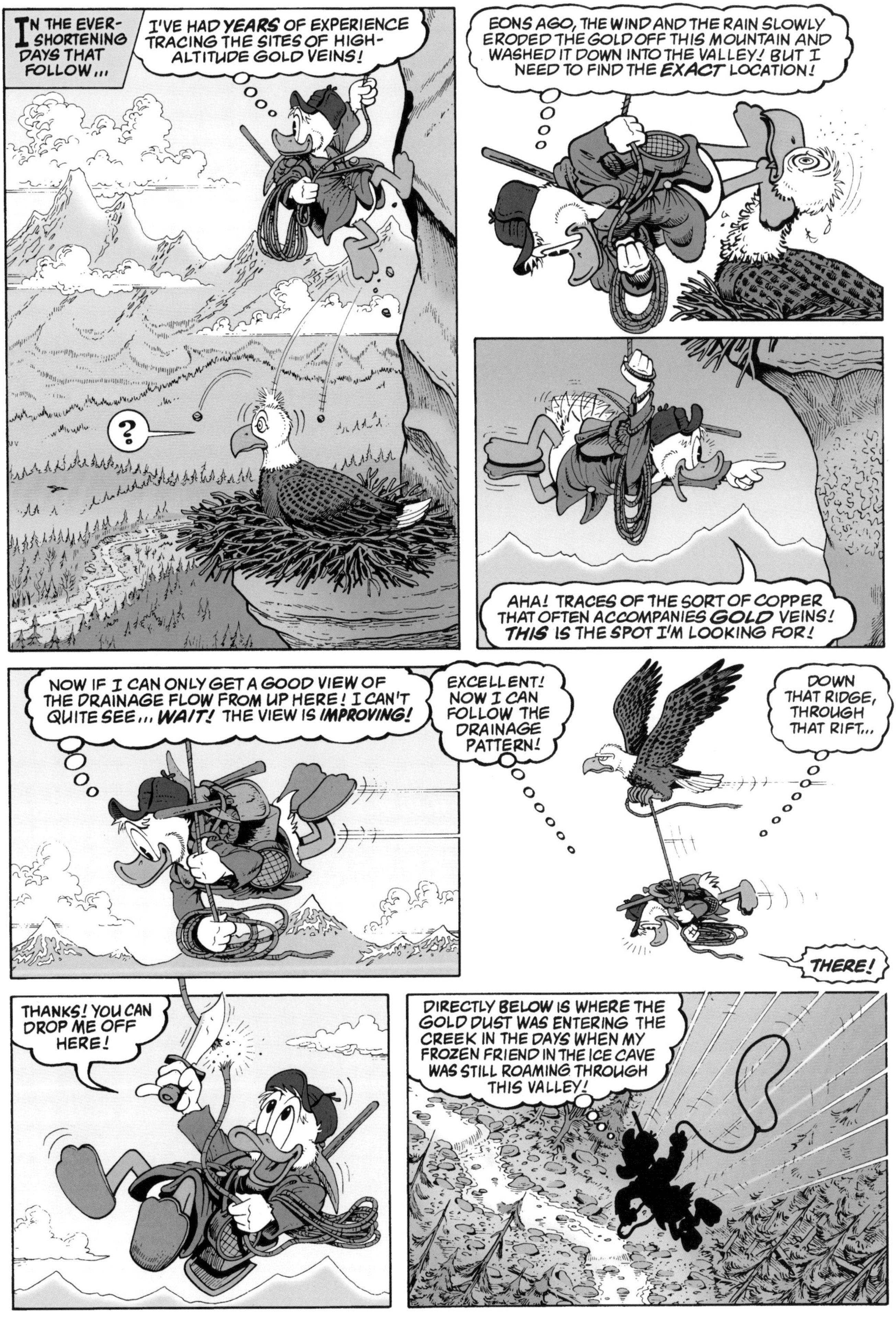

IN THE EVER-SHORTENING DAYS THAT FOLLOW...
I'VE HAD YEARS OF EXPERIENCE TRACING THE SITES OF HIGH-ALTITUDE GOLD VEINS!
?
EONS AGO, THE WIND AND THE RAIN SLOWLY ERODED THE GOLD OFF THIS MOUNTAIN AND WASHED IT DOWN INTO THE VALLEY! BUT I NEED TO FIND THE EXACT LOCATION!
AHA! TRACES OF THE SORT OF COPPER THAT OFTEN ACCOMPANIES GOLD VEINS! THIS IS THE SPOT I'M LOOKING FOR!
NOW IF I CAN ONLY GET A GOOD VIEW OF THE DRAINAGE FLOW FROM UP HERE! I CAN'T QUITE SEE... WAIT! THE VIEW IS IMPROVING!
EXCELLENT! NOW I CAN FOLLOW THE DRAINAGE PATTERN!
DOWN THAT RIDGE, THROUGH THAT RIFT...
THERE!
THANKS! YOU CAN DROP ME OFF HERE!
DIRECTLY BELOW IS WHERE THE GOLD DUST WAS ENTERING THE CREEK IN THE DAYS WHEN MY FROZEN FRIEND IN THE ICE CAVE WAS STILL ROAMING THROUGH THIS VALLEY!

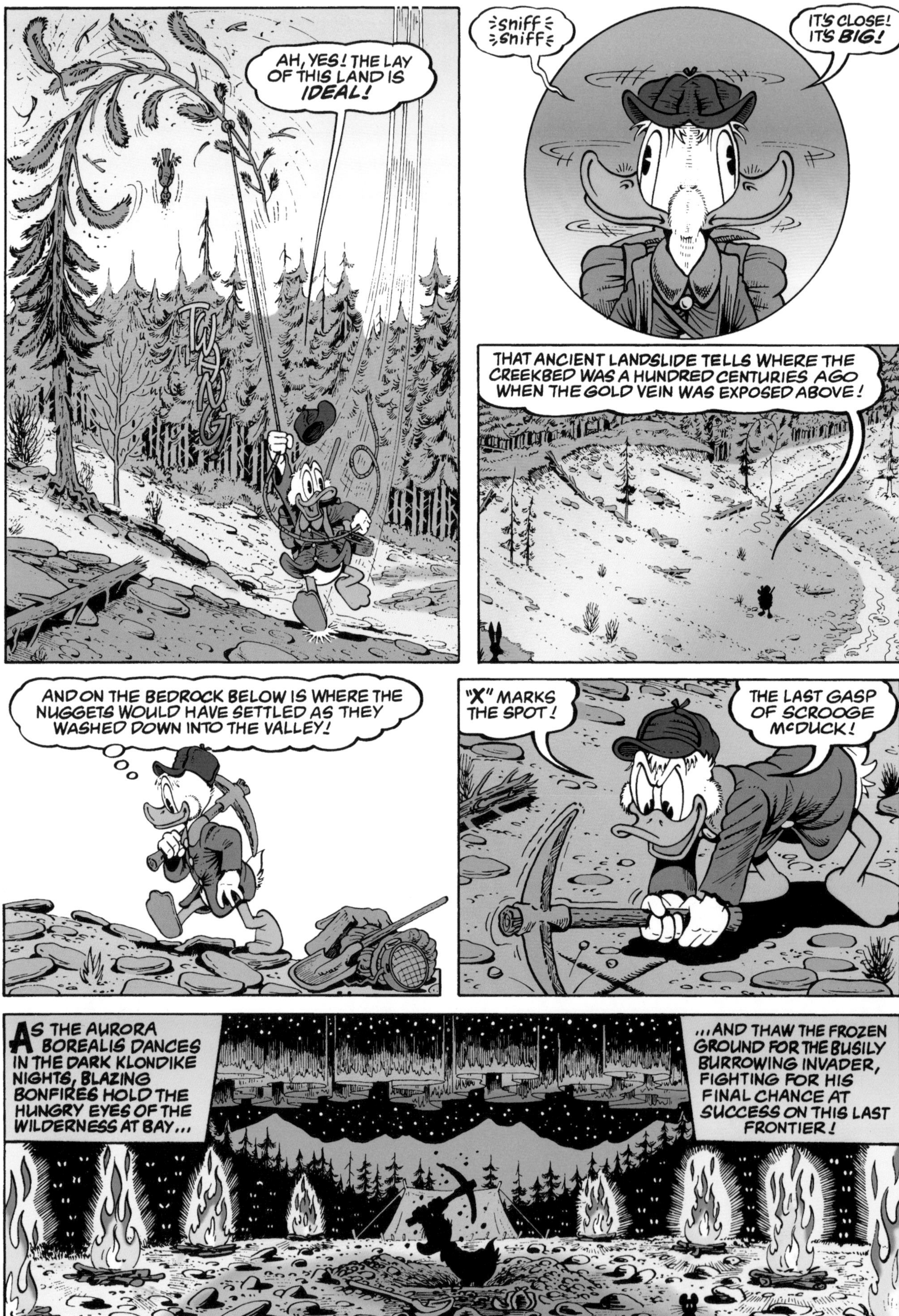
AH, YES! THE LAY OF THIS LAND IS IDEAL!
TWANG
sniff sniff
IT'S CLOSE! IT'S BIG!
THAT ANCIENT LANDSLIDE TELLS WHERE THE CREEKBED WAS A HUNDRED CENTURIES AGO WHEN THE GOLD VEIN WAS EXPOSED ABOVE!
AND ON THE BEDROCK BELOW IS WHERE THE NUGGETS WOULD HAVE SETTLED AS THEY WASHED DOWN INTO THE VALLEY!
"X" MARKS THE SPOT!
THE LAST GASP OF SCROOGE McDUCK!
AS THE AURORA BOREALIS DANCES IN THE DARK KLONDIKE NIGHTS, BLAZING BONFIRES HOLD THE HUNGRY EYES OF THE WILDERNESS AT BAY...
...AND THAW THE FROZEN GROUND FOR THE BUSILY BURROWING INVADER, FIGHTING FOR HIS FINAL CHANCE AT SUCCESS ON THIS LAST FRONTIER!

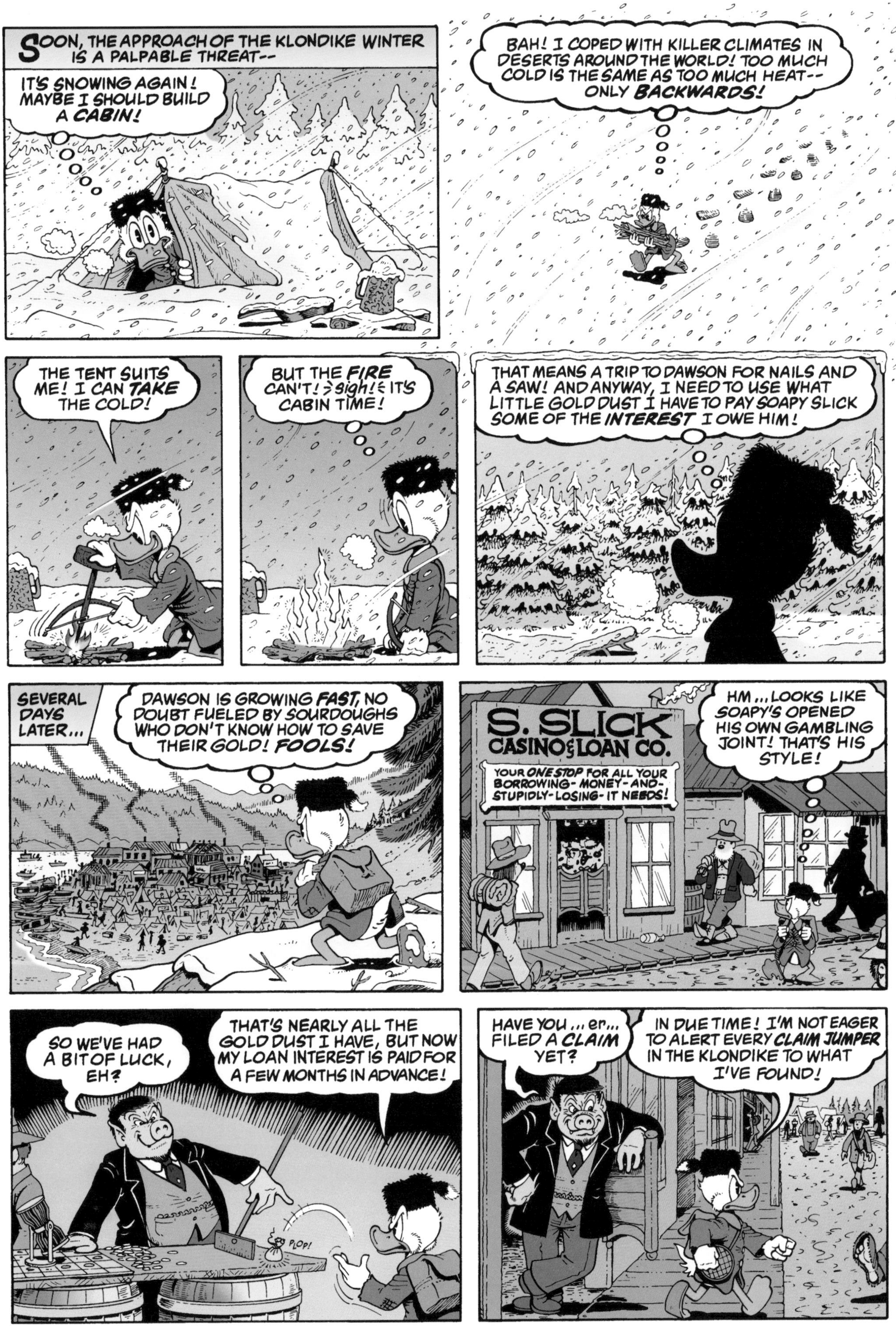
SOON, THE APPROACH OF THE KLONDIKE WINTER IS A PALPABLE THREAT--
IT'S SNOWING AGAIN! MAYBE I SHOULD BUILD A CABIN!
BAH! I COPED WITH KILLER CLIMATES IN DESERTS AROUND THE WORLD! TOO MUCH COLD IS THE SAME AS TOO MUCH HEAT-- ONLY BACKWARDS!
THE TENT SUITS ME! I CAN TAKE THE COLD!
BUT THE FIRE CAN'T! *sigh!* IT'S CABIN TIME!
THAT MEANS A TRIP TO DAWSON FOR NAILS AND A SAW! AND ANYWAY, I NEED TO USE WHAT LITTLE GOLD DUST I HAVE TO PAY SOAPY SLICK SOME OF THE INTEREST I OWE HIM!
SEVERAL DAYS LATER...
DAWSON IS GROWING FAST, NO DOUBT FUELED BY SOURDOUGHS WHO DON'T KNOW HOW TO SAVE THEIR GOLD! FOOLS!
S. SLICK CASINO & LOAN CO.
YOUR ONE STOP FOR ALL YOUR BORROWING-MONEY-AND-STUPIDLY-LOSING-IT NEEDS!
HM... LOOKS LIKE SOAPY'S OPENED HIS OWN GAMBLING JOINT! THAT'S HIS STYLE!
SO WE'VE HAD A BIT OF LUCK, EH?
THAT'S NEARLY ALL THE GOLD DUST I HAVE, BUT NOW MY LOAN INTEREST IS PAID FOR A FEW MONTHS IN ADVANCE!
PLOP!
HAVE YOU... er... FILED A CLAIM YET?
IN DUE TIME! I'M NOT EAGER TO ALERT EVERY CLAIM JUMPER IN THE KLONDIKE TO WHAT I'VE FOUND!

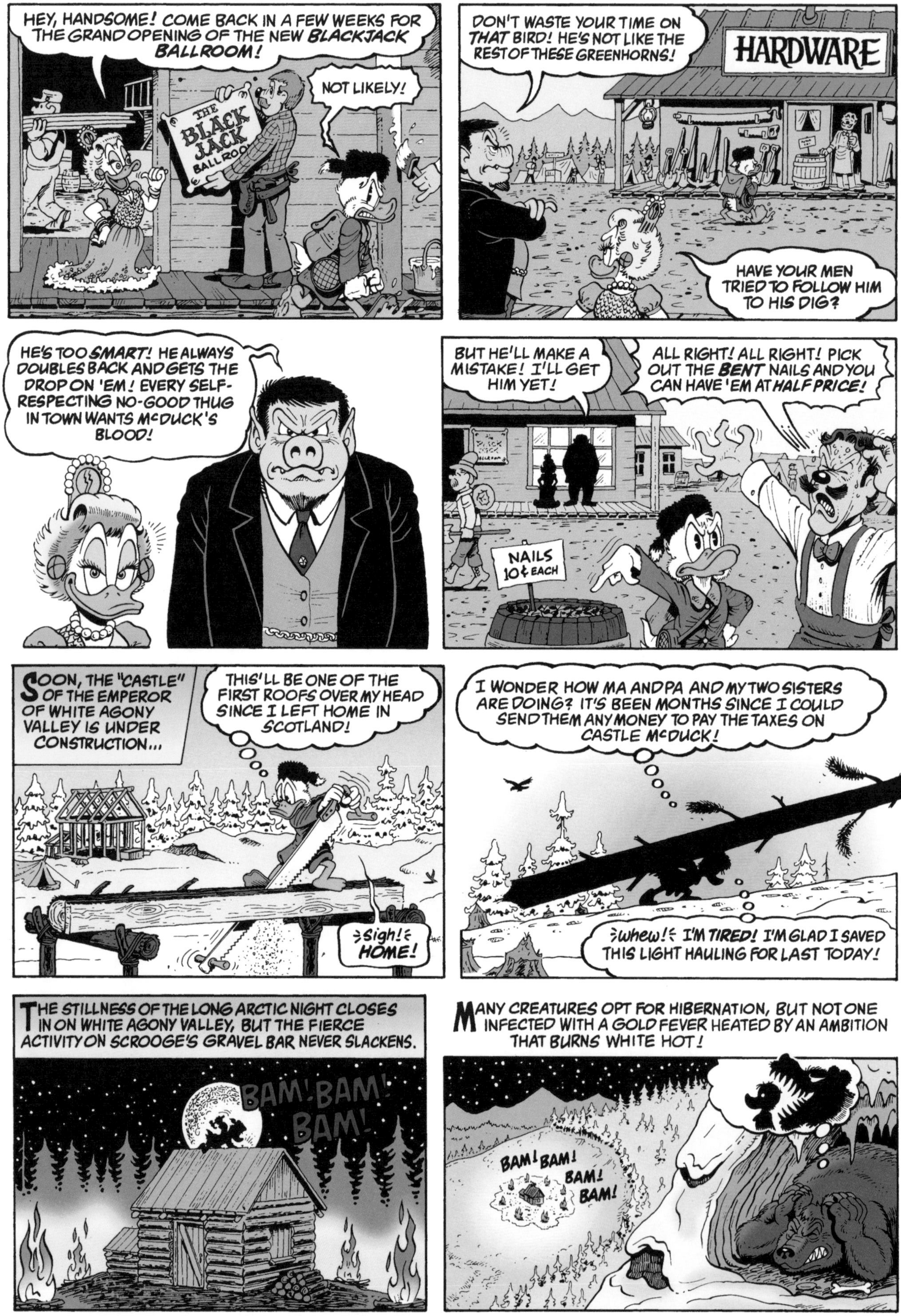

HEY, HANDSOME! COME BACK IN A FEW WEEKS FOR THE GRAND OPENING OF THE NEW BLACKJACK BALLROOM!
THE BLACK JACK BALLROOM
NOT LIKELY!
DON'T WASTE YOUR TIME ON THAT BIRD! HE'S NOT LIKE THE REST OF THESE GREENHORNS!
HARDWARE
HAVE YOUR MEN TRIED TO FOLLOW HIM TO HIS DIG?
HE'S TOO SMART! HE ALWAYS DOUBLES BACK AND GETS THE DROP ON 'EM! EVERY SELF-RESPECTING NO-GOOD THUG IN TOWN WANTS McDUCK'S BLOOD!
BUT HE'LL MAKE A MISTAKE! I'LL GET HIM YET!
ALL RIGHT! ALL RIGHT! PICK OUT THE BENT NAILS AND YOU CAN HAVE 'EM AT HALF PRICE!
NAILS 10¢ EACH
SOON, THE "CASTLE" OF THE EMPEROR OF WHITE AGONY VALLEY IS UNDER CONSTRUCTION...
THIS'LL BE ONE OF THE FIRST ROOFS OVER MY HEAD SINCE I LEFT HOME IN SCOTLAND!
Sigh! HOME!
I WONDER HOW MA AND PA AND MY TWO SISTERS ARE DOING? IT'S BEEN MONTHS SINCE I COULD SEND THEM ANY MONEY TO PAY THE TAXES ON CASTLE McDUCK!
whew! I'M TIRED! I'M GLAD I SAVED THIS LIGHT HAULING FOR LAST TODAY!
THE STILLNESS OF THE LONG ARCTIC NIGHT CLOSES IN ON WHITE AGONY VALLEY, BUT THE FIERCE ACTIVITY ON SCROOGE'S GRAVEL BAR NEVER SLACKENS.
BAM! BAM! BAM!
MANY CREATURES OPT FOR HIBERNATION, BUT NOT ONE INFECTED WITH A GOLD FEVER HEATED BY AN AMBITION THAT BURNS WHITE HOT!
BAM! BAM! BAM! BAM!

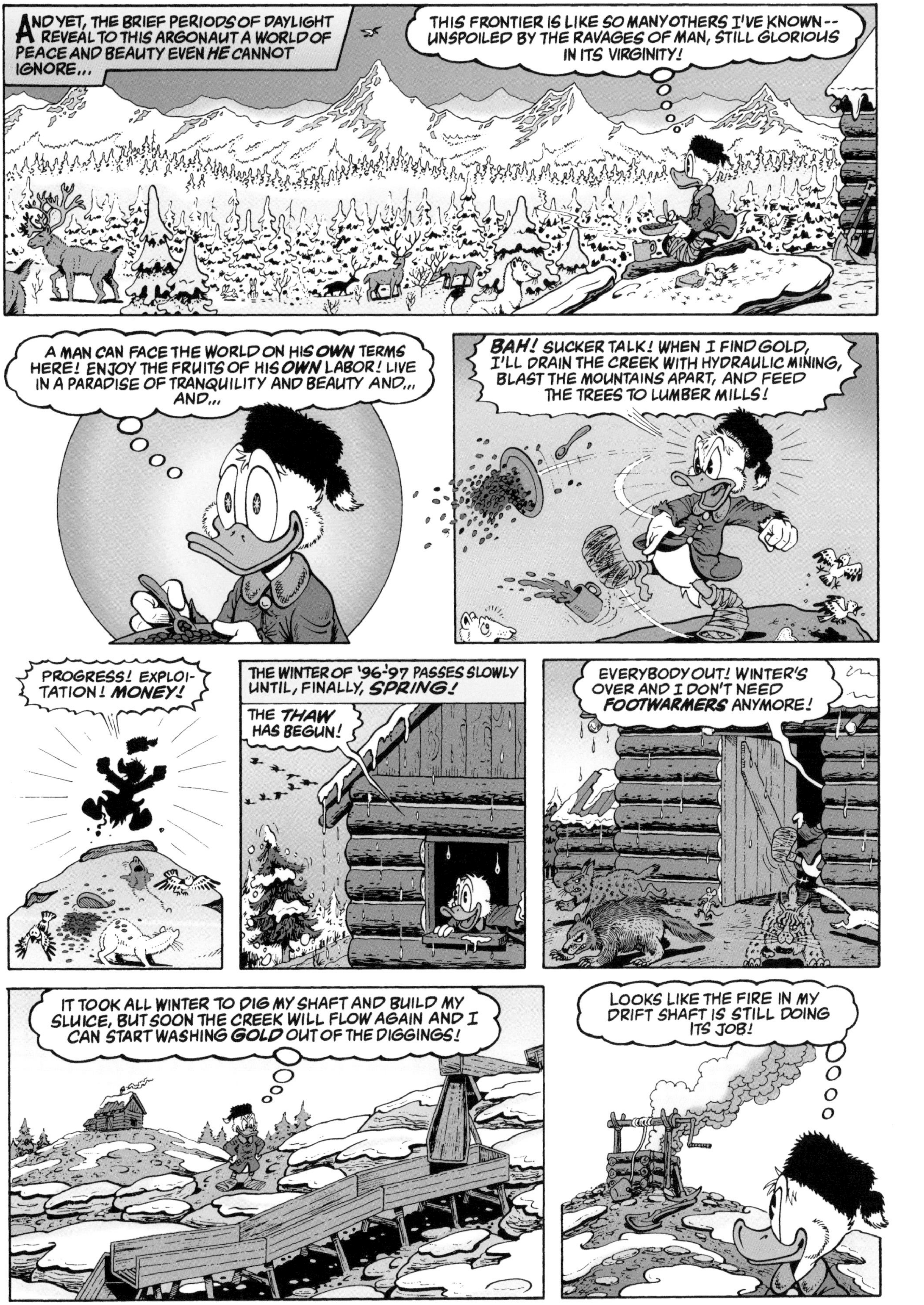
AND YET, THE BRIEF PERIODS OF DAYLIGHT REVEAL TO THIS ARGONAUT A WORLD OF PEACE AND BEAUTY EVEN HE CANNOT IGNORE...
THIS FRONTIER IS LIKE SO MANY OTHERS I'VE KNOWN-- UNSPOILED BY THE RAVAGES OF MAN, STILL GLORIOUS IN ITS VIRGINITY!
A MAN CAN FACE THE WORLD ON HIS OWN TERMS HERE! ENJOY THE FRUITS OF HIS OWN LABOR! LIVE IN A PARADISE OF TRANQUILITY AND BEAUTY AND... AND...
BAH! SUCKER TALK! WHEN I FIND GOLD, I'LL DRAIN THE CREEK WITH HYDRAULIC MINING, BLAST THE MOUNTAINS APART, AND FEED THE TREES TO LUMBER MILLS!
PROGRESS! EXPLOI-TATION! MONEY!
THE WINTER OF '96-'97 PASSES SLOWLY UNTIL, FINALLY, SPRING!
THE THAW HAS BEGUN!
EVERYBODY OUT! WINTER'S OVER AND I DON'T NEED FOOTWARMERS ANYMORE!
IT TOOK ALL WINTER TO DIG MY SHAFT AND BUILD MY SLUICE, BUT SOON THE CREEK WILL FLOW AGAIN AND I CAN START WASHING GOLD OUT OF THE DIGGINGS!
LOOKS LIKE THE FIRE IN MY DRIFT SHAFT IS STILL DOING ITS JOB!

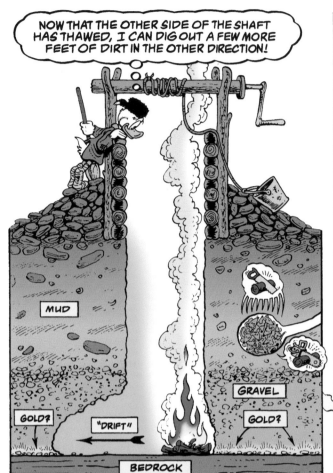

NOW THAT THE OTHER SIDE OF THE SHAFT HAS THAWED, I CAN DIG OUT A FEW MORE FEET OF DIRT IN THE OTHER DIRECTION!
MUD
GRAVEL
GOLD?
"DRIFT"
GOLD?
BEDROCK
SHORTLY...
HEY! I TOLD YOU TO CLEAR OUT! I HAVE WORK TO DO!
EEP!
CRASH!
HAH! THIS IS THE RICHEST PAYDIRT I'VE EVER SEEN! BUT IT MIGHT BE A "GLORY-HOLE" WITH ONLY A DAB OF SUCH GOLD!
IT'S TIME TO GO INTO DAWSON AND FILE MY CLAIM! AND PAY MY LOAN INTEREST TO SOAPY SLICK! MAYBE I'LL SOON BE DONE WITH HIM!
YEP! WHITE AGONY CREEK JUST MIGHT BE THE END OF MY RAINBOW!
SEVERAL DAYS LATER SCROOGE REACHES DAWSON, BUT IT IS A NEW DAWSON, UNLIKE ANY TOWN THE WESTERN HEMISPHERE HAS EVER KNOWN!
HE IS ABOUT TO ENTER INTO THE WILDEST, MOST LAWLESS AND JUST PLAIN CUSSEDEST SETTLEMENT IN NORTH AMERICA!
BAR
CASINO
SALOON
HOTEL
CAFE
HE IS ALSO ABOUT TO ENTER INTO LEGEND!

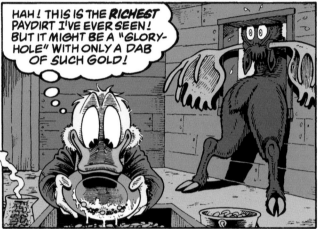

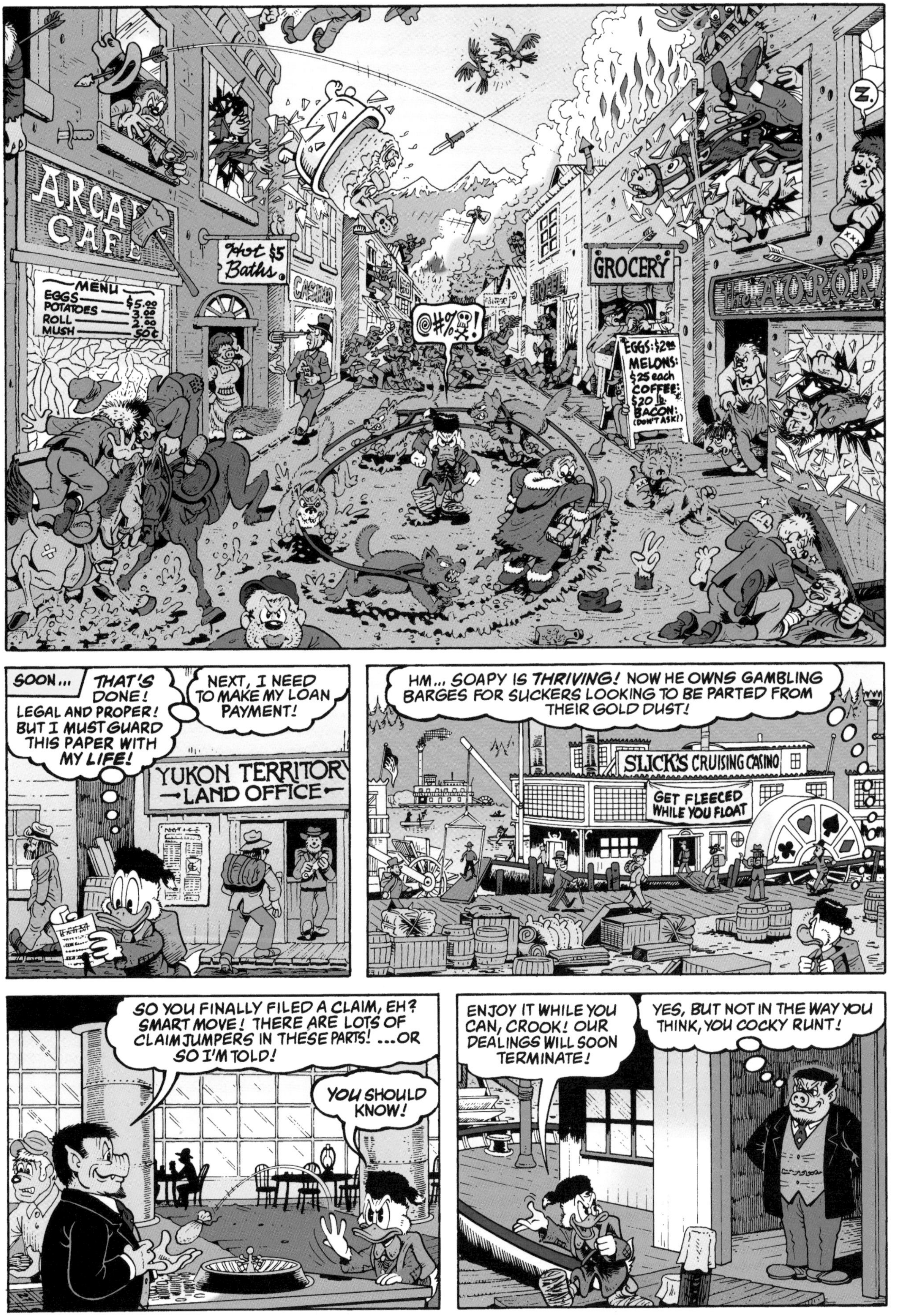
ARCA
CAFE
MENU
EGGS $5.00
POTATOES 3.00
ROLL 2.00
MUSH 50¢
Hot $5 Baths
GROCERY
EGGS: $2 ea
MELONS: $25 each
COFFEE: $20 lb.
BACON: (DON'T ASK!)
SOON...
THAT'S DONE! LEGAL AND PROPER! BUT I MUST GUARD THIS PAPER WITH MY LIFE!
NEXT, I NEED TO MAKE MY LOAN PAYMENT!
YUKON TERRITORY
→LAND OFFICE←
HM... SOAPY IS THRIVING! NOW HE OWNS GAMBLING BARGES FOR SUCKERS LOOKING TO BE PARTED FROM THEIR GOLD DUST!
SLICK'S CRUISING CASINO
GET FLEECED WHILE YOU FLOAT
SO YOU FINALLY FILED A CLAIM, EH? SMART MOVE! THERE ARE LOTS OF CLAIM JUMPERS IN THESE PARTS! ...OR SO I'M TOLD!
YOU SHOULD KNOW!
ENJOY IT WHILE YOU CAN, CROOK! OUR DEALINGS WILL SOON TERMINATE!
YES, BUT NOT IN THE WAY YOU THINK, YOU COCKY RUNT!

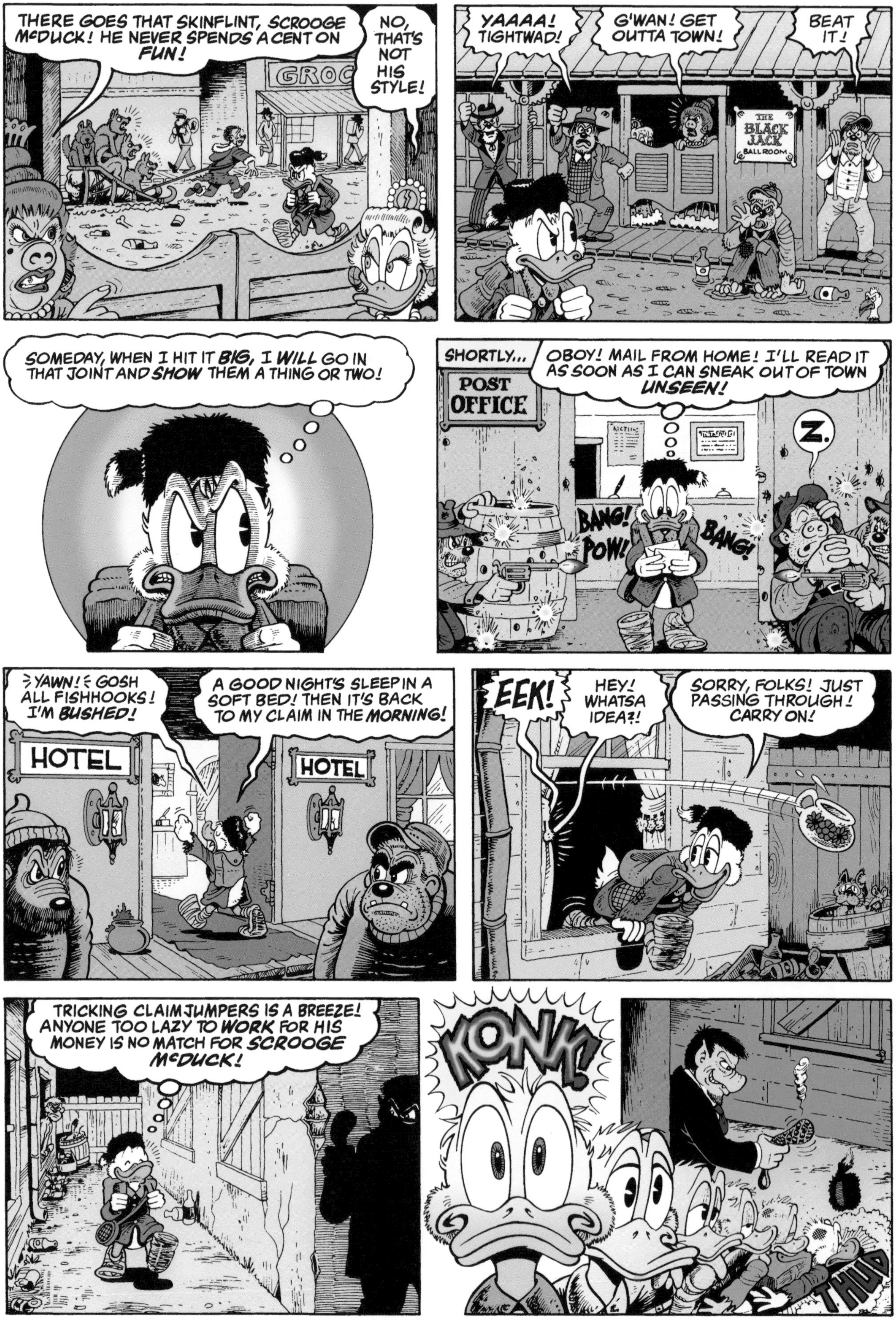
THERE GOES THAT SKINFLINT, SCROOGE McDUCK! HE NEVER SPENDS A CENT ON FUN!
NO, THAT'S NOT HIS STYLE!
GROC
YAAAA! TIGHTWAD!
G'WAN! GET OUTTA TOWN!
BEAT IT!
THE BLACK JACK BALLROOM
SOMEDAY, WHEN I HIT IT BIG, I WILL GO IN THAT JOINT AND SHOW THEM A THING OR TWO!
SHORTLY...
OBOY! MAIL FROM HOME! I'LL READ IT AS SOON AS I CAN SNEAK OUT OF TOWN UNSEEN!
POST OFFICE
Z.
BANG!
POW!
BANG!
YAWN! GOSH ALL FISHHOOKS! I'M BUSHED!
A GOOD NIGHT'S SLEEP IN A SOFT BED! THEN IT'S BACK TO MY CLAIM IN THE MORNING!
HOTEL
HOTEL
EEK!
HEY! WHATSA IDEA?!
SORRY, FOLKS! JUST PASSING THROUGH! CARRY ON!
TRICKING CLAIM JUMPERS IS A BREEZE! ANYONE TOO LAZY TO WORK FOR HIS MONEY IS NO MATCH FOR SCROOGE McDUCK!
KONK!
THUD

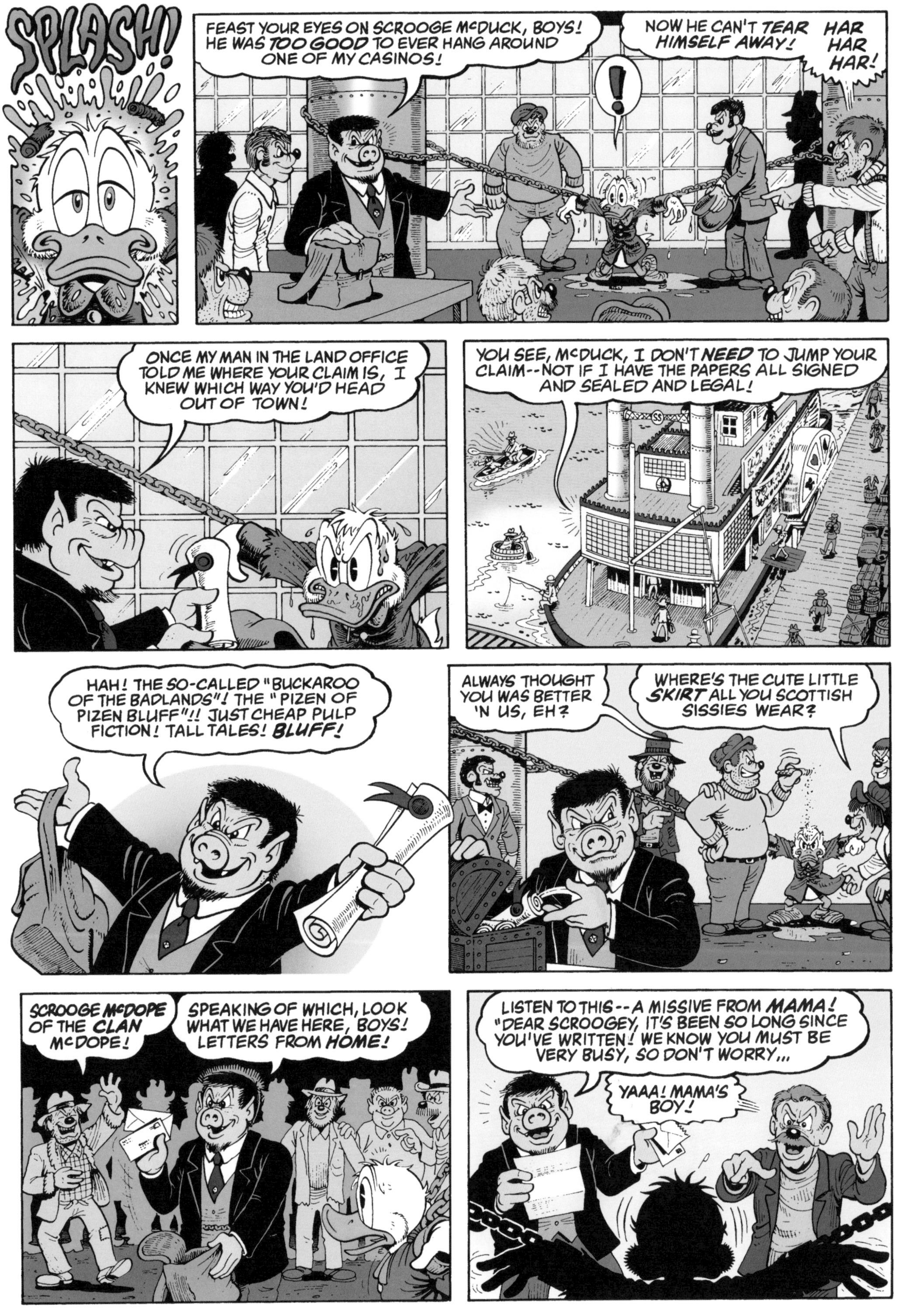
SPLASH!
FEAST YOUR EYES ON SCROOGE McDUCK, BOYS! HE WAS TOO GOOD TO EVER HANG AROUND ONE OF MY CASINOS!
NOW HE CAN'T TEAR HIMSELF AWAY!
HAR HAR HAR!
!
ONCE MY MAN IN THE LAND OFFICE TOLD ME WHERE YOUR CLAIM IS, I KNEW WHICH WAY YOU'D HEAD OUT OF TOWN!
YOU SEE, McDUCK, I DON'T NEED TO JUMP YOUR CLAIM--NOT IF I HAVE THE PAPERS ALL SIGNED AND SEALED AND LEGAL!
HAH! THE SO-CALLED "BUCKAROO OF THE BADLANDS"! THE "PIZEN OF PIZEN BLUFF"!! JUST CHEAP PULP FICTION! TALL TALES! BLUFF!
ALWAYS THOUGHT YOU WAS BETTER 'N US, EH?
WHERE'S THE CUTE LITTLE SKIRT ALL YOU SCOTTISH SISSIES WEAR?
SCROOGE McDOPE OF THE CLAN McDOPE!
SPEAKING OF WHICH, LOOK WHAT WE HAVE HERE, BOYS! LETTERS FROM HOME!
LISTEN TO THIS--A MISSIVE FROM MAMA! "DEAR SCROOGEY, IT'S BEEN SO LONG SINCE YOU'VE WRITTEN! WE KNOW YOU MUST BE VERY BUSY, SO DON'T WORRY...
YAAA! MAMA'S BOY!

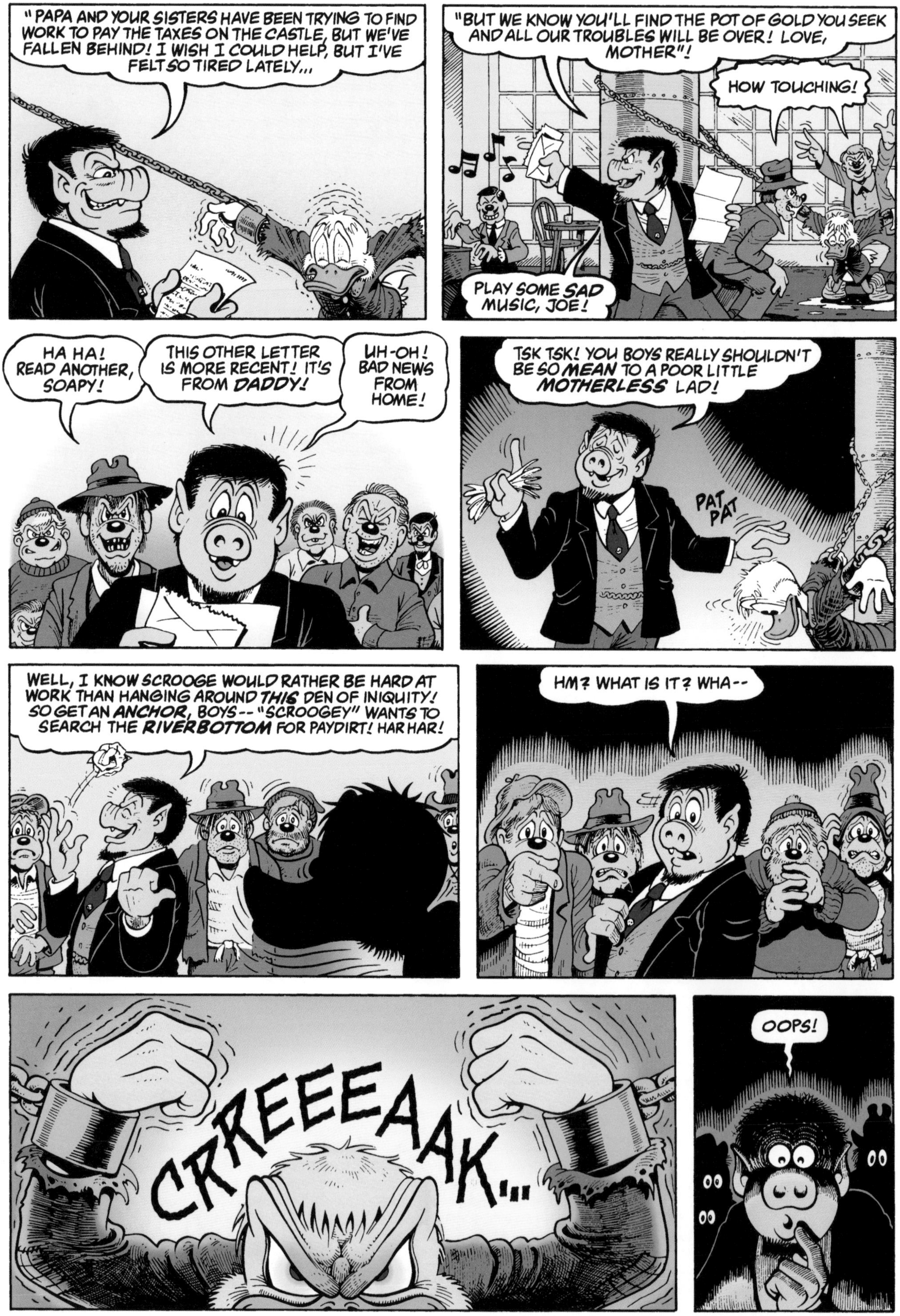
"PAPA AND YOUR SISTERS HAVE BEEN TRYING TO FIND WORK TO PAY THE TAXES ON THE CASTLE, BUT WE'VE FALLEN BEHIND! I WISH I COULD HELP, BUT I'VE FELT SO TIRED LATELY...
"BUT WE KNOW YOU'LL FIND THE POT OF GOLD YOU SEEK AND ALL OUR TROUBLES WILL BE OVER! LOVE, MOTHER"!
HOW TOUCHING!
PLAY SOME SAD MUSIC, JOE!
HA HA! READ ANOTHER, SOAPY!
THIS OTHER LETTER IS MORE RECENT! IT'S FROM DADDY!
UH-OH! BAD NEWS FROM HOME!
TSK TSK! YOU BOYS REALLY SHOULDN'T BE SO MEAN TO A POOR LITTLE MOTHERLESS LAD!
PAT PAT
WELL, I KNOW SCROOGE WOULD RATHER BE HARD AT WORK THAN HANGING AROUND THIS DEN OF INIQUITY! SO GET AN ANCHOR, BOYS-- "SCROOGEY" WANTS TO SEARCH THE RIVERBOTTOM FOR PAYDIRT! HAR HAR!
HM? WHAT IS IT? WHA--
CRREEEAAK...
OOPS!

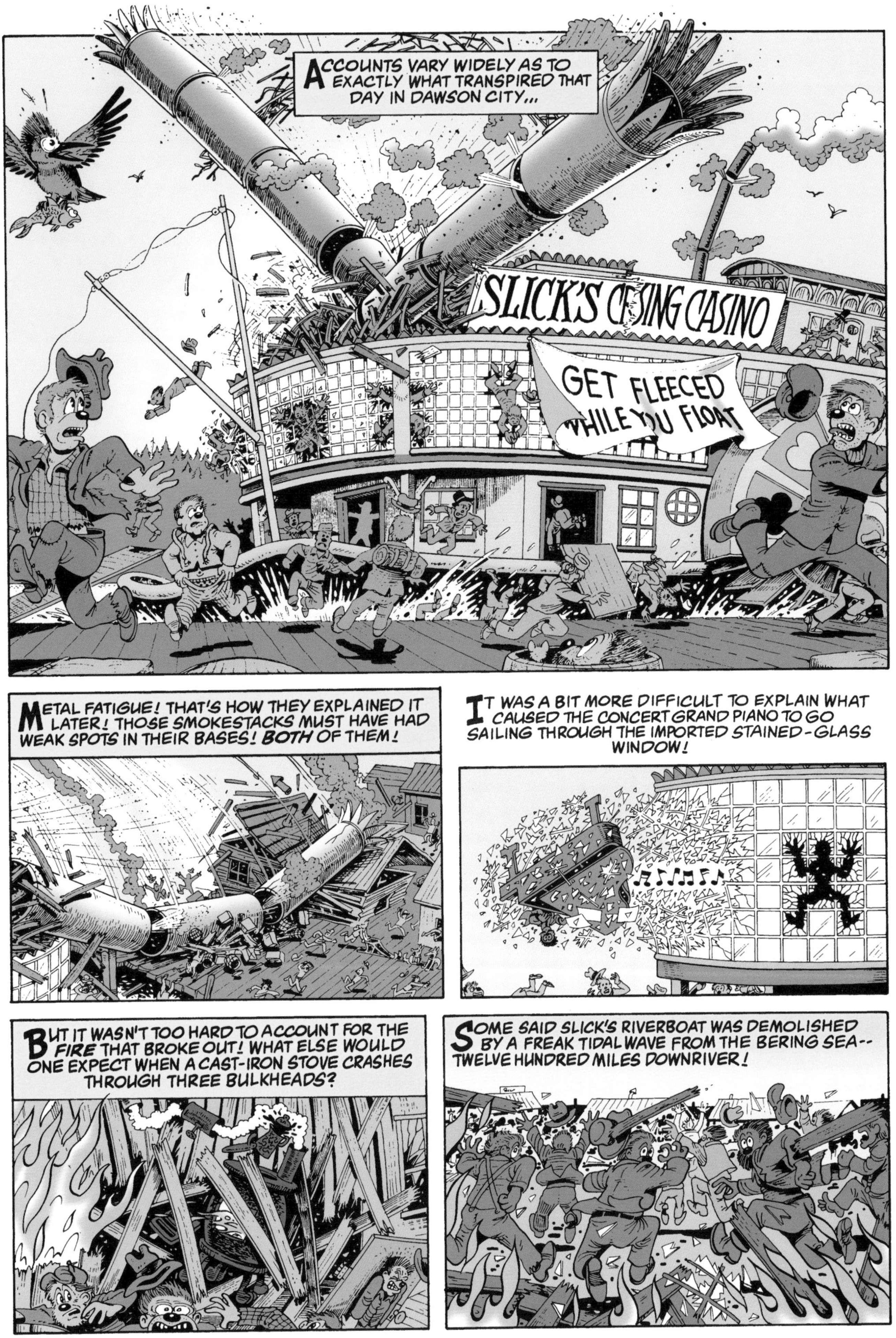
ACCOUNTS VARY WIDELY AS TO EXACTLY WHAT TRANSPIRED THAT DAY IN DAWSON CITY...
GET FLEECED
METAL FATIGUE! THAT'S HOW THEY EXPLAINED IT LATER! THOSE SMOKESTACKS MUST HAVE HAD WEAK SPOTS IN THEIR BASES! BOTH OF THEM!
IT WAS A BIT MORE DIFFICULT TO EXPLAIN WHAT CAUSED THE CONCERT GRAND PIANO TO GO SAILING THROUGH THE IMPORTED STAINED-GLASS WINDOW!
BUT IT WASN'T TOO HARD TO ACCOUNT FOR THE FIRE THAT BROKE OUT! WHAT ELSE WOULD ONE EXPECT WHEN A CAST-IRON STOVE CRASHES THROUGH THREE BULKHEADS?
SOME SAID SLICK'S RIVERBOAT WAS DEMOLISHED BY A FREAK TIDAL WAVE FROM THE BERING SEA-- TWELVE HUNDRED MILES DOWNRIVER!

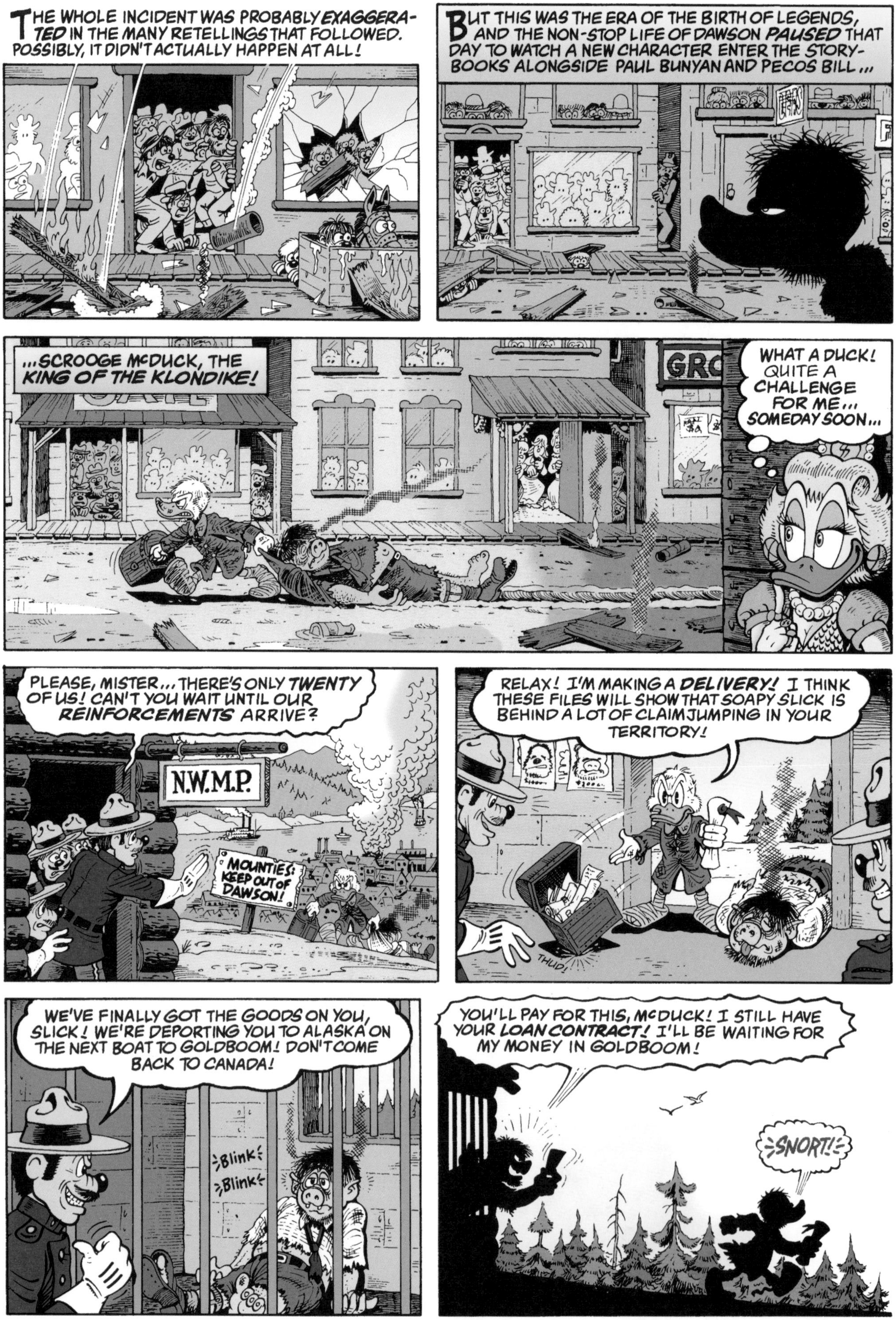

THE WHOLE INCIDENT WAS PROBABLY EXAGGERATED IN THE MANY RETELLINGS THAT FOLLOWED. POSSIBLY, IT DIDN'T ACTUALLY HAPPEN AT ALL!
BUT THIS WAS THE ERA OF THE BIRTH OF LEGENDS, AND THE NON-STOP LIFE OF DAWSON PAUSED THAT DAY TO WATCH A NEW CHARACTER ENTER THE STORY-BOOKS ALONGSIDE PAUL BUNYAN AND PECOS BILL...
...SCROOGE McDUCK, THE KING OF THE KLONDIKE!
GRO
WHAT A DUCK! QUITE A CHALLENGE FOR ME... SOMEDAY SOON...
PLEASE, MISTER... THERE'S ONLY TWENTY OF US! CAN'T YOU WAIT UNTIL OUR REINFORCEMENTS ARRIVE?
N.W.M.P.
MOUNTIES: KEEP OUT OF DAWSON!
RELAX! I'M MAKING A DELIVERY! I THINK THESE FILES WILL SHOW THAT SOAPY SLICK IS BEHIND A LOT OF CLAIMJUMPING IN YOUR TERRITORY!
THUD!
WE'VE FINALLY GOT THE GOODS ON YOU, SLICK! WE'RE DEPORTING YOU TO ALASKA ON THE NEXT BOAT TO GOLDBOOM! DON'T COME BACK TO CANADA!
Blink
Blink
YOU'LL PAY FOR THIS, McDUCK! I STILL HAVE YOUR LOAN CONTRACT! I'LL BE WAITING FOR MY MONEY IN GOLDBOOM!
SNORT!

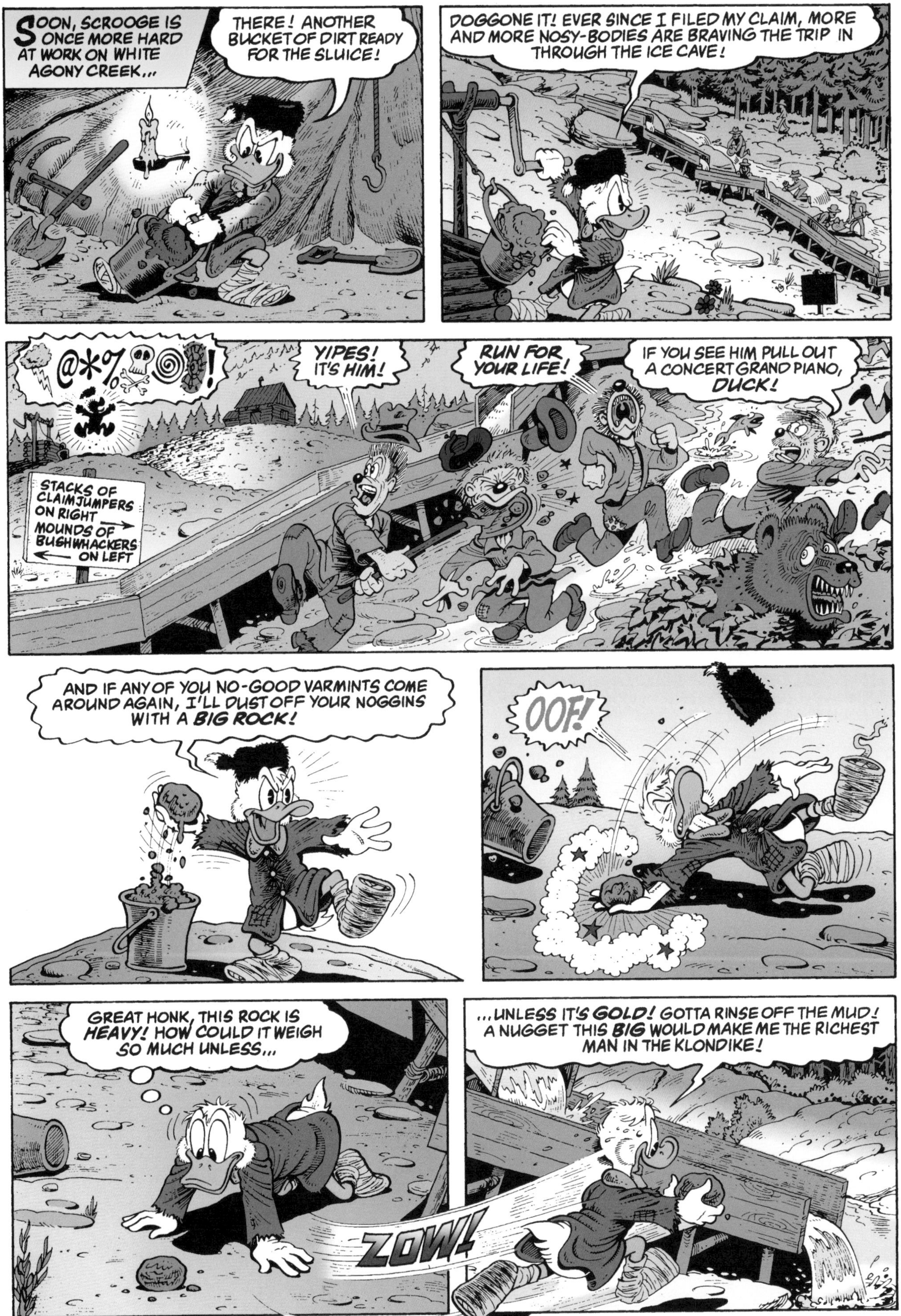
SOON, SCROOGE IS ONCE MORE HARD AT WORK ON WHITE AGONY CREEK...
THERE! ANOTHER BUCKET OF DIRT READY FOR THE SLUICE!
DOGGONE IT! EVER SINCE I FILED MY CLAIM, MORE AND MORE NOSY-BODIES ARE BRAVING THE TRIP IN THROUGH THE ICE CAVE!
@*%!
YIPES! IT'S HIM!
RUN FOR YOUR LIFE!
IF YOU SEE HIM PULL OUT A CONCERT GRAND PIANO, DUCK!
STACKS OF CLAIMJUMPERS ON RIGHT
MOUNDS OF BUSHWHACKERS ON LEFT
AND IF ANY OF YOU NO-GOOD VARMINTS COME AROUND AGAIN, I'LL DUST OFF YOUR NOGGINS WITH A BIG ROCK!
OOF!
GREAT HONK, THIS ROCK IS HEAVY! HOW COULD IT WEIGH SO MUCH UNLESS...
...UNLESS IT'S GOLD! GOTTA RINSE OFF THE MUD! A NUGGET THIS BIG WOULD MAKE ME THE RICHEST MAN IN THE KLONDIKE!
ZOW!

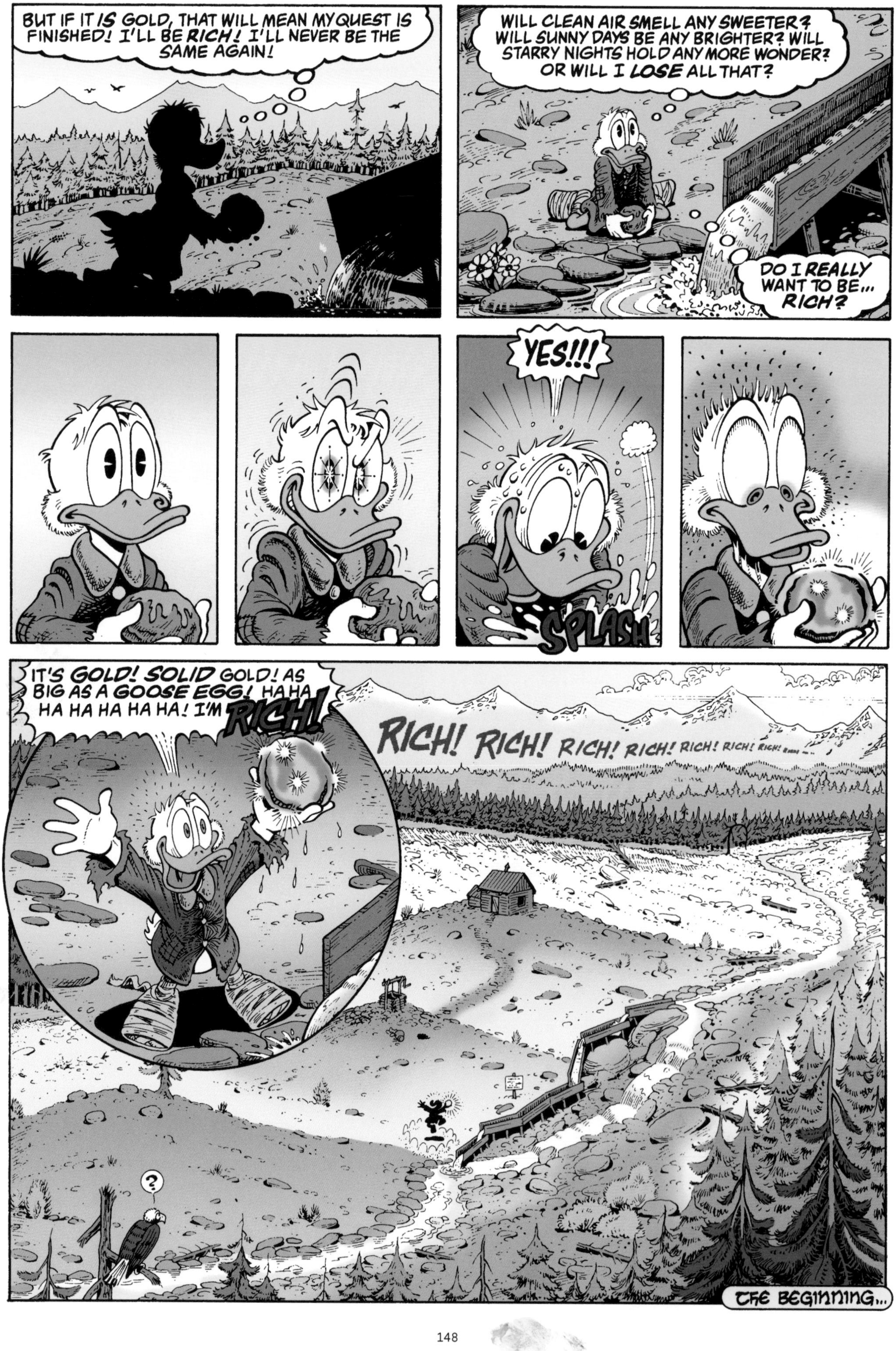
BUT IF IT IS GOLD, THAT WILL MEAN MY QUEST IS FINISHED! I'LL BE RICH! I'LL NEVER BE THE SAME AGAIN!
WILL CLEAN AIR SMELL ANY SWEETER? WILL SUNNY DAYS BE ANY BRIGHTER? WILL STARRY NIGHTS HOLD ANY MORE WONDER? OR WILL I LOSE ALL THAT?
DO I REALLY WANT TO BE... RICH?
YES!!!
SPLASH
IT'S GOLD! SOLID GOLD! AS BIG AS A GOOSE EGG! HA HA HA HA HA HA HA! I'M RICH!
RICH! RICH! RICH! RICH! RICH! RICH!
?
THE BEGINNING...

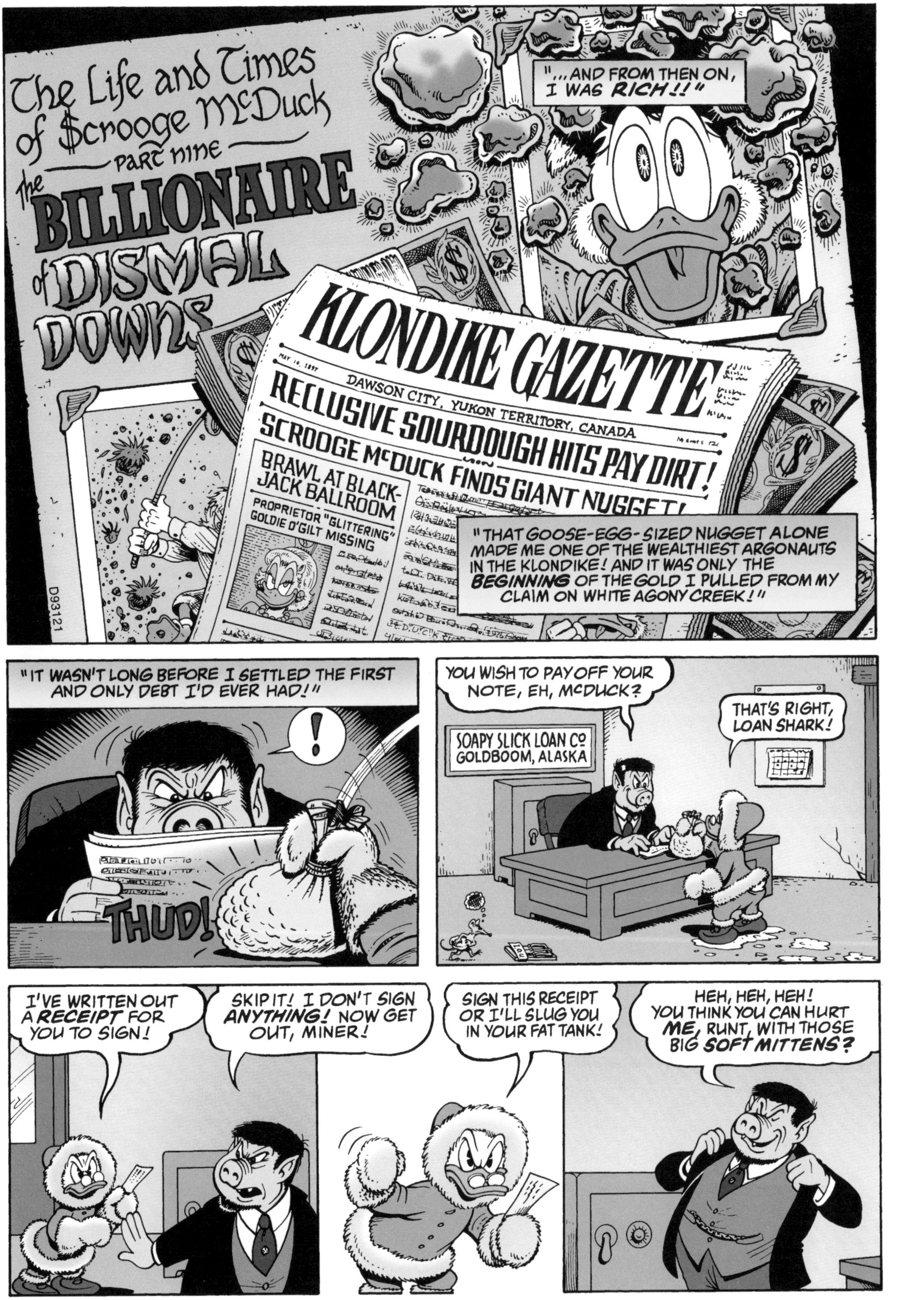
The Life and Times of $crooge McDuck
— PART NINE —
the BILLIONAIRE of DISMAL DOWNS
"...AND FROM THEN ON, I WAS RICH!!"
KLONDIKE GAZETTE
DAWSON CITY, YUKON TERRITORY, CANADA
RECLUSIVE SOURDOUGH HITS PAY DIRT!
SCROOGE McDUCK FINDS GIANT NUGGET!
BRAWL AT BLACK-JACK BALLROOM
PROPRIETOR "GLITTERING" GOLDIE O'GILT MISSING
"THAT GOOSE-EGG-SIZED NUGGET ALONE MADE ME ONE OF THE WEALTHIEST ARGONAUTS IN THE KLONDIKE! AND IT WAS ONLY THE BEGINNING OF THE GOLD I PULLED FROM MY CLAIM ON WHITE AGONY CREEK!"
D93121
"IT WASN'T LONG BEFORE I SETTLED THE FIRST AND ONLY DEBT I'D EVER HAD!"
!
THUD!
YOU WISH TO PAY OFF YOUR NOTE, EH, McDUCK?
THAT'S RIGHT, LOAN SHARK!
SOAPY SLICK LOAN Co
GOLDBOOM, ALASKA
I'VE WRITTEN OUT A RECEIPT FOR YOU TO SIGN!
SKIP IT! I DON'T SIGN ANYTHING! NOW GET OUT, MINER!
SIGN THIS RECEIPT OR I'LL SLUG YOU IN YOUR FAT TANK!
HEH, HEH, HEH! YOU THINK YOU CAN HURT ME, RUNT, WITH THOSE BIG SOFT MITTENS?

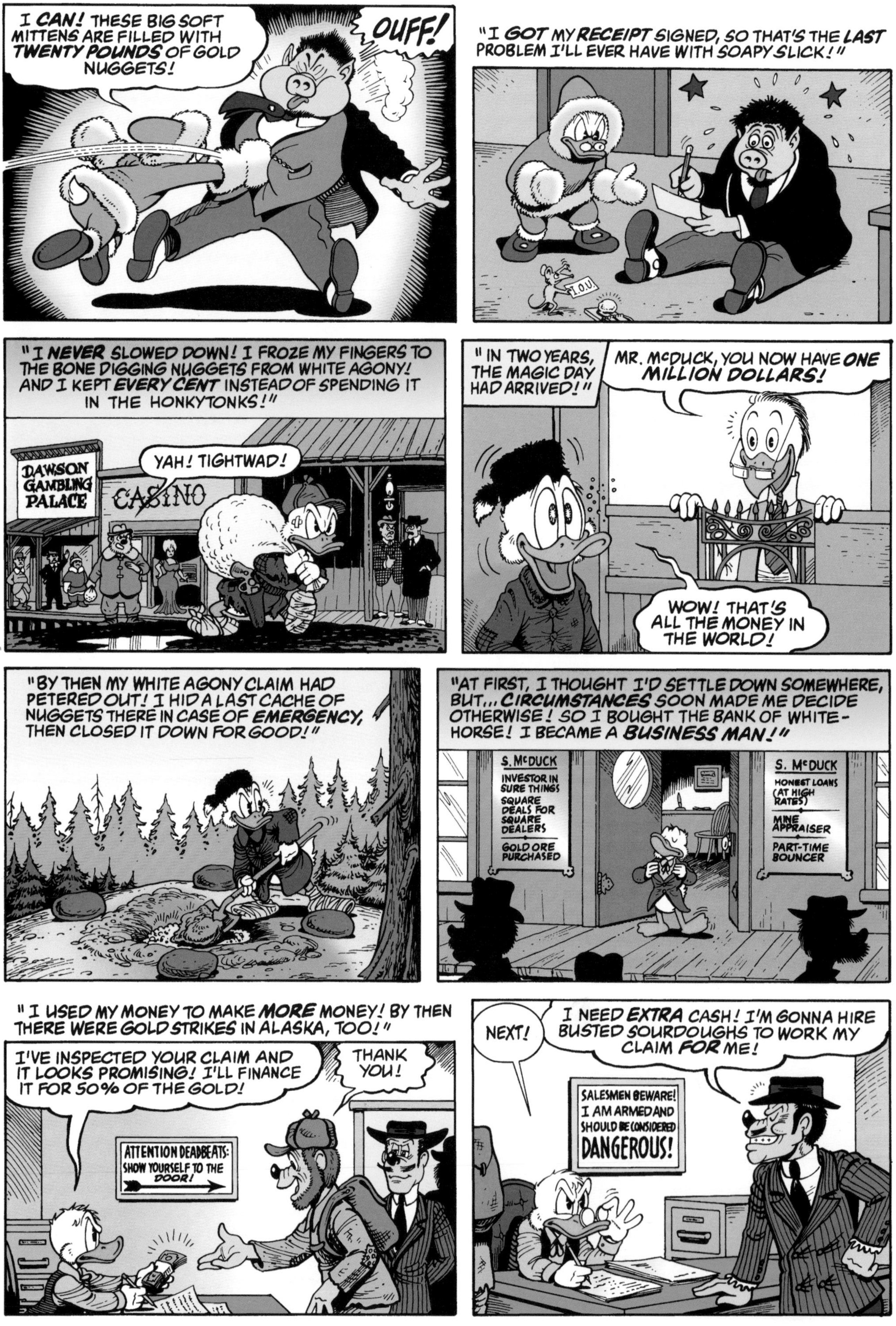
I CAN! THESE BIG SOFT MITTENS ARE FILLED WITH TWENTY POUNDS OF GOLD NUGGETS!
OUFF!
"I GOT MY RECEIPT SIGNED, SO THAT'S THE LAST PROBLEM I'LL EVER HAVE WITH SOAPY SLICK!"
I.O.U.
"I NEVER SLOWED DOWN! I FROZE MY FINGERS TO THE BONE DIGGING NUGGETS FROM WHITE AGONY! AND I KEPT EVERY CENT INSTEAD OF SPENDING IT IN THE HONKYTONKS!"
DAWSON GAMBLING PALACE
CASINO
YAH! TIGHTWAD!
"IN TWO YEARS, THE MAGIC DAY HAD ARRIVED!"
MR. McDUCK, YOU NOW HAVE ONE MILLION DOLLARS!
WOW! THAT'S ALL THE MONEY IN THE WORLD!
"BY THEN MY WHITE AGONY CLAIM HAD PETERED OUT! I HID A LAST CACHE OF NUGGETS THERE IN CASE OF EMERGENCY, THEN CLOSED IT DOWN FOR GOOD!"
"AT FIRST, I THOUGHT I'D SETTLE DOWN SOMEWHERE, BUT... CIRCUMSTANCES SOON MADE ME DECIDE OTHERWISE! SO I BOUGHT THE BANK OF WHITE-HORSE! I BECAME A BUSINESS MAN!"
S. McDUCK
INVESTOR IN SURE THINGS
SQUARE DEALS FOR SQUARE DEALERS
GOLD ORE PURCHASED
S. McDUCK
HONEST LOANS (AT HIGH RATES)
MINE APPRAISER
PART-TIME BOUNCER
"I USED MY MONEY TO MAKE MORE MONEY! BY THEN THERE WERE GOLD STRIKES IN ALASKA, TOO!"
I'VE INSPECTED YOUR CLAIM AND IT LOOKS PROMISING! I'LL FINANCE IT FOR 50% OF THE GOLD!
THANK YOU!
ATTENTION DEADBEATS: SHOW YOURSELF TO THE DOOR!
NEXT!
I NEED EXTRA CASH! I'M GONNA HIRE BUSTED SOURDOUGHS TO WORK MY CLAIM FOR ME!
SALESMEN BEWARE! I AM ARMED AND SHOULD BE CONSIDERED DANGEROUS!

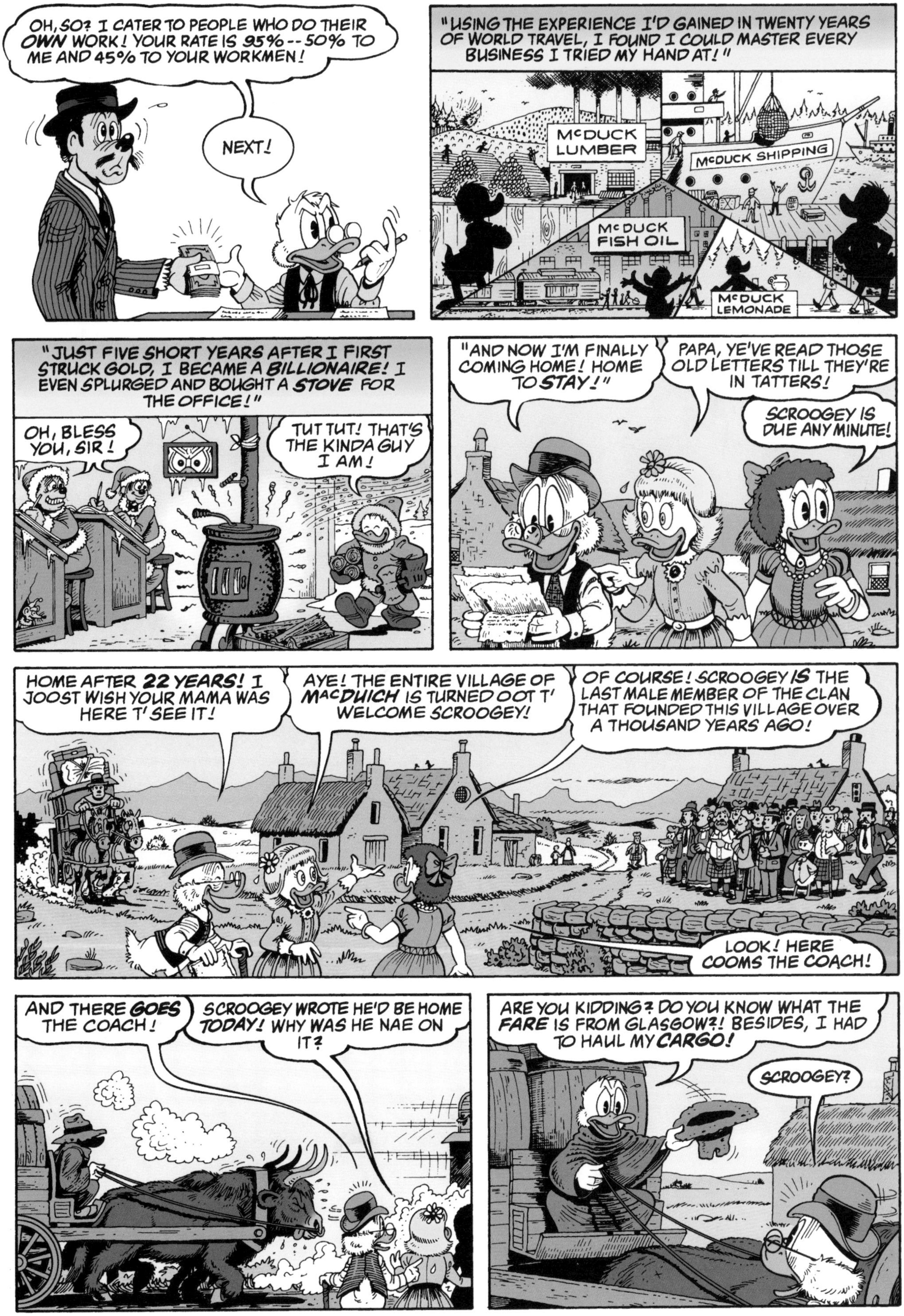
OH, SO? I CATER TO PEOPLE WHO DO THEIR OWN WORK! YOUR RATE IS 95% -- 50% TO ME AND 45% TO YOUR WORKMEN!
NEXT!
"USING THE EXPERIENCE I'D GAINED IN TWENTY YEARS OF WORLD TRAVEL, I FOUND I COULD MASTER EVERY BUSINESS I TRIED MY HAND AT!"
McDUCK LUMBER
McDUCK SHIPPING
McDUCK FISH OIL
McDUCK LEMONADE
"JUST FIVE SHORT YEARS AFTER I FIRST STRUCK GOLD, I BECAME A BILLIONAIRE! I EVEN SPLURGED AND BOUGHT A STOVE FOR THE OFFICE!"
OH, BLESS YOU, SIR!
TUT TUT! THAT'S THE KINDA GUY I AM!
"AND NOW I'M FINALLY COMING HOME! HOME TO STAY!"
PAPA, YE'VE READ THOSE OLD LETTERS TILL THEY'RE IN TATTERS!
SCROOGEY IS DUE ANY MINUTE!
HOME AFTER 22 YEARS! I JOOST WISH YOUR MAMA WAS HERE T' SEE IT!
AYE! THE ENTIRE VILLAGE OF MacDUICH IS TURNED OOT T' WELCOME SCROOGEY!
OF COURSE! SCROOGEY IS THE LAST MALE MEMBER OF THE CLAN THAT FOUNDED THIS VILLAGE OVER A THOUSAND YEARS AGO!
LOOK! HERE COOMS THE COACH!
AND THERE GOES THE COACH!
SCROOGEY WROTE HE'D BE HOME TODAY! WHY WAS HE NAE ON IT?
ARE YOU KIDDING? DO YOU KNOW WHAT THE FARE IS FROM GLASGOW?! BESIDES, I HAD TO HAUL MY CARGO!
SCROOGEY?

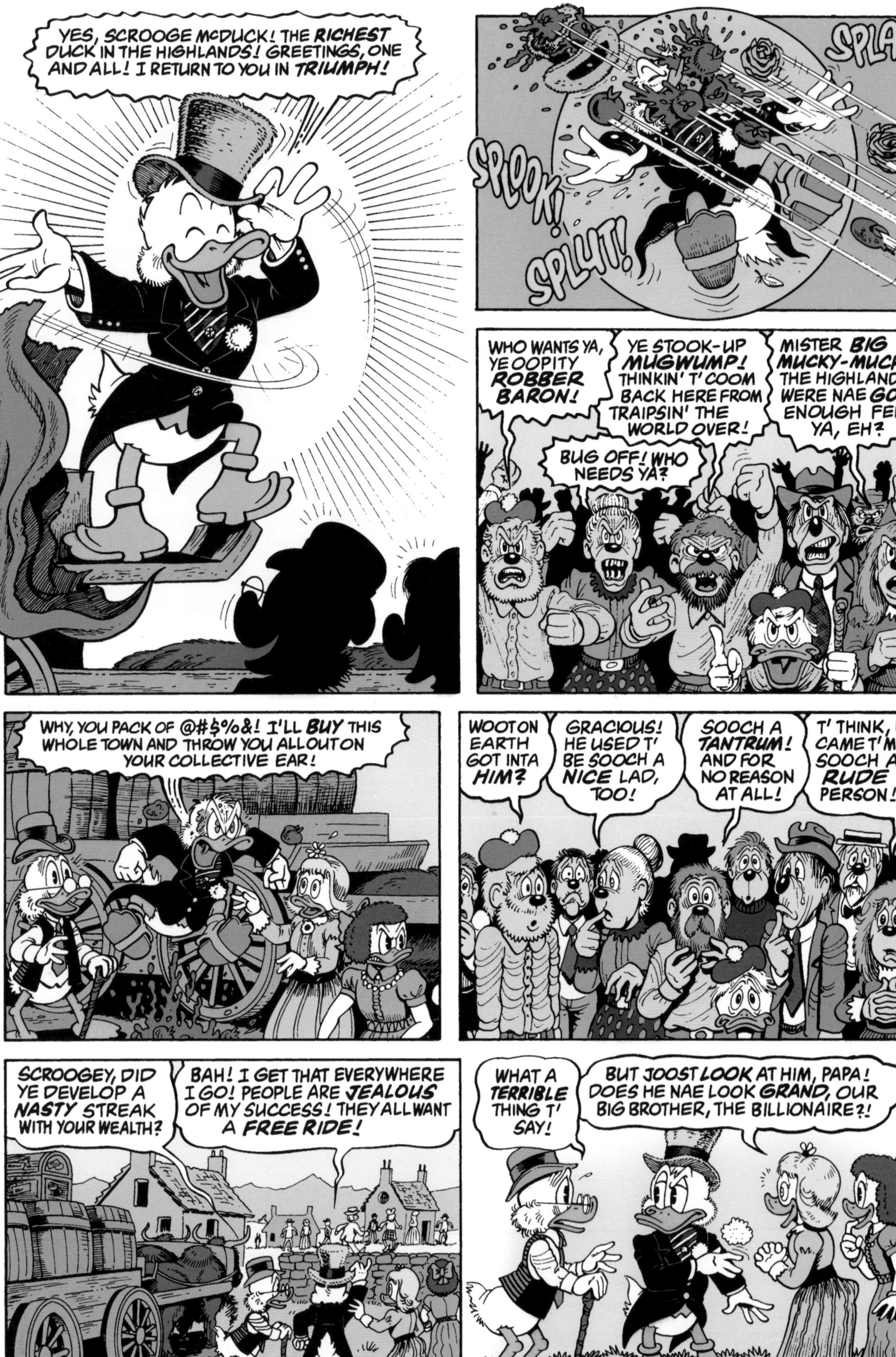
YES, SCROOGE McDUCK! THE RICHEST DUCK IN THE HIGHLANDS! GREETINGS, ONE AND ALL! I RETURN TO YOU IN TRIUMPH!
SPLAT!
SPLOOK!
SPLUT!
WHO WANTS YA, YE OOPITY ROBBER BARON!
YE STOOK-UP MUGWUMP! THINKIN' T' COOM BACK HERE FROM TRAIPSIN' THE WORLD OVER!
MISTER BIG MUCKY-MUCK! THE HIGHLANDS WERE NAE GOOD ENOUGH FER YA, EH?
BUG OFF! WHO NEEDS YA?
WHY, YOU PACK OF @#$%&! I'LL BUY THIS WHOLE TOWN AND THROW YOU ALL OUT ON YOUR COLLECTIVE EAR!
WOOT ON EARTH GOT INTA HIM?
GRACIOUS! HE USED T' BE SOOCH A NICE LAD, TOO!
SOOCH A TANTRUM! AND FOR NO REASON AT ALL!
T' THINK, WE CAME T' MEET SOOCH A RUDE PERSON! TSK!
SCROOGEY, DID YE DEVELOP A NASTY STREAK WITH YOUR WEALTH?
BAH! I GET THAT EVERYWHERE I GO! PEOPLE ARE JEALOUS OF MY SUCCESS! THEY ALL WANT A FREE RIDE!
WHAT A TERRIBLE THING T' SAY!
BUT JOOST LOOK AT HIM, PAPA! DOES HE NAE LOOK GRAND, OUR BIG BROTHER, THE BILLIONAIRE?!

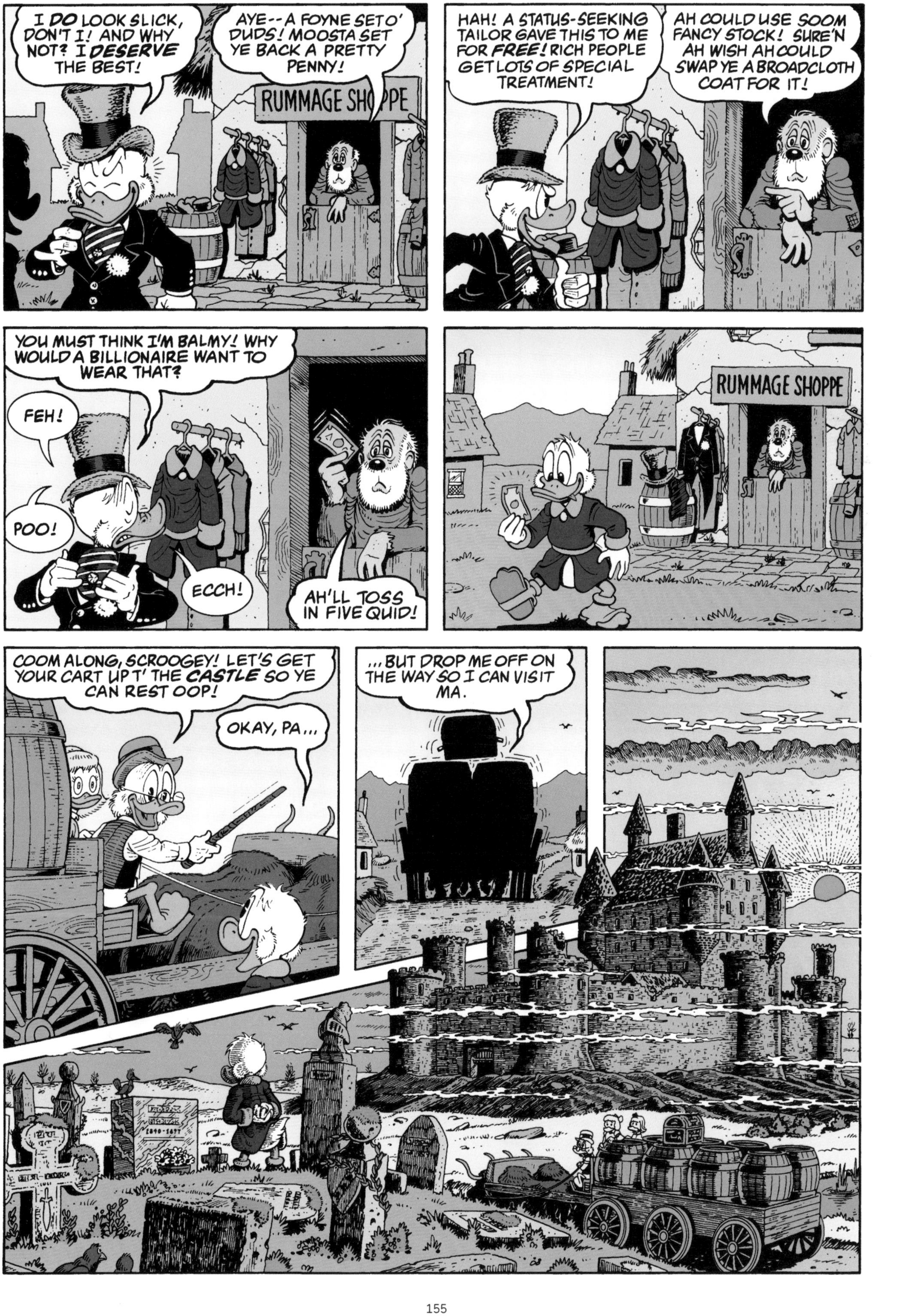
I DO LOOK SLICK, DON'T I! AND WHY NOT? I DESERVE THE BEST!
AYE--A FOYNE SET O' DUDS! MOOSTA SET YE BACK A PRETTY PENNY!
RUMMAGE SHOPPE
HAH! A STATUS-SEEKING TAILOR GAVE THIS TO ME FOR FREE! RICH PEOPLE GET LOTS OF SPECIAL TREATMENT!
AH COULD USE SOOM FANCY STOCK! SURE'N AH WISH AH COULD SWAP YE A BROADCLOTH COAT FOR IT!
YOU MUST THINK I'M BALMY! WHY WOULD A BILLIONAIRE WANT TO WEAR THAT?
FEH!
POO!
ECCH!
AH'LL TOSS IN FIVE QUID!
RUMMAGE SHOPPE
COOM ALONG, SCROOGEY! LET'S GET YOUR CART UP T' THE CASTLE SO YE CAN REST OOP!
OKAY, PA...
...BUT DROP ME OFF ON THE WAY SO I CAN VISIT MA.

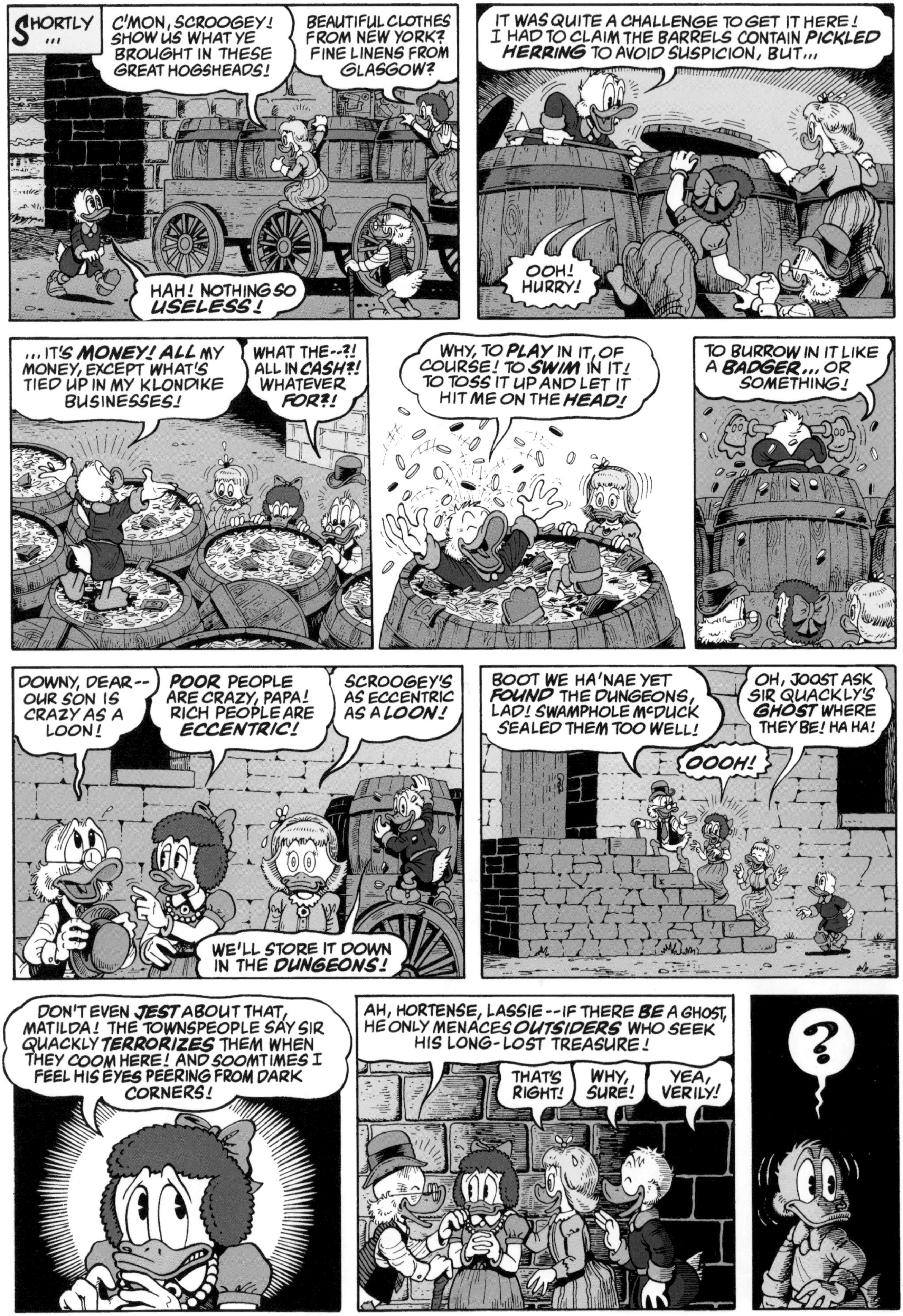

SHORTLY ...
C'MON, SCROOGEY! SHOW US WHAT YE BROUGHT IN THESE GREAT HOGSHEADS!
BEAUTIFUL CLOTHES FROM NEW YORK? FINE LINENS FROM GLASGOW?
HAH! NOTHING SO USELESS!
IT WAS QUITE A CHALLENGE TO GET IT HERE! I HAD TO CLAIM THE BARRELS CONTAIN PICKLED HERRING TO AVOID SUSPICION, BUT...
OOH! HURRY!
...IT'S MONEY! ALL MY MONEY, EXCEPT WHAT'S TIED UP IN MY KLONDIKE BUSINESSES!
WHAT THE--?! ALL IN CASH?! WHATEVER FOR?!
WHY, TO PLAY IN IT, OF COURSE! TO SWIM IN IT! TO TOSS IT UP AND LET IT HIT ME ON THE HEAD!
TO BURROW IN IT LIKE A BADGER... OR SOMETHING!
DOWNY, DEAR-- OUR SON IS CRAZY AS A LOON!
POOR PEOPLE ARE CRAZY, PAPA! RICH PEOPLE ARE ECCENTRIC!
SCROOGEY'S AS ECCENTRIC AS A LOON!
WE'LL STORE IT DOWN IN THE DUNGEONS!
BOOT WE HA'NAE YET FOUND THE DUNGEONS, LAD! SWAMPHOLE McDUCK SEALED THEM TOO WELL!
OH, JOOST ASK SIR QUACKLY'S GHOST WHERE THEY BE! HA HA!
OOOH!
DON'T EVEN JEST ABOUT THAT, MATILDA! THE TOWNSPEOPLE SAY SIR QUACKLY TERRORIZES THEM WHEN THEY COOM HERE! AND SOOMTIMES I FEEL HIS EYES PEERING FROM DARK CORNERS!
AH, HORTENSE, LASSIE--IF THERE BE A GHOST, HE ONLY MENACES OUTSIDERS WHO SEEK HIS LONG-LOST TREASURE!
THAT'S RIGHT!
WHY, SURE!
YEA, VERILY!
?

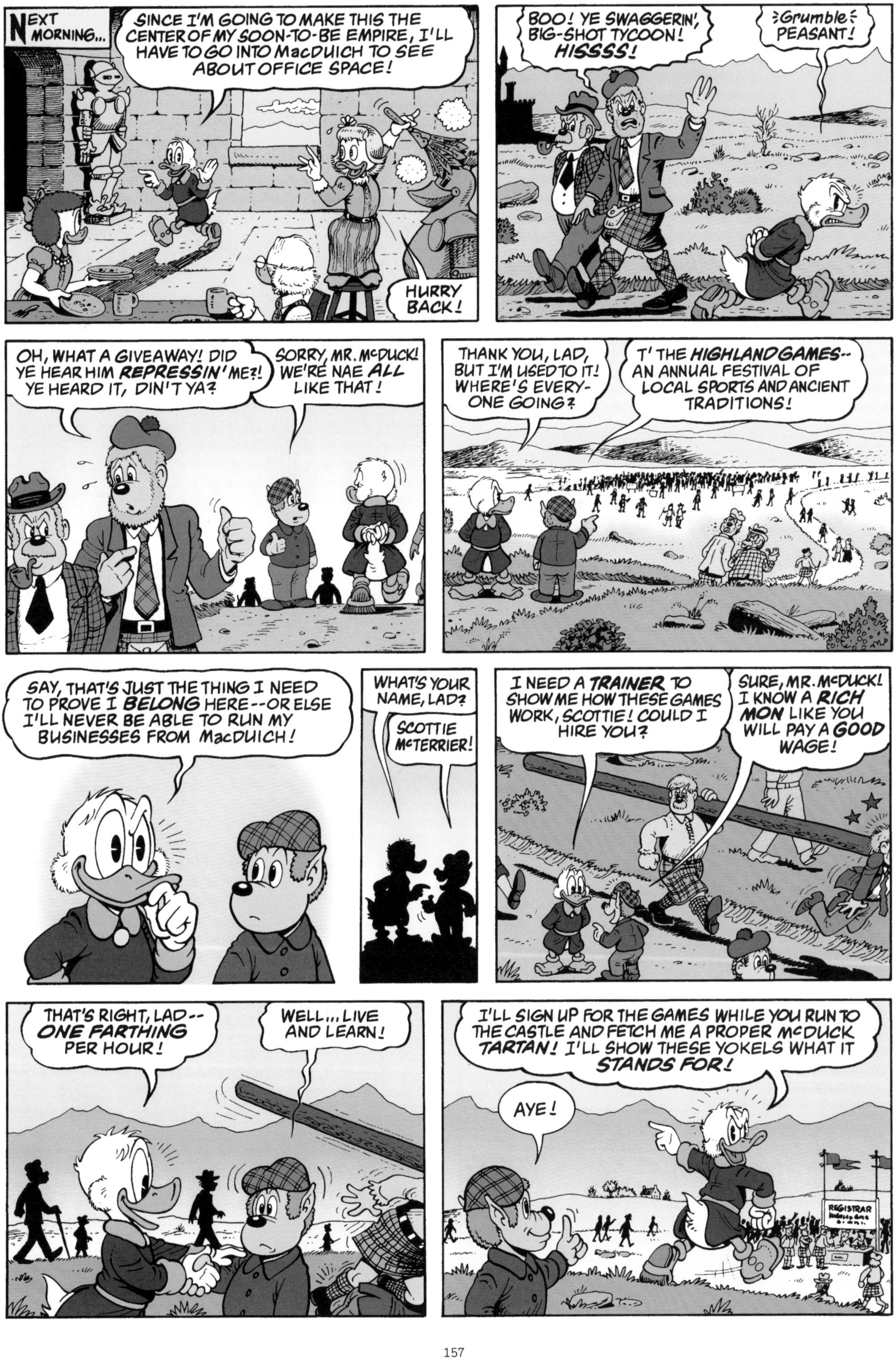
NEXT MORNING...
SINCE I'M GOING TO MAKE THIS THE CENTER OF MY SOON-TO-BE EMPIRE, I'LL HAVE TO GO INTO MacDUICH TO SEE ABOUT OFFICE SPACE!
HURRY BACK!
BOO! YE SWAGGERIN', BIG-SHOT TYCOON! HISSSS!
Grumble PEASANT!
OH, WHAT A GIVEAWAY! DID YE HEAR HIM REPRESSIN' ME?! YE HEARD IT, DIN'T YA?
SORRY, MR. McDUCK! WE'RE NAE ALL LIKE THAT!
THANK YOU, LAD, BUT I'M USED TO IT! WHERE'S EVERY-ONE GOING?
T' THE HIGHLAND GAMES-- AN ANNUAL FESTIVAL OF LOCAL SPORTS AND ANCIENT TRADITIONS!
SAY, THAT'S JUST THE THING I NEED TO PROVE I BELONG HERE--OR ELSE I'LL NEVER BE ABLE TO RUN MY BUSINESSES FROM MacDUICH!
WHAT'S YOUR NAME, LAD?
SCOTTIE McTERRIER!
I NEED A TRAINER TO SHOW ME HOW THESE GAMES WORK, SCOTTIE! COULD I HIRE YOU?
SURE, MR. McDUCK! I KNOW A RICH MON LIKE YOU WILL PAY A GOOD WAGE!
THAT'S RIGHT, LAD-- ONE FARTHING PER HOUR!
WELL... LIVE AND LEARN!
I'LL SIGN UP FOR THE GAMES WHILE YOU RUN TO THE CASTLE AND FETCH ME A PROPER McDUCK TARTAN! I'LL SHOW THESE YOKELS WHAT IT STANDS FOR!
AYE!
REGISTRAR

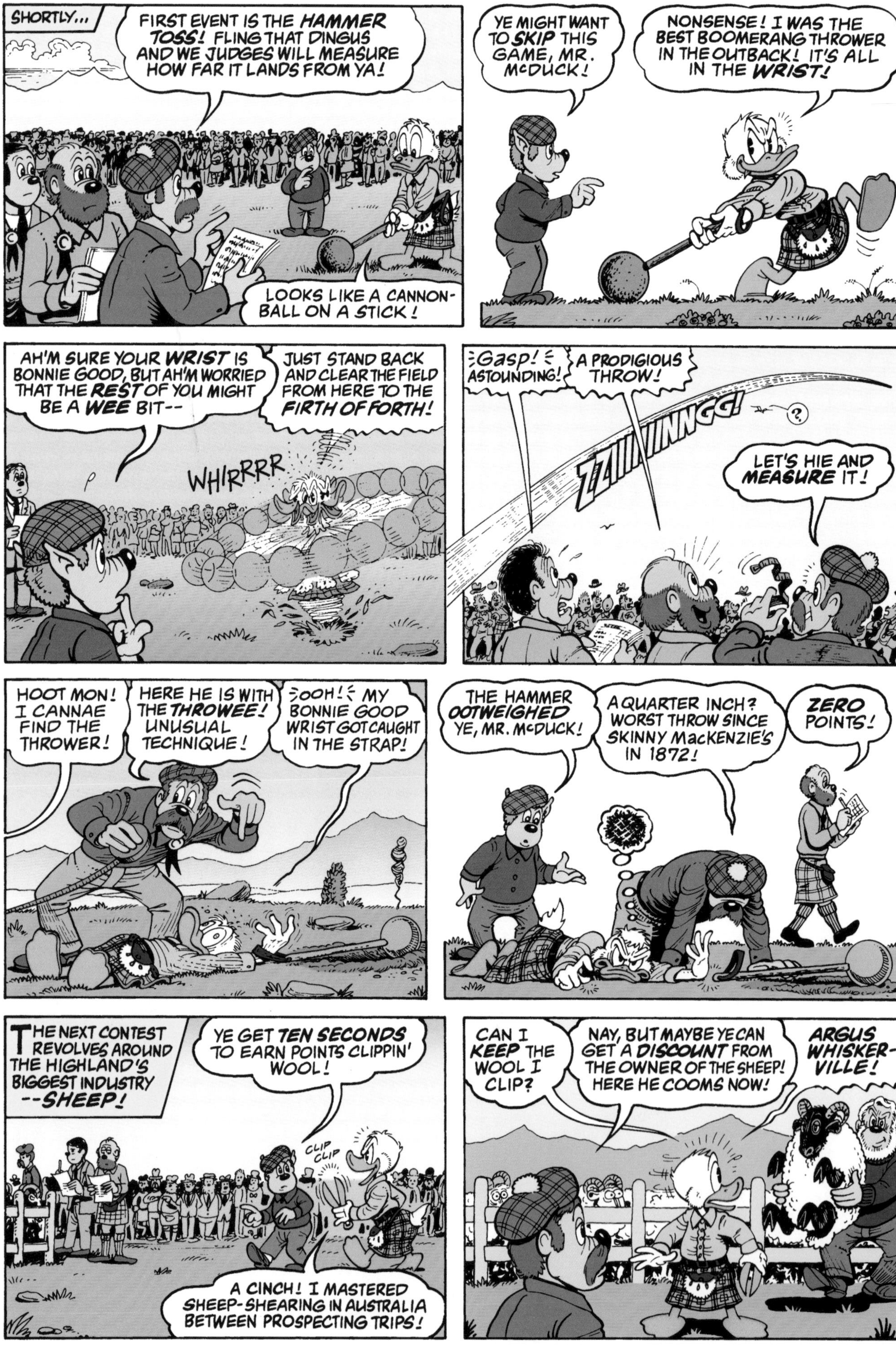
SHORTLY...
FIRST EVENT IS THE HAMMER TOSS! FLING THAT DINGUS AND WE JUDGES WILL MEASURE HOW FAR IT LANDS FROM YA!
LOOKS LIKE A CANNON-BALL ON A STICK!
YE MIGHT WANT TO SKIP THIS GAME, MR. McDUCK!
NONSENSE! I WAS THE BEST BOOMERANG THROWER IN THE OUTBACK! IT'S ALL IN THE WRIST!
AH'M SURE YOUR WRIST IS BONNIE GOOD, BUT AH'M WORRIED THAT THE REST OF YOU MIGHT BE A WEE BIT--
JUST STAND BACK AND CLEAR THE FIELD FROM HERE TO THE FIRTH OF FORTH!
WHIRRRR
Gasp! ASTOUNDING!
A PRODIGIOUS THROW!
ZZIIIIIINNGG!
LET'S HIE AND MEASURE IT!
HOOT MON! I CANNAE FIND THE THROWER!
HERE HE IS WITH THE THROWEE! UNUSUAL TECHNIQUE!
OOH! MY BONNIE GOOD WRIST GOT CAUGHT IN THE STRAP!
THE HAMMER OOTWEIGHED YE, MR. McDUCK!
A QUARTER INCH? WORST THROW SINCE SKINNY MacKENZIE'S IN 1872!
ZERO POINTS!
THE NEXT CONTEST REVOLVES AROUND THE HIGHLAND'S BIGGEST INDUSTRY --SHEEP!
YE GET TEN SECONDS TO EARN POINTS CLIPPIN' WOOL!
CLIP CLIP
A CINCH! I MASTERED SHEEP-SHEARING IN AUSTRALIA BETWEEN PROSPECTING TRIPS!
CAN I KEEP THE WOOL I CLIP?
NAY, BUT MAYBE YE CAN GET A DISCOUNT FROM THE OWNER OF THE SHEEP! HERE HE COOMS NOW!
ARGUS WHISKER-VILLE!

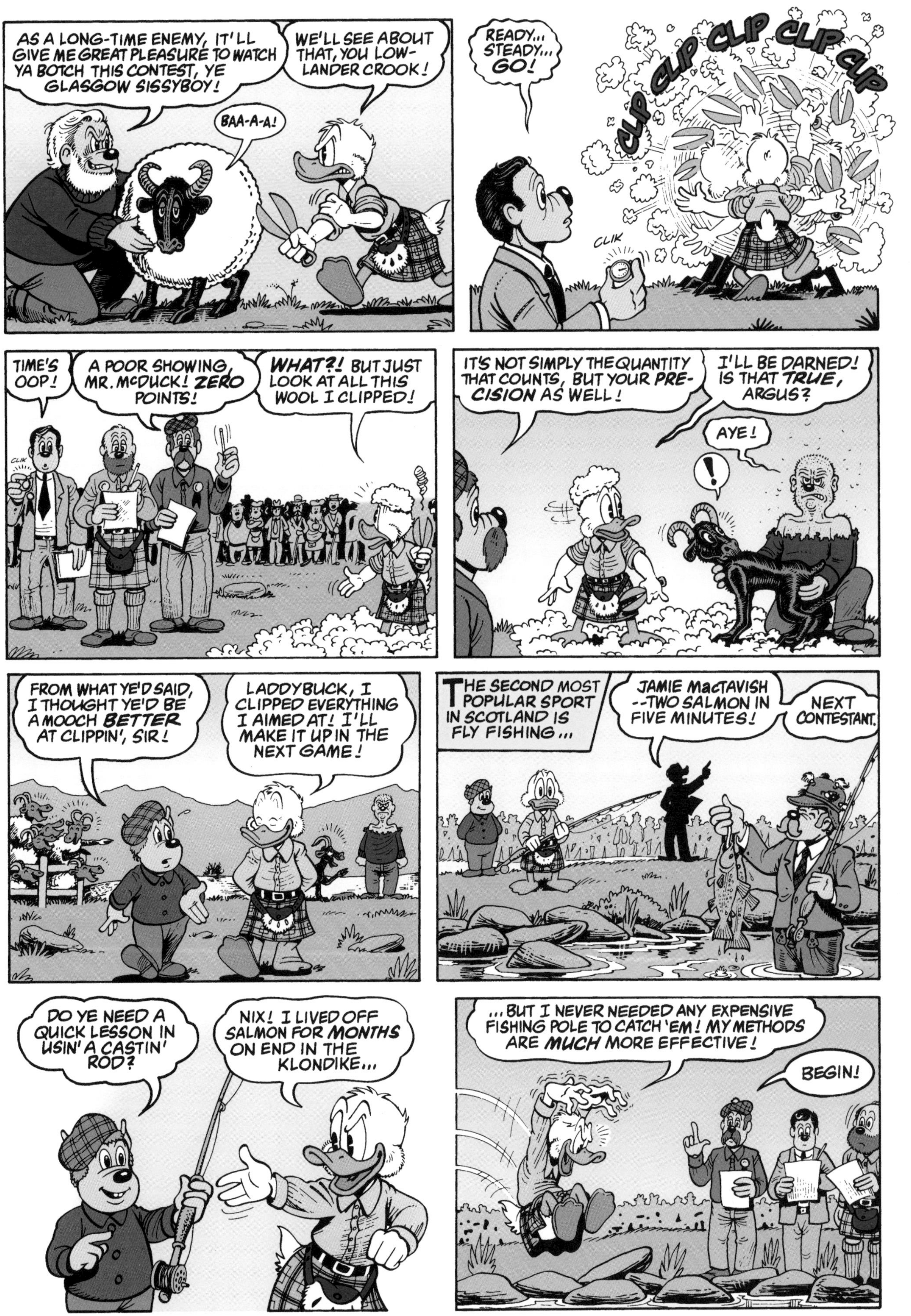
AS A LONG-TIME ENEMY, IT'LL GIVE ME GREAT PLEASURE TO WATCH YA BOTCH THIS CONTEST, YE GLASGOW SISSYBOY!
BAA-A-A!
WE'LL SEE ABOUT THAT, YOU LOW-LANDER CROOK!
READY... STEADY... GO!
CLIP CLIP CLIP CLIP CLIP
CLIK
TIME'S OOP!
A POOR SHOWING, MR. McDUCK! ZERO POINTS!
WHAT?! BUT JUST LOOK AT ALL THIS WOOL I CLIPPED!
CLIK
IT'S NOT SIMPLY THE QUANTITY THAT COUNTS, BUT YOUR PRE-CISION AS WELL!
I'LL BE DARNED! IS THAT TRUE, ARGUS?
AYE!
!
FROM WHAT YE'D SAID, I THOUGHT YE'D BE A MOOCH BETTER AT CLIPPIN', SIR!
LADDYBUCK, I CLIPPED EVERYTHING I AIMED AT! I'LL MAKE IT UP IN THE NEXT GAME!
THE SECOND MOST POPULAR SPORT IN SCOTLAND IS FLY FISHING...
JAMIE MacTAVISH --TWO SALMON IN FIVE MINUTES!
NEXT CONTESTANT.
DO YE NEED A QUICK LESSON IN USIN' A CASTIN' ROD?
NIX! I LIVED OFF SALMON FOR MONTHS ON END IN THE KLONDIKE...
...BUT I NEVER NEEDED ANY EXPENSIVE FISHING POLE TO CATCH 'EM! MY METHODS ARE MUCH MORE EFFECTIVE!
BEGIN!

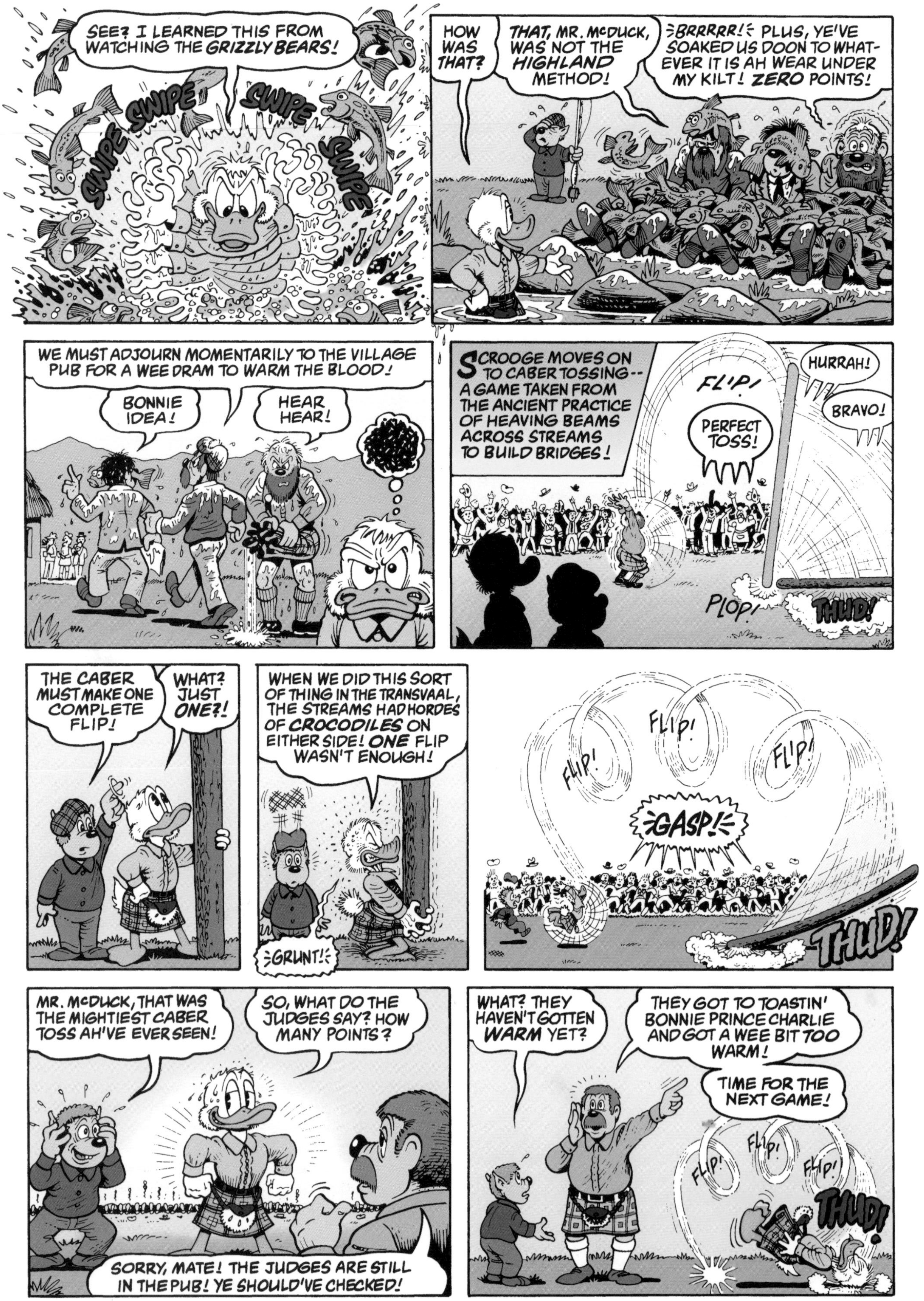
SEE? I LEARNED THIS FROM WATCHING THE GRIZZLY BEARS!
SWIPE SWIPE SWIPE SWIPE SWIPE
HOW WAS THAT?
THAT, MR. McDUCK, WAS NOT THE HIGHLAND METHOD!
BRRRRR! PLUS, YE'VE SOAKED US DOON TO WHATEVER IT IS AH WEAR UNDER MY KILT! ZERO POINTS!
WE MUST ADJOURN MOMENTARILY TO THE VILLAGE PUB FOR A WEE DRAM TO WARM THE BLOOD!
BONNIE IDEA!
HEAR HEAR!
SCROOGE MOVES ON TO CABER TOSSING-- A GAME TAKEN FROM THE ANCIENT PRACTICE OF HEAVING BEAMS ACROSS STREAMS TO BUILD BRIDGES!
FLIP!
PERFECT TOSS!
HURRAH!
BRAVO!
PLOP!
THUD!
THE CABER MUST MAKE ONE COMPLETE FLIP!
WHAT? JUST ONE?!
WHEN WE DID THIS SORT OF THING IN THE TRANSVAAL, THE STREAMS HAD HORDES OF CROCODILES ON EITHER SIDE! ONE FLIP WASN'T ENOUGH!
GRUNT!
FLIP! FLIP! FLIP!
GASP!
THUD!
MR. McDUCK, THAT WAS THE MIGHTIEST CABER TOSS AH'VE EVER SEEN!
SO, WHAT DO THE JUDGES SAY? HOW MANY POINTS?
SORRY, MATE! THE JUDGES ARE STILL IN THE PUB! YE SHOULD'VE CHECKED!
WHAT? THEY HAVEN'T GOTTEN WARM YET?
THEY GOT TO TOASTIN' BONNIE PRINCE CHARLIE AND GOT A WEE BIT TOO WARM!
TIME FOR THE NEXT GAME!
FLIP! FLIP! FLIP!
THUD!

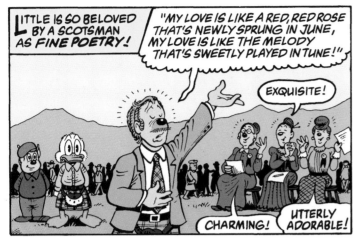

LITTLE IS SO BELOVED BY A SCOTSMAN AS *FINE POETRY!*

"MY LOVE IS LIKE A RED, RED ROSE THAT'S NEWLY SPRUNG IN JUNE, MY LOVE IS LIKE THE MELODY THAT'S SWEETLY PLAYED IN TUNE!"

EXQUISITE!

CHARMING!

UTTERLY ADORABLE!

DO YE KNOW ANY POETRY, MR. McDUCK?

DO I EVER! HERE'S ONE I HEARD BACK IN DAWSON ...≷ahem≷...

NEXT!

"THERE ONCE WAS A BARMAID IN NOME AND A GOLD MINER LONELY FOR HOME. HE HAD THE BREATH OF A MOOSE AND SHE COULDN'T GET LOOSE SO SHE PULLED OUT HER KNIFE AND..."

!!!!!!

HM... THEY LOVED THAT ONE AT THE BLACK JACK BALLROOM! IS IT TOO...*ROUGH-HEWN* FOR THE LOCALS?

WE COULD ASK THEM WHEN THEY COME TO-- BUT MAYBE WE'LL JOOST *MOVE ON* TO THE NEXT GAME!--

TWITCH!

--WHICH IS *GOLF* --THE MOST BELOVED SPORT IN SCOTLAND OVER THE LAST 500 YEARS! ARE YE GOOD AT GOLF *ALSO,* MR. McDUCK?

OH, SURE! WE HAD *LOADS* OF GOLF COURSES IN THE KLONDIKE!

UM... BETTER USE THE *OTHER* END OF THE CLUB, SIR, AND GIVE THE BALL A GOOD LICK!

WHACK!

PLOK.

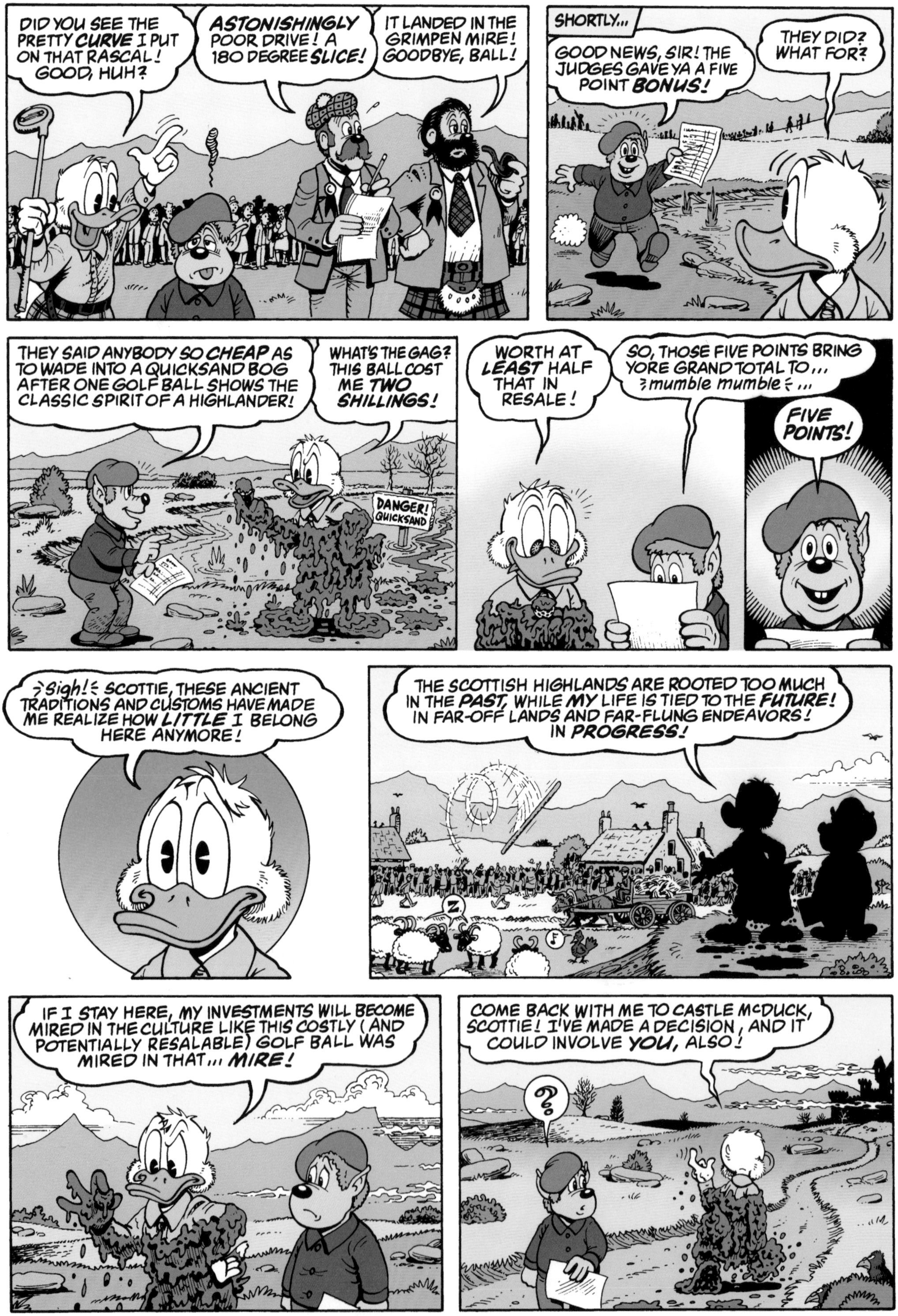
DID YOU SEE THE PRETTY CURVE I PUT ON THAT RASCAL! GOOD, HUH?
ASTONISHINGLY POOR DRIVE! A 180 DEGREE SLICE!
IT LANDED IN THE GRIMPEN MIRE! GOODBYE, BALL!
SHORTLY...
GOOD NEWS, SIR! THE JUDGES GAVE YA A FIVE POINT BONUS!
THEY DID? WHAT FOR?
THEY SAID ANYBODY SO CHEAP AS TO WADE INTO A QUICKSAND BOG AFTER ONE GOLF BALL SHOWS THE CLASSIC SPIRIT OF A HIGHLANDER!
WHAT'S THE GAG? THIS BALL COST ME TWO SHILLINGS!
DANGER! QUICKSAND
WORTH AT LEAST HALF THAT IN RESALE!
SO, THOSE FIVE POINTS BRING YORE GRAND TOTAL TO... mumble mumble ...
FIVE POINTS!
Sigh! SCOTTIE, THESE ANCIENT TRADITIONS AND CUSTOMS HAVE MADE ME REALIZE HOW LITTLE I BELONG HERE ANYMORE!
THE SCOTTISH HIGHLANDS ARE ROOTED TOO MUCH IN THE PAST, WHILE MY LIFE IS TIED TO THE FUTURE! IN FAR-OFF LANDS AND FAR-FLUNG ENDEAVORS! IN PROGRESS!
Z
IF I STAY HERE, MY INVESTMENTS WILL BECOME MIRED IN THE CULTURE LIKE THIS COSTLY (AND POTENTIALLY RESALABLE) GOLF BALL WAS MIRED IN THAT... MIRE!
COME BACK WITH ME TO CASTLE McDUCK, SCOTTIE! I'VE MADE A DECISION, AND IT COULD INVOLVE YOU, ALSO!
?

SOON...

I HAVE SOMETHING IN THIS SAFE DEPOSIT BOX FROM MY WHITEHORSE BANK THAT'S THE *KEY* TO OUR FUTURE!

SEVERAL YEARS AGO, WHEN I BRIEFLY CONSIDERED SETTLING DOWN, I BOUGHT THIS *LAND GRANT* FROM A SOURDOUGH NAMED *CASEY COOT!*

?

WHAT'S THIS LOCK OF HAIR, SCROOGEY?

NOTHING!

THIS PAPER MAKES ME THE OWNER OF A TEN-ACRE HILL IN AMERICA!

SCROOGEY'S GOT A *GIR-RUHL!* SCROOGEY'S GOT A *GIR-RUHL!*

THE GIRL--I MEAN, THE *LAND*--IS IN THE STATE OF GOLDIESOTA--I MEAN *CALISOTA*-- IN A SMALL SETTLEMENT CALLED GOLDIEBURG --I MEAN *DUCKBURG!* DRAT!

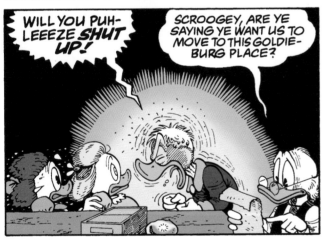

WILL YOU PUH-LEEEZE *SHUT UP!*

SCROOGEY, ARE YE SAYING YE WANT US TO MOVE TO THIS GOLDIE-BURG PLACE?

YES! *NO! DUCK-BURG!* YES! MOVE! ≥ pant pant ≤

MOVE TO *AMERICA?* JUST THINK, HORTENSE! HOW EXCITING!!

COWBOYS AND INDIANS AND COWBOYS AND SKYSCRAPERS!

AND *COWBOYS!*

SCOTTIE, YOU'RE AN HONEST LAD--COULD I HIRE *YOU* TO BE CARETAKER OF OUR FAMILY ESTATE?

LIVE IN THIS HISTORIC CASTLE? HOOT MON, *YES,* MR. MCDUCK! EVEN FOR WHAT *YE'D* PAY!

FINE, THAT'S SETTLED AND--

SAY! WHAT WAS *THAT* CRACK SUP-POSED TO MEAN?!

WHAT'S WRONG, PAPA?

LASS, AH'M TOO OLD AND WEARY T' BE MOVING AGAIN! *THIS* IS MY HOME NOW!

BUT, PAPA--WE CANNAE LEAVE YE HERE *ALONE!*

YOUNG SCOTTIE WILL BE HERE! AND MAYBE *SIR QUACKLY* WILL WATCH O'ER ME AS WELL!

SCROOGE, TAKE YOUR SISTERS TO A NEW LIFE IN AMERICA! YE'RE RIGHT --YE'VE OOTGROWN THE LIFE *AH'VE* KNOWN!

BUT--

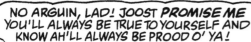

NO ARGUIN, LAD! JOOST *PROMISE ME* YOU'LL ALWAYS BE TRUE TO YOURSELF AND KNOW AH'LL ALWAYS BE PROOD O' YA!

I....UH....YESSIR, PA....SURE!

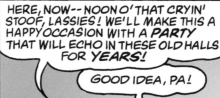

HERE, NOW-- NOON O' THAT CRYIN' STOOF, LASSIES! WE'LL MAKE THIS A *HAPPY* OCCASION WITH A *PARTY* THAT WILL ECHO IN THESE OLD HALLS FOR *YEARS!*

GOOD IDEA, PA!

SO GOODBYES AND FAREWELLS AND SONGS OF "AULD LANG SYNE" DRIFT OUT ACROSS DISMAL DOWNS AND FAR, FAR INTO THE NIGHT.

EARLY NEXT MORNING...

PAPA WAS RIGHT! AH'M GLAD WE SAID ALL OUR GOODBYES LAST NIGHT!

AYE! IT'S EASIER T' LEAVE WHILE HE'S STILL ASLEEP!

LOOK! PA *DID* GET UP TO SEE US OFF AFTER ALL! THERE HE IS WAVING FROM HIS WINDOW!

GOODBYE, PAPA! I PROMISE WE'LL COME BACK TO VISIT!

'BYE, PA!

G'BYE!

WHO'S THAT WAVING *WITH* HIM?

SCOTTIE, WHO ELSE?

G'BYEEEEEE!

G'BYE, PAPA!

WHEEE! WE'RE ON OUR WAY!

GOLDIEBURG, HERE WE COME-- EH, MATILDA?

⸮Giggle!⸮

DUCKBURG, DOGGONE YA! *DUCKBURG!*

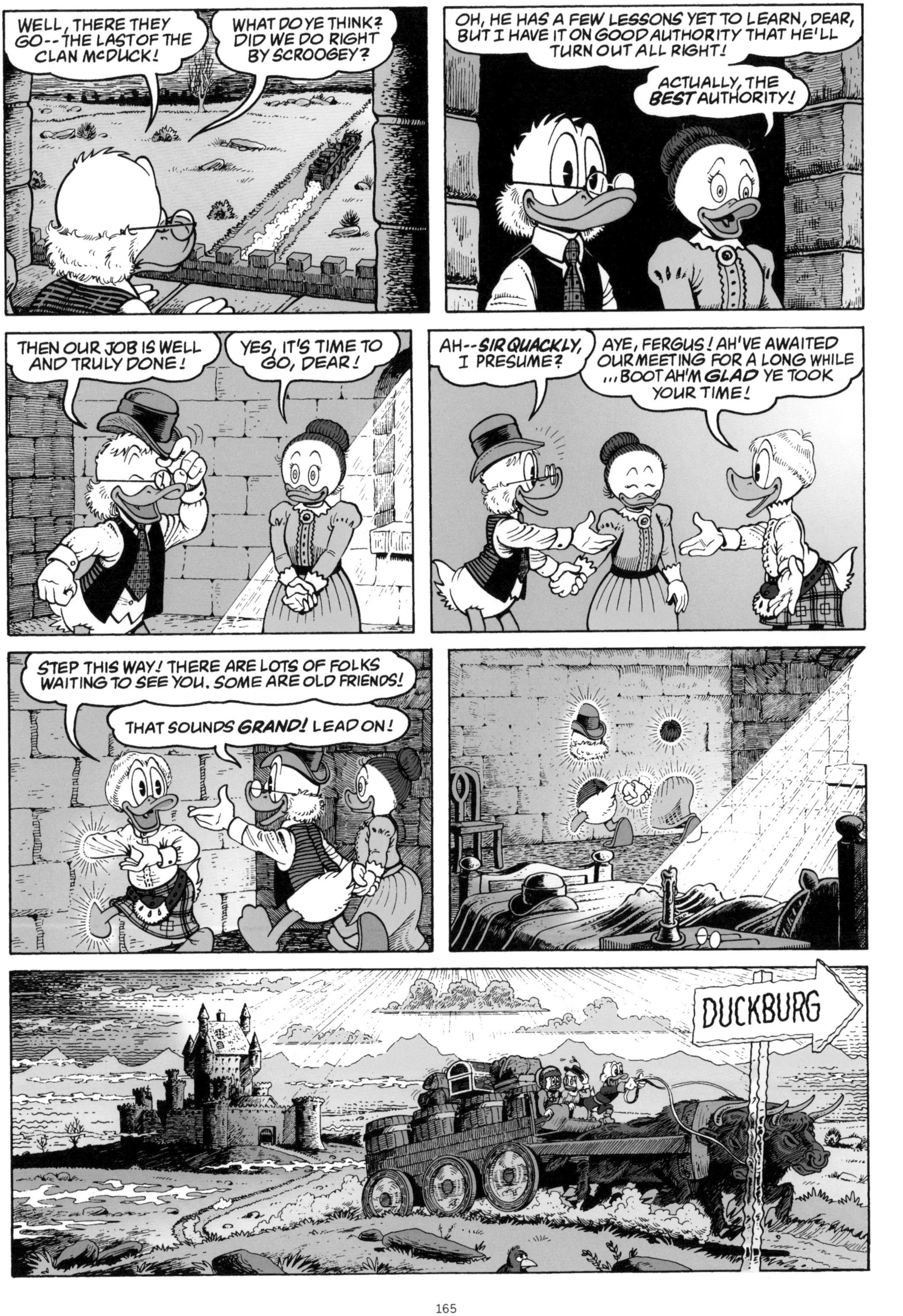

WELL, THERE THEY GO--THE LAST OF THE CLAN McDUCK!
WHAT DO YE THINK? DID WE DO RIGHT BY SCROOGEY?
OH, HE HAS A FEW LESSONS YET TO LEARN, DEAR, BUT I HAVE IT ON GOOD AUTHORITY THAT HE'LL TURN OUT ALL RIGHT!
ACTUALLY, THE BEST AUTHORITY!
THEN OUR JOB IS WELL AND TRULY DONE!
YES, IT'S TIME TO GO, DEAR!
AH--SIR QUACKLY, I PRESUME?
AYE, FERGUS! AH'VE AWAITED OUR MEETING FOR A LONG WHILE ...BOOT AH'M GLAD YE TOOK YOUR TIME!
STEP THIS WAY! THERE ARE LOTS OF FOLKS WAITING TO SEE YOU. SOME ARE OLD FRIENDS!
THAT SOUNDS GRAND! LEAD ON!
DUCKBURG

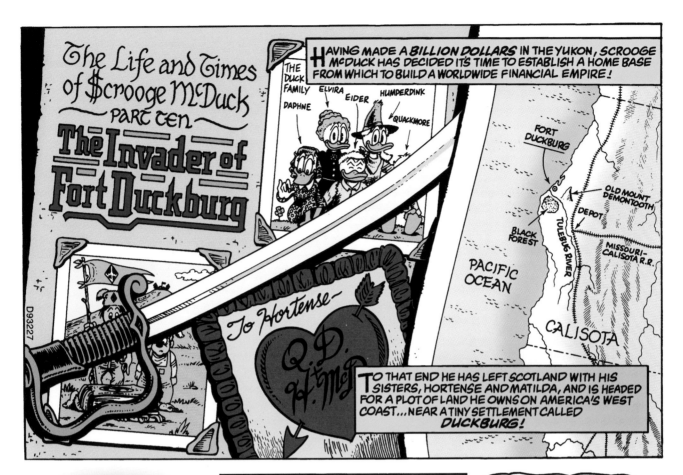

The Life and Times of $crooge McDuck — PART TEN —
The Invader of Fort Duckburg

THE DUCK FAMILY
DAPHNE ELVIRA EIDER HUMPERDINK QUACKMORE

To Hortense—
Q.D. H.McD

HAVING MADE A *BILLION DOLLARS* IN THE YUKON, SCROOGE McDUCK HAS DECIDED IT'S TIME TO ESTABLISH A HOME BASE FROM WHICH TO BUILD A WORLDWIDE FINANCIAL EMPIRE!

FORT DUCKBURG
OLD MOUNT DEMONTOOTH
DEPOT
BLACK FOREST
TULEBUG RIVER
MISSOURI-CALISOTA R.R.
PACIFIC OCEAN
CALISOTA

TO THAT END HE HAS LEFT SCOTLAND WITH HIS SISTERS, HORTENSE AND MATILDA, AND IS HEADED FOR A PLOT OF LAND HE OWNS ON AMERICA'S WEST COAST...NEAR A TINY SETTLEMENT CALLED *DUCKBURG!*

THE CALISOTA COUNTRYSIDE IS DOUBLY SERENADED BY A STRANGE SHAPE MOVING ALONG THE DUSTY BACK ROADS...

PIP PIP PIP PIP PIP PIP

@#%!

OH, SCROOGEY! QUIT *GRIPING!*

I CAN'T HELP IT! I NEVER SHOULD HAVE BOUGHT THIS INFERNAL CONTRAPTION!

PIP PIP PIP PIP

HOW COME YOU DIDN'T *KNOW* IT ONLY RUNS ON A MIXTURE OF KEROSENE AND WHALE OIL? DIDN'T YOU *READ* THE FINE PRINT?

I COULDN'T *SEE* THE FINE PRINT! SIX YEARS OF YUKON SNOW ALL BUT *RUINED* MY EYES! I'M NOT EVEN SURE WHAT WAS ON THE LIST OF COSTLY *OPTIONS* I REJECTED!

PIP PIP PIP

WE'RE *LOST,* TOO! I'D BETTER STOP AND ASK THAT FARMER FOR DIRECTIONS TO FORT DUCKBURG!

!

ASK HIM IF THERE ARE ANY HANDSOME *COWBOYS* AROUND!

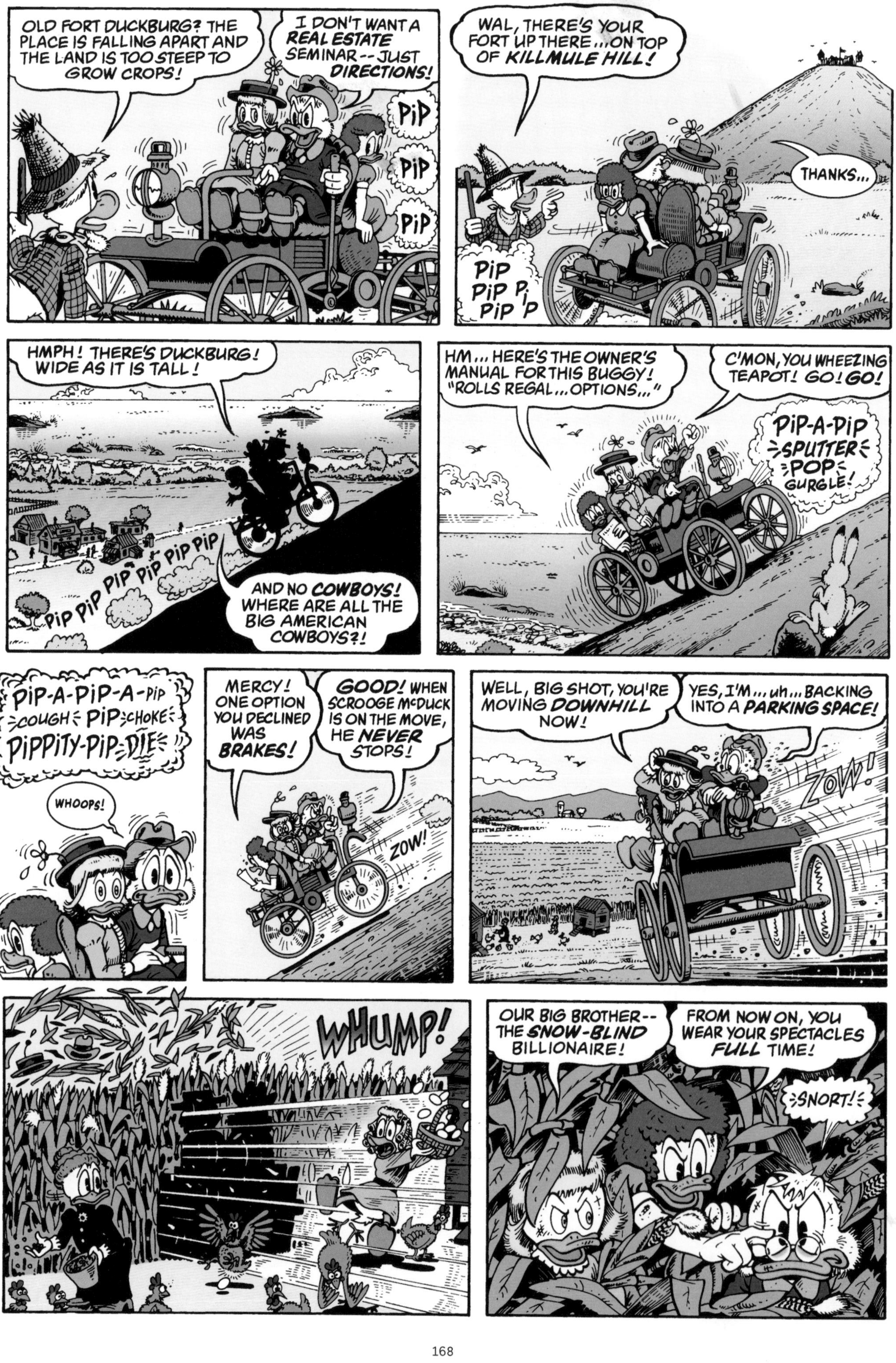

OLD FORT DUCKBURG? THE PLACE IS FALLING APART AND THE LAND IS TOO STEEP TO GROW CROPS!
I DON'T WANT A REAL ESTATE SEMINAR -- JUST DIRECTIONS!
PIP
PIP
PIP
WAL, THERE'S YOUR FORT UP THERE... ON TOP OF KILLMULE HILL!
THANKS...
PIP PIP PIP P P
HMPH! THERE'S DUCKBURG! WIDE AS IT IS TALL!
PIP PIP PIP PIP PIP PIP
AND NO COWBOYS! WHERE ARE ALL THE BIG AMERICAN COWBOYS?!
HM... HERE'S THE OWNER'S MANUAL FOR THIS BUGGY! "ROLLS REGAL... OPTIONS..."
C'MON, YOU WHEEZING TEAPOT! GO! GO!
PIP-A-PIP SPUTTER POP GURGLE!
PIP-A-PIP-A-PIP COUGH PIP CHOKE PIPPITY-PIP-DIE
WHOOPS!
MERCY! ONE OPTION YOU DECLINED WAS BRAKES!
GOOD! WHEN SCROOGE McDUCK IS ON THE MOVE, HE NEVER STOPS!
ZOW!
WELL, BIG SHOT, YOU'RE MOVING DOWNHILL NOW!
YES, I'M... uh... BACKING INTO A PARKING SPACE!
ZOW!
WHUMP!
OUR BIG BROTHER -- THE SNOW-BLIND BILLIONAIRE!
FROM NOW ON, YOU WEAR YOUR SPECTACLES FULL TIME!
SNORT!

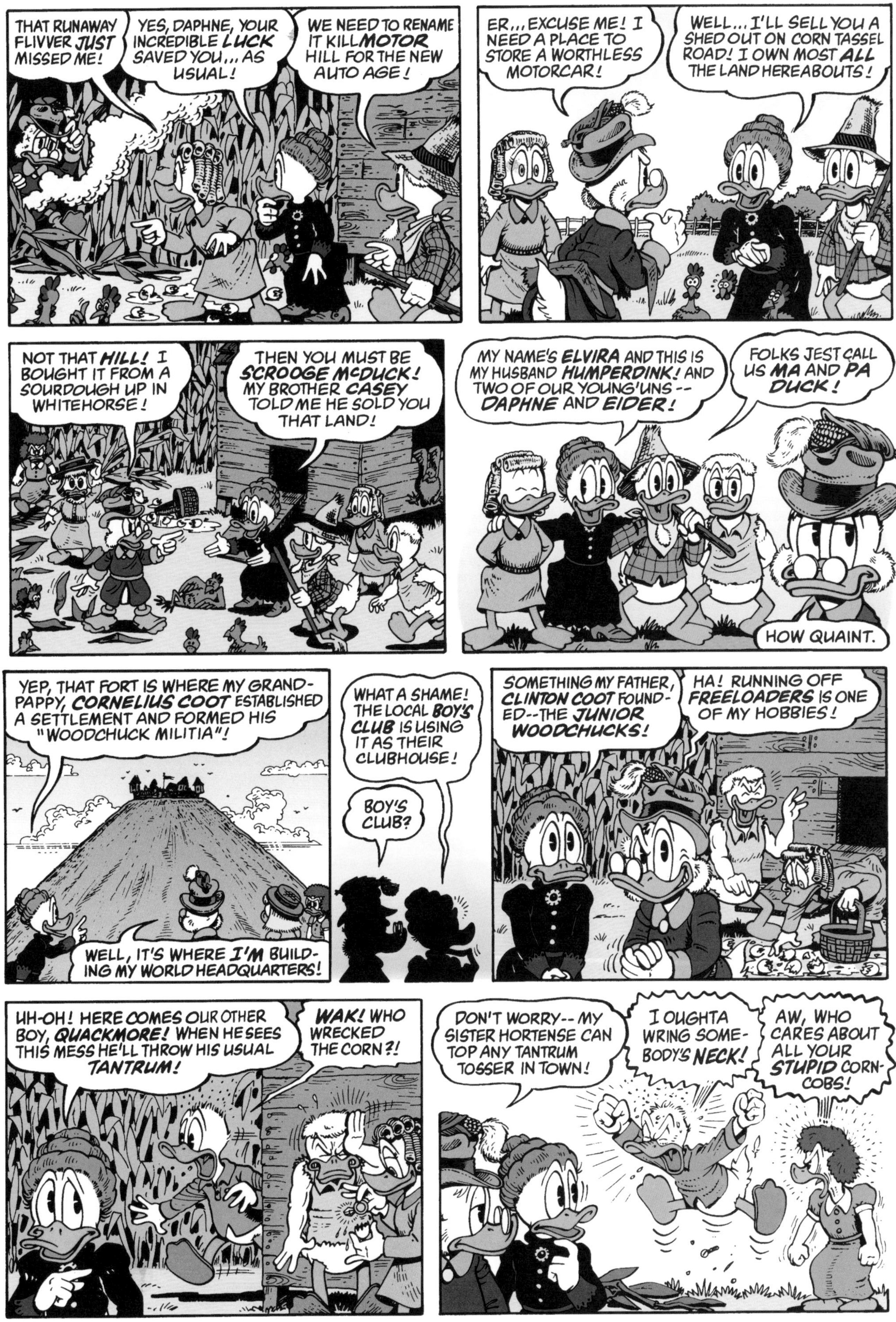
THAT RUNAWAY FLIVVER JUST MISSED ME!
YES, DAPHNE, YOUR INCREDIBLE LUCK SAVED YOU... AS USUAL!
WE NEED TO RENAME IT KILLMOTOR HILL FOR THE NEW AUTO AGE!
ER... EXCUSE ME! I NEED A PLACE TO STORE A WORTHLESS MOTORCAR!
WELL... I'LL SELL YOU A SHED OUT ON CORN TASSEL ROAD! I OWN MOST ALL THE LAND HEREABOUTS!
NOT THAT HILL! I BOUGHT IT FROM A SOURDOUGH UP IN WHITEHORSE!
THEN YOU MUST BE SCROOGE McDUCK! MY BROTHER CASEY TOLD ME HE SOLD YOU THAT LAND!
MY NAME'S ELVIRA AND THIS IS MY HUSBAND HUMPERDINK! AND TWO OF OUR YOUNG'UNS -- DAPHNE AND EIDER!
FOLKS JEST CALL US MA AND PA DUCK!
HOW QUAINT.
YEP, THAT FORT IS WHERE MY GRAND-PAPPY, CORNELIUS COOT ESTABLISHED A SETTLEMENT AND FORMED HIS "WOODCHUCK MILITIA"!
WELL, IT'S WHERE I'M BUILD-ING MY WORLD HEADQUARTERS!
WHAT A SHAME! THE LOCAL BOY'S CLUB IS USING IT AS THEIR CLUBHOUSE!
BOY'S CLUB?
SOMETHING MY FATHER, CLINTON COOT FOUND-ED--THE JUNIOR WOODCHUCKS!
HA! RUNNING OFF FREELOADERS IS ONE OF MY HOBBIES!
UH-OH! HERE COMES OUR OTHER BOY, QUACKMORE! WHEN HE SEES THIS MESS HE'LL THROW HIS USUAL TANTRUM!
WAK! WHO WRECKED THE CORN?!
DON'T WORRY-- MY SISTER HORTENSE CAN TOP ANY TANTRUM TOSSER IN TOWN!
I OUGHTA WRING SOME-BODY'S NECK!
AW, WHO CARES ABOUT ALL YOUR STUPID CORN-COBS!

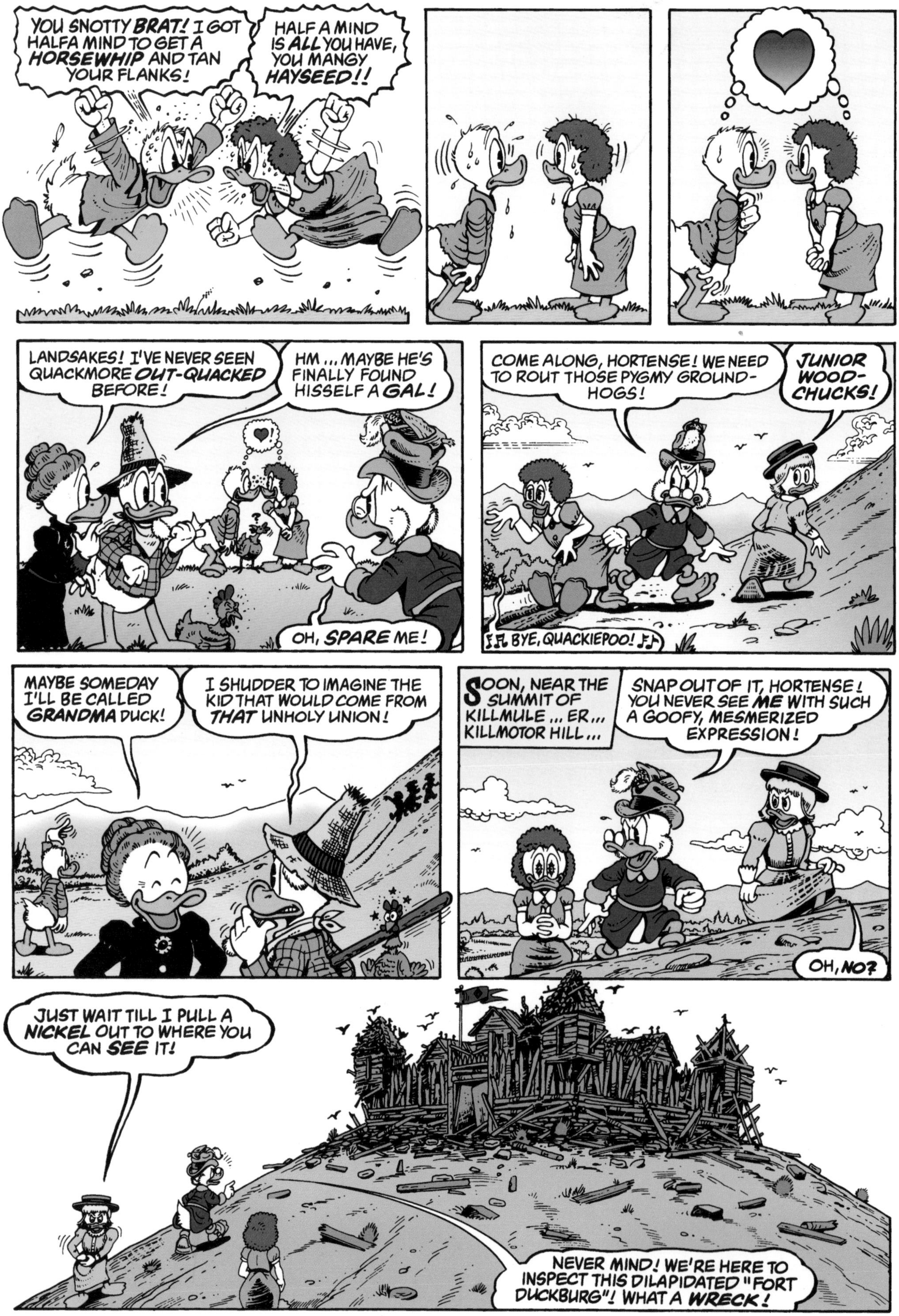
YOU SNOTTY BRAT! I GOT HALFA MIND TO GET A HORSEWHIP AND TAN YOUR FLANKS!
HALF A MIND IS ALL YOU HAVE, YOU MANGY HAYSEED!!
LANDSAKES! I'VE NEVER SEEN QUACKMORE OUT-QUACKED BEFORE!
HM ... MAYBE HE'S FINALLY FOUND HISSELF A GAL!
OH, SPARE ME!
COME ALONG, HORTENSE! WE NEED TO ROUT THOSE PYGMY GROUND-HOGS!
JUNIOR WOOD-CHUCKS!
BYE, QUACKIEPOO!
MAYBE SOMEDAY I'LL BE CALLED GRANDMA DUCK!
I SHUDDER TO IMAGINE THE KID THAT WOULD COME FROM THAT UNHOLY UNION!
SOON, NEAR THE SUMMIT OF KILLMULE ... ER ... KILLMOTOR HILL ...
SNAP OUT OF IT, HORTENSE! YOU NEVER SEE ME WITH SUCH A GOOFY, MESMERIZED EXPRESSION!
OH, NO?
JUST WAIT TILL I PULL A NICKEL OUT TO WHERE YOU CAN SEE IT!
NEVER MIND! WE'RE HERE TO INSPECT THIS DILAPIDATED "FORT DUCKBURG"! WHAT A WRECK!

CAREFUL! I'VE SPENT ENOUGH TIME ON THE WORLD'S WILDEST FRONTIERS TO KNOW THAT THE EARLY SETTLERS WERE A ROUGH AND READY BUNCH!

THEY MAY HAVE SET HIDEOUS *BOOBY TRAPS* AS DEFENSES AGAINST ATTACKS BY INSURGENTS!

SPLOSH!

HORRORS! OUR POOR BROTHER, IN THE VERY PRIME OF HIS LIFE, WHEN SUDDENLY, WITHOUT WARNING--*DRENCHED!* O, CRUEL FATE!

AWRIGHT, AWRIGHT!

SOMEONE'S COMING!

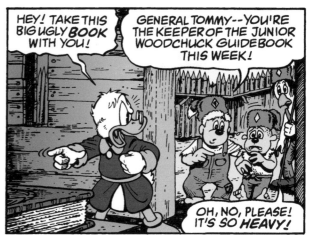

DUCKBURG CHARTER TROOP--PREPARE TO REPEL INVADER!!

IT'S THE MIDGET GOPHERS!

JUNIOR WOOD-CHUCKS!

CLINK!

THIS IS *MY* PROPERTY! GET OFF MY LAND --*NOW!!*

GENERAL FULTON--WE'VE LOST OUR CLUBHOUSE! NOTIFY THE *REST* OF OUR WORLDWIDE ORGANIZATION!

HE *KNOWS*, GENERAL BILLY! HE'S RIGHT BEHIND ME!

HEY! TAKE THIS BIG UGLY *BOOK* WITH YOU!

GENERAL TOMMY--YOU'RE THE KEEPER OF THE JUNIOR WOODCHUCK GUIDEBOOK THIS WEEK!

OH, NO, PLEASE! IT'S SO *HEAVY!*

SOMEDAY WE'VE JUST *GOT* TO MAKE POCKET-SIZE COPIES OF THIS MONSTER!

AND YOU RUNT CHIPMUNKS CAN *STAY* OUT!

JUNIOR WOOD-CHUCKS!

NEVER MIND! THIS IS AN *IDEAL* SPOT FOR MY HOME BASE! NOW WE CAN HEAD BACK TO THE TRAIN DEPOT AND GET MY *MONEY BARRELS!*

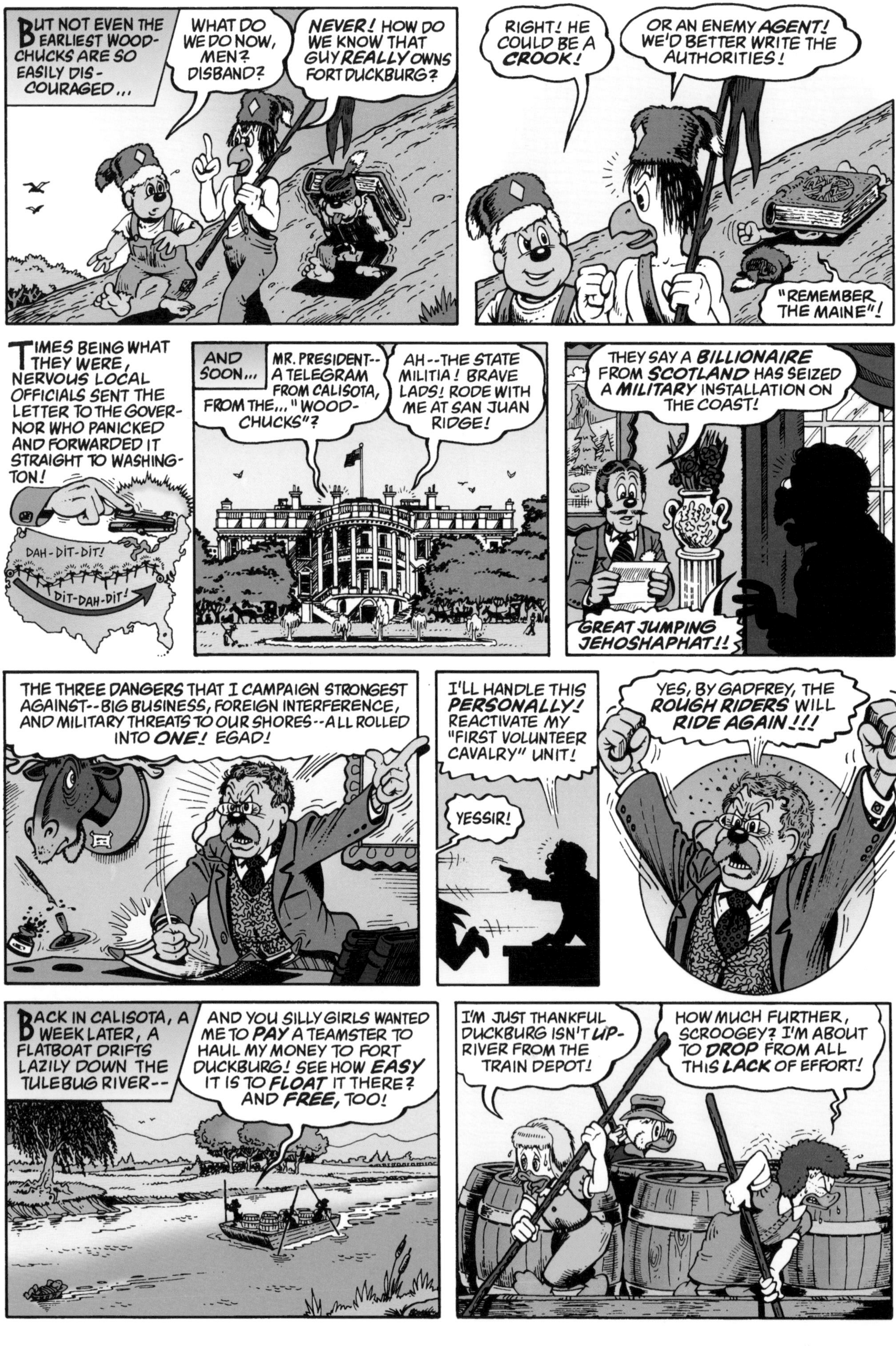
BUT NOT EVEN THE EARLIEST WOODCHUCKS ARE SO EASILY DISCOURAGED...
WHAT DO WE DO NOW, MEN? DISBAND?
NEVER! HOW DO WE KNOW THAT GUY REALLY OWNS FORT DUCKBURG?
RIGHT! HE COULD BE A CROOK!
OR AN ENEMY AGENT! WE'D BETTER WRITE THE AUTHORITIES!
"REMEMBER THE MAINE"!
TIMES BEING WHAT THEY WERE, NERVOUS LOCAL OFFICIALS SENT THE LETTER TO THE GOVERNOR WHO PANICKED AND FORWARDED IT STRAIGHT TO WASHINGTON!
DAH-DIT-DIT!
DIT-DAH-DIT!
AND SOON...
MR. PRESIDENT-- A TELEGRAM FROM CALISOTA, FROM THE... "WOODCHUCKS"?
AH--THE STATE MILITIA! BRAVE LADS! RODE WITH ME AT SAN JUAN RIDGE!
THEY SAY A BILLIONAIRE FROM SCOTLAND HAS SEIZED A MILITARY INSTALLATION ON THE COAST!
GREAT JUMPING JEHOSHAPHAT!!
THE THREE DANGERS THAT I CAMPAIGN STRONGEST AGAINST--BIG BUSINESS, FOREIGN INTERFERENCE, AND MILITARY THREATS TO OUR SHORES--ALL ROLLED INTO ONE! EGAD!
I'LL HANDLE THIS PERSONALLY! REACTIVATE MY "FIRST VOLUNTEER CAVALRY" UNIT!
YESSIR!
YES, BY GADFREY, THE ROUGH RIDERS WILL RIDE AGAIN!!!
BACK IN CALISOTA, A WEEK LATER, A FLATBOAT DRIFTS LAZILY DOWN THE TULEBUG RIVER--
AND YOU SILLY GIRLS WANTED ME TO PAY A TEAMSTER TO HAUL MY MONEY TO FORT DUCKBURG! SEE HOW EASY IT IS TO FLOAT IT THERE? AND FREE, TOO!
I'M JUST THANKFUL DUCKBURG ISN'T UP-RIVER FROM THE TRAIN DEPOT!
HOW MUCH FURTHER, SCROOGEY? I'M ABOUT TO DROP FROM ALL THIS LACK OF EFFORT!

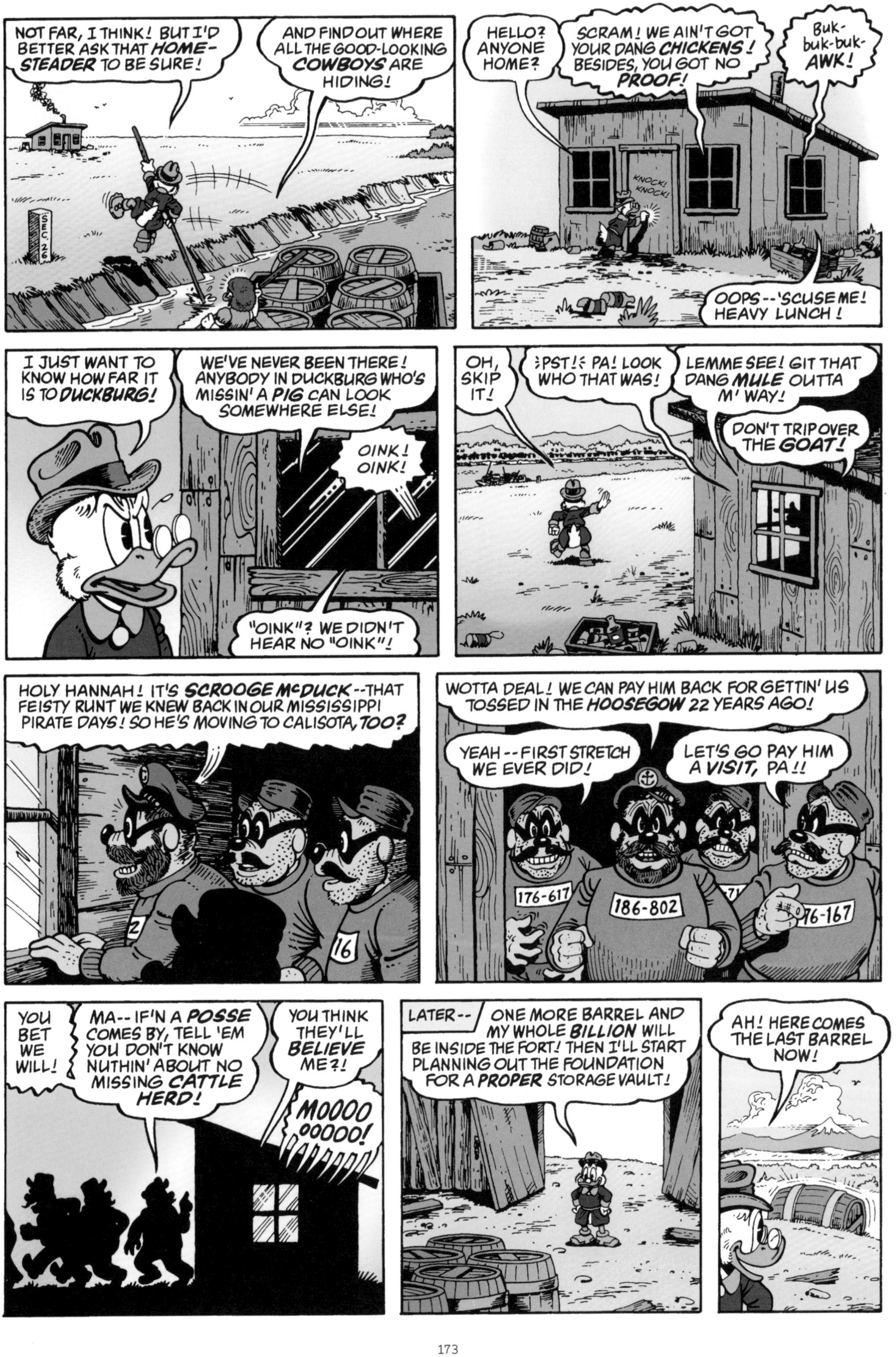
NOT FAR, I THINK! BUT I'D BETTER ASK THAT HOMESTEADER TO BE SURE!
AND FIND OUT WHERE ALL THE GOOD-LOOKING COWBOYS ARE HIDING!
SEC. 26
HELLO? ANYONE HOME?
KNOCK! KNOCK!
SCRAM! WE AIN'T GOT YOUR DANG CHICKENS! BESIDES, YOU GOT NO PROOF!
Buk-buk-buk-AWK!
OOPS--'SCUSE ME! HEAVY LUNCH!
I JUST WANT TO KNOW HOW FAR IT IS TO DUCKBURG!
WE'VE NEVER BEEN THERE! ANYBODY IN DUCKBURG WHO'S MISSIN' A PIG CAN LOOK SOMEWHERE ELSE!
OINK! OINK!
"OINK"? WE DIDN'T HEAR NO "OINK"!
OH, SKIP IT!
PST! PA! LOOK WHO THAT WAS!
LEMME SEE! GIT THAT DANG MULE OUTTA M' WAY!
DON'T TRIP OVER THE GOAT!
HOLY HANNAH! IT'S SCROOGE McDUCK--THAT FEISTY RUNT WE KNEW BACK IN OUR MISSISSIPPI PIRATE DAYS! SO HE'S MOVING TO CALISOTA, TOO?
WOTTA DEAL! WE CAN PAY HIM BACK FOR GETTIN' US TOSSED IN THE HOOSEGOW 22 YEARS AGO!
YEAH--FIRST STRETCH WE EVER DID!
LET'S GO PAY HIM A VISIT, PA!!
176-617
186-802
76-167
YOU BET WE WILL!
MA--IF'N A POSSE COMES BY, TELL 'EM YOU DON'T KNOW NUTHIN' ABOUT NO MISSING CATTLE HERD!
YOU THINK THEY'LL BELIEVE ME?!
MOOOO OOOOO!
LATER--
ONE MORE BARREL AND MY WHOLE BILLION WILL BE INSIDE THE FORT! THEN I'LL START PLANNING OUT THE FOUNDATION FOR A PROPER STORAGE VAULT!
AH! HERE COMES THE LAST BARREL NOW!

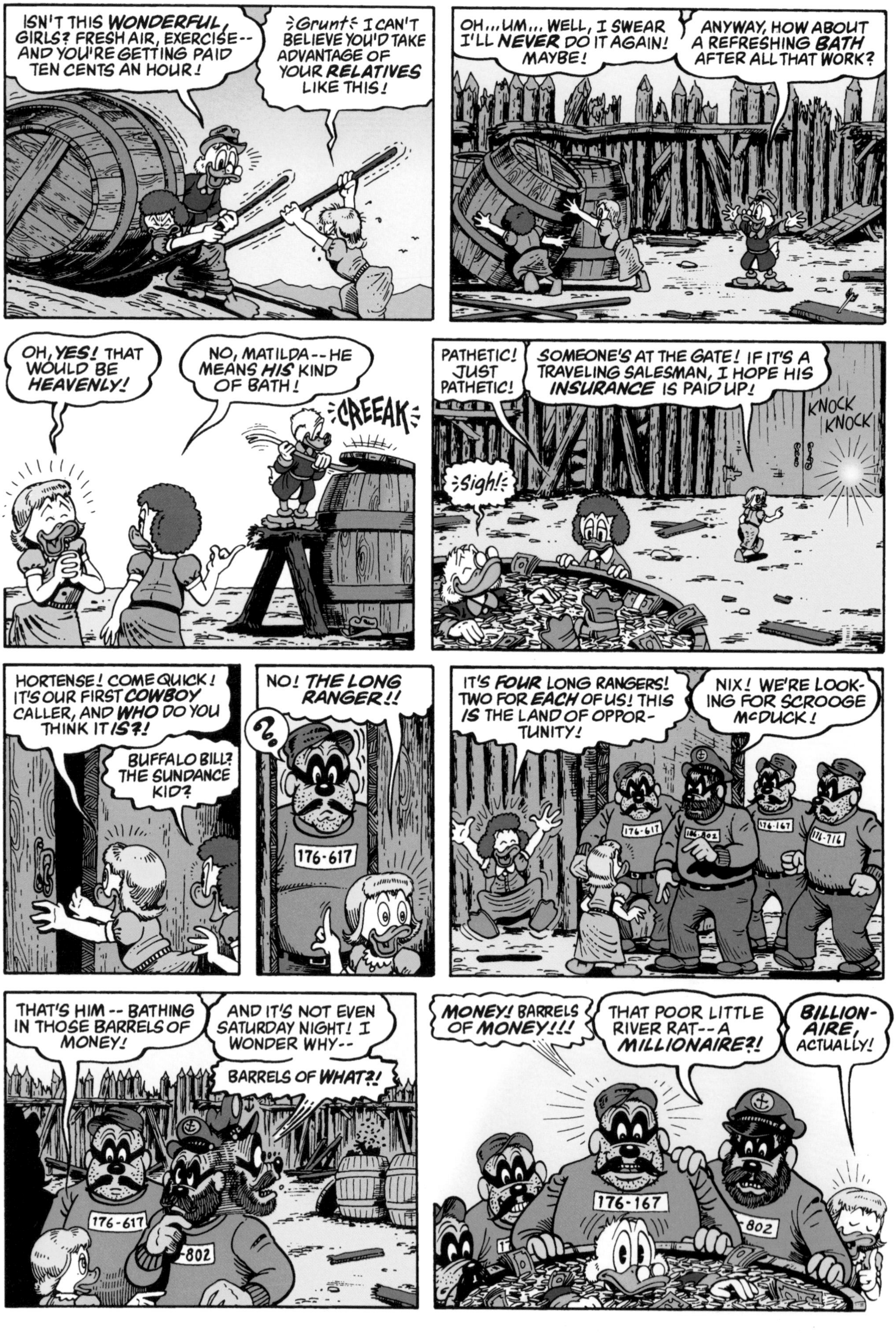

ISN'T THIS WONDERFUL, GIRLS? FRESH AIR, EXERCISE-- AND YOU'RE GETTING PAID TEN CENTS AN HOUR!
GRUNT I CAN'T BELIEVE YOU'D TAKE ADVANTAGE OF YOUR RELATIVES LIKE THIS!
OH... UM... WELL, I SWEAR I'LL NEVER DO IT AGAIN! MAYBE!
ANYWAY, HOW ABOUT A REFRESHING BATH AFTER ALL THAT WORK?
OH, YES! THAT WOULD BE HEAVENLY!
NO, MATILDA--HE MEANS HIS KIND OF BATH!
CREEAK
PATHETIC! JUST PATHETIC!
SOMEONE'S AT THE GATE! IF IT'S A TRAVELING SALESMAN, I HOPE HIS INSURANCE IS PAID UP!
KNOCK KNOCK
SIGH!
HORTENSE! COME QUICK! IT'S OUR FIRST COWBOY CALLER, AND WHO DO YOU THINK IT IS?!
BUFFALO BILL? THE SUNDANCE KID?
NO! THE LONG RANGER!!
176-617
IT'S FOUR LONG RANGERS! TWO FOR EACH OF US! THIS IS THE LAND OF OPPORTUNITY!
NIX! WE'RE LOOKING FOR SCROOGE McDUCK!
176-617
176-802
176-167
176-716
THAT'S HIM -- BATHING IN THOSE BARRELS OF MONEY!
AND IT'S NOT EVEN SATURDAY NIGHT! I WONDER WHY--
BARRELS OF WHAT?!
176-617
-802
MONEY! BARRELS OF MONEY!!!
THAT POOR LITTLE RIVER RAT--A MILLIONAIRE?!
BILLIONAIRE, ACTUALLY!
176-167
-802

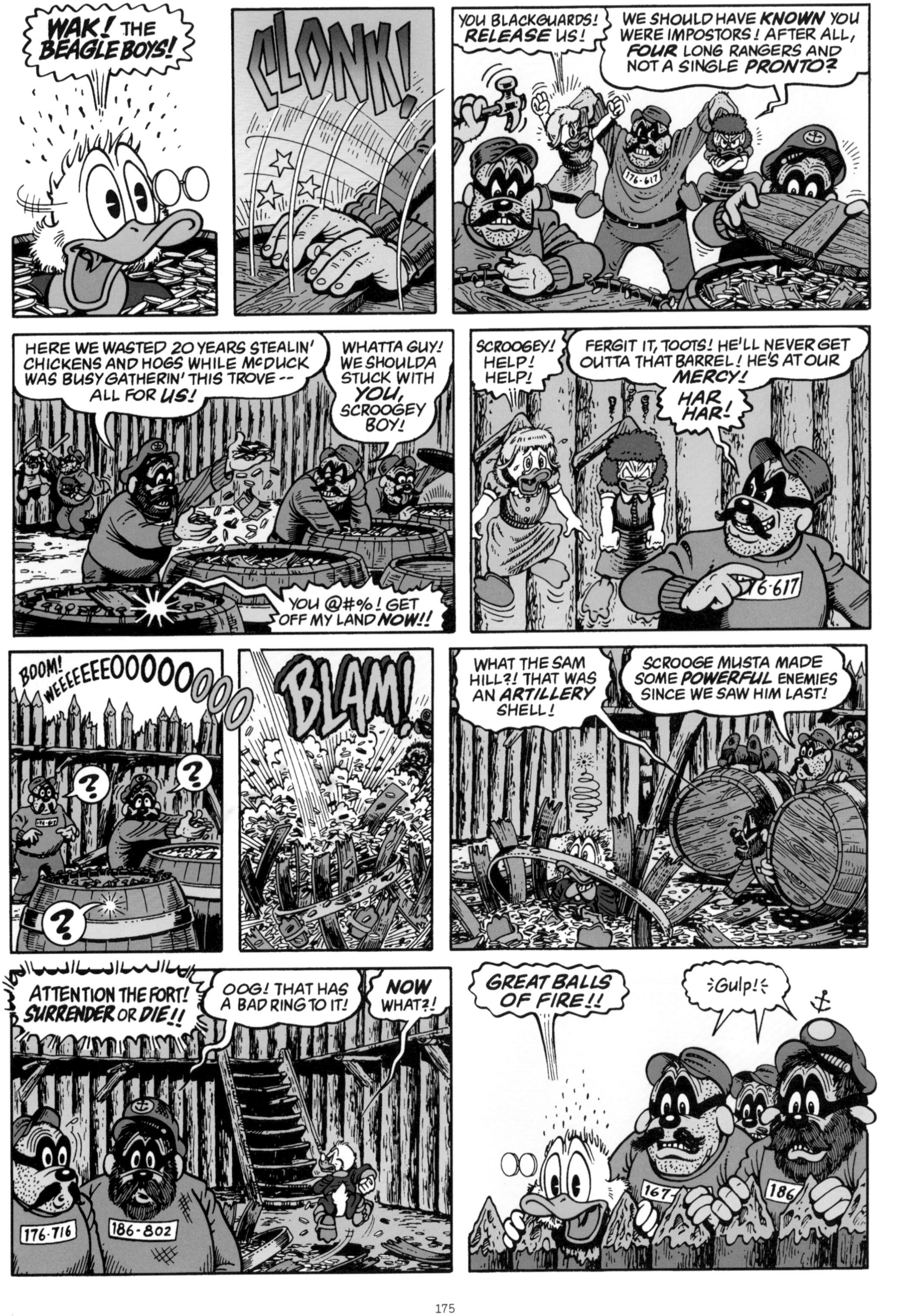
WAK! THE BEAGLE BOYS!
CLONK!
YOU BLACKGUARDS! RELEASE US!
WE SHOULD HAVE KNOWN YOU WERE IMPOSTORS! AFTER ALL, FOUR LONG RANGERS AND NOT A SINGLE PRONTO?
176-617
HERE WE WASTED 20 YEARS STEALIN' CHICKENS AND HOGS WHILE McDUCK WAS BUSY GATHERIN' THIS TROVE -- ALL FOR US!
WHATTA GUY! WE SHOULDA STUCK WITH YOU, SCROOGEY BOY!
YOU @#%! GET OFF MY LAND NOW!!
SCROOGEY! HELP! HELP!
FERGIT IT, TOOTS! HE'LL NEVER GET OUTTA THAT BARREL! HE'S AT OUR MERCY!
HAR HAR!
176-617
BOOM! WEEEEEEEOOOOOOOOO
?
?
?
BLAM!
WHAT THE SAM HILL?! THAT WAS AN ARTILLERY SHELL!
SCROOGE MUSTA MADE SOME POWERFUL ENEMIES SINCE WE SAW HIM LAST!
ATTENTION THE FORT! SURRENDER OR DIE!!
OOG! THAT HAS A BAD RING TO IT!
NOW WHAT?!
176-716
186-802
GREAT BALLS OF FIRE!!
Gulp!
167-
186

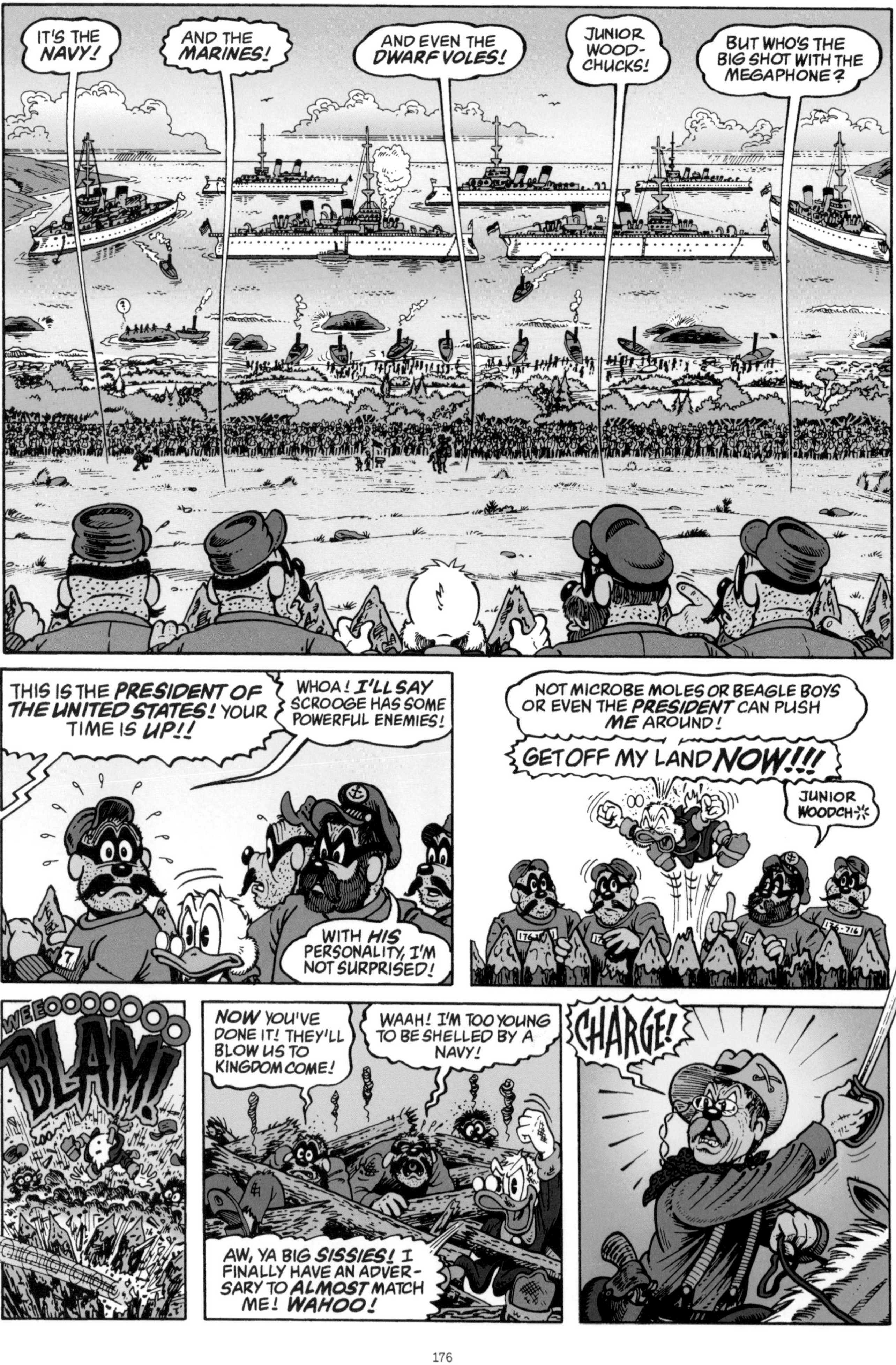
IT'S THE NAVY!
AND THE MARINES!
AND EVEN THE DWARF VOLES!
JUNIOR WOOD-CHUCKS!
BUT WHO'S THE BIG SHOT WITH THE MEGAPHONE?
THIS IS THE PRESIDENT OF THE UNITED STATES! YOUR TIME IS UP!!
WHOA! I'LL SAY SCROOGE HAS SOME POWERFUL ENEMIES!
WITH HIS PERSONALITY, I'M NOT SURPRISED!
NOT MICROBE MOLES OR BEAGLE BOYS OR EVEN THE PRESIDENT CAN PUSH ME AROUND!
GET OFF MY LAND NOW!!!
JUNIOR WOODCH
WEEOOOOOOOO
BLAM!
NOW YOU'VE DONE IT! THEY'LL BLOW US TO KINGDOM COME!
WAAH! I'M TOO YOUNG TO BE SHELLED BY A NAVY!
AW, YA BIG SISSIES! I FINALLY HAVE AN ADVER-SARY TO ALMOST MATCH ME! WAHOO!
CHARGE!

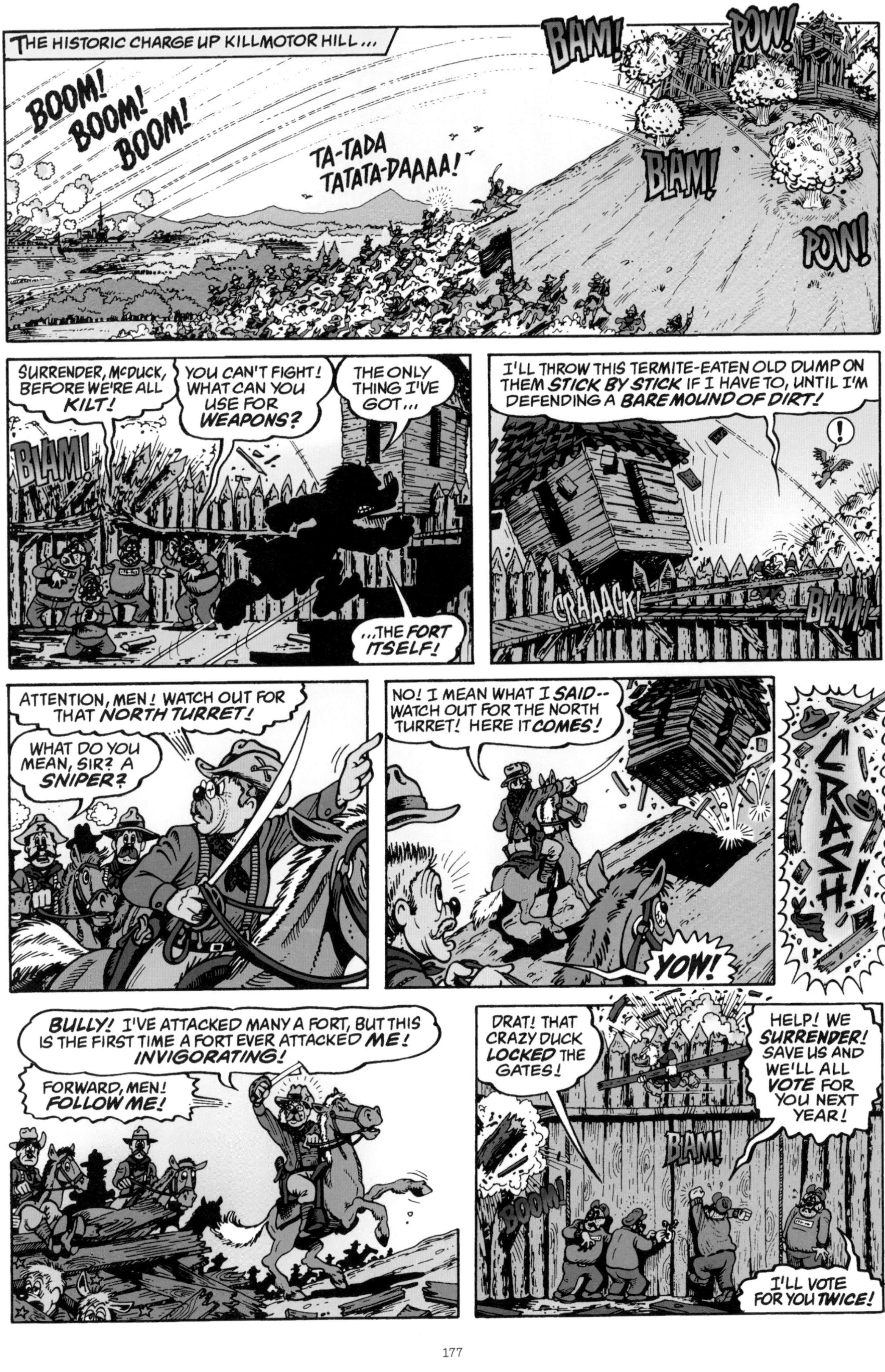
THE HISTORIC CHARGE UP KILLMOTOR HILL...
BAM! POW!
BOOM! BOOM! BOOM!
TA-TADA TATATA-DAAAA!
BLAM!
POW!
SURRENDER, McDUCK, BEFORE WE'RE ALL KILT!
YOU CAN'T FIGHT! WHAT CAN YOU USE FOR WEAPONS?
THE ONLY THING I'VE GOT...
BLAM!
...THE FORT ITSELF!
I'LL THROW THIS TERMITE-EATEN OLD DUMP ON THEM STICK BY STICK IF I HAVE TO, UNTIL I'M DEFENDING A BARE MOUND OF DIRT!
!
CRAAACK!
BLAM!
ATTENTION, MEN! WATCH OUT FOR THAT NORTH TURRET!
WHAT DO YOU MEAN, SIR? A SNIPER?
NO! I MEAN WHAT I SAID-- WATCH OUT FOR THE NORTH TURRET! HERE IT COMES!
YOW!
CRASH!
BULLY! I'VE ATTACKED MANY A FORT, BUT THIS IS THE FIRST TIME A FORT EVER ATTACKED ME! INVIGORATING!
FORWARD, MEN! FOLLOW ME!
DRAT! THAT CRAZY DUCK LOCKED THE GATES!
HELP! WE SURRENDER! SAVE US AND WE'LL ALL VOTE FOR YOU NEXT YEAR!
BAM!
BOOM!
I'LL VOTE FOR YOU TWICE!

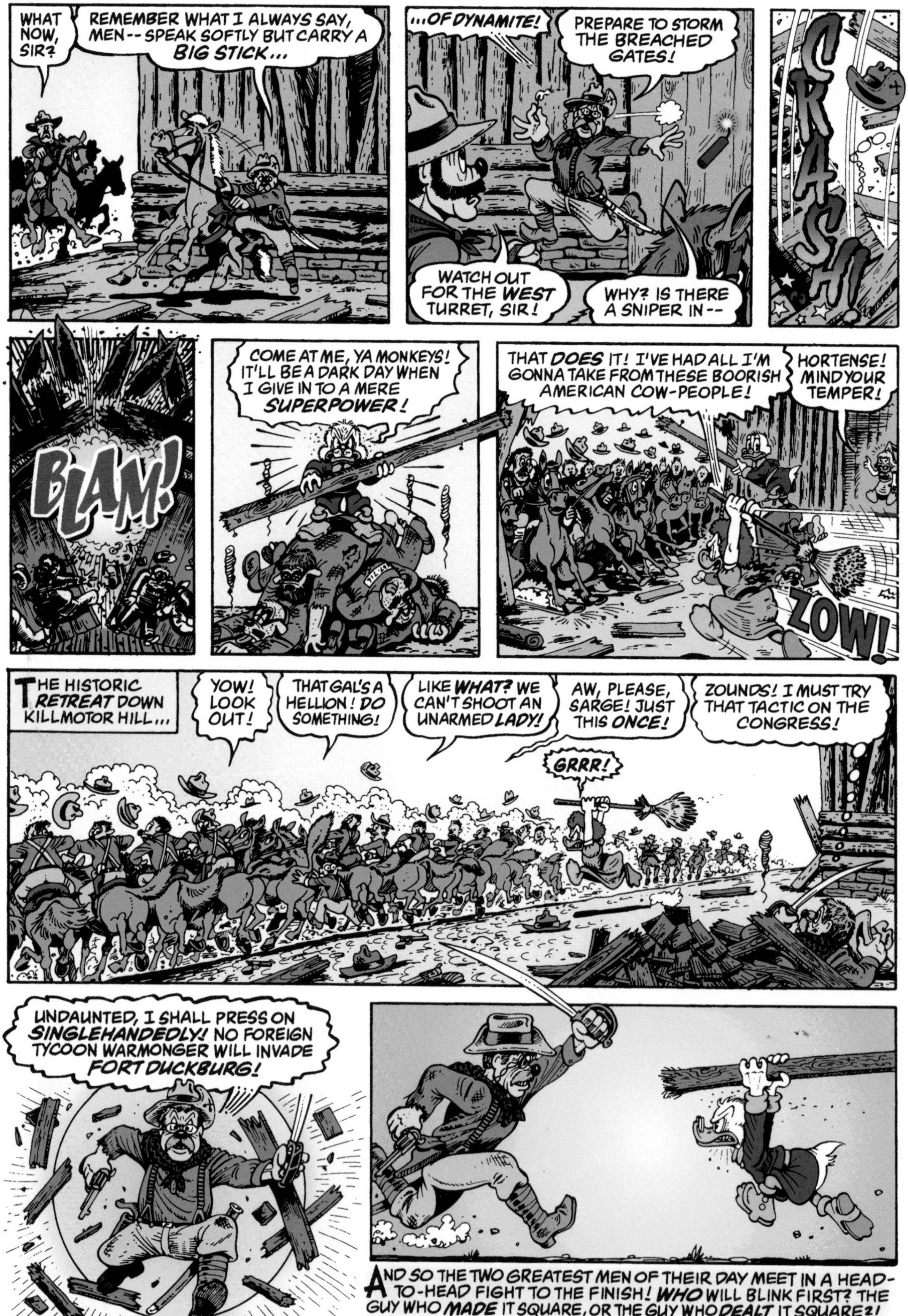
WHAT NOW, SIR?
REMEMBER WHAT I ALWAYS SAY, MEN -- SPEAK SOFTLY BUT CARRY A BIG STICK...
...OF DYNAMITE!
PREPARE TO STORM THE BREACHED GATES!
WATCH OUT FOR THE WEST TURRET, SIR!
WHY? IS THERE A SNIPER IN --
CRASH!
BLAM!
COME AT ME, YA MONKEYS! IT'LL BE A DARK DAY WHEN I GIVE IN TO A MERE SUPERPOWER!
THAT DOES IT! I'VE HAD ALL I'M GONNA TAKE FROM THESE BOORISH AMERICAN COW-PEOPLE!
HORTENSE! MIND YOUR TEMPER!
ZOW!
THE HISTORIC RETREAT DOWN KILLMOTOR HILL...
YOW! LOOK OUT!
THAT GAL'S A HELLION! DO SOMETHING!
LIKE WHAT? WE CAN'T SHOOT AN UNARMED LADY!
AW, PLEASE, SARGE! JUST THIS ONCE!
ZOUNDS! I MUST TRY THAT TACTIC ON THE CONGRESS!
GRRR!
UNDAUNTED, I SHALL PRESS ON SINGLEHANDEDLY! NO FOREIGN TYCOON WARMONGER WILL INVADE FORT DUCKBURG!
AND SO THE TWO GREATEST MEN OF THEIR DAY MEET IN A HEAD-TO-HEAD FIGHT TO THE FINISH! WHO WILL BLINK FIRST? THE GUY WHO MADE IT SQUARE, OR THE GUY WHO DEALT IT SQUARE?!

WHY... YOU'RE **BUCK McDUCK** FROM MONTANA!

AND YOU'RE THAT **RANCHER** I MET YEARS AGO IN THE **DAKOTA BADLANDS**!

HAH! I THOUGHT **YOU** WERE SOME COWARDLY INTERLOPER! HOW **ABSURD**!

I NEVER GUESSED **YOU** ENDED UP THE **PRESIDENT**!

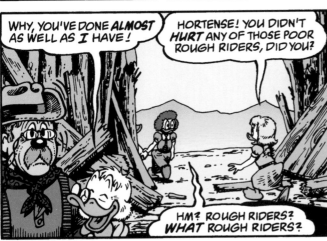

WHY, YOU'VE DONE **ALMOST** AS WELL AS **I** HAVE!

HORTENSE! YOU DIDN'T **HURT** ANY OF THOSE POOR ROUGH RIDERS, DID YOU?

HM? ROUGH RIDERS? **WHAT** ROUGH RIDERS?

YOU **KNOW** WHAT ROUGH RIDERS! THE ONES I HAD TO PULL YOU **OFF** OF BEFORE YOU **WHACKED** 'EM SILLY!

OH, GO TILL YOUR **TURNIPS**, YOU BUMPKIN! NOBODY ASKED YOU TO MEDDLE!

HM... DO I HEAR WEDDING BELLS... OR **DO** I?

I ALMOST MADE A TRAGIC MISTAKE, BUCK! WHY DIDN'T YOU ANSWER MY FIRST HAIL?

I WAS HAVING SOME **MOMENTARY** TROUBLE WITH THOSE CROOKS!

ALLOW ME!

YOU BOYS GO FIND AN **UNWHACKED** ROUGH RIDER AND TELL HIM I PUT YOU UNDER **ARREST**!

WOW! YOU BET!

IMAGINE! ARRESTED BY THE PRESIDENT OF THE UNITED STATES! WAIT TILL WE TELL MA!

AND WHEN WE GET OUTTA JAIL, WE'LL KNOW WHERE **SCROOGE** WILL BE WITH ALL THAT **MONEY**!

BUT ARE JUST THE FOUR OF US A MATCH FOR **THAT** DUCK?

YOU BOYS NEED TO START RAISING **FAMILIES**! WE NEED **MORE** BEAGLE BOYS!

UH... YOU GUYS SEEN A GAL WITH A **BROOM**?

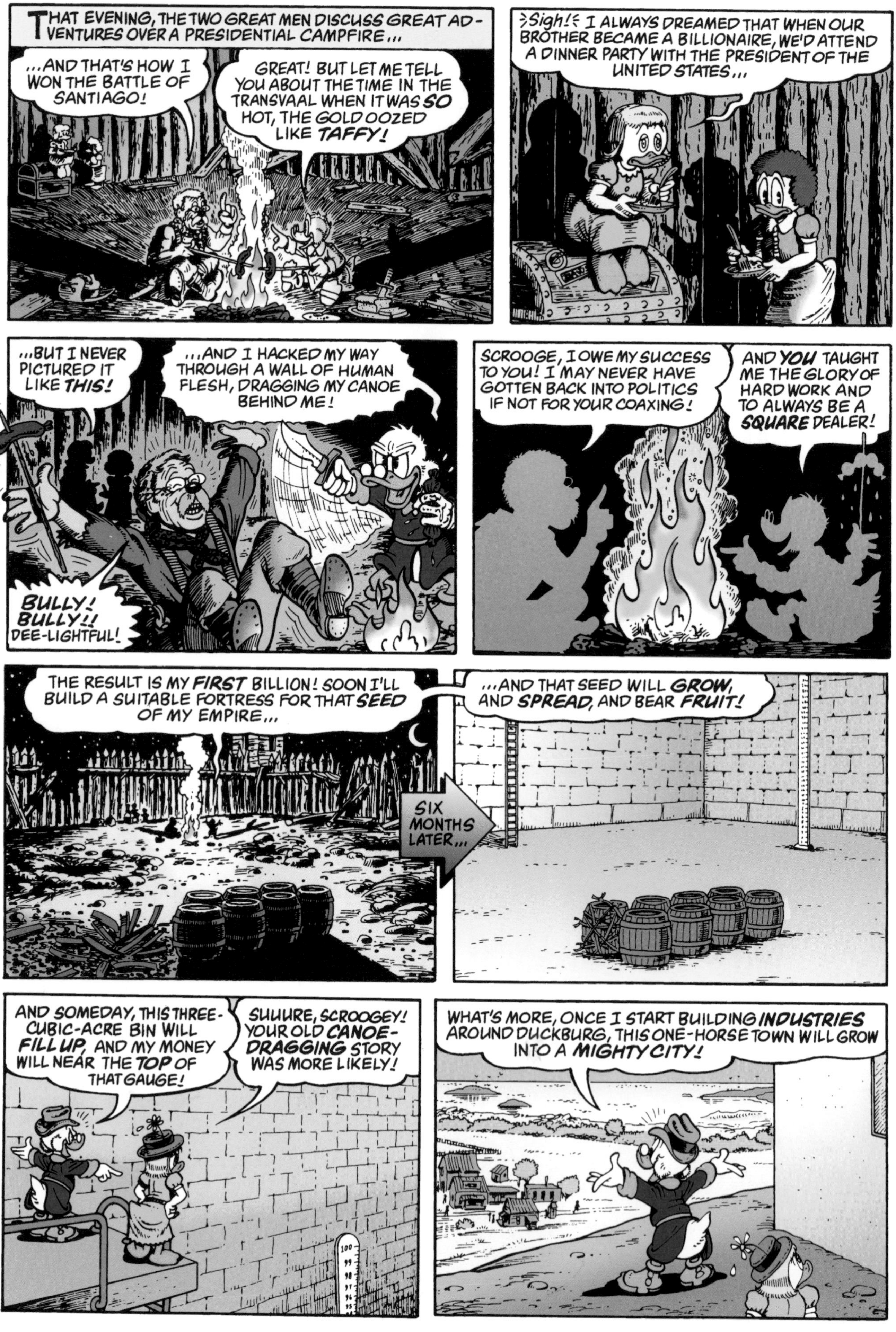

THAT EVENING, THE TWO GREAT MEN DISCUSS GREAT ADVENTURES OVER A PRESIDENTIAL CAMPFIRE...
...AND THAT'S HOW I WON THE BATTLE OF SANTIAGO!
GREAT! BUT LET ME TELL YOU ABOUT THE TIME IN THE TRANSVAAL WHEN IT WAS SO HOT, THE GOLD OOZED LIKE TAFFY!
>Sigh!< I ALWAYS DREAMED THAT WHEN OUR BROTHER BECAME A BILLIONAIRE, WE'D ATTEND A DINNER PARTY WITH THE PRESIDENT OF THE UNITED STATES...
...BUT I NEVER PICTURED IT LIKE THIS!
...AND I HACKED MY WAY THROUGH A WALL OF HUMAN FLESH, DRAGGING MY CANOE BEHIND ME!
BULLY! BULLY!! DEE-LIGHTFUL!
SCROOGE, I OWE MY SUCCESS TO YOU! I MAY NEVER HAVE GOTTEN BACK INTO POLITICS IF NOT FOR YOUR COAXING!
AND YOU TAUGHT ME THE GLORY OF HARD WORK AND TO ALWAYS BE A SQUARE DEALER!
THE RESULT IS MY FIRST BILLION! SOON I'LL BUILD A SUITABLE FORTRESS FOR THAT SEED OF MY EMPIRE...
SIX MONTHS LATER...
...AND THAT SEED WILL GROW, AND SPREAD, AND BEAR FRUIT!
AND SOMEDAY, THIS THREE-CUBIC-ACRE BIN WILL FILL UP, AND MY MONEY WILL NEAR THE TOP OF THAT GAUGE!
SUUURE, SCROOGEY! YOUR OLD CANOE-DRAGGING STORY WAS MORE LIKELY!
WHAT'S MORE, ONCE I START BUILDING INDUSTRIES AROUND DUCKBURG, THIS ONE-HORSE TOWN WILL GROW INTO A MIGHTY CITY!

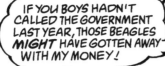

LOOK! THE JUNIOR WOOD-CHUCKS!

WOOD-CHUCKS! HUH? OH... SORRY!

HELP US BUILD A CLUBHOUSE!

IF YOU BOYS HADN'T CALLED THE GOVERNMENT LAST YEAR, THOSE BEAGLES *MIGHT* HAVE GOTTEN AWAY WITH MY MONEY!

MAY I MAKE A DONATION TOWARD YOUR NEW CLUB-HOUSE?

HELP US BUILD A CLUBHO! JEEPERS--SURE!

A *USED DOOR-KNOB?*

DUCKBURG WILL NEVER BE THE SAME WITH MR. McDUCK AROUND!

NOT BY A JUGFUL!

HEY, BUDDY! I HEAR SOME *TYCOON* MOVED INTO TOWN AND THERE'S GONNA BE LOTS AND LOTS OF NEW *JOBS!*

THAT'S RIGHT!

WELL, MABEL--THIS IS WHERE WE'LL BUILD OUR HOMESTEAD!

YES, BUT NOT NEAR *THAT* THING! WHAT A *MONSTROSITY!*

YOU'D BETTER GET *USED* TO THAT "MONSTROSITY", MA'AM...

...IT'S HERE TO *STAY!*

HANDS OFF!! THIS MEANS YOU!

WHY YOU *MALLETHEAD!* WHAT SORT OF A *STUPID* NAME FOR A KID IS *DONALD?!* NO SON OF MINE WILL *EVER* BE BLAH BLAH BLAH BLAH BLABETY BLABETY BLAH BLAH....

181

The Life and Times of $crooge McDuck
Part Eleven
"The Empire-Builder from Calisota"

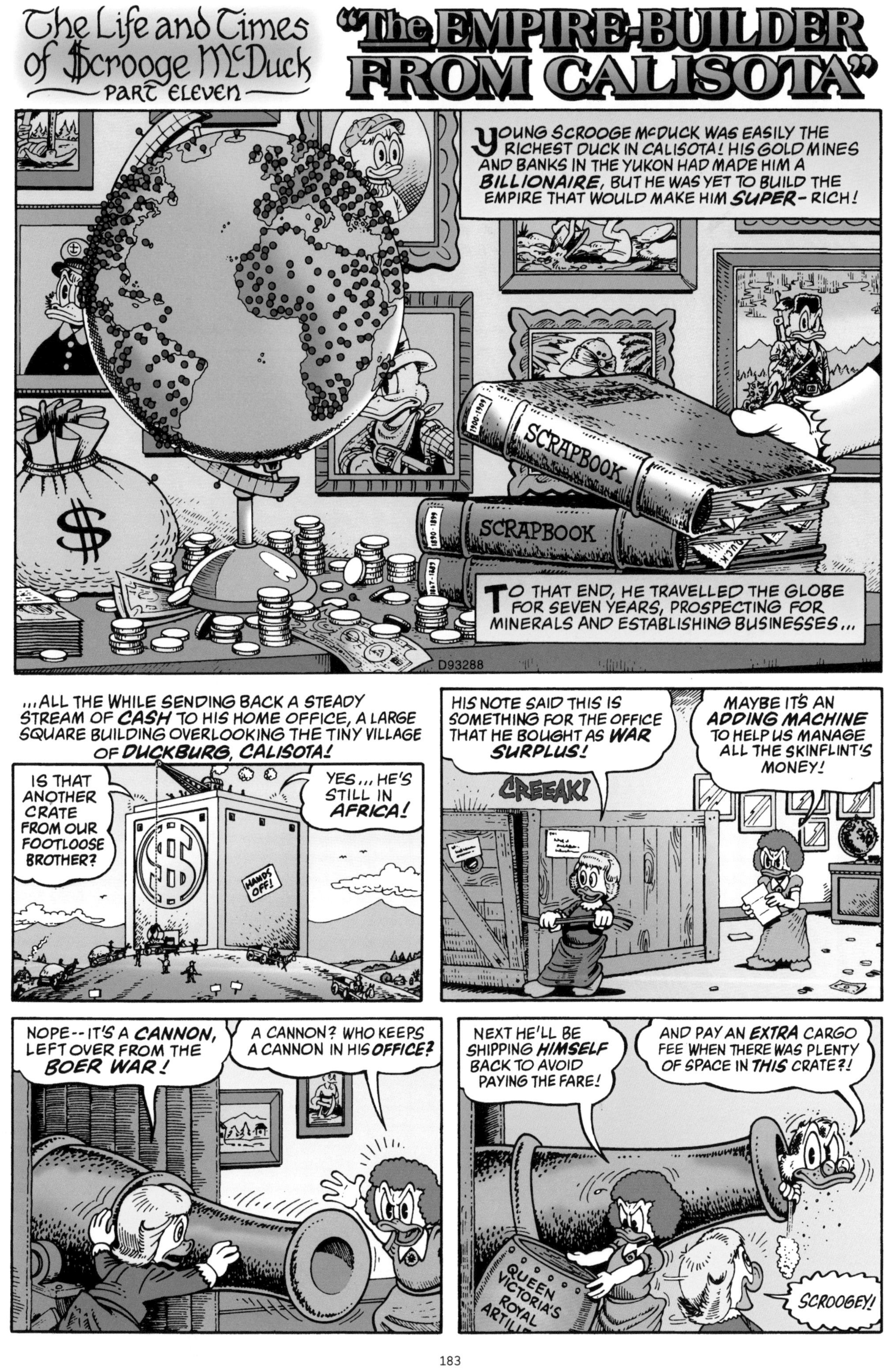
YOUNG SCROOGE McDUCK WAS EASILY THE RICHEST DUCK IN CALISOTA! HIS GOLD MINES AND BANKS IN THE YUKON HAD MADE HIM A BILLIONAIRE, BUT HE WAS YET TO BUILD THE EMPIRE THAT WOULD MAKE HIM SUPER-RICH!
SCRAPBOOK
1900-1909
SCRAPBOOK
1890-1899
1867-1883
TO THAT END, HE TRAVELLED THE GLOBE FOR SEVEN YEARS, PROSPECTING FOR MINERALS AND ESTABLISHING BUSINESSES...
D93288
...ALL THE WHILE SENDING BACK A STEADY STREAM OF CASH TO HIS HOME OFFICE, A LARGE SQUARE BUILDING OVERLOOKING THE TINY VILLAGE OF DUCKBURG, CALISOTA!
IS THAT ANOTHER CRATE FROM OUR FOOTLOOSE BROTHER?
YES... HE'S STILL IN AFRICA!
HANDS OFF!
HIS NOTE SAID THIS IS SOMETHING FOR THE OFFICE THAT HE BOUGHT AS WAR SURPLUS!
MAYBE IT'S AN ADDING MACHINE TO HELP US MANAGE ALL THE SKINFLINT'S MONEY!
CREEAK!
NOPE--IT'S A CANNON, LEFT OVER FROM THE BOER WAR!
A CANNON? WHO KEEPS A CANNON IN HIS OFFICE?
NEXT HE'LL BE SHIPPING HIMSELF BACK TO AVOID PAYING THE FARE!
AND PAY AN EXTRA CARGO FEE WHEN THERE WAS PLENTY OF SPACE IN THIS CRATE?!
QUEEN VICTORIA'S ROYAL ARTIL
SCROOGEY!

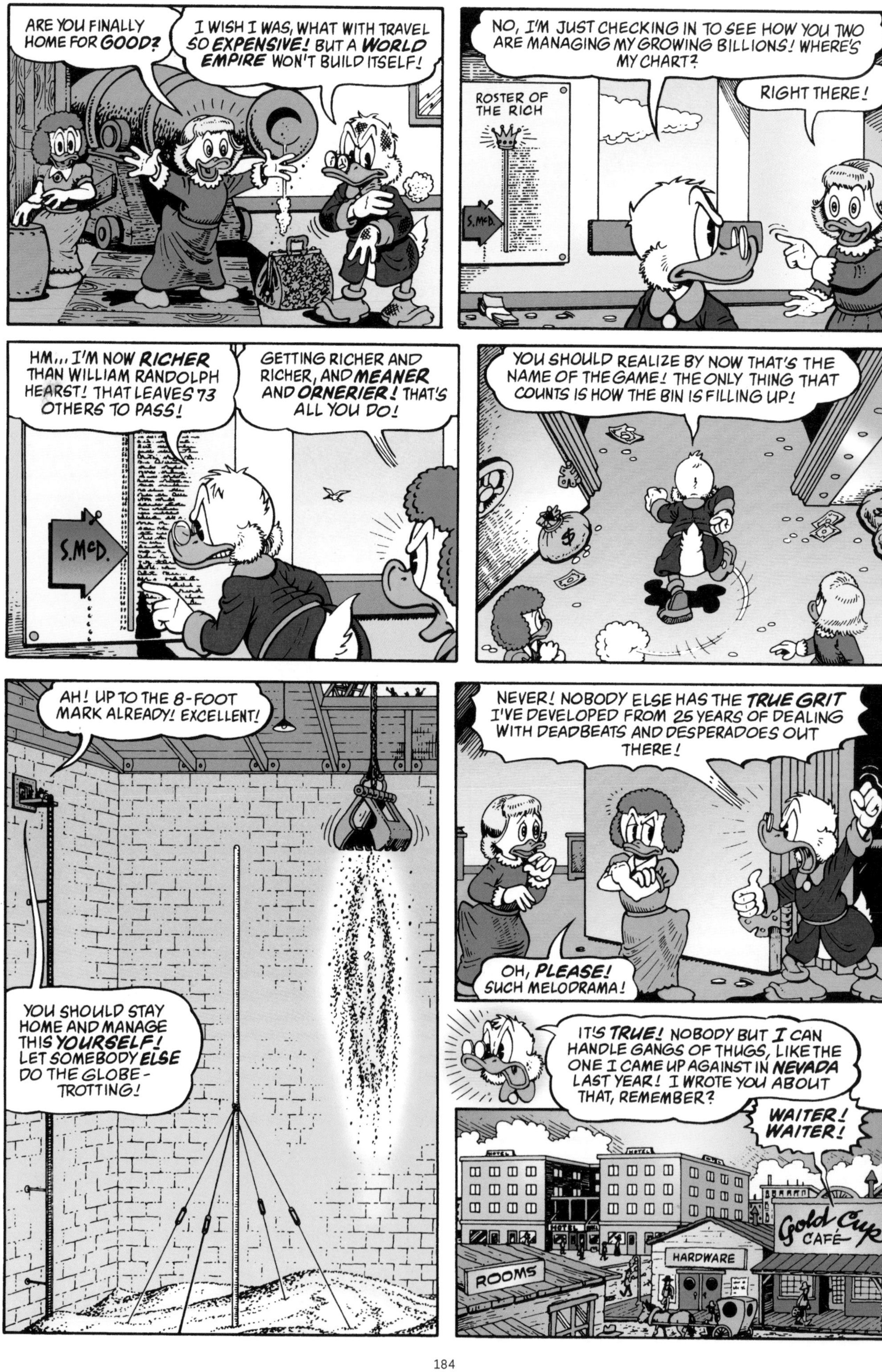
ARE YOU FINALLY HOME FOR GOOD?
I WISH I WAS, WHAT WITH TRAVEL SO EXPENSIVE! BUT A WORLD EMPIRE WON'T BUILD ITSELF!
NO, I'M JUST CHECKING IN TO SEE HOW YOU TWO ARE MANAGING MY GROWING BILLIONS! WHERE'S MY CHART?
ROSTER OF THE RICH
S. McD.
RIGHT THERE!
HM... I'M NOW RICHER THAN WILLIAM RANDOLPH HEARST! THAT LEAVES 73 OTHERS TO PASS!
GETTING RICHER AND RICHER, AND MEANER AND ORNERIER! THAT'S ALL YOU DO!
S. McD.
YOU SHOULD REALIZE BY NOW THAT'S THE NAME OF THE GAME! THE ONLY THING THAT COUNTS IS HOW THE BIN IS FILLING UP!
AH! UP TO THE 8-FOOT MARK ALREADY! EXCELLENT!
YOU SHOULD STAY HOME AND MANAGE THIS YOURSELF! LET SOMEBODY ELSE DO THE GLOBE-TROTTING!
NEVER! NOBODY ELSE HAS THE TRUE GRIT I'VE DEVELOPED FROM 25 YEARS OF DEALING WITH DEADBEATS AND DESPERADOES OUT THERE!
OH, PLEASE! SUCH MELODRAMA!
IT'S TRUE! NOBODY BUT I CAN HANDLE GANGS OF THUGS, LIKE THE ONE I CAME UP AGAINST IN NEVADA LAST YEAR! I WROTE YOU ABOUT THAT, REMEMBER?
WAITER! WAITER!
HOTEL
HARDWARE
ROOMS
Gold Cup CAFÉ

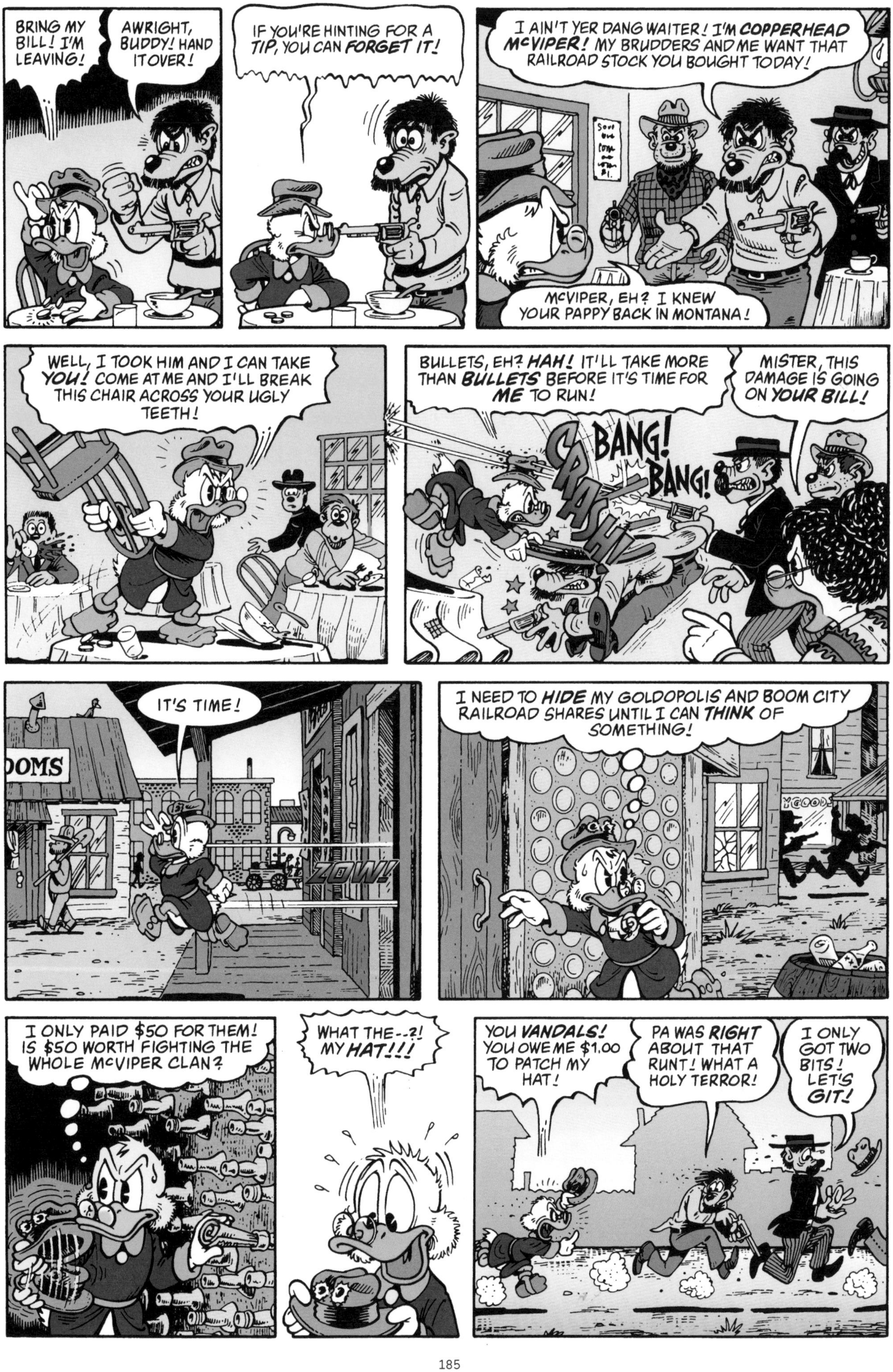
BRING MY BILL! I'M LEAVING!
AWRIGHT, BUDDY! HAND IT OVER!
IF YOU'RE HINTING FOR A TIP, YOU CAN FORGET IT!
I AIN'T YER DANG WAITER! I'M COPPERHEAD McVIPER! MY BRUDDERS AND ME WANT THAT RAILROAD STOCK YOU BOUGHT TODAY!
McVIPER, EH? I KNEW YOUR PAPPY BACK IN MONTANA!
WELL, I TOOK HIM AND I CAN TAKE YOU! COME AT ME AND I'LL BREAK THIS CHAIR ACROSS YOUR UGLY TEETH!
BULLETS, EH? HAH! IT'LL TAKE MORE THAN BULLETS BEFORE IT'S TIME FOR ME TO RUN!
MISTER, THIS DAMAGE IS GOING ON YOUR BILL!
BANG! BANG!
CRASH!
IT'S TIME!
OOMS
ZOW!
I NEED TO HIDE MY GOLDOPOLIS AND BOOM CITY RAILROAD SHARES UNTIL I CAN THINK OF SOMETHING!
I ONLY PAID $50 FOR THEM! IS $50 WORTH FIGHTING THE WHOLE McVIPER CLAN?
WHAT THE--?! MY HAT!!!
YOU VANDALS! YOU OWE ME $1.00 TO PATCH MY HAT!
PA WAS RIGHT ABOUT THAT RUNT! WHAT A HOLY TERROR!
I ONLY GOT TWO BITS! LET'S GIT!

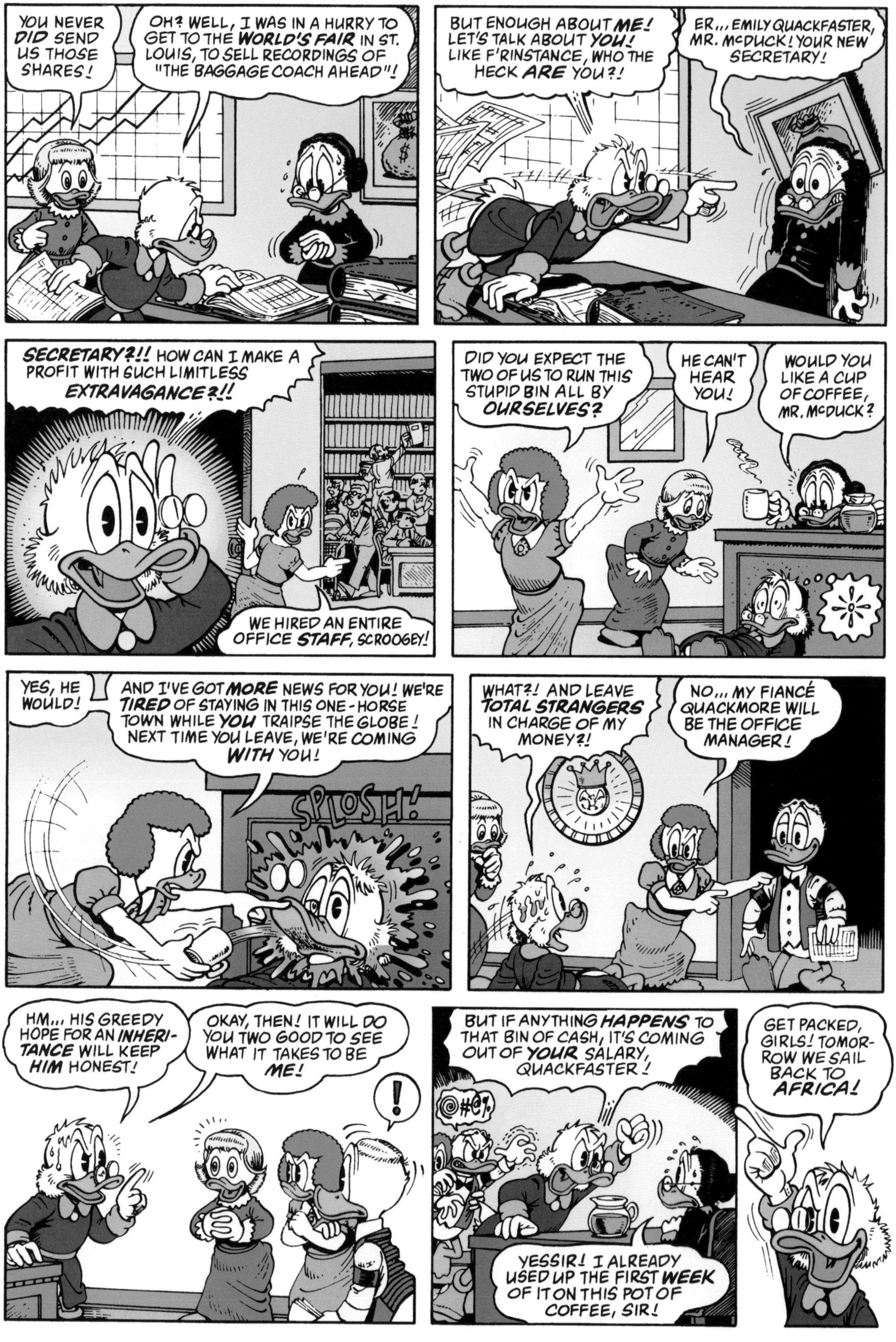
YOU NEVER DID SEND US THOSE SHARES!
OH? WELL, I WAS IN A HURRY TO GET TO THE WORLD'S FAIR IN ST. LOUIS, TO SELL RECORDINGS OF "THE BAGGAGE COACH AHEAD"!
BUT ENOUGH ABOUT ME! LET'S TALK ABOUT YOU! LIKE F'RINSTANCE, WHO THE HECK ARE YOU?!
ER... EMILY QUACKFASTER, MR. McDUCK! YOUR NEW SECRETARY!
SECRETARY?!! HOW CAN I MAKE A PROFIT WITH SUCH LIMITLESS EXTRAVAGANCE?!!
WE HIRED AN ENTIRE OFFICE STAFF, SCROOGEY!
DID YOU EXPECT THE TWO OF US TO RUN THIS STUPID BIN ALL BY OURSELVES?
HE CAN'T HEAR YOU!
WOULD YOU LIKE A CUP OF COFFEE, MR. McDUCK?
YES, HE WOULD!
AND I'VE GOT MORE NEWS FOR YOU! WE'RE TIRED OF STAYING IN THIS ONE-HORSE TOWN WHILE YOU TRAIPSE THE GLOBE! NEXT TIME YOU LEAVE, WE'RE COMING WITH YOU!
SPLOSH!
WHAT?! AND LEAVE TOTAL STRANGERS IN CHARGE OF MY MONEY?!
NO... MY FIANCÉ QUACKMORE WILL BE THE OFFICE MANAGER!
HM... HIS GREEDY HOPE FOR AN INHERITANCE WILL KEEP HIM HONEST!
OKAY, THEN! IT WILL DO YOU TWO GOOD TO SEE WHAT IT TAKES TO BE ME!
!
BUT IF ANYTHING HAPPENS TO THAT BIN OF CASH, IT'S COMING OUT OF YOUR SALARY, QUACKFASTER!
YESSIR! I ALREADY USED UP THE FIRST WEEK OF IT ON THIS POT OF COFFEE, SIR!
GET PACKED, GIRLS! TOMORROW WE SAIL BACK TO AFRICA!

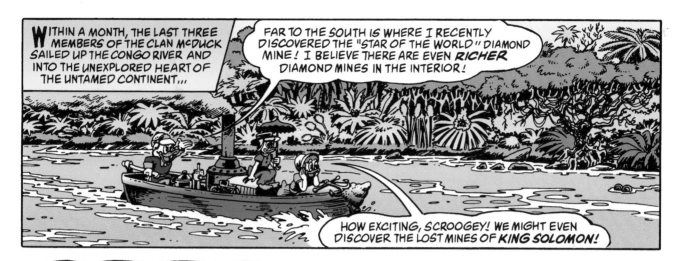

WITHIN A MONTH, THE LAST THREE MEMBERS OF THE CLAN MCDUCK SAILED UP THE CONGO RIVER AND INTO THE UNEXPLORED HEART OF THE UNTAMED CONTINENT...

FAR TO THE SOUTH IS WHERE I RECENTLY DISCOVERED THE "STAR OF THE WORLD" DIAMOND MINE! I BELIEVE THERE ARE EVEN *RICHER* DIAMOND MINES IN THE INTERIOR!

HOW EXCITING, SCROOGEY! WE MIGHT EVEN DISCOVER THE LOST MINES OF *KING SOLOMON!*

MAYBE SOMEDAY, BUT RIGHT NOW WE'RE HEADING INTO THE MUMBO JUMBO RIVER! YOU'LL SOON SEE WHAT A *GENIUS* YOUR BIG BROTHER IS!

DAYS LATER, IN A SHADY PART OF DARKEST AFRICA, SCROOGE MCDUCK BEGAN A DAY THAT WOULD LIVE IN *INFAMY!*

...AS A SYMBOL OF OUR TREATY, HERE IS A MINIATURE WAR DRUM!

WHAT SIMILAR TREASURE WILL YOU GIVE THE QWAK QWAK TRIBE FOR OUR KACHOONGA DIAMOND MINE?

I OFFER THIS, CHIEF...

...A *MINIATURE PORTRAIT* OF THE CHIEF OF *MY* VILLAGE!

OOO,... CHIEF "QUARTER-DOLLAR"! MOST IMPRESSIVE!

TELL ME, CHIEF BOOGER-BOOBOO-- ANY *OTHER* VALUABLE LAND IN THESE PARTS?

OH, YES, SOME EXCELLENT RUBBER PLANT LAND! BUT THE *VOODOO TRIBE* BELIEVES IT IS SACRED TO THEIR GODS! THEY WILL NOT SELL,...

...NOT EVEN FOR SUCH A PRIZE AS *THIS!*

OH, SO? WELL, MAYBE I'LL MAKE THEM AN OFFER THEY *CAN'T* REFUSE!

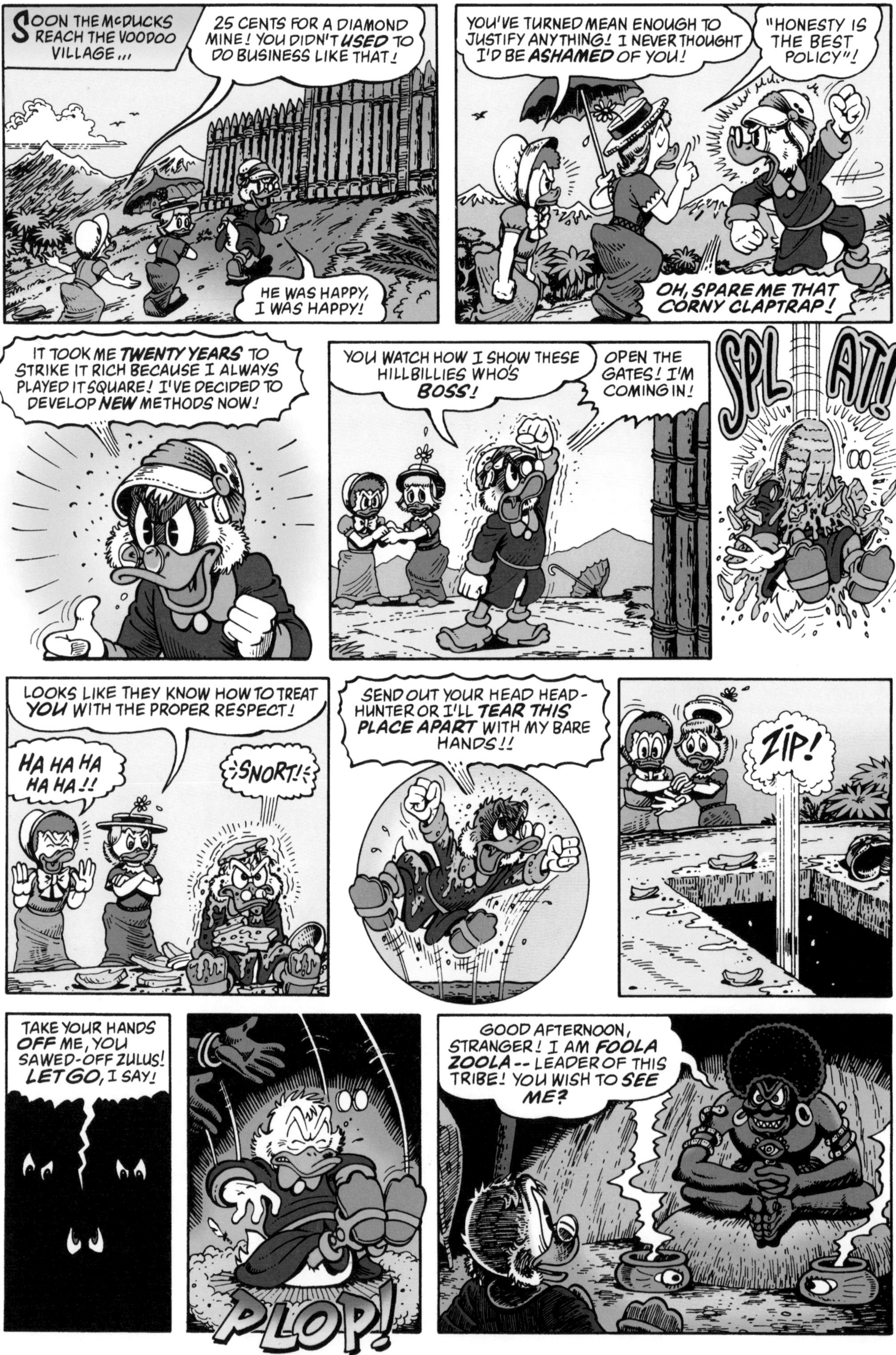

SOON THE McDUCKS REACH THE VOODOO VILLAGE...
25 CENTS FOR A DIAMOND MINE! YOU DIDN'T USED TO DO BUSINESS LIKE THAT!
HE WAS HAPPY, I WAS HAPPY!
YOU'VE TURNED MEAN ENOUGH TO JUSTIFY ANYTHING! I NEVER THOUGHT I'D BE ASHAMED OF YOU!
"HONESTY IS THE BEST POLICY"!
OH, SPARE ME THAT CORNY CLAPTRAP!
IT TOOK ME TWENTY YEARS TO STRIKE IT RICH BECAUSE I ALWAYS PLAYED IT SQUARE! I'VE DECIDED TO DEVELOP NEW METHODS NOW!
YOU WATCH HOW I SHOW THESE HILLBILLIES WHO'S BOSS!
OPEN THE GATES! I'M COMING IN!
SPLAT!
LOOKS LIKE THEY KNOW HOW TO TREAT YOU WITH THE PROPER RESPECT!
HA HA HA HA HA!!
SNORT!
SEND OUT YOUR HEAD HEAD-HUNTER OR I'LL TEAR THIS PLACE APART WITH MY BARE HANDS!!
ZIP!
TAKE YOUR HANDS OFF ME, YOU SAWED-OFF ZULUS! LET GO, I SAY!
PLOP!
GOOD AFTERNOON, STRANGER! I AM FOOLA ZOOLA -- LEADER OF THIS TRIBE! YOU WISH TO SEE ME?

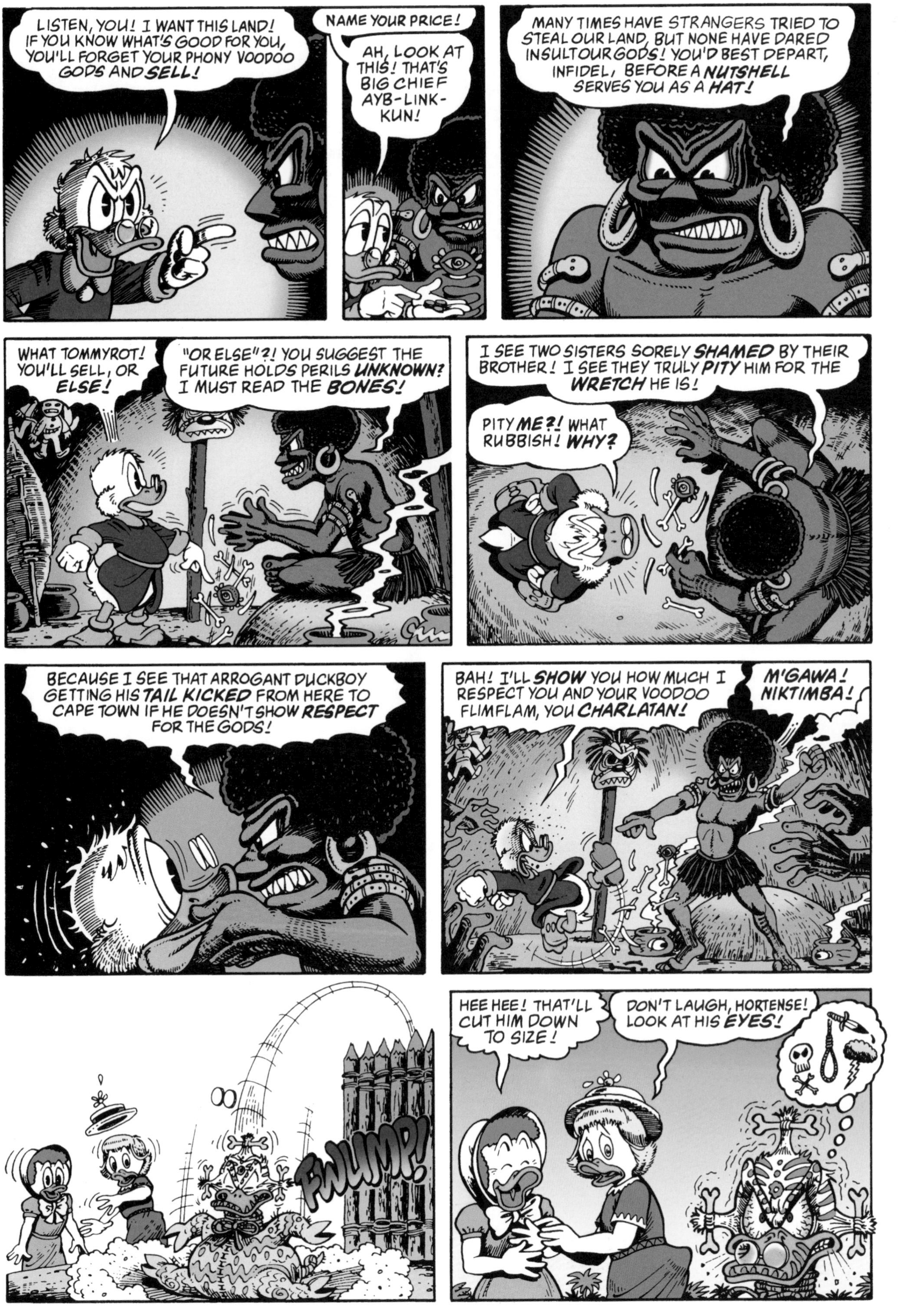
LISTEN, YOU! I WANT THIS LAND! IF YOU KNOW WHAT'S GOOD FOR YOU, YOU'LL FORGET YOUR PHONY VOODOO GODS AND SELL!
NAME YOUR PRICE!
AH, LOOK AT THIS! THAT'S BIG CHIEF AYB-LINK-KUN!
MANY TIMES HAVE STRANGERS TRIED TO STEAL OUR LAND, BUT NONE HAVE DARED INSULT OUR GODS! YOU'D BEST DEPART, INFIDEL, BEFORE A NUTSHELL SERVES YOU AS A HAT!
WHAT TOMMYROT! YOU'LL SELL, OR ELSE!
"OR ELSE"?! YOU SUGGEST THE FUTURE HOLDS PERILS UNKNOWN? I MUST READ THE BONES!
I SEE TWO SISTERS SORELY SHAMED BY THEIR BROTHER! I SEE THEY TRULY PITY HIM FOR THE WRETCH HE IS!
PITY ME?! WHAT RUBBISH! WHY?
BECAUSE I SEE THAT ARROGANT DUCKBOY GETTING HIS TAIL KICKED FROM HERE TO CAPE TOWN IF HE DOESN'T SHOW RESPECT FOR THE GODS!
BAH! I'LL SHOW YOU HOW MUCH I RESPECT YOU AND YOUR VOODOO FLIMFLAM, YOU CHARLATAN!
M'GAWA! NIKTIMBA!
FWUMP!
HEE HEE! THAT'LL CUT HIM DOWN TO SIZE!
DON'T LAUGH, HORTENSE! LOOK AT HIS EYES!

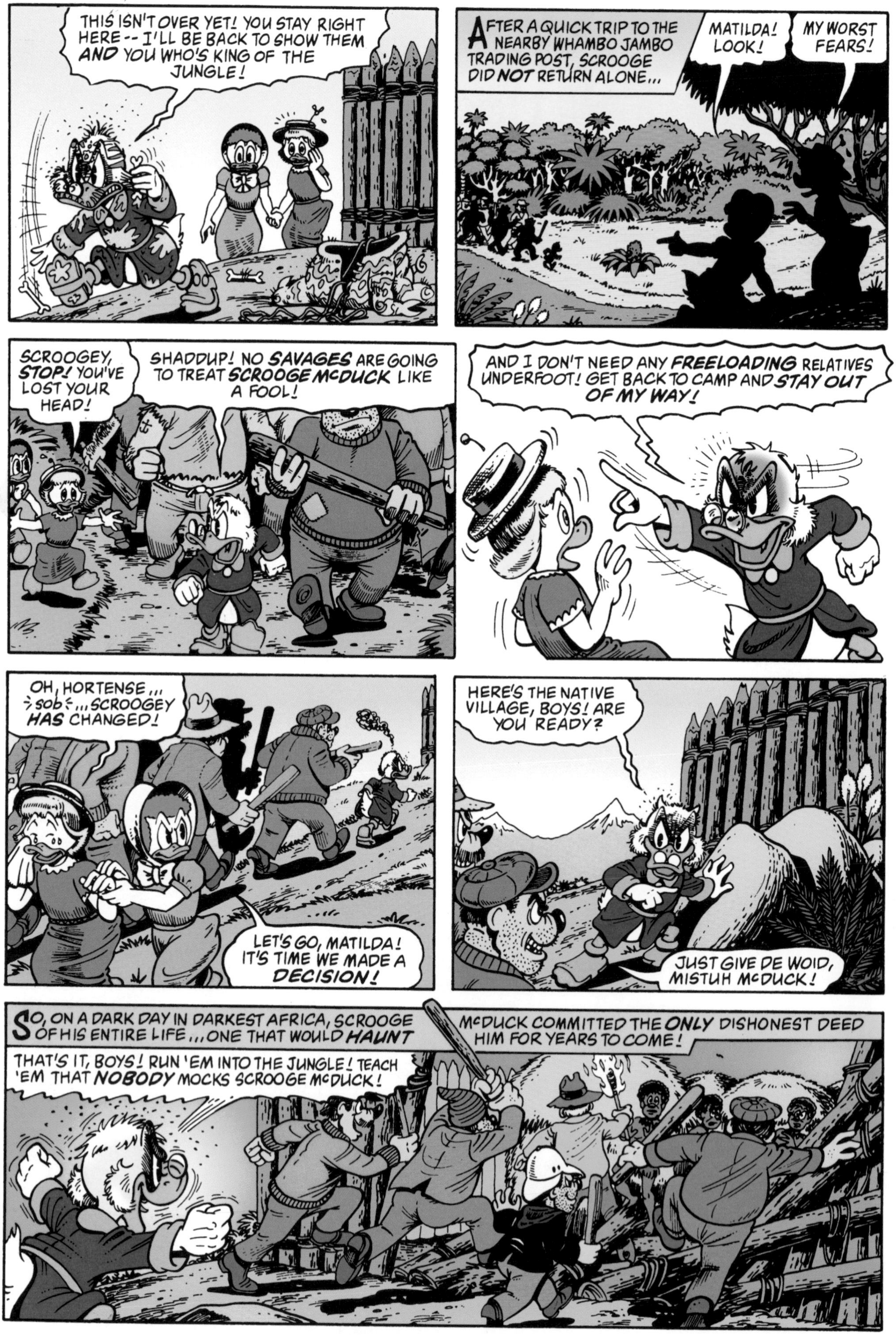
THIS ISN'T OVER YET! YOU STAY RIGHT HERE -- I'LL BE BACK TO SHOW THEM AND YOU WHO'S KING OF THE JUNGLE!
AFTER A QUICK TRIP TO THE NEARBY WHAMBO JAMBO TRADING POST, SCROOGE DID NOT RETURN ALONE...
MATILDA! LOOK!
MY WORST FEARS!
SCROOGEY, STOP! YOU'VE LOST YOUR HEAD!
SHADDUP! NO SAVAGES ARE GOING TO TREAT SCROOGE McDUCK LIKE A FOOL!
AND I DON'T NEED ANY FREELOADING RELATIVES UNDERFOOT! GET BACK TO CAMP AND STAY OUT OF MY WAY!
OH, HORTENSE... ~sob~ ... SCROOGEY HAS CHANGED!
LET'S GO, MATILDA! IT'S TIME WE MADE A DECISION!
HERE'S THE NATIVE VILLAGE, BOYS! ARE YOU READY?
JUST GIVE DE WOID, MISTUH McDUCK!
SO, ON A DARK DAY IN DARKEST AFRICA, SCROOGE McDUCK COMMITTED THE ONLY DISHONEST DEED OF HIS ENTIRE LIFE... ONE THAT WOULD HAUNT HIM FOR YEARS TO COME!
THAT'S IT, BOYS! RUN 'EM INTO THE JUNGLE! TEACH 'EM THAT NOBODY MOCKS SCROOGE McDUCK!

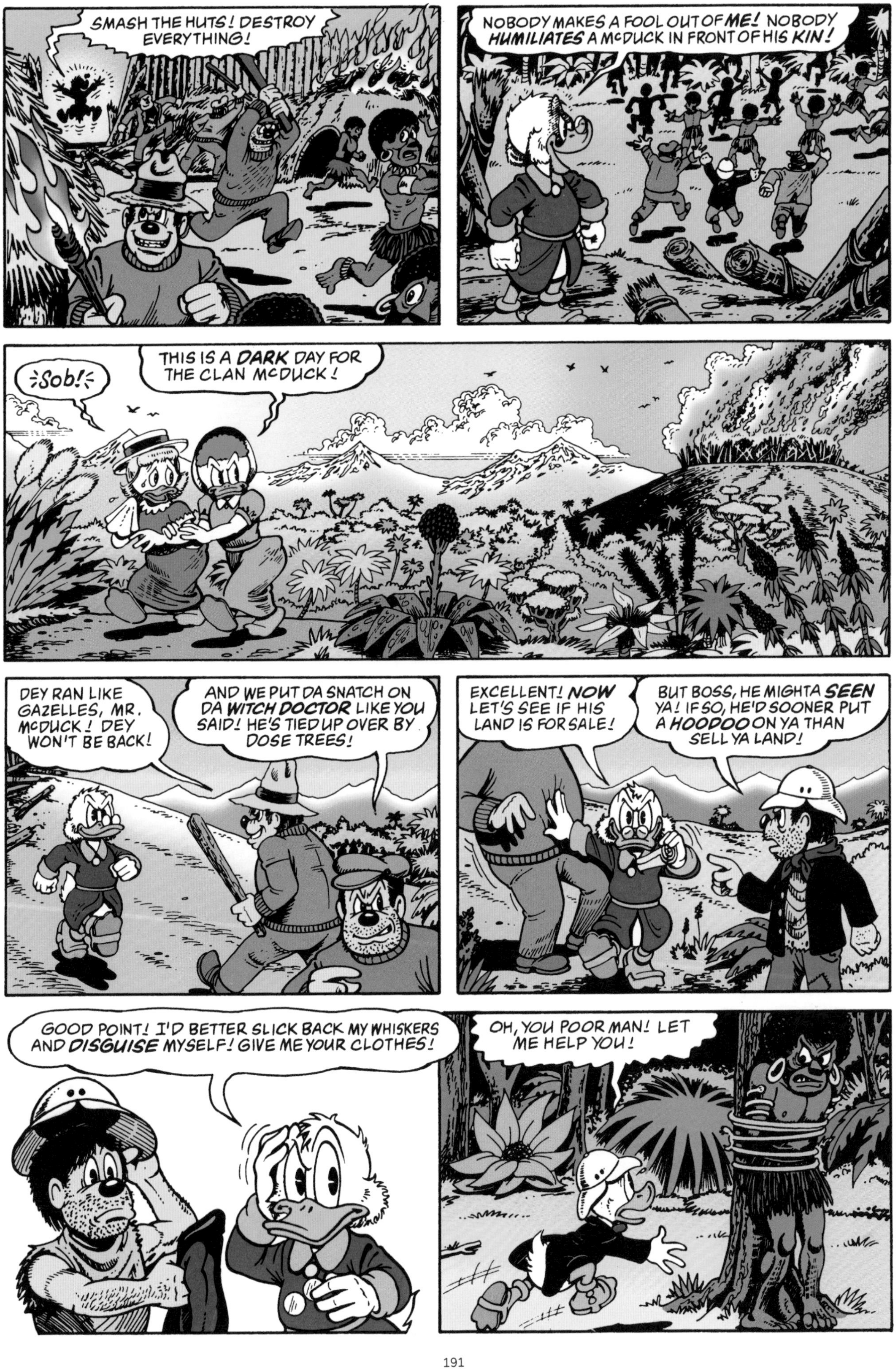
SMASH THE HUTS! DESTROY EVERYTHING!
NOBODY MAKES A FOOL OUT OF ME! NOBODY HUMILIATES A McDUCK IN FRONT OF HIS KIN!
Sob!
THIS IS A DARK DAY FOR THE CLAN McDUCK!
DEY RAN LIKE GAZELLES, MR. McDUCK! DEY WON'T BE BACK!
AND WE PUT DA SNATCH ON DA WITCH DOCTOR LIKE YOU SAID! HE'S TIED UP OVER BY DOSE TREES!
EXCELLENT! NOW LET'S SEE IF HIS LAND IS FOR SALE!
BUT BOSS, HE MIGHTA SEEN YA! IF SO, HE'D SOONER PUT A HOODOO ON YA THAN SELL YA LAND!
GOOD POINT! I'D BETTER SLICK BACK MY WHISKERS AND DISGUISE MYSELF! GIVE ME YOUR CLOTHES!
OH, YOU POOR MAN! LET ME HELP YOU!

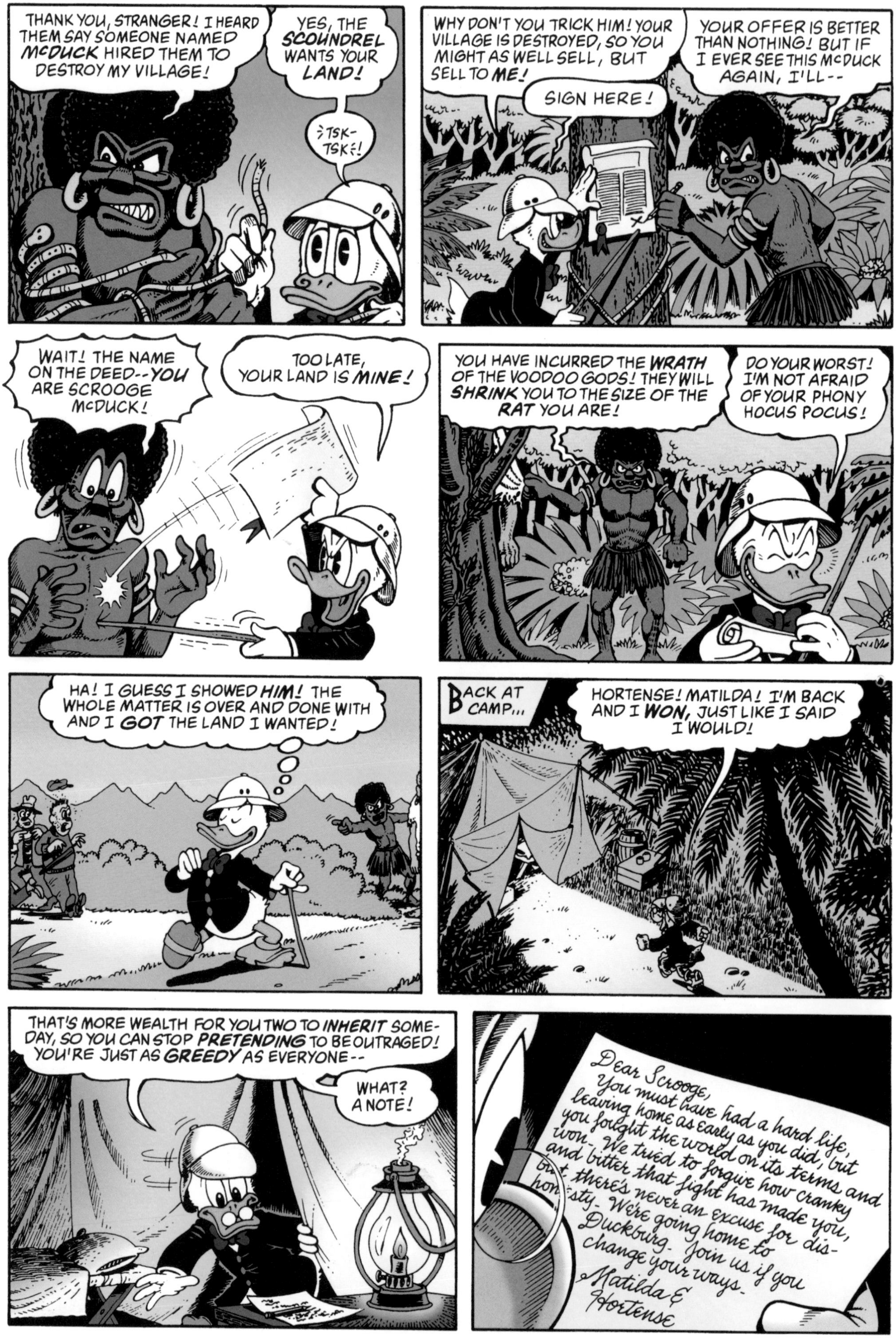
THANK YOU, STRANGER! I HEARD THEM SAY SOMEONE NAMED McDUCK HIRED THEM TO DESTROY MY VILLAGE!
YES, THE SCOUNDREL WANTS YOUR LAND!
TSK-TSK!
WHY DON'T YOU TRICK HIM! YOUR VILLAGE IS DESTROYED, SO YOU MIGHT AS WELL SELL, BUT SELL TO ME!
SIGN HERE!
YOUR OFFER IS BETTER THAN NOTHING! BUT IF I EVER SEE THIS McDUCK AGAIN, I'LL--
WAIT! THE NAME ON THE DEED--YOU ARE SCROOGE McDUCK!
TOO LATE, YOUR LAND IS MINE!
YOU HAVE INCURRED THE WRATH OF THE VOODOO GODS! THEY WILL SHRINK YOU TO THE SIZE OF THE RAT YOU ARE!
DO YOUR WORST! I'M NOT AFRAID OF YOUR PHONY HOCUS POCUS!
HA! I GUESS I SHOWED HIM! THE WHOLE MATTER IS OVER AND DONE WITH AND I GOT THE LAND I WANTED!
BACK AT CAMP...
HORTENSE! MATILDA! I'M BACK AND I WON, JUST LIKE I SAID I WOULD!
THAT'S MORE WEALTH FOR YOU TWO TO INHERIT SOMEDAY, SO YOU CAN STOP PRETENDING TO BE OUTRAGED! YOU'RE JUST AS GREEDY AS EVERYONE--
WHAT? A NOTE!
Dear Scrooge, You must have had a hard life, leaving home as early as you did, but you fought the world on its terms and won. We tried to forgive how cranky and bitter that fight has made you, but there's never an excuse for dishonesty. We're going home to Duckburg. Join us if you change your ways. Matilda & Hortense

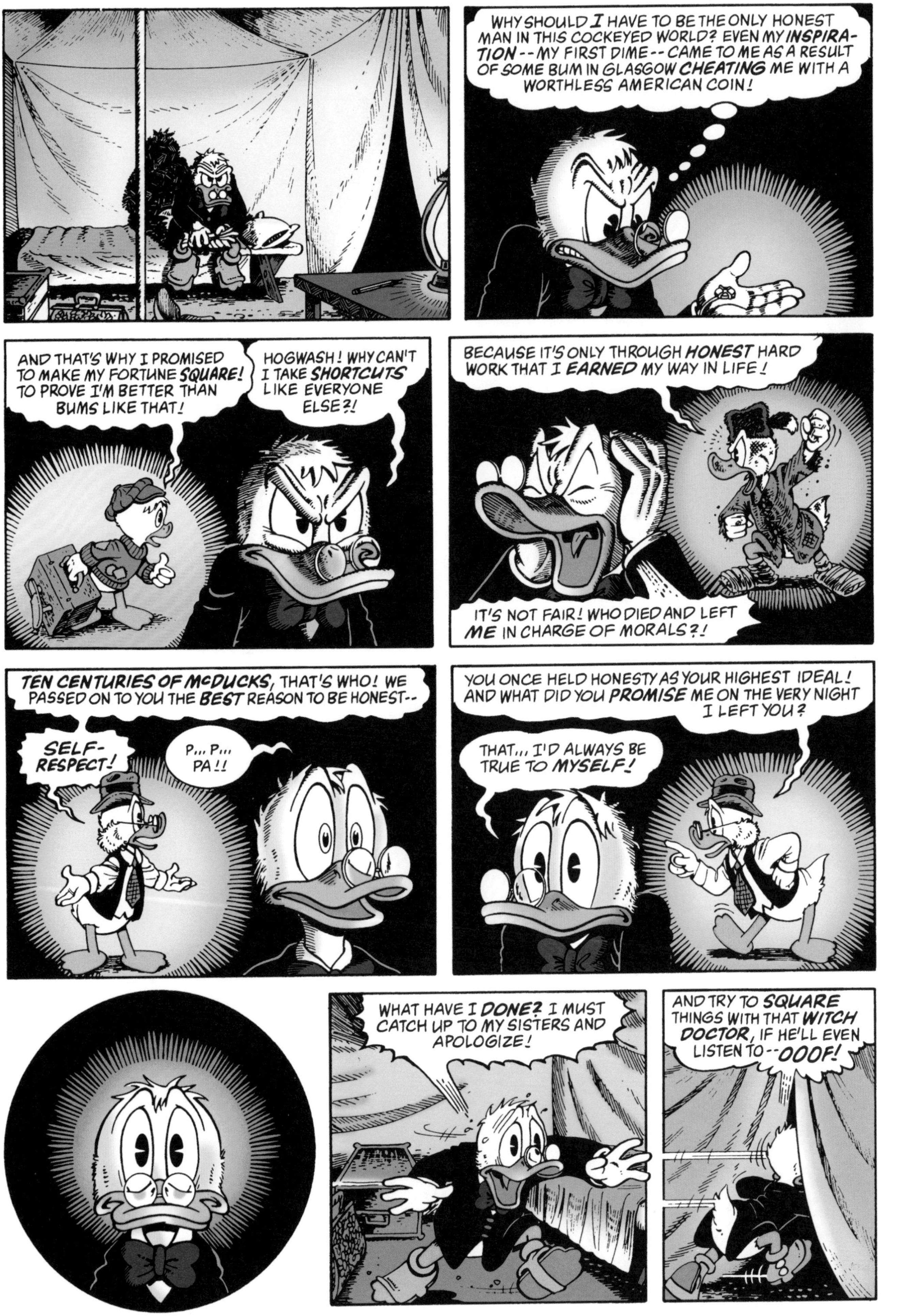
WHY SHOULD I HAVE TO BE THE ONLY HONEST MAN IN THIS COCKEYED WORLD? EVEN MY INSPIRATION -- MY FIRST DIME -- CAME TO ME AS A RESULT OF SOME BUM IN GLASGOW CHEATING ME WITH A WORTHLESS AMERICAN COIN!
AND THAT'S WHY I PROMISED TO MAKE MY FORTUNE SQUARE! TO PROVE I'M BETTER THAN BUMS LIKE THAT!
HOGWASH! WHY CAN'T I TAKE SHORTCUTS LIKE EVERYONE ELSE?!
BECAUSE IT'S ONLY THROUGH HONEST HARD WORK THAT I EARNED MY WAY IN LIFE!
IT'S NOT FAIR! WHO DIED AND LEFT ME IN CHARGE OF MORALS?!
TEN CENTURIES OF McDUCKS, THAT'S WHO! WE PASSED ON TO YOU THE BEST REASON TO BE HONEST--
SELF-RESPECT!
P... P... PA!!
YOU ONCE HELD HONESTY AS YOUR HIGHEST IDEAL! AND WHAT DID YOU PROMISE ME ON THE VERY NIGHT I LEFT YOU?
THAT... I'D ALWAYS BE TRUE TO MYSELF!
WHAT HAVE I DONE? I MUST CATCH UP TO MY SISTERS AND APOLOGIZE!
AND TRY TO SQUARE THINGS WITH THAT WITCH DOCTOR, IF HE'LL EVEN LISTEN TO--OOOF!

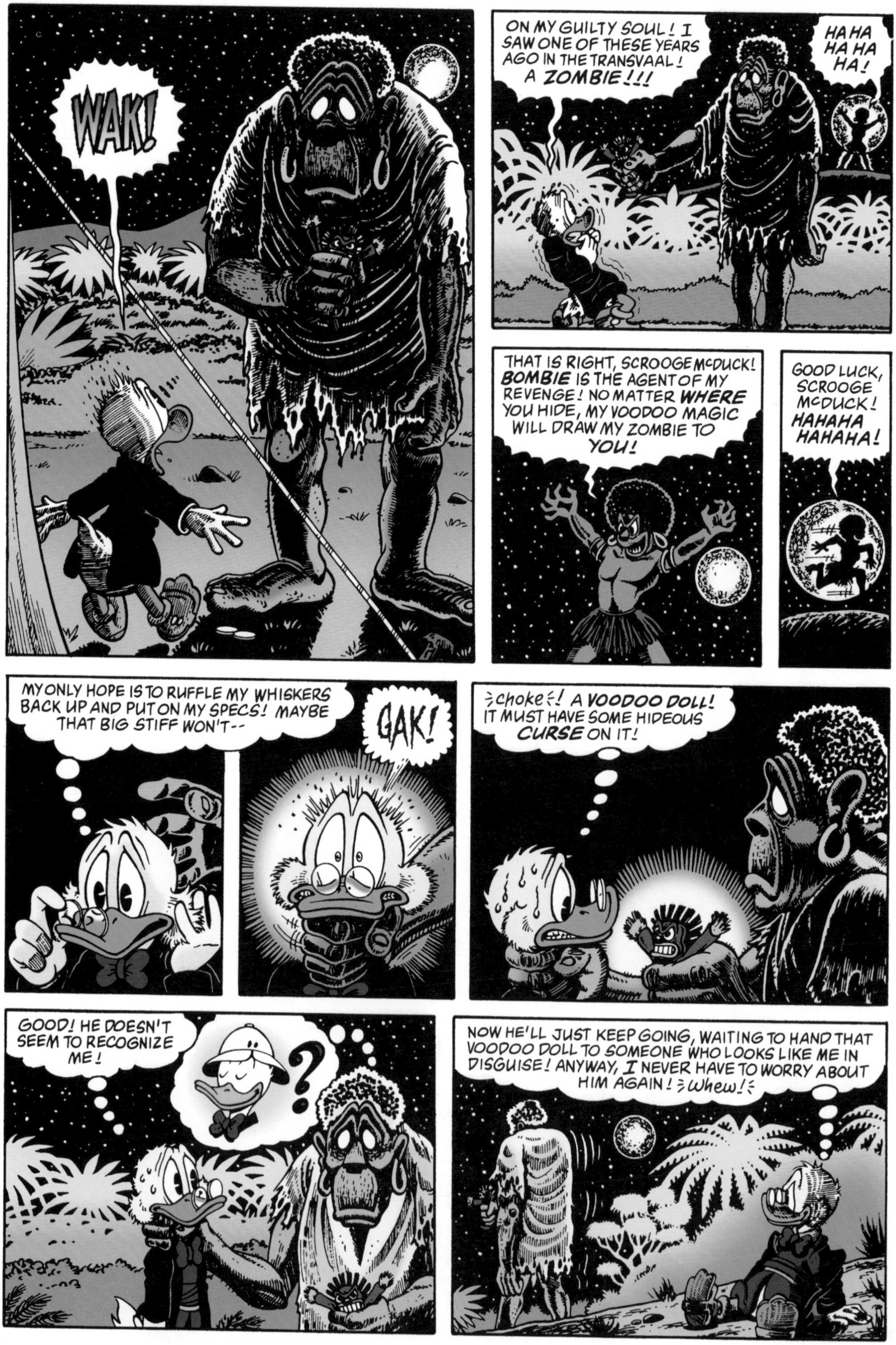

WAK!
ON MY GUILTY SOUL! I SAW ONE OF THESE YEARS AGO IN THE TRANSVAAL! A ZOMBIE!!!
HA HA HA HA HA!
THAT IS RIGHT, SCROOGE McDUCK! BOMBIE IS THE AGENT OF MY REVENGE! NO MATTER WHERE YOU HIDE, MY VOODOO MAGIC WILL DRAW MY ZOMBIE TO YOU!
GOOD LUCK, SCROOGE McDUCK! HAHAHA HAHAHA!
MY ONLY HOPE IS TO RUFFLE MY WHISKERS BACK UP AND PUT ON MY SPECS! MAYBE THAT BIG STIFF WON'T--
GAK!
choke! A VOODOO DOLL! IT MUST HAVE SOME HIDEOUS CURSE ON IT!
GOOD! HE DOESN'T SEEM TO RECOGNIZE ME!
?
NOW HE'LL JUST KEEP GOING, WAITING TO HAND THAT VOODOO DOLL TO SOMEONE WHO LOOKS LIKE ME IN DISGUISE! ANYWAY, I NEVER HAVE TO WORRY ABOUT HIM AGAIN! Whew!

UNABLE TO FIND FOOLA ZOOLA, SCROOGE SET OFF TO PATCH THINGS UP WITH HIS SISTERS...
YES, A HORTENSE AND MATILDA McDUCK WERE HERE, BUT YOU JUST MISSED THEM! THEY TOOK THE TRAIN TO THE COAST!
THEN GIVE ME A TICKET ON THE NEXT TRAIN!
WHAMBO JAMBO
BUT THAT TRAIN IS HEADING NORTH TO JOIN THE ORIENT EXPRESS IN ISTANBUL! THE NEXT TRAIN TO THE COAST WON'T LEAVE FOR A WEEK!
HMM... THE ORIENT EXPRESS GOES THROUGH CONTINENTAL EUROPE! LOTS OF BUSINESS OPPORTUNITIES THERE! I CAN ALWAYS CATCH UP WITH MY SISTERS A LITTLE LATER! HMM...
OF COURSE, BOAT FARES ARE CHEAPER FROM EUROPE!
SOLD! I MAY BE HONEST, BUT I DIDN'T JUST GET STUPID!
OVER THE NEXT YEAR SCROOGE WAS CONTINUALLY SIDE-TRACKED ON HIS WAY HOME! HE SOLD LAWNMOWERS IN THE SAHARA, SALT IN EGYPT, RAINHATS IN ADEN...
ORIENT EXPRESS
ARABIA
SAHARA DESERT
ADEN
...AND SO ON AND SO ON, FROM TURKEY TO HOLLAND! WHILE SELLING WIND TO WINDMILL MAKERS ON THE ZUYDER ZEE, SCROOGE LEARNED OF A UNIQUE OPPORTUNITY...
AMSTERDAM EXTRA!
SO, TAKING ONE LAST DETOUR ON HIS WAY TO AMERICA, SCROOGE STOPPED OFF IN GREENLAND FOR A RENDEZVOUS ON THE POLAR ICE CAP...
HALLO! ARE YOU ROBERT PEARY?
YES! WHAT DO YOU WANT?
I WANT TO SPONSOR YOUR EFFORTS TO REACH THE NORTH POLE!
WHY? DO YOU REPRESENT A UNIVERSITY OR A GEO-GRAPHIC SOCIETY?
NO! I INTEND TO BUY THE NORTH POLE! EVERY TIME ANYONE LOOKS AT A COMPASS, THEY'LL HAVE TO PAY ME A STIFF ROYALTY!
NOT TO MENTION THE HEFTY SURCHARGE I'LL SLAP ON KIDS' LETTERS TO SANTA!

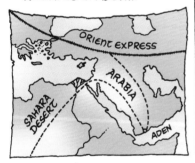

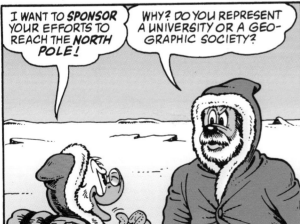

I'M BACK WITH THE NEW BEARERS I HIRED, MISTER PEARY!

I'LL BE RIGHT THERE.

AS FOR YOU, SIR, *BEGONE!* THIS IS A *SCIENTIFIC* EXPEDITION!

YOU'LL REGRET THIS, PEARY!

MARK MY WORDS-- SOME DAY YOU'LL COME CRAWLING TO ME TO FINANCE SOME OTHER-- ⸘OOF!⸬

ACK! BOMBIE THE *ZOMBIE!!*

THE QUIET GUY'S A *ZOMBIE,* EH? THAT MIGHT EXPLAIN WHY HE'S WEARING ONLY A *TORN SHROUD* WHEN IT'S 60° BELOW!

NEXT TIME, HIRE A *WEREWOLF!* AT LEAST HE'D BE *DRESSED WARMLY!*

FOOLA ZOOLA WASN'T KIDDING! HIS MAGIC DRAWS BOMBIE TO ME *WHEREVER* I AM!

LOOK! I'M NOT *ME!* I'M SOME OTHER GUY!

CRACK!

WOOSH!

WHAT A BREAK! HE FELL INTO A CREVICE AND GOT SEALED DEEP IN THE ICE! THAT'S THE *END* OF MY ZOMBIE TROUBLES!

CRUNCH!

CREAK!

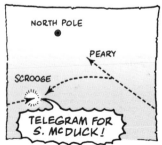

ONCE AGAIN ON HIS WAY TO RECONCILE WITH HIS SISTERS, SCROOGE WAS STOPPED WHEN A MESSAGE REACHED HIM...

NORTH POLE

PEARY

SCROOGE

TELEGRAM FOR S. MᶜDUCK!

⸘ahem!⸬

WOW! I'VE BEEN GRANTED THE *ROYAL AUDIENCE* I'VE SOUGHT FOR YEARS! I'VE GOT TO *RUSH TO RUSSIA* BY THE *SHORTEST* ROUTE!

SO ONCE AGAIN, SCROOGE'S JOURNEY HOME WAS POSTPONED...

LOOK! THERE IT IS! I'LL BE THE *FIRST* TO REACH THE NORTH POLE!

NORTH POLE

SCROOGE

PEARY

⸬GRUMBLE!⸬ NO TIP!

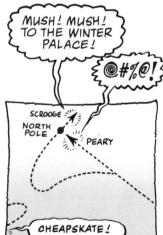

MUSH! MUSH! TO THE WINTER PALACE!

@#%@!

SCROOGE

NORTH POLE

PEARY

CHEAPSKATE!

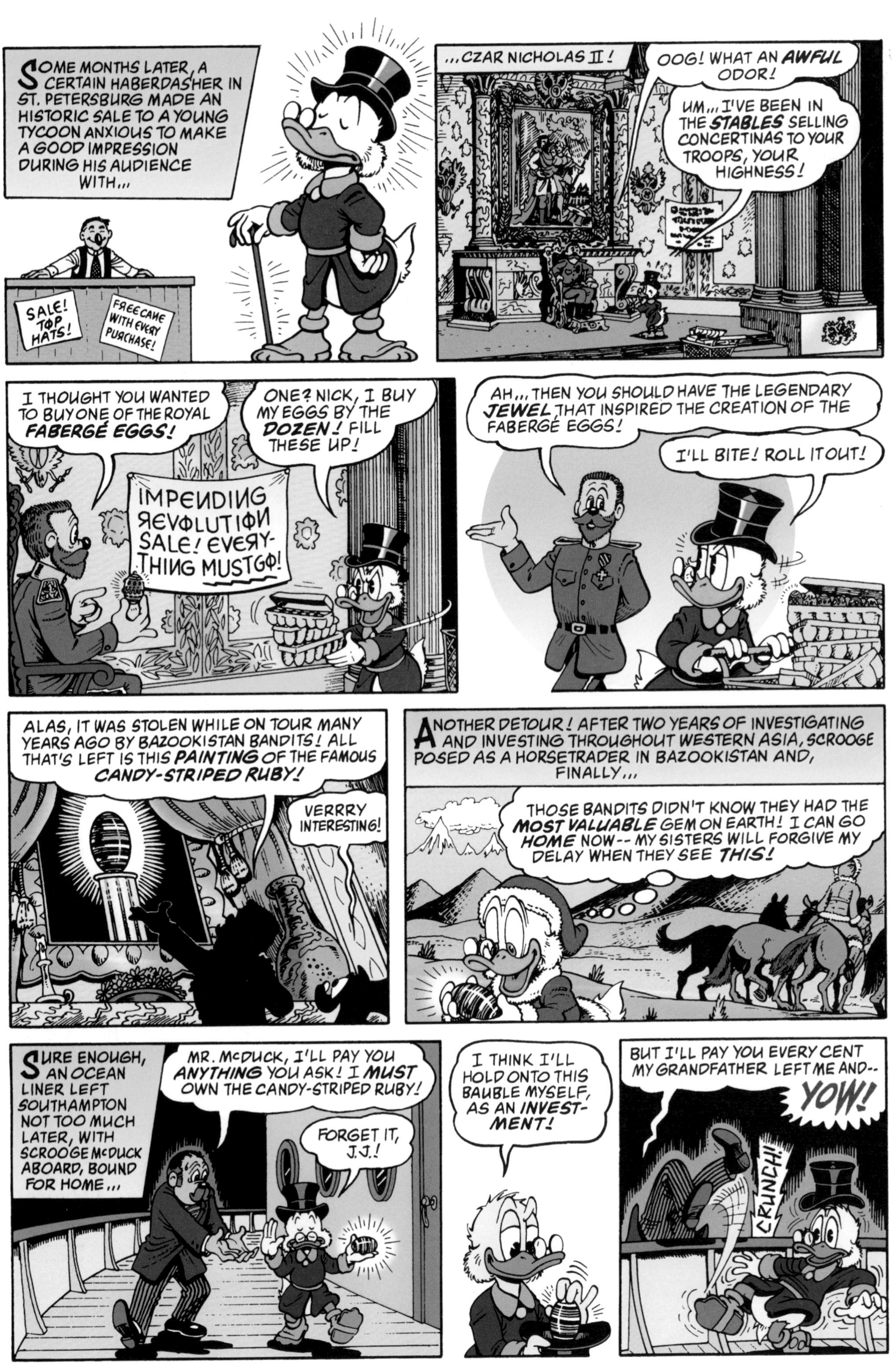
SOME MONTHS LATER, A CERTAIN HABERDASHER IN ST. PETERSBURG MADE AN HISTORIC SALE TO A YOUNG TYCOON ANXIOUS TO MAKE A GOOD IMPRESSION DURING HIS AUDIENCE WITH...
SALE! TOP HATS!
FREE CANE WITH EVERY PURCHASE!
...CZAR NICHOLAS II!
OOG! WHAT AN AWFUL ODOR!
UM... I'VE BEEN IN THE STABLES SELLING CONCERTINAS TO YOUR TROOPS, YOUR HIGHNESS!
I THOUGHT YOU WANTED TO BUY ONE OF THE ROYAL FABERGÉ EGGS!
ONE? NICK, I BUY MY EGGS BY THE DOZEN! FILL THESE UP!
IMPENDING REVOLUTION SALE! EVERYTHING MUST GO!
AH... THEN YOU SHOULD HAVE THE LEGENDARY JEWEL THAT INSPIRED THE CREATION OF THE FABERGÉ EGGS!
I'LL BITE! ROLL IT OUT!
ALAS, IT WAS STOLEN WHILE ON TOUR MANY YEARS AGO BY BAZOOKISTAN BANDITS! ALL THAT'S LEFT IS THIS PAINTING OF THE FAMOUS CANDY-STRIPED RUBY!
VERRRY INTERESTING!
ANOTHER DETOUR! AFTER TWO YEARS OF INVESTIGATING AND INVESTING THROUGHOUT WESTERN ASIA, SCROOGE POSED AS A HORSETRADER IN BAZOOKISTAN AND, FINALLY...
THOSE BANDITS DIDN'T KNOW THEY HAD THE MOST VALUABLE GEM ON EARTH! I CAN GO HOME NOW-- MY SISTERS WILL FORGIVE MY DELAY WHEN THEY SEE THIS!
SURE ENOUGH, AN OCEAN LINER LEFT SOUTHAMPTON NOT TOO MUCH LATER, WITH SCROOGE McDUCK ABOARD, BOUND FOR HOME...
MR. McDUCK, I'LL PAY YOU ANYTHING YOU ASK! I MUST OWN THE CANDY-STRIPED RUBY!
FORGET IT, J.J.!
I THINK I'LL HOLD ONTO THIS BAUBLE MYSELF, AS AN INVESTMENT!
BUT I'LL PAY YOU EVERY CENT MY GRANDFATHER LEFT ME AND--
YOW!
CRUNCH!

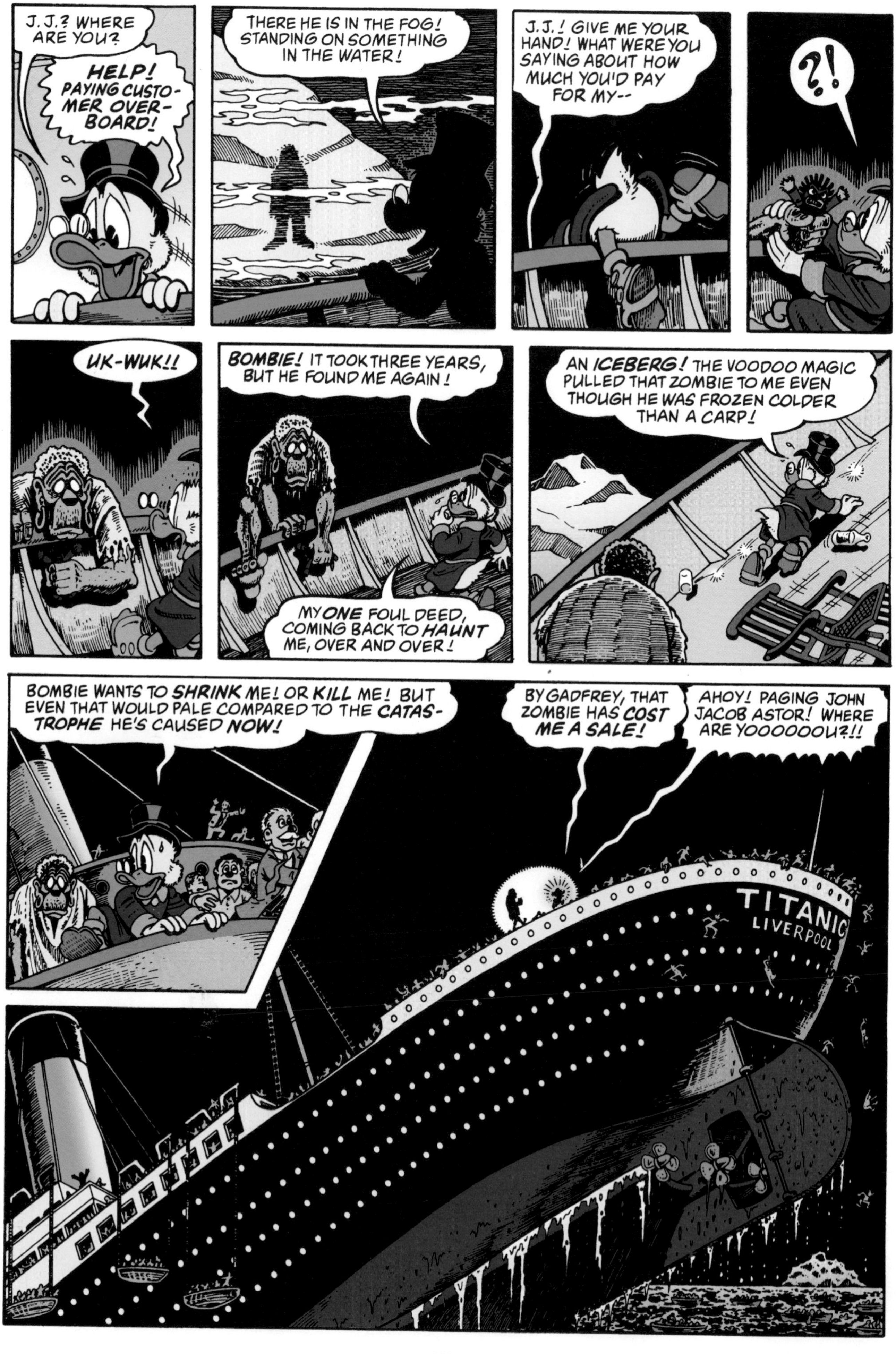
J. J.? WHERE ARE YOU?
HELP! PAYING CUSTOMER OVERBOARD!
THERE HE IS IN THE FOG! STANDING ON SOMETHING IN THE WATER!
J. J.! GIVE ME YOUR HAND! WHAT WERE YOU SAYING ABOUT HOW MUCH YOU'D PAY FOR MY--
?!
UK-WUK!!
BOMBIE! IT TOOK THREE YEARS, BUT HE FOUND ME AGAIN!
MY ONE FOUL DEED, COMING BACK TO HAUNT ME, OVER AND OVER!
AN ICEBERG! THE VOODOO MAGIC PULLED THAT ZOMBIE TO ME EVEN THOUGH HE WAS FROZEN COLDER THAN A CARP!
BOMBIE WANTS TO SHRINK ME! OR KILL ME! BUT EVEN THAT WOULD PALE COMPARED TO THE CATASTROPHE HE'S CAUSED NOW!
BY GADFREY, THAT ZOMBIE HAS COST ME A SALE!
AHOY! PAGING JOHN JACOB ASTOR! WHERE ARE YOOOOOOU?!!
TITANIC
LIVERPOOL

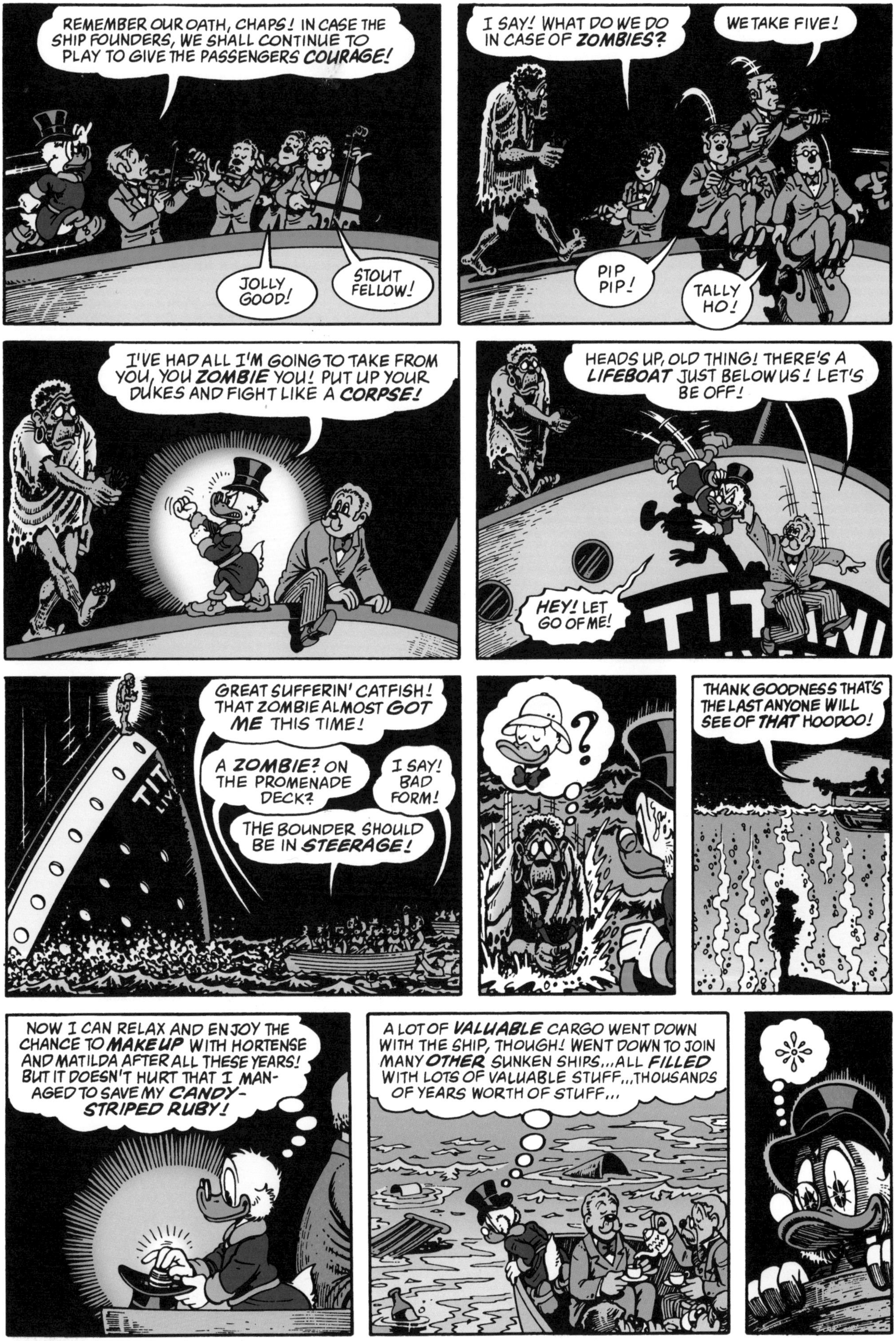
REMEMBER OUR OATH, CHAPS! IN CASE THE SHIP FOUNDERS, WE SHALL CONTINUE TO PLAY TO GIVE THE PASSENGERS COURAGE!
JOLLY GOOD!
STOUT FELLOW!
I SAY! WHAT DO WE DO IN CASE OF ZOMBIES?
WE TAKE FIVE!
PIP PIP!
TALLY HO!
I'VE HAD ALL I'M GOING TO TAKE FROM YOU, YOU ZOMBIE YOU! PUT UP YOUR DUKES AND FIGHT LIKE A CORPSE!
HEADS UP, OLD THING! THERE'S A LIFEBOAT JUST BELOW US! LET'S BE OFF!
HEY! LET GO OF ME!
GREAT SUFFERIN' CATFISH! THAT ZOMBIE ALMOST GOT ME THIS TIME!
A ZOMBIE? ON THE PROMENADE DECK?
I SAY! BAD FORM!
THE BOUNDER SHOULD BE IN STEERAGE!
THANK GOODNESS THAT'S THE LAST ANYONE WILL SEE OF THAT HOODOO!
NOW I CAN RELAX AND ENJOY THE CHANCE TO MAKE UP WITH HORTENSE AND MATILDA AFTER ALL THESE YEARS! BUT IT DOESN'T HURT THAT I MANAGED TO SAVE MY CANDY-STRIPED RUBY!
A LOT OF VALUABLE CARGO WENT DOWN WITH THE SHIP, THOUGH! WENT DOWN TO JOIN MANY OTHER SUNKEN SHIPS... ALL FILLED WITH LOTS OF VALUABLE STUFF... THOUSANDS OF YEARS WORTH OF STUFF...

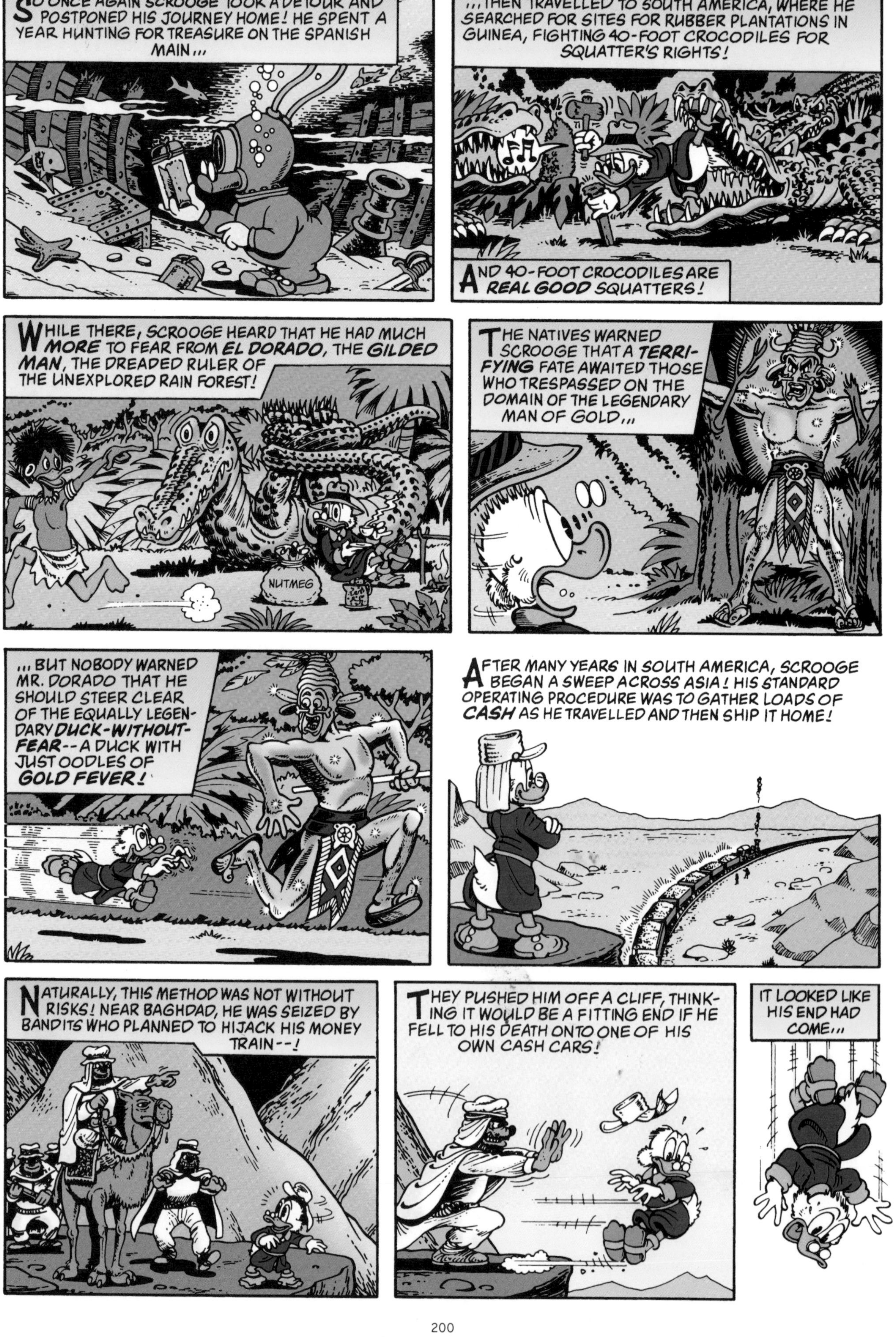

SO ONCE AGAIN SCROOGE TOOK A DETOUR AND POSTPONED HIS JOURNEY HOME! HE SPENT A YEAR HUNTING FOR TREASURE ON THE SPANISH MAIN...
...THEN TRAVELLED TO SOUTH AMERICA, WHERE HE SEARCHED FOR SITES FOR RUBBER PLANTATIONS IN GUINEA, FIGHTING 40-FOOT CROCODILES FOR SQUATTER'S RIGHTS!
AND 40-FOOT CROCODILES ARE REAL GOOD SQUATTERS!
WHILE THERE, SCROOGE HEARD THAT HE HAD MUCH MORE TO FEAR FROM EL DORADO, THE GILDED MAN, THE DREADED RULER OF THE UNEXPLORED RAIN FOREST!
NUTMEG
THE NATIVES WARNED SCROOGE THAT A TERRIFYING FATE AWAITED THOSE WHO TRESPASSED ON THE DOMAIN OF THE LEGENDARY MAN OF GOLD...
...BUT NOBODY WARNED MR. DORADO THAT HE SHOULD STEER CLEAR OF THE EQUALLY LEGENDARY DUCK-WITHOUT-FEAR--A DUCK WITH JUST OODLES OF GOLD FEVER!
AFTER MANY YEARS IN SOUTH AMERICA, SCROOGE BEGAN A SWEEP ACROSS ASIA! HIS STANDARD OPERATING PROCEDURE WAS TO GATHER LOADS OF CASH AS HE TRAVELLED AND THEN SHIP IT HOME!
NATURALLY, THIS METHOD WAS NOT WITHOUT RISKS! NEAR BAGHDAD, HE WAS SEIZED BY BANDITS WHO PLANNED TO HIJACK HIS MONEY TRAIN--!
THEY PUSHED HIM OFF A CLIFF, THINKING IT WOULD BE A FITTING END IF HE FELL TO HIS DEATH ONTO ONE OF HIS OWN CASH CARS!
IT LOOKED LIKE HIS END HAD COME...

...BUT HE MIRACULOUSLY FOUND THAT HE COULD DIVE THROUGH THE HARD METAL COINS AS IF THEY WERE LIQUID, AND HE WAS LIKE...

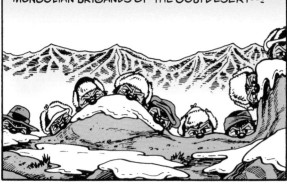

...LIKE A PORPOISE!

APPARENTLY, HIS YEARS OF BATHING AND BURROWING THROUGH HIS MONEY HAD TAUGHT HIM SOME INSTINCTIVE TRICK...

...THOUGH IT WORKS ONLY IN CASH!

BANDITS! HIT THE THROTTLE!

OTHER PERILS INHERENT IN TRAVELLING THROUGH THE HINTERLANDS WITH SUCH A CARGO SOON PRESENTED THEMSELVES -- PERILS SUCH AS THE MONGOLIAN BRIGANDS OF THE GOBI DESERT --!

A LONE MERCHANT PROMISED TO LEAD THEM TO SCROOGE'S MONEY CARAVAN IF THEY WOULD HELP HIM TRANSPORT HIS CARGO OF LICHEE NUTS TO PEKING...

THE MERCHANT WOULD NEVER HAVE BEEN ABLE TO GET HIS WAGONS THROUGH THAT RUGGED FRONTIER WITHOUT THOSE FEROCIOUS BRIGANDS' HELP AS GUARDS AND TEAMSTERS...

...BUT WHEN CHINESE SOLDIERS CHASED THE BRIGANDS OFF ON THE OUTSKIRTS OF PEKING, THERE WAS NO ONE AROUND TO SEE THE MERCHANT'S TRUE CARGO!

AS THE YEARS PASSED, SCROOGE CONTINUED HIS GLOBAL SWEEP ALONG THE PACIFIC RIM! THERE HE ESTABLISHED A THRIVING PEARL TRADE USING TRAINED CORMORANTS AS DIVERS!

THEN ONE DAY, ON THE TINY ISLAND OF RIPPAN TARO IN THE SOUTH PACIFIC --

I CAN MAKE YOU A GENEROUS OFFER FOR ALL YOUR COCONUTS, CHIEF!

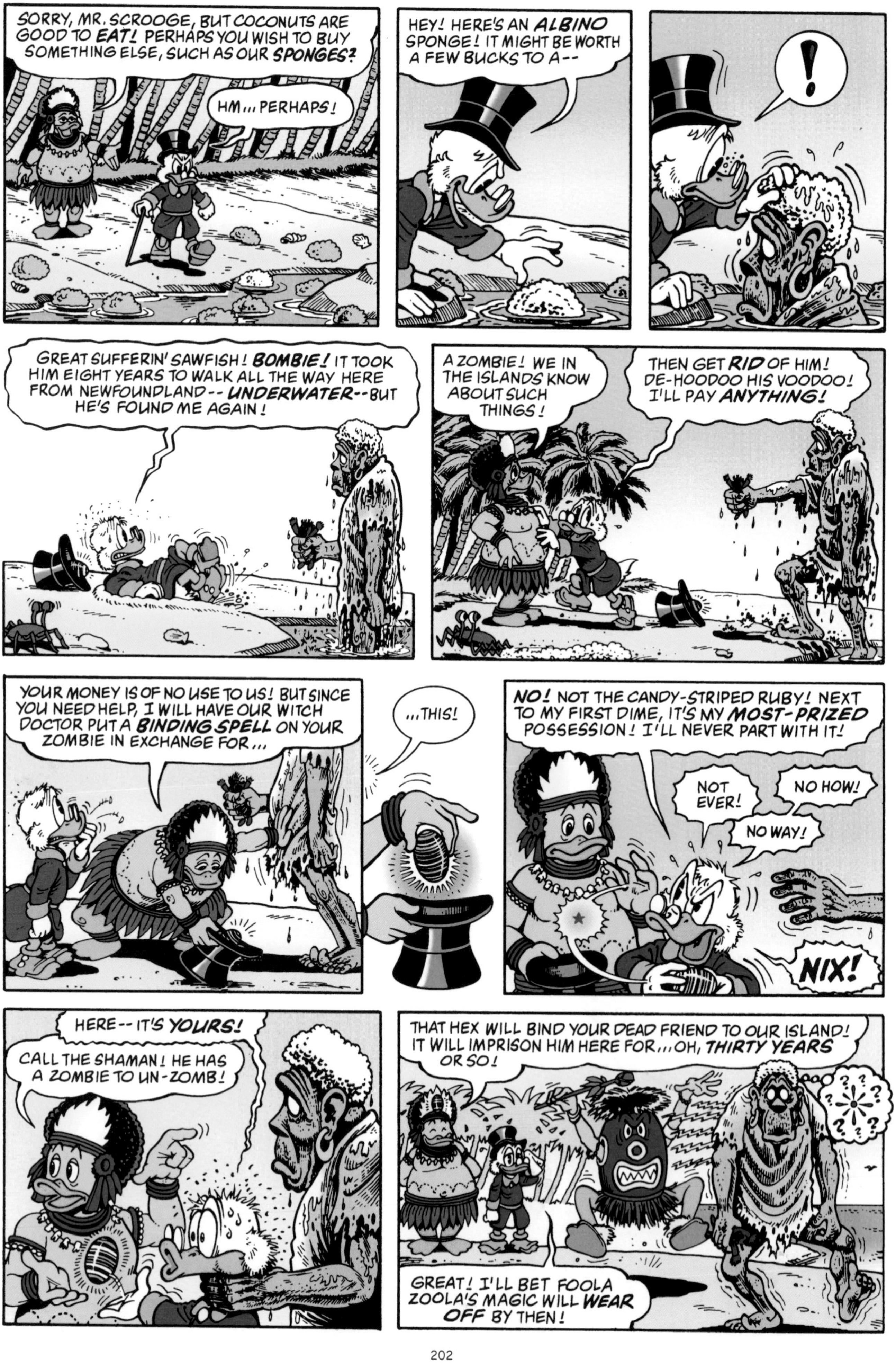
SORRY, MR. SCROOGE, BUT COCONUTS ARE GOOD TO EAT! PERHAPS YOU WISH TO BUY SOMETHING ELSE, SUCH AS OUR SPONGES?
HM... PERHAPS!
HEY! HERE'S AN ALBINO SPONGE! IT MIGHT BE WORTH A FEW BUCKS TO A--
!
GREAT SUFFERIN' SAWFISH! BOMBIE! IT TOOK HIM EIGHT YEARS TO WALK ALL THE WAY HERE FROM NEWFOUNDLAND--UNDERWATER--BUT HE'S FOUND ME AGAIN!
A ZOMBIE! WE IN THE ISLANDS KNOW ABOUT SUCH THINGS!
THEN GET RID OF HIM! DE-HOODOO HIS VOODOO! I'LL PAY ANYTHING!
YOUR MONEY IS OF NO USE TO US! BUT SINCE YOU NEED HELP, I WILL HAVE OUR WITCH DOCTOR PUT A BINDING SPELL ON YOUR ZOMBIE IN EXCHANGE FOR...
...THIS!
NO! NOT THE CANDY-STRIPED RUBY! NEXT TO MY FIRST DIME, IT'S MY MOST-PRIZED POSSESSION! I'LL NEVER PART WITH IT!
NOT EVER!
NO HOW!
NO WAY!
NIX!
HERE--IT'S YOURS!
CALL THE SHAMAN! HE HAS A ZOMBIE TO UN-ZOMB!
THAT HEX WILL BIND YOUR DEAD FRIEND TO OUR ISLAND! IT WILL IMPRISON HIM HERE FOR...OH, THIRTY YEARS OR SO!
GREAT! I'LL BET FOOLA ZOOLA'S MAGIC WILL WEAR OFF BY THEN!

FREE TO CONTINUE HIS GLOBAL CONQUEST, SCROOGE CRISS-CROSSED THE WORLD MANY MORE TIMES OVER THE NEXT TEN YEARS!

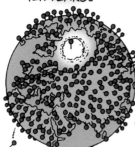

HE ARRIVED ON WALL STREET JUST AFTER THE *GREAT CRASH* AND MANAGED TO CORNER THE MARKET-- ON *EVERYTHING*-- BY PAYING ONLY A PENNY ON THE DOLLAR FOR HARD-HIT COMPANIES!

THAT'S RIGHT! I'M BUYING!

HE TRUSTED NO ONE, CONDUCTING ALL HIS BUSINESS USING HIS TRAINED CORMORANTS AS MESSENGERS, EARNING HIM THE TITLE OF "BIRDMAN OF WALL STREET"!

OUT

NO MOULTING ON COMPANY TIME!

IN

THEN FINALLY, AFTER 27 YEARS ON THE ROAD, HE MADE A LONG-DELAYED JOURNEY...

Duckburg Times

SCROOGE McDUCK RETURNS!! *Globetrotting Patriarch Home to Stay*

McDUCK GAS   McDUCK MOTORS   McDUCK FOODS   McDUCK HOTEL   McDUCK-INK-   McDUCK WIDGETS   McDUCK OIL

McDUCK PAPER   McDUCK TIRES   McDUCK ELECTRIC

A *NEW* DUCKBURG TURNED OUT TO GREET ITS LEADING CITIZEN! NO LONGER A SLEEPY LITTLE SHACKTOWN, IT HAD BECOME A THRIVING AND GLORIOUS *CITY*, ITS ECONOMY FUELED BY McDUCK INVESTMENTS--!

BUT SCROOGE WAS NOT IMPRESSED! HIS HARD-FOUGHT STRUGGLE FOR WEALTH IN A WORLD HE BELIEVED TO BE POPULATED BY DEADBEATS AND LOAFERS HAD TAKEN ITS TOLL...

KEY TO THE CITY-- *BAH*! I ALREADY OWN ALL THE *LOCKS*!

"HOME IS THE HUNTER, HOME FROM THE HILL!" BUT THIS HUNTER'S HEART WAS HARDENED TO THE FOREST CREATURES AFTER FIFTY YEARS ON THE HUNT--!

THE WORLD OWES ME A LIVING!   HELP!!!!! HAVEN'T EATEN SINCE LUNCH!   GIMME!   FUND TO ABOLISH FUNDS   AID TO THE LAZY   GIMME!

ONCE, THE LAD WHO SHINED SHOES FOR FIVE PENCE A PAIR ON THE STREETS OF GLASGOW WOULD HAVE BEEN MOVED BY PLEAS FOR HELP, BUT THIS WAS ALTOGETHER A *DIFFERENT* SCROOGE McDUCK!

HERE HE COMES!

GET READY!

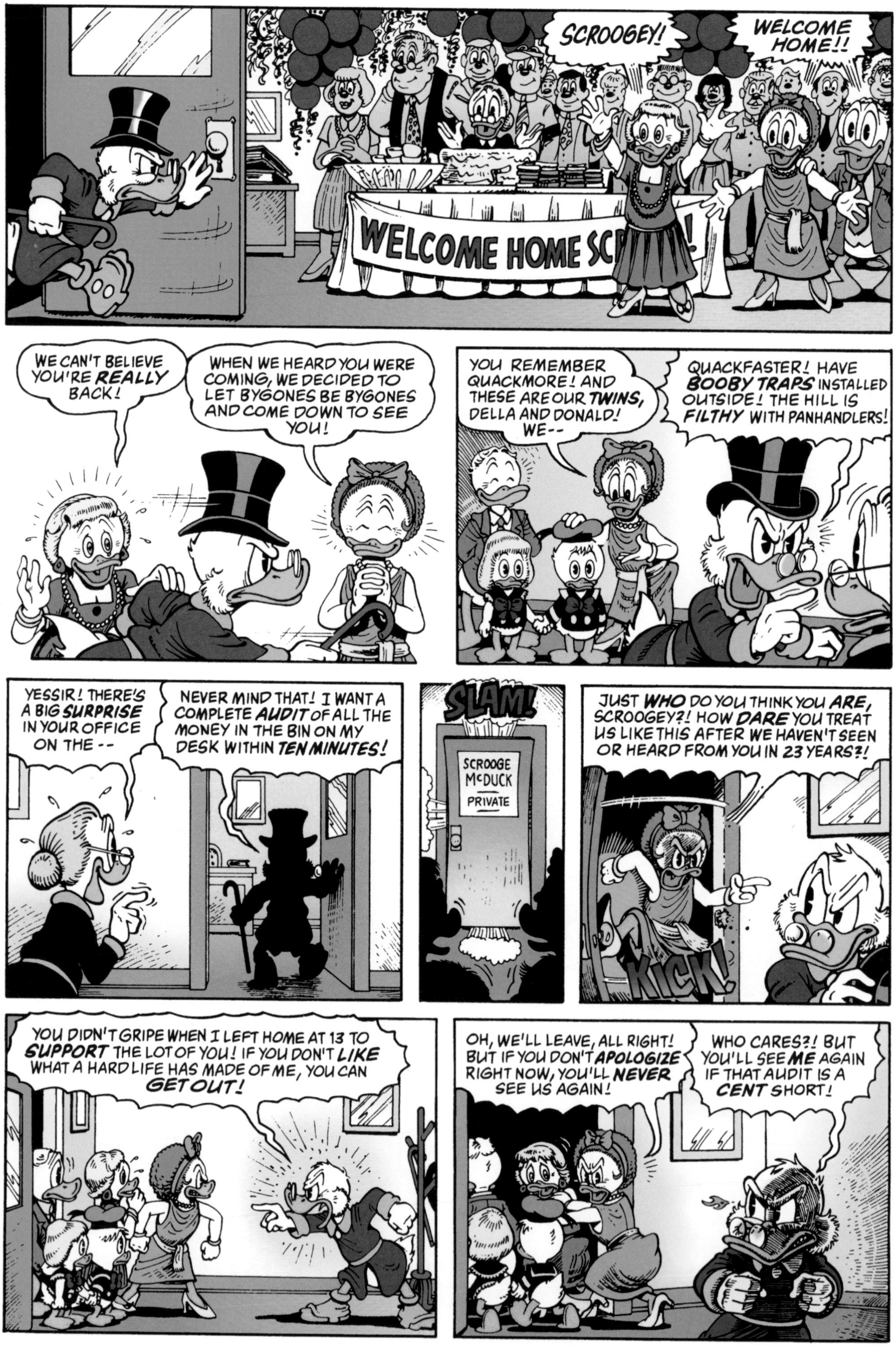
SCROOGEY!
WELCOME HOME!!
WELCOME HOME SC
WE CAN'T BELIEVE YOU'RE REALLY BACK!
WHEN WE HEARD YOU WERE COMING, WE DECIDED TO LET BYGONES BE BYGONES AND COME DOWN TO SEE YOU!
YOU REMEMBER QUACKMORE! AND THESE ARE OUR TWINS, DELLA AND DONALD! WE--
QUACKFASTER! HAVE BOOBY TRAPS INSTALLED OUTSIDE! THE HILL IS FILTHY WITH PANHANDLERS!
YESSIR! THERE'S A BIG SURPRISE IN YOUR OFFICE ON THE --
NEVER MIND THAT! I WANT A COMPLETE AUDIT OF ALL THE MONEY IN THE BIN ON MY DESK WITHIN TEN MINUTES!
SLAM!
SCROOGE McDUCK PRIVATE
JUST WHO DO YOU THINK YOU ARE, SCROOGEY?! HOW DARE YOU TREAT US LIKE THIS AFTER WE HAVEN'T SEEN OR HEARD FROM YOU IN 23 YEARS?!
KICK!
YOU DIDN'T GRIPE WHEN I LEFT HOME AT 13 TO SUPPORT THE LOT OF YOU! IF YOU DON'T LIKE WHAT A HARD LIFE HAS MADE OF ME, YOU CAN GET OUT!
OH, WE'LL LEAVE, ALL RIGHT! BUT IF YOU DON'T APOLOGIZE RIGHT NOW, YOU'LL NEVER SEE US AGAIN!
WHO CARES?! BUT YOU'LL SEE ME AGAIN IF THAT AUDIT IS A CENT SHORT!

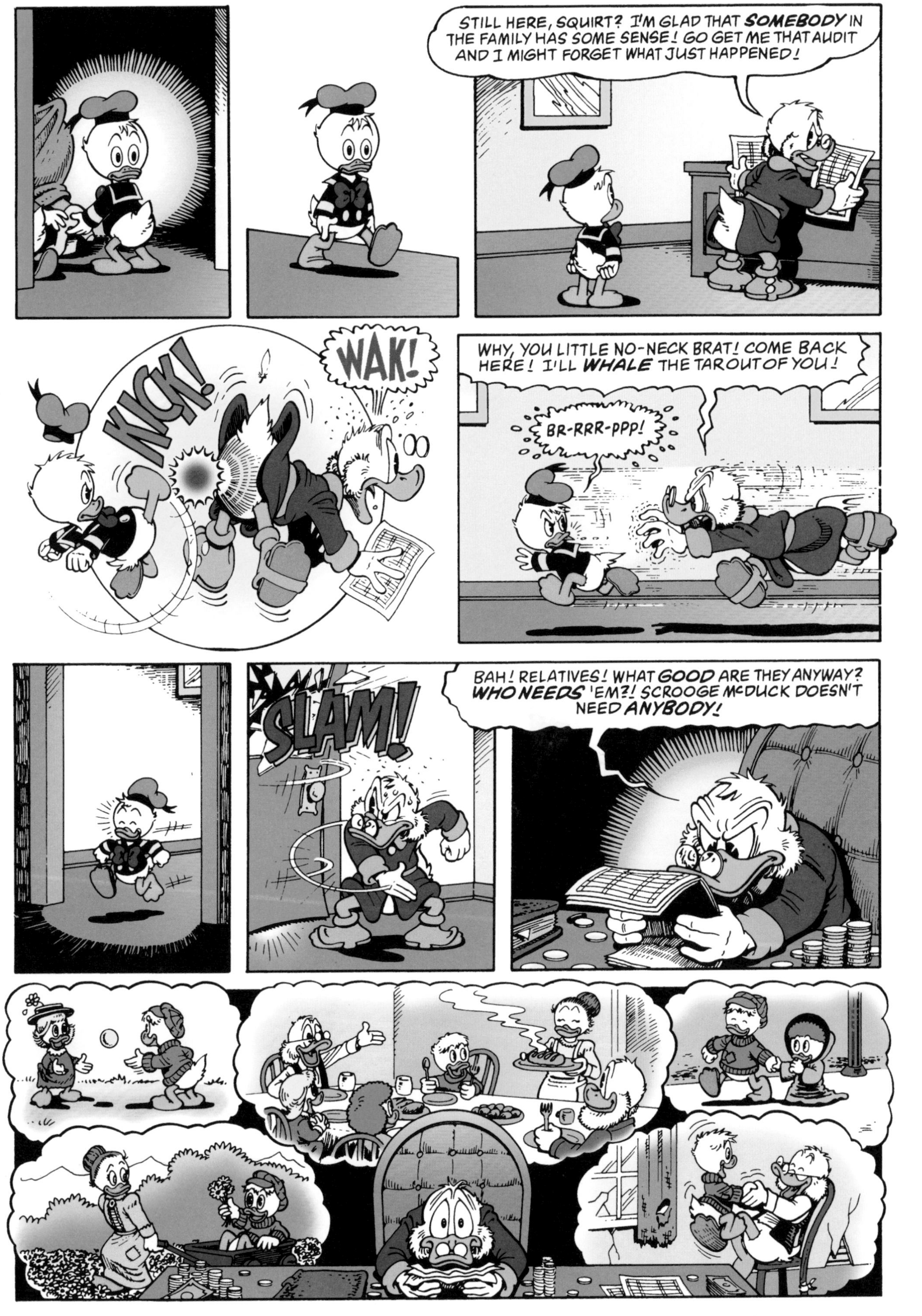
STILL HERE, SQUIRT? I'M GLAD THAT SOMEBODY IN THE FAMILY HAS SOME SENSE! GO GET ME THAT AUDIT AND I MIGHT FORGET WHAT JUST HAPPENED!
KICK!
WAK!
WHY, YOU LITTLE NO-NECK BRAT! COME BACK HERE! I'LL WHALE THE TAR OUT OF YOU!
BR-RRR-PPP!
SLAM!
BAH! RELATIVES! WHAT GOOD ARE THEY ANYWAY? WHO NEEDS 'EM?! SCROOGE McDUCK DOESN'T NEED ANYBODY!

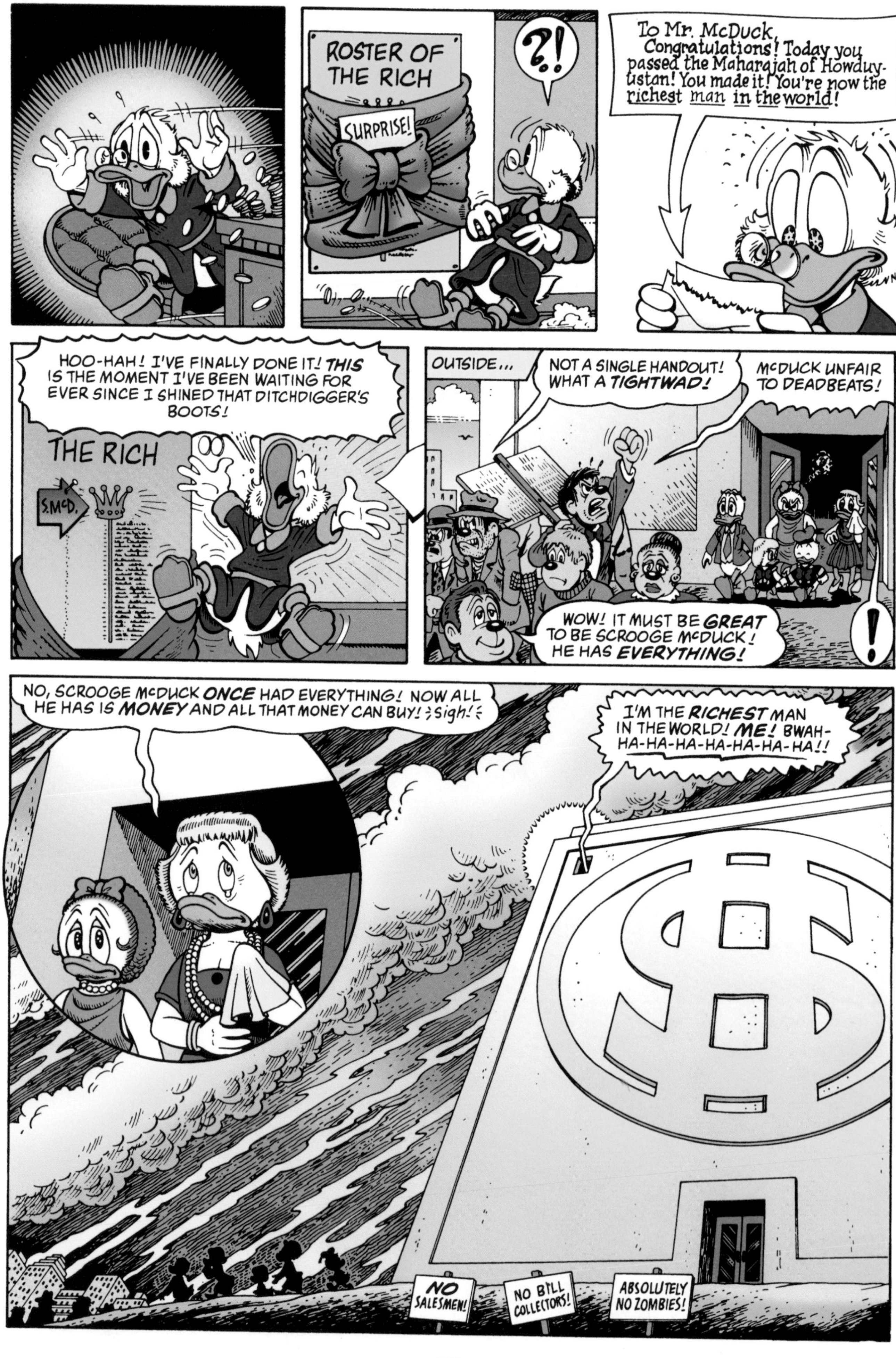
ROSTER OF THE RICH
SURPRISE!
?!
To Mr. McDuck, Congratulations! Today you passed the Maharajah of Howduyustan! You made it! You're now the richest man in the world!
HOO-HAH! I'VE FINALLY DONE IT! THIS IS THE MOMENT I'VE BEEN WAITING FOR EVER SINCE I SHINED THAT DITCHDIGGER'S BOOTS!
THE RICH
S.McD.
OUTSIDE...
NOT A SINGLE HANDOUT! WHAT A TIGHTWAD!
McDUCK UNFAIR TO DEADBEATS!
WOW! IT MUST BE GREAT TO BE SCROOGE McDUCK! HE HAS EVERYTHING!
!
NO, SCROOGE McDUCK ONCE HAD EVERYTHING! NOW ALL HE HAS IS MONEY AND ALL THAT MONEY CAN BUY! *sigh!*
I'M THE RICHEST MAN IN THE WORLD! ME! BWAH-HA-HA-HA-HA-HA-HA-HA!!
NO SALESMEN!
NO BILL COLLECTORS!
ABSOLUTELY NO ZOMBIES!

The Life and Times of $crooge McDuck PART TWELVE

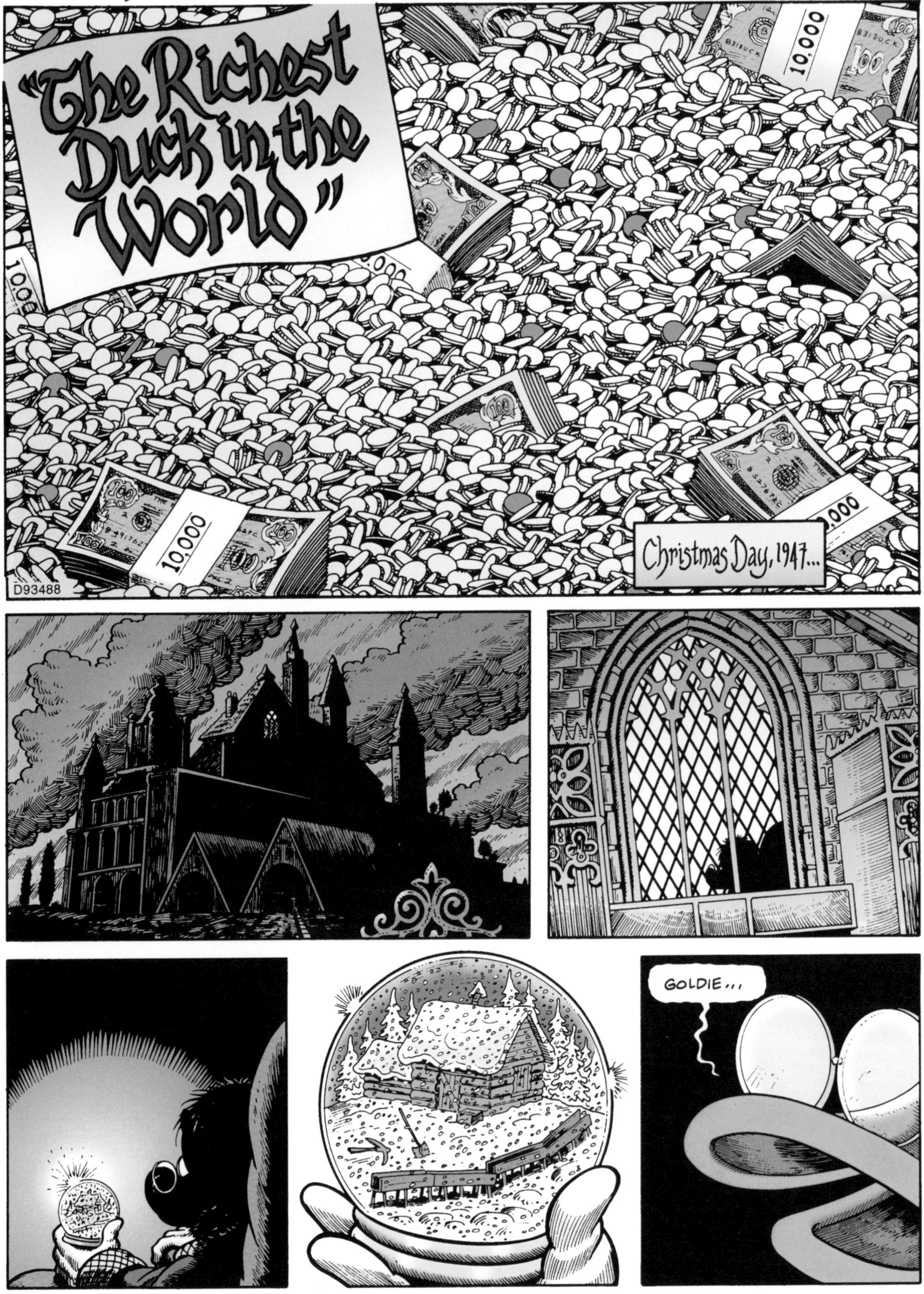
"The Richest Duck in the World"
Christmas Day, 1947...
D93488
GOLDIE...

NEWS ON THE MARCH

"*LEGENDARY* WAS FORT DRAKEBOROUGH, WHERE SIR FRANCIS DRAKE ESTABLISHED HIS AMERICAN OUTPOST... AND WHERE THE GREAT *CORNELIUS COOT* FOUNDED DUCKBURG!"

"EQUALLY LEGENDARY IS THE MODERN OWNER OF THAT SITE AND MOST OF THE THRIVING METROPOLIS THAT HAS SPRUNG UP AROUND IT--THE RICHEST MAN IN THE WORLD AND FIRST CITIZEN OF DUCKBURG..."

"...*SCROOGE McDUCK!!*"

"*FAMED* IN LOCAL LEGEND IS THE ORIGIN OF THE McDUCK FORTUNE! THE McDUCKS, DESCENDANTS OF A ONCE NOBLE SCOTTISH CLAN, HAD FALLEN ON HARD TIMES!"

"YET THE YOUNG McDUCK LAD WAS SOMEHOW INSPIRED TO SEEK HIS FORTUNE! AT THE AGE OF 13 HE SIGNED ON AS A CABIN BOY ON A CATTLE BOAT AND SAILED AWAY FOR PARTS UNKNOWN!"

"FARFLUNG RUMORS SUGGEST THIS RUGGED YOUTH TRAVELED THE WORLD'S WILDEST FRONTIERS, MASTERING MANY SKILLS, YET MEETING WITH *FAILURE* FOR *TWO DECADES!*"

"EVIDENCE OF HIS EVENTUAL *TRIUMPH* HAS RECENTLY BEEN FOUND IN NEWSPAPER FILES OF THE YUKON GOLD RUSH!"

KLONDIKE GAZETTE
SCROOGE McDUCK STRIKES IT RICH!!!

KLONDIKE GAZETTE
McDUCK BUYS WHITEHORSE BANK!

McDUCK A BILLIONAIRE!

"*SCROOGE McDUCK* FIRST APPEARED IN LOCAL HISTORY 45 YEARS AGO WHEN HE CAME TO CALISOTA WITH HIS TWO SISTERS AND BUILT ON THE SITE OF FORT DUCKBURG OUR MOST FAMOUS LANDMARK -- THE McDUCK OFFICE BUILDING!"

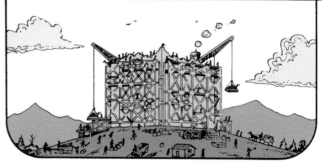

"FEW DETAILS ARE KNOWN OF McDUCK'S ENSUING LIFE! HIS SISTERS, THE ONLY WITNESSES TO HIS RISE TO RICHES, HAVE LONG SINCE DISAPPEARED FROM PUBLIC LIFE! THEY WERE LAST SEEN IN THIS NEWSREEL FOOTAGE TAKEN 17 YEARS AGO!"

"THE FACT THAT McDUCK HAS LONG BEEN RECLUSIVE IS CONFIRMED IN THE MEMORIES OF SOME OF OUR OLDEST CITIZENS..."

THE LAST TIME I SAW SCROOGE WAS WHEN I SOLD HIM ALL OF MY GRANDFATHER CORNELIUS COOT'S LAND, EXCEPT MY *FARM* HERE!

NO, MUM... REMEMBER WHEN HE CAME AND FORECLOSED ON THE CHICKEN COOP!

"EVEN HIS RELATIVES KNOW LITTLE! DISTANT RELATIVE BY MARRIAGE AND LOCAL BON VIVANT, *GLADSTONE GANDER*..."

NO, BUT IF I EVER *DID* MEET THE OLD BOY, I'D ASK TO SEE HIS *LUCKY DIME*, THE CHARM THAT MADE HIS FORTUNE FOR HIM!

SOME PEOPLE NEED *CHARMS* FOR LUCK! HA!

"HIS CLOSEST RELATIVE AND LOCAL TOP BLOWER, *DONALD DUCK*..."

NO COMMENT! AND IF YOU QUOTE THAT LINE ABOUT "TOUGHER THAN THE TOUGHIES" AND "MAKING IT SQUARE" JUST *ONCE* MORE, I'LL *BLOW MY TOP!*

"SEE WHAT WE MEAN?"

"SUDDENLY, FIVE YEARS AGO, THE AGED FINANCIER CLOSED DOWN HIS ENTIRE EMPIRE, CLAIMING THERE WAS NO ONE *WORTHY* TO INHERIT OR MANAGE HIS FORTUNE!"

The Duckburg Times
McDUCK RETIRES!
CANTANKEROUS TYCOON WILL BE MISSED BY FEW...
...IF ANY...

McDUCK FINANCE CO.
CLOSED
McDUCK CANNERY
CLOSED
CLOSED
McDUCK MANUFACTURING
CLOSED

"AFTER MOVING TO A PALATIAL MANSION UNCHARACTER-ISTIC OF HIS FORMER FRUGAL LIFESTYLE, SCROOGE McDUCK CEASED TO BE SEEN IN PUBLIC!"

NO TRESPASSING!

NEVER MIND DOGS-- BEWARE OF OWNER!

"YET HIS ABANDONED OFFICE BUILDING ON KILLMOTOR HILL REMAINS A LOCAL LANDMARK! BUT *IS* IT A WARE-HOUSE FILLED WITH DUSTY LEDGERS, AS HAS LONG BEEN ASSUMED?"

CLOSED!
HANDS OFF
GO AWAY
SCRAM!
BEAT IT!

CANDID TALKS WITH FORMER EMPLOYEES HINT OTHER-WISE! COULD THIS EDIFICE ACTUALLY CONTAIN... *THREE CUBIC ACRES OF CASH?!*

MORE ON TOMORROW'S *NEWS ON THE MARCH!*

FOR SALE! NEW 1948 MODEL TV SETS!

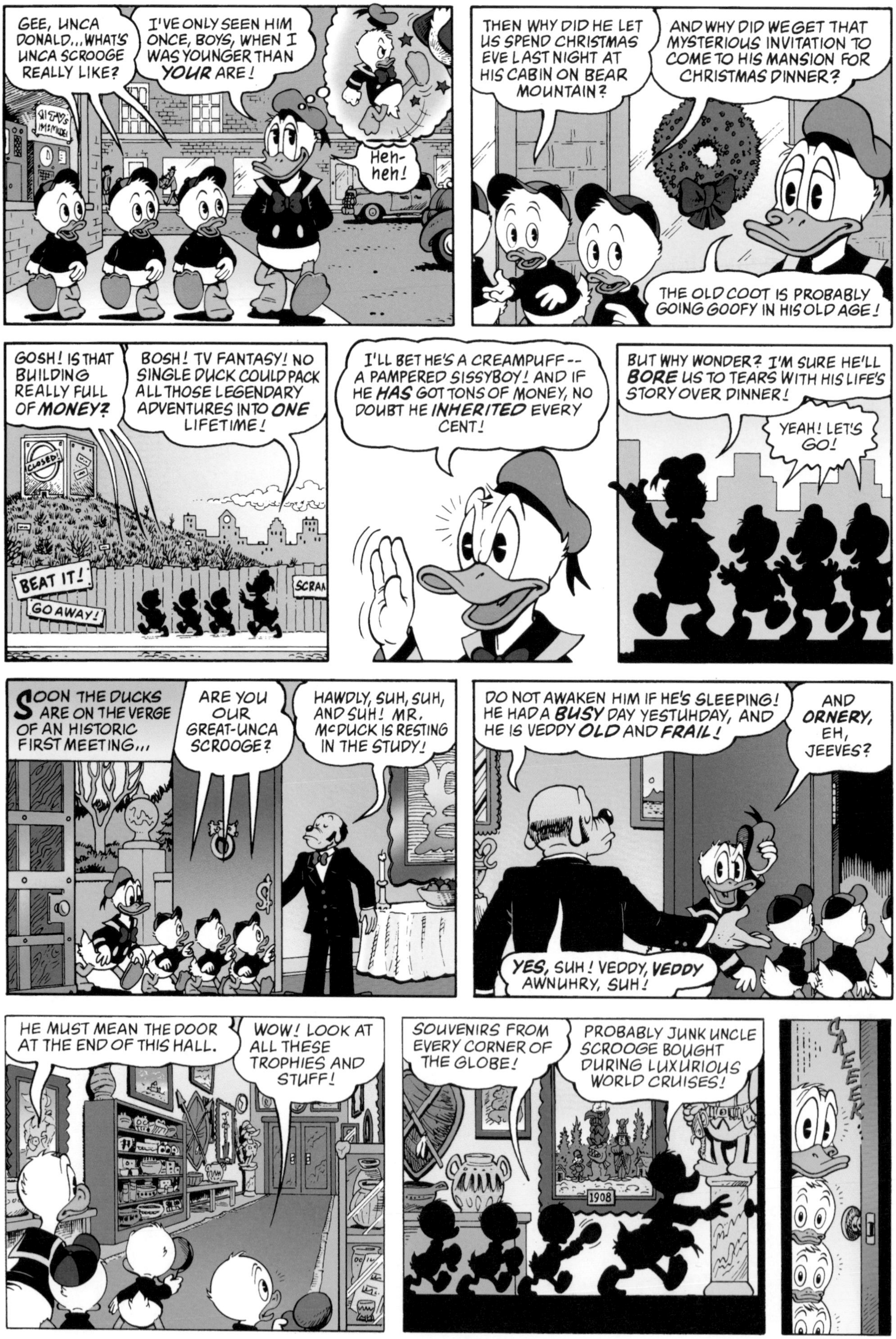
GEE, UNCA DONALD... WHAT'S UNCA SCROOGE REALLY LIKE?
I'VE ONLY SEEN HIM ONCE, BOYS, WHEN I WAS YOUNGER THAN YOUR ARE!
Heh-heh!
THEN WHY DID HE LET US SPEND CHRISTMAS EVE LAST NIGHT AT HIS CABIN ON BEAR MOUNTAIN?
AND WHY DID WE GET THAT MYSTERIOUS INVITATION TO COME TO HIS MANSION FOR CHRISTMAS DINNER?
THE OLD COOT IS PROBABLY GOING GOOFY IN HIS OLD AGE!
GOSH! IS THAT BUILDING REALLY FULL OF MONEY?
BOSH! TV FANTASY! NO SINGLE DUCK COULD PACK ALL THOSE LEGENDARY ADVENTURES INTO ONE LIFETIME!
CLOSED!
BEAT IT!
GO AWAY!
SCRAM
I'LL BET HE'S A CREAMPUFF -- A PAMPERED SISSYBOY! AND IF HE HAS GOT TONS OF MONEY, NO DOUBT HE INHERITED EVERY CENT!
BUT WHY WONDER? I'M SURE HE'LL BORE US TO TEARS WITH HIS LIFE'S STORY OVER DINNER!
YEAH! LET'S GO!
SOON THE DUCKS ARE ON THE VERGE OF AN HISTORIC FIRST MEETING...
ARE YOU OUR GREAT-UNCA SCROOGE?
HAWDLY, SUH, SUH, AND SUH! MR. McDUCK IS RESTING IN THE STUDY!
DO NOT AWAKEN HIM IF HE'S SLEEPING! HE HAD A BUSY DAY YESTUHDAY, AND HE IS VEDDY OLD AND FRAIL!
AND ORNERY, EH, JEEVES?
YES, SUH! VEDDY, VEDDY AWNUHRY, SUH!
HE MUST MEAN THE DOOR AT THE END OF THIS HALL.
WOW! LOOK AT ALL THESE TROPHIES AND STUFF!
SOUVENIRS FROM EVERY CORNER OF THE GLOBE!
PROBABLY JUNK UNCLE SCROOGE BOUGHT DURING LUXURIOUS WORLD CRUISES!
1908
CREEEK

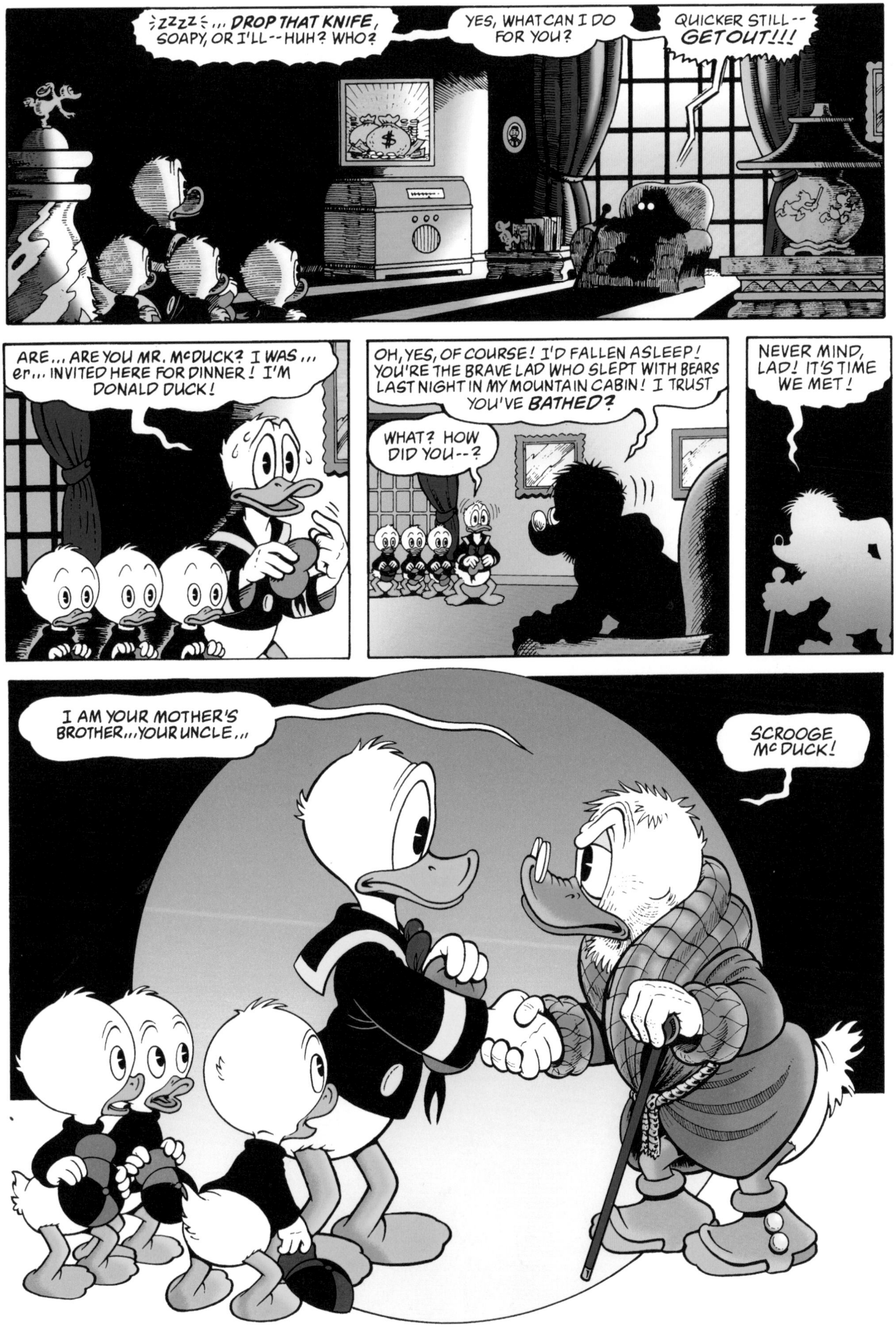
ZZZZ ... DROP THAT KNIFE, SOAPY, OR I'LL -- HUH? WHO?
YES, WHAT CAN I DO FOR YOU?
QUICKER STILL -- GET OUT!!!
ARE... ARE YOU MR. McDUCK? I WAS... er... INVITED HERE FOR DINNER! I'M DONALD DUCK!
OH, YES, OF COURSE! I'D FALLEN ASLEEP! YOU'RE THE BRAVE LAD WHO SLEPT WITH BEARS LAST NIGHT IN MY MOUNTAIN CABIN! I TRUST YOU'VE BATHED?
WHAT? HOW DID YOU --?
NEVER MIND, LAD! IT'S TIME WE MET!
I AM YOUR MOTHER'S BROTHER... YOUR UNCLE...
SCROOGE McDUCK!

YES -- AND YOU'RE OUR *GREAT* UNCLE!

HUEY, DEWEY, AND LOUIE, IS IT? YOU'LL EXCUSE ME -- I'M NOT USED TO *CHILDREN!* I NEVER HAD TIME TO BE ONE MYSELF!

I'M NOT USED TO *RELATIVES,* EITHER! THE FEW I HAD SEEM TO HAVE... DIS-APPEARED!

WE KNOW HOW *THAT* FEELS, UNCA SCROOGE!

WE'RE SO GLAD TO HAVE ANOTHER UNCLE, UNCA SCROOGE!

HERE, NOW! NONE OF THAT RUBBISH!

BAH! DON'T PRETEND WE HAVE ANYTHING IN *COMMON!* I ONLY INVITED YOU TO GET YOUR *MEASURE,* AND YOU ONLY CAME TO SEE HOW *RICH* YOU'LL BE WHEN I'M *GONE!*

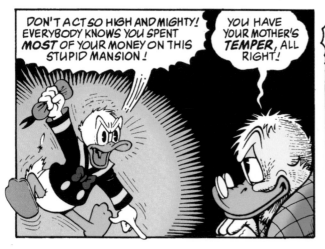

DON'T ACT SO HIGH AND MIGHTY! EVERYBODY KNOWS YOU SPENT *MOST* OF YOUR MONEY ON THIS STUPID MANSION!

YOU HAVE YOUR MOTHER'S *TEMPER,* ALL RIGHT!

BUT I'LL *SHOW* YOU HOW MUCH I HAVE LEFT! I'LL SHOW YOU YOUNGSTERS AND YOUR LAZY GENERA-TION!

EDGERTON! GET ME DRESSED! WE'RE GOING TO THE *BIN!*

"BIN"?

LET'S JUST *HUMOR* HIM! ALL THIS HOKEY JUNK PROVES HE'S... WELL... ECCENTRIC!

SEE? ONE OF THOSE GAG PHOTOS THEY MAKE FOR TOURISTS! WOTTA PHONY SCENE!

HM. LOOKS REAL TO ME!

1897

HA! THEN HOW DO YOU EXPLAIN *THIS?!* OBVIOUSLY ALL FAKES!

COME ALONG, NEPHEW!

WILL EISNER COMICS INDUSTRY AWARD

"The Life and Times of Scrooge McDuck"

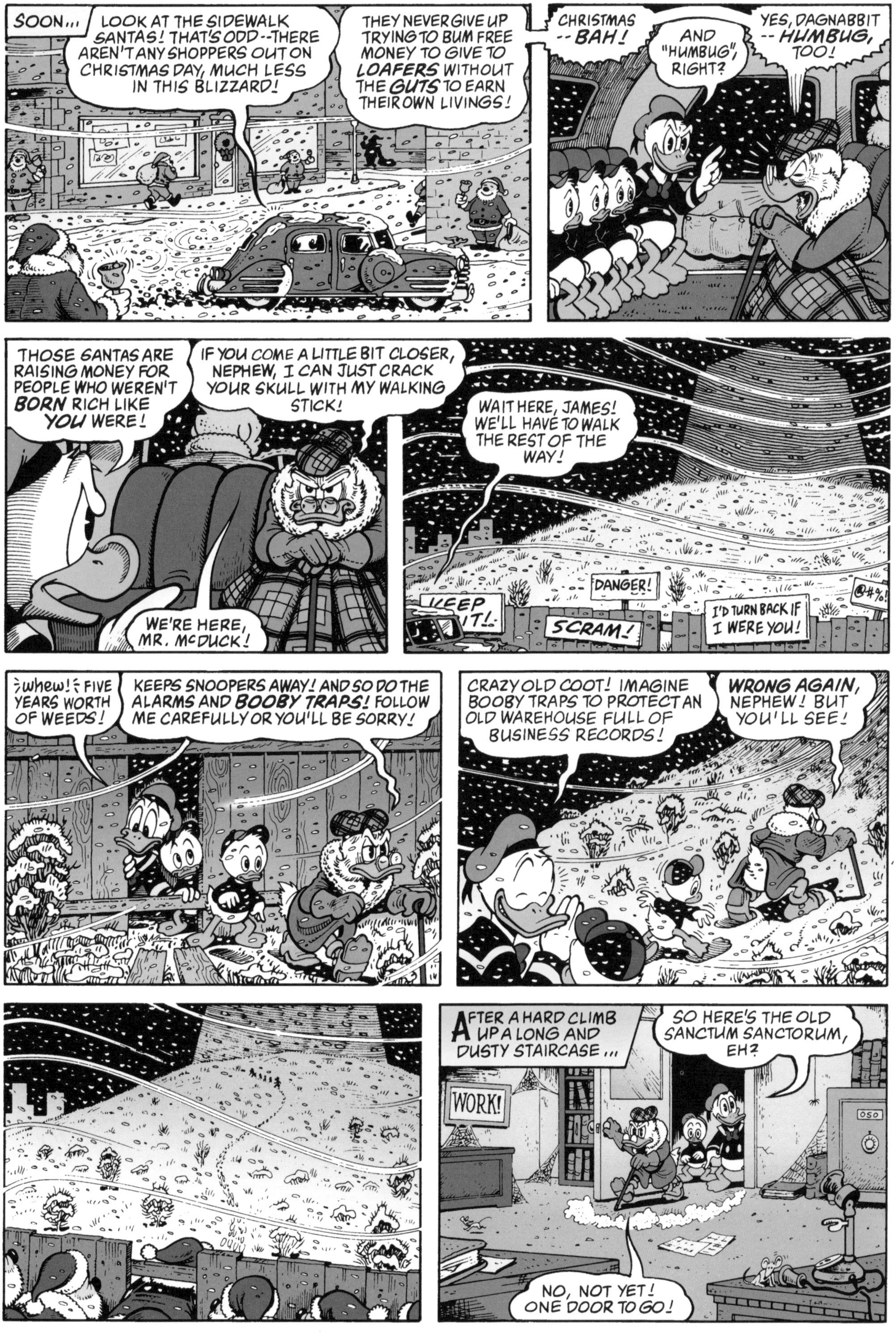

SOON...
LOOK AT THE SIDEWALK SANTAS! THAT'S ODD--THERE AREN'T ANY SHOPPERS OUT ON CHRISTMAS DAY, MUCH LESS IN THIS BLIZZARD!
THEY NEVER GIVE UP TRYING TO BUM FREE MONEY TO GIVE TO LOAFERS WITHOUT THE GUTS TO EARN THEIR OWN LIVINGS!
CHRISTMAS --BAH!
AND "HUMBUG", RIGHT?
YES, DAGNABBIT --HUMBUG, TOO!
THOSE SANTAS ARE RAISING MONEY FOR PEOPLE WHO WEREN'T BORN RICH LIKE YOU WERE!
IF YOU COME A LITTLE BIT CLOSER, NEPHEW, I CAN JUST CRACK YOUR SKULL WITH MY WALKING STICK!
WE'RE HERE, MR. McDUCK!
WAIT HERE, JAMES! WE'LL HAVE TO WALK THE REST OF THE WAY!
DANGER!
KEEP
SCRAM!
I'D TURN BACK IF I WERE YOU!
@#%!
whew! FIVE YEARS WORTH OF WEEDS!
KEEPS SNOOPERS AWAY! AND SO DO THE ALARMS AND BOOBY TRAPS! FOLLOW ME CAREFULLY OR YOU'LL BE SORRY!
CRAZY OLD COOT! IMAGINE BOOBY TRAPS TO PROTECT AN OLD WAREHOUSE FULL OF BUSINESS RECORDS!
WRONG AGAIN, NEPHEW! BUT YOU'LL SEE!
AFTER A HARD CLIMB UP A LONG AND DUSTY STAIRCASE...
SO HERE'S THE OLD SANCTUM SANCTORUM, EH?
WORK!
NO, NOT YET! ONE DOOR TO GO!

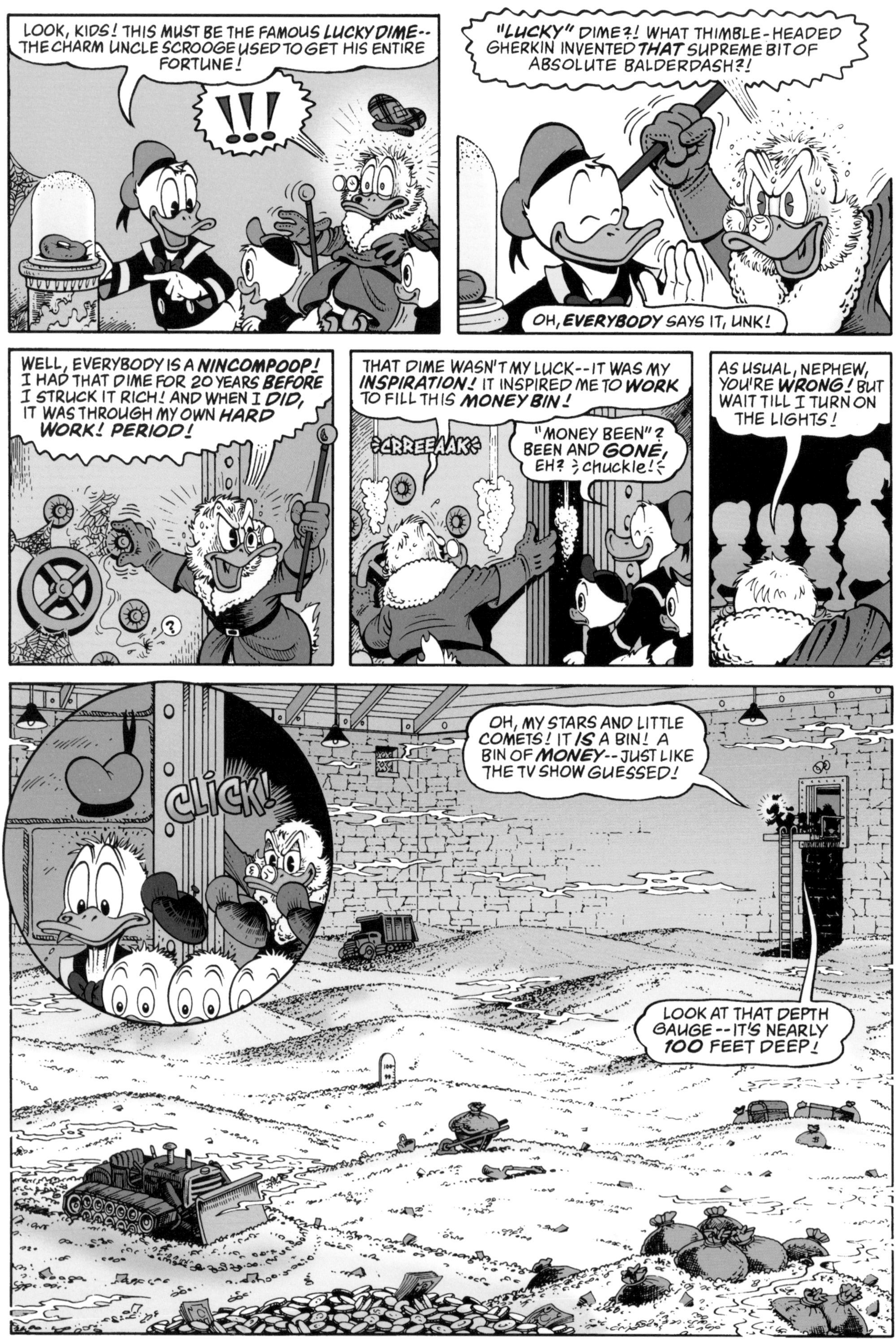

LOOK, KIDS! THIS MUST BE THE FAMOUS LUCKY DIME--THE CHARM UNCLE SCROOGE USED TO GET HIS ENTIRE FORTUNE!
!!!
"LUCKY" DIME?! WHAT THIMBLE-HEADED GHERKIN INVENTED THAT SUPREME BIT OF ABSOLUTE BALDERDASH?!
OH, EVERYBODY SAYS IT, UNK!
WELL, EVERYBODY IS A NINCOMPOOP! I HAD THAT DIME FOR 20 YEARS BEFORE I STRUCK IT RICH! AND WHEN I DID, IT WAS THROUGH MY OWN HARD WORK! PERIOD!
THAT DIME WASN'T MY LUCK--IT WAS MY INSPIRATION! IT INSPIRED ME TO WORK TO FILL THIS MONEY BIN!
CRREEAAK
"MONEY BEEN"? BEEN AND GONE, EH? chuckle!
AS USUAL, NEPHEW, YOU'RE WRONG! BUT WAIT TILL I TURN ON THE LIGHTS!
CLICK!
OH, MY STARS AND LITTLE COMETS! IT IS A BIN! A BIN OF MONEY--JUST LIKE THE TV SHOW GUESSED!
LOOK AT THAT DEPTH GAUGE--IT'S NEARLY 100 FEET DEEP!

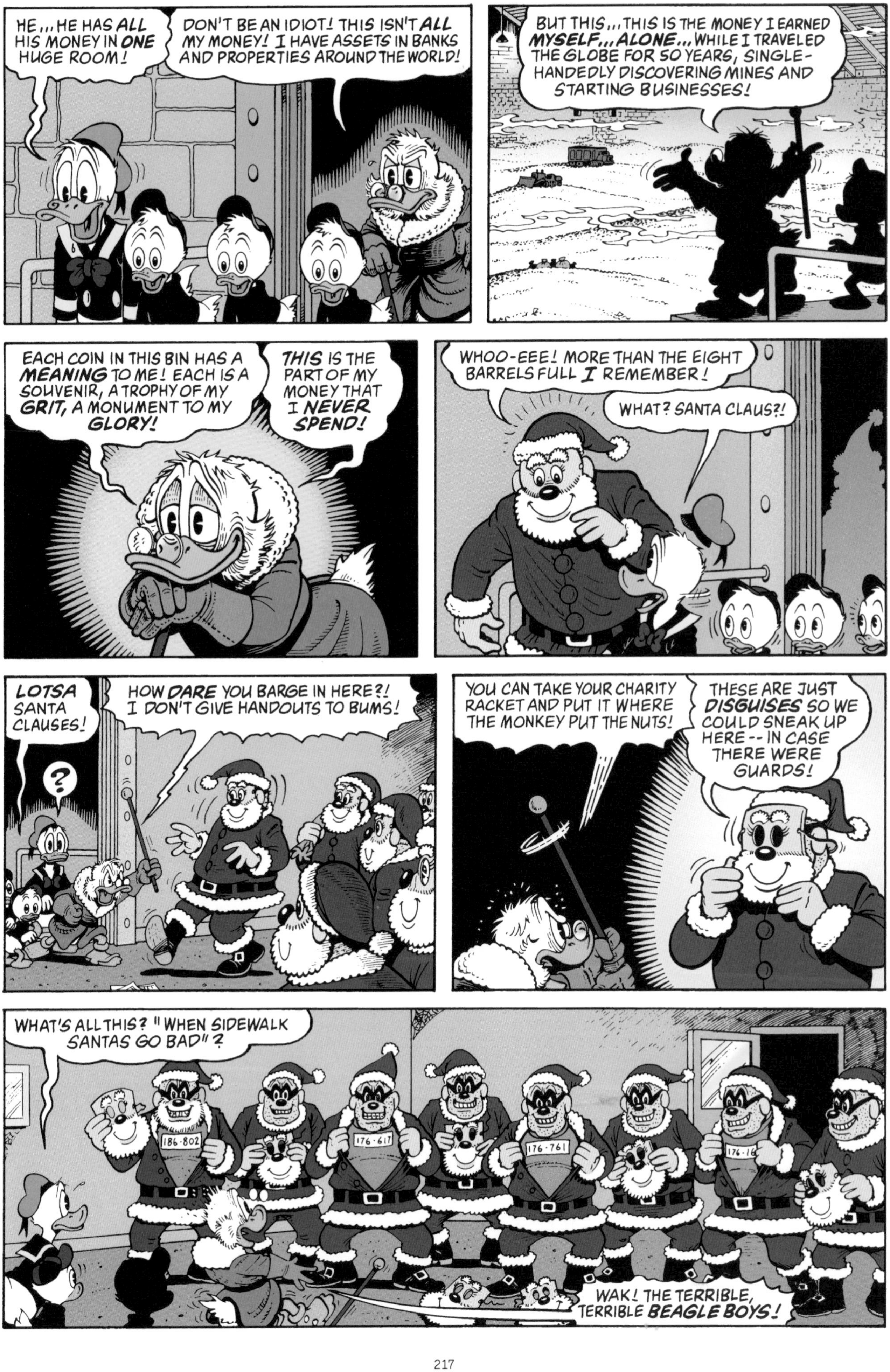
HE,,, HE HAS ALL HIS MONEY IN ONE HUGE ROOM!
DON'T BE AN IDIOT! THIS ISN'T ALL MY MONEY! I HAVE ASSETS IN BANKS AND PROPERTIES AROUND THE WORLD!
BUT THIS,,, THIS IS THE MONEY I EARNED MYSELF,,, ALONE,,, WHILE I TRAVELED THE GLOBE FOR 50 YEARS, SINGLE-HANDEDLY DISCOVERING MINES AND STARTING BUSINESSES!
EACH COIN IN THIS BIN HAS A MEANING TO ME! EACH IS A SOUVENIR, A TROPHY OF MY GRIT, A MONUMENT TO MY GLORY!
THIS IS THE PART OF MY MONEY THAT I NEVER SPEND!
WHOO-EEE! MORE THAN THE EIGHT BARRELS FULL I REMEMBER!
WHAT? SANTA CLAUS?!
LOTSA SANTA CLAUSES!
HOW DARE YOU BARGE IN HERE?! I DON'T GIVE HANDOUTS TO BUMS!
?
YOU CAN TAKE YOUR CHARITY RACKET AND PUT IT WHERE THE MONKEY PUT THE NUTS!
THESE ARE JUST DISGUISES SO WE COULD SNEAK UP HERE -- IN CASE THERE WERE GUARDS!
WHAT'S ALL THIS? "WHEN SIDEWALK SANTAS GO BAD"?
186-802
176-617
176-761
WAK! THE TERRIBLE, TERRIBLE BEAGLE BOYS!

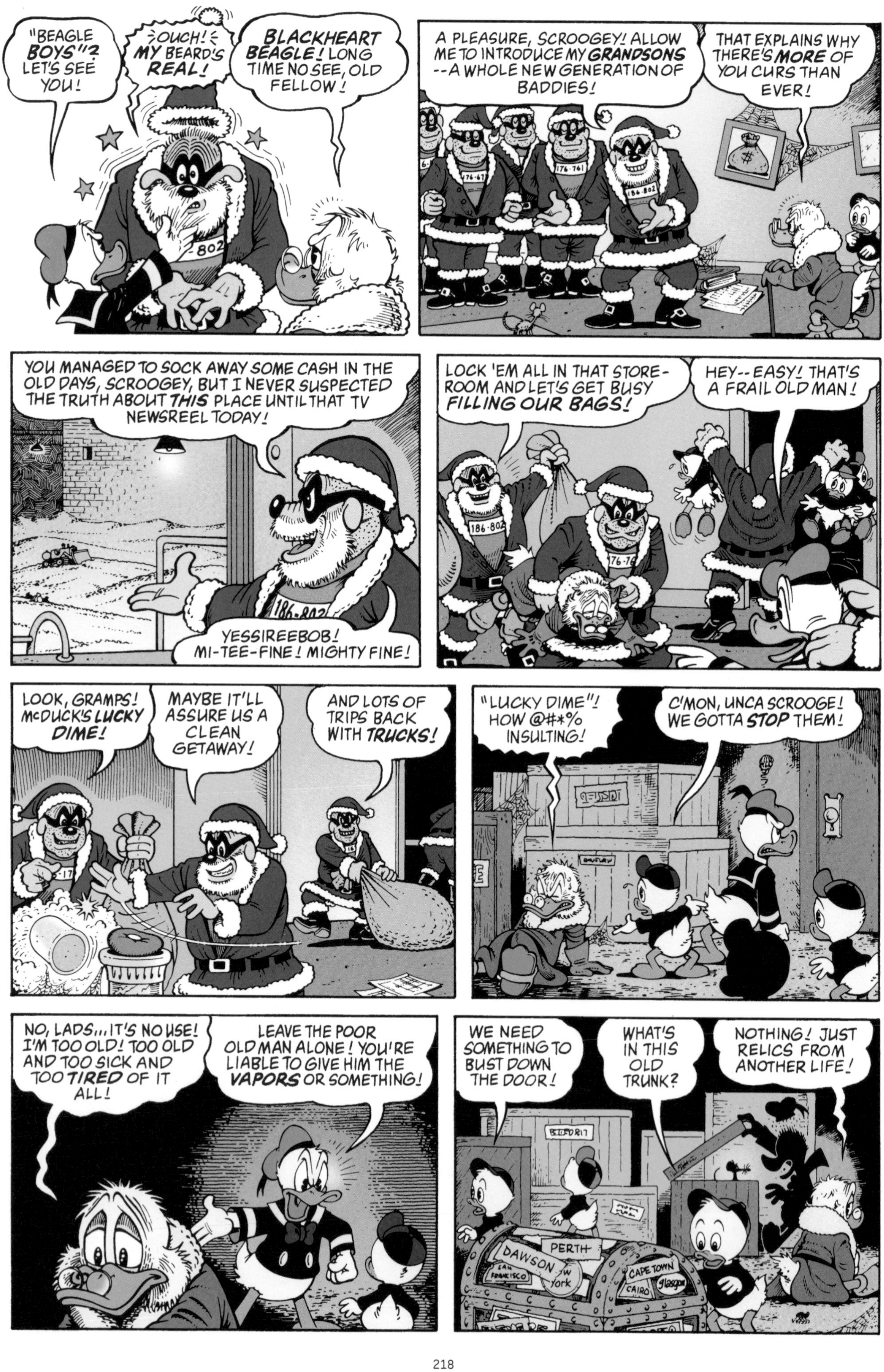
"BEAGLE BOYS"? LET'S SEE YOU!
OUCH! MY BEARD'S REAL!
BLACKHEART BEAGLE! LONG TIME NO SEE, OLD FELLOW!
A PLEASURE, SCROOGEY! ALLOW ME TO INTRODUCE MY GRANDSONS --A WHOLE NEW GENERATION OF BADDIES!
THAT EXPLAINS WHY THERE'S MORE OF YOU CURS THAN EVER!
YOU MANAGED TO SOCK AWAY SOME CASH IN THE OLD DAYS, SCROOGEY, BUT I NEVER SUSPECTED THE TRUTH ABOUT THIS PLACE UNTIL THAT TV NEWSREEL TODAY!
YESSIREEBOB! MI-TEE-FINE! MIGHTY FINE!
LOCK 'EM ALL IN THAT STORE-ROOM AND LET'S GET BUSY FILLING OUR BAGS!
HEY-- EASY! THAT'S A FRAIL OLD MAN!
LOOK, GRAMPS! McDUCK'S LUCKY DIME!
MAYBE IT'LL ASSURE US A CLEAN GETAWAY!
AND LOTS OF TRIPS BACK WITH TRUCKS!
"LUCKY DIME"! HOW @#*% INSULTING!
C'MON, UNCA SCROOGE! WE GOTTA STOP THEM!
NO, LADS... IT'S NO USE! I'M TOO OLD! TOO OLD AND TOO SICK AND TOO TIRED OF IT ALL!
LEAVE THE POOR OLD MAN ALONE! YOU'RE LIABLE TO GIVE HIM THE VAPORS OR SOMETHING!
WE NEED SOMETHING TO BUST DOWN THE DOOR!
WHAT'S IN THIS OLD TRUNK?
NOTHING! JUST RELICS FROM ANOTHER LIFE!
DAWSON
PERTH
CAPE TOWN
CAIRO

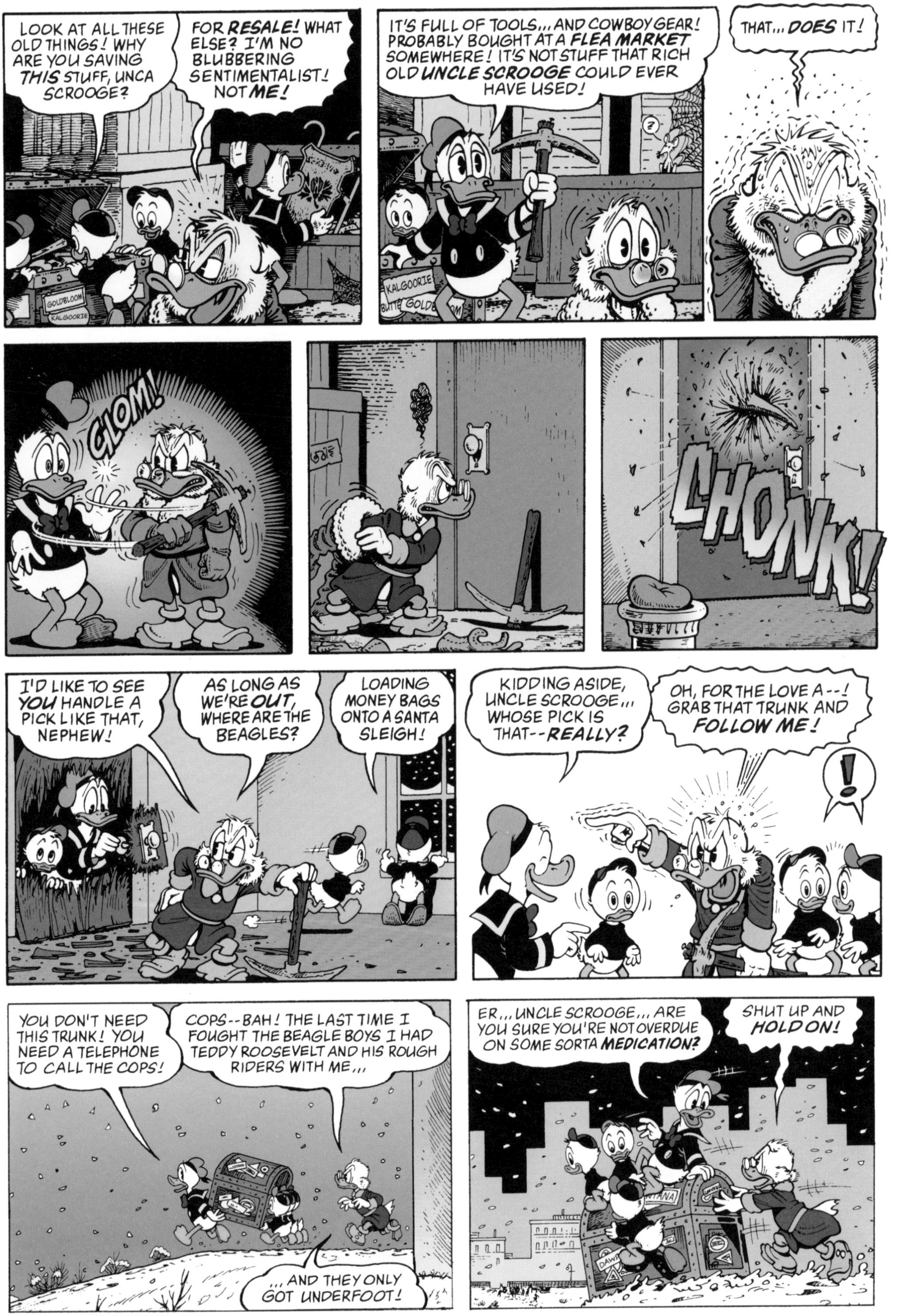
LOOK AT ALL THESE OLD THINGS! WHY ARE YOU SAVING THIS STUFF, UNCA SCROOGE?
FOR RESALE! WHAT ELSE? I'M NO BLUBBERING SENTIMENTALIST! NOT ME!
GOLDBLOOM
KALGOORIE
IT'S FULL OF TOOLS,,, AND COWBOY GEAR! PROBABLY BOUGHT AT A FLEA MARKET SOMEWHERE! IT'S NOT STUFF THAT RICH OLD UNCLE SCROOGE COULD EVER HAVE USED!
KALGOORIE
THAT,,, DOES IT!
GLOM!
CHONK!
I'D LIKE TO SEE YOU HANDLE A PICK LIKE THAT, NEPHEW!
AS LONG AS WE'RE OUT, WHERE ARE THE BEAGLES?
LOADING MONEY BAGS ONTO A SANTA SLEIGH!
KIDDING ASIDE, UNCLE SCROOGE,,, WHOSE PICK IS THAT--REALLY?
OH, FOR THE LOVE A--! GRAB THAT TRUNK AND FOLLOW ME!
!
YOU DON'T NEED THIS TRUNK! YOU NEED A TELEPHONE TO CALL THE COPS!
COPS--BAH! THE LAST TIME I FOUGHT THE BEAGLE BOYS I HAD TEDDY ROOSEVELT AND HIS ROUGH RIDERS WITH ME,,,
,,, AND THEY ONLY GOT UNDERFOOT!
ER,,, UNCLE SCROOGE,,, ARE YOU SURE YOU'RE NOT OVERDUE ON SOME SORTA MEDICATION?
SHUT UP AND HOLD ON!

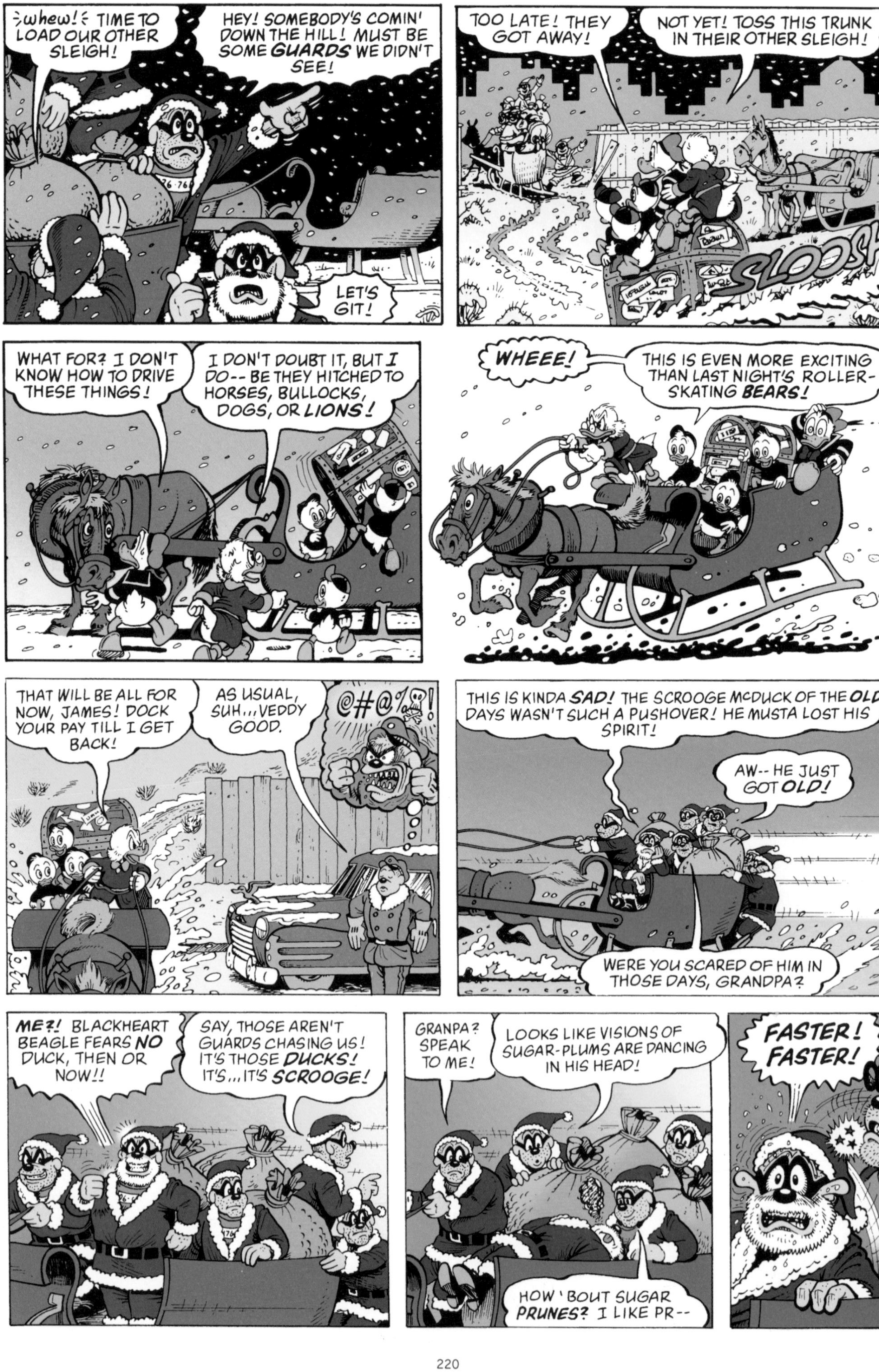

whew! TIME TO LOAD OUR OTHER SLEIGH!
HEY! SOMEBODY'S COMIN' DOWN THE HILL! MUST BE SOME GUARDS WE DIDN'T SEE!
LET'S GIT!
TOO LATE! THEY GOT AWAY!
NOT YET! TOSS THIS TRUNK IN THEIR OTHER SLEIGH!
SLOOSH
WHAT FOR? I DON'T KNOW HOW TO DRIVE THESE THINGS!
I DON'T DOUBT IT, BUT I DO-- BE THEY HITCHED TO HORSES, BULLOCKS, DOGS, OR LIONS!
WHEEE!
THIS IS EVEN MORE EXCITING THAN LAST NIGHT'S ROLLER-SKATING BEARS!
THAT WILL BE ALL FOR NOW, JAMES! DOCK YOUR PAY TILL I GET BACK!
AS USUAL, SUH... VEDDY GOOD.
@#@%!
THIS IS KINDA SAD! THE SCROOGE McDUCK OF THE OLD DAYS WASN'T SUCH A PUSHOVER! HE MUSTA LOST HIS SPIRIT!
AW-- HE JUST GOT OLD!
WERE YOU SCARED OF HIM IN THOSE DAYS, GRANDPA?
ME?! BLACKHEART BEAGLE FEARS NO DUCK, THEN OR NOW!!
SAY, THOSE AREN'T GUARDS CHASING US! IT'S THOSE DUCKS! IT'S... IT'S SCROOGE!
GRANPA? SPEAK TO ME!
LOOKS LIKE VISIONS OF SUGAR-PLUMS ARE DANCING IN HIS HEAD!
HOW 'BOUT SUGAR PRUNES? I LIKE PR--
FASTER! FASTER!

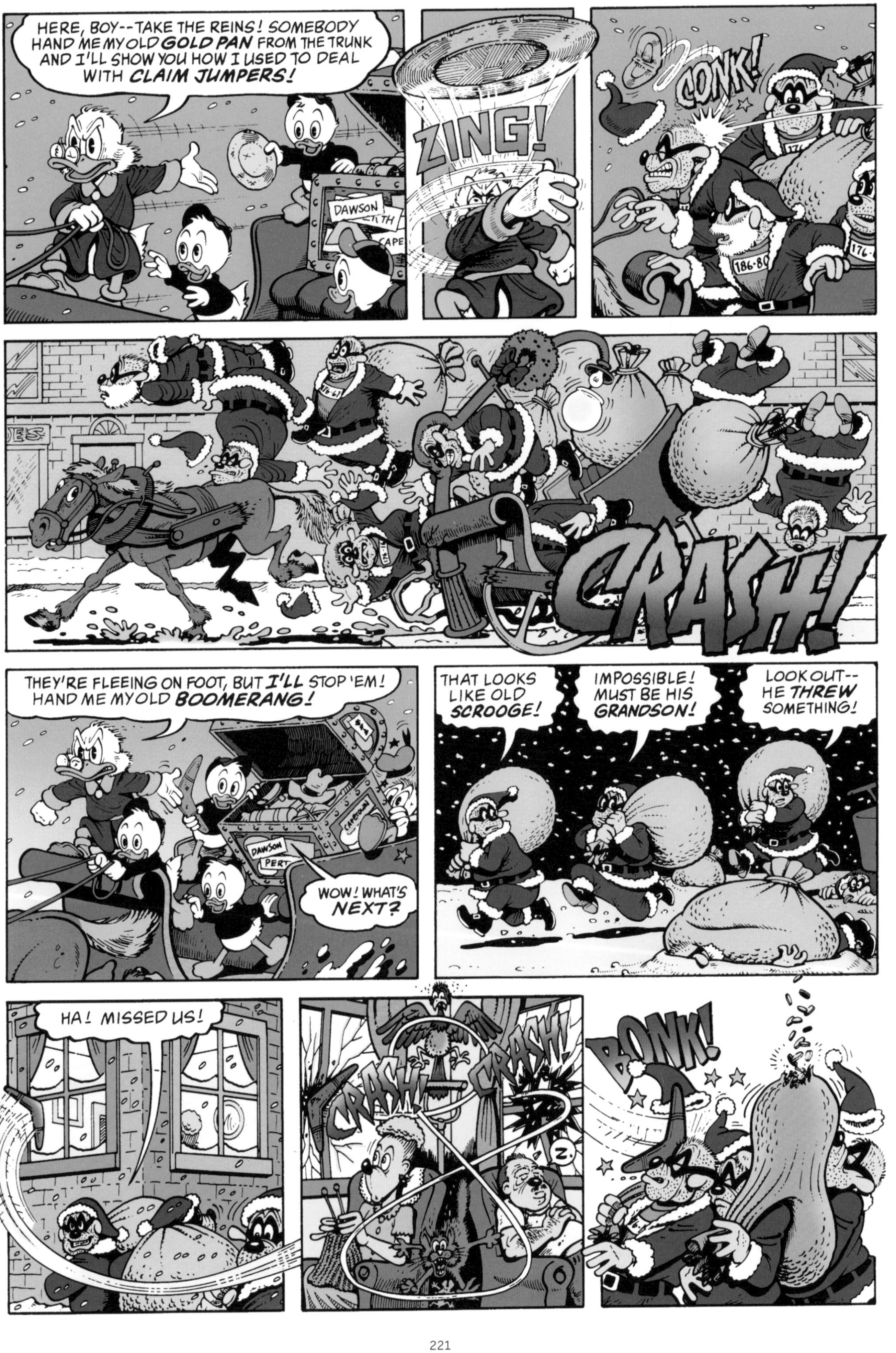
HERE, BOY--TAKE THE REINS! SOMEBODY HAND ME MY OLD GOLD PAN FROM THE TRUNK AND I'LL SHOW YOU HOW I USED TO DEAL WITH CLAIM JUMPERS!
DAWSON
ZING!
CONK!
186-80
CRASH!
THEY'RE FLEEING ON FOOT, BUT I'LL STOP 'EM! HAND ME MY OLD BOOMERANG!
DAWSON
PERT
CAPETOWN
WOW! WHAT'S NEXT?
THAT LOOKS LIKE OLD SCROOGE!
IMPOSSIBLE! MUST BE HIS GRANDSON!
LOOK OUT-- HE THREW SOMETHING!
HA! MISSED US!
CRASH!
CRASH!
Z.
BONK!

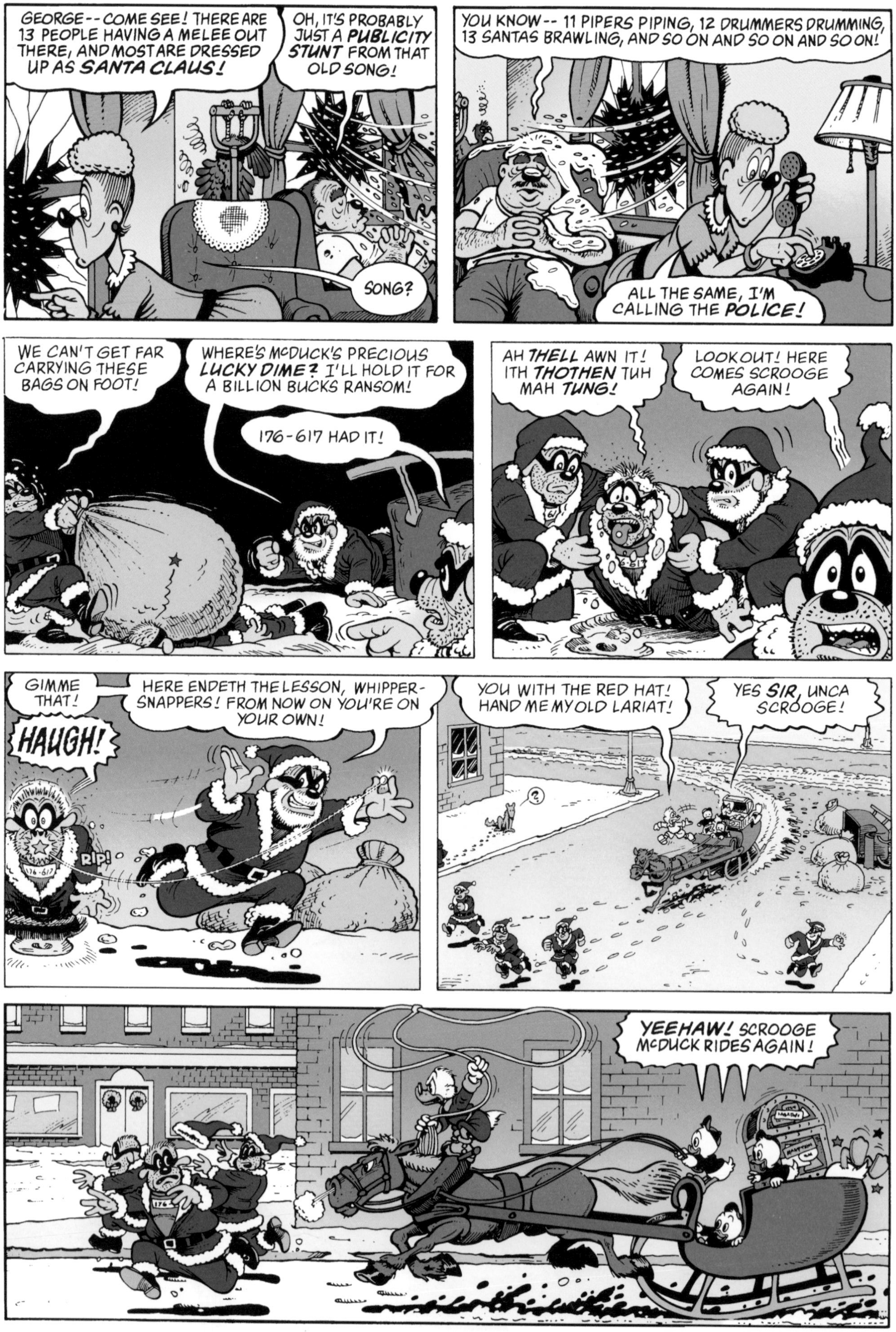
GEORGE -- COME SEE! THERE ARE 13 PEOPLE HAVING A MELEE OUT THERE, AND MOST ARE DRESSED UP AS SANTA CLAUS!
OH, IT'S PROBABLY JUST A PUBLICITY STUNT FROM THAT OLD SONG!
SONG?
YOU KNOW -- 11 PIPERS PIPING, 12 DRUMMERS DRUMMING, 13 SANTAS BRAWLING, AND SO ON AND SO ON AND SO ON!
ALL THE SAME, I'M CALLING THE POLICE!
WE CAN'T GET FAR CARRYING THESE BAGS ON FOOT!
WHERE'S McDUCK'S PRECIOUS LUCKY DIME? I'LL HOLD IT FOR A BILLION BUCKS RANSOM!
176-617 HAD IT!
AH THELL AWN IT! ITH THOTHEN TUH MAH TUNG!
LOOK OUT! HERE COMES SCROOGE AGAIN!
GIMME THAT!
HAUGH!
HERE ENDETH THE LESSON, WHIPPER-SNAPPERS! FROM NOW ON YOU'RE ON YOUR OWN!
RIP!
176-617
YOU WITH THE RED HAT! HAND ME MY OLD LARIAT!
YES SIR, UNCA SCROOGE!
?
YEEHAW! SCROOGE McDUCK RIDES AGAIN!

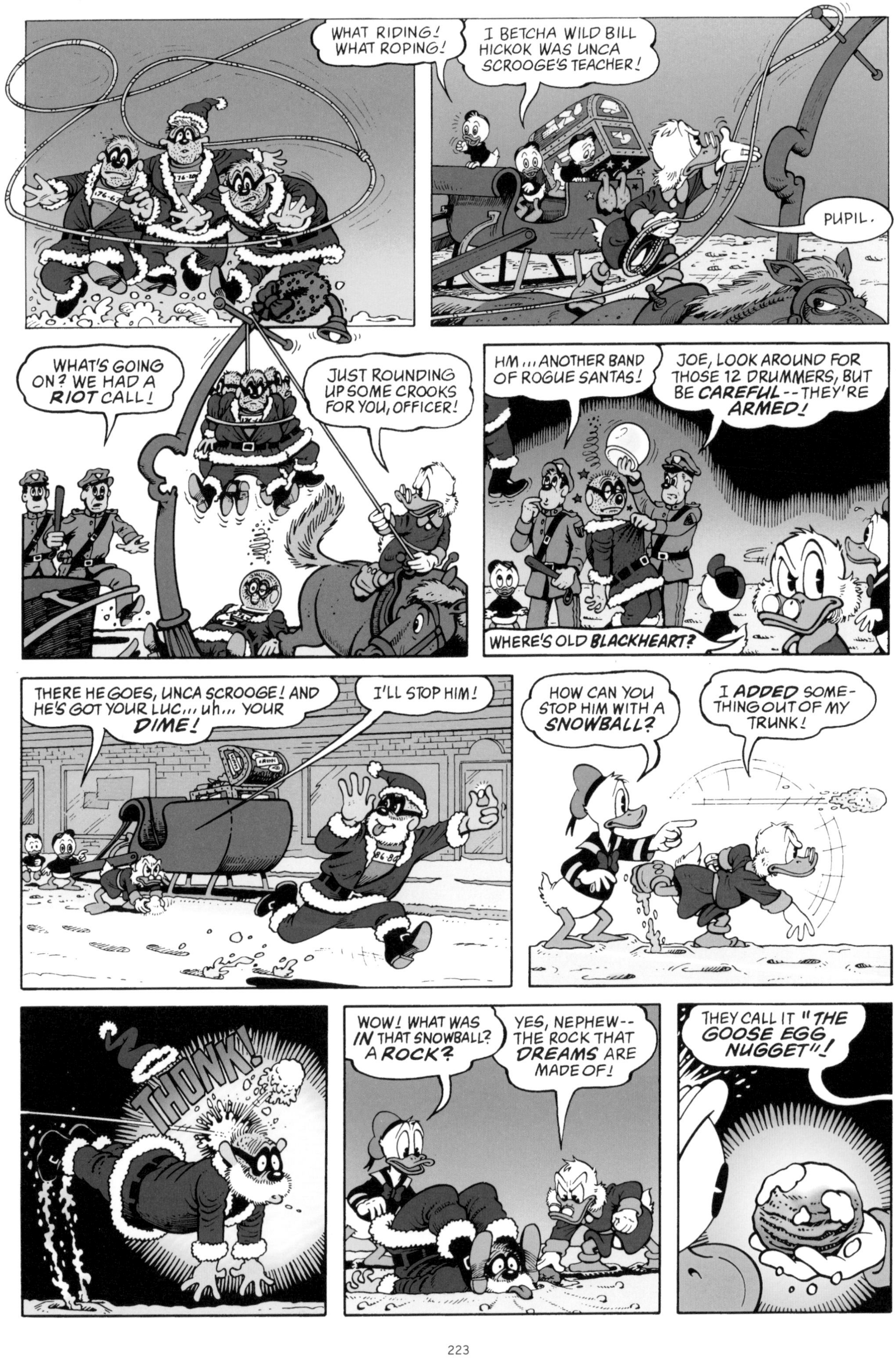
WHAT RIDING! WHAT ROPING!
I BETCHA WILD BILL HICKOK WAS UNCA SCROOGE'S TEACHER!
PUPIL.
WHAT'S GOING ON? WE HAD A RIOT CALL!
JUST ROUNDING UP SOME CROOKS FOR YOU, OFFICER!
HM ... ANOTHER BAND OF ROGUE SANTAS!
JOE, LOOK AROUND FOR THOSE 12 DRUMMERS, BUT BE CAREFUL -- THEY'RE ARMED!
WHERE'S OLD BLACKHEART?
THERE HE GOES, UNCA SCROOGE! AND HE'S GOT YOUR LUC... uh... YOUR DIME!
I'LL STOP HIM!
HOW CAN YOU STOP HIM WITH A SNOWBALL?
I ADDED SOMETHING OUT OF MY TRUNK!
THONK!
WOW! WHAT WAS IN THAT SNOWBALL? A ROCK?
YES, NEPHEW-- THE ROCK THAT DREAMS ARE MADE OF!
THEY CALL IT "THE GOOSE EGG NUGGET"!

>sigh!< I THINK IT'S TIME TO RETIRE!

WHOEVER SAYS THIS IS A "LUCKY" DIME IS A *NITWIT!*

THANKS FOR THE TESTIMONIAL!

186-80?

THAT WILL BE THE LAST TIME *THAT* BUNCH BOTHERS YOUR BIN, EH, UNCLE SCROOGE?

NOT IF I KNOW THE BEAGLE CLAN, NEPHEW! NOT BY A LONG SHOT!

ANYWAY, HELP ME GET THESE SACKS OF *CASH* BACK INTO MY BIN!

AARGH -- I'LL BE SORE TOMORROW!

*S*OON, ALL IS RESTORED TO ORDER....

MAN! THAT WAS A *GREAT* ADVENTURE!

WHO'D HAVE GUESSED OUR UNCA SCROOGE LEADS SUCH AN *EXCITING* LIFE!

NO, LADS... NOT ANYMORE...

I'M A FOSSIL OF A BYGONE AGE... WHEN A MAN COULD LIVE ON HIS *OWN* TERMS... BE AN INDIVIDUAL!

MAYBE *TOO MUCH* OF AN INDIVIDUAL, UNCA SCROOGE!

BUT *WE'LL* BE YOUR FAMILY NOW!

NO.... IT'S TOO LATE! THAT'S THE *ONE* EXPERIENCE I'VE NEVER HAD! YET... THERE WAS A TIME WHEN I ...ALMOST...

BUT YOU *THRIVE* ON NEW EXPERIENCES! JUST LOOK AT THE LIFE YOU'VE LED!

MY LIFE *WAS* A DOOZY, ALL RIGHT, BUT IT'S *BEHIND* ME NOW! ALL I HAVE LEFT IS ENDLESS DAYS OF BOREDOM IN THAT *GLOOMY* MANSION!

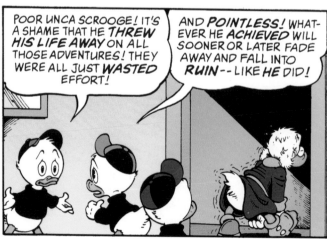

POOR UNCA SCROOGE! IT'S A SHAME THAT HE *THREW HIS LIFE AWAY* ON ALL THOSE ADVENTURES! THEY WERE ALL JUST *WASTED* EFFORT!

AND *POINTLESS!* WHATEVER HE *ACHIEVED* WILL SOONER OR LATER FADE AWAY AND FALL INTO *RUIN* -- LIKE *HE* DID!

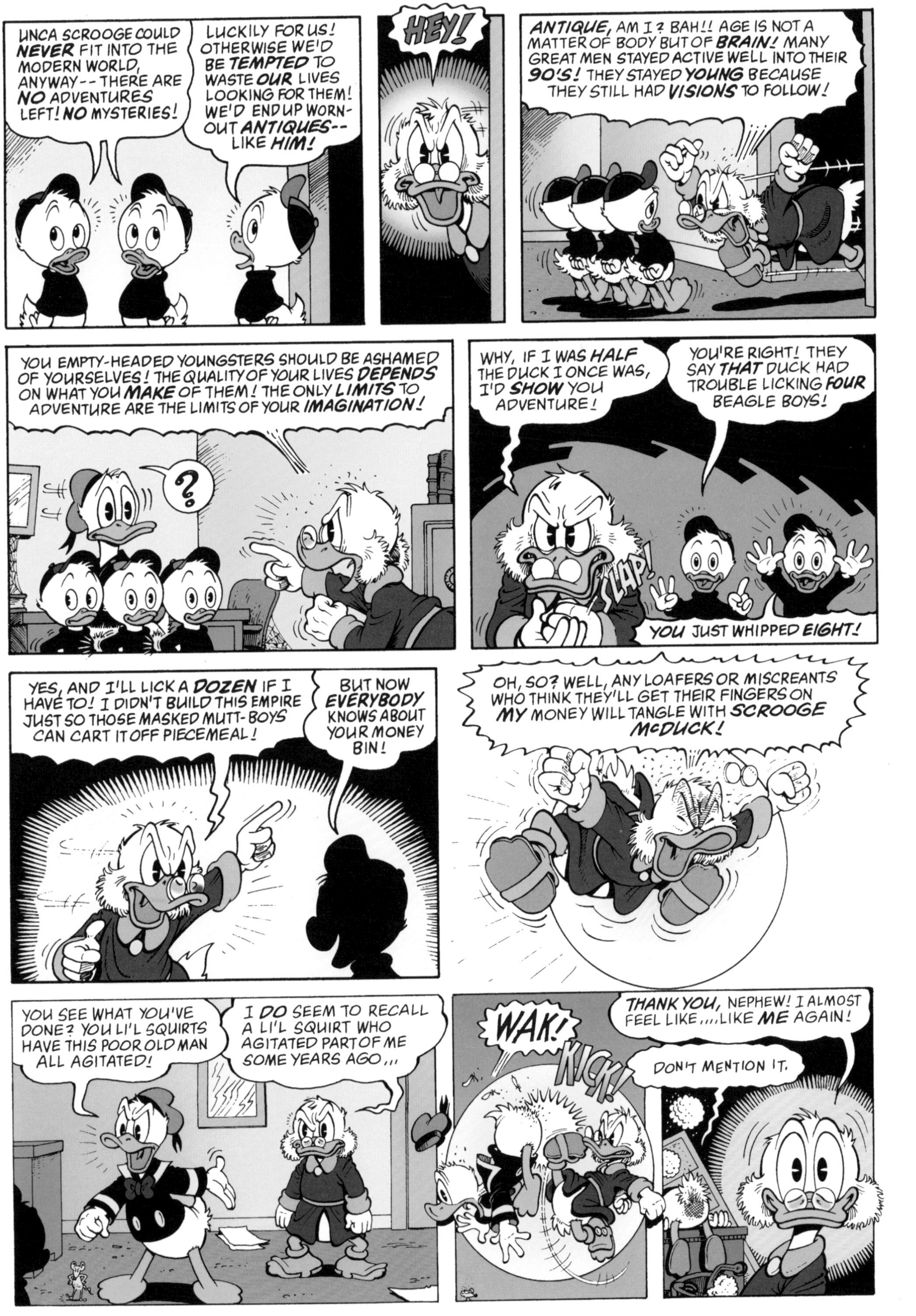
UNCA SCROOGE COULD NEVER FIT INTO THE MODERN WORLD, ANYWAY-- THERE ARE NO ADVENTURES LEFT! NO MYSTERIES!
LUCKILY FOR US! OTHERWISE WE'D BE TEMPTED TO WASTE OUR LIVES LOOKING FOR THEM! WE'D END UP WORN-OUT ANTIQUES-- LIKE HIM!
HEY!
ANTIQUE, AM I? BAH!! AGE IS NOT A MATTER OF BODY BUT OF BRAIN! MANY GREAT MEN STAYED ACTIVE WELL INTO THEIR 90'S! THEY STAYED YOUNG BECAUSE THEY STILL HAD VISIONS TO FOLLOW!
YOU EMPTY-HEADED YOUNGSTERS SHOULD BE ASHAMED OF YOURSELVES! THE QUALITY OF YOUR LIVES DEPENDS ON WHAT YOU MAKE OF THEM! THE ONLY LIMITS TO ADVENTURE ARE THE LIMITS OF YOUR IMAGINATION!
?
WHY, IF I WAS HALF THE DUCK I ONCE WAS, I'D SHOW YOU ADVENTURE!
YOU'RE RIGHT! THEY SAY THAT DUCK HAD TROUBLE LICKING FOUR BEAGLE BOYS!
SLAP!
YOU JUST WHIPPED EIGHT!
YES, AND I'LL LICK A DOZEN IF I HAVE TO! I DIDN'T BUILD THIS EMPIRE JUST SO THOSE MASKED MUTT-BOYS CAN CART IT OFF PIECEMEAL!
BUT NOW EVERYBODY KNOWS ABOUT YOUR MONEY BIN!
OH, SO? WELL, ANY LOAFERS OR MISCREANTS WHO THINK THEY'LL GET THEIR FINGERS ON MY MONEY WILL TANGLE WITH SCROOGE McDUCK!
YOU SEE WHAT YOU'VE DONE? YOU LI'L SQUIRTS HAVE THIS POOR OLD MAN ALL AGITATED!
I DO SEEM TO RECALL A LI'L SQUIRT WHO AGITATED PART OF ME SOME YEARS AGO,,,
WAK!
KICK!
THANK YOU, NEPHEW! I ALMOST FEEL LIKE,,,,LIKE ME AGAIN!
DON'T MENTION IT.

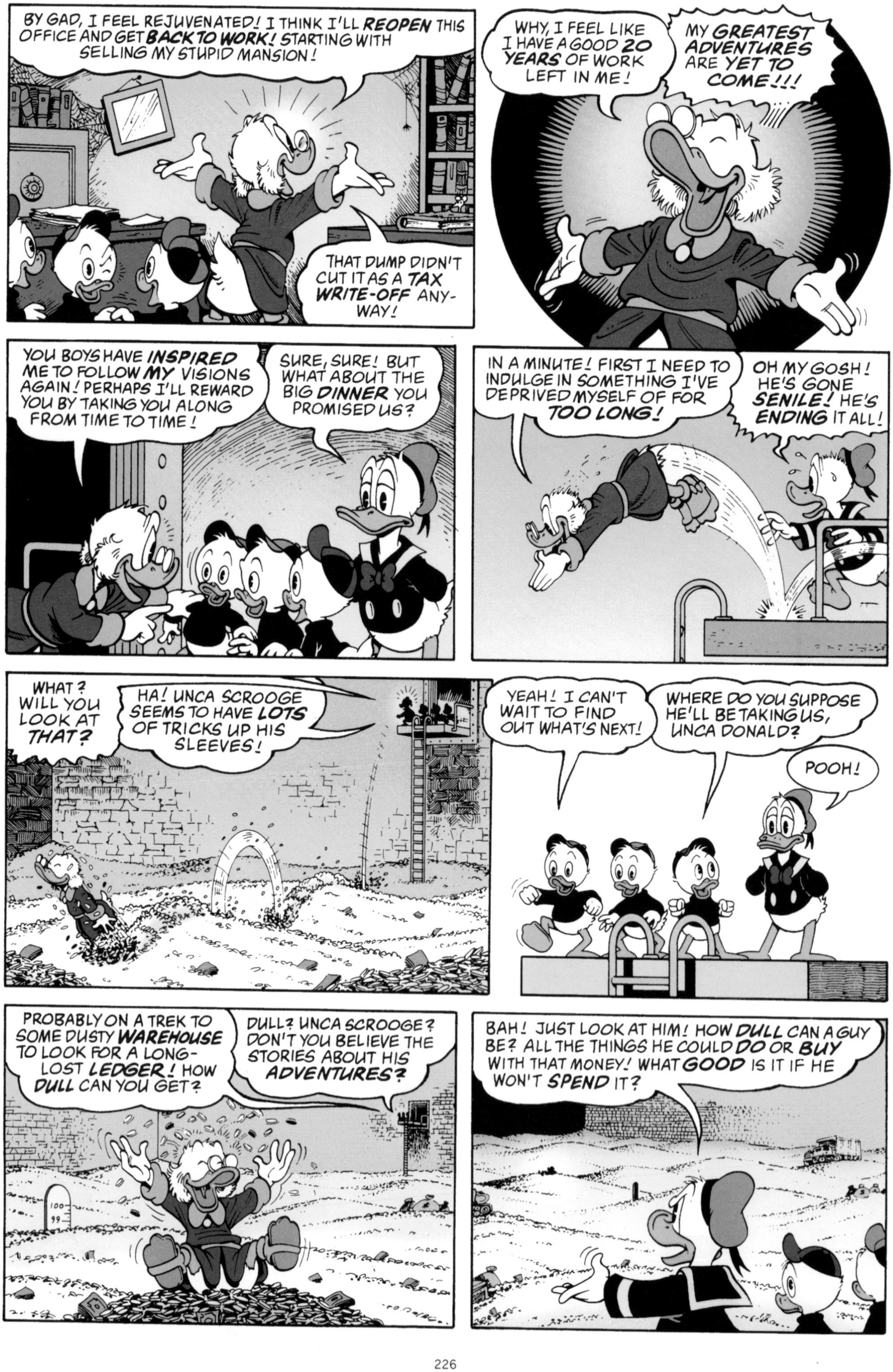
BY GAD, I FEEL REJUVENATED! I THINK I'LL REOPEN THIS OFFICE AND GET BACK TO WORK! STARTING WITH SELLING MY STUPID MANSION!
THAT DUMP DIDN'T CUT IT AS A TAX WRITE-OFF ANYWAY!
WHY, I FEEL LIKE I HAVE A GOOD 20 YEARS OF WORK LEFT IN ME!
MY GREATEST ADVENTURES ARE YET TO COME!!!
YOU BOYS HAVE INSPIRED ME TO FOLLOW MY VISIONS AGAIN! PERHAPS I'LL REWARD YOU BY TAKING YOU ALONG FROM TIME TO TIME!
SURE, SURE! BUT WHAT ABOUT THE BIG DINNER YOU PROMISED US?
IN A MINUTE! FIRST I NEED TO INDULGE IN SOMETHING I'VE DEPRIVED MYSELF OF FOR TOO LONG!
OH MY GOSH! HE'S GONE SENILE! HE'S ENDING IT ALL!
WHAT? WILL YOU LOOK AT THAT?
HA! UNCA SCROOGE SEEMS TO HAVE LOTS OF TRICKS UP HIS SLEEVES!
YEAH! I CAN'T WAIT TO FIND OUT WHAT'S NEXT!
WHERE DO YOU SUPPOSE HE'LL BE TAKING US, UNCA DONALD?
POOH!
PROBABLY ON A TREK TO SOME DUSTY WAREHOUSE TO LOOK FOR A LONG-LOST LEDGER! HOW DULL CAN YOU GET?
DULL? UNCA SCROOGE? DON'T YOU BELIEVE THE STORIES ABOUT HIS ADVENTURES?
BAH! JUST LOOK AT HIM! HOW DULL CAN A GUY BE? ALL THE THINGS HE COULD DO OR BUY WITH THAT MONEY! WHAT GOOD IS IT IF HE WON'T SPEND IT?

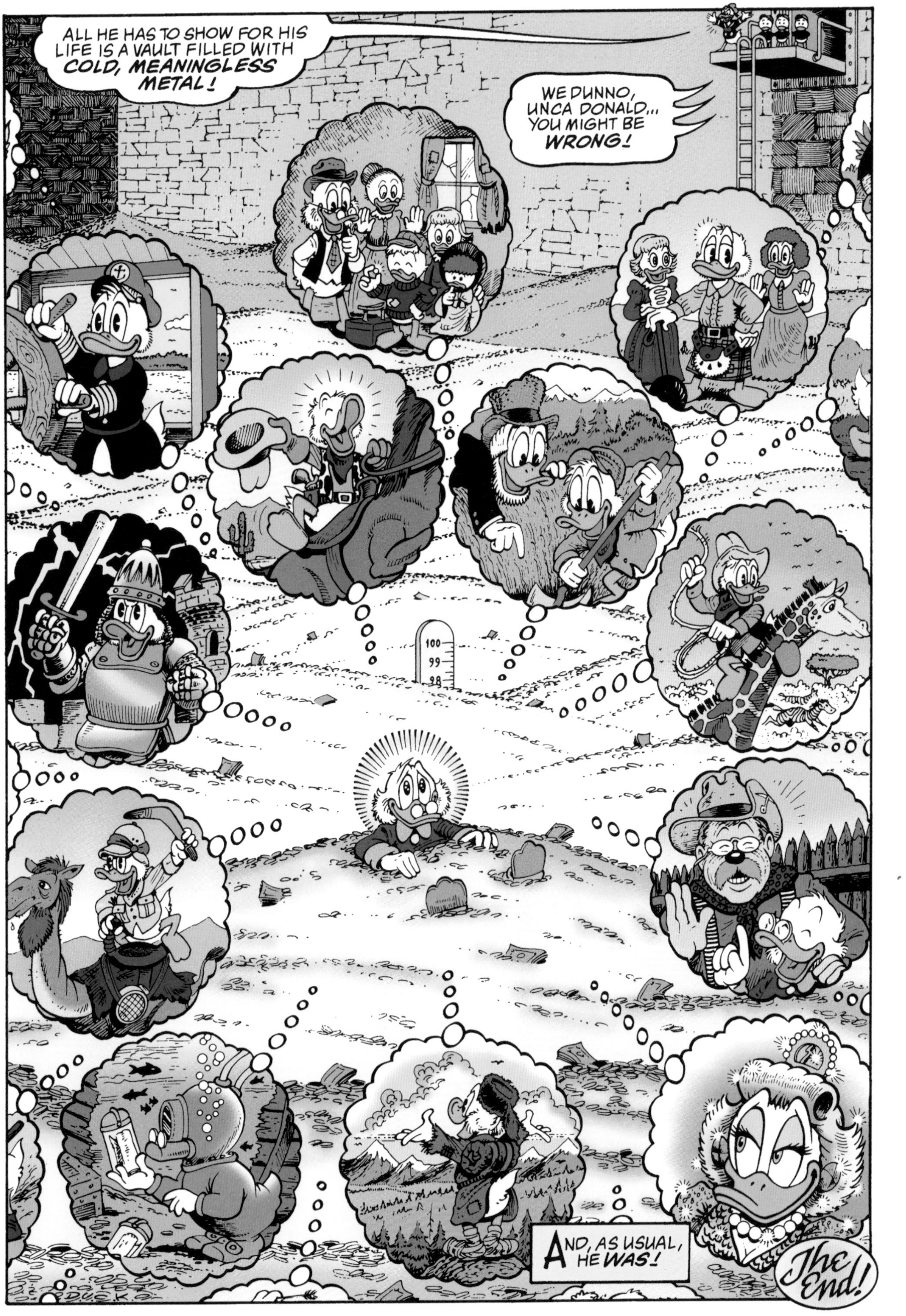
ALL HE HAS TO SHOW FOR HIS LIFE IS A VAULT FILLED WITH COLD, MEANINGLESS METAL!
WE DUNNO, UNCA DONALD... YOU MIGHT BE WRONG!
100
99
98
AND, AS USUAL, HE WAS!
The End!

Now Available!

Now you can own the complete Duck works of internationally acclaimed cartoonist Don Rosa — in ten luxurious volumes — collecting every Disney Duck story he drew, from his first ("The Son of the Sun") to his last ("The Prisoner of White Agony Creek")!

Printed and bound to last a lifetime, each full-sized, full-color hardcover book in this collection features a treasure trove of Don's stories and art, generously supplemented by the most comprehensive set of behind-the-scenes extras available anywhere.

Faithfully reproduced under the watchful eye of the artist himself, this is the definitive collection of Don Rosa's Uncle Scrooge and Donald Duck adventure classics!

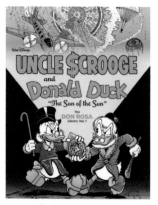

VOL. 1 • *The Son of the Sun*

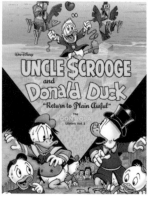

VOL. 2 • *Return to Plain Awful*

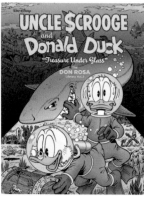

VOL. 3 • *Treasure Under Glass*

VOL. 4 • *The Last of the Clan McDuck*

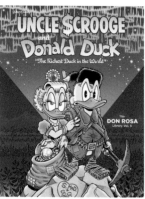

VOL. 5 • *The Richest Duck in the World*

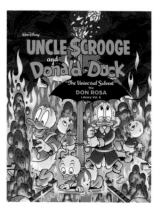

VOL. 6 • *The Universal Solvent*

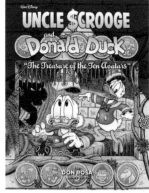

VOL. 7 • *The Treasure of the Ten Avatars*

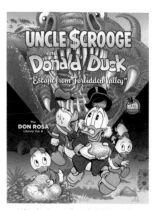

VOL. 8 • *Escape From Forbidden Valley*

VOL. 9 • *The Three Caballeros Ride Again!*

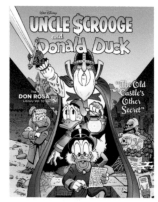

VOL. 10 • *The Old Castle's Other Secret*

Also Available!

Wait! You thought Scrooge's story was finished? But Don Rosa is just getting warmed up! He still has more secrets to reveal from Scrooge McDuck's legendary past — including a rollicking Yukon adventure involving Glittering Goldie (that might just break your heart!) — in this special collection featuring "in-between" untold tales!

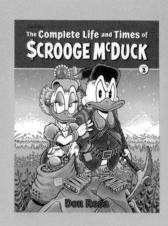

The Complete Life and Times of Scrooge McDuck Volume 2